A Stranger to Herself

Hilary Bailey was born near Bromley. She now lives in West London, not far from Portobello Road. She is the author of about twenty short stories, and her first novel, *Polly Put the Kettle On*, was published in 1975. Her other novels include *Mrs Mulvaney* and *As Time Goes By*. She has also written *Hannie Richards*, a thriller about a woman smuggler; a short biography of Vera Brittain; and the best-selling family saga *All the Days of My Life*.

Also by Hilary Bailey
in Pan Books

All the Days of My Life

Hilary Bailey

A STRANGER TO HERSELF

Pan Books
in association with Macmillan London

For Fanny Blake,
my editor,
and Mabel Longford,
September 13th 1887–September 3rd 1979

First published 1989 by Macmillan London Ltd

This edition published 1990 by
Pan Books Ltd, Cavaye Place, London SW10 9PG
in association with Macmillan London Ltd

1 3 5 7 9 8 6 4 2

ISBN 0 330 31605 2

Printed in England by Clays Ltd, St Ives plc

CONTENTS

ONE

Kate Higgins, March 14th, 1991

I got the job of writing Violet Levine's biography in the early spring of 1991, just over a year after she died at the age of ninety-three. I was commissioned by Askew and Askew, an old-established firm of London publishers, who had employed Henry James as a reader and also William Makepeace Thackeray, Thomas Love Peacock and, for all I knew, Chaucer's uncle. They commissioned me because I was the first person to suggest the biography to them, because no one else seemed to be doing it, because I had no track record so I would work for little money and because I knew Roger Littlebrown, who was senior person there, due to the fact that I was sleeping with his cousin Andy. 'Seeing' or 'having a relationship with' his cousin Andy might be a more conventional way of putting it but I have my standards and even then I wouldn't have liked to claim I was having a relationship with Andy. Most of the time I didn't and when I did I had no idea what it was. After what happened I now have even less idea, of course. Still, I knew Roger, via Andy, so I'd contacted him to discuss the idea of a biography about Violet.

We had lunch at a place called La Somnambule, just off the Haymarket, where there were Raffles Hotel-style fans in the ceiling and on the walls old stills of French thirties and forties films showing Jean Gabin in a pulled-down fedora and Simone Signoret in a slinky evening gown. We ate tiny portions of food nicely arranged on plates and in the ladies the notice telling you not to put sanitary towels down the lavatory was in French. What about women who didn't understand French, I wondered? Still, it was bright at La Somnambule, and pretty clean, though I noticed Roger Littlebrown, a big, fair man, built on Danish invader lines, was giving his curly lettuce and teeny bit of duck an old-fashioned look. He would probably have been happier in one of those grubby restaurants where old men in old waiters' costumes plonk down heavy portions of British food and insult you. He was an 'I'll have the steak and kidney' man, an 'Oh good – treacle tart' chap.

The food was neither here nor there to me – I had no appetite and was probably better off eating at La Somnambule, where there was hardly any food, than trying to get down a steak somewhere else. I was worried about meeting. I wanted to write the biography, all right, but I wasn't sure I could. Andy had told me I couldn't, for starters, pointing out that I'd never done anything like it before and hadn't the right gifts for it anyway. In the meanwhile, the atmosphere at the restaurant was not kind to the shabby and unsuccessful and unconfident, and I was all three.

I might sound, now, as if I was pretty smart in those days. Knowing, office-wise, hard to shake, rattle or generally disconcert. In fact, I'm not that, even now. Then, I was a mere babe in the wood. This story is, among other things, about how they separate the girls from the women these days; and, I think, about how I started, at thirty-five years old, as one and ended up not long after as the other.

I looked at Roger, frowning at the menu in search of carbohydrates. I'd met him several times, the first time about eighteen months earlier, just after I found Andy at a press do for a book about the Gulf War, which had been written by a friend of his. I'd gone along at the instigation of Dave Gottlieb, who was the deputy editor of *The Mag*, a weekly I sometimes did a little, badly paid work for, and was glad to get it. So, about a week after Andy and I began our affair, and I thought I must be the luckiest, if the most nervous, woman in the world, Andy said, 'Do you mind coming along to a pub to meet my cousin Roger? He's a dull publisher. I'm going to be the best man at his wedding. Got to discuss the arrangements in as little detail as possible. I think his fiancée's coming too. You'll probably have to hear about the dress and the mortgage and so forth. I'm sorry about this. I've been dodging it for ages, but there you are . . . '

The evening passed much as expected. Roger and Sarah, his future wife, were formidable in their size, blondness and good humour. There was a point where they were laughing about having exchanged contracts on their new house, at a price they couldn't really afford, just as the sitting-room ceiling collapsed on their heads, when I felt a pang of envy at their unity go through me. Like a knife-stab. I reminded myself that I loved Andy. He was better looking, more intelligent, more interesting than Roger. We were both, perhaps, more complicated than Roger and Sarah. And, I told myself, the last thing I wanted was marriage, a house in rising Dalston, with rising damp, original features and two years' work in it, a plump baby. I wanted magic, even if it meant sleepless nights, anxieties, jealousies and jumping for the phone when it rang.

The next time I saw Roger was at the wedding a few months later. My presence went down fairly badly in Chichester, since the family, especially Roger's parents and Andy's mother, and many of their friends, knew Andy had left his wife Miriam and was being unreliable about money for her and the baby. They assumed, since it improved the plot, I suppose, and in order to have someone to blame other than Andy, their golden boy, that it was for me that he had left his wife and that I was the woman eating big meals on his credit cards, going on holidays and telling him Miriam could easily go out and get a job. It wasn't true – I'd met him months after he left Miriam and some of the information about the money was news to me, and not welcome news either. Anyway, there's no anonymity at a small wedding in a country town, nor any of the complicitous chat of city life either. All they needed was a scarlet woman from the metropolis, especially if she was divorced, and they got her – it was me. Afterwards I accused Andy of having brought me to take the heat off him – I certainly thought he shouldn't have invited me to go. He said that without me he would have been too miserable to play the part of Roger's best man properly. This might have been true.

We saw Roger and Sarah occasionally after that, and paid a visit to the maternity hospital when their child, Thomas, was born. We should never have gone because when we left the maternity ward Andy was green in the face and sweating heavily. I knew he hadn't wanted a child by Miriam, that he didn't like children, but I'd never realised it was a fierce aversion. If he'd acted like that every time he saw a baby, while all the time his wife wanted one, then she must have had problems. It also accounted for why he never went to see her and was being so mean about money – he felt she had betrayed him by getting pregnant and having his child. After that there were sporadic meetings with Roger and Sarah but I never got to know them any better and thought I never would, even if we went on meeting in the same way for the next ten years. Not that I imagined we would, since I always doubted if Andy and I would be together for the next ten months, or even weeks.

Nevertheless, it was Andy who seized on my remark, when I saw in the paper that Violet Levine had died, that I'd always wanted to know more about her, and perhaps now someone would write a biography of her, and said, 'Well, if you're interested, why don't you do it? You're always saying you want to get your teeth into something more than what you're doing.'

Violet Levine was one of those figures who inhabit the landscape of your brain a bit like ghosts – Josephine Baker, Ernest Bevin, King Zog, Albert Chevalier, Madame Blavatsky – you know they're there, you think you know all about them but when you think about it, you don't. People used to say of her, 'Wasn't she involved with the suffragettes? She became an MP when she was quite old, didn't she – then there was scandal . . . ?' They would eventually say, 'She's dead, isn't she?' and then look puzzled and try to remember if she was or not. She'd written her autobiography, *I Affirm*, in 1957. It was still in print, in paperback in fact, and many people, mostly women, read it. I had myself, twice, but it had a mysterious way of seeming to tell you everything while leaving you, somehow, doubtful at the end. In retrospect I can see it wasn't chiefly the quality of the information – though Violet was a specialist in leaving gaps where she didn't want to go into details, and cunningly masking the gaps, as if spreading branches over a pit. It was just as often the quality of emotion in her narrative, or rather the lack of it. Quite often Violet's account of her life was impassive and neutral, rather as if she hadn't been the main protagonist. Later, of course, I understood why. Anyway, she seemed to have come and gone without achieving the semi-mythological status some people acquire, often those with less claim to fame than Violet Levine. Her long life had made her, publicly, an historical figure who was still alive. Her ambiguous position vis-à-vis eternity did nothing for her image. You'd see her name in the lists of December birthdays in the newspaper and feel amazed she was still alive.

Andy's remark about my doing the biography, was partly made to point out my habit of complaining and doing nothing, but it made me haul myself up in bed. 'Why not? I'll see if anybody wants me to. I know,' I said, looking at the unbelievably handsome face, slightly tanned, with very blue eyes and quite long, rumpled black hair, glossy as an Indian's, 'I'll suggest it to Roger – it won't be so bad if he tells me to get lost.'

Andy heaved himself up also and, muttering, 'Leave the filofax till later,' kissed me and bore me down. There's no way of conveying the effect he had on me – I was like a little pile of iron filings poured in front of a magnet, every bit of me moving irresistibly towards him. Some men are like that, some women, too, and they can have a fearsome effect on those who have little else to cling to.

I still don't know why, that morning, I made my absurd statement about intending to write a biography of a woman I knew almost nothing about, or how, that afternoon, I stood in the hall and made my call to a rather startled Roger Littlebrown, who paused, said, 'Er . . . ' and then, having thought it over, fixed a date to meet me. It feels like fate now, but it probably came from a desperation I was only half aware of. To date, at the age of thirty-five, I'd been married, which meant following my husband, an army officer, about, moving every two years, always to somewhere beginning with B – Berlin, Belize and, in the end, Belfast – and I'd had a child and managed to write two novels, somewhat reviewed, totally unprofitable and now out of print. Then I'd left for freedom with my eight-year-old son, who was now ten and living with my parents in Brighton while I shared my friend Di Carter's council flat in west London and did bits for mags and papers. The relationship, if I have to call it that, with Andy Littlebrown, vibrant radical foreign correspondent for *The Witness*, liberal Sunday newspaper, had the effect of taking my mind off my undefined life, while at the same time somehow focusing my attention on it. There's nothing like being with a man with an airbag, deadlines, international phone calls and an armful of injections against nasty tropical diseases to make you notice an almost complete lack of movement in your own life.

At the same time I knew what was happening to me, more or less. Also, I knew I was up against it. I wasn't earning enough to keep my child, which puts a woman in a dreadful situation. I could barely keep myself, in fact. I didn't have a proper job. I didn't have the qualifications or track record to get one which would pay me decently. I didn't live with Andy, except when he was in London. Then I sometimes stayed at his flat, sometimes Di's. I had half a career, half a child, half a man and half a home. Everything was on terms. I couldn't see any way of changing the situation.

That was why, when I met Roger Littlebrown of Askew and Askew, I lacked confidence and intensity and why, I now know, he mentally cut the amount of money he might have been prepared to pay me by a third during the course of our lunch. I hadn't done any homework on the subject and to him I was only his cousin's girlfriend, not a solid status since the whole family obviously said to each other, 'Well, we all know what Andy's like.' As the meal progressed I could see, too, that he was very tired. Shared parenthood was taking it out of him, evidently. In fact it turned out that he, Sarah and the au pair were all dog-tired, a far cry from a few years back when one individual, the mother, used to be suicidally tired by a young child, or, if she was rich enough, only a servant was exhausted. This, as it turned out, was one of the secrets of Violet Levine's brilliant career – servants, and plenty of them. It wasn't something she'd stressed in her autobiography.

But tired though he was, the moment came when Roger leaned forward, keen, or mimicking keenness as publishers have to, and said to me, 'Tell me exactly why you want to write Violet Levine's biography.'

I put down my glass and adopted the lively expression of the successful interviewee – intelligent and practical, but dedicated, as if about to start work in a run-down leper colony with an austere order of nuns. Perhaps I shouldn't have had the second glass, though, because the expression faded almost at once and I just said, 'She was born in the same year as my grandmother, as it happens, but she's only just died. She was a suffragette. She had three children, a political career. She was a writer. She was active in two world wars – well, I've seen it said she was a spy in the Second World War and she must have been in her mid-forties by then. She stood up for good causes all her life from the vote to CND. What more do you want? It's all there, isn't it?' Roger must have seen the point but, from me, he needed more. I leaned forward. 'But I have no idea what she was really like – I don't think anybody has. That's what I want to find out.' (And I did find out, by God, I did, more than I ever wanted to know.) I made my eyes glitter at the thought. Roger's glittered spasmodically back. As I saw the light go out I said, 'There isn't another biography of her, you know. This is the first.' And I saw the glitter turn to a steadier gleam. We were on. As I'd spoken I realised I really wanted to write the biography and would have been very upset if Roger had just gone off saying, 'I'll let you know.'

People might wonder about my basic seriousness and more, perhaps, about Roger Littlebrown's attitude to publishing, and, more specifically, to publishing biography. Why did he so placidly hire his cousin's mistress to write the biography of a famous national figure? Why didn't he ask more questions? I think the truth is that he had to give me a crack at it because I'd thought of it first. In the meanwhile he had first call on the idea. If I didn't work out, he could get rid of me and get someone else to do it instead.

Roger said, 'I think we'd like to do this,' and asked the name of my agent. I didn't have one so he said he'd put a proposal in the post to me. In the end he offered me fifteen thousand pounds, half payable in advance, and the book to be completed in less than a year. It seemed like a long time and a lot of money then.

I gave up teaching the evening class in GCSE history that afternoon, leaving the pupils in the lurch. Andy left for Ho Chi Minh City that evening. He congratulated me when I told him Roger was interested in the book, and said, 'I hope you're not biting off more than you can chew.' But as he picked up his bag, visa, passport, wallet and letters of introduction I suppose he was quite pleased I didn't sit there, watching him getting ready to move, with the unspoken words hovering in the air, 'Do you love me? Is there another woman? Is she in London, is she in Vietnam, New York? When will you be back?' My air of being a dog left behind in the hall always made him uneasy. Though I did say, 'When will you be back?' and he replied, 'Two weeks, possibly.' He turned in the doorway, the tailor's dream, bronzed throat coming out of the open-necked white shirt from a superior shirtmaker, his shiny hair hanging a little low on to the collar of his cream suit, a flash of the blue eyes over the shoulder. He was saying, 'I'll ring you when I can.' I'll always remember that moment – it's nice to know you had the teen dream, the housewife's Mills and Boon, just once in your life. Of course, the price was high, as it turned out.

I left his Notting Hill Gate flat, which was the top floor of two houses made into one, a dream of pale carpets, huge windows looking over little crooked roofs and full of sky, everything convenient and luxurious and taken care of by the daily, Mrs Connelly, including the plants and the unneutered cat, Rupert, who roamed his ginger way over the rooftops, raping and terrorising.

'Cheerio, Rupert,' I said to the battered cat, who lay stretched out on the pale carpet. He opened an eye at me and closed it again. I walked down the five flights to the bottom, my head filled with yearning for handsome Andy, and little did I realise, when I went into a bookshop on my way back to Henry Thackery House and spent my last five pounds on a new copy of Violet Levine's autobiography, *I Affirm*, exactly what I was letting myself in for.

TWO

Violet Crutchley, 1913
Kate Higgins, March 29th, 1991

My family, father, mother, three sisters and two brothers, was what could only be described as poor but honest. My father, a police constable, had joined the Metropolitan police as a young man. We lived in south London in that lower-middle-class atmosphere where it is of paramount importance to pay bills promptly and cleanliness is always considered to be next to godliness. I cannot describe my early life as either intellectually or culturally stimulating, but it instilled in me from an early age an ability to work hard and steadily at any task allotted to me, be it humble or elevated. I am convinced it was the patience of my mother, who brought up five children on very little money and died, I believe, mostly as a result of putting everyone else before herself, literally working herself to death, which inspired my strongest feelings of resentment against any system which can allow this to happen, taking the lives of such women very much for granted and indeed often holding them up to others as an example.

Picture me, then, one morning in 1913, in a park adjacent to my home, taking my younger brothers for a walk to keep them occupied while my mother was going through the exhausting annual ritual of spring cleaning. I think I was bending down to do up a little boy's shoelace, when I heard a voice say, 'I believe your other little charge is running towards the pond. You might allow me to go after him and bring him back.' I gratefully accepted this offer and soon observed the gentleman's lean, athletic figure in pursuit of the naughty boy. When he brought him back I regret to say that I forgot my mother's constant exhortations on the subject of the danger of talking to men whom I did not know in public places and, to cut a long story short, very soon Mr Frederick Levine, the kindly stranger who had been strolling in the park after attending to some properties he had in the neighbourhood, became a regular visitor at my family's little house in Ferndale Road . . .

I Affirm, Violet Levine, 1957

It was cold in the narrow iron-framed bed in which Violet Crutchley lay early one February morning in 1913. There were ten beds, containing ten young women, in the dormitory under the eaves of Hammonds of Kensington and hers was furthest from the door, hard up against the slightly flaking whitewash of the far wall, and five beds away from the softly glowing coke stove which stood against the opposite wall in the middle of the room. Nevertheless, Violet, lying there chilled with a plume of cold breath coming out of her mouth, was quite happy in the narrow bed she had all to herself and looking forward to the breakfast – porridge, bread, margarine and marmalade and strong cups of tea – she and the other twenty young women from the Hammonds dormitories would share in the chilly dining-room next door. In the meanwhile she lay with the faintest of early light coming through the frosty window above her head, listening to the clopping horses of early delivery vans, the squeak of cartwheels, someone walking along the pavement whistling a ragtime tune.

It was luxury for her, this narrow bed in the narrow, clean room. No more Norah in the bed with her, breathing heavily through her mouth, no screech from the battered alarm clock on the trunk next to the bed, urging her up on to a patch of holed linoleum, gritty underfoot, and down the two flights of frayed stair-carpet to the kitchen, where the remains of some snack meal would still be lying on the table. Then she would have to rake out the ashes from the bottom of the long black stove, opening the draught, taking the coal-scuttle out into the yard, a coat over her nightdress and her feet thrust into the pair of old boots of her father's which were kept in the scullery doorway. At this time of year an icy wind would be scouring the yard while she opened the bottom of the coal-bunker and thrust in the long, cylindrical hod, rattled it to fill it with coal, then carried it back to the kitchen to feed the stove. Then the ashes would have to go into a metal bucket and out into the yard, by the back door. Then she would take the big kettle from the top of the stove to the scullery tap, fill it with water and haul it back to put on the range to heat, for washing in the kitchen sink, and for the breakfast tea. After that she'd brush the polish from the row of boots and shoes standing on sheets of newspaper beside the range and then, in winter, stand huddled over the stove for warmth, or, in summer, go and stand in the back doorway, looking at the sky and the thin sycamore which struggled in a corner of the garden.

The next event would usually be the arrival of her sister Norah, thumping downstairs, usually in a temper, or else her mother, tired, in an old wrapper, hair straggling on her shoulders. Her mother would haul the heavy frying pan on to the range and start looking in the larder for eggs, bacon or sausages to fry for her father's breakfast. Then the younger ones – Alice, a tall fourteen-year-old, her blonde hair still in yesterday's frayed plaits, and Frank and Ben, twelve and seven, would arrive together. Soon the kitchen would be full of children asking where their clothes were, all trying to wash in the sink at once.

Violet stretched her thin body in its flannel nightdress. No cup of tea to be carried upstairs to Father, lying there with his big black moustache and red face on the pillow, no nasty pinch on the arm as she bent over him saying, 'Dad. Dad, breakfast is nearly ready. Time to get up.' No smell of stale beer or sweat either, for here she was in her own bed and soon they would all get up and wash properly in basins of heated water brought by a proper servant and put on the little chests of drawers opposite their beds. Then they would put on their black dresses and perhaps a drop of cologne, Quelques Fleurs or lavender, for those who could afford the luxury, and get their hair well pinned up with hairpins and tortoiseshell combs, the only adornment other than a neat white collar and cuffs, cotton or linen, *not* lace, permitted to the women who worked behind the superior mahogany counters at Hammonds. There'd be no rubbing behind dirty boys' ears, or having to listen to Father's complaints and Mother's excuses, or Norah borrowing her stockings because she hadn't mended her own, or her trying to go to school while her mother argued with her, saying she needed her at home today, because it was washday, because the stairs needed cleaning or the kitchen wanted a thoroughly good scrub. Norah had a job in a local shop and was bringing home wages, so she didn't have to help but she, Violet, being the next oldest girl, had always been expected to miss school to aid her mother in the ceaseless battle against grease, soot, dust and sweat. After she left school she had a job in a local grocer's. She'd hated cutting bacon and serving broken biscuits, and had to give it up anyway when her mother miscarried a baby.

It had been the best day of her life when she'd written to Hammonds asking if they wanted any young ladies for the store and gone off, without telling her parents, in her best coat and skirt for the interview. She was neat and tidy, good at figures and writing and she'd got the job on the spot. Her wages were half a guinea a week, and all found, and her parents, with the promise of half her wages and more room in the house, had been obliged to give in. Now, here she was with a nice, clean job as a young lady assistant in a smart London store. And today she even had a half day off, due to working all weekend at stocktaking. She could go over to see Tom Rawlinson and get him to take her to the Corner House for supper.

In fact, she thought, she might as well try to get Celia Hardwick, who had been feeling ill last night with her monthly pains, she said, to stay in bed for today and let her tell the floor manager that Celia had asked her to take over the gentlemen's glove counter until lunch-time. She'd done it once before and proved to be just forward enough to please customers without being too bold or too retiring. They needed a girl to make them feel comfortable and happy when they tried their gloves on, the gentlemen, and she, Violet, knew how to manage them. She felt more pleasure about the prospect of a day behind the glove counter, with all its opportunities for discreet flirtation and contact with real gentlemen than she did at the thought of the afternoon in Camberwell with Tom Rawlinson. What could he offer her but the usual scuffle in bed, which she knew gave him more fun than it did her, and then a tram-ride to the Strand and a poached egg before she had to return to Hammonds by ten at night? And she knew well where it all might lead – to marriage, children, the coal-bucket, the scrubbing board and the washtub, wet or fine, sick or well. Her mother's tired face, sagging figure and old clothes told the whole tale.

Anyway, here she was, with the day ahead. She jumped up, got her shoes from under the chest of drawers, clean underclothes from the top drawer and pattered to the bathroom. The water in the wash-jugs was warm when it came, but Violet fancied a good all-over wash today, even if the water in the bathroom would be cold. As she stood in the bath, throwing cold water over her shivering frame, there came the sound of heavy banging on the door.

'Let me in, miss, whoever you are. I've got to get the jugs and basins out of the cupboard.'

'In a minute. In a minute,' cried Violet, throwing more water over herself.

'I haven't got a minute,' wailed the young servant. 'I need them jugs now.'

'I'm coming,' said Violet, wrapping her towel round her cold body and getting out of the bath. She began to dry herself.

'Oh, please come out, miss, or unlock the door and let me in. I'll catch it if I'm late. Why couldn't you wait with the others? That water's stone-cold, anyway.'

'I'm just getting dressed,' said Violet irritably, pulling black lisle stockings over her shapely legs.

'Just open the door,' the girl said desperately.

'All in God's good time,' Violet called, tying the tape of her knee-length cotton drawers round her waist. Then she pulled on her chemise, with the real lace at the yoke and the bottom, put on her white petticoat and tied it, pushed her feet into her sturdy black shoes with two-inch heels, and unlocked the door.

The girl, in a black uniform and large white pinafore, her hair in a rough bun from which locks were escaping, looked at her furiously before pushing past her, saying, 'I'll remember you, mark my words.'

There was a furious clattering of enamel basins and jugs as Violet walked calmly back to the dormitory thinking, I can do that whenever I like and stopped in the doorway, adding to herself, I'm going to be a lady. She had little information about the world except what she was told or she read in sensational novels, full of dukes and servant girls, fires, abductions and stolen legacies, but she had a sense of what a lady was – a woman who wore silk in summer and fur in winter, whose shoes were made of good, soft leather, who rode in carriages and went to balls, who was waited on by servants, whose parcels were carried home by other people, whose hair was done by a maid, whose back was straight and voice clear, who was treated with respect and said 'please' and 'thank you' and 'if you don't mind' only if she felt like it. But however clean you kept your gloves, however often you mended your stockings, however much you protested about coarse subjects or language and the thickness of the crockery on which your meals were served, even if you knew your tables perfectly from two to twelve, could name all the parts of speech and all the capital cities of the world (and Violet did know all these things), the one great distinction between you and these privileged women was cash. They called it 'background' or 'breeding' or 'culture', but Violet, who had heard ladies in Hammonds swearing like market porters, seen them with the hems of their petticoats well below the level of their dresses and their hair all anyhow, on occasions, knew it was the money which made all the difference. She also knew instinctively that the passport to a better world was her looks and her wits and that the territory she wanted to enter was controlled by men.

Later, clean and tidy, she stood by the immaculate counter, beside the brass stand showing a selection of men's gloves, and assessed herself. She was small, slender, with a head of thick, glossy hair, slightly wavy, large hazel eyes, which sometimes looked a very dark blue, a small pink mouth and an ivory skin. She had a tiny waist, small well-shaped hands and feet, slender wrists and ankles. Her hands had improved a great deal since she had left the grates and the washtub behind. They were soft and white and she rubbed cream into them every evening. Her feet, she knew, would soon be ruined, like the feet of her mother and her friends as they sat easing them in basins of hot water, revealing lumps, callouses, corns and bunions, all, like medals, proof of valiant shopping and carrying heavy burdens in ill-fitting shoes.

Her own shoes were hard and painful. Still, happily the fashion for tall, curved, lush high-coloured blonde women was going, as had the fashion for bustled dresses, stressing bosom and hips.

The woman of 1913, as Violet read in magazines, was active and well-informed, a true companion and helpmeet to her husband. Violet was sceptical about this, knowing that gentlemen still showed a preference for young women like Celia Hardwick, golden-haired, curvaceous, flirtatious and about as well-informed, Violet reflected, as the mahogany counter in front of her.

The first customers were beginning to filter through the big doors. Many were maids in plain coats and hats and thick stockings, obviously sent to purchase items for their employers, but among them were a few well-dressed women in fur coats, men in black overcoats and bowler-hats. That was the trouble with Hammonds, thought Violet, you saw too many of the better sort in front of the counter. The next thing was you thought you were like them, or could be. It wasn't as easy as that.

'Miss Crutchley,' came Henry Gummidge's voice behind her, 'would you go down to the stock-room and get half a dozen gentlemen's gloves in white cotton, in sizes seven and a half and eight.'

'None down there, sir, I'm afraid,' Violet replied promptly. 'Only one pair of cream, size eight, slightly marked, sir.'

'Can it be possible? Go down and talk to Miss Abrahams and tell her I must have them.'

'I already did, sir, when we were stocktaking,' Violet told him. 'She says they were ordered from Purvis's in Manchester last week, but they haven't arrived yet.'

Gummidge, an anxious man, gave her a piercing look. 'I'll go down there and look myself,' he said. 'But woe betide you if you've sent me there on a fool's errand.'

After he had gone a tall, dark man in a black overcoat, carrying a bowler-hat, came up and leaned over the counter.

'Can I assist you, sir?' asked Violet. She looked into large dark eyes.

'I need some cotton gloves, white ones. I think it's size eight. For some reason mine appear to have been destroyed at the laundry.'

'How unfortunate,' murmured Violet. 'If you'd be good enough to give me your hand I'll assure myself of the size.'

Straightening up, he gave her his hand and while she was bent over the brass measure, checking the size, he gazed down on her glossy head. Violet prolonged the contact a little, for he was a good-looking man and not very old, perhaps in his mid-twenties, then said, 'Size eight it is, sir. We're just bringing up stocks of those particular gloves— '

'Oh, good Lord,' he said, 'you'd think a place this size could produce a pair of perfectly normal gloves straight away. I haven't got time to wait about.'

'I can have them sent round . . . ' said Violet.

'Very good,' he said. 'Make it three pairs. Levine, Cavendish Square. You'll have the details – but I must have them for tonight.'

'We'll have them before three, sir,' Violet assured him.

He smiled, thinking her a very pretty girl, and quick, too. 'Good. Then I'll be off – thank you.'

Violet sighed when he had gone. Lovely eyes, even if he did look a bit weak about the mouth. Hand-made shoes, too. Cavendish Square.

'Dreaming, Miss Crutchley?' came Henry Gummidge's voice as he came up to her.

'No, sir,' she said. 'A customer came in for gloves and I offered to deliver them.'

'What?' he said. 'Really, Miss Crutchley – are you a delivery girl now?'

'It was a Mr Levine from Cavendish Square,' she told him. 'He came in for those very white cotton gloves, size eight. I told him we'd make sure he got them. I thought it best, sir, even if we have to get them from elsewhere.'

Henry Gummidge puffed irritably and turned to Violet. 'If you noticed while stocktaking that there were insufficient cotton gloves, Miss Crutchley,' he told her, 'I would have appreciated it if you could have pointed it out to me. A certain amount of initiative is expected of Hammonds staff.'

Violet saw that it would be pointless to mention that at the time she had been employed in another department. She said, 'Yes, Mr Gummidge.'

'As to the other matter. You'd better purchase Mr Levine's gloves at Finnegan's during your dinner-break. I'll get them there in the afternoon.'

'I'll take them,' Violet offered. 'It's my afternoon off.'

'Afternoon off,' complained Gummidge. 'How I'm supposed to manage I do not know. And while we're on the subject, are there any further catastrophes you have to report?'

'The drawers on the left-hand side of the counter are sticking. I think there's a screw loose in the casing,' reported Violet. 'And we'll shortly be out of small driving gloves. There are only three pairs left.'

'Thank you, Miss Crutchley,' said Gummidge and walked off to inspect the collar counter.

Violet sulked. Henry Gummidge walked about like a king. If anything went all right he got all the credit. It wasn't as if she couldn't do his job standing on her head but it would go to young Mr Bradley or someone, not her, ever, because she was a woman. Too much cleverness, and she'd wind up being watched like a hawk, in case she'd found a cunning way of getting money out of the till without being detected or otherwise taking advantage of the situation. Keep your eyes to yourself and keep your place, that was the motto, thought Violet, looking at Henry Gummidge's back as he made the black-coated assistant on the collar counter check through the drawers while he watched. Still, she had the afternoon off, and after dinner she'd get a chance to look into one of those big houses round Cavendish Square when she delivered the gloves.

By two she was walking up the marble steps, with her little brown parcel of gloves swinging from a string from her finger. She stood under the portico and rang the brass bell. She had only a brief glimpse of a huge marble-tiled hall, with a big white marble fireplace in it, a great sweep of stairs and many pictures on the wall before the fat, pale butler sent her down to the basement, to the servants' entrance.

'Beg your pardon, I'm sure,' Violet said mockingly, before turning round and skipping down the steps. Above her old long black coat she was wearing a new red tam o'shanter which cheered her up.

Even the servants' entrance had a brass door-knocker, she

observed, as she banged on it. Above her, beyond the railings, people's feet went to and fro. A hoop bowled along, followed by a pair of small boots. A girl in a white cap and apron answered the door. 'Yes? What do you want?' she asked.

'I'd better come in,' Violet said. 'It's important.' And she walked forward into the long kitchen about the size of the whole ground floor of her family's house in south London. Twelve servants sat round a table big enough for twenty, enjoying an after-dinner cup of tea. There was the remains of a vast apple pie on the table, and a big jug which must have custard in it. On the wall behind the table a huge range burned brightly. If this was how the servants lived, Violet thought, God knows what kind of luxury their employers had upstairs.

A parlourmaid in a black dress and small, frilly apron stood up and went across to Violet saying, in no friendly way, 'Yes? What do you want?'

Violet knew herself to be the daughter of a police constable, and one who owned his own house. He'd bought it when he married on the strength of a legacy from an uncle. Violet, daughter of a respectable guardian of the law and ratepayer, looked haughtily at the girl and said, 'I've come with an urgent delivery for Mr Levine.'

'Oh,' said the girl in her starched cap and apron. 'And what might this important delivery be?'

'Gloves,' Violet said with authority.

'Oh, my goodness,' said the girl. 'This isn't just a message from the bank in Vienna or a few diamonds from Hatton Garden. This is a pair of gloves, is it? Now I can see why you had to push in here and disturb us at our dinner.'

'Mr Levine seemed to think this morning it was quite important to have a couple of pairs of gloves for a ball this evening,' remarked Violet. 'Unless you want your guv'nor to get a reputation for putting his sweaty hands all over nice young ladies' backs, which I'm sure you don't, what with this being a respectable and well-conducted household. These things can make or break a young man, as you know. So, if you don't mind, I'd like to put this parcel into reliable hands and be on my way. I've other things to do.'

'I'll take it,' said the girl.

Violet considered, then said, 'All right. Don't drop it in the custard.'

She had gained the sympathy of the table, from the housekeeper at the top, in a black dress, to the very small girl in a striped dress and tight white collar at the bottom, trying not to grin. She'd cheered them all up on a stuffy February afternoon. She added, 'I hope you'll make sure Mr Levine is given these gloves. We don't require any inefficiency or muddling in this matter.'

The girl seized the parcel.

Violet remarked, 'Thank you, I'm much obliged. Good afternoon to you all,' turned on her heel and left.

Following her to the door the girl said, 'Next time Hammonds has a parcel to deliver we'd appreciate it if they sent a proper messenger.'

'Don't bank on it,' said Violet. 'I may be back,' and skipped up the basement steps as the door slammed behind her.

Silly chit, thought Violet to herself as she tripped along the pavement, her ankles, even in the horrible shoes, drawing some attention from passing gentlemen in top-hats, and two workmen in caps, carrying a ladder between them. That maid was a fool to bandy words with her, Violet Crutchley, who had more words in her than the dictionary. 'Your tongue will hang you,' her mother used to declare after their verbal battles, in which Violet always came off best. When Violet lost her terrifying temper she changed this to 'Your temper will hang you.'

Violet caught a bus, then changed for a tram which would take her to Camberwell. As it rattled and bumped along the sunshine changed to cloud and the streets suddenly became dark. Perhaps she shouldn't keep on giving way to him, Tom Rawlinson, Violet thought, but if she didn't he sulked and nagged and if she did he was nice to her afterwards, and tried to please her. The trouble was, he was used to having his way with her, a bit like a dog, Violet thought, used to getting its dinner from the same plate at the same time.

Kate Higgins, March 29th, 1991

Happily these days we are less snobbish; there are fewer discrepancies between wealth and poverty than existed in those days. For much of this new spirit in Britain we have to thank the activities of the post-war Labour government, which I was privileged to serve. We live in much more democratic times now, but when I married Frederick Levine the social distinctions were like so many huge fortifications, heavily guarded and impossible to breach. It was not only a matter of a financial discrepancy between the classes, although that had a strong bearing on the matter, but that the members of each class, by education, by tradition, by upbringing, were as strange to each other as so many different tribes, each with their differing cultures, all living within the boundaries of one country.

I Affirm, Violet Levine, 1957

Well, what would you say to it all now, Violet, I thought, reading *I Affirm* lying on my bed at eleven thirty in the morning.

The flat was on the second floor of the four-storeyed Henry Thackery House, next door to a row of substantial Victorian buildings also mostly split up. Henry Thackery House reached to the corner, occupying the space where three or four houses, bombed in the last war, must have stood. All I could see, lying down and looking through the slightly steamed-up steel-framed windows was some pale blue, early spring sky, the church spire and the tops of some trees which lay behind the high wall of the school opposite. All I could hear from my room was the faint roar of traffic along the main road a hundred yards away. There was a tree on the pavement outside the flats. Di kept an old banger in the street and lay under it a lot of the time.

I'd been re-reading the book since nine, making notes. Having to read it now drew my attention to the elusive quality of some parts. So many episodes, when you looked closely, appeared almost surreal. One minute, so to speak, we were in the park with the youthful Violet, the next, she was married. Six months later, a mother. No real comment, for example, about what it must have been like for a policeman's daughter to find herself part of a rich Anglo-Jewish family before the First World War. How had she got on? Had they accepted her arrival without any demur? Then, her second marriage took place all of a sudden – no explanations of where, when, why or how. There were times when all seemed vivid, like her account of her nursing in France. She was lively on her part in the post-war parliament. At other points a series of flat statements or, where other people were concerned, fulsome clichés gave the impression that Violet, in some manner, had been separated from her own story. It may have been partly how she wrote – her literary style had always been awkward and by 1957, when she was sixty, it seemed to have stiffened into old age. Yet rumour had it, she'd been a lively and sought-after public speaker. The House of Commons had filled to hear her in the forties, and it wasn't just to look at her legendary hats, subject of so many cartoons and radio jokes. She'd been good on a soapbox, platform or debating chamber, a strong speaker at the factory gates of her northern constituency, a spellbinder in draughty halls, ready-witted in working men's clubs. I guessed that the blanks were where I'd have to concentrate, to find my story.

I'd had enough of Violet's autobiography after two hours and stopped reading to stare round the room, my narrow bed with the white, bobbled counterpane and the pink stippled walls. The beige curtains hung there depressingly. Hadn't I been a keen cook, interior decorator, upholsterer and gardener once? I wasn't these days. Now I was a mystery to myself.

I made a Nescafé in the kitchen and moved into the living-room to think and escape Violet's remorseless voice. Di had seen to all this: there was a good mirror on the mantelpiece in a carved frame she had picked up somewhere, and some plants in brass pots, some oriental fabrics over the two, slightly battered sofas. I began to feel depressed. How had all this happened? I was in my mid-thirties and I didn't seem to have anything, not even a lamp. It must be my fault.

Down in Brighton my son Ray, now ten, conceived in Aldershot and born in Berlin and deprived of his father in Belfast, two years ago, when I left on the morning ferry with three suitcases, was going back to the classroom after break. My mother, meanwhile, in boots, overcoat and scarf was probably starting off some seedlings in the greenhouse or coming back from the shops with the dog, and a few chops for the family supper. She and my father took it for granted that I was here in London, while Ray stayed with them. They'd missed a lot of his childhood because his father and I spent so much time posted overseas. I think they were also more anxious about me, and my future, keen to help, but unable to see why I didn't train as a teacher, which they both were. Then I could get a job in Brighton. I felt I ought to, but I didn't like teaching and wasn't any good at it. 'There are enough teachers in the world, only in it for the short hours and because it fits in with the children's holidays,' I told my father, rather speciously. He'd only just retired as head of the modern languages department of a comprehensive (what was left of it, as his classrooms had been slowly filled with computers few knew how to handle, or teach, properly) so he could hardly quarrel with me over that. Nor could my mother, who'd been a primary school teacher all her life until the school had been shut down a few years ago. They'd both seen enough poor teaching to last them the rest of their lives.

The truth was that I didn't want, at my age, to live with them, or do a job I didn't like. Well, Violet seemed to have pulled off two happy marriages (she said), three children and a successful career, so why not me? Armies of servants had helped a lot, of course, but even they couldn't do everything. It was hard work, motivation, resolution and excellent health, I suspected, that had really pulled her through. And of the four I suspected I only had one – good health. Then, suddenly, as if the defence counsel in my brain had suddenly sprung to his feet during a particularly rough cross-examination by the prosecution I remembered – in extenuation, m'lud – why I was here now.

I recalled sitting by the window in the army house in Belfast, in a quiet, tree-lined little street of suburban houses with clean curtains at every window and an armoured truck parked at each end, there to guard the women and children the Ministry of Defence dearly wished had stayed behind on the mainland. The rain. Small rooms with regular army embossed cream/pale green/pale blue/pale pink wallpaper. Kissed goodbye in the morning by a husband going off to work in khaki and a child going off to school in a jeep full of children, two soldiers with rifles hanging on the sides of the vehicle. I was acting out, for Sam, my husband, Ray, my son, and the British army, the part of a suburban housewife, while off the set there was a war going on. I had to go on, I was part of the *matériel*, that great weapon as important as bombers and weapons, army morale.

As time went on I felt less and less able to understand anything, there, only a couple of hundred miles from Manchester, hardly any further to London, where the enemy looked the same as us, spoke the same language, were living in their own homes five miles away. I began to feel like part of an army of occupation. There were times, shopping in Belfast with my credit card, having come easily through the barriers manned by soldiers with machine-guns while others were having their cars searched, when I realised I hadn't the stomach for being a consort of a colonial army, or an army holding down a foreign city. I wished I'd had nursing qualifications instead of a history degree – perhaps that way I'd have found something useful to do. And all the time I was afraid for all of us and at the same time desperately bored. I'll never forget that little road, Wellingford Avenue.

'Ulster will fight and Ulster will be right,' they used to say in Violet's day, before the First World War, when the army was on the verge of mutiny since they were about to be ordered to shoot civilians – Protestants this time – when they rebelled against Home Rule. Nothing was right then, and almost eighty years later it still wasn't. My life was greeting my husband in the early hours of the morning, knowing some other woman might still be trying to get her children back to sleep, pick her broken ornaments off the floor, perhaps wedge shut a kicked-in door. Sam's life was coming home having seen inside her kitchen cupboard and her wardrobe, and not having known, when he flung open her doors, whether he would be faced by a man in a crouch, with a machine-gun, an old grandmother in bed, or a teenage girl starting up, screaming, with the blankets clutched to her chest. I could talk about it to him. He was doing his duty, it was necessary, but it wasn't a burning crusade for him, how could it be?

Practically the last thing I remember before leaving was watching a soldier who was, in turn, watching some other soldiers searching a bus. He stood with his rifle in the rain. His great-great-grandfather might have been African, his great-grandfather was probably Caribbean, also his grandfather, but his father lived in Coventry, or Cardiff, or London and for all I knew his mother or his mother's mother might have been Irish, also from Coventry, Cardiff or London. Now he was here in khaki searching an Irish bus on behalf of the British government. It says a lot for the human race that it can face these contradictions and still get to the disco or the film show, but I couldn't take the last days of empire any more, and not a week later added myself to the statistics of army marriages, failed, Northern Ireland Division.

It wasn't just Ireland, of course, or the army. I'd married at twenty-four because I met a handsome and lively young man. I'd had a child at twenty-five, written my books a few years later and saw my husband become a solid and conscientious soldier but, even so, if the army hadn't been turning him into a model officer and been trying to turn me into a model officer's wife, it was quite likely his company, whichever it was, would have been turning him into a solid company man and me into his reliable consort. Sam had to keep us so he had to change. On a day-to-day basis I could have managed, but I saw the next twenty years and I despaired.

So Ray and I battled across the Irish Channel like any immigrants, leaving behind husband and father risking his life for his country and actually, as I drank my Nescafé, and lit a Silk Cut from a packet of ten at Thackery House, I suddenly felt better. Even if I was a flop, I was a flop with possibilities. I was not backing one of Her Majesty's officers as he went about his duties, not fearing death for all of us, not bringing up a child whose Daddy came home in an armoured car in case someone else's Daddy shot him, who went to school in a tank, as he now described it to his friends at school.

Well, they hadn't managed to keep Violet Levine at home during two world wars, I thought. She'd been forty miles from the trenches of northern France by Christmas 1915, wearing a nurse's hat which hung down behind, a skirt barely above the ground, thick black stockings and boots, cutting bloodstained tunics and trousers off wounded soldiers, unwinding puttees stained with mud and blood, holding a hurricane lamp up high when the power failed so that the surgeons could ram back in intestines, sew up abdomens and amputate limbs at lightning speed. She'd left a two-year-old daughter behind her. What she'd done, again in northern France, in 1942 and 1943, in her late forties, was not quite clear in *I Affirm*. My letter to the Ministry of Defence, asking for access to information giving the details, was obviously still in someone's pending tray. But plainly she'd delivered some messages, organised some escapes across the Channel and had, at one point, fallen into the hands of the Germans and talked her way out of it. But as I mentally congratulated her for boldness, I had the nasty idea, suddenly, that this quest for Violet Levine was going to take me down some dark alleys where things were waiting to spring out at me. As I was about to leave the flat for the British Library to check on Violet's published work, the phone rang.

'They tell me you're writing Violet Levine's biography,' a high, slightly cracked voice said, without preamble. 'I wonder if I could have a word in your ear, my dear.'

'Yes, of course.' I couldn't tell, from the timbre of the voice, whether it was a man or a woman. It was not a young voice, nor did it seem to belong to anyone very old.

'She was a dreadful woman,' said the voice, confidently. 'But perhaps you haven't got to the stage of noticing that, yet?'

'I haven't got very far. But there are some mysteries— '

'Nothing but, my dear. Nothing but, where Violet's concerned. You're reading what she wrote, but what happened and what Violet wrote about it are often two very different things.'

'I see.' Then, like a well-behaved dog out for a walk when it suddenly smells a rabbit, I became keen. Of course, I was meant to. 'Then, what do you suggest I concentrate on?'

'I don't want you to start smearing Violet.'

Stung, I replied, 'That's not my intention at all. I only want to get at the truth.'

The person at the other end gave a little laugh. 'Very

commendable. But of course there are many ways of dealing with the truth. What do you suppose your approach will be?'

I didn't like the turn the conversation was taking. I might easily be dealing with a lunatic, and a lunatic who had my telephone number, which he or she could not have found in the directory as it was in the book under Di's name, not mine.

I replied, 'I don't know – it's early days. My approach will have to be dictated by the information. By the way, may I ask who you are?'

I might not have spoken. The voice said, 'Well, you're obviously young and intelligent and I'm sure you'll make an absolutely splendid job of it. It's a big opportunity for you. Well, to cases, to cases – so, where to begin?'

'I'm hoping to talk to Violet's children, and, of course, ask if they have any photographs or letters— '

'I'll be very surprised if they see you,' said the caller. 'They don't want this to happen, I can assure you of that.'

'Why not?'

'Too much to hide. To begin with, Pamela, the eldest, is not Frederick Levine's child.'

'What?' I said. 'Does she know?'

As if I hadn't spoken the voice said, 'The infant Pamela, born in November, Frederick Levine and Violet having first slept together in April, weighed in at almost seven pounds – very large for a premature baby. You have a child?' the voice enquired. It was chilling, because, I realised, the usual enquiry is 'Have you got any children?' Did this person actually know I had a child, one child, Ray?

'Yes. A boy of ten,' I answered. 'Who was the father of the child then?'

'He was nobody. He died in the first war. It was the same old story – an unmarried girl expecting a baby . . . '

'And who are you?' I asked again, hoping to catch him/her off guard.

It didn't work. The voice went on coolly, 'I should talk to Rose Johnson about her career in the Labour Party. And I believe that you might manage to get Jack Christian-Smith, Violet's grandson, to talk to you. None of the others will, not even his twin sister.'

'What are they hiding?' I asked.

There was a peculiar laugh. 'A lot. Some of it nasty. It's high time an eye was cast on the myth of Violet Levine. Perhaps it's more important now – there are many aspects of her life I think might bear examination, which I won't mention now. I'll ring again if anything occurs to me, with your permission . . .'

'I'd be very grateful,' I said. 'Naturally, anything you can tell me— '

'Well, there we are then,' the voice said comfortably. In the distance I heard another voice saying something at a distance. 'Goodness, is that the time?' replied my informant, then, to me, 'I must go. So nice talking to you. I'm sure you'll make a wonderful job of Violet's life story. My best wishes are with you. Goodbye.'

'Goodbye,' I replied, stunned, wanting to shout, 'Wait a minute, there's something else— '

'Until we speak again,' the voice said warmly, and the receiver began to purr next to my ear. I stood and stared at it, as if it were a poisonous snake. It was a shock to think there might be a lot to uncover about Violet Levine – more than I thought, and some of it nasty. It was a shock to think I might get no co-operation at all from the Levines, not one interview, family photograph, old letter. I wondered if the business wasn't going to be more difficult than I'd thought, optimistically, at the start.

Certainly the mysterious caller had been in charge of the conversation. I hadn't stood a chance. But who was it – and why? It seemed fairly certain that the person knew something, probably quite a lot about Violet. But was I being put on a false trail or set on the right one? And if the latter, why wouldn't the caller declare him or herself and just see me in the normal way?

I rang Roger Littlebrown at Askew and Askew's to ask if anyone had been on to him about the book. He said no. Then had, I asked, anyone phoned for my telephone number? Not, he said, as far as he knew. Had he announced the coming book anywhere? No, he said. I told him about the caller.

He said seriously, 'I should be careful. It could be a hoaxer.

Someone trying to lead you up the garden path.' But he couldn't guess why. 'Any news of Andy?' he asked.

I told him I hadn't heard anything.

'Ah well,' he said, 'he's a busy lad.'

I put the phone down, thinking that the last thing I needed for my brilliant career was to be having an unsuccessful love affair with my publisher's cousin. Men like Roger are still back in the Dark Ages, where a woman's either protected by a man another man respects, or fair game. And being disrespectfully treated by her protector also makes her fair game. Not that Roger would make passes at me. He'd just assume I was weak, too weak, to get away from Andy or make him behave, and that would affect his attitude to me. If I'd been an unknown man he'd probably have announced he was publishing a brand new biography, the first ever, of Violet Levine. But not if I was his cousin's bit of stuff, over whom this fascinating relation was riding roughshod. 'Get out, now,' I advised myself when the phone rang and it was the fascinating relation himself, Andy, saying he'd missed me in Ho Chi Minh City and was now missing me in Thailand. He'd be back in two days and we must meet on Thursday when he'd come round to collect me at eight. But since it was Monday I had to assume he'd be elsewhere on Wednesday, probably with my rival, Vanessa Hume. Dave Gottlieb, editor of *The Mag* told me her bills tended to be paid by the man who owned the big chains of foodstores where nearly all of us paid our money, or foodstamps, for our groceries. He said – and goodness knows how a man in a woolly hat on a bike managed to keep in touch with what was happening in palaces and pigsties alike – that in spite of lovely Vanessa's blonde streaks and permanent holiday tan, all funded by Sir Harold Treblesave and his special offers on past-selling-date commodities (no liability) – Vanessa only wanted Andy. So I was back on the old bone-shaker of love again and pedalling myself furiously towards the cliff.

Now I was standing in Di's flat, shaking like a leaf because I'd had a funny phone call from a stranger and another one from a returning lover. I pulled myself together though, and managed to get to St Catherine's House at lunch-time, competed there with a horde of people trying to find their roots or prove their immigration status and ordered as many Levine and Crutchley birth certificates as I could fight for. Afterwards I soldiered through sleet to the British Library, to collect the books I'd ordered and spend the afternoon, like a good student, in the library.

Violet Crutchley, 1913

Violet peered up at the misty gas mantle as Tom Rawlinson pumped away. Second time, she thought, with no pleasure, and she hoped he'd finish soon. It must be eight o'clock by now. She had to be back at Hammonds by ten and if this went on there'd be no time for a light supper and a cup of tea at the Corner House.

Raising himself on his hands Tom looked down at her out of big blue eyes in a reddened face and said, 'Oh, Violet. I love you so much.'

'I love you too, Tom,' she said, but it was not true. She liked him, always had, since they'd been to school together, but it wouldn't do for her, this place in Camberwell with the landlady cooking kippers downstairs for her husband's tea, as anyone across the street could tell, and Tom's job as a postman – who'd want to be a postman's wife? – and Tom's aspiration to be a music-hall star. So far he'd only been bottom of the bill at the Brixton Empire and the Clapham Empire. At the Clapham Empire he'd come on after a boy of fourteen who did bird imitations. Tom Rawlinson, the Singing Postman, following a kid and a woman doing tricks with an old seal, then – nothing. He wasn't going to succeed on the halls, Violet knew it. His voice wasn't strong enough and his songs weren't funny enough, and comics like George Robey could make you laugh just by standing there, raising their eyebrows, or their little finger. ('Shall I wait for you, Violet, dear?' asked Tom. 'No, Tom dear, don't trouble.') She lay there as he heaved up and down, the words of his own song going oddly through her head:

Well, I am the singing postman –
Tra la, tra la, tra la,
And I wouldn't want to boast ma'am –
Tra la, tra la, tra la,
But the ladies they all wait for me as I go up the street
And a little cup of tea and a little slice of cake
    are always quite a treat.
Oh dear, I don't want to go too far
But the ladies they all wait for me
To go tra la la la la.

'Be careful, Tom,' she whispered and, as he reached his climax she lay poised, ready to twist away like an eel if he showed signs of losing control and releasing his seed into her. This time he withdrew in time and lay on her now, saying, 'Violet. I love you so.'

'I love you too, Tom, but you're far too heavy for poor little me,' said Violet and he rolled off and buried his face in her hair. Violet stared up at the ceiling.

'Violet,' he whispered. She knew what he would say. 'Violet, dear Violet, come on – say you'll make me a happy man.'

'I would, Tom. I would.' Violet told him, mingling truth with falsehood as she normally did. 'But I'm oh so frightened of finishing up like my poor Mum.'

'We could manage, Violet,' Tom said. 'With my wages and what I can get on the stage. And I've got getting on for a hundred and fifty pounds put by. It's a steady job and with any luck I'll give it up one day and go full time into the profession. And, come to that, your Mum's life's not so terrible. She's got a home and kids and it won't be too long before you're all grown up, and bringing something in. Your Dad's in a good job— '

'That's what you say,' said Violet. 'She's not happy. She really isn't. She cries a lot,' she added untruthfully. 'I grew up with my mother's sobs in my ears. She got married at eighteen and then it was us, and Father and the house . . . ' Her voice trailed off. Tom wasn't interested. Why should he be? 'Fire needs more coal,' she said. 'I'll put some on.' Tom groaned when she left him, but she threw her coat over her naked body and went to the fireplace and put on more coal. She turned up the gas and thought of the women she knew who had not married. Miss Phibbs, the corsetière at Hammonds, who lived with her mother in Ealing and talked about her customers as if they were her own family. Poor old Phibbsy, thought Violet, in love with the Baptist clergyman, the one with the blond hair at the church she went to every Sunday, and otherwise only thinking what to give her mother for supper when she got home. Miss Phibbs in corsets, Miss Wallace in ladies' tailoring and Miss Reilly in linens, who'd been jilted by a bank manager and still slept in the linen sheets she'd bought for her trousseau – everyone pitied them for the lives they led. It was all right being single if you were on the stage. You could have plenty of gentlemen friends and no husbands or babies and no one cared. But for ordinary girls marriage was the best they could do.

Tom, watching Violet in the gaslight, said, 'Come on, Vi. Be a sport. You'll regret it if you don't. I'll make you ever so happy. Come back to bed for a minute and I'll show you.'

Violet, smoothing his hot forehead by the bed told him, 'Tom, I've got to get back.'

'Tell 'em to put the job where the monkey put the nuts,' he said. 'Look at this. I'm bursting.' He guided her hand to his erect penis. 'I can't get enough of you, and that's a fact. Stay here tonight. We'll tell the landlady in the morning we're getting married and she can make the best of it. You can tell Hammonds you're not coming back.'

But Violet just wanted to get away, into a nice café, back to her narrow bed. 'Oh, Tom,' she said, 'I've got to go. I haven't had anything to eat since dinner-time and I'm feeling ever so faint.'

'Oh, all right, Vi,' he said, getting out of bed. 'Corner House is it?'

'Oh, yes,' she said. 'You're ever so good to me.'

Soon they were sitting squeezed together on top of the tram going through narrow streets where smoke came from all the chimneys of small houses and gas lamps glowed through the smoky air, and shone down on women taking their children home to bed through chilly streets. Men were coming home late from work and clusters of youths, their breath coming in clouds out of their mouths, were talking and laughing round the lampposts, stamping their boots and shaking their fingers to keep warm. Then the lights grew brighter and more frequent and the streets wider as they entered the centre of London. There were couples in cars, in evening dress, going to the theatre. There were two Guardsmen in red coats on high-stepping horses. Men were strolling to their clubs, brightly dressed women went confidently up to men on their own, addressing them as if they were friends, moving on when rejected.

There were crowds of people, going to the cinema, going to dances, going to parties – Violet felt excluded, somehow, sitting there beside Tom. If he ever made a name for himself on the halls then she would be part of a world where women wore silks and crêpe, lawn and muslin, had expensive scent, rouged their lips and had jewellery to make them glow, and men in evening dress bent over them caressing their shoulders, whispering in their ears . . . But he wouldn't make a name for himself, Violet thought disconsolately, never in a million years. What he was offering was the job of a postman's wife, serge in winter, cotton in summer, a sewing machine to make her own and the children's clothes; if she was lucky, a life of what they liked to call honest toil. She turned to Tom, kissed him on the cheek and said, 'It's ever so nice of you to take me out like this,' but as she spoke she thought of going to the races in a big car, with a hamper at the back, going to plays every week, wearing silk stockings on her legs, kid pumps on her lively little feet. She wanted music, lights and laughter. She was only sixteen and if she married Tom now she could kiss the world goodbye. In any case, she thought, she didn't love him. Not that love, in real life, seemed to help a woman much, unless she was lucky enough to fall in love in the right direction. Still, she wished she was in love. For the moment, though, she just wished for a poached egg and a cup of tea and her bed at Hammonds.

But at four in the morning she was still lying awake, deeply frightened. The only person in the room when she'd come in at a quarter to ten had been Celia Hardwick, sitting on the edge of her tightly made bed at the other end of the room from Violet's. Violet remembered the others had gone off to see

Irene Vanbrugh in a new play by J. M. Barrie, followed by the Russian ballet. It had been organised by one of the directors of the firm, who wanted to expand the minds of his young ladies. Violet, who would have preferred *Everybody's Doing it!* or George Formby playing the ukelele at the London Pavilion or even the film of Captain Scott's expedition, had cried off. So while all the others were watching Irene Vanbrugh, Violet and Celia were alone in the long, echoing top floor of Hammonds.

The beds were all made, sheets tidily tucked in, blankets tucked in afterwards, washing bowls all neatly in the centre of the chests of drawers opposite the beds. Violet stood by the stove in the middle of the room, warming her hands, turning round to warm her behind. Celia sat still on the edge of her bed. 'Hello, Celia! Cat got your tongue?' Violet cried cheerily. She was nettled that Celia hadn't greeted her when she came in.

Celia looked at her and simply said, 'He's down in the country with his people. I waited for ages. Then I rang the house. He must have forgotten to tell me.'

'You don't half look pale,' Violet told her. 'Is it still the curse?'

'Not that,' Celia said.

'What then?' asked Violet. 'You ill? Shall I see if Mrs Henderson's about? I can't remember if she went with the others.'

'That's the last thing,' said Celia.

'I should get into bed, then,' said Violet, briskly taking out *The Heart's Awakening* and beginning to read. The mansion containing Sir Edward's will leaving everything to the orphan Cynthia, and Cynthia's little boy, Hereward, had just been ignited by Sir Edward's cousin, Roland Devereux, who, if the will were destroyed, would inherit everything. Cynthia had plunged into the flames to save her child. By the time Cynthia had rescued the child but Roland Devereux had turned her out into the wild night, Violet looked up, having heard a sound. Celia was still sitting on her bed, but was doubled over now, seemingly in pain. Her black-stockinged legs were sprawled out at an ungainly angle. Her piled-up golden hair was falling down over the shoulders of her lavender dress. Violet tucked a piece of paper into her book, closed it, stuffed it under her pillow and went over to her.

'Here, are you all right, Celia?' she asked.

'Can't stand up,' muttered Celia. 'There's blood all over the back of my skirt. And the bed,' she added.

'What's going on?' asked Violet. 'I thought you said . . . Oh,' she said, understanding. 'You've gone and done something to yourself, haven't you? I'm going to get Mrs Henderson.'

'No. No,' said Celia.

'I'll have to,' declared Violet quickly. She didn't want to get involved. It was too dangerous.

'Don't call Mrs Henderson,' pleaded Celia. 'It'll be all right.'

'Don't look like it,' said Violet. 'What's been happening anyway?'

'He drove me to the doctor in his carriage this morning. In Kilburn. He's got to announce his engagement on Monday. He's in debt and his fiancée's got money. There was no other way— ' She winced. 'Christ, this hurts. That doctor never told me. He said it'd be all over by tonight.' She paused. 'But he said he'd meet me in Trafalgar Square at eight o'clock and I waited there ever so long. It was ever so cold. Then when I phoned the house, which he doesn't like me to do, the maid said they'd all gone to the country.' She paused again. 'He's not his own master, now, I suppose.'

'Well, what did this doctor do?' asked Violet.

'What do you think? Got rid of the kid, of course. He has to marry. He can't afford any doubt to be cast on him until the ceremony's over. Now I'm bleeding – I don't know what to do.'

'Well, whatever it is, you can't do it here,' declared Violet.

Doubled over again Celia gasped, 'God, you're a hard bitch, Violet.'

'I didn't ask for all this,' Violet pointed out. 'I came back here after a quiet evening with my gentleman friend and what do I find? You here, looking ready to die.'

'He had to do it,' Celia said. 'It could have ruined his engagement.'

'Pity he's not here now, then, isn't it?' remarked Violet, standing up. 'I've had enough of this. I'm going to find somebody.'

'Think of something else, Violet,' Celia said. 'Help me. You could help me to the hospital in a cab— '

'What? And get arrested for procuring abortions?' said Violet angrily. 'Oh no.'

Celia's head dropped again as a spasm of pain struck her and when she raised it again she saw Violet, in stockinged feet, going out.

Within moments Mrs Henderson, a bulky woman in black silk, was back with Violet. To emphasise her innocence of such matters Violet had told the housekeeper a confusing story, with enough detail to lead her to the truth. 'She says she's been to a doctor. A gentleman friend took her in his carriage. Now she's in pain, and ever so frightened,' Violet had reported, which was enough to get the housekeeper, who had been writing to her niece on a desk in her cosy room, up from her chair in an instant.

'Silly girl. Silly girl,' said Mrs Henderson, kneeling beside Celia. She looked up at Violet, standing in confusion at the end of the bed. 'Violet! Run straight out and find a cab!'

'All right, Mrs Henderson,' said Violet meekly. 'I'll just have to get my boots on.'

'Hurry up, then,' said the housekeeper. As Violet laced her boots she saw the woman pull Celia to her feet. 'Get some monthly towels, Violet, and bring them here.' Violet reluctantly pulled three of the cotton-wool sanitary towels she used for her monthly periods from a drawer and brought them over. 'Now, run for it,' ordered Mrs Henderson as she handed them over.

Ten minutes later Celia Hardwick and Mrs Henderson had gone and the maid was stripping the sheets and blankets from Celia's bed. She came back for the mattress.

'That bad, eh?' said Violet, on her bed with *The Heart's Awakening* again.

The maid, who had failed to stop Violet's early morning ablutions and was having to get up earlier to get her hot-water jugs filled in time, made no reply. She thought it was typically hard-hearted for Violet to be lying on a bed reading a book when another young lady had been taken to hospital in a cab, however wicked and misguided that young woman had been.

Nevertheless, Violet went peacefully to sleep after finishing her book, having told the girls who came in what had happened. But at three she was woken by a nightmare, suddenly aware of the risk she was running herself. She saw Celia's chalky face, the dark circles under her eyes, her fear, and all the blood. She knew what happened to girls who slept with men they weren't married to; her mother had told her often enough. But Violet's mother, with her lined face, thickened body, untidy skirts and old boots, her hands roughened by hot water, scrubbing and ashes, was an all too vivid picture of what happened to women who slept with men to whom they were married. Violet had scarcely heeded the warnings. Now she saw the danger she was in from Tom Rawlinson's erect member and agonised, pleading looks. It was all very well, she thought, messing about on the railway embankment as kids, when one thing had led to another, on hot summer nights. She'd been fourteen, then, and Tom seventeen. She'd been lucky so far, but luck didn't last for ever. Look at Celia, who might die, and, if she didn't, wasn't going to be allowed to set foot in Hammonds again. Celia's fate would lead her to hanging round stations looking for men. Probably in the end she'd die of a nasty disease. If she, Violet, got pregnant, she'd have that to look forward to too, or a speedy marriage to Tom, which she didn't want. Deeply frightened, alone in the dark, Violet didn't entirely lose her nerve. That was a habit she'd abandoned at eight years old, seeing her sister Norah blubbering under her father's blows because she'd panicked and not had the presence of mind to blame next door's cat for the breaking of a teapot. At that point Violet decided never to lose her head. Now she decided that never again would Tom Rawlinson make love to her, however much he pleaded.

Celia Hardwick was never seen again. Mrs Henderson refused to give any information about her but it was because Celia had gone for good that Violet got her permanent position on the gentlemen's glove counter in Mr Gummidge's department, and it was only four days later when Frederick Levine looked in again.

'Hello,' he said, 'I wanted to thank you for bringing me my gloves in time. They told me you came yourself. But unfortunately I've spoiled one pair and left another in a cab – I've come to pester you again.'

'You'd better take a dozen, the giddy life you're leading,' said Violet, knowing a young woman could be pert to a gentleman who was young enough, or old enough, as long as Mr Gummidge was out of hearing.

'Make it a dozen then,' he said. 'But only if you'll have supper with me tonight. Otherwise I'll have one pair today, another tomorrow and another the day after, just to see you again. You'd better accept my invitation or I'll be haunting your counter like a ghost.'

Violet smiled at him, showing her pretty, even teeth. She had lost her temper with Tom the night before, fallen into one of those uncontrollable rages which hit her like a storm when they occurred. She'd learned to use the threat of these tempers to good effect, when her mother wanted her to stay home from school, for example, or when asked to do household tasks while making herself a dress, but the truth was that the real thing, surging over her, terrified her as much as it frightened the victims and witnesses. They came less often than in childhood, when she had screamed, torn her own clothes, attacked bystanders, once stabbing her brother Frank deeply in the arm with a pair of scissors before being dragged off by her mother and Norah. Violet in a rage, they said at home, seemed possessed by the devil. The real reason was probably that ordinarily Violet maintained an iron control over her own behaviour, while living in a world which never gave her what she wanted. Sometimes it was all too much for her; sometimes she exploded.

That night in Camberwell, Tom had tried to put his arms round her. She'd burst out, 'You said we were going to the pictures. Now you want to start messing about with me as usual. You'll give me a baby yet, you bastard.'

'Violet, Violet,' he said, startled. 'I love you so much. I want you so— '

And Violet had screamed, 'Don't you dare come near me again,' glaring at him. 'I'll kill you if you do. I hate you.'

And even now, as she spoke quietly to Frederick Levine, she had only the fear, but no real recollection of what she'd done in Tom's room the night before. She'd stamped and raged about. She remembered breaking the photograph of Tom's dead mother which stood on the mantelpiece in a silver frame. At one point the landlady had come up and banged on the door, and Tom had opened it and spoken to her. She recalled Tom holding her at arm's length, while she kicked out at him, and his sudden grimace as she hit him, followed by his incredulous expression as, suddenly, he seemed to realise exactly what was going on. She'd smashed a vase and told him nothing made her feel sicker than that horrible thing in his trousers, she'd rather handle dog's mess, she'd told him in a scream, he'd never make a success on the halls, unless he joined a troupe of performing monkeys. She remembered him sitting on the bed with his head in his hands, saying, 'Go away, Violet. Go away. I can't stand you being in the room any more.' She'd left the mess and Tom's sobs and jumped straight on a tram. She was shaking violently, but had only the faintest of qualms about what she'd just done. Sometimes such a feeling of darkness and oppression came over her that she knew if she didn't release them she would die.

She woke next morning feeling fresh and light, as if the world had started anew, but uncertain about herself, who had done all these things. Now here was a gentleman inviting her to supper, not one of your mashers, not the sort who usually hung round actresses, or milliners, or girls who worked in shops. He was quite diffident, really, thought Violet. The sort you could handle. She smiled at him and said, 'If you insist, sir.'

'I'll collect you at . . . When does the store close tonight?'

'At seven,' Violet said primly.

'I'll pick you up then,' he said.

'I shall have to be back by ten,' she said.

'Oh – do you live here, then?' he asked.

'During the week,' she said. 'I spend the weekends with my family.'

He nodded, put on his black homburg and walked, tall, straight and tidy, to the door of the shop. He had tact, she thought, didn't hang round the counter chaffing and laughing and making Mr Gummidge suspicious. The only question in her mind was why he had invited her at all. He wasn't a womaniser, so why was a gentleman like him handing out invitations to a girl like her?

Meanwhile Frederick Levine, in the back of the car taking him to the Levine-Schreft bank, was slightly agitated. As Violet had seen, he wasn't a man who went out with girls who worked in shops, made presents to dancers, picked girls up at fairs. Now twenty-three, he had little experience of women. His brother Laurence had taken him to Mrs Leslie's brothel in Half Moon Street on the evening before his sixteenth birthday, though he was dragging about the house after a pretty maid at the time, a girl whom he imbued with all the virtues his sentimental nature led him to invent, or perhaps, detect, for he never got to know her well since his mother discharged her not long after. At Half Moon Street he was taken by a good-natured woman, heavily powdered and scented, unlike all the other women he knew, who entertained him in a gilt and plush bedroom, on a big brass-knobbed bedstead. He was half-frightened by her ample, very white bosom and hips. His immature body had performed, but although Laurence would have laughed if he had told him, he blamed his brother for taking him to Mrs Leslie's and making sure his first sexual experience had been a challenge, loveless and almost masturbatory.

He returned to Mrs Leslie's from time to time. He'd made regular, half-termly visits when at Oxford and now rationed his trips there to one a month, after he had been at his club. It was, he knew, damaging to a man's health to suffer too many erections without relief and he had been told as a boy that masturbation was harmful and weakening. He was sure about the first part, less sure of the second, but saw his visits to places like Half Moon Street as necessary, as well as pleasant, where you entered what looked like a respectable hall, were ushered into what looked like a conventional drawing-room, where young ladies, fully dressed in the latest styles, sat on well-upholstered furniture – sometimes one played Chopin, or some drawing-room piece on the piano – and finally found yourself upstairs with a naked woman. The sexual act was intended to mean no more to you than ordering tea from a waitress in a tea-shop.

After some years of this, at Mrs Leslie's and one or two establishments of the same kind, he began to associate the women he met there with friendship, of a kind, and sexual release, and the unmarried girls he met at dances with chaste, tepid companionship. They had, after all, been brought up in sheltered surroundings. They revealed few views, if they had any, showed their characters, if they had any, hardly at all. Certainly, they showed no signs of knowing anything about the relations between men and women. If they did, they concealed it successfully. In their mothers, often, Frederick Levine sensed a kind of ease and acceptance of life, some of the sharp perceptions he had found among the prostitutes in the brothels. They attracted him more than the daughters, Frederick knew, but could not face making approaches to them, even when he suspected the approaches might not be unwelcome, and could feel nothing for the girls he danced with at balls, with their white dresses and the flowers in their hair. He supposed other men found ways of courting these girls, who seemed to him to be more like grown-up children, whom he took in to supper or who poured his tea on sunny lawns – his brother had married one after all – but it seemed to him that there was no way of finding out who they actually were, so carefully had their upbringing taught them to conceal themselves.

As the car drew closer and closer to the bank, he wondered what on earth he was going to do with that small, pretty girl from behind a shop counter this evening. What would they talk about? What was the point? He wasn't planning to seduce an honest working girl – he didn't even want to. He decided he'd have to go through with the evening somehow, then let her down lightly at the end. Send her some flowers, then, goodbye, he thought. The chauffeur opened the door, he got out, pondering how far the bank should be investing in the new Russian railway line. The loan would produce four and a half per cent. There were industrial disturbances in Russia but then, so there were in Britain. The loan was guaranteed by the Tsar – perhaps that was good enough. On the whole, he thought, a good idea to invest heavily. He'd get an opinion from his Uncle Leopold.

Not long after Frederick Levine had sat down in his office and asked his secretary to ask his chief assistant, Henry Sturgess, to come in, Violet was in the bathroom upstairs at Hammonds, feeling for the five guineas in half sovereigns she had taped under the back slat at the top of the cupboard, behind a roll of purple oilcloth which no one liked to throw away, but for which no use could be found. Then she got off the chair, with the money in her hand, and raced back to her counter, telling Mr Gummidge she had been to the stock-room.

At dinner-time she spent two guineas, a whole month's wages, on a pair of black kid shoes, with small heels and a bar across the foot, shoes far too fragile for a young woman who spent her time walking in muddy streets and getting on and off buses and trams. She bought a lawn petticoat with lace at top and bottom for half a guinea, spent five shillings and sixpence on lace-fringed drawers, another five and six on a matching camisole and got, for five shillings, two pairs of black silk stockings. This left her with less than a pound. She bought a pair of leather gloves, in black, and taped the remaining half guinea back under the shelf. For the money she had spent she could have bought herself a good dress, or a costume, but Violet knew that a real lady dresses properly from the skin outwards and was in any case concentrating on enhancing the effect of her pretty little hands and feet. While Frederick Levine had dismissed Violet from his thoughts as soon as he got to his office, Violet spent the day dreaming of her own body, in its expensive underwear, her legs in silk and her hands in their dainty little gloves.

The hands of the clock on the wall opposite her counter slowed down after dinner, crawled after four, and from five onwards seemed stationary for long periods. Violet thought she would die if the afternoon went on any longer. At a quarter to seven she hid six pairs of stitched leather gloves at the back of a drawer used for exchanged or damaged gloves and told Mr Gummidge she had better go to the stock-room for more. As there were few customers about he agreed. The assistants were forbidden to go into their dormitory during business hours unless they were ill, so Violet had hidden all her new things in a large cupboard containing shelves of huge, old-fashioned corsets, huge, pink shapes of canvas, elastic and whalebone, designed to control and enlarge ample bosoms and bottoms of an earlier generation. There, in the dim light coming through a transom above the cupboard door she quickly stripped naked and slipped into her new underclothes and put her outer clothes on again. She put her camisole, drawers and cotton petticoat in a bag on the shelf and stuffed her own narrow corset on a shelf with the others, resolving never to wear it again. During the last ten minutes of her dinner-break, after she had finished shopping, she had tidily sewn four stocking suspenders from four pieces of elastic, attached to a broad belt of elastic round her waist. It felt lighter, more comfortable, and she felt freer. She put on the new, soft shoes and, sucking a scented purple cachou to sweeten her breath, she strolled back to her counter, the replacement gloves in her hands, looking much as she had done when she left, although, in her new shoes, she felt like dancing.

Kate Higgins, April 1st, 1991

Andy picked me up outside the flat on Thursday. He'd said over the phone that he wouldn't come up. 'I don't want to have to chat to your flatmate,' he said. 'The trip was a real bastard.' I knew he didn't like Di, who was exactly the sort of woman he objected to. She ran a small print shop with some other women. He said this was bread and circuses on the rates designed to keep the community happy and employed, defusing discontent which ought to be expressed openly. It was true that though the place ran at a profit a lot of their work came from people wanting posters for gigs they were holding in council-sponsored halls and from various local organisations. He actually told her his views of her work during a supper party which I organised so that we could all be friendly, but where Andy made it obvious he was not happy with the food and company. Di told him that if he wanted discontent openly expressed perhaps he'd like to lead the movement from the front, and try some rubber bullets and CS gas on for size. Andy was so startled by her rudeness and also by being accused, implicitly, of being too cowardly to face the police, that he scarcely replied. Wherever he went everyone knew he was brave. It was never mentioned, but the three days and nights pinned down by Iraqi fire in a cave with the Kurdish partisans, the siege of Lesotho, the river-run across the Rio Grande with illegal immigrants, guards and searchlights on the other bank, had not been forgotten. You didn't accuse Andy Littlebrown of leading from the rear, and Di had.

It wasn't just Di's job to which Andy objected, but the

fact that she spent much of her free time helping people fight landlords or trying to get funding to set up crèches, or stop the closure of the local casualty ward or compiling statistics about the suicide rate in tower blocks. Andy supported all these things but he couldn't stand Di's style, which consisted of going on doggedly and unglamorously, expecting no fame or money for her efforts, and certainly not getting any. Nor could he bear her assumption, never expressed, that people with surplus income must automatically be doing something morally wrong. Putting them together was like throwing a dog and a cat into a small room.

Anyway, I got into the car outside the flats and we drove off. Andy maintained an intimidating male silence, implying that he had important matters on his mind and might lose his temper if those thoughts were interrupted. Sitting in a vehicle filled with this deadly nerve gas I began a weak monologue intended to interest and cheer, but not overexcite or make any demands. I said I'd met an old friend of his who'd hoped he'd get in touch and I mentioned my mystery caller about Violet Levine. I told him I'd rung Roger to see if he knew who the caller was.

Andy said only, 'I hope you didn't give him my phone number,' of the friend I'd met and, of the mystery caller, 'I wouldn't keep on ringing him up – Roger – he's not keen on authors' phone calls. I mean, if you've taken on the job, just do it, eh.'

After this I said, 'Stop the car. It's obvious you're not in the best of moods. Let's call it a day, shall we? You'd probably feel better if you went to the pub and had a drink with Don and the lads.'

Still driving, Andy said, 'What do you mean, bad mood? I'm in a perfectly good mood. I'm a bit tired, that's all. It's not too surprising. It's been a long trip, or it seemed one, and I've just come away from one of the most horrible office meetings of my career. If I seem tense I'm sorry. Let's just go and eat, shall we?'

But it was a silent meal, followed by silent viewing of a film on TV at his flat. Undemanding companionship was what he needed, though I couldn't help wondering if he'd be better off hiring a faithful labrador when he was in London. In bed things improved, as they always did. I knew he loved me, that I loved him – funnily enough, I could never really see it as 'we loved each other' – and I realised that he was tired, after a frustrating time in Vietnam, and the editor was making a pig of himself. It was then that he suggested a weekend away and I agreed, though guiltily, since I'd said I would go to Brighton to see Ray and my parents. I rang them straight away. My mother said it might be better the week after – Ray would be out all Sunday with the local Scouts. I was relieved but at the same time I could see my own figure becoming smaller and smaller on Ray's landscape until I dwindled into a tiny dot waving my arms at him from too far away.

As if to compensate for this in some way, I was up bright and early next morning to go on with my work, leaving Andy's black head on the pillow, a long, brown arm trailing over the edge of the bed. 'Where to?' he mumbled. I dashed back to make him a cup of tea, sat on the edge of the bed while he drank it. 'Ruining my sex life, she is,' he muttered.

I might have stayed, then, but I noticed two parallel scratches on his back and, knowing I hadn't made them, wasn't sure if he'd got them while crawling through the jungle or somewhere in darkest Pimlico, from an English rose. This doubt was enough to get me through the door and out into the cold but sunny street, where I took a bus to the British Library and found what I should have seen weeks before. On the list of Violet's publications were two books, described as novels, which she herself had never mentioned. The first, *A Simple Rose*, was published in 1914, the second, *The Discarded Blossom*, in 1915. It was a discovery, of a sort. I couldn't have the books immediately, so ordered them, then went and, quite by chance, discovered *Turnings*, her novel of 1923, in a second-hand bookshop. Encouraged, I went into Hyde Park and sat on a bench in my gloves and scarf and started reading it. *Turnings*, a novel Violet had not suppressed, followed Rosamund Beckett from her dreamlike childhood in a big house in Wiltshire to her marriage to Julian Vane, a damaged war hero, who went mad during the course of the book. I got to the point where Rosamund was obviously, in desperation, going to join the fast-lane set of the twenties when I began to think Violet was taking the readers, and me, for a bit of a ride. It wasn't bad but it was like so many other books of the period.

I got the impression that Violet had not been so much inspired by her themes as jumping on the bandwagon. I wanted to think well of Violet but literary integrity didn't seem to be one of her attributes. The trouble was, if she wrote false novels, could you believe her autobiography was utterly sincere? By now it was really cold. I stood up and walked back to the flat, thinking I'd finish reading the book somewhere warm. As I went along I wondered all over again what it must have been like for a policeman's daughter, found in the park by the second son of a family of prominent Jewish bankers, or bankers of Jewish extraction (I was not sure how Jewish the family actually was when Violet joined it) and then courted, then married, then taking up residence in the family house in Cavendish Square.

> For our own reasons neither Frederick nor I wanted a wedding full of pomp and ceremony to surround what we mutually saw as an essentially private pledge of our love and in consequence we married in a small chapel attached to Lambeth Palace in June, 1913, in the last year of peace the country would enjoy for a long time to come.

Thus Violet, in *I Affirm*.

On the way home I noticed the police had surrounded a bus, and seemed to be searching everyone on it. For me, George V was on the throne, Asquith the Prime Minister, the mutiny of British troops threatened in Ireland, the suffragettes in jail, a world war more than a year off, and Violet Levine married to Frederick Levine. Suddenly I saw people pulled off the bus and searched on the pavement outside Notting Hill Gate tube station and at first it didn't seem real. Then I saw a thin, afraid young man, pockets turned out, his arms in suppliant position and I left 1913 for 1991, walking past the scene, not looking, the way you do.

Back at the flat, I flopped down with *Turnings* by the gas-fire. Di had nipped home at lunch-time to collect the shopping money from the jar in the kitchen and was eating a cheese sandwich and watching the news on TV. The Home

Secretary, Adrian Critchlow, was explaining why it would be a good idea for everyone voluntarily to carry a plastic ID card with name, address and National Insurance number on it, also their blood group, in case of an accident. 'Voluntary today, compulsory tomorrow,' Di observed.

'All it'll mean is that someone who's got one is either a solid citizen or a well-prepared bad guy,' I said.

'I suppose people will be queueing to get them,' Di observed gloomily.

'Kids will,' I told her. 'Ray'd love a piece of plastic with his picture on the card.'

'You all right?' she asked.

'Freezing,' I said. 'I was sitting in the park reading Violet Levine's novel.'

'Any good?'

'Rotten,' I told her. 'Everything gets more mysterious by the minute. If only I could talk to her children.'

'If they'll talk to you,' Di said prophetically.

THREE

The Levines, April, 1991

In another part of London a telephone rang. 'Pam,' said a man's voice, 'I've just got the copy of that letter you sent me. Look, you'll have to get rid of this woman, Kate Higgins. Obviously, no one wants to talk to her, but it'll look better coming from you – well, I'll be writing from here to say it's impossible. But— '

'I told Jack I felt he should deal with it,' Pamela Christian-Smith broke in. 'He told me he didn't want to have anything to do with it either way.'

'Very helpful,' said her brother. 'You'd better tell him if he won't help you, he'd better make bloody sure he doesn't help her.'

'I'm sure he won't. But I wish you'd deal with all of it.'

'It'd look extremely odd – me writing from New York to say you can't see her. Who is she anyway?'

'I asked Jack if he could find out but he told me he couldn't ask round casually from the Amazon. I could hardly quarrel with that. The truth is he's too far away at the moment to know or care.' Pamela Christian-Smith looked round her drawing-room, at the narcissi, the curtains, hanging in stiff folds by the long windows, through which could be seen the leaves on the trees of the square opposite. Then she glanced nervously upwards at the portrait of a small, dark woman, well lipsticked and marcel-waved, wearing a pale green chiffon evening dress and a string of pearls. She said, after a pause, 'Jack said I should get Anna to write saying that Harry died six months ago and I was not ready to talk to her and then make up an excuse, like that she's moving with Ben and the boys to Rio. What do you think, Bobbie? I can't think at all. And Jack was somewhere off the map and the phone went off before we could discuss it properly.'

'It doesn't look very good, frankly,' said Robert Levine, Violet's son, to his sister. 'Perhaps it would be better if you saw the woman, briefly . . . '

'I can't, Bobbie. I just can't. It would be too much, with Harry gone and Jack out of the country. I mean, Mother practically ruined my marriage one way and another – I couldn't trust myself not to say too much. Why couldn't you come back and talk to her? Or find a time when you're coming to London anyway?'

'And start up hares that'd never stop running?' said Robert Levine.

'Oh, Bobbie,' said Pamela Christian-Smith pitifully.

'What's going on?' said her daughter Anna, coming into the room and hearing her mother's helpless voice. She was a tall, robust woman in her mid-forties.

'Uncle Bobbie,' her mother told her.

'What, is it this Higgins woman – the book about Grandmother?'

Pamela nodded as she said into the phone, 'Oh, I'm sure it would be much better if you or Jack— '

'Let me talk to him,' said her daughter, taking the telephone. She said, 'Uncle Robert? Listen, Mother really can't manage this. I can't see why we don't just write to the woman and tell her we don't want a biography of Grandmother. It was her personal wish that no one should ever write one and that's what we'd prefer. We therefore, with regret, can't give any co-operation. What's the matter with that?'

'Nothing, if she's easily put off,' her uncle said. 'And everything if she isn't. I've more experience of prying journalists than you have, and so has your mother, for that matter. What we went through over Mackinnon hardly bears thinking about, even now, and that wasn't all. There are things even you don't know . . . '

'Well, if you can't think of anything better – I certainly can't – then we'll simply have to adopt Jack's suggestion— '

'It'll do,' said Robert Levine, not pleased. 'For the meanwhile, at any rate. We'll just have to see what happens next. You'd better write, say your mother can't help at the moment, your own movements are uncertain for the next six months but in all probability you'll be travelling on business with your husband. You might add you scarcely knew Violet anyway. And make it plain that your poor Aunt Joanna's in a clinic and has been for many years.' He paused. 'I must say I never anticipated this – and so soon.'

'I suppose Grandmother poisoned all about her for so long it's not surprising she's having a final try from beyond the grave,' remarked Anna.

'That sort of attitude isn't going to get us very far. Look, try to look after your mother. This is very upsetting. It brings back all sorts of unpleasant memories.'

Anna Schreft glanced at her mother, who was staring carefully at the fireplace, as if trying not to hear what was going on. 'All right, Uncle Robert,' she said. 'I'll try. I suppose if all fails you'd better step in and buy the publishers.'

'Even that occurred to me,' he said. 'But for the time being it's sensible not to over-react. Just keep a careful eye on what's happening. You know what I'm really worried about, of course— '

'A promise was given— '

'Promises have been broken. Still, I think I can cope with all that.'

After he had said goodbye to his niece and told her to give his love to his sister, Robert Levine swivelled his chair round and looked across the vista of skyscraper tops. He sighed deeply and then pressed a button, telling his assistant to get him a number in Connecticut.

In London, Anna Schreft put the receiver down and told her mother, 'All right. It's agreed I'm writing roughly as Jack suggested. In the meanwhile, I'm getting this rubbish off the wall. It was never a good portrait and now Grandmother's dead I can't see any reason for having it here.' Standing on a chair she heaved down Violet Levine's picture, stood it with its face to the wall and went to the door and shouted, 'Felipe! Felipe! Can you come here straight away?'

Pamela, from her chair, said, 'Now there's a patch on the wallpaper. And where are we going to put the picture?'

'I'd burn it,' advised her daughter. 'But shall I take it away with me – stick it in our attic?'

'I think in her will she offered it to the National Portrait Gallery,' said Pamela Christian-Smith.

'Well, they don't seem to have wanted it. And anyway, who cares? She's dead now. She's got no say in the matter. Honestly, Mother,' she said, staring at her mother's face, 'what this place needs is no pictures of Violet, a decorator to get rid of the patch on the wallpaper and if all that fails, an exorcist.'

'Don't joke,' said her mother. 'I sometimes think she's still here.'

'That's because of this bloody woman and her bloody little book,' said Anna. 'Felipe, here's the keys. Can you get this picture into the back of my car?'

He nodded and trundled it on to the landing. He and his wife carried it downstairs. His wife shuddered and said something about witches and would probably have crossed herself if she'd had her arms free.

FOUR

Violet Crutchley, 1913
Kate Higgins, April 9th, 1991

Violet Crutchley, in the Café Royal, a spotless white cloth, coffee cups and a brandy glass in front of her, and Frederick Levine opposite, was making no effort whatsoever to entertain. They had been to see *Nell Gwynne* at the Lyceum, where she had sat entranced by the lively heroine, the horrible murder and the Frenchies' plot to bring her and the country down. Frederick had himself been more entranced by her pretty face, open mouth and small gasps of excitement and horror and wished that the little hand with which she gripped him when the story became particularly thrilling would stay on his arm for ever. Then they had got into Frederick's car, which had been waiting for them outside the theatre when the show ended, and gone to the Café Royal. Frederick had muttered a word or two to the waiter, who had seated them at the back, out of sight of the men and women in evening dress who were filtering in after the theatre or parties they had attended.

It had, Violet admitted, been a bit embarrassing to walk down the aisle of the theatre to the fifth row of the stalls when everyone else was wearing penguin suits, or evening dresses and jewellery. Frederick was just wearing an ordinary suit, with a waistcoat, and she was in her drab, everyday coat and skirt with a big green hat which suited her, but had seen better days. Nevertheless, borne up by the new shoes and stockings, Violet had sailed down the aisle with a straight back, pretending to herself she was a lady who'd just returned from the East End where she'd been bringing comfort to the poor, wearing her oldest clothes so's not to make them feel bad about themselves, or that she'd just gone off in disguise to a suffrage meeting so her high-born family would not be exposed to shame when she was recognised.

For herself, Violet hardly cared one way or another about the vote. She couldn't see the point of throwing vitriol over golf courses. It would only annoy men, even the ones like her father who'd never been near a golf course and quite likely never would. Everybody knew men got angry when you defied them – it was no surprise to her that they were throwing perfect ladies into jail and knocking them about. When it came to women, men stood together. This was not quite what she said when Frederick referred to the blowing up by suffragettes of a house Lloyd George was having built for himself in Surrey, near the golf links. 'Picked the locks with a hatpin,' he said, half-admiringly, 'and made a couple of bombs with gunpowder, fuses – the lot. One even went off. It shows a good deal more technical ingenuity than one would normally accuse ladies of having. What think you, Violet? Are you planning to join the Amazons?'

Violet remarked sensibly that if the bombs had gone off twenty minutes later they might have killed a large number of workmen due on the site but not Mr Lloyd George, or Mr Asquith, so she couldn't see the point of it. She added, 'Of course they say women's brains aren't up to politics. I know mine aren't.'

'Be good, sweet maid, and let who will be clever,' pronounced Frederick.

Violet nodded. 'That's about the size of it,' she agreed and allowed a silence to fall, for she knew that if she could concentrate on Frederick in the right way, and make him concentrate on her, she would have him in the palm of her hand. A discussion of politics was not what she wanted. He had to think about her. She gazed into his pleasant brown eyes and concentrated, quite relaxed, big-eyed, gentle, like a cat sitting on the grass contemplating a bird pecking worms nearby. Many men later were to say Violet Levine had a powerful effect on them, though they could never quite describe what it was. When she wasn't concentrating on you she was a woman you appreciated for her looks, her clothes, her style, grace, conversation. When she was paying the other kind of attention you seemed to sink into those remarkable violet-hazel eyes, be surrounded by her melodious voice and the strange charm she could exert. She now said softly, 'I suppose the really important thing for a woman is to concern herself with a man.'

'Most definitely,' said Frederick. 'And what could be nicer for both of them, particularly when the young lady concerned is you, Miss Crutchley?'

'Well, then,' said Violet. 'Then I'll have to make sure I'm concentrating on you, Mr Levine.'

'And you must begin by calling me Frederick,' he told her.

'Frederick,' she assured him softly. The sounds of the restaurant came back to her, the music of the orchestra, the sounds of people talking, the odd burst of laughter. 'Oh, I can't think when I've enjoyed an evening more. That silly play, I did enjoy it and this lovely place – oh, it's like a dream.'

He was touched. 'We must do it again, then.'

Violet had, as she could, bathed the situation in warmth and affection. Her glances spelt sympathy and admiration. Frederick, who had been, from birth, the less favoured son of a redoubtable mother, relaxed in her warm company. Meanwhile Violet said, 'Oh, do let's if you can spare the time for a little one. But, please tell me the time. I may be late.' As it happens, Violet was one of those people who always know what time it is. She had, in fact, been due back at Hammonds half an hour earlier, but was relying on a good record on time-keeping and the tale of a mishap at home to keep her out of trouble with the housekeeper. Frederick squeezed her hand when they parted outside the store and told her he must see her again soon.

Thinking the evening over in her narrow bed, she counted herself lucky. He wasn't a bad-looking fellow and he wasn't a brute, and he was probably quite clever in whatever line he was in – at a bank, he'd said, and not just shovelling money in and out of bags either. She could do worse – better than staying on at Hammonds until she was an old shoe, or marrying somebody like Tom and dropping down dead over the washtub. She saw the white shirt-fronts, heard the orchestra, felt the chauffeur close the door of a car behind her. That was the life. If she'd been born to the purple she'd have had it all without worrying. The problem was, if she gave in to Frederick, for that was the next step, she could have a baby. Oh Gawd, thought Violet to herself. Damn and blast babies. A girl could have a perfectly nice time if it wasn't for babies. Still, if she played her cards right she could end up with a nice little shop in a superior area. Selling flowers, or hats, or scents, perhaps. With a nice big plate-glass window and gold letters above the door. Violette's, she thought, for that was the name of the heroine of a romance she'd recently read. Lovely name – Violette. Plenty of others had done it, why not her? Violette, Violette, she thought, and fell fast asleep.

Kate Higgins, April 9th, 1991

A bad dream woke me: a woman with no face, just a black space above her shoulders moving towards me with arms outstretched, down a long room with trees outside. Why she was reaching for me wasn't obvious, but I lay terrified in my room which was faintly lit by the street lamp a few feet away along the pavement and the guard lights on the wall of the school opposite. What had really woken me, I realised, was not the dream, but the sound of the front door opening and someone creeping in. I was aware, first, of a person coming out of the bathroom and then of the door to the spare room near the front door opening (the flat was so big because Di had moved in on the basis that she and her brother and sister would all be living there – now, for council purposes, I was her sister). Then the spare room door opened and I heard her whispering, though I couldn't hear the replies. It was three in the morning.

I rolled over and tried to go back to sleep. At eleven that morning I was due in Hampstead to see Rosie Johnson, as my mystery caller had suggested. Rosie was the redoubtable ex-MP, who had known Violet during her parliamentary days after the Second World War. Then I was going down to Brighton. Andy had accepted this news somewhat glumly and said something about a party he thought we'd both be going to, but I told myself that if I couldn't expect too much of him then he couldn't really expect too much of me. And with that, I went to sleep.

That morning I was having a slice of toast and a cup of instant when a letter arrived. On thick paper headed The Old Rectory, Potterfield, Gloucester, Violet's granddaughter Anna Schreft wrote, telling me that due to the recent death of her husband her mother was unable to help. She herself was about to embark on a six-month business trip with her husband. Her brother was in Latin America, making a TV documentary and would not be back for several months. (I knew this, having phoned Jack Christian-Smith's office. My letter asking for an interview now lay in a no doubt huge pile of correspondence he would attend to when he returned.) Anna Schreft added, too, that her Aunt Joanna, Violet's daughter, was in a clinic. There was no suggestion that she or her mother would be prepared to see me at some other time, no offer of a peep at letters, albums of photographs or other documents. There was no offer, full stop. I imagined that Robert Levine's letter, when he replied from the USA, would be much the same. It was an enormous blow but it proved one thing. My anonymous caller was right. The Levines didn't want to help me.

Di came in eating a slice of toast and started to put on her earrings in front of the mirror. 'You still going to see Rosie Johnson?' she asked.

I said I was and told her about the letter from Anna Schreft.

'I suppose it's almost as interesting that they *don't* want to see you as if they met you and told you everything,' she said.

'It's interesting in a way,' I said. 'But they could just be people who hate publicity. I suppose it's their right. Maybe I just look like a vulture, homing in on the body.'

'Oh,' she said, having fixed the earrings, and turning round. 'There's a friend of mine, Jim Williams, in the spare room. He missed the last train back to Leeds last night. He's still asleep, I expect. Are you still going to Brighton, or is it old war-torn Andy Littlebrown again?'

I told her my plans.

Then she said, 'They've done it again.'

On the TV, which was on at a mutter, there was a picture of Horse Guards Parade, covered in bits of masonry and glass, the shattered side of a building, Whitehall cordoned off, windows up and down Whitehall broken, men in helmets with visors walking in the rubble. I turned the sound up. A bomb planted in the shadow of a wall had gone off at six in the morning. The IRA had admitted responsibility. Di pushed the rest of her toast on the windowsill for the birds, shut the window, went out of the room and came back in her coat. 'That's the second in a month,' she said.

'Must be the third since just before Christmas. There was that store in Oxford Street, then the ICA, now this. I wonder why the IRA wanted to blow up the ICA.'

'Close to Buckingham Palace as they could get,' Di suggested. She pulled down a woolly hat and wound a long coloured scarf round her neck. 'You won't be here, so it doesn't matter – still, when you come back, might as well get a cab from the station. A young black man died in custody last night and there's going to be a lot of tension on the estate. They're already talking about a protest march on the police station. You could run into it accidentally and who knows what's going to happen? There could be trouble.' She went to the door and said, 'I'm working at the pub tonight, so I won't be back till late, but can you leave the mortice off when you go out? Otherwise Jim won't be able to get out. I'll just have to chance the Yale, for once.'

'Take care,' I said.

'You too,' she replied, leaving in a rush with her blonde hair flapping over the back of the big scarf. I was thinking it would be nice if Di could find someone – she was still in love with a man in prison in South Africa. Once upon a time she used to bring the odd man back to the flat for the night, to give it a whirl, but she'd lost heart, that was obvious. But she couldn't go on pining for the South African. I couldn't really say anything. It wasn't my business and would only give her an excuse to mention Andy yet again on a look-who's-talking basis. 'The Radical Centrefold,' she called him, adding, 'You can't go on running with the hare and hunting with the hounds for ever, like Andy does. In the end it doesn't work any more. Not these days anyway.'

I set off to see Rosie Johnson, now eighty years old, first elected to parliament for a northern constituency in 1935, marched all the way from Jarrow to London in 1936, became a minister in 1948 and, sacked by Harold Wilson in 1964, stayed on the back benches until 1979, when she retired. On the way to Hampstead the train sped right through Paddington without stopping, leaving passengers, many with luggage, standing baffled at the doors. At the next station a notice, chalked on a blackboard on the platform read, 'No trains to Paddington. Passengers advised to cancel journeys from Paddington Station mainline until further notice.'

'It's getting like New York,' said one disgruntled man with a suitcase to another.

I trudged half a mile up a long, tree-lined street in cold April rain and arrived at a big house, set back from the road behind a tall privet hedge. I rang the bell marked Johnson and after a delay a voice called, 'Who is it?'

'Kate Higgins. I've got an appointment,' I called back, and after a certain amount of chain rattling I was let in by a short, thin old lady with a grey bun who said, 'Come in. Come in,' and set off down a wide passageway with a light, quick step.

In a living-room full of chintz-covered armchairs, and a sofa, and photographs everywhere – on the walls, on several small tables, on a grand piano at the end of the room looking on to the street – we sat down near a window overlooking the garden.

Rosie Johnson, settling in her chair, said, 'Irene Bell will bring us in some coffee. She's been my secretary for fifty years and I like to keep her in work, especially now I'm past it.' I thought Rosie Johnson looked past nothing at all, except childbearing. 'And how do you come to be saddled with this job,' Rosie Johnson asked, 'writing about Violet? Did the family ask you?'

'Far from it,' I told her. 'I don't think they like the idea; at least, that's the impression I'm getting.'

'Family not co-operating?' Rosie Johnson said in her high voice. She had a North Country accent, not very marked, but even if she'd been able to change her accent she had the wrong timbre for the mystery caller. Though, I thought, she might be able to guess who it could be.

'I've just had a letter from Anna Schreft, Violet's granddaughter, saying the family can't co-operate with me.'

'What about Violet's son Robert?' asked Rosie Johnson.

'I haven't heard from him yet. But I don't expect anything different. Do you think they're just shy, or are they trying to conceal something? I hope they don't think I'm trying to dig up dirt. I'm not.'

'I don't suppose you are. But they're a proud lot, the Levines. They've had money for generations, lived in society since Queen Victoria's times. Old Mrs Levine was a real snob to the last. Frederick was the best of them, funnily enough, and in some ways the brightest, though not where Violet was concerned. She made a fool of him, but I can remember people saying that when it came to the economic sort-out after the Second World War, when Frederick was on the Commission, he turned out to be very clear-sighted, honest, disinterested – everyone ended up by respecting him. Herbert Morrison was a supporter of Frederick Levine's. He had a good heart, too, unlike some of the other Levines. I suppose Violet must have been a shock to them from the start. Then that terrible divorce. And Mackinnon must have been the last straw. I only knew her from the forties on. They said she got a lot of money from her ex-mother-in-law, Sophie Levine, after the war, but as far as I know the Levines never spoke to her after the divorce.'

A large woman of about Rosie Johnson's age came in with a tray. Rosie took a number of photographs off a small table and said loudly, 'Down there, Irene. Why haven't you brought yourself a cup?'

'I'll have mine in the kitchen. You know there are subjects I don't have to get involved in, these days.'

'Well, Violet Levine was a dreadful woman,' Rosie Johnson said placidly. Raising her voice she said, 'Dreadful, wasn't she – Violet?'

'Oh, dreadful,' agreed Irene. 'She couldn't resist trying to get you into trouble. She ignored me, until she realised how useful I was. Then she tried to bribe me away from you – that's right, isn't it, Rosie? Then when I wouldn't go to her she made my life a living hell while Charlie was ill. You remember, don't you, Rosie?' Irene Bell had small blue eyes and ruddy cheeks. She looked quite crumpled when she spoke of Violet's perfidy.

'Irene's husband was dying for two years while all this was going on,' Rosie Johnson explained, raising her voice.

'She tried to get rid of you, too,' said Irene. She shook her head. 'Well, I'll go off. I don't want to have to remember all this.'

She went out, leaving me disconcerted. I said the first thing that came into my head: 'Why was she so horrible?'

'Well, she was ambitious,' said the old woman. 'And in the post-Mackinnon era she was fighting for her political career. It was hopeless, of course.'

'And did you know Mackinnon?' I asked.

Rosie Johnson nodded. 'I saw him about for years, from before the war. He had a lot of charm. No wonder Violet fell for him. He was a terrible womaniser, Duncan,' she said, 'and he drank. I don't think I ever saw him sober. He got worse and worse, too. But what a handsome man he was – it was that kind of handsomeness with the lock of hair over the eyes, and a very soft mouth, like a woman's. He was clever but weak. She was like iron herself. I remember him best when Violet was living at Cheyne Walk – butler, champagne, the lot. No wonder she needed Levine money. The Party didn't like it. One minute she's elected for a constituency in Sunderland, next she's running pseudo-ambassadorial functions. The Labour Party didn't like it, but they had to put up with it because she was there in the constituency every weekend while the House was sitting, and a lot of the time when it wasn't. She knew every council department, every factory, every foundry. She got things done. She was an effective speaker in the House. She did her homework. There were a lot worse Labour MPs than Violet Levine, even if they drank brown ale and only had one suit. It's a pity she didn't enter parliament earlier. As a woman she was a bitch. As a mother she was – well, I'm glad she wasn't my mother, but she had energy, plenty of guts, and a lot of intelligence. She wasn't Karl Marx, but I'm not sure I'd have picked him as my MP, or for Transport Minister either.'

'You wouldn't have wanted her to be your mother . . . '

'I don't think she took much interest in her children – but I'm really thinking about Joanna. There was something wrong with Joanna, not just Violet's jealousy, God knows what it was. She reminded me of some of the girls I went to school with in Widnes. That's a bad sign, of course, when a woman, even a young one, reminds you of a thirteen-year-old you once knew when you were thirteen; you'll be too young to see what I mean, but one day you will . . . ' She smiled at me, then said, 'I'm a chatty person, too chatty. This habit of mine, nattering on, didn't help me in Cabinet, I can tell you.'

'They loved you,' I told her.

'Oh aye, they loved me as much as a politician can love anybody. Never stopped them from stabbing me, though, when it suited them.'

'Joanna?' I said. 'What was it? The girls she reminded you of . . . ?'

'She had no confidence, but that's not it.' Rosie groped for an idea. 'I suppose she was carrying a burden, trying not to let it show. Maybe she thought everyone was the same. The girls I was talking about – one had parents who drank. The other one's mother was on the streets. You couldn't put your finger on the problem, but there was something – Then, of course, during Violet's party-giving days she was always showing Joanna up. Little asides: "You look pale today. Oh, I thought you'd wear the white dress. I always think green makes most women look so sallow." Then you'd notice Violet was wearing green herself. She could be very spiteful, especially to women. If you had anything she wanted, if she thought you were making any progress, she'd sabotage it if she could.

'It was cruel, how she got that seat at Sunderland. The sitting member there was an old chap, about seventy, Jack Armitage, and I'm not saying he wasn't past his best. But he'd started in a steelworks at twelve and he'd fought and struggled for the Labour movement all his life and by that stage, well, he liked a drink and he wasn't as young as he had been – he'd have had to go, sooner or later. But Violet wanted that seat and the Normandy landings were hardly over before she was on the train to Sunderland getting the goods on old Jack. She searched out some constituents who'd gone to Jack's surgery and found him useless with drink, found out about a contract for some municipal building which had gone, wrongly, to Jack's brother-in-law – that sort of thing. Then straight back, and tipping it all into the right ears. They might have been waiting for a tactful moment to get him to resign, but not long after Violet started her campaign old Jack was out of the way and Violet was up there banging on doors and opening jumble sales. Not nice, you see,' said Rosie. 'Not nice at all.' She offered me another cup of coffee. I got up and poured us both one. 'Putting you off, am I?' she asked.

I licked my lips – I remember doing it – and said, 'I don't know.'

'There'd be a reason why she was like she was,' said Rosie. 'There always is, isn't there? She started life from a humble home. In fact, the more she got on in the movement the more humble her home became. We used to wonder how much humbler it could get before it became a hole in the ground. Nonetheless, she had to make her way. And she was brave . . . '

'Did she ever mention her war service?'

'First World War, yes. She used to get round the voters in Sunderland by finding a one-legged man in the crowd and saying she wondered if he was the man whose leg she'd finished amputating in France when the surgeon fell unconscious in the middle of an operation in 1917. She'd done it, of course – she'd nerves of steel. She never said much about the Second World War. Everyone knew she'd been on Special Ops but I smell a bit of a mystery there. It's never what people say . . . '

'Especially when it's Violet Levine. Her book, *I Affirm—* '

'She was always a one for organising her own publicity, was Violet,' said Rosie drily. 'And when it came to her life story, well, she must have thought she'd write it herself and make sure the author said what she wanted.' She got out of her chair and went to the window, crumbled a biscuit and put it out for the birds, then shut the window.

As she did this, just what Di had done earlier, I said, 'I've had an anonymous phone call about Violet's life – the caller won't give a name. English, but I don't know whether it's a man or a woman. This person told me Pamela, Violet's daughter, wasn't Frederick Levine's child. She couldn't have been conceived at the right time – the affair began in April, said the caller, and Pamela was born in November. Apparently Violet said the baby was premature.'

Rosie turned round. 'She wouldn't be the only woman in

the world who ever told a man a baby was his when it wasn't. Anonymous calls, eh?'

'I suppose you wouldn't have any idea . . . ?' I asked.

She shook her head. 'If it's genuine, then it must be someone from a long way back. It's not very nice, but I once had an anonymous call which saved my bacon. They can be useful.'

The photographs all round the room showed a large family. Edwardian couples posed at the seaside with children in sailor hats. There were weddings outside bleak-looking northern churches. Two little boys in thick boots grinned outside a workman's cottage in a low row of similar houses. There was the young Rosie Johnson, in a pretty hat, arms clasped above her head on election night, then standing in her coat and gloves on a box outside some factory gates. Drab men in old-fashioned suits who had once led the country walked together down steps or sat at tables. The young Rosie, in a new-look skirt and tiny hat smiled at Hugh Gaitskell. Aneurin Bevan sat in a restaurant, grinning broadly with a brandy glass in front of him. On the grand piano was a photograph in a silver frame of Rosie Johnson, in a war-time suit, and a man with a moustache. They were on the steps of what looked like a town hall. Rosie had a bouquet, both were smiling into the camera.

Rosie, turning to watch a robin on the sill eating biscuit crumbs, said, 'It seems wrong somehow, to speak ill of her, now she's dead, but as a politician there she was, solid for public ownership, a ferocious republican – she'd have been called a militant and thrown out of the Party these days, I shouldn't wonder. But she had to cover up, pretend to be perfect.'

I thought Rosie was getting tired.

She went on, 'I think there was a lot to hide. She gave you the impression she was always troubled, always torn, under the surface. Never really happy.'

I said, 'I'm very grateful to you for seeing me.'

Then she rallied a bit, telling me, leaning forward slightly, 'Perhaps I haven't been of much help. You must ask me again, if there's anything you need to know. But I'll be honest. In a long life I've developed a nose for trouble. I can smell it here. If you begin to have doubts, remember I told you. Remember I said there's only one thing worse than backing off from trouble and that's not knowing when trouble's too big for you.'

'Any idea what sort?' I asked.

She touched the middle of her forehead, thinking, then shook her head. 'The thirties. She never said much about what happened after she got divorced – not until we got to her special missions during the Second World War. Violet's life was all edited highlights. Gordon Stone was in there somewhere.'

Irene Bell came in and said warningly, 'Rosie.'

I stood up. 'I was just leaving. Thank you again, Mrs Johnson.' Irene Bell took me to the door. 'I'm very grateful,' I said.

Irene Bell, recalling Violet, it seemed, said, 'She gave us all a lot of pain. You be careful of her. The past isn't a door you slam and lock behind you, you know.'

'Thanks,' I said, thinking, Phew! I was getting a picture of Violet I'd never got from *I Affirm*.

It was cold outside. I realised I had to go back to the flat for a thick sweater and my anorak. By the time I got to Thackery House I was frozen. As I walked through the front door I just heard the door of the spare room, which was on the right as I walked in, close silently. I half expected the person who'd gone into the room to come out and say, 'Hello,' but he didn't, so I put the kettle on for a warming cuppa – I was frozen – and while waiting for it to boil rang *The Mag*, the magazine I sometimes worked for and asked for Dave Gottlieb.

I said, 'Dave, I've been commissioned to write a book about Violet Levine. I've just been to see Rosie Johnson. She mentioned someone called Gordon Stone. Does the name ring any bells?'

'Why do you want to know – oh, Violet Levine,' said Dave. 'Well, I can't say I know anything about a Gordon Stone, Kitty, and that's a fact.'

'Pity. Never mind. Just thought I'd ask.'

'How's Rosie? She must be eighty.'

'You'd never believe it.'

'Wonderful woman,' Dave said. 'I hope the book's going well.'

'Marvellous. It's a wonderful story. Look, I've got to go and catch a train . . . '

'I was wondering if you could review a couple of films

for us. I've been ringing around – everybody's got the flu.'

'I'll come in and get the press passes next week. Is Monday, around twelve, all right?'

'I'll tell them to give them to you. On my desk – I'll put your name on the envelope.'

I went and made myself a cup of tea and stood staring at the tea-bag floating in the cup. Because the phone at *The Mag* was constantly tapped, presumably by Special Branch, the staff never talked about anything which might interest the authorities over the phone. The warning to stay off certain subjects was given when one side of the conversation said the other person's name in a form they never used. When Jim became James, Dave Gottlieb D.G., Elizabeth Betsy or, in my case, Kate became Kitty, the alarm bell was ringing. Dave had told me he didn't want anyone listening to think he was interested in Gordon Stone. Though he must be in his seventies now and fairly unlikely to be actively involved in Dave's areas – government infiltration of the unions, leaked documents, secret installations, ministerial cover-ups, that sort of thing.

I drank my tea, packed a larger bag, put on the anorak and left the flat. It was only when I got outside the door that I thought about the man in the spare room. I'd feel a fool if it turned out he wasn't a shy friend, but a burglar who'd opened the door with a credit card and nipped into a side room when he heard me coming. On the other hand, I thought, if I went back and it was a burglar he might hit me over the head and maim me for life, so, bearing in mind that I had a train to catch, I hoped for the best and went to the station.

I was sitting in the pictures with Ray that afternoon, not really watching a glossy spacecraft with glossy men hunched over the controls swooshing through space, shooting beams of light at each other. We'd just had a blowy walk along the front. I was seeing the photographs of the dowdy men who'd nationalised coal, steel, the railways, invented the health service and school milk, standing in their photograph frames in Rosie's flat, the robin pecking crumbs on the windowsill of Rosie's flat, the sparrows eating Di's toast on our windowsill at Henry Thackery House. I thought of the man behind the spare room door, the train, the tossing sea, the grate of pebbles, the wind.

Violet Crutchley, February, 1913

Violet, walking back to Hammonds through Hyde Park on a quiet February evening, shyly held Frederick Levine's gloved hand.

They were quite alone. Frederick had climbed the railings in Bayswater Road and gallantly helped Violet over. 'You're a very pretty girl, Violet,' he had said, dropping a kiss on her brow as he held her and, as he lowered her to the ground, he added, 'and a very nice one.' They walked under leafless trees. A car honked its horn in the distance. A solitary bird woke as they passed and began to twitter. Frederick squeezed her hand.

'I'm ever so fond of you, Frederick,' said Violet, shyly. 'Though we don't know each other all that well you seem to be so – strong. You know what I mean – you're so firm and in control of yourself.'

Frederick said nothing, but Violet knew he was pleased. In fact she did not at all believe what she had told him about himself. Frederick had the assurance of a gentleman, she saw, but that was no wonder; in his world they didn't sack you on the spot, or dress you down in front of everybody. You touched your cap to no one and you always had some money. Underneath, she knew, he was uncertain about large areas of his life. He had said he lived with his widowed mother, his brother Laurence and Laurence's wife – she assumed this wasn't because they couldn't afford to live separately – but somewhere there was a bully, and Frederick the victim. She imagined being a Jew didn't help, because nobody liked the Jews, no matter how much money they had. None of these thoughts attracted her to Frederick. Where she came from a man was expected to be a bit rough, and, as she saw it, they had to be. They had to keep their families under control, which meant they had to be ready to dole out threats, and the odd blow, if necessary, when the domestic situation got out of hand. They had to go out and get the money and that was usually enough to ensure that at home they got what they wanted. Men who didn't were weak, pushed around and called cissies by other men. So men had to be strong and women had to manage them so that they didn't know they were being manipulated. That was Violet's understanding and the fact that she couldn't stand her father and thought her mother's life a misery made no difference to her. Frederick Levine did not command Violet's respect, as a man, but she saw he needed confidence and thought she could give it, and in that way secure her position with him.

Now, she looked up at him as they walked and said, 'I feel so safe with you.'

'A tiny kiss, then,' said Frederick, stopping in the darkness, some distance from the park railings, which they had to cross to get back on to the road. 'Just a tiny, feathery kiss?' he said, turning to her and putting his arms round her. 'To show what friends we are?'

'Just a little, teeny, weeny one,' said Violet, turning up her pretty face, crowned by the big, green hat.

He bent and just brushed her cheek. 'There,' he said, 'that didn't hurt my little Violet, did it?'

'Not even a little bit,' said Violet. 'But let's walk on, Frederick dear, just in case the little tiny kiss grows into a bigger, bigger one . . . '

His arm now round her shoulders he exclaimed, as they walked to the park railings, 'What a darling you are! What a little duck!'

Violet giggled. Before they reached the railings he kissed her again, brushing her lips with his. 'Naughty Frederick,' she said, 'and his bristling moustache. I'm ashamed of him, I really am.'

'But the worst of it is, little Violette,' he said, giving her name the French pronunciation which for her now represented her new identity, her new future, access to what she dreamed of, 'the worst of it is – your naughty Frederick will have to leave his little Violet alone for a week or two.'

Violet concealed the sudden sinking of the heart this news gave her. She was making headway with Frederick, she knew it, and now he was going away, or perhaps just pretending to. Perhaps this was his way of saying he'd never see her again. 'Oh!' she cried. 'Away! Oh, what a shame. Where are you going?'

'Vienna,' he said. 'I've got to go and see some ugly men on business and I'll bring my Violet back a present when I've seen them and come home. There are big things going on in the world, my dear, perhaps not very nice ones you shouldn't have to think about, but we men have to.'

'Poor men,' she sighed. 'Poor women, who have to see them go.' A family like that, she thought to herself, might have lined up half a dozen Austrian princesses and duchesses for him to marry! He could go away free and come back engaged, then where would she be? They said Austrian women were the most charming in Europe. She sighed. 'I expect you'll have a lovely time, while you're not talking to the important men, but I'll be thinking of you and I hope you'll just once or twice think of little me.'

As he lifted her over the railings he kissed her again. The women walking up and down the pavement beside the railings gave them a clear berth. A man in a top-hat got out of a taxi on the other side of the road, some distance up from where Violet and Frederick stood, spoke to a young woman in a low-cut dress and a cloth jacket. She tapped across the road beside him and they both got into the cab. Meanwhile Violet turned her face up to Frederick's in the lamplight, rather sadly, but giving a little smile.

'It's not for long,' he said. 'When I come back we'll go to Kew Gardens and see the beginnings of spring. How would you like that?'

'I should love to,' she told him. 'All the flowers and trees – I love nature.'

Frederick, almost carried away by the vulnerable, sweetly upturned face, nearly said, 'And I love my little Violet,' as he wanted to, and was perhaps meant to, but caution held him back. He brushed her lips again, imagining what it would be like to hold the small body, trembling, naked in his arms, then tucked her arm in his and marched her up the road to Hammonds. As he told her, 'You'll be the prettiest flower there, my blushing Violet, my little primrose by the river's brim, but let's hurry or you'll be late again and the nasty housekeeper will be cross.'

Violet, in her white flannel nightdress, rubbing hand-cream into her delicate hands, now softened by having no contact with the fireplaces or pots and pans of home, lay in bed alarmed. Two weeks, which could easily turn into three, or even four, might be enough to make Frederick forget her altogether. He could easily come under anyone's influence in Vienna, from a duchess to a tart, not to mention some young cousin. He'd said he'd be staying with relations. Wine, women and song, that's what Vienna was like. The women were beautiful and gay, they had lovely clothes, everyone danced and sang and no one had any morals. The thought of losing him made Frederick seem more desirable in her eyes. He was good-looking, in a dark way, rich and kind. She decided that she loved him.

If she wasn't going to see him for a few weeks she would make sure that when he returned she would be ready for him. She would find out all she could about the world he inhabited and the kind of life he led. Accordingly, each day she purchased for threepence a copy of *The Times* from the news-vendor who stood on the corner near Hammonds. Each evening, after supper, she sat in the crowded sitting-room with the other girls, who were mending their stockings, giving themselves manicures, drying their long hair in front of the fire. There, she read the newspaper solidly, while they tittered and made jokes, 'Looking for the announcement of your engagement, Vi?' 'Can I help you out with the hard words, Vi?' She read doggedly on, from the advertisements on the first page to details of steamer sailings at the end.

The contents astonished her. Dr Barnardo's had sent 24,536 orphans to the colonies already, and now appealed for donations of ten pounds from readers, each ten pounds being the price of despatching another orphan to Canada, or Australia, or New Zealand. A clergyman wanted money for hot dinners every day for four hundred poor children in the dock area of London; there were plans for another sugar beet factory in Norfolk. Harrods corsets, thigh to shoulder, were fifty-nine shillings and sixpence, though the ones with removable whalebone cost less. William Knight demanded that someone stop the suffragettes and put an end to 'this mad struggle which is doing irreparable injury to the wellbeing of women and of men'. In the meanwhile there was an appeal for ten thousand pounds to celebrate the fiftieth anniversary of Queen Alexandra's arrival in Britain. All over Britain people were reporting German airships overhead, though the Germans denied sending any airships and experts said that they could not have come so far. There were many advertisements asking for the relatives of men and women who had died all over the empire to get in touch with solicitors in order to hear something to their advantage.

It was bewildering, but for Violet it produced some vague outlines of a larger picture of the world than had been revealed to her during her sixteen years. Money was coming in from all over the world – the gold mines in South Africa, the rubber plantations of Malaya. Bridges, railways and hospitals were being built. The Germans were being watched as they, and the French, built up armies and navies. Ladies were giving balls all over London and titled people were setting off for somewhere called Cannes. She didn't plan to reveal all this reading to Frederick on his return. She was studying the lair while the beast was off hunting. He was not meant to notice, when he got back, that she had intruded into it. She searched the paper for clues about why Frederick had gone to Austria, but found none.

Frederick had in fact been despatched to Vienna by his Uncle Leopold on behalf of Levine-Schreft. His brother Laurence preferred to stay at home with his wife and small son, enjoying a life centring on his club, friends, social life and home. For some years, Leopold had seen the possibility of a war with Germany, and now had to act to preserve the banks. The main banking houses of Levine-Schreft were based in Vienna, Paris and London, still chiefly, for historical reasons, under the control of the Viennese bank. In the event of a European war the old Austrian-based system would no longer work. The small branch in New York was already almost autonomous. Now it seemed to Leopold that the three European banks should be officially separated, so that major decisions were no longer referred to Austria by the other two. If war came, whichever side won, at least one branch of Levine-Schreft would be on the winning side, and might find it easier to salvage the others. The complex business of altering the administration of the banks, as well as taking into account all the arguments and ambitions of the different but related families which ran them would be a challenge for anyone who undertook it. Leopold was ill – too ill to travel, too tired to undertake the gruelling two or three weeks the inception of the plan would demand. 'It must be swiftly arranged now,' he had told Frederick, in his guttural accent, somewhere between German and Russian. 'I wish I could go myself but, as you know, I am not well.'

He did not say that he was dying and did not need to, for Frederick knew, they all did, that Leopold's doctor had given him only a year to live. He did not say he considered Frederick's brother Laurence ought to have been readier to give up his London pleasures and the comfortable life in Cavendish Square to go abroad with Frederick. He did not say that in his opinion the contemporary Levines knew too little of their own family history. They had been European since the fourteenth century, but always ready to pack up and go at short notice when a wave of anti-Semitism came over the city they were living in. His brother Samuel, Laurence's father, had been a little too keen to put that behind him, Leopold thought. It was understandable that he would wish to spare his children this knowledge, now the Levines, the Schrefts, the Zwemmers, the Waldsteins, were so pleasantly ensconced in the hearts of the big cities of Europe. It was excellent that this generation was able to relax, that Laurence especially and then his son, would be able to live the life of confident, blond innocence of the British upper class they, seemingly effortlessly, seemed to belong to. This generation considered itself different from the Jews of the shtetls in Russia, the Jews of the ghettos of Salerno, Rome, Hamburg, the Jews of the slums of the East End of London. Very good, thought Leopold Levine, just as long as the people among whom these families lived accepted them and went on describing men like Laurence, as 'not an obvious Jew' and marrying their dowryless daughters to them. 'Remember, Frederick,' he told his nephew, 'when times become difficult the Jew is blamed. When they become even more difficult, the Jew is punished.'

Frederick's visit to Vienna consisted of business which had to be handled with tact. Joshua Schreft, who had come from Paris, and his brother-in-law, Joseph Waldstein, who conducted the affairs of the great Vienna bank, were less than happy at losing complete control. Frederick spent long days and restless nights on the large walnut bed at the Waldsteins. There were many visits to relatives, large dinners, and musical evenings when Julie and Aimée Waldstein, the daughters of the house, played the harp, more to show off Julie's white arms, and the piano, more to show off Aimée's white fingers than for the sake of the music itself. Leopold had already told Frederick that Joseph and Rebecca Waldstein's daughters were charming, rich and of marriageable age. But Frederick, with no stomach for huge family dinners and no ear for music, even when it was good, and tired by the heavy demands of the work, was having a hard time of it in the heavily furnished homes of his relations' large houses until captured by his cousins, Rudolph and Hanno Waldstein, twin brothers of the musical Julie and Aimée, and dragged round the cafés, bars and brothels of the city. 'Come, Frederick, we're taking you to the opera – again,' cousin Rudolph had threatened with a grin, and promptly led him to a beautiful house full of beautiful whores, where he ended up in a bedroom with a red-headed woman lovely enough for a painting by Rossetti and whose sexual skills seemed to him to make the girls of Half Moon Street seem like nuns. He left Vienna sadly, feeling that he had found its real pleasures too late, the brothels, the little cafés, the beauty of the great streets and buildings at night as he strolled arm-in-arm with his cousins, laughing and sometimes singing for sheer joy.

After leaving the pleasures of Vienna he went to Berlin, staying with a young cousin who had married into the minor German aristocracy. It was here that he began to see clearly why Leopold thought it so urgent to divide the banks up before war came. 'It's obvious we have to smash Britain, or they will smash us,' his cousin's husband had explained across a heavily laden dinner table. His blue eyes were cold, his own passion made him forget that he was speaking to an Englishman. 'They want our trade, our colonies. One of us must triumph, the other yield. We can endure no more.' Over wine later he apologised, hoping Frederick would forgive him his lack of manners. Yet, listening to a pianist playing Chopin nocturnes in the drawing-room that evening Frederick felt he knew now why Leopold thought war would come. The atmosphere in the room seemed oppressive.

At the back, against the door, stood his host's brother and a friend, both in cadet uniform, and all Frederick could think as he looked at the healthy sixteen-year-olds, at the dignified men and women in evening dress listening to the music and the host's pretty sister in her pink silk dress, was that a cloud was gathering over all their heads. He prayed for a swift campaign and a victory for Britain as he sat in Berlin, with the music in his ears.

When he reached England three weeks later he had been in Austria, Germany and Paris, he had worked out most of the details of the changes for the bank and felt satisfied that he had left the family in a reasonably contented mood. He spent a week with Leopold in London and a week in the country with the family of one of his university friends. When he sent Violet a note, asking her out to the theatre, and got her reply saying she would like to come, he was a man much more confident and, perhaps, harder than the man who had set out for Austria five weeks before. He was not particularly conscious of the fact, but he was now a man who wanted a woman.

In that spring of 1913 the balance of power between Frederick and Violet shifted. Frederick was strong and confident. Violet knew she was pregnant.

She had known, by mid-March, that Frederick must have returned. She waited and waited, then took the step of telephoning Cavendish Square and asking for him. She was told that he was away, staying with friends in the country. It was as she put the receiver back on its hook that a dreadful fear struck her. Her period was four days overdue. She had to face the fact that on the evening she had decided she would never risk Tom making her pregnant again, she might have conceived. This awful thought drove out thoughts of Frederick's not getting in touch with her after he came back. It was no more than she had expected. Now, one leaden day passed into another and heavy, dream-disturbed sleeps led inexorably to more days behind the counter. She felt terrified and angry. A strong dose of cascara had given her a day of diarrhoea and left her weak and trembling. It had not brought on a period. Still smacking cold water all over her body in the mornings, the bracing, tingling effect only worked on her skin. Inside she felt heavy, tired, invaded.

The obvious answer was to tell Tom, marry him and begin the life of bearing children, scrimping and scraping, slaving twelve hours a day over grates, a washtub and a stove. Another choice was to try to get an abortion, and risk ending up like Celia, or worse, because at least Celia was alive, they said, and she, Violet, might die. But then, she could die in childbirth anyway, many did. She could have the child and leave it in an orphanage, but she'd be sacked as soon as Hammonds knew she was pregnant. She'd have to go home, in disgrace, the family would mock and insult her because of her previous pretensions, she'd be talked about in the street. In the end her mother might even try to persuade her to keep the baby; from then on she'd be the lowest of the low in her own home, the daughter who'd brought the family down. A job in a factory, ten hours a day putting the filaments in light bulbs or making shirts, while her mother took care of both children, that's what it would be. She'd got to decide, and soon. The problem wouldn't go away. It was the one secret you couldn't keep for more than a few months. Finally, she supposed, it might have to be Tom.

After an unbearable week she got a letter in her fourteen-year-old sister's careful copperplate hand.

Dear Vi,

Mum says you ought to know Tom Rawlinson is angry with you, says you are a bad-tempered b-t-h and that he is going around with a girl from a tea-shop with red hair. She says to tell you if you want to see Tom again you better get over there and apologise quick. Try to make it up with him. I thought I'd best to let you know. All well here and hope you are the same. Mum's angry with you too. Sorry to be the bearer of bad tidings, your loving sister,

Allie

Violet's little cold heart warmed to Allie; the best of the bunch, she thought, and very nice of her to have taken the trouble. Still, it was discouraging news, for somebody who might have to marry a man, to find out he was courting somebody else.

When Frederick Levine, driven by desire and full of confidence, turned up at her counter on a late spring day in March, he found Violet, keeping perfect control of her nerves, but underneath badly shocked, glum and not far from desperation.

Kate Higgins, April 11th, 1991

When the phone rang, we were all having tea in Brighton, scrambled eggs and fruit cake, before I left to get on the train to go back to London. My father answered it. It was Andy. He very much wanted me to have dinner with him that night. He was sorry to have been out of touch for so long because of pressure at work. Of course, I said yes, told him I would meet him at eight; but, as I went, suppressing my joy, back into the living-room, where a bright fire burned, and my mother was cutting more cake on the trolley, I felt, under the pleasure, slightly rotten. My parents' decent faces and cardigans, my son's rosy face, growing body, big feet in trainers, seemed to reproach me. There they were, mature autumn harvest on one side, advancing spring on the other, while my own situation seemed more like a long, tiring summer, when the sun is shining but the ground is drying and the plants are fading. Not too late to marry again, provide a stable home for Ray, have another child. That would please everyone.

Ten years before, when I married the first time I had felt enthusiastic about the prospect; not now. When I explained all this to my parents my father only nodded, conscious of the fact that my mother's career might have gone further than his own, if she had not had the responsibility of a home and children. She said only, 'Good luck to you, if you can do it, Kate.'

Andy's flat was full of people when I arrived. I saw Vanessa Hume, my probable rival, if that was the term, looking tall, blonde and well-dressed, and a couple of Africans in suits, probably politicians, and a few journalists from Andy's paper. Cousin Roger, my publisher, was sitting in a corner while his baby crawled after Andy's cat. Andy greeted me with a big hug and a kiss in the middle of the room, then said, 'Roger's over there. Why don't you go and be nice to him?'

Conscious of Vanessa's eyes on my back I went over and said, 'Hello, Roger. Want to hear the news about the book?'

He looked as if he'd forgotten I was writing one, or that he was the publisher, then said, 'Not the right moment. Looking forward to it, though.'

It didn't seem the right moment, either, to tell him the Levines had declined to co-operate with me, though I was very worried. 'Is Sarah here?' I asked, looking round for his wife.

'No, she's gone to visit her sister. It's my turn with the baby.' His expression was glum.

Rupert had dangled his tail provocatively over the edge of a low table. Roger went across the room and unclenched the baby's hand from the tail while Rupert, the cat, thwarted of a good scene, turned his back, lashing his tail, and Roger returned carrying the wailing baby. 'Wringing wet,' he said. 'I'd better go and change him.' He plodded off.

Andy put a drink in my hand. 'Come and meet everybody,' he said, and I did. Vanessa was distant. I felt she had me under observation and I wondered what was going on. I talked to a few people and not long after Roger came back with the baby, which began to cry.

'He's over-tired. I'll have to get him home,' he said. 'I've rung, but Sarah's not back yet.'

I thought it was not so much that he couldn't look after the baby, or didn't want to. He loved his baby but it was hard and lonely work, somebody had to do it and sometimes he wished it wasn't him.

'They shouldn't have them if they aren't prepared to look after them,' observed Andy's friend non-judgmentally.

'Some of us are at least trying,' Roger said, plainly knowing the other man's disreputable history.

'And we're right behind you, Roger,' said the journalist unremorsefully, 'and downwind a bit.'

'I've just changed him,' said Roger, indignantly, off guard and glancing at the back of the baby's red dungarees.

I couldn't help grinning though I knew it was wrong.

Andy said, 'Right, you lot. We're off. Stay and drink up, but don't let the cat out through the front door when you go. He's on antibiotics and he's got to stay in till he's finished the course.' He took my arm and hurried me out. 'We'd be all night getting rid of that lot,' he said on the stairs. 'I hope they'll be gone when we get back.'

Vanessa was one of those left behind.

'What's wrong with Rupert?' I asked.

'He got in another fight and it went septic,' Andy said. We were going to eat at a fish restaurant off Regent Street, but there was a police cordon at the top and parked police vans and ambulances, lights flashing, and after making a wide detour we found cordons all round Piccadilly Circus.

'What's happening?' said Andy to an officer in a peaked cap.

'We're cleaning up Leicester Square, sir,' said the policeman, observing Andy's press sticker in the window of the car. 'Getting rid of the rats as you might say. Sorry about the inconvenience.'

'Drugs, rent boys spreading AIDS,' said Andy, going down towards Trafalgar Square. There was a cordon round the South African Embassy and another outside Downing Street and, as we went round Parliament Square, more policemen, vans and flashing lights, all round the Houses of Parliament. We ended up in Chelsea.

'Adrian Critchlow's a busy chap these days,' he said, 'what with all this trouble in Morecambe. There're four thousand police there all the time, now.' There had been some trouble on the drilling rigs, too many accidents, not enough safety precautions. The men had tried to unionise, and been stopped.

I didn't say anything. During my time in Northern Ireland the Home Secretary, Adrian Critchlow, with his new jails and his refusal even to open an enquiry on any outrage whatsoever, had come to figure in many of my nightmares, a bully figure with black eyebrows and a heavy black moustache.

I felt I couldn't talk about it to keen-brained Andy Littlebrown, prominent international journalist, always steady under shot and shell, the man who had done six months in Parkhurst for refusing to divulge his sources over an exposé of carelessness at nuclear power stations, and subsequent cover-up. Here was a man who had been in jail for his beliefs, who was standing on the windy beach, constantly defending the sea wall against tides of Fascism. How could I discuss my nightmares about Critchlow under the matrimonial duvet in the avenue in Belfast with this expert on terror, sadism and repression?

'How are you getting on with Roger's book?' he asked.

I told him about Rosie Johnson and the Levine family's apparent refusal to co-operate. 'There's still Joanna, the youngest child,' I said hopefully.

'The letter told you she's in a clinic,' said Andy. 'Everybody knows. No way you'll get any answers out of her.'

'What's supposed to be wrong with her?' I asked.

'Paranoid depressive, that's what somebody told me. I just happened to mention Violet Levine and that's what the guy said.' It was frustrating that Andy always knew somebody who knew something.

'I'll try to see her anyway, if I can,' I declared.

'Well,' said Andy, shrugging, 'I wouldn't. In fact with the Levines out I wonder if you can do the thing at all. Maybe you should reconsider the whole thing.'

'She could be in a lucid patch. Anyway, it might be enlightening, one way or another. And I'm not getting any co-operation so far from Violet's other children, Robert Levine or Pamela Christian-Smith.'

Andy stared at me. 'I'll finish that meat, if you're not going to eat it,' he said.

I passed him my half-eaten steak. Chewing, he asked, 'Any other progress?'

'No,' I said. 'It's like digging out a boulder which is blocking your path. You dig and dig. There's more and more mud, and every time you push it, it still won't shift.'

'That's what I've been saying,' he told me. 'You can't get far if the family won't see you. Inevitably they're your most important source of information. Then there's the aspect of privacy to consider: are you really prepared to continue when the dead woman's relatives so obviously don't want you to?'

'That's a funny statement, coming from you,' I said. 'Your job depends on getting people to tell you what they don't want to say.'

'I'm talking about people's private lives,' he said. 'I deal in news. I think you're being carried away by all these publishing tales of gallant biographers carrying on against all the odds— '

'She was a public figure,' I retorted, stung. 'She wrote her autobiography – one of the points she made was that even her private life was partly a reflection of the times.' But I didn't feel as confident as I was trying to sound. I'd just left the family in Brighton and given my mother money for Ray. Even then I knew I wasn't doing enough to cover the expenses of a ten-year-old boy. I asked if Sam had sent his part of Ray's maintenance and my mother was forced to say he hadn't, telling me this was probably because he'd suddenly been posted back to Belize.

And then there was Vanessa Hume. I felt I was meant, somehow, to mention Vanessa to Andy. We were nudging each other's feet and knees under the table, staring into each other's eyes, but we hadn't, I felt, dealt with Andy's hidden agenda. To avoid the discussion we were meant to have, I rattled on: 'Oh, well, there's a mystery man called Gordon Stone. I rang Dave Gottlieb at *The Mag* and he wouldn't talk over the phone. Anyway, I'm meant to see him tomorrow and he'll tell me. You don't know anything about him, do you?'

'I don't think so' Andy said. 'I should be careful of Dave Gottlieb. He's paranoid about the phones being bugged at that magazine. He thinks he's followed everywhere. He'd arrange a meet at the Round Pond to discuss the weather. Coffee at my place?'

'Let's hope the crowd's cleared.' I let him pay. I was too broke to preserve my independence. Next time we'd have to go to Macdonalds, I thought, but Andy wouldn't so what could I do? Bring sandwiches?

That night Andy said the words I longed to hear, 'I love you.' I was joyful but I dreamed of being hunted through the mist by the army. I knew I was able to fly, and escape, but when I tried, I couldn't and stood on the edge of a cliff, flapping my arms and trying to lift off, while they came up behind me. I could hear them shouting instructions to each other, through the mist, but I couldn't take flight.

Violet Crutchley, March, 1913

A lad in battered boots and an old bowler brought Violet a message at her counter. 'Miss Violet Crutchley – gent gimme 'arf a crahn to bring you this quick.'

Violet took it from him and said, ' 'Oppit, you.' When the urchin showed signs of waiting for a further tip she said, 'Get out, or else. I'm warning you.'

He then ducked down one of the carpeted aisles and disappeared. Violet looked round to see if Mr Gummidge had noticed. He had, but he couldn't reprimand her as he was selling some kid gloves to a gentleman in a top-hat. She stared at the envelope, seeing Frederick's writing but noting also that he had not come himself, or sent a message by a maid. He had found a casual street urchin, given him money to deliver the note, hardly caring, it seemed, if the boy fulfilled the task or not.

Covertly, she opened the note, scrawled in Frederick's copperplate:

Dearest Vi,

Are you free tonight? I should *love* to see you,

Frederick

The heat of the shop and the smell of leather gloves were nauseating to her. It was a smell she was never afterwards able to bear. Hastily written, no protestations, no request, no pleases and thank yous, she thought, deciding she'd go anyway; he'd probably throw her over, but who cared, she told herself, crushed by this ordinary fate, which had altered the lives of her mother and all the women she knew. Upstairs, the smart ladies were purchasing cotton and lace, silk and lace camisoles and knickers to go under their slender gowns, silk stockings for their exposed ankles, and all too soon she, Violet, would be bulging and swelling. She'd probably have to marry Tom Rawlinson, the Singing Postman, and give him an even better excuse than the average man for making her life a misery. She could hear him now, shouting, 'I had to marry you,' across a cramped kitchen.

And even that wasn't certain, now he'd taken up with someone else. He could always play the villain, say the child wasn't his and not marry her. He had all the power now.

That evening Violet met Frederick in her black shop dress, not even bothering to change the starched white collar and cuffs, slightly soiled by the day's work, for another set. She took off her stockings, and the belt supporting them, rammed her bare feet into her shoes, stuck her old black coat over the lot. She brushed out her long, glossy hair but lacked the energy to pin it up again. She just tied it back with a black bow, put her big wide-crowned, wide-brimmed green hat on top, and walked a mile to the corner of Cavendish Square, where she waited in drizzling rain. She had done this before, but that time she had been excited by the illicit feeling of the situation. His family, in their mansion, were not to know that on a street corner nearby, in the lamplight, waiting for him, was the humble girl he truly loved, she had told herself, in the style of the romances she and the other girls at Hammonds read out to each other in the evenings while they dried their hair or mended their underwear, or pinned up each other's hair in new styles. Now, standing under the lamp on the corner, she realised what kind of girls really stood about in the street waiting for men and dreaded becoming one of them.

When Frederick came to meet her, in a dark suit, carrying his gloves, cane and a light coat, he was five minutes late. Nor, as he took her arm, did he apologise for this or, as last time, for meeting her in the street. 'Lovely to see you, Vi,' he said. 'Let's go to Cummings.' They took a cab to the chop-house in the Strand, where there were booths with high wooden backs, wooden seats and waiters in long white aprons racing about in a smoky, steamy atmosphere, with huge silver platters loaded with food. Seized by a frantic hunger, Violet ate a plate of chops, cabbage and mashed potato with enthusiasm.

She asked him what had happened in Austria, guessing easily that his trip had given him the manly confidence which, in her circles, usually meant an equally manly disregard for the feelings of women. She questioned him sharply. She commented. Finally, in a burst of intuition she said, 'What you mean is you're moving the business here, in case there's a war with Germany.'

'I didn't say that,' protested Frederick. 'Come off it, Vi. You sound like Mrs Pankhurst. Let's go and have a drink and I'll let you quiz me on what the ladies are wearing.'

Which you know, down to their skins, I bet, thought Violet vengefully, and then, in a rallying tone, said it.

Frederick laughed. Violet was a tartar tonight, he thought. She was showing an unexpected side to her nature, and one, in his mood, he was happy to see. 'Where to, then?' he said.

'The Variety,' she responded. They sat in a box, drank champagne all through the jugglers, comedians and singers and came out into a fierce wind. Violet was a bit drunk. Her skirt blew up.

In the hansom cab he put his arm round her shoulders, on her breast, and said, 'Won't you come somewhere else with me?'

And Violet, with nothing to lose and not caring, said, 'The night is young.'

'What about— ' Frederick asked, meaning what about explaining her absence overnight at the store.

'My Mum's been suddenly taken sick,' declared Violet. 'I can feel it in my bones.'

Frederick laughed. 'I hope that's not all you feel.'

'Oh, no,' she responded quickly. 'I feel a lot more than that.'

'You're a sport, Vi,' Frederick said. He was even a little alarmed by Violet's sudden change from a quiet shopgirl from a respectable family to a working girl on the spree, but he saw he was getting what he came for; he was enjoying himself, that was what mattered. It seemed that Violet needed no persuading, urging, protestations of love.

Violet was taking off her clothes in the bedroom in a hotel in Leinster Gardens, where no questions were asked and she thought, Perhaps, perhaps this is no bad thing.

Frederick came up behind her, stark naked, as she stood only in her drawers, and clasped her breasts. 'You've done this before,' he declared.

'Only twice, when I was just a girl and didn't know any better,' Violet declared.

'That's what you say,' he told her, and as she protested, showing the last remnants of common sense – 'No, Frederick, I swear, I was taken advantage of when I didn't know any better' – he carried her to the bed, and took her, rapidly and unceremoniously.

As he lay, panting, beside her, Violet wept a little. Frederick felt relieved, and a little remorseful. She wasn't a tart, after all, little Vi. Perhaps he'd been a shade brusque. She did look very tiny, crying there, with her black hair spread over her little breasts. He turned to her and took her in his arms. 'Poor little Violet, my poor little flower. Was your Frederick a beastly man to you, just then? Come, let's kiss it better.'

And this time he wooed her, while Violet feigned surprised arousal, tentative love, and as Frederick whispered endearments to her, gave little gasps and exclamations. 'Oh, that's lovely, Frederick.' This excited him more and more. Soon he was in her, Violet clinging to him, nibbling his neck, exclaiming, while feeling little but a pain in her pelvic bone caused by his previous violent assault, and her usual distaste when she felt a bulky man on top of her. Frederick, it had to be admitted, smelt better than Tom Rawlinson, for he bathed more often, and used better soap, and his hair was slightly scented with musky pomade, but his skin was not so smooth and his moustache tickled. Soon he was moving faster, crying out. Violet grasped his buttocks, squeezed them, gasped herself, and then it was over. Frederick smiled at her as she smiled shyly at him and confessed, 'Oh, Frederick. I didn't know . . . this . . . could be like that. It was so horrible – before – when it happened to me before, when – well, I won't talk about it.'

That night Frederick Levine told her he would like to find somewhere for her to live, a pleasant little house where he could visit her. The part of Violet which knew you couldn't trust a man's promises after he'd done that to you didn't believe him. Another part of her almost trusted him. Next morning, when she woke, there was a note on the dressing-table.

Dearest little Violet,

My darling, I am engaged all day. Mr Sturgess, at my office, will be finding you a sweet little house where we can be alone together all the time. Beloved, will you meet me tonight so we can go to look at our nest? My heart is full of love for you,

Your Frederick

Violet put the note in her bag, dressed, jammed her hat on her head, passed the woman who was still at the desk without a word, went to work and reached her counter by ten that morning. She didn't really believe Frederick's desire for her would last, she didn't quite believe in the little house, or Sturgess. What she knew was that she needed her week's wages, and the following week's, until she knew for sure whether she had a home with Frederick Levine, or would have to find Tom Rawlinson and tell him that she was pregnant by him. She had only a few weeks. Tom could get married if she didn't get to him soon. In the meanwhile, she had to work and look after herself as best she could.

That was the day the suffragettes attacked Hammonds. During the afternoon, the hour when ladies are normally taking tea, the assistants close to the front of the store saw, through the plate-glass windows, a crowd of twenty women, dressed in mainly dark coats and hats, outside the store, and heard them shouting. At her counter at the back of the shop Violet heard the faint noise, heard young Mr Bradley, the junior assistant, shout in a very un-Hammonds tone, 'Blimey! It's the suffragettes!'

After glancing up at the shout, Mr Gummidge, Violet noted, fell to putting two pairs of gentlemen's black gloves tidily back in a sliding drawer beneath the counter, a look of confusion on his face.

Young Bradley then made up for his vulgarity by shouting, 'Get everybody away from the windows,' and suiting the deeds to the words, rushed to the huge plate-glass windows and began to push staff and customers to the back of the store.

Violet, fired by the excitement, ran from her counter to join him, yelling, 'All get back, all get back. They're going to break the windows,' which the women, grabbing hammers from their large handbags and shouting, 'Votes for women', duly did, shattering, in less than three minutes, the six large plate-glass windows of the store. Violet herself pushed a large woman away from a toppling wax figure wearing a green barathea model at four guineas, and concluded her work by seizing a boy of five, who had escaped his nurse and was standing staring at the sight of women – one in her sixties, Violet noted, with the appearance of a respectable housekeeper, one a very pretty girl in an expensive blue coat with a fur collar – who were smashing the windows. In a flash the women were gone, still calling, as they ran, 'Votes for women – tell Asquith'.

They were succeeded by a stunned-looking police constable, who stared through the broken windows, across the toppled models, the fragments of a displayed dinner service, a walnut table, covered in broken glass, at the customers crowded at the back of the store.

'Catch them, man! Go after them and catch them,' called the woman Violet had pushed aside, as she removed her hat, which was askew, and put it back again, pushing in the hatpins. 'My God,' she said, turning to the man beside her, 'no wonder these women get away with murder if this is the kind of policeman we have to count on.'

The floor manager was now on the pavement talking to the policeman. Young Mr Bradley was organising a team to sweep up the broken glass, while the customers, not without careful looks up and down the pavement beforehand, were leaving.

'Outrageous,' Henry Gummidge was saying with an attempt at firmness. 'How they think this will impress anybody I don't know. Termagants.' He looked at Violet sternly. 'Miss Crutchley, you're covered in blood.'

Violet put her hand on her face and brought it away, bloody. 'Bit of glass must have caught me,' she said weakly.

'Not too bad I don't think,' said a man's voice behind her. 'With your permission, sir, I'll take Miss Crutchley home and give her some assistance. A cup of tea, perhaps. She's been very brave, I'm sure you'll agree.'

Violet turned to see a short, portly man in a bowler-hat, with a black moustache.

'It is Miss Crutchley, isn't it? Miss Violet Crutchley? I'm Mr Sturgess, Henry Sturgess, personal clerk to Mr Levine of the banking house, Levine-Schreft. I happened to be looking for you when this incident occurred. I believe Mrs Wilson, the housekeeper at Cavendish Square, would be only too happy to attend to you. If you agree, that is,' he said, then turning to Mr Gummidge, 'and if your superior will allow you to go.'

'Miss Crutchley can hardly attend to the customers in that condition,' Gummidge said. He had shown want of leadership in the crisis, and knew it. 'On consideration, it might be best if she goes somewhere and tidies up while we restore order here.'

'Thank you,' Henry Sturgess said, touching his bowler.

He took Violet's arm and steered her over the carpet, past one young woman assistant, weeping, with others trying to comfort her, another angrily shaking a shoe in which some glass had lodged, a furious man rapping on a counter selling silk scarves with his cane saying, 'Is no one serving here? I haven't got all day,' and several women sweeping glass into dustpans under the eye of young Mr Bradley.

In the street Sturgess hailed a cab, saying, 'Best not to brave Cavendish Square at the moment. If you'll trust me, Miss Crutchley, I'll take you to my own home, where Mrs Sturgess can help you tidy yourself a little, and give you a nice cup of tea. A visit to Mrs Wilson, formidable housekeeper of Cavendish Square, and her strong-minded accomplice, Mr Arthur Brough, the butler, might not be opportune at this moment.'

'Righty ho,' agreed Violet, getting into the cab, which drove off to the less fashionable area of Notting Hill Gate, on the wrong side of Holland Park. 'So what's all this?' she said. Henry Sturgess, she quickly saw, was not a gentleman, more of a non-commissioned officer, and a very clever one, she thought. There would be no point in play-acting with him, or trying to pull the wool over his eyes. He reminded her of the headmaster of the school she'd been to, who presided over his brick and asphalt kingdom with a keen eye and an ever-ready cane.

'I came to collect you at dinner-time,' he said, 'to see over a property I had selected for Mr Levine, on your behalf. If you liked it, I proposed to conclude the transaction this afternoon. I prefer to deal with matters speedily, as they arise. I dislike clutter. I'm asked to inform you that the house, a very nice, compact premises near Swiss Cottage, with a garden, four bedrooms, dining-room, drawing-room, small but with a charming outlook and the usual offices, all extremely modern, would be yours to live in once the usual formalities had been completed.'

'Oh,' said Violet.

'You're a fortunate young woman,' Sturgess said. 'And here we are.' They had stopped at a small house in a quiet street.

Walking up the path he whistled, then stood at the door, waiting. 'Mrs Sturgess has been kind enough to look over the house – a woman's eye you know – and expressed herself delighted, only wished she had the chance to live in it. Oh, there you are,' he said, as a parlourmaid opened the door.

'Sorry, sir,' she said, 'I wasn't expecting you.'

'Not the point, Betty, not the point,' Sturgess said. 'Be prepared, that's the motto. Please remember, in life, the unexpected always occurs. There you are, dearest,' he said, as a plump woman in a dark woollen dress came down the stairs, with a large child in her arms.

'Oh, my goodness, it must be Miss Crutchley,' she said, 'and covered in blood. Betty, take Miss Crutchley to the bathroom and bring up hot water immediately. Call Effie and tell her I want her to take the baby.' She had the same small blue eyes as her husband. So, Violet noticed, had the baby, a little girl of about a year old in a red dress and shoes. The parlourmaid disappeared, came back with an enamel bowl of water, followed by a girl in a print dress and apron. 'How did this happen?' Mrs Sturgess asked Violet, setting the child on its feet with the instruction, 'Go to Effie, darling.'

'Suffragettes,' Violet said.

'Oh dear, oh dear,' said Mrs Sturgess placidly. 'Well, never mind, you follow Betty upstairs to the bathroom and I'll ask cook to get us a cup of tea.'

In the glass in the bathroom Violet noted that she was very pale and her hair was falling down. She had a streak of blood on one cheek which had stained her white collar.

'Give the collar to me. I'll give it a good soak and a wash, then I'll iron it dry. Be ready in half an hour,' said the parlourmaid. Taking the collar she said, 'These suffragettes, they'll be the death of us all before they're done. That and the Fenians. My sister works at the house of a member of the Cabinet. He has two policemen outside his house night and day. Shocking, isn't it? Still, she's marrying one of them, so I suppose every cloud has a silver lining.' Showing all the speed which seemed characteristic of this household she whisked off with the collar before Violet could reply.

Violet washed her face and hands, brushed out her hair and pinned it up again, trying to collect her thoughts. Everything had happened too quickly. The sudden present of the house near Swiss Cottage was the biggest surprise, but, she thought gloomily, what good was it to her, when she was expecting another man's child? It was rotten luck, thought Violet. No point in moving in; she'd be out on her ear in a month or two. Going downstairs, the thought, obvious really, struck her. Of course, she could try to make Frederick Levine believe the child was his.

Kate Higgins, April 14th, 1991

'So, why do you want to know about Gordon Stone?' Dave Gottlieb asked.

We hadn't used the pub the magazine staff normally went to but had gone, at Dave's suggestion, to a wine bar off Piccadilly, full of potted plants and thirty-year-old upwardly mobile men and women. It didn't seem typical of Dave. He explained with some satisfaction, 'They wouldn't expect us to come here, and if they did, they'd stand out like a sore thumb. That's the secret of dealing with plain-clothes policemen: if you're somewhere where you look out of place yourself, the only other person who looks out of place is your tail. They're dressed to mingle with my crowd, not a load of word processor operators, hair stylists and investment consultants.'

'Are you sure you aren't getting it a little bit out of proportion?' I asked him, remembering Andy's remarks about Dave's paranoia.

'None of you lot knows what it's like,' Dave replied. 'We have to get the office debugged by a security firm every week. Needless to say, our mail's opened. My flat was burgled three times last year. They're improving – the last one looked nearly like a real burglary. I'm not sure it wasn't a real break-in.

'What we've got now is a nasty little case, some leaked

papers from Trade and Industry about a small company working on non-oil-fuelled vehicles. If the invention's any good it'll throw the oil industry into confusion. The firm's already had to fight two bankruptcy petitions, both organised to hit them when their credit was at its lowest, the MD's been photographed picking up what they thought was a callgirl and going back to her house – the woman was his ex-wife. Meanwhile, a mystery buyer's bought up all the available shares, so now the company's forty per cent in unknown hands, plus the top R and D man's getting calls threatening his family – what a mess. Our question is, who's behind the original leak? Who's pushing who? I get twenty-four-hour surveillance, my flat's searched, phone tapped – and characters like you and Andy say I'm paranoid.' He looked at me sharply through horn-rimmed spectacles. 'My mother's house in Rotherham had a break-in and, believe it or not, my grandad's ashes, stored in an urn on the mantelpiece, prior to dispersal over the sea off Harrogate, get tipped on the floor – searched for microdots, I suppose.'

'Rotten,' I said. 'How are your nerves, by the way?'

'If they were cracking, I wouldn't tell you,' he said, 'in case you passed it on. You get used to it, like you got used to living in Belfast, I suppose. Anyway, why do you want to know about Gordon Stone?'

'I'm writing a biography of Violet Levine. I saw Rosie Johnson. She said this Stone was part of Violet's life. He's not in her autobiography.'

'I'm not surprised. I'd keep away from him as much as possible. Concentrate on something else.'

I told him Andy hadn't heard of Stone.

'Well . . . ' said Dave, seeming at a loss.

The well-trimmed, upwardly mobile suits, the spike heels, coiffures and short voluminous coats began to disappear through the door of the wine bar. 'People have got to live,' he seemed to remind himself, then said suddenly, 'The best thing in life is not to be on one of Adrian Critchlow's lists. Once you're seriously on the computer at the Home Office you can't move without scrutiny – break-ins, taps, bugs; if you drive too fast, if you get pushed over in a fracas outside a pub, the cop in the car taps out your name and number on the car computer and you're assisting the police with their enquiries down at the station for hours on end, if not in court on some minuscule charge. Once you're on the list life's one big problem. Critchlow's a genius. He seems to be protecting Stone. So don't draw his attention by contacting Stone. Why not, you ask? That's the problem,' said Dave, his eyes on the door. Then he turned to me and said rapidly, 'I don't like that man and woman who came in. Talk to me for a bit about nothing, see where they sit, then we'll switch if they look as if they can lip-read me.'

'There's a bit of a problem – the family, the children that is, won't see me,' I said. 'Well, if they won't I'll just plod on. The great thing, as I see it, is not Violet's great contribution to twentieth-century life and thought, but the way she reflected her own times. She was more moulded than a mould-maker, if you see what I mean.'

Dave glanced at his watch.

'Have you got to go?'

'I'm expecting a phone call in half an hour. It's okay for a bit. Another drink?'

'No, I've got to get back.'

'I'll drop you,' he said.

In the street we got into a taxi. 'Sorry,' he said. 'I decided not to risk that pair in the corner. Now the point is – all I know about Stone is that he's on a Critchlow list, not for observation but protection. At one point we got into a government computer, found a mysterious list, thousands of names. We tried ringing up about a few, and every time a shutter went down. Ask an official anything about them and just giving the name triggers a response on the computer. They don't know about them. They say you'll be rung back. Only you aren't. Our conclusion was that all the people on that list are under cover, in major or minor positions, working for firms with defence contracts, running small businesses in dodgy ghettoes where trouble might break out, infiltrators into left-wing movements, or CND, teachers at schools near nuclear installations – ordinary people, leading ordinary lives, but they put in a report if anything interests them. They're sleepers. They lie doggo until something happens. Operation Nemo, it's called, Latin for nobody, bit of classical education somewhere. These listed individuals are supposed to be nobody, but they're in touch with somebody – and that somebody, at quite a high level, protects them by denying any knowledge of them, so they can go on being nobody in peace. The point is, Stone's on that list. I don't know why, so even more reason to stay away. Otherwise you could be in for trouble.'

As he got out of the taxi, I gave him a kiss. He seemed not to notice. He pushed some money for the fare into my hand, and went into the doorway of the gloomy Victorian building in Farringdon Street, where the magazine had two floors. I took the cab on to the tube station and went back to the flat, looking down the carriage as I went along to see if anyone looked like a spook. Of course everyone did, from the lady knitting a green jumper with the balls of wool in a Tesco bag on the floor to the black kid with headphones in his ears. I couldn't see how Dave could stand it.

Di was in a temper when I came back. She said I'd drunk all the coffee and when I produced the fresh jar I'd bought and put it on the table she started on about toilet paper, and when I showed her where I'd put a new pack of four rolls she said how was she supposed to find it and wondered if I'd be at Andy's place that night. When I told her I didn't know, she suggested, predictably, I should stop allowing my plans to be dictated by that bastard. I said if she'd like me to be out she had only to tell me so. 'Is there something on your mind?' I said. 'Is there something that needs airing? If so, let's have it.'

This reasonable approach seemed to make her angrier. Then the phone rang and she answered it. 'For you,' she snapped.

The same high, slightly cracked voice – it was another call from my anonymous informant.

'She was a shopgirl when she met Frederick Levine – sold gloves.'

'Why didn't she say so?'

'The suffragette attack on the shop – she was inside it, serving at the counter, not outside the shop shouting "Votes for women".'

'How can I prove it, though?' I asked.

'Ah,' said the peculiar voice.

'I suppose you don't want to tell me who you are?'

'Not now. Perhaps never.'

'Very well,' I went on quickly, realising that the important thing to do was keep the voice talking. 'Why didn't she tell the truth about these incidents— '

'Why do you think?' asked the voice.

'To make herself look better.'

'Just so – and she had a lot to hide.'

'You mean, a lot of what she said in *I Affirm* is not true?'

'Not all of it.' I heard a click, like a cup going into a saucer. I could hear traffic behind the voice. But it could have been traffic anywhere – Edinburgh, Rome, Toronto.

'The difficulty is proof,' I said. 'You must see my point of view. If I could see you, and quote what you say to me . . . '

'I don't think so.'

'Violet's daughter, Joanna,' I said desperately. 'I'm trying to find her . . . ' For all I knew, I was speaking to her.

'She's mostly at a place called the Priory, in Rye.'

'Do you think she'll talk to me?'

There was a pause. 'She might,' the voice said finally. 'Why don't you go and see?'

'Who's Gordon Stone— ?' I started to ask, but there was a click, and the phone began to purr.

Di was standing in the doorway. She said quickly, 'I think we need a break from each other. Honestly, it might be best.' She still looked angry.

I stared at her, thinking about the phone cutting off like that and half-taking in the small skinny figure and small furious face. I felt baffled and annoyed. It wasn't fair. 'I don't understand, Di. I mean – I just don't understand. How come things have changed so quickly? All I can say is – I'm going to Rye and if you want me out when I come back, tell me then. And what it's all about. There's more to this – I've known you a long time, Di. Nothing fits.' I knew I was right – and she knew I knew. 'I'll get my stuff together. I'll be back in a few days.'

And I packed some books and clothes. I was due to see Andy that night but I left a message on his answering machine saying I had to go away. I'd phone that evening. I wasn't happy. I knew Andy would take offence about my cancelling at short notice. Di had flustered me. I was being pushed out.

Di listened to the call and said, 'I suppose you're going to tell him about this.'

'Maybe not,' I told her. 'He likes little spats between the girls. He resents our relationship, our independent lifestyle, our friendship between women, our mutual support system . . . ' I couldn't help adding, 'No need for me to tell him it's a fuck-up.'

Di just went away. Then I left the flat. I went down to Rye and took a room in a B and B. I was still feeling confused about Di, who, as far as I could see, had rushed on me unexpectedly, or had simply been living in a state of suppressed fury about me which I hadn't noticed for months. Neither thought was comfortable to live with and I had to assume that, if we couldn't sort out our differences I might shortly be homeless.

I made my call to the Priory where Joanna Levine was supposed to be from a pay-phone in the long, narrow hall. I knew the landlady was listening behind the door. I was put through to the director of the clinic, Dr Alan Findlater, who told me I could see Joanna Levine tomorrow. For once I seemed to be making progress.

Next day, with my notebook and recorder, I took a bus through Rye and beyond it, and walked in a strong wind up a long road where large houses surrounded by trees overlooked an expanse of flats and sea. The tide was far out. The rock-scattered beach was covered for a mile in big pools of sea-water. The Priory was yet another large Edwardian seaside house in its own grounds behind a high wall. There were little balconies upstairs, lots of ornately carved wood and it was surrounded by a long verandah running right round the house, on which one or two cane chairs were set. Whether it was an old folks home or a clinic was unclear. The notice-board set on the lawn beside the drive read, The Priory Convalescent Home, Director, Dr Alan Findlater, MD.

A nurse in a cap and white uniform let me in. 'I'll take you to Dr Findlater,' she said, and led me along a corridor Marley-tiled in brown, with the black track of wheelchairs and trolleys down the centre. It wasn't very clean. Nothing was. The pot plant on a bamboo table in a corner under a window looking out on a couple of big, bare trees had dusty leaves. The air smelt stale and institutional. Through the open door of the day-room I saw a woman in an overall hoovering a speckled red carpet, without moving the chairs. Dr Findlater was sitting at his desk in a small office on the right, opposite the day-room. I went in. He stood up and shook my hand, a big man in a white coat who looked as if he was in with the local bank manager, played a few rounds on Saturdays with the local house agent, would probably, if I'd been a man, have given me a Masonic handshake. 'So you've come to see our Joanna,' he said. 'What's the book about?'

I was about to become an anecdote at the golf club bar, I could sense it. 'I've been commissioned by a publisher, Askew and Askew,' I said, 'to write a biography of Violet Levine, Joanna Levine's mother.'

'Very interesting. Have you done this sort of thing before?' he had to ask.

Tempted to reel out a string of imaginary biographies I answered, 'Not exactly like this.'

'A challenge, then,' he said. 'Well, I'm not sure how much change you'll get out of Joanna. She gets very confused and withdrawn sometimes.' He consulted a file. 'This seems to be one of her better patches – it might be all right.'

'What's wrong with her?' I asked.

'I could put a label on it,' Dr Findlater told me, 'but it wouldn't mean anything. Basically, since adulthood she's been subject to depression, paranoid delusions, and so forth. I needn't tell you some of what she says can't be taken too literally.'

'What sort of delusions?'

'Paranoiacs aren't very original – enemies from outer space, rays of various kinds coming from various sources, Hitler— '

'Hitler?' I asked.

'Yes, yes,' he told me, standing up, 'it's a common fantasy. I'll let Sister lead you to her. If there's anything else I can do . . . '

'Thank you,' I said.

He pressed a button on the internal communicator. 'Sister James,' he said, 'Miss Higgins for you.'

Following the nurse's broad white back down the passageway, the day-room was still empty but for the woman cleaning.

'Where is everybody?' I asked the nurse.

'What?'

'Well – the patients.'

'Residents,' she corrected me. 'There are only four here at the moment. Joanna's in the small sitting-room.'

'Why so few?' I asked.

'Ask Dr Findlater – he admits them.'

I was, by now, nervous. This almost empty house looking over the sea frightened me slightly. And I was about to see a real link with Violet Levine, not Rosie Johnson, who had known her, professionally more than personally, when she was nearly fifty, but a child she had borne, who had lived with her in the same house during her most impressionable years. I was by now so thoroughly confused about what Violet was like, that what her daughter said, even her actual presence, even the fact that she contained the real Violet Levine's DNA was enough to encourage me. I hoped something would start to make sense. I dreaded that what I might hear would throw me into worse confusion. And of course I was wondering if she was my informant, my secret caller.

The woman sat in the big window overlooking the flats, where birds swooped down over the sands. She was tall and fairly big, not fat, with long well-shaped legs shod in expensive brown shoes stuck out in front of her. She wore a brown skirt and a tan twinset with a string of pearls. Her fair hair was permed, I thought, and probably dyed. She wore whitish powder and red lipstick.

The nurse settled herself comfortably at the back of the room. Whether this was in order to eavesdrop, observe, or because her patient might need controlling I didn't know.

I sat down in the chair opposite Violet's daughter. Now seventy, Joanna had bright blue eyes, a fair-skinned, comparatively unlined face. She did not look like either Violet or Frederick, both dark, but she might have resembled her Uncle Laurence, who had been big and fair, judging from his photograph. I leaned forward and said, 'Miss Levine. I'm writing a biography of your mother. I'd like to ask you some questions about her, if you don't mind.'

'Dr Findlater said I could speak to you about my famous

mother,' she said, and again I was surprised by how easy it all was, since the other Levines were refusing to see me at all. 'Though of course I didn't live with her much in my teens. Usually with Father and my stepmother – and Granny. Mother was living in Cheyne Walk.'

I risked a difficult question and asked her, 'Was it a shock, when your parents divorced? You were only twelve.'

She took it without surprise. 'Not really,' said Joanna Levine. 'Robert and Pamela had been predicting it for years, I'm afraid. I grew up with the idea that it was going to be not so much a question of "if" but "when". And Mother was a wonderful woman, but we never saw that much of her, she was always so busy, with parties and politics and things like that. And the books she wrote. It was mostly – well, the nurse, and then the governess – then school. I was away during term-time anyway . . . '

In spite of the hesitations she was perfectly controlled, completely lucid, although slow, but her face had the look of someone either utterly calm, or on heavy drugs, and judging by where she was, I suspected the latter. I didn't know how long I would be able to talk to Joanna before the doctor, or nurse, sent me away. How could I get close to finding out the truth, some truth? Almost more important, how could I gain some sense of Violet Levine as a real person? Now I was here, I hardly knew what to ask.

The only question I could think of was, 'What was she like?'

'Well, she was really rather wonderful,' came the light, upper-class voice. 'She was very busy, interested in things. She knew interesting people . . . ' Her voice trailed off a little. It was almost as if she couldn't think what to say. Yet she'd lived with Violet for the first twelve years of her life; I wasn't certain what had happened afterwards.

'Wonderful clothes,' she said. 'So well turned out – I think Pamela still has lots of her things in her house.'

No point in mentioning I was never going to see Pamela's things – or Pamela herself, if she could help it. I wasn't getting very far with Joanna, either.

'She was always busy,' came the soft voice, 'with committees, and so forth, and entertaining . . . ' Her voice was trailing now, words coming slowly. I thought perhaps the drugs they gave her were uncertain in their effects.

She looked out at the beach, where a man in a raincoat was throwing sticks for an Alsatian. Something was disturbing her, perhaps memories of nervous collapses, perhaps something else. I did not like to press. 'Of course,' she said, 'when I left home I took qualifications as a librarian. I had a job, with Westminster Council. Then I had a breakdown, for quite a long time.'

'Your mother says, in *I Affirm*, how loyal you were to her during that very difficult period in the fifties.'

The lipsticked lips closed, forming a tight red line, but the blue eyes still seemed expressionless. 'She was nice to say that,' said the high voice. It was not just the voice, but the intonations, I realised, which reminded me of a much younger woman. Certainly it was not the experienced voice of my mystery caller.

'What was your childhood like?' I said.

The lips relaxed. 'It was fun. We used to laugh and sing a lot in the nursery. We went to theatres, often very unsuitable performances. We had a Scottie, called Keir, after Keir Hardie, you know. He was the god of the nursery. We used to put his picture up, Nanny used to keep taking it down. We went to France, Normandy, or Brittany, on holiday . . . '

'I can't imagine your mother paddling in the Channel,' I said, rather hoping to see a different Violet, a woman making sand-castles, going for windy walks, eating ice-cream.

There wasn't going to be one, for Joanna said promptly, 'Oh no, she didn't. Often she didn't come. Father came.'

'Father came?' I said.

'Of course it wasn't the same when Mother left.'

'Although she seems not to have been there very much,' I remarked.

'It wasn't Mother, really,' Joanna said in a low voice.

I looked at her and she avoided my puzzled expression.

She looked at me carefully, then seemed to get back on course again. 'To be truthful,' she said, 'Mother blighted the fun, really. She was very anxious, always. She was frightened, I think. Children can sense it. They don't like it. And of course, my grandmother didn't like her. I think my Aunt Caroline had a sneaking liking for her though.'

'And what happened to Caroline?' I asked.

'Her son Jo-Jo became a soldier. After Uncle Laurence died in the First World War Caroline married again. I couldn't go to the wedding, I was ill. Then he died, too, so she married again. That one was killed in the Battle of Britain . . . '

'History certainly did its worst with her husbands,' I commented.

'Yes. My mother, on the other hand, came out of every world war with an enhanced reputation.' It was a dry joke.

'And what happened to Jo-Jo?' I raced on.

Here she seemed to slump back into confusion. 'I'm not sure. He was a soldier.'

I let it drop, thinking I'd been stupid not to have thought of tracking down Joseph Levine, Violet's nephew. I was also beginning to see that Joanna's confusions might not have been to do with her mental condition but a way of dealing with matters she didn't want to discuss. I deliberately mentioned a difficult subject: 'What happened when Duncan Mackinnon disappeared?' I asked.

Joanna just stared at me. 'I don't want to talk about that,' she said.

I said nothing.

Her voice rose. 'That's what you've come to talk about, really, isn't it? Well, I won't, I won't – I'll never talk about him, never, never. I thought you wanted to talk about Mother— '

'I did,' I interrupted, wondering if the question about Mackinnon's disappearance had upset her badly.

The nurse was sitting watching closely. And Joanna had jumped out of her chair.

Standing, she cried agitatedly, 'Mother was a dreadful woman. She was a Nazi. She knew Hitler – she was his mistress, before the war. Not many people know that, but I do. And Duncan made her do it. He was a German agent. No one knows about that either, but I saw him, in the dark— '

The nurse came over. 'Joanna. Calm down. The lady doesn't want to hear all this.'

'Oh, doesn't she?' said Joanna. 'Well, I know she does.

She's come to find out what I know. And then she's going to report back and then they'll – do something to me. They'll have to, you see – I know too much.'

I said, 'Please believe me. I'm only interested in your mother's life. I'm nothing to do with anybody— '

'You'd have to say that – so they'd let you in. You can't fool me. I know. I've known it all for years. I'm on to them. They know it. Well, I've been silly. I've told you something I shouldn't. I know you've been signalling to that man on the beach, with the dog. He's probably heard every word we said, but I swear I'll never repeat it. I swear it. I've put myself in danger— '

I broke in, 'Honestly . . . ' realising that I'd made a mistake. The gaps in Joanna's memories, her evasions, were not accidental. They were ways of dodging the parts of the past which, like so many pathways, led her into her elaborately constructed fantasy world. Now she'd slipped into this second life she led.

'Honestly,' she said. 'That's funny, coming from you.'

'I'm so sorry.' I looked at the nurse, now holding Joanna by the upper arm.

The nurse replied coldly, 'I'm not surprised at this. I was surprised Dr Findlater allowed the interview. It's no good when she talks about her family, or the past.' To Joanna she said, 'Come on, Joanna. Dr Findlater wants to see you now.'

'I expect he does,' she said. 'So he can give me an injection to make me forget. That's what it's all about.' She went with her nurse. She halted and looked back at me, very frightened. 'I won't say anything. I promise I won't say anything.'

I stood looking out of the window for a moment. There was no point in going to find Dr Findlater. If Joanna was with him, she would think I was chasing her. So I left the house, seeing no one, hearing nothing, and walked back down the long, empty road, where the big houses stood blindly behind their trees, hedges, banks of rhododendrons. I'd done Joanna no good, but I didn't imagine I had done her any further harm, only provided another piece of material for her long-standing fantasies. She would have found them somewhere else anyway: in a newspaper, a TV programme, from watching someone walk past the house. I'd only triggered the fantasies. For myself, I'd gained some picture of the Levine nursery. I'd sensed the cheerful child she had been before her collapse in adolescence. But something jarred me, as I went along, buffeted by the wind. At first I thought it was sadness about Joanna's fate and guilt about having stirred up the trouble in her head. Then I realised part of my mind was occupied with her appearance – the rather long, tweedy skirt, the short, permed hair. I bet myself that under the tweedy skirt she had stockings, held up by suspenders. Silk stockings? Women sometimes keep the style of the time when they were happy, and sometimes of the time when life stopped for them. Where was Joanna? In the thirties or forties somewhere? And if she was still there – why? I pushed on in the wind, knowing I'd found nothing but another mystery.

FIVE

Violet Crutchley, 1913

Kate Higgins, April 18th, 1991

Violet moved into 3 Whittington Gardens, Belsize Park, in early April 1913, when the small, square garden, with the green gate set in the high wall around it, was beginning to grow again. There were buds on the apple and plum trees by the bottom wall, new grass was growing on the lawn. The house itself, two main storeys, with attics for the servants, was furnished in opulent, elaborate style. There were thick, patterned carpets, sofas with large, claw feet and tassels around the bottom, a heavily carved table in the dining-room. But the kitchen was modern, with a new gas stove, hygienic white-tiled larder and a vast copper for boiling clothes, and the house came equipped, or had probably been equipped in advance, by Henry Sturgess, with a cook and two maids.

A week after the move, which consisted of Violet getting into a cab with Henry Sturgess, greeting the servants in the hall with hauteur and ordering the cook to produce a steak and kidney pie 'and all the trimmings', Violet now lay with her shoes off on a white lace counterpane, in a big bed with a bronze embossed bedstead. On it was a chain of nymphs, in draperies, dancing, and, at each end, a satyr peeping out of an embossed bush. She had quickly noted, in fact, that there were touches about the house hinting it had been previously the house of a mistress, not a wife. The bathroom had two huge gilt, full-length mirrors and very long walnut shelves which had, no doubt, contained expensive jars of many kinds. There were uninteresting oil paintings of nude women on the walls of the small upstairs sitting-room. Violet, putting her hand down the side of the sofa, had pulled up an amber cigarette holder with a small band of diamonds round it. The previous occupant, Violet concluded, had not been an honest wife and mother. Now she lay in her chemise, with lace at bosom and ankle, smoking a Balkan Sobranie, using the holder. She felt quite cheerful. Ever since the night at the hotel with Frederick and the sudden move to Belsize Park her nausea had diminished. The slight swelling and puffing of her well-knit little body, which had upset her so much, seemed to have vanished and she thought that in three weeks it would be worth risking telling Frederick she was pregnant by him. She had no choice.

All in all the week following her installation had been a strain. She had been concerned not to reveal she was unaccustomed to servants and had practically no idea how a household with staff conducted itself. She had managed to work out what was supposed to happen by a mixture of native wit and the complicity of the staff, who, she decided realistically, must have been primed by Henry Sturgess for an inexperienced mistress. Then she had to equip herself for her new life. Henry Sturgess had opened accounts for her at several London stores, but she had no money, other than her savings, for her personal use, so had to face long bus journeys to endure the ordeal of ordering sheets, table-cloths and towels, and her own clothes, from big stores like Gamages, saying, 'Put it on the account of Mr Frederick Levine,' to young assistants whom, she thought, from her own personal experience, knew her position – that of 'kept woman' – precisely. Then would come the return journey on the bus, without so much as a cup of tea and a bun in a tea-shop. She didn't dare spend the money even on that. It was all very wearying, but her fatigue came chiefly from attending to her main duty, that of making everything pleasant for Frederick. This involved further study, for it meant giving him the right drink when he came in from the bank, and the right dinner later, at which she had to say the right things, and then seducing him nightly in the big bed with the bronze nymphs. She decided Frederick's needs were in essence not unlike her father's – a beer, a hot dinner when he came home, a bit of peace and quiet, a smile from his wife. And, as with her father, Violet concluded, the effect had to be managed with no apparent strain.

Now she lay back, half asleep, listening to the birds in the trees outside the window, thanking her stars that

Frederick had needed to go back to Austria. He might fall in love, or find another woman there, but the relief of having some time to herself almost made her forget this anxiety. When the parlourmaid, Dorothy, knocked at the door and told her tea was ready in the drawing-room she said, 'Put it on a tray and bring it up. I'm not feeling very well. And put some more coal on the fire, would you?'

'Shall I open the window, madam?' asked the girl.

'No, thanks,' said Violet emphatically. She was getting up a good old fug, cigarette smoke and smoke from the fire, and enjoying it. She thought about demanding a kipper for her tea, and decided she couldn't afford to lower herself too much in front of the servants. After tea, she had a doze and, by six, when it was dark, she began to feel bored. There wasn't a book in the house. She'd ordered a gramophone the day before, but it hadn't arrived. When she heard the doorbell ring she was pleased, thinking it might be the postman, with a letter, or even a parcel, from Frederick. As soon as she heard the front door shut she came downstairs in a white lawn wrapper, with a pink silk sash, to find the maid, Dorothy, in the hall with a girl of fourteen in a rusty navy-blue skirt and coat, no gloves, sagging black stockings and old boots. A mass of fair hair hung down her back and a big tartan tam o'shanter sat on her head. The girl looked up. 'Vi!' she called.

Violet ran down the stairs, grabbed the girl's arm and hustled her into the dining-room opposite the stairs. It was cold, for the fire had not been lit. She said, 'That'll be all, Dorothy,' and shut the door. Dragging the girl across the room to the window she said in a low voice, 'What the hell are you doing here? What's the matter?'

'You might fetch me a cup of tea, Vi,' the girl said crossly. 'It's taken me all day to find you. I'm dropping. Why the hell couldn't you have sent a bleeding postcard? It's not much to ask.'

'I've only been here a week and I've had a lot to do. Anyway, what's it all about? Why are you suddenly so keen to find me? Months have passed without anybody wondering if I was alive or dead.'

'I wish you'd get that servant to fetch a cup of tea,'

the girl said. She was very pretty, although her face was grubby. Her cheeks had a rosy flush, her eyes were big and blue, her eyebrows and eyelashes dark, although her hair was almost white.

Violet said, 'All right. Come in the drawing-room. I'll get you some tea and cake but I've got to say it – I don't want you all coming round here. You know where I am now, so that's that. This is your first and last visit, Allie.' She led her sister into the drawing-room overlooking the garden and rang the bell.

Allie sat down. 'Well, very nice,' she said, settling in her well-stuffed armchair. 'I can see you fell on your feet. Mind you, Ma'll go crazy when I tell her. And I don't fancy Pa when I tell him you're being kept by a Yid, which I've found out.'

'If you tell either of them, Allie— ' Violet said fiercely, breaking off as Dorothy came in. 'A pot of tea,' she said with a question-defying stare, 'and some of that fruit cake I had today.' When Dorothy had gone she turned back to Allie and said, 'Like I said, you tell Ma and Pa where I'm living, or who with, and I'll make you pay, I swear it.'

'Threats you can't carry out don't mean a lot, Vi,' her sister remarked coolly. 'Try bribery, and you might be getting somewhere.'

'You're a nice sister, and no mistake,' Violet told her sourly. 'And as for bribery, chance'd be a fine thing, I must say. I've hardly a penny to my name.'

Allie, looking round the room, said, 'Well, even so, I suppose it's better than working for a living. Or is it?'

'I don't know,' said Violet, recalling her undisclosed pregnancy. 'All I'm telling you, Allie, is that if a great gang of relations starts coming round, I'm done for. All I need is Pa coming round breathing fire and slaughter about his damaged daughter, and trying to get compensation for my ruin, or Ben and Frank treating it as a place to stop off for tea after a tram ride – all that could get me in bad trouble here and if you've got any sense or feeling for me at all, Allie, you'll keep your mouth shut. At least till I'm more established here.' If I ever am, she thought to herself.

Allie pulled a face. 'Well, I've got to tell them something, or the next thing they'll do is have the police out trying to find you, in case you've been murdered, or white-slaved— '

'Anyway, why are you here?' Violet interrupted. Dorothy knocked at the door and brought in the tea, and a cake, but not the fruit cake Violet had asked for. When she had left Violet poured tea for her sister. She asked again, 'Allie, why are you here?'

'Mum wanted you to know she'd fallen for another baby,' Allie told her with her mouth full of cake. 'She wrote you a letter to Hammonds but you never came round so she sent me to come and tell you at the shop. 'Course, when that snobby Mr Gummidge told me you didn't work there no more, you'd gone off unexpected, leaving no address, I had to get angry with him and I made him tell me . . . '

As Allie went on with her saga of a journey to the City to find Levine-Schreft and the hour and a half she'd waited for Henry Sturgess to attend to her, Violet's mood became blacker. Her mother was expecting a baby, too, her sixth, at forty years of age. It was impossible that she wanted it, but she was going to have to put up with it, and her father's tempers when it woke at night. She and her mother had been caught in the same trap. Her mother would be feeling beaten, yet again. She, Violet, would not. She had to make Frederick think the child was his. She broke in on Allie's description of how she'd found her and said, 'So the long and short is, she wants me back home to help? That's it, isn't it?'

'Don't go losing your temper, Vi,' said Allie in alarm.

'What's happened to Norah, then?'

'Norah's getting married to Harry Felper,' Allie said.

'Thought she didn't like him?'

'She's making him marry her now – she's got to – says he forced her, one day at his house when his ma and pa were out. Whether it's love or not, she's getting married; just as well, with Ma how she is. So it's you or me, Vi, at home, helping Ma— ' Allie broke off, then said, 'I can't stand it. I just can't stand it, Vi. Before all this I'd got Ma and Pa to say I could get some training as a lady typist, I was going to start in a month. Now I can't. I wanted to get a nice job in an office, get some decent clothes, have something to spend on myself for once.'

'Why can't Ma just manage? It'd only be Ben and Frank and the new baby— '

'She reckons at her age it'd be too much for her.'

'Other women have thirteen,' Vi said.

'She says she's not well already . . . '

Vi was angry. 'She's never had any spirit, that's her trouble.'

'Well, maybe she did once, but Pa knocked it out of her,' Allie said, defending her mother.

'Can't have been much there to break in the first place,' Violet said.

'That doesn't help me, does it? I can't learn the typewriter because Pa won't pay the twelve guineas for six months' training. Look here, Vi. It's your own family you're talking about. Ma's expecting your new brother or sister, and someone's got to help.'

'Well, it won't be me,' Violet said promptly. 'I don't care if she's having triplets. See here, Allie, I may need a month or two. You sling your hook, say you couldn't find me. You've spent the day at the Salvation Army, the hospitals, no one could help – just give me a little bit of time, to see what I can manage, that's all I'm asking.' If things didn't work out, Violet reflected, she'd have to go home, expecting a baby, and she and her mother would have to settle down together with squalling babies, two out-of-hand hooligan brothers, an angry husband and father, while Allie, now, would be the one who escaped to a good job in an office and a bit of dignity.

'If I do this for you, what about the typewriting?' Allie said implacably.

'I promise I'll see what I can manage.'

'Well, I'm not stopping, anyway,' said Allie. 'I'll go into service, I'll do anything to get away. You can't imagine what Pa's like with this latest little bit of news. You'd think Ma'd done it on her own, just to spite him. He hit Ma the other day. He's always walloping the boys. I'll be next, I know it. The worst thing is, another man got promoted to be a sergeant when he thinks it should have been him. Ma's very tired – she can hardly do anything. I'd help, honest I would, Vi, but if I do, what's to become of me?' She looked around the pleasant sitting-room, cut herself another slice of cake and said, 'All right. I'll help you out. I'll say I never found you. But don't forget Pa'll get you traced through the police, if he can. He'll keep after you and God help me if they find you and it comes out I knew all along.'

'I've never seen you,' said Violet. 'You push off. You know the address now – don't write it down. If you want to get in touch with me, write me a letter or a telegram. I'm known as Mrs Frazier – remember that. I'll reply, I swear it, but you can see for yourself I could be more use to you in the end sitting here than sweeping the steps at home.'

Allie took the shilling Violet offered her and left. Violet, in a panic, went into the kitchen, where the cook was knitting by the kitchen range, and the two maids sitting at the table, having a cup of tea with a fruit cake on a plate between them.

'I'll see the accounts, now,' she announced, 'and also that fruit cake I asked for just now.'

'Mr Sturgess said he was to see the accounts monthly,' said the cook.

'That's not to say I can't see them whenever I want,' said Violet. 'I'm not sure things are going right here.'

The cook stood up. 'Mrs Frazier, the bills haven't been put in order yet.'

'I'll take them before you've had a chance to fudge them,' Violet told her. 'So find them.'

'I'll bring them to you,' said the cook.

'I'll wait,' said Violet, sitting down at the kitchen table. 'And don't bother to carry that cake off,' she said to the maid who had stood up with the plate from the table, 'because I can easily see you've been eating cook's fruit cake, while I've been eating shop-bought seed cake.'

'It's not the practice in good houses to offer a cut cake to guests— '

'It's not the practice in good houses for the servants to scoff their employers' grub in the kitchen, either,' Violet told her. 'And send up the bought seed cake to the drawing-room.'

'If I had known *two* cakes would be required today . . . ' the cook countered, implying that the better sort of people did not ring all day long for cups of tea and pieces of cake.

'Just produce those bills,' Violet demanded.

The bills were taken from a kitchen drawer, and one from the cook's basket. Scrutinising them, Violet could find little wrong. Obviously, the servants were eating well, the grocer and butcher were charging high prices. They might well have been embarking on the usual arrangement whereby they charged the cook more for goods supplied or not supplied at all, and split the difference with her, but this system, if it existed, was still in its infancy. Violet made a fuss about an error of sixpence on one butcher's bill, said that of the two pounds of cheese which had come into the house she had seen none, mentioned the cake again, and dismissed the staff.

'I'm stopping this rot before it starts,' she declared.

The cook and two maids were stunned. 'You've no right to do this,' Dorothy said, nearly in tears.

'I shall speak to the agency, and Mr Sturgess,' said the cook.

'Speak to who you like,' said Violet.

'I believe we're being discharged on account of that visitor you had, while Mr Frazier is absent,' she said, 'and I shall say so.'

'I shall say,' Violet told her, 'that my visitor was an informant, shocked by your dishonesty, who took it on herself to let me know what was going on in my house.' She stood up. 'All out, first thing tomorrow morning, and references will be supplied, by Mr Sturgess, on my report, which means you won't be wanting to give any trouble, doesn't it?'

And she left the kitchen, went upstairs to her bedroom, and went to bed, where she cursed Allie for turning up, her mother and father for fools, and Tom Rawlinson for ignorantly leaving his seed in her. She did not think about her own part in all this, for when the chips were down Violet Crutchley had hot blood, steel teeth and claws and no tendency to self-criticism. She was fighting for survival now.

Next day she presented herself prettily in a blue cloak and hat, clutching a small blue reticule, at the office of Mr Sturgess at Levine-Schreft. The servants, she said, had seized the opportunity of Mr Levine's absence to be rude and inattentive to her, and she had reason to believe some, if not all, were dishonest. Henry Sturgess, who had already had the woman who ran the domestic agency on the telephone, expressing faith in the servants for whom she found employment, and, implicitly, doubts about the lady of the house's suitability as an employer, now sympathised with Violet and said he would send fresh staff to the house for her to interview. Violet might or might not be the innocent young woman she seemed to be, but Sturgess was not going to challenge her. She was at present a force to be reckoned with in his employer's life.

His wife had cautioned him against Violet. 'There's something wrong behind her eyes,' Mrs Henry Sturgess had said by the fireside as she sewed buttons on the baby's new velvet coat. Then, picking up a roll of elastic and beginning to make a fresh set of garters for the baby's stockings, 'I don't know what it is, but it's not what you'd expect. And talking of expecting, Henry, I wouldn't rule out the possibility— '

'What?' Sturgess had said, staring at his wife in alarm.

'I don't know,' she replied, cutting a thread with a small pair of gold scissors, which, with a gold thimble, had been a Christmas present from Frederick Levine. 'All I'm saying is, where Miss Violet Crutchley's concerned, Henry dear, I'd advise you to be very careful.'

So Sturgess, who had no feelings about Violet, but every concern for his employer, accepted Violet's story. Fresh staff arrived for interview that afternoon.

Violet took on two plain maids, sisters, refused two cooks, whose strength, she guessed, was cooking, and the next morning hired an elderly French chef whose weakness, she could tell, was drink. 'I'll put it like this,' she said. 'Any bad habits you have will be tolerated as long as the food's on time, up to scratch and the maids aren't interfered with. I also want ice kept in the shed, winter and summer. That way you can cool the wine and, if you've got any sense, keep something in a basin you can hot up at short notice, if you're not feeling too well. It's up to you. And I'll need you to teach me French, one hour a day, in the mornings, when I give you your orders.'

'Teach you French?' he said, startled.

'Yes. And German too, if you know it. During the afternoons I'll get a proper lady in to teach me. In the mornings, on weekdays, you can stand here and talk to me.'

'Very well, Madame,' he said.

'Come on a week's trial, starting tomorrow,' she said. 'And this business about the French is between you and me.'

'*Très bien*, Madame,' he said, beginning to see the point of Violet's request, but privately not thinking her appearance and manners up to the task of becoming a truly successful adventuress, the mistress of a peer, or a famous politician. Violet was not really planning any such future, only dreaming, still, of her flower shop, Violette's, where a knowledge of French and German might be useful for dealing with a better kind of customer.

Before the week was out she had also hired an elderly lady who had been a governess in the family of Russian aristocrats. She would come in for an hour on two afternoons a week to teach her French and German, so long as Frederick was not there, seeking her attention. Violet then joined a circulating library, so as to keep up her reading, and, still profiting from Frederick's absence, found a local seamstress to make the clothes she wanted, and alter others to her requirements. She also moved the furniture and started an account with a local florist, so that the house was always full of hothouse blooms.

Yet in spite of all these occupations she was still gnawed by anxiety. Each evening her last thought before she slept was of keeping her pregnancy a secret until she could tell Frederick the child was his, of how she would tell him, and how he would respond. Another month would have to pass before she could dare to hint she might be expecting a child. By then she would be actually over three months pregnant. She pushed aside the thought that by November she would bear a child she would have to claim to be almost two months premature. She could only take one step at a time, and her sole ambition now was to get Frederick to believe the child was his. As bad luck would have it the nausea she had barely noticed for the past fortnight returned at full strength the day before Frederick was due to return. She was sick in the morning, and dizzy with illness in the afternoon, and she knew she would have to conceal all this discomfort for several weeks more.

It was almost a relief when Frederick did not return. Instead a telegram arrived, saying he would be delayed until the middle of the following week, and, next day, a small parcel, containing a gold bangle, inscribed inside, 'for Violet from her loving F'. Violet, pricing it at no more than thirty pounds, hid it with the telegram in the tissue paper under a new hat in a hat-box and reflected that a man who didn't send a more expensive gift, or put his name in full upon it, seemed to be acting with a suspicious caution. She began to fear, again, that he would find a new lover in Vienna. She had imagined at first that Frederick Levine was a man with a good position at a bank and, perhaps, a little financial help from a well-off family. She was amazed when a visit to the bank showed the name of Levine above the door. That certainly explained the speed with which everything had been arranged by Henry Sturgess, the sudden rallying of attention in shops when Mr Frederick Levine's name was mentioned – Frederick did not work for the bank. He owned it. The family's resources were beyond anything she could imagine. This told her that Frederick could get anything he wanted with money. And the question after that became, why then, would he want her, and for how long? It was not a reassuring thought for a penniless, pregnant seventeen-year-old.

Although nervous, she was also extremely bored and spent days without talking to anyone, except Felix, the chef, in French, which was a matter of remarking that it was a fine day today and she had seen a bird eating bread in the garden.

Nevertheless, on Wednesday, the day of Frederick's return, she put on underclothes, drawers and chemise in heavy crêpe-de-chine, an excellently cut frock in very pale, light wool, silk stockings and little cream patent leather shoes with buckles. She added a careful touch of rouge to revive her pale complexion. She got Felix to cook some veal and make a custard and sat by the fire in a flower-filled room reading and trying to compose herself. When the door opened she pushed the book under a chair and ran to greet Frederick.

He embraced her, saying, 'Fourteen hours for the crossing from Amsterdam. What a storm,' then let her put him in a chair. She poured him a brandy but he waved it away. 'I drank all the way. It's supposed to make you feel better, but I'm not so sure. That's it – if there are any more trips like that I'll hire an aeroplane, and get there in half a day, not two days in trains and boats.' He gave her a pale smile. 'Would you like to come with me?'

'Oh, Frederick,' she said, expressing timidity and excitement, like a child. 'I'd be so frightened.'

'Ring for some tea, there's a good girl. Then come and sit on my knee.'

He did not notice that the maid had changed. Violet sat on his knee, asking, 'Did you manage all you had to, clever Frederick?'

'I think there'll be a war.'

Violet was alarmed, thinking of her own concerns. 'When?' she said. 'You won't have to go for a soldier, Frederick?'

He smiled. 'Not so soon. Plenty of time for us. Shall we go upstairs? I've missed you, my little flower.'

Violet, thinking of the servants, who would know what they were doing if they went up now, and of Felix's joint of meat in the oven, did not demur, but said, 'Oh yes, Frederick. Yes.' The nightmare of the Austrian countess receded.

He was on her as soon as they reached the bedroom, gobbling her neck, pulling at the buttons down the back of her dress; she heard the stitching on her chemise rip. Her breasts were very sore and she felt extremely sick. A long hour of pretence passed for her. Finally, as he attempted to make love to her for the second time, she had to get up and go to the bathroom, where as silently as possible, she vomited, rinsed her mouth with cologne and came back into the bedroom, wishing only that he would get up and leave her alone, in bed, with the curtains drawn. While he had been gone she had missed him, enjoying the sensation of being like the heroine of the novels she enjoyed, but now he was back she resented him. He was hard work, like a baby who needed a lot of attention, but didn't appreciate the effort. It was a pity. He was a handsome man and good-natured, but underneath he was just like her father, and she supposed all men were: Mr Asquith, King George, probably even terrible Fenian men, whom she imagined coming in with their faces all black with gunpowder and bloody shirts falling in chairs even after blowing people up, so poor women would still be rushing with cups of tea, and boiling up water so they could wash themselves, putting bloody shirts in buckets of cold water to soak. And when you added on the physical side – well, Violet thought, it made you wonder how married women stayed on their feet and weren't all dead of exhaustion or lying in hospitals. Slipping back into bed, she murmured and moaned while Frederick made love to her again. Then he, to her relief, fell asleep. Some women, she'd heard, enjoyed all this, but she knew from her experience with Tom Rawlinson that she was not one of them.

She lay restlessly in the darkness, then got quietly out of bed and dressed. She went downstairs to tell Felix to prepare a cold supper and go. He was itching for his visit to the pub, where he went every evening, and she could tell he had already had a glass or two. As if he had anticipated the cancellation of supper, he produced chicken in jelly, a chocolate mousse, and began rapidly to slice cold beef and ham into thin slices. He even produced a lettuce, beat up a salad dressing, poured it into a small silver jug and told her to stir it and pour it over the lettuce just before they ate it. Violet was suspicious of this, but decided to trust him. The whole thing took five minutes as Violet watched him fascinatedly.

'*Pas mal?*' he remarked, catching her look. '*Vous voulez aussi des leçons de cuisine?*'

'Jolly good,' came Frederick's voice beside her. He was standing there in his dressing-gown.

'This is Felix, the new cook,' Violet said.

Felix bowed. 'Mr Frazier.'

'You can go now, Felix,' Violet said with dignity.

'Thank you, madam,' Felix responded.

'Well, the maids seem to have disappeared, so let's carry it in ourselves,' said Frederick, putting slices of beef and chicken on a plate. 'I must say I'm ravenous. He's a good thing that Mr Felix. I suppose he's only standing in for the other one.'

'He's permanent,' said Violet. 'I've discharged cook and maids.'

'Up to you,' said Frederick. 'Mind you, I don't hold with changing the staff every five minutes myself.'

'I think I'm suited now,' said Violet with dignity.

Frederick laughed, took her in his arms and spun her round. 'To the manner born, Violet. What a little wonder you are.' He held her off and examined her. 'What a lucky chap I am to have found you.'

'Aren't you?' Violet teased, resolving that once he'd eaten she'd ask him for some money. Apart from anything else, a guinea and the promise of more to come might help Allie to keep her mouth shut. Her plan collapsed when, as soon as the meal was over, the doorbell rang and she let in Henry Sturgess, who greeted her cordially and went straight into the study with Frederick to write some letters.

'Would you arrange some coffee and brandy for us, Violet, my dear?' Frederick asked.

Violet went into the kitchen, didn't know what to do, boiled a kettle, made coffee like tea, poured some out, decided it was too weak, made it again, decided it was too strong and took it into the study on a tray anyway, interrupting a conversation about shares in a button factory. She heard Frederick say, 'I count on you to manage the affair slowly – nothing to startle the horses, Sturgess.' And heard Henry Sturgess reply, 'You may count on that, Mr Levine.'

Later she said to Frederick, 'Why did Mr Sturgess come over so late just to talk about buttons?'

'Oh – buttons? Oh, buttons – well, Violet, even buttons have their significance to bankers.'

Violet smiled, still wondering. Then she asked a question more on her mind than buttons. 'Do your family know you're back?'

'I imagine so,' he replied. 'I telegraphed from Belgium and France to say I was on my way back.'

'Won't they be expecting you at home?'

'I told them I was coming here,' he said.

'So they know about this – about me?'

'Not in any detail,' he said. 'But naturally I told them I'd taken the lease on a house, where I would be spending a good deal of my time in future.'

Violet hesitated. 'Just in those very words?' she questioned.

'More or less,' he told her.

There was an awkward pause, during which Frederick was embarrassed, for no reason he could define, and Violet momentarily wondered whether his family knew of her, and what they thought about his absences. But she knew Frederick could not be allowed to feel discomfort on the subject of herself and his family and so said, 'That's nice, then. You must be so tired, after all that travelling and then Mr Sturgess. It's after one. Let's go to bed.'

He slept. She got up and was sick again, wondering, her head hanging wearily over the prettily decorated lavatory pan, how long she could go on concealing her nausea, worrying if her figure was beginning to betray her condition, always acting a part and somehow managing not to scream. They get paid for this at the Lyceum, she thought with a little surge of hope. Maybe I should go on the stage. Playing what? The pregnant daughter who gets thrown out of the house? said the other voice inside her. Another spasm took her. Then she stood up, dizzy, and bathed her sweating face with cologne, rinsed her mouth and went back to bed.

The next few weeks were slightly easier. Frederick went to the bank at ten and returned ordinarily at five in time for tea, although he was plainly working hard at that point and was sometimes later. He spent one Sunday in two with his family, saying nothing about it when he returned. Violet was made uneasy by this, being fairly sure someone, probably Frederick's mother, whose power she feared, had been criticising his constant absence from the house. She explained to Frederick she had no money. He'd given her ten guineas from his pocket, and she sent two to Allie at her friend's house with instructions not to write back unless the matter was urgent.

Meanwhile Violet acted on, day after day, suffocating with boredom and fear, all of which she had to disguise, until at last the moment came when she felt it safe to hint that she might be pregnant. Frederick had again left that Sunday to visit his mother. When he returned, looking awkward, sensing but not expressing the tension between his relationship with Violet and the more substantial parts of his life, she greeted him as submissively as ever. Her fear of Frederick's mother was not based on any information, but on Frederick's obvious dread of complaints and criticisms from women, even herself. She suspected the source of this to have been the strong-minded Mrs Sophie Levine, who, she felt sure, also favoured Frederick's older brother, Laurence. The result was that Frederick could bear almost no comment from her, and was only reassured by the kind of faith and love from her a loyal dog, hand-reared by its owner, might give. To Violet's mind the odd thing was that this sensitive person was a shrewd businessman, with enormous power outside the home. As far as she could judge by secretly reading the correspondence he sometimes left on the study table, he financed large industries, even small states, and, on occasion, could break them by refusing credit. If he ever applied the same rules to her that he applied to, say, the Gateshead Small Arms Factory, where he had evidently decided a loan should be repaid, and, in spite of the owner's pleas, had finally bankrupted the firm and thrown seven hundred men and women out of work, then she, Violet, would be looking at an altogether different Frederick Levine.

She had also noticed that although he denied her nothing in the way of clothes, or domestic expense, he instinctively disliked the idea of her having any ready money. After the gift of the ten guineas he had not suggested any regular payments to her, nor had he given her any expensive presents. They had not been out in the evening since the move to Belsize Park. Frederick was luxuriating, she felt, in the kindly nursery he had never had. Consequently, Violet, offering him a whisky and water and telling him it had been warm enough to spend the afternoon reading in the garden, was terrified of the effect of announcing her pregnancy, which she now had to do.

Therefore, as dinner was announced by the maid, she fainted. She was never sure afterwards whether it had been a real faint, or a simulated one, but as she blinked her eyes open on the sofa to which Frederick had carried her, she was so unnerved by her own loss of control she burst into tears. Frederick, at a loss, cradled her in his arms saying, 'No, no, Violet. Don't cry. Please don't cry. What is it, my little darling?'

She gazed up at him, pleadingly. There was no turning back now. 'I've been feeling so strange,' she said.

'I'll send for a doctor,' he said.

Violet went cold with fear, and almost lost consciousness again, knowing the doctor might tell Frederick how long she'd been pregnant. She clung to him. 'Oh, no. I don't think I'm ill. Not ill.'

'Then what?' he said, looking down at the slender little body in the white lace dress, at her small face and huge eyes. 'How can you not be ill?' With some relief and some dread Violet saw his face go blank with realisation.

'I think . . . I think,' she murmured, 'I think I'm expecting your child.'

Greatly to her amazement, Frederick's eyes filled with tears. He knelt down and covered her face with kisses. 'Oh, Violet, my little love. What have you done for me? What have you done for my sake?'

She dropped her head to the side, looking at him as he knelt. 'I thought . . . I didn't like to tell you – I thought you might be angry with me.'

But he was not, he was weeping with pleasure and something like remorse. It was as if he had done her an injury, and she had made a sacrifice. It was not the view her father, Arthur Crutchley, had ever taken in the same circumstances. Violet, stunned, realised that Frederick actually felt happiness. She was healing him, helping him to recover from his mother's favouring of his brother, a life of only half-concealed dislike of his race, at school, where he had been unable, like Laurence, to gain acceptance. She realised if she was careful from now on, she'd be all right. She embraced Frederick Levine in genuine relief and gratitude.

Kate Higgins, April 18th, 1991

I got back tired from Brighton, where I'd gone to after my visit to Rye on another overcast, windy day. I felt depressed all the way on the train, not helped by a view of the big open prison just outside Bromley, where you could see the Portacabin-style factories where the inmates worked, the prisoners in the gardens and armed guards patrolling the perimeters. Last year, when it opened, the *Daily Mail* had demanded why commuters, not to mention visitors from Europe, should be faced with this spectacle from the windows of trains approaching London. Andy's paper, *The Witness*, had complained about the increasing numbers of detention centres, mostly containing remand prisoners and those serving short sentences, being set up all over the country. The Home Secretary, Adrian Critchlow himself, had responded that the high security jails had to be freed for terrorists and violent criminals, while unconvicted men, or those convicted of minor crimes, were better off in the new centres than old, overcrowded jails. As to the siting of these places, there was no reason to transport people sentenced in London courts for great distances to places where they could not be visited by their families. Nevertheless, it was a gloomy spectacle – perhaps it was meant to be – and did little for my mood.

I got on the bus at Victoria. It had to detour a cordoned-off street where apparently the Active Democrats, a left-wing group, had succeeded in half-burning down the Passport Office. Last week it had been Tottenham Court Road tube station, a month ago there had been a minor fire in the ladies underwear section of the Edgware Road Marks and Spencer. There'd been similar episodes in Liverpool, Glasgow and Dundee. It didn't make sense, just caused uneasiness everywhere and a lot of grumbling in front of the TV in the evenings.

I pushed through the wind to the flat, dreading that Di's mood would be the same as when I left. But when I arrived she wasn't in. I'd just put my bag down on the floor when the phone rang. It was Andy. 'Darling,' he said, 'I've got ten days until I go to Belize for the elections; they think the Marxists might get in – then a revolution. I don't know when I'll be back. Please come to Spain with me. If you haven't got any money I'll lend it to you and put pressure on Roger to pay up. All right?'

'All right,' I said, my depression lifting in spite of the fact that my ex-husband, Ray's father, was already in Belize, where there might be danger. That's obsessive love for you. I'd planned to read Violet's pseudonymous novels in the British Library next week – I was wondering why she hadn't mentioned them in *I Affirm* – but this was more appealing. And Di wasn't going to miss me, that was for sure. It was cold, wet and windy here but it might be spring in Salamanca, and the suggestion must mean Andy loved me. So I said I'd go. A bit later I found a note on the kitchen table from Di saying, 'Really sorry about what I said. I've taken my Easter break early, gone to Paris. Will bring you back a stick of rock.' But, as I put my washing for the launderette in the plastic holdall, along with various tea-towels, which should have gone a week ago, I still knew there was an explanation for Di's attitude and I still didn't know what it was.

Somehow, we were both living on the margin, I suddenly thought. Then I opened my letters. The truth was I was so excited about my holiday I was behaving like a child on its birthday. In fact, not having to look after Ray made it easy to go back to childhood, or adolescence. I had no fixed hours, except those professionally dictated, no domestic responsibilities except the shared maintenance of a flat, no one to sustain or care for but myself. I hadn't noticed, because Andy was exactly the same, though Di, somehow, wasn't.

The post consisted of an overdue library card, a letter about my overdraft and a letter from the woman I had expensively hired to check birth and death certificates registered at St Catherine's House. Some of the information I already knew. Violet's mother, Emily Crutchley, had died in December 1913, Arthur Crutchley, Violet's father, had died in 1940, her brother Frank had died in 1916, Ben, it seemed, had married and there was no record of his death, although by now he would be eighty-five. Norah, Violet's older sister, had married Harold Felper in 1913 and died in 1953. There was no record of Violet's sister Allie's death. The accompanying letter warned me that the information from St Catherine's House only dealt with recorded births, marriages and deaths in England, Scotland and Wales, and wondered if I required any further services. I did, but I couldn't afford them. I could spend time checking the question of whether Ben and Norah had had any children, who might have information for me, whether even Allie was still alive. At ninety-three years old it seemed unlikely, but then, her sister Violet had lived to be ninety-three, her brother Ben appeared to be alive, so perhaps they were all like parrots, or tortoises, and just went on longer than anybody else. There were many things I could do, and probably would, but I realised what I needed, for speed's sake, was a chat with my mystery informant, Deep Throat, who might have some idea where everybody, including Violet's missing nephew, Jo-Jo, might be. The skeins were tangled. It was just a question of having the patience to disentangle them, but I knew that kind of patience was not my forte. I supposed that now it had to be. But a call from D.T. would help – where was he or she, now I needed him or her?

The time was ripe for going to the launderette, where a woman can think as her laundry circles round and round before her eyes. But in the launderette I only thought of Andy, though it occurred to me at one point, as I loaded everything into the drier and slammed the door, that if in 1913 Violet's sister had married, her mother had died, and she herself had married and had her daughter then 1913 must have been a year of years for the Crutchleys. My secret informant had stressed the business of Violet's marriage being so close to the birth of her child. I'd thought it rather old-fashioned to dwell on the scandal of the bride-with-a-baby. But there might be more to the story than that. Again, Violet, war-heroine and later Labour politician had, in her teens, hooked a millionaire. What did that imply? What had the Levines thought about it? The situation had been covered in one of Violet's bland paragraphs, in *I Affirm*:

> The Levines greeted their rather unexpected in-law cordially, and after the birth of my lovely daughter, Pamela, with her striking resemblance from the first to my husband's brother, Laurence Levine, who was later killed in action, all difficulties ended.

But, I wondered, had the Levines been quite so relaxed about Frederick marrying a sixteen-year-old policeman's daughter from south London?

I stood surrounded by the dead, as the fishmonger handed me a pound and a half of cod in wet newspaper and I turned my mind from Violet's life to mine. Maybe, I thought, I'd just conceive a baby myself and damn the consequences. I was quite surprised to be thinking this. Previously, the idea of having another child had been connected with some future state of stability I might be able to achieve with a nameless husband.

Suddenly I was thinking irresponsibly about it. Andy would be furious. Perhaps I should just do it. But my parents would be anxious for me. I thought of Ray, having a baby, no money, and nowhere to live. Of course, I could go on working, but at present I wasn't earning nearly enough to get somewhere decent to live, and pay for child care. Perhaps all this was about trying to reject my research, my involvement in the past, all the problems. Perhaps.

And a few days later I was riding round Spain: mountains, and plains, walled cities, quiet village squares with statues of the Virgin in the middle, great olive groves, above everything a mild blue sky. And the day before we had to leave I was sitting with Andy, looking out over the sea, knowing I'd lived a dream, like something out of a romantic novel, but it had been true, and for a time I'd been able to forget my guilt about my flight from Northern Ireland, and leaving Ray with my parents, and my unwillingness to make amends by trying for a straightforward marriage or job.

Andy leaned forward a bit and put his hand over mine. 'We ought to get married, some time,' he said. 'I'm mad not to ask – supposing I lost you?'

'You won't lose me,' I told him.

'You look so much better. You were getting peaky, living in that flat and dashing about worrying all the time about the book. Now you look wonderful. Why don't you give it up fast, before Roger pays you?'

'I've been thinking about it,' I said. 'It's getting very complicated, and every time I think I'm finding something out, I run up against another brick wall. My only ally seems to be the mysterious caller and I can't rely on that.'

'It's too hard if you haven't got the co-operation of the next of kin. No letters, papers, snapshots, no direct testimony. It's like the story you can't get, because no one will talk to you. And there's no one like these influential upper-middle-class families for clamming up. They stick together like glue when they feel threatened.'

'I'm no threat,' I said.

'Well, obviously they don't want a biography. How would

you feel if it was your mother? Anyway, with them against you, there's no way forward.'

'It's been done, though.'

'I thought you said you were having second thoughts anyway.'

'I am. I don't like to be driven off.'

'I suppose they've got a perfect right— '

'They've a perfect right to anything. So have I.'

'It's too tough. After all, look what Roger's paying you. You'll barely make a profit. It's not as if Violet Levine's life is going to sell a lot of copies.'

There was a pause. I said, 'I know. But you were the person who encouraged me at the start— '

'I didn't anticipate all these problems. Look,' he said, 'if you want to do it, think of someone else. Get Roger to switch the contract. I'll back you.'

'It's not a bad idea.'

'Of course it isn't,' he said. 'This one's giving you aggravation, making you nervous— '

'Your job makes you nervous,' I said.

'We don't need two lots of bad nerves. Look how happy we've been this week.'

'Yes,' I said. The sun was going down.

'Ring him when you get back,' Andy said, as we went arm in arm along the beach. Andy appeared happier now I seemed to be giving up the idea of writing Violet's biography. In the end what I learned from her life was that we never know what the results of our actions will be. She didn't. I didn't. If I'd rung Roger and cancelled the project when I got back to London whatever else I lost I would have kept my innocence.

Violet Crutchley, 1913

In Belsize Park, Violet, relieved of the burden of concealment, was able to relax to some extent, while Frederick urged her to take glasses of claret and rest more, checking that she had not, during the day, exerted herself too much. He was very distressed that Violet would not see a doctor, but Violet was frightened that any doctor, particularly one known to Frederick, would reveal she'd been pregnant for a lot longer than a month. She told him she was embarrassed, since she and Frederick were not married, but knew that sooner or later she'd have to satisfy him. Finally she found a shabby surgery a bus ride away and, putting on her plainest dress, which unfortunately was not very plain, being a rosebud-sprinkled cotton from Paris, with a big rose-coloured sash, she slid off there one morning. She gave her false name to the overworked maid who let her in, and sat on a frayed leather chair in front of Dr Malcolm Smith, who turned out to be a lean young man in a shabby suit. 'I think I've fallen for a baby,' she said.

'How long do you think you've been pregnant, Mrs Frazier?' he asked.

Violet looked at him sharply, noting the old suit was well cut and his manner gentlemanly. What she had needed was a rough-and-tumble, unfussy doctor in a poor area, not this keen-eyed young man. 'I don't know. Too long, I think. Would you have to tell my husband?' She studied his face, which remained calm.

'Well, Mrs Frazier,' he said, 'doctors are bound by an oath which forbids them to reveal their patients' secrets to anyone else, though in the case of married women it's usual for the doctor to be quite frank with their husbands. And were your husband to ask me directly, I would feel bound to give him a truthful answer . . . '

'That's nice, isn't it?' said Violet. 'It doesn't apply the other way about, does it – when the husband's picked up a nasty disease from a woman and doesn't want his wife told?'

He studied her with his intelligent eyes and said, 'I didn't make the world, Mrs Frazier. Perhaps I'd better just examine you, to make sure you really are expecting a baby, and how far along you are. Would you like to step behind the screen and just take off your lower garments?'

Violet endured this examination patiently, though with a feeling of outrage, then put her drawers, shoes and stockings on again, while he washed his hands.

He told her she was over three months pregnant, and in

good health, as far as he could tell. 'I imagine this was what you didn't want to hear,' he said.

'You couldn't – arrange anything?' she said. 'I've got plenty of money.'

He said, 'No, I can't. And I advise you strongly not to go to anyone who can. It's illegal and dangerous. You do understand that, don't you?'

'Couldn't you tell him the baby came too soon?' Violet demanded.

Dr Smith stood up. 'Mrs Frazier,' he said, 'I've told you I cannot lie to your husband. I'm afraid you and I have nothing further to say to each other. The fee is five shillings and I imagine you might prefer to pay me now.' Relenting, he said, 'I'm sorry. I can't help you in the way you want.'

Violet stood up obediently. 'If I told you I wasn't married . . . ' she suggested.

'It would make very little difference,' he said, still standing. 'If you're a churchwoman, perhaps it would help to see your clergyman.'

Violet, tears of rage and despair suddenly in her eyes, opened her bag, took out two half crowns and put them on the desk. He had pressed her stomach, thrust his fingers into her body, refused to help her and now he was suggesting she saw the vicar. Moreover she now knew no doctor would do anything else, except the kind of doctor she guessed Frederick would find undesirable at first glance, and never let in the house again. She was opening the surgery door when she turned back. Dr Smith was studying her back, not unsympathetically. 'Oh, well, I've got to have someone,' she said, as much to herself as him. 'You'd better hear the whole story,' she said.

He shook his head. 'No, Mrs Frazier,' he told her. 'I think I'd better not.' It was almost as if he was afraid of her.

'I can pay you,' she said.

In front of him, Dr Malcolm Smith saw a small, pretty girl, with eyes the colour of amethysts, wearing a new, well-laundered dress and expensive shoes, no older, he guessed, than his sister Grace, who was still at school in Huntingdon, but, he could tell from her accent and behaviour, from a background which had not been so sheltered. No river at the bottom of the garden for her, he thought, no books, no piano, however much in need of French polishing, no room to herself, with old blue wool curtains at the windows in winter, chintz in summer.

He said, 'You must understand that members of the medical profession are bound by an oath – there are rules we have to keep. If doctors don't keep them they are struck off, discharged; they aren't allowed to practise any more. You do understand me?'

'Yes,' said Violet. She'd made up her mind to have him. She'd have to agree with him up to a point and that was that. In the meantime, she listened, because you didn't interrupt men when they were speaking, even if what they said was off the point, or you knew what they were going to say already. She stood attentively by the door as he continued and watched a beam of sunlight dancing on his narrow brown head, as he sat at the desk.

'Now, if you wish to become my patient you cannot ask me to break the rules governing my conduct. Or try to persuade me to bend them, Mrs Frazier, for your convenience. Whatever your needs, as you see them, these rules were made for the benefit of all, for the common good, and I must maintain them.' He privately reflected that these rules, which had once imparted such inspiration, were harder to stand by in practice than in theory. His was a poor neighbourhood, girls of thirteen bore children by their own fathers, women nearing fifty, already worn out by large families, embarked on pregnancies which could kill them, the infant or both of them, leaving behind widowers and helpless children. Here was yet another bitter story, he felt sure. The girl had already told him she was not married. At that age, with a baby on the way and no wedding ring, she was already on the road to tragedy. He frowned and said, 'If you assure me you've understood what I've told you, I'll accept you as a patient.'

Had he finished? wondered Violet. It looked like it. 'All right,' she said, sitting down and adopting a respectful tone. 'I do need a doctor. I seem to understand that you don't have to tell my . . . my friend how far along I am, unless he asks. That'll have to do. Can you get me a midwife, and so forth, for when the baby comes?'

'I can attend to all that,' said Dr Smith. 'I ought also to call on you at regular intervals to make sure that all is as it should be.'

Violet guessed that this was what well-off women did, and what Frederick would expect. 'You could come in the afternoons,' she said.

That evening she told Frederick she had found a doctor.

Frederick was doubtful. 'I'd like to see him when he visits you,' he told her. 'Ask him to come next Saturday afternoon.' Without admitting it to himself he was relieved Violet had appointed a doctor on her own, since otherwise he would have had to find one, almost inevitably consulting Henry Sturgess, to whom he was not keen to reveal Violet's pregnancy.

Violet, disguising her reluctance, agreed. If he lets on, she thought grimly to herself, I'm o-u-t. And, she added to herself just as grimly, Frederick Levine is going to keep me under wraps as far as his family's concerned. I'm a bit of fluff tucked away in Belsize Park to him, and all his lovey-dovey business don't mean a thing. If he falls under a brewer's dray tomorrow I'd be nobody from nowhere as far as the Levines were concerned, even if it was his baby.

Kate Higgins, April 28th, 1991

After we got back from Spain I stayed at Andy's flat for a few days. On Wednesday he was due to go off to cover the elections in Belize. After the results were declared, there might be trouble. Andy, as usual, was due to get injured, captured, killed. He decided to give a party the day before he left. I organised it. Fifty people drank champagne, ate snacks provided by caterers amid banks of flowers supplied by florists in his luxurious flat overlooking the church, and the charming little streets of North Kensington. From above, the women with pushchairs, the little knot of black young men outside the domed community centre, the children playing in the square, all looked small and picturesque in the bright spring dusk, as in an old print of Montmartre in the nineties. That all this charm was maintained from a police station built like a fortress, with a yard behind it stuffed with reinforced buses, cars, a basement full of police vans, riot gear and supplies of CS gas, was not worth commenting on. Everybody at the party knew all this, knew the lines they were treading. Everybody, as the saying goes, knew and nobody said.

Dave Gottlieb was there, in an old Fair Isle cardigan, a cap and grey trousers which had seen better days. 'So how's Violet Levine?' he asked me, standing in the window, looking down.

I hesitated, feeling a bit embarrassed to confess to diligent, high-minded Dave that I was planning to give up the project.

Andy came by and put a hand on my shoulder. 'She's packing it in,' he said.

Dave's eyes went from him to me, back to Andy, in the space of half a second. His face registered nothing. Then he said, 'Well. It's a tough proposition. With no co-operation from the heirs. Still, with or without, it would have made an interesting book.'

'Askew and Askew'll have to find another sucker,' said Andy, moving over to another group, saying, 'Kev. I'm glad you're here. I want you to tell me . . . '

I'd told Andy yesterday I was going to ring Roger and tell him I was giving up the biography. But I hadn't done it.

Dave's bespectacled eyes circled the room vaguely as he said, 'Seems a shame. Why don't you just tell Askew and Askew the family won't help, but you'll do it anyway?'

'It's not the family, or the publisher,' I said, and then stuck, realising that I was about to explain what was preventing me from going on with Violet's biography – except that I didn't know what to say. It had something to do with Andy, I knew. But what? Then, I suddenly realised, I'd become afraid of what I was doing. But why? I looked at Dave. I think my mouth was open.

Dave, his head on one side, said, 'Something wrong?'

'I think so. Maybe I'm not giving it up after all.' I felt afraid as I spoke.

'Stay away from Gordon Stone, that's all,' said Dave.

All I knew, without even thinking about it, was that I couldn't decide whether I really wanted to go on with the biography until Andy was gone, and that meant that he was putting pressure on me to give up. Then he claimed me and dragged me off, saying I had to meet someone on his paper, which was either a proposal of marriage, or he was trying to get me a job. It turned out to be the latter. Next thing, I was talking to the editor of the women's page, suggesting a problem column.

'A good idea,' praised Andy in the cab to the airport.

'Whoever said I could deal with anyone's problems? It could be fatal,' I said.

'Just common sense,' he declared. 'And a pack of experts . . . ' He hugged me. 'I'll be back to watch you start it. You can move into a better flat.'

I didn't say anything, partly because I was concerned about his assignment – anything could happen. Three years as the wife of a soldier in Belfast had taught me not to express my fears.

After he left I went back to the flat. Next day Di had a morning off. I told her about the problem page.

'Sounds very good,' she said. 'I'm sure you could do an upmarket feminist problem page. What about women having ethical differences with a marriage guidance counsellor, or whether it's right to start a family quarrel on Christmas Day when your brother says he's going to vote Conservative . . . ' Then she started to laugh. 'At least you could give up the biography.'

'That's what Andy thinks,' I told her. 'But, I feel queasy about – everything. I can't explain it. As if I'm going the wrong way. D'you know what I mean? Your life's all of a piece— '

'Oh, *yes*. Of course,' said Di. 'It's wonderful.' She didn't mean it.

'No, you know what you're doing, and what you think is worthwhile,' I went on earnestly. 'Whatever happens you know you're doing right— ' I broke off. Di's rather small face was frightening. She looked grim, terrifying, very anxious. 'Well, that's what it looks like,' I ended feebly. 'Perhaps it doesn't look like that to you . . . '

'You couldn't know,' she said. She grabbed her bag off the floor and began to roll a cigarette. In a moment she said, 'You don't want this job, even if it exists. But do you think you want to do the biography? Because if it's important to you, you should. On balance, the *Witness* job is a better earner. Regular pay. And you could go on for another six months with the biography and find somehow you still can't do it. But there's such a thing as doing what you've got to do . . . '

Di was thinner, rather frail-looking. Her face was pale under her mat of fair hair. She'd looked awful all winter, but she ought to have been picking up by now. Was she worried? Wasn't she eating enough? Was she ill?

'You're looking peaky,' I said. 'There's nothing wrong, is there? Next time I go to Brighton, do you want to come too, rest and recuperation, sea air, quiet weekend?'

'Are you going next weekend?' she asked.

'Yes.'

'Friday night to Sunday night?'

'I was thinking – coming?'

'I can't, this weekend.'

She'd tried to help me with my dilemma over the jobs, but that obviously didn't mean she wanted me in the flat for the weekend. If I irritated her, if she was sleeping with a lover, a married man, another woman, even if she was sleeping with my ex-husband, if she was practising the steel drums, running a poker school, forging bank notes, why the hell didn't she tell me? What hadn't we told each other over the years? Or was it all my imagination that she wanted me gone? And what could I say? Nothing.

I told her tentatively, 'Andy said if I took the *Witness* job I could get another place.'

'I need your rent,' said Di, smiling. Then, 'Just like Andy to try to break up our beautiful relationship.'

Then the phone rang, but no one spoke, so I put the receiver down. It happened from time to time. When it rang again before I went back into the front room I expected the same thing but it was Roger Littlebrown. He began angrily, 'I'm quite disappointed, in fact I'm very disappointed, Kate. I really think if you were planning to break our contract, you might have discussed it with me first.'

'Roger— ' I said.

'Frankly I find it rather discourteous. This isn't the sort of thing you want to hear from a third party. In any case,' he said, softening his tone, 'if there are problems I would have thought the first thing to do would be to discuss them with me— '

I took advantage of his lowered tone to shout, 'Roger! What's this all about?'

He paused, then said, 'Well, Andy rang me to say goodbye before he went to Belize and told me you'd decided to give up the biography. Naturally, I was very upset. You see, Kate, we think here it could be a very interesting book. We were really looking forward to having it on our list.'

'When did he ring you?' I asked.

'Yesterday afternoon, just before five. I tried to call you several times yesterday evening but you weren't in. He didn't mention it?'

'No, actually he didn't,' I told him. 'And as a matter of fact I haven't quite decided what to do. It's a bit annoying of Andy to have rung you without telling me.'

'Yes. So I'd have thought . . . ' Roger said, coldly.

'Does he usually ring to say goodbye before he goes off?' I asked.

'No, this time he asked me to visit Aunt Jocelyn – his mother – while he was away. But, Kate, if you're thinking of giving up the book, please come and see me first. Let's have lunch soon.'

After we rang off I stood looking round the hall, staring at the anoraks on Di's old-fashioned hatstand and her stupid woolly hat on a brass peg, feeling angry with Andy. He must have felt that having virtually got me the job in the first place he had to take the responsibility for resigning me from it. He didn't even think he needed to mention it to me. It was a cheek. I went and told Di. She shook her head in amazement. 'I'll never understand him. What are you going to do?'

'God knows,' I said. 'It's getting confusing.'

Violet Crutchley, November, 1913

Violet lay weakly in the bronze-figured bed at Belsize Park, while the doctor said, 'A healthy little girl, Mrs Frazier,' the midwife pushed her stomach to release in a final spasm of pain the afterbirth, then her assistant set about washing her legs and rolling her over to change the sheet. The midwife bustled about in a corner to the sound of a baby crying. Violet pulled herself up to see what was going on. 'Lie flat, Mrs Frazier,' Dr Smith said, but Violet didn't and observed her bloodied sheet and the undersheet being bundled away by a tidy girl in a huge, bloodied apron and in the corner a middle-aged woman in a long blue overall, with her hair covered in a white scarf knotted at the back, plunging a small blue and red form into a large enamel basin on a table, then pulling it out, as all the time it yelled a high, agonised cry. She swathed the baby in a big white towel from a wooden airer in front of the fire. The curtains were drawn, although it was only six thirty in the evening, and fog was seeping round the corners of the stiff red brocade. Now she was being put into a clean nightdress. 'Well done, Mrs Frazier,' said Dr Malcolm Smith, bending over her. 'Taken it like a trooper. Anyone would think you'd done it before.'

'And I won't be doing it again,' responded Violet, falling back on the pillows. She hadn't believed there could be such pain.

The midwife, who had dried the baby and dressed it in a nappy, a soft vest and a flannel nightdress with a sash, placed it on her shoulder, and said, 'There you are, Mrs Frazier.'

Violet stared at the bawling face, gingery hair and bright blue eyes, looking exactly like Tom Rawlinson, only older, and thought, Oh, Christ, all this – for that.

'You'd better put your baby to the breast, Mrs Frazier,' said the woman. She had seen the tough little body and Violet's small face distorted with pain and determination during the birth. It had been an awe-inspiring sight, as had been Violet's utter lack of reliance on her, the girl and even her own doctor, as the struggle went on. She knew instinctively that here was a woman who could give birth as easily as a cat, and would show less concern for her children than the cat would for her kittens. She opened the laces of Violet's nightdress and put the baby to her breast. 'She'll do the rest,' she remarked easily. She glanced at the doctor. He knows there's something up, she thought.

'Couldn't someone open the window?' remarked Violet. 'I'm stifling. And what about a cup of tea?'

'Shall I telephone your husband now?' asked Dr Smith, and it was scarcely a question. Violet had only sent her parlourmaid with a note at four o'clock. The doctor had not received it until he came in at five. When he told his servant he'd like a pot of tea and some toast before he set out, she told him that Violet's parlourmaid had said that she thought the doctor ought to come quickly.

Dr Smith guessed Violet had been trying to pretend to herself that the baby, officially due near Christmas, was not being born on November 5th. She may even have thought she could hold it back. Young women did. He had got into his car, providentially found the midwife at home, giving her children their tea, and driven them both as fast as thick fog would permit to Whittington Gardens.

He'd run up the stairs two at a time with the midwife hard behind him. After one look at Violet, clinging to the mantelpiece in front of the unlit grate, the midwife was calling for hot water, sheets and hot coals from the top of the stairs. Twenty minutes later, the baby was born. The doctor suggested her husband should be sent a message telling him he was shortly to be a father, but Violet, her face contorted, had gasped, 'No. Wait till it's born.'

Now Dr Smith was again asking her to tell Frederick. 'I'd like a quiet word,' she said.

Dr Smith nodded the two women out of the room. When they had gone he said, 'Yes?'

'Is it always going to look like this?'

Dr Smith, astonished, looked at the baby at Violet's breast, then at Violet. He couldn't understand the question.

Violet sighed. 'All right,' she said. 'Does this baby look premature to you?'

'Frankly, Mrs Frazier, no, she doesn't,' said Smith.

Violet hauled herself up. 'You won't tell him?' The baby,

jolted from the breast, began crying and thrashing on the pillow.

Smith replied firmly, 'Summon your husband immediately, Mrs Frazier. Delay will only make things look worse. And please lie down. I can't answer for the consequences if you keep agitating yourself like this.' He rang the bell.

The midwife returned and wordlessly put the baby to Violet's other breast.

'Wonderful business, this, isn't it?' said Violet to the doctor. 'Your body's suddenly everybody's. Get me a pen and paper.' She scribbled the note, addressed the envelope, said, 'Make sure that gets to Mr Frederick Levine at Cavendish Square directly. Mr Levine, and only Mr Levine.'

Dr Smith was surprised. He had doubted the identity of this 'Mr Frazier' who, due to Violet's skilled manipulation of events, he had only met once, in the hall. He had imagined him to be a stockbroker or lawyer living under an assumed name with his young mistress. After the maid left he could not resist asking, 'Is the gentleman to whom you sent the note Mr Frederick Levine, the banker?'

Violet nodded. Suddenly tired, Violet murmured, 'If only someone would fetch me a cup of tea. What's that noise?'

'Fireworks,' said Dr Smith. 'It's Guy Fawkes night. Nurse, I think we should take the baby away and let Mrs Frazier have some food and rest. Have you no nurse for the child?' he asked Violet. 'Oh, no – perhaps you weren't prepared.'

At that moment the maid came up with a telegram in her hand and a tray of tea. Violet opened the telegram. It read:

> Mum had a little boy last Wednesday. Not well. Can you come and help please. Love Allie.

She put it down near her and said to Smith, 'It'll be managed.'

'Good,' Smith replied, bewildered by the hardening of Violet's face as she read the telegram.

'Mrs Jellicoe could perhaps be persuaded to stay until tomorrow, to hold the fort?' he enquired. And Mrs Jellicoe nodded, not liking what she heard or saw in this household but at least reassured by the word 'banker' that her payment would be forthcoming.

'Excellent,' said Smith. He looked uncertainly at Violet, the baby, the abandoned telegram, thought of a maid on her way to the Levines at Cavendish Square. He recalled his sister Grace, now probably reading a book by the fire with her spaniel beside her, or coming in fresh and a little muddy round the shoes and stockings from a country walk. 'Get Mrs Frazier a cup of tea,' he said to the midwife.

At Cavendish Square Frederick Levine sat opposite his mother in the drawing-room, listening to her reading in German. He wore the evening clothes he kept at the house, with all his other clothes, in the dressing-room next to his bedroom. His mother ceased to read, lowering the book in her hand. 'Beautiful,' she said.

'Beautiful,' Frederick agreed.

His sister-in-law, Caroline Levine, who was leaning back against the cushions of a sofa opposite the fire, said nothing. She found the atmosphere in the Levine drawing-room extremely boring. 'Deadly,' she told her mother. 'All incomprehensible names and foreign languages, and never a laugh in sight.'

'Well,' Lady Despencer had said, 'it's only to be expected.'

Frederick got up and poured another whisky, then settled back in his chair. 'And so, how have you passed the day, Caroline?'

Caroline roused herself. The house was always too hot, she thought, no wonder she was always half asleep. She replied, 'The usual things. Some shopping in the morning. Jo-Jo in the afternoon. Nanny and I took him to the Round Pond and fed the ducks, but then the fog came down, so we came home.' Privately, she reflected that Frederick was turning up more often at Cavendish Square in the evenings, and wondered if life in the love-nest at Belsize Park, which he'd told his brother about, was beginning to pall. When Laurence had told her, she'd laughed. 'Old Fred,' she said, 'keeping a woman in a house in Belsize Park – who'd have believed it.'

'Fred's twenty-three,' her husband had said. 'He was bound to break out some time.'

'Who's the woman?' Caroline asked. 'I hope it's not a grasping chorus girl who will ruin him. Or,' she added, widening her eyes in mock horror, 'a diseased prostitute.'

Laurence, who loved his brother, and sometimes found Caroline's pitiless Despencer humour trying, said only, 'He doesn't seem to want to talk about it. Of course, he hasn't told Mother but I think she guesses. He seems very happy – happier than he's been for a long time. Whoever she is, she's not bad for him.'

Caroline felt snubbed but put a good face on it. She countered, 'Nevertheless, he ought to get married soon. Your Uncle Leopold was asking me about it.'

'Heavens. I'd have thought he had a good few years to run before he turns into a crusty old bachelor,' Laurence said.

Mrs Levine looked at the clock on the mantelpiece. 'Where on earth is Laurence?' she asked. 'It's almost dinner-time.'

'He said he was stopping at the club on the way home, but he promised he'd be punctual this time,' Caroline told her.

'Brough told me he'd arrived twenty minutes ago,' Frederick said. 'I expect he's changing. Hello, Laurence,' he said, as the door opened. 'We were just betting on whether you'd be late again or not. I bet a guinea at 100 to 1 you would be, but Caroline stuck by you like a loyal wife, so now I owe her 100 guineas.'

'We were in it together,' Laurence said comfortably, pouring himself a whisky. 'We were going to buy a racehorse with the winnings.'

'Dinner's just about to be served,' Caroline pointed out.

'Time for a drink, though,' Laurence told her.

Caroline, suspecting he'd already had a few whiskies while dressing, said, 'Not unless you take it in one swallow. Honestly, Laurence, you're a trial sometimes.'

As Brough came in with a note on a tray, Mrs Levine reflected that the rough manners of young Englishwomen were not, in her opinion, designed to keep their husbands happy and comfortable. Brough took the note to Frederick, who, frowning slightly, opened it. Then he stood up, looking extremely startled, said, 'Excuse me. There's someone I must speak to downstairs,' and left the room rapidly.

'What's all that about?' wondered Caroline. Mrs Levine said nothing and Laurence said, 'Business, no doubt.'

Brough, returning, announced that dinner was ready.

'We'll begin without Mr Frederick,' said his mother, and they walked downstairs, passing Frederick, in conversation with a young, rather tousled girl who looked like a servant. While they were being served their soup at the long dining-table Frederick came into the room in his overcoat, carrying his hat and said, 'I'm extremely sorry, Mother, I have to go out.'

Mrs Levine, from the head of the table, nodded and said only, 'Of course.'

She knows it's a domestic disturbance, thought Caroline – the kept woman's poisoned herself with valerian, or the pipes have burst all at once. A disturbance in Belsize Park, and a split between Frederick and his mistress might be the best opportunity yet to push the interests of her sister, Rosalind, she thought. Why shouldn't Fred marry Rosalind? He was nice-looking, kind, didn't drink or use his fists on the servants, and she was well brought up, healthy and good-natured and would bring a bit of fresh air into his life. There was even a chance, if Fred married, that she might be able to get Laurence to move away, into their own house. It would be Rosalind's turn to put up with the stultifying atmosphere at Cavendish Square.

As if she read Caroline's mind, Sophie Levine spoke. 'The table looks very big tonight. Perhaps one's more conscious of it because Frederick should have been here. At any rate, it's high time we invited some guests – it would be very pleasant if your parents and Rosalind could be with us, Caroline.'

'I'm sure they'd be most pleased,' said Caroline, fingering the large pearls which looped twice round her throat, hung over her bosom – Sophie Levine's mother's pearls, a wedding gift from her mother-in-law.

Upstairs Brough, checking that the drawing-room was ready for the return of the family, found the note Frederick had crumpled on the arm of his chair. He read it and put it on the fire.

Frederick, sitting nervously in a cab, ploughing its way through silent, foggy streets, with the sound of the engine unnaturally loud where he sat, clenched his hands with excitement and apprehension. The parlourmaid sat silently opposite. 'Your daughter born at six thirty this evening,' Violet had scribbled. 'Both well. Come soon, my darling.' Now that the moment had come he hardly knew what he felt. 'My daughter,' he said to himself experimentally. But pity seized him for the new life. She was only a girl and she would not have the rights of even a girl born in wedlock. He'd have to protect her, make arrangements, give Sturgess some instructions in the morning.

He'd have to tell Laurence, too, though, as he thought of it he shuddered. The child's being a girl would, somehow, count against him. As ever, he'd seem to be lagging behind Laurence, not capable of siring a son like Jo-Jo, who'd inherited the old cradle they'd both slept in as children, who had first claim now on all the Levines possessed. But, dear little Violet, he thought. And now her baby. He tapped on the window with his stick. 'Are we lost?' he called.

'Please, sir,' pleaded the driver, 'I'm doing my best.' He doubted if he'd get back to Putney through this, would probably have to sleep in the cab by the roadside tonight. His wife would lie awake worrying.

Inside the house Violet had slept, woken and was suckling her child vigorously, thinking that somehow the milk, taken internally, would erase the lineaments of Tom Rawlinson from the baby's face. She was sitting up when Frederick burst in, and, tears starting in his eyes, fell on his knees beside her and the child, gazing into his daughter's eyes. 'She's beautiful,' he told her. 'What a shock – six weeks too soon.' He looked up at her as she lay against the pillows. 'Oh my dear, good little Violet, did you suffer much?'

'It was worth it,' said Violet gently. 'But, oh, dear Frederick, tell me truly. Did you really want a son?'

'No, my love. A daughter, just like her mother.' He embraced her, drawing deep breaths, repressing a sob. Violet looked over his head, almost sighing aloud with relief.

At Cavendish Square Sophie Levine put down her spoon and smiled at her son and daughter-in-law. 'I'm tired tonight,' she said. 'Perhaps it's this stifling fog, but for me, the day seems to be over. I think I'll go to my room.'

'Goodnight, then, Mother,' said her son, and 'Goodnight, Mama,' echoed her daughter-in-law.

As soon as she had gone Caroline asked, 'Whatever got into Fred tonight? Imagine bolting out in a fog like this. I wonder if even now he's managed to get to where he was going.'

'Dirty work at B.P.,' he said, the initials being their joke term for the Belsize Park ménage.

In her room, on the heavy dressing-table, framed in ebony stood a photograph of a clean-shaven, middle-aged man, who was Samuel, Sophie Levine's late husband, father of Laurence and Frederick. Sophie Levine sat in a chair by the fire, one lamp burning behind her on the draped table crowded with ornaments and silver-framed photographs of family and friends. She said to the butler, 'Will you bring me coffee here, Brough? I'll read a little before I retire. I think you might lock up now.'

'Very good, Mrs Levine,' said Brough.

As he was going Sophie Levine drew a breath and said calmly, 'Mr Frederick left a note behind when he went out,' she said. 'What happened to it?'

Brough turned and looked at her steadily. 'I took it and burned it, Mrs Levine. I hope that was the right thing to do.'

It would be quite wrong for her to ask him about the contents of a note. He was not supposed to have read it. She was not supposed to find out what her sons did not choose to tell her. Had there been any other means of discovering what the letter said, she would have employed it. As it was, Brough knew she would ask and she knew he was expecting the question. 'Did you happen to see what it said, before you burned it?' she asked.

Brough said, without expression, 'Your daughter born at six thirty this evening. Both well.' He left out the end of Violet's message, and, tactfully, her name.

'Thank you, Brough,' said Sophie Levine.

'Thank you, Mrs Levine. I shall send the maid with your coffee.' As he left the room she was picking up her book, and putting on her spectacles.

After the door closed she took off the glasses, looked at the fire, turned to glance at her late husband's photograph on the dressing-table. Frederick had been a silly young fool, she thought. But after all, the child was a girl and if the woman was sensible, when the affair died a natural death, she'd be glad to accept a reasonable financial settlement from Frederick for herself and the child. No harm would be done. Young men would, after all, sow their wild oats. Meanwhile she must make an earnest effort to get Frederick married and settled down. Even if it meant Rosalind. Much as she dreaded the Despencers, with their terrible English philistinism, their horseplay, those awful 'jokes' and their unassailable belief in the superiority of their own education, cuisine, housing and bloodlines, at least Rosalind was, like Caroline, healthy, and reasonably well brought up. And with that thought, Sophie Levine picked up her book and read some soothing passages from Heine. An hour and a half later, she summoned her maid, who assisted her to undress, brushed her long black-grey hair, plaited it for the night, and went to bed.

For the next month there was nothing to disturb her sense that Frederick's life was following a satisfactory course. During his now-infrequent visits to the house, he seemed placid and happy. Laurence, whom Sophie Levine had told about the child, although she did not reveal how she had got the information, just laughed when he heard.

Only Caroline, when he told her, took it more seriously. 'I'd like to see her,' she said. 'If you get the address from Sturgess I'll call there, pretending I'm looking for somebody else.'

Laurence was shocked. 'Frederick is not to know that we know,' he said. 'Leave him alone for God's sake. Let him enjoy his happiness.'

But Caroline returned to the topic again one afternoon, as she sat, sewing a shirt for her son, while Sophie wrote one of her many letters in German or French to the vast network of relatives spread all over Europe. 'May I interrupt you for a moment, Mama-in-law?' she asked.

'Of course,' said Sophie Levine, laying down her pen and dreading what this robust, bored, twenty-one-year-old was about to propose. She hoped the news would be that Caroline was having another child, but guessed she was not.

'I rather wondered if you'd like me to go and visit Frederick's . . . friend – on a pretext, and find out what she's like.'

Sophie Levine disliked this crude approach, although she could not deny the common sense behind the idea. She also thought that if anyone was going to investigate Frederick's mistress it should not be Caroline. She replied calmly, 'Thank you, my dear. But I think we should allow Frederick's private life to remain private, until he decides he'd like to take us into his confidence.'

'If I were his mother, I believe I would like to know what kind of a woman she was.'

'You may discover,' responded Mrs Levine, 'as you grow older, that what a mother would like and what she receives are two very different things.'

This snub infuriated Caroline. She wished, not for the first time, that she was at home in the country with her brothers and sisters, with Rosy combing the dogs and taking off the postmistress in that killing way she had, and one of the boys just in from a ride. With a winter afternoon to endure then a family dinner followed by an evening at Covent Garden Opera looming, she hardly knew how to contain herself. She bit her lip and said, sulkily, 'Oh, very good. If that's what you prefer.'

A fortnight later, Violet Crutchley struck. Having got Frederick to accept the pregnancy, and the child, Pamela, as his own and register her as such, no longer weighed down by anxiety or pregnancy, she was feeling confident and discontented.

Since they had moved to Belsize Park eight months before they had hardly been out and she had seen no one but him, the servants, Dr Smith, and the woman who came in on several afternoons a week to teach her French and German. It was obvious that even with the baby fully in charge of a nursemaid Frederick still planned to stay in the snugness of the little home, having himself all the stimulus of his working life and of family and friends at Cavendish Square when he chose, treating the house at Belsize Park as a place of relaxation, comfort and support. She read a lot and Malcolm Smith, half-appalled, half-fascinated by her, often dropped in at tea-time, and spoke of his political beliefs; they discussed what she was reading and Violet began to perceive the depths of her ignorance.

Nevertheless, she was not used to quietness or solitude; it began to prey on her and she could see no end to it. She began by looking disconsolately at Frederick and speaking little during dinner.

Afterwards, as they sat by the fire he asked, 'What is

it, Violet? Are you unwell, or a little depressed? Is the baby tiring you?'

'It's the thought of Christmas,' Violet said, dabbing her eyes with a little handkerchief. 'I can't go home, as things are, to see my family. And you'll want to go to Cavendish Square without me. What am I to do? I'll be here with baby all by myself. Even the nurse will be visiting her sister. It'll be so lonely without you.'

Frederick had already allowed his mother to assume he would be present for the family party on Christmas Eve, when several Schrefts and Waldsteins, including the pretty cousins from Vienna, would be staying at Cavendish Square over Christmas. Now he felt uncomfortable.

'It's very awkward,' he told her. 'Mother expects me for a family party on Christmas Eve— '

Violet suppressed a sob at this.

'Oh, Violet,' he burst out, 'aren't I enough for you?'

'It's just thinking about Christmas,' she said. 'I love you so much, Frederick, and baby, but with you gone at Christmas, what have I got – and who? All over the place people high and low will be sitting down with their friends and family. No matter how poor they are, there'll be something. It's a special day. And I can't go home . . . ' And she began to sob, although, the truth was that it would have taken little negotiation for her to have gone home. She had heard from Allie that her mother was still unwell after the birth of the baby. Her older sister Norah, pregnant and not fit herself, had no thought of helping. Allie, in spite of protests from Norah, and her father, who said it was selfish to continue the typing course with her mother ill and a new brother to take care of, not to mention two growing boys, was still doggedly attending the course so that she could get her diploma. Between the lines of Allie's letter, Violet could easily see that the arrival of a sister with energy and money at Christmas or any other time would be a boon. There might be complaints about her situation for the sake of respectability but far from being the fallen daughter turned out into the snow on Christmas Eve, she'd probably be welcomed in with open arms. But she wasn't planning to go. She had to maintain Frederick's refuge, the cosy home at Belsize Park. She certainly didn't want her family to forgive her and start turning up at Belsize Park. And they were still in touch with Tom Rawlinson. Even if Frederick couldn't count how many months it took to have a baby, Tom could. So could her mother. She would no more have crossed the Thames to south London at Christmas than thrown herself into the river. Nevertheless, she sobbed on.

Meanwhile Frederick gazed into the fire, seeing no way out. He did not want to disappoint his mother, but he couldn't bring Violet and, presumably, the baby, unexpectedly to a family Christmas party. Somehow, that evening, he patched it up with Violet, although, unknown to him, but not to her, she had managed now to establish herself as the young woman who had sacrificed all for him. Next evening at Cavendish Square he was anxious about Violet, alone at Belsize Park, excluded from this family occasion, as she would be over Christmas. The distinguished singer, who had come to perform after dinner, sang songs by Schubert and Hugo Wolf. Laurence, sitting next to his brother at the back of the room murmured, 'Are you all right, Fred? You look a bit down in the mouth.'

'Violet's a little sad I'm not with her, poor girl,' replied Frederick.

Laurence nodded sympathetically.

In bed that night, as Laurence lay with his head dreamily on Caroline's shoulder, she said, 'Your mother should have let me go to see her.'

'I don't know,' replied Laurence comfortably. 'No real need, was there? A moping woman doesn't keep her man, that's a fact of life.'

'If she mopes well enough,' Caroline said fiercely, thinking of Rosalind's chances with Frederick, 'she ends up with the family jewels.'

At Belsize Park Frederick was temporarily comfortable again with his compliant Violet, innocently sensual, simple and loving. She, however, was hiding an increasing fury, a mixture of intense boredom and frustration. The baby, Pamela, interested her from time to time, but remained mostly as a reminder of the stratagems she had had to employ, and was still employing, just to survive in what began to feel like a comfortable prison. She could see no way out.

One dark afternoon she went into one of her uncontrollable rages. She had flown at the maid, flung a tea-tray through the window, screamed and screamed at the girl standing there, appalled, and finally plucked a hot coal from the fire with her bare hands and thrown it at her head. She continued to scream and choke as the cook, Felix, rushed from the kitchen, took one horrified look at her and went and telephoned Dr Smith on the newly installed telephone. Then with difficulty, he held Violet as she kicked, struggled and swore. 'It was over a piece of cake,' he gasped, as the doctor came into the room. 'She's gone mad, I think.'

Malcolm Smith, producing a blue medicine bottle from his bag, poured some liquid into a glass and, staring into Violet's eyes with a look such as someone might give a dog about to attack, said, 'Drink this.'

Violet, the fit abating, and knowing from his expression that his next gesture would be to slap her face hard, which was what her mother had always done, drank the liquid, and was soon lying down upstairs, drowsily, while the servants downstairs cleared up the mess.

'What brought this on?' he asked.

'I was going to kill the baby,' she muttered.

'What brought it on?'

'Nothing.'

Malcolm Smith's training had stressed the unaccountable nature of women, their wombs being in control of their bodies and emotions. He told her these fits were connected with her sex and gave her a bottle of valerian, with instructions to take three drops, in water, when attacks threatened. But, as he drove away, he found his mind, again, on his sister, almost seventeen, like Violet, but leading a very different life.

Before Frederick came home Violet gave Felix money for himself and the maids, to ensure their silence. Felix's reaction, during the scene, had been to assume that, reluctant as he was to leave a good job, where Violet tolerated his weakness for drink, he might soon be looking for another position. This event, he reasoned, would be followed by others, and the relationship between his master and mistress would break up as she became more demanding and difficult.

Ten days before Christmas Frederick came back, on Sunday night, all the servants being out, to find Violet stretched under the Christmas tree, a half-empty bottle of valerian in her hand, at her side a note saying, 'Frederick, I love you so much but I cannot go on like this.' Upstairs his daughter was screaming in her cradle.

On his knees beside her bed later, Frederick said to Violet Crutchley that they must marry. And Violet, smiling, holding his hand, half-fainting on her pillow, agreed.

She spent Christmas alone at Belsize Park since Frederick decided he had better spare his family the news of a secret wedding until after Christmas. Alone on Christmas morning, Violet looked into her baby's cot and said, 'Well Pamela, my girl. Next year I won't be a kept woman and you won't be a bastard. Let the Levines chew on that one.' The nursemaid, coming in, caught her doing a little, triumphant dance round the room. Felix, in the kitchen, heard the story and smiled.

Kate Higgins, April 30th, 1991

It was arranged I'd have lunch with Roger Littlebrown two days after his angry phone call. He'd managed to squeeze time for lunch with an obscure, first-time author, writing a biography of a known, but not very important woman, into a programme of entertainments which stretched into the following year and made Louis XIV look like a hermit.

I overslept that morning and by the time I'd got organised I'd only just time to join Roger for our rendezvous at La Somnambule. Rushing, I noticed the postcard Di must have propped up on the mantelpiece that morning from Andy, saying, '*Ich liebe dich*' sent from a stop-over in Munich. This made me feel nervous. I suspected I might be going to do what he didn't want at lunch-time today: I might tell Roger I'd go on with the book. There might be a terrible row when he got back from Belize. He might tell me he never wanted to see me again. He seemed to resent the demand on my time and interest the book was making and which I knew, and I suppose he did too, would get even greater as I got deeper and deeper in. Attitudes to Andy were implicitly understood by both of us. His editor, after the party, had said, 'Look after him,' to me. Roger, Andy's many other women supporters, everybody, really, always asked after Andy, his career, his health and state of mind, never about me. The feeling was that Andy was incredibly gifted, a hero of the left, a public saviour and benefactor who risked his life daily in the cause of truth, and that my priority ought to be looking after him. Di was one of the few people who didn't believe this but, swayed by public opinion, I half-believed myself that if Andy wanted me to give up the book, I should. Standing there, feeling confused, I noticed the envelope which Di had put behind the postcard. I was just opening it when the telephone rang and I carried it to the phone.

'Hello,' said my friend Deep Throat in that high, cracked voice. 'Have you got my letter?'

'No,' I said, startled, 'unless it's the one I'm just opening.'

'Open it,' said the voice.

And I opened it. Between two bits of cardboard held together with a paper-clip was the picture of a tall young man in a dark suit, a young woman in a pale dress and a big deep crowned hat with lace round the edge, he looking gravely down at her, she smiling up at him, submissively, prettily. A clergyman, to the side, smiled at both of them.

'Violet's wedding?' I said.

'Looks like the cat looking at the canary, doesn't she?' asked Deep Throat nastily. 'Innocent, butter wouldn't melt, but the cage door has been left open, and it's only a matter of time . . . '

'You're no friend of Violet's,' I said.

'I told you, didn't I?' the other person replied tetchily. 'She was a dreadful woman. She did a lot of damage. Turn the photograph over.'

But I already had and saw the photographer's stamp, 'Hans Klemer, 10 Bond Street, W1' and in the space underneath, in old-fashioned writing, faded and authentic, the initials H.K. and the date, December 21st, 1913.

'Six months after she says, in *I Affirm*,' I said.

'And six weeks after Pamela was born. She was under-age. She forged the letter of consent from her father – you should know better than to take Violet's book as the truth. It's what she thought should have happened, not what did. Some of it was written to make herself look more acceptable, respectable, more noble – all that sort of thing. But I think one of her motives was to retell her own past as she wished it had happened.'

'I suppose we'd all like to do that.'

'Yes, but we know we can't. A person has to be very neurotic, or have an ego like a Sherman tank, to try.'

'Which do you think?' I asked quickly. The reply, if it came, might tell me who the speaker was, or give me a clue.

But the quiet, rather whistly voice (asthma, I wondered? A lifelong smoker?) ignored the question. There was a silence.

Terrified the caller would ring off I hastily took another tack. 'I've got to see my publisher,' I said hastily. 'All the Levines have refused to co-operate, as you predicted. I very much hope Jack Christian-Smith will see me – I think you thought he might. Otherwise there's a chance this book will never be written. If you would come forward and agree to help me – I wouldn't even need to identify you – I'd be able to feel some confidence. At present I'm hesitating. And after all, the Levine family has some right to a say in the matter.'

'No, they haven't,' my caller assured me. 'If I thought they had I wouldn't be assisting you.'

'Why do you believe they haven't?' I asked.

'I can't tell you,' said the cracked voice. 'I can't come forward. There are reasons. Perhaps I shouldn't be speaking to you . . . '

'Why?'

'I can't tell you,' the voice said again. I heard someone else now, speaking faintly in the background. 'Yes,' replied my caller to the other person. Then, to me, 'I've been reminded you should find Violet's boss in Special Operations – Aurelia Jenks-Davidson. I don't know much about what happened, except that all wasn't as it seemed, not unusual where Violet was concerned as you'll be discovering. You know,' the voice went on, after a pause, 'I don't think the true story of Violet's life would really harm her.'

'I hope not,' I said. 'But all these secrets . . . What's the matter with Joanna Levine?'

'Poor Joanna,' said the voice. 'Poor, poor Joanna.'

There was another pause. I asked quickly, 'Who's alive? Who'll speak?' I knew I was being driven to show how desperate I was. I didn't dare ask, yet again, 'Who are you?'

'Joseph Levine's still alive, as far as I know. He was in the Household Cavalry – or was it the Grenadier Guards? Something with a smart uniform. He served in the Second World War anyway. As a regular army officer he ought to be easy to trace.'

'If he shares the family desire for secrecy he won't be much good. What about the Crutchleys? Are there any left?'

'Ben. Frank died on the Somme in 1916. You must have forgotten. It's in *I Affirm* – the loss sustained by Violet, and so forth. He only joined up to get away from home, poor boy. He was only fifteen. He told them he was older.' The voice was sad. 'Ben'll talk to you. He lives in a village in Kent – Oathouses, it's called.' The voice paused. 'Radleigh Cottages.'

'Thanks,' I said. 'Thanks a lot. He'll be . . . eighty-five, of course.'

'I expect he's all right.' Another pause. 'They're a long-lived lot, the Crutchleys.'

'Thank you,' I said. 'This is very kind . . . '

'You seem a nice young woman,' the voice said reflectively. 'You want to know the truth. Perhaps I want it told. I must go now. Goodbye.'

I was becoming used to these sudden cut-offs. But I still hadn't talked about Gordon Stone, or got an opinion about Joanna Levine. I thought, somehow, Deep Throat must be an older person. The voice wasn't definably old or young, and the vocabulary and phrasing ranged curiously from the old-fashioned to the modern.

Now I was late for my meeting with Roger Littlebrown at La Somnambule, so I got my coat and left, still clutching Violet and Frederick's wedding photograph.

To Roger, over one of those ambiguous little plates of food, I said, 'I don't know, Roger. I was getting nowhere. There's an enormous amount of hidden material, I know that, but the relatives, Violet's children, are keeping me at bay – no letters, no documents, no photographs, and, after all, they're the primary source. And everything else was a blind alley. I was warned off speaking to someone— '

'Who?'

'Gordon Stone?'

'Rings a bell,' said Roger. 'Who's he?'

'I don't know. A former friend of Violet's in the thirties.'

'I must say it shook me when Andy said you were off the project . . . '

'I can't think why he did that. So you mean he rang you up?'

'Well, yes,' said Roger.

I was annoyed. 'I told him I was stuck,' I said. 'He told me it was too much for me. I'm a bit surprised he rang up— '

'It was partly to say goodbye before he went off.'

'I suppose so,' I said.

'I wouldn't take any notice of Andy,' Roger responded easily. 'I shouldn't say this, but he likes one hundred per cent attention – always has. That may be why he wanted you to give up this book. You shouldn't take all that much notice of him. I mean, if it's a question of money, we might be able to— '

'I haven't had anything yet, Roger,' I told him.

'You haven't?' he said, appalled. 'I don't believe it. Look, I'll get on to accounts as soon as I get back. We'll send it round – by messenger.'

'All right,' I agreed. 'I'll keep going. I've got a few more leads. But if those peter out, I don't know . . . The trouble is, I'm going to go up blind alley after blind alley.'

'Everybody,' Roger said emphatically, 'everybody who tries to do what you're doing has the same experience. Don't let it worry you. Look, is there any chance of a few pages . . . '

'I've hardly even made any notes.'

Roger was crestfallen. 'I'm getting some interest in America. Two firms have called,' he said. 'Think about it.'

I left, in fact, far deeper in than I was when I arrived. Up to now I'd had an arrangement with someone's cousin and no money. Now I was expecting a messenger with a cheque. I could see Roger wanted me to go on, if publishers in the USA were interested. He'd even given me the name of a literary agent to approach. I went back to the flat and wrote letters to Ben Crutchley at the village in Kent, and to Joseph Levine, whom I'd tracked down in *Who's Who*.

I turned on the radio while I made a spaghetti bolognese, thinking Di might be glad of a meal when she got back. I missed the first items, and just got a government minister explaining why councils were being instructed not to consider women who had left their husbands, taking children, as priority cases when allocating council flats. They'd have to join the list like anyone else, the Minister of Housing explained reasonably. It wasn't fair on couples with children who had been waiting for years to be continually pushed back by cases of domestic emergency. Three months before, unmarried women with children had been similarly taken off the priority list. Which meant never getting housed. Disciplinary measures were being taken against female revolutionaries who had babies out of wedlock, or left their husbands.

As ever, the government seemed to be telling me personally to find a breadwinner, forget Violet Levine and go home to take care of everybody. I was a one-woman attack on the family, as seen officially, a threat to the state, an anarchist with a bomb in my skirt. Well, I thought, Violet might have been no angel, she might have lied about her wedding, but she'd never minced her words on such topics. She'd written:

> So long as society in its wisdom declares that every woman, married or unmarried, must stay at home, guarding the foyer, tending the welfare of whole families, from the cradle to the grave, without respect or payment or honour, except in the form of lip-service unsupported by any tangible reward or serious marks of respect, it is guaranteed an unfailing source of bitterness and resentment, neurasthenic ailments and narrow domestic strife, which will subtly poison all the individuals involved, corrupting all the men, women and children who come in contact with it. We will not be able to measure the kind of damage this imprisoning of women in their homes, for the sole purpose of serving others, has done until the day, and may it come soon, when we live in a society where women are free to follow their own inclinations, to work, not to work, to

marry, not to marry, to have many children, or few, or none at all, whatever it may be, without censure, hindrance or fear.

Violet was no great original thinker, I thought. Her gift was simply for seeing her own experience, and generalising from it intelligently. To put it bluntly, if you kicked Violet on the shin, first she hopped about clutching her leg, then she came up with a general theory on leg-kicking. Then she'd probably start campaigning against it. During the twenties she'd stood up for the right of women civil servants and teachers to keep their jobs after marriage. Red Vi, they'd called this party-going, campaigning banker's wife. In the forties and fifties she'd fought for public nursery schools and equal pay; in the sixties she'd signed letters in the papers in favour of liberalising abortion. She'd been in CND. I wondered what she'd be supporting now, if she was young.

I decided to have her photograph blown up and framed. I'd put it on the wall. Somehow, I'd agreed with Roger that I'd try to go on. Somehow I'd regained my enthusiasm for Violet, and I wondered if the enlarged photograph would tell me anything.

Violet Levine, December, 1913

The family, initially surprised by the arrival in their home of a young woman from south London, daughter of an officer in the London police force, as wife of one of the sons of the house, soon took me and our baby daughter to their hearts.

I Affirm, Violet Levine, 1957

These proud bankers, with their aristocratic connections, hated this girl from the pavements of the city who had entrapped their young relative. They saw her for what she was, a cunning woman who had seduced the innocent Frederick. They dedicated their lives to discovering ways of tormenting her. They mocked her speech and culture. They found a hundred ways of making her life troublesome. It would have resembled the torments endured by the virtuous young girls in fairy stories, if it had not been for the character of the victim. She was not virtuous. They did not know, as I did, that the child she brought with her to the house was not her husband's, did not carry his blood.

Memoirs, C. F. Lamier, 1958

It was after dinner and two glasses of port on Boxing Day that Frederick Levine, who had not enjoyed his pheasant, had the courage to tell the menfolk of his family that he was married. The women were in the drawing-room. His Uncle Leopold, looking very ill, was at the head; next to him on the right was his cousin Louis, Joshua Schreft's son, dark and quick-eyed. The two Waldstein cousins, Hanno and Rudolph, were at the end of the table with Laurence.

To his uncle, Frederick said, in a low voice, 'Uncle Leopold, I have an announcement to make – I married before Christmas.'

Louis Schreft, who heard the words, after a short pause, said, 'May I congratulate you, Frederick.' Leopold, at the top of the table, nodded in agreement. Meanwhile, Laurence had caught the words from his end and said loudly, 'What?' Hanno and Rudolph, slightly drunk, caught the mood of the table late, realising something was happening, stared at Laurence, who was now gazing at Frederick. Then they, too, looked at Frederick, who felt the whole weight of the panelled room heavy on him. He had ruined the announcement. Even the portraits seemed to be staring at him. As Laurence said again, 'What – what, Frederick? Married, did you say?' and stood up, Leopold Levine simply said, 'Then, why is your wife not with us?' Hanno, grasping what was happening, muttered an explanation to Rudolph.

All five men felt something unusual about the situation. Something seemed to be wrong. The Levines, Schrefts and Waldsteins were expected on the whole to marry young women they knew, who had been studied by the older members of the family as possible wives, desirable or undesirable. Engagements were announced, financial agreements drawn up between the parents involved, houses arranged, presents sent and acknowledged. Finally, after months of preparation, frequently involving religious considerations, the wedding would take place in church or synagogue, before hundreds of invited guests, followed by a ball or at least a large reception. Yet here was Frederick suddenly announcing a hole-in-corner marriage to goodness knew whom. And, they realised, he had not yet told his mother. Nor, as Leopold had said, was his wife among them.

'I wanted to prepare the family first,' Frederick told his uncle, realising the delay in informing them simply showed how embarrassed he was about his marriage, and his new wife.

Leopold nodded. 'Mm . . . '

Laurence broke in. 'Who is it?' he said in a voice just short of outright challenge.

Leopold, shocked though not surprised, said, 'So we must congratulate you.' The others murmured congratulations, as he added, 'And your mother – you haven't yet told her, I imagine.'

'Yes, Frederick,' Laurence said grimly. 'You haven't really, have you?'

'There no need to take that tone, Laurence,' Frederick said. 'I shall tell Mother immediately.'

'Why not before?' Laurence demanded. 'Surely she had the right to know first. And, may I ask you again, who have you married? Don't you think you ought to tell us?' He knew perfectly well that Frederick had married the woman he was keeping in Belsize Park. He was furious. A marriage like that would make the whole family look ridiculous, he considered. Caroline's family would see it as bizarre; would make jokes about it. Leopold would be angry, and it was a bad idea to antagonise the major shareholder of the bank, who was on the point of death and had not yet made his will. Apart from anything else, it was not pleasant to see your younger brother trapped into marriage by an ambitious woman.

Frederick, fearful but annoyed by Laurence, told him, 'Of course. I'll tell you who I've married.' He knew his marriage to Violet was indefensible in Levine terms. If she had been Jewish the position might have been somewhat better. A well brought-up Jewish girl, even if her background was humble, would have been acceptable to the older Levines, although they were far from devout. The younger Levines practised no religion. Laurence's child, Joseph, had been christened in the Church of England. It had not pleased either Leopold, or his sister-in-law, Sophie, the baby's grandmother, but they had to admit that being a member of the established Church had its advantages, particularly for a boy. So the disadvantages of being a Jew were not as great, obviously, as they had been in previous times, but they existed. Who, after all, could claim that anywhere in the world except among other Jews being Jewish was an advantage? So, the opposition to Joseph's christening was not wholehearted. Nevertheless, Violet would have been more acceptable if she'd come of humble, but Jewish parents, Frederick considered. Now he tried to control his temper – Laurence had no right to be so instantly hostile, nor was it discreet to put the situation on a war footing in front of many ambitious relatives, openly demonstrating his hot temper and suggesting he thought Frederick a fool. Leopold Levine, with half an hour to go before his next injection, and in considerable pain, was silently thinking the same thing. Frederick might, or might not, have made a wise choice of bride, probably not, he considered, but Laurence was behaving badly. What was done was done. The future was what mattered.

'My wife's name is – was – Violet Crutchley,' said Frederick. 'She is the mother of my child. I love her. That is why I married her.'

Spoken like a man, reflected Leopold, though it would have been better to have told his mother first. Still, the bride might be a good young woman, which was what mattered. Laurence was like most of the younger generation, marrying the Baronin von This and the Honourable That, proving they could be accepted by aristocratic Christian families. But if things began to go badly what mattered in a wife was courage, steadiness and loyalty. Blue blood didn't count – Laurence's Caroline would do, he thought, whatever her faults. She was strong and determinedly loyal to her husband and child. He hoped this wife of Frederick's might be the same, and anyway there was nothing he could do now the news had been broken, so he stood, his face expressionless, gripping the table with one hand, saying, 'Very well. My congratulations again, Frederick, on your marriage and on the birth of your little daughter.' The child was not a son, he knew, or Frederick would have called him 'my son'. 'I hope you will introduce your wife to me very soon. Now I must go and find my nurse.'

Frederick got up and put his arm round him, helping him from the room. 'Thank you, Uncle Leopold,' he said, profoundly grateful for Leopold's acceptance of the situation.

Outside the door he told Brough to call the nurse and Leopold murmured, as they waited, 'You may find your mother difficult. This secret marriage will upset her.'

Unfortunately, as he spoke, Caroline was coming out of the drawing-room opposite. She heard the words, stopped, her hand went to her pearls and dropped, she stepped forward. 'Frederick! What is this? How exciting. You must tell us.'

Frederick dropped his head. He muttered to the nurse, 'My uncle would like to go to bed, I think.' He and Caroline stood in silence while the nurse helped Leopold upstairs, by which time the long silence convinced Caroline that what she thought she had overheard was true. She had also had time to compose herself.

Once the nurse and Leopold had managed the long first flight and reached the landing she was smiling and said, 'So – are we to congratulate you? Why didn't you let us know? Mama will be very disappointed at being cheated of the chance to invite people from all the corners of Europe. Tell me everything.'

Now Laurence was standing impatiently in the doorway. He said to his brother, 'It's time for some explanations.'

'Perhaps I should fetch your mother,' said Caroline. 'It seems wrong that everyone in the house should hear of Frederick's marriage before she does.' Both men knew Caroline was doing this to stir up trouble. Neither, at that moment, could think of any way to stop her. As she bustled off, full of mischief, she could not resist looking over her shoulder and saying to Frederick, 'Where is she? When shall we see her?'

Frederick had evidently been tricked into marrying the schemer in Belsize Park, she thought. Sophie should have let her go and see the woman. There would presumably now be children to rival her Jo-Jo. The woman could be anybody. The family would be humiliated. Concealing her anger, she hurried into the room full of women, all in jewels, silk and velvet, all talking. There'd be a shenanigans now. She bent over her mother-in-law's chair, saying, 'Mama. Frederick tells me he would like to see you rather urgently on a family matter.' Having spoken she felt a frisson of fear.

Sophie Levine stood up, betraying no sense of urgency, and followed her from the room.

Laurence and Frederick were still standing in the hall. 'We'd better go to the library,' Laurence said grimly.

'Perhaps first you'd ask the gentlemen if they would like to join the ladies,' said Sophie. If there were to be a long conference she was anxious not to leave the two separate groups, the men with their port, the women with their sweet wine and coffee, speculating separately about what could be going on. Her heart was already sinking. She had an inkling, seeing Frederick pale and crestfallen, Laurence angry, what kind of news she was about to hear. She prayed it was not something to do with that woman in Belsize Park, and knew it probably was. She hoped Frederick had not made too much of a fool of himself. She braced herself ready to plan, meet arguments, manipulate events, as she entered the library. Caroline, eager to miss nothing, followed. No one could ask her not to come, though she knew she should have left the Levines to themselves at that point. 'Where's Leopold?' she asked Laurence, as she sat down.

'He was unwell. He went up with his nurse,' replied Frederick. 'I apologise for disturbing you now, Mother, but I felt I had to tell you before Christmas ended.' He looked into his mother's calm face, touched by a pleasant half-smile, and was seized with guilt, remorse, and, suddenly, some rage. Surely, in the end, it was his business whom he married? He seemed to be confessing, not making an announcement, and what was there to confess? That he'd found the woman he loved? That she'd borne his child? That he'd married her? Violet was not the kind of wife his mother had wanted for him. Was she seeing the Levines as a great dynasty, protecting their blood and keeping up their fortunes by making suitable marriages? Thomas Despencer, founder of the Despencers, had made the family's fortune by being the lover of Edward II – was that better or worse than his marrying the woman he loved?

'Well, Frederick?' his mother asked. 'Tell me your news.'

The anger he felt was making him confident. 'Please sit down, Mother.'

'No,' she told him. She would meet the crisis on her feet. The clock ticked loudly on the mantelpiece. Coals in the fire cracked. There was complete silence. Nothing moved in the street outside.

Frederick took a deep breath.

Caroline, suddenly merciful, acting on the impulse of the big sister of younger brothers, came to his rescue. Now, having looked forward to the discomfiture of the Levines, she found she couldn't bear watching Frederick floundering. She said, 'I believe my dear old brother-in-law is trying to tell you, Mama, that he's gone off and got himself married. Isn't that horrible of him – to deprive us all of a wedding? And where, we ask, is the bride?' Her assumed cheerfulness cut no ice.

Sophie, her face unchanging, as Caroline spoke, said instantly to her son, 'Is this true, Frederick?' Inwardly she was shocked this had gone so far, so fast, without her knowledge.

Frederick, ashamed and angry, said, 'I'm so sorry, Mother. I couldn't face a fuss. I wanted to marry Violet as quickly as possible. In any case, Violet has my child, a daughter.'

'A child,' said Sophie flatly.

'A daughter,' added Caroline, quick to point out that she, having borne a son, was the dominant female.

Everyone expected Sophie to speak, but she was calculating angrily. Divorce? Or just the crushing of the new little wife?

Laurence broke into this intimidating silence, 'When did this happen, Frederick?'

Frederick looked at him coolly.

'Come on,' he said, 'speak up. My God, I need a large drink. Mother, will you sit down, take something?'

'I think not,' said Sophie Levine. 'Well,' she said to Frederick, 'perhaps you will tell us something about all this.'

'A brandy, Laurence, please,' said Caroline in a mutter. More loudly she said, 'Perhaps we might all sit down now. Mama?'

And so Sophie Levine finally sank into a leather chair on one side of the fire. Caroline took the opposite one. Laurence maintained a position by the drinks tray in the window, Frederick by the big desk over which hung the portrait of his father, a plump man, with a dark moustache.

'Violet's a simple girl from an ordinary home,' Frederick began, in a steady voice. 'She left it because her father, a policeman, was cruel to her and her mother. I met her when she was working in a shop. I fell in love with her. In November she had our child, Pamela, and I began to realise that I couldn't leave a girl of almost— '

'Seventeen,' Sophie Levine broke in. It was a statement and a question.

'Yes, seventeen,' Frederick confirmed. 'As I say, I could not leave her, and my child, in a defenceless position. And so, a few days ago I married her by special licence. I know it isn't what you all would have preferred, but my heart is satisfied, which is more than enough for me, and I hope I can trust you to welcome Violet here, as my wife.'

It sounded to Laurence as if he had rehearsed this stiff little speech.

A policeman's daughter, thought Sophie Levine. And now a child. It all sounded unbearable, and she was tired, having entertained nine relatives for ten days, and several more to go. It would be fatal to say the wrong thing, antagonise Frederick, make him hostile to her before she had met the girl and assessed the situation. In any case, if the girl was only seventeen, had her parents given permission? She smiled, patiently and pleasantly, said, 'This is so exciting, and so unexpected. I really feel quite – tired. I shall go to bed now. Tomorrow we must discuss our plans.'

Well fielded, Sophie Levine, Caroline said to herself. Just enough to make Frederick feel bad, but enough to give you time to think. Frederick, having said goodnight to his mother, scanning her face for signs of anger, or illness, then left the house to return to Belsize Park.

Alone in the library with Caroline, Laurence, pouring yet another whisky, quoted Sir George Askwith, 'There may be movements in this country coming to a head of which recent events have been a small foreshadowing.'

Caroline, whose father and uncles had spent the last few years of strikes and industrial unrest predicting that the country was on the verge of something like the French Revolution, that their heads would soon be held up in front of jeering crowds if drastic action wasn't taken quickly, gave a shudder. 'Don't joke, Laurence,' she said. 'But what do you think your mother will do now? If Frederick and this Violet and the baby are to come here, shouldn't we think of moving to a house of our own?'

Laurence suspected that once he and Caroline had what she called 'a dear little house of their own' Caroline would fill it with dogs and a healthy crowd of Despencers, such as her brother Tommy who was a Coldstream Guard and never came home before two, or alone, or until he was drunk, and her sister Rosalind with whom she could giggle all day and swap Despencer jokes. Then there was, not unnaturally, her mother, who would start a civil war by trying to take over the servants and make every effort to marry Rosalind from the house, with consequent expenditure on dinner parties, and deliveries of flowers and suitors calling at all hours. And her father, who wanted everybody flogged whom he didn't want to hang, and any Despencer who happened to be up for Henley, back from a rubber plantation in Malaya or from governing New South Wales, or had a daughter coming out, or had just popped up from Cumberland for the dentist and some shopping in the Army and Navy – Laurence knew his wife found the house in Cavendish Square dull and his mother difficult, but he preferred the situation as it was. 'Well,' he said easily, 'we have twelve bedrooms here, a large nursery with five rooms, an extra drawing-room which is never used and seems to be full of discarded furniture and servants taking a few moments off from their duties – I should have thought we could somehow squeeze Frederick and his wife into a house big enough for a regiment.'

None of this, he thought, was getting to the heart of the problem of Frederick's marriage, but then, with Sophie and Leopold in bed, and the chief protagonist, Frederick, on the way back to his seventeen-year-old policeman's daughter, there was nothing much to be said at present. 'I suppose I'll have to go out and tell the relations,' he groaned. 'After all, we've got to explain why we all disappeared, and they'll have to know sooner or later. Good manners have been at a discount in this business. I don't think my mother will ever forgive the impulsive way in which you broke the news to her. Your choice of words wasn't very appropriate, either.'

'It was kinder to say something. You and Fred would have left her waiting for hours,' Caroline said. 'Now for the others . . . ' Taking his arm and assuming the air of someone with good news to impart, she drew him from the room, wondering at the same time if Frederick's marriage was going to be either useful to her, or very amusing after all. The beginning had not been promising.

Kate Higgins, May 3rd, 1991

Radleigh Cottages, Oathouses, West Kent, was a row of modern brick cottages, each with a little garden in front. Two days after my letter to Ben Crutchley, I got a typed letter back, letter-headed Soames, Needham, Cottwell, Murchison, and James which was a large advertising agency, with many major commercial accounts, and some with the government. Their current advertising campaign was to persuade people to carry identity cards. Large black and white posters and full-page advertisements showed friendly policemen thankfully accepting evidence of people's identities, with a background showing a siege, an explosion, a fire. Others showed friendly doctors at the scenes of accidents, equally grateful to be able to identify obviously fairly unhurt victims rapidly. Other friendly characters smiling at the ID cards of others were shop assistants, restaurateurs and airline officials. It was a soft sell.

The brief, business-like letter was from an account executive, Jessica Fellwell. She said her grandfather, Ben Crutchley, had died the previous week. She had read my letter to him and was interested in the idea of a book about her Great-Aunt Violet Levine, formerly Crutchley. She was Ben's only grandchild, and as he had died the previous week, she was now sorting out his effects, her parents being in Australia. If I would like to come to the cottage, she would be pleased to tell me anything she could and would in fact be grateful for any help in identifying photographs. So I made an appointment to join her at the weekend at Radleigh Cottages and found the house on a council estate on the outskirts of a pretty village, an old man's home, with forget-me-nots straggling in the front garden and net curtains in all the windows. There was a smart Rover parked in front, Jessica Fellwell's, I assumed. I rang the bell and a small woman of about forty opened the door. She had Violet's spare figure and the tight little face of Violet in her later photographs. Earlier ones were posed and in them she wore the romantic and soulful expression each enjoined on the women of the time when they were photographed. It was in the later news photographs when you saw her alertly pointing out something to Barbara Castle or smiling at a foreign dignitary, that you noticed her intelligence and her tension.

Jessica Fellwell led me past an old-fashioned hatrack in the hall, where a tired mac and a cap hung despondently by a walking stick. She suggested a cup of coffee, which she made in the kitchen where enamelled containers read, in nearly obliterated lettering, TEA, COFFEE, SUGAR. An ancient bread-board, covered in cuts, stood scrubbed, propped on the draining-board. Jessica then carried a tray into the living-room, where I sat in a stuffed chintz chair gazing at the giant TV screen and, past it, to the back garden where the outlines of an untended vegetable plot could be seen at the bottom of a little, uncut lawn. Poor old Ben had been forced to give up the garden a few years ago, I reflected, looking at the straggling roses. A starling alighted on the lopsided birdbath in the middle of the lawn.

'I didn't know what to keep and what to throw away,' Jessica Fellwell told me. 'I really don't think my parents are interested, but I feel I ought to save something for my daughter. And I suppose Violet was a national figure.'

'Did you see much of her?' I asked.

'I never met her,' said Jessica. 'Well, perhaps you didn't know. She never saw any of her family after she married – except Great-Aunt Allie of course. Allie kept in touch with the family until the war. That's how they got news of Violet. But never any personal contact.'

'Why was that?' I asked.

'Oh,' she said, surprised, 'I thought you knew. Still, how could you? No, Violet just cut off from the Crutchleys when she married Frederick Levine. In fact, I don't think they ever saw her after that. Apparently they tried to get in touch when their mother died. I think Norah and Allie had some idea she'd help them out. From what I gather, there they were, Norah married, Allie, the other sister, only about fourteen, the two boys – well, what, Grandfather was born in 1906. He must have been about seven. His brother, Frank, was a bit older – twelve. He was the one who lied about his age, joined up and got killed on the Somme when he was only fifteen. The father was a bit of an old sod, drank, didn't spare the rod, so when the mother died the family was in trouble. There was no one to take care of the boys or the mother's new baby. Violet didn't want to know. Understandable, I suppose. She was on top. She'd made it. She didn't want to be dragged back.'

I asked, 'What happened after that?'

'The old man remarried a year later. It must have been the only answer. But the stepmother was pretty cruel. Allie left not long after, but what did she want with two big boys – and a baby. She would have been a drudge – and that wasn't all. Grandfather had welts on his back to the day he died, my mother told me, all from the beatings his father gave him. According to my mother what made Ben so bitter was the way his brother joined the army because he had to get away from home. And of course Frank died – and the baby died . . . '

'This baby you mentioned?' I asked.

'Well, my great-grandmother had a baby, just before she died. I suppose that was effectively what killed her. So she left a three-month-old baby which must have been why my grandfather remarried in haste. But the child didn't make it— ' She broke off. The recollection of these old, sad events was depressing her. 'Rightly or wrongly, they blamed Violet for Frank and the baby's deaths,' said her great-niece.

'Wait a minute – if the older sister Norah was married, and Allie left, wasn't she responsible, too? Allie might have done something if she'd stayed. Why was it all Violet's fault?'

Jessica Fellwell looked at me, surprised. She said, 'Allie was living with Violet at the Levines. Violet took her in. That was what they thought was so awful – the brothers stuck with a brutal father and stepmother. Both the parents were drinking heavily by that stage. While Violet and Allie were living like princesses in a palace in Cavendish Square. I think Allie tried to help, but she was Violet's plaything, as far as you can tell from these stories. Violet took her in and Violet could fling her out again. Allie bought her brothers clothes and toys, Grandfather said. But of course she wasn't there. You can see her point of view. Violet offered her a new life. What was she supposed to do?' She paused. 'It's a terrible story, really. You ought to talk to my mother, or write to her, at any rate. She knows more about all this than I do.'

I was startled at the news that Allie had lived with the Levines. Violet just hadn't mentioned it in *I Affirm*. I said, 'You probably think I'm very ignorant. I'm not getting any co-operation from the Levine side of the family.'

'They've got a lot to hide,' declared Jessica Fellwell vigorously. 'My impression is that Violet was a dreadful woman. She had guts, give her that. She had to be like she was to get where she did, but from what I've heard I wouldn't have liked to have been at her mercy.'

'What do you think the Levines have got to hide?' I asked Jessica.

'The sheer awfulness of their mother, to start with,' declared Jessica. 'Don't forget she's a national myth.' She was a quick, efficient woman, not pleased, I suppose, by having to spend Saturday looking through a dead old man's effects. 'As to the rest, I don't know. They don't want anything to do with us, that's for sure. My mother went to the trouble of finding out Violet's daughter's address, and wrote to her – Pamela Christian-Smith – just to tell her that Grandfather was ill, terminally ill. He spent most of last year in and out of hospital, finally in a hospice. She felt she ought to tell her, because Ben was Violet's only surviving brother but there wasn't a whisper from the Levine end. But it's not just that – I'm sure there are mysteries. It's only an instinct. But if they haven't got anything to hide, why aren't they helping you?'

'Protecting their privacy,' I suggested.

She looked doubtful. 'Could be. But be careful. They're influential. Levine-Schrefts is a powerful institution. The Christian-Smith family have been big noises in the Conservative government for years. Jack Christian-Smith works for the BBC

– television. I should be very careful what I unearthed, and what use I made of it. You never know.'

I looked at her across Ben's little sitting-room and she looked back at me. She knew the world she dealt with, I realised. I also noticed I was studying her as if she might be an enemy, someone who might betray me, or cause me harm.

She said, 'Come on. There's a box of old photographs and stuff I bundled together and put upstairs. If you can help me identify a few I could lend them to you for the book.'

'Right,' I said, jumping up. One old album and a couple of old biscuit tins of snapshots came out from the bottom of a stale-smelling wardrobe. I said, 'This is a real goldmine for me. Have you read the letters?'

'No,' she said. 'No time. I was going to take them home. I'll lend them to you. You realise you can't reproduce them without permission.' She opened the album. There they were, the Crutchleys, probably on a day out at Brighton, photographed on the promenade. It must have been about 1910. Violet's mother, in a print dress and a straw hat, holding a grinning small boy in a sailor suit by the hand, the bright-faced lad who ended up, somehow, as an old widower, in a half-dead village in Kent. There was Violet's father, a big man with a black moustache, holding a taller, thinner, raw boy of about eight or nine – Frank, who was going to die in France only a few years later. Then, next to Frank, a fat girl with dark hair and a sulky expression, and next to her a much smaller, thin girl of fifteen, dark hair hanging down under her sailor hat, black stockings and shoes, her chin up, she smiled challengingly at the camera, holding by the hand a fair girl, staring not at the camera but at something to the side. Dark Violet and fair Allie. Allie who had moved in with the Levines when her mother died. What had happened to her?

I identified the children for Jessica Fellwell. She looked mournful.

'Two of them didn't have long to live even then,' Jessica said. She was trying to distance herself from this situation, I thought. It didn't fit with the advertising woman, one child, husband, jacuzzi and time-shares in California, Portugal, Berlin, all tax-deductible. But the situation had got to her.

That night I wrote to Jessica Fellwell's mother in Australia.

SIX

Kate Higgins, May 5th, 1991
Violet Levine, 1914

Two days later I went to the British Library to read the two novels Violet had written in 1914 and 1915 and then suppressed. But I was curious. What had this under-educated, though intelligent young woman been doing writing novels shortly after her marriage to Frederick Levine? And could I read between the lines and find some clues which would help me to find out what she'd been feeling at the time?

Of the two, the first was the worst. *A Simple Rose* was the story of Arthurina Jessop, a country girl brought up in humble surroundings by a woman she had been told was her aunt. Not so; by a series of accidents and wild coincidences she discovers she is rich and well born and leaves the cottage with the roses round the door to join her new family in their mansion. But, alas, she discovers she was betrothed at birth, for unexplained dynastic reasons, to a Balkan count from a world full of painted women, loud laughter, playing cards flung carelessly to the table and vast sums won and lost. Her marriage is a struggle, but eventually her honest heart and simple beauty conquer the vices of the sinister Count Alucard and all ends happily. This book bore the marks of Violet's self-education and was pretty banal, full of purple passages drawn from the sensational fiction of the time. Nevertheless, it had a lot of energy, and if it wasn't the work of a well-educated woman, you had to admire the large strides she must have taken, even by that time.

The Discarded Blossom (she must have been planning a series of books all with botanical titles) showed improvement. It was more sensibly written and the backgrounds more plausible, but it was, so to speak, the downside of the tale of Arthurina Jessop. Here the heroine, Corinthia James, is the proprietor of a little flower shop; she touches fingers one day with Sydney Faunt, Lord Daubeny, over a bunch of roses he is buying for his mother, the haughty Lady Daubeny. One thing leads to another and they marry, although the family is furious because of her lowly birth. Here follows a skilful exposure of the ways in which Lady Daubeny and her equally evil sister and her daughter torment, harass and finally try to kill the pregnant Corinthia while her husband is away attending to business in the West Indies. Their final attempt is to damage the stairs leading from Corinthia's room in the tower, then set light to the floor below, so that she'll be burned to death, or kill herself trying to escape. Corinthia's husband arrives to rescue her in the nick of time. The plot is revealed; the evil women sent away.

It was strongly portrayed and fairly revealing. The details of the female persecutions over the tea-cups were vivid. In real life I don't suppose Sophie Levine had been unsubtle enough to set fire to Violet's room, but she must have tried pretty hard to drive her out in other ways.

Violet Levine, 1914

Violet Crutchley, who had now been Levine for more than two months, sat alone in her bedroom in Cavendish Square, a room about twice the size of the parlour all the Crutchleys fitted into at Sunday tea-time, a room she'd had entirely redecorated in lemon and pale green, as a criticism of the rather dark furnishings of the rest of the rooms at Cavendish Square. She was obstinately repeating French and German verbs to herself. '*Je vais*, *ich gehe*, I go, *tu vas*, *du gehst*, you go, or thou goest, *il va*, *er geht*, he goes,' she recited. Her teacher, who came twice a week from Belsize Park, had just left. She knew Frederick's mother and sister-in-law were laughing at her exploits behind her back. They knew languages, or Sophie Levine did. Caroline had been taught French but Violet could tell she didn't know much. Nevertheless, she persisted. '*Nous allons*, *wir gehen*, we go, *vous allez*, *Sie gehen*, you both go, *ils vont*, *sie gehen*, they go.'

It was hard work, but she struggled on.

Then she began to stare at the silver and green flowers on the wallpaper opposite. She got off the bed with its elaborate tapestry cover, stared into the gilt mirror and saw her own same small, pretty face staring, palely, back. She brushed her hands down her elegant pink woollen dress, paced round the room, stared ferociously at a pair of gilt chairs placed on either side of a wide net-draped window, an equal inch and a half from the folds of brocade curtain, looped back from the window with gold cords. She sighed. 'A bird in a bleeding gilded cage,' she said. She would have loved a cup of tea but that meant joining her mother-in-law and Caroline in the small drawing-room. She believed they'd rather be alone, although she did not know that in a sense they almost enjoyed her arrivals at lunch and tea. Her unwelcome presence drew them together while her absence made them recall their differences. She dared not call for tea in her room, or Sophie would talk pointedly about giving the servants extra work. Meanwhile, she sat down by the fire with a little book, *Jean et Pierre*, and turned to page ten. '*Vous irez au parc, n'est-ce pas?*' Jean and Pierre's father was asking, when Brough, the butler, knocked at the door.

'A visitor's called for you, Mrs Levine,' he told her. 'I was not sure where you would wish to receive her.'

'Who is it?' asked Violet, surprised. She knew no one who would come here to see her.

'Miss Alice Crutchley, madam,' said Brough.

'Better bring her up here, then,' said Violet ungraciously. She had written to Allie, telling her of her marriage and asking her to keep it a secret, and not to tell her family where she was. When she was better established at Cavendish Square, she'd told her sister, she'd see what she could do for her. Now she was angry, imagining that Allie had disobeyed her instructions and arrived to ask a favour before she wanted to grant it, or had any power to do so. And if she gave her any money, she reasoned, Allie would come back and back for more. Not that she had anything but a dress allowance from Frederick, and that wasn't much, when you considered the vast range of clothing required to maintain her new position as Mrs Frederick Levine, and exactly how often during the day everyone here changed clothes – morning dresses to be worn with no jewellery, dresses for lunch and the afternoon with some jewellery, evening dresses for dining at home, evening dresses for going to concerts or the theatre to be worn with more jewellery than in the afternoons. Then there were macintoshes for when it rained, opera cloaks for the opera, the right shoes, stockings and gloves. The hair adornments, nightdresses, chemises, drawers, tea-gowns for relaxing at home, and an entirely different set of clothes to be worn in the country, at the Levines' house in Shropshire, where she had so far not been. It was hard to keep up the style, Violet thought, on her allowance, so if Allie had come for money she'd better think again.

She was shocked at Allie's appearance. She was pale and disturbed, dressed in mourning in a dusty black coat and hat. Violet stood up. 'Oh, God, Allie, what's happened? Is it Frank or Ben?'

Allie began to cry. 'It's Mum,' she said. 'She's dead.'

Brough who had timed his departure to seem natural, but delayed long enough to hear what was going on, was closing the door. 'You'd better bring some tea, pronto,' Violet told him brusquely.

As he walked quietly down the back stairs he wondered if another disturbance was due to start at Cavendish Square. There'd been no shortage of those since Violet's arrival as a mysterious bride with a mysterious child. 'No more Mr Frederick's little girl than I am,' his ally, Mrs Wilson, the housekeeper, had declared. He had not commented. He needed no word or glance from Mrs Sophie Levine to tell him she also had doubts about the child's paternity. Then there were the problems involved in coping tactfully with a common little baggage who had no more idea of the ways of a good house than a savage. (The Pygmy Queen, one of the footmen had christened her and the name had stuck, though Brough pretended not to know about it.) A further exercise in tact was required to ignore the fact that Mrs Levine the older disliked her new daughter-in-law more than she disliked the old one, that Mrs Laurence Levine thought her a bad joke, and that Laurence Levine was torn between rage and mirth whenever she spoke. Meanwhile poor Mr Frederick was angry and mortified when he came across any signs of these feelings in his family. The final awkwardness was that Mrs Wilson had recognised, in the new Mrs Frederick Levine, the chit they had all snubbed when she came, only a few months before, with a parcel of gloves. Rose, the parlourmaid she had bandied words with, was so embarrassed she left for a job in another household soon after Mrs Frederick Levine's arrival.

'She said she'd be back,' Mrs Wilson recalled, 'and little did we know how soon that would be. It tickles my sense of humour in a way, her arriving in that red tammie with her "important delivery" one day and swanning in on Mr Frederick's arm the next, with the nursemaid behind carrying a baby all done up in silks and lace. And I can't help thinking the mistress and Mrs Laurence are a bit hard on her. Whichever way you look at it, she's Mr Frederick's wife now and it would be kinder and more sensible to encourage her and bring her on. She can learn. She's willing to – but this way they'll never be able to bring her out in public.'

'Gentlemen in high places do marry all kinds of ladies these days – ladies from the chorus, American ladies, all sorts,' said Brough consideringly. 'The peerage can manage.'

'That's because they *are* the peerage,' Mrs Wilson said, and at that point both he and Mrs Wilson knew that the conversation, if it should ever have started, had gone quite far enough.

Now he said to a parlourmaid in the kitchen, 'Tea, for Mrs Levine and her guest upstairs in her room, Briggs.'

'All right, Mr Brough,' said the young woman lethargically.

'I will take it up,' said the second cook, now Felix, who had been brought into the house by Violet on the grounds that Frederick was enthusiastic about his cooking and tolerated by Sophie Levine for that reason. 'I'm off duty in half an hour, anyway.'

Brough said, 'Well, if you like.' He would continue to conduct his household in a proper manner, but that meant accepting random factors like Felix. Flexibility was the secret of real success in his position, and he knew it paid to have friends above and below stairs, for the balance of power inside big houses could change quickly, a fact appreciated more readily by servants than their masters.

Upstairs Violet spoke rapidly to Allie. 'I'm not coming back.

I've got a husband and a baby here. I'm sorry about Ma, and the baby, and the whole lot of you, but Dad's got to get some sensible woman in to take care of things. And to answer the next question, I haven't got much money, and I'm certainly not giving any to Dad because I don't know he'll spend it on all of you anyway. He can get a woman to help, and then he can look round for a new wife.'

'That's it, is it?' said Allie.

'That's it.'

'You hard-hearted bitch,' said Allie with tears in her eyes. 'Aren't you even coming to the funeral?'

'No,' said Violet.

'My God, your own mother's funeral,' Allie said. 'Who could believe it? Violet, I don't care now if I never see you again.'

'You will,' Violet promised her.

Felix knocked at the door and came in. 'Felix, this is my sister Alice,' Violet said in French.

Felix bowed over his tray. '*Enchanté, mademoiselle.*'

'Shut up, you bloody bitch,' said Allie. 'I won't wait for tea and thank you very much, Violet, for your help and sympathy. I hope you burn in hell. And if ever you need any help, remember – don't come to me.'

'Write to me, Allie,' Violet said to her retreating back. 'Put the tea on the table, Felix. Thank you.'

Felix, imperturbably, did so. To think he'd assumed she was learning languages in order to qualify herself as a *poule de luxe*, while all the time she'd had it in mind to marry a Jewish bank, he reflected, with some respect. Not that her life here was a happy one, but he suspected that somehow or other she would change all that.

Violet picked up her French book again, but could not concentrate. Poor old Ma, she thought, that was the reward she got for all her hard work, respectability, worrying about the neighbours, worrying about the children. Whoever wrote the rules about what a good woman did with her life it couldn't have been a woman. A melancholy, reinforced by the silence of Cavendish Square, overcame her. But she shed no tears.

For something to do, and to avoid the after-tea visit of

the nanny to the drawing-room with the children, an occasion which caused tension of many kinds, she went up to the nursery, to discover Jo-Jo, who had not taken to little Pamela's arrival, hurling bricks at the legs of her crib. As Violet opened the door she heard the smack of bricks on the carpet and saw Nanny knitting by the fire. 'What's going on?' said Violet as a brick hit the crib legs.

'It's the rain, madam. We weren't able to go for our walk today,' Nanny Thwaite replied calmly. Nanny held up a spider's web of knitting and said, 'Look, I'm on the second of Pamela's little vests. She'll be so much more comfortable in these.'

'No she won't, Nanny. Wool brings her out in a rash as you know. We've seen it often enough,' retorted Violet. 'And Jo-Jo, if you're thinking of throwing that brick at me, kindly think again.'

'I'm sure Jo-Jo has no such idea in his mind,' said Nanny Thwaite, 'and as to the vests, all my babies wear wool next to the skin. There's nothing like clean, softly washed wool.'

'Nanny, please. We've already seen the child red raw and crying, with a chest like a beetroot.'

'I've seen many grow out of that. It's just a phase.'

Meanwhile, Jo-Jo hurled the brick in the direction of the cot. It fell on the patterned carpet near to the crib.

'Stop all that, Jo-Jo,' said Violet sharply. 'You'll hit the baby's cot.'

Jo-Jo began to cry and Nanny went to him. Violet looked round the big cream nursery. The rooftops opposite were visible through net curtains at the windows. She stared at the immaculate white-painted crib and sighed, as Nanny comforted Jo-Jo. His big blue eyes, overhung with a white fringe of hair, caught hers over Nanny's back as she knelt on the floor.

'He was deliberately aiming at Pamela's crib, Nanny,' she said. 'I think you ought to have given him a smack before, not start kissing and cuddling him now.'

Nanny straightened up. 'I have my methods, Mrs Levine,' she said.

Violet, unable, as Nanny knew, to control her at all, could say nothing. She had been Caroline's nanny and had become a domestic institution. Her blatant favouring of Jo-Jo, the son and heir, over the doubtful Pamela, daughter of the doubtful wife of Frederick Levine, went unchecked. There was nothing Violet could do. She had protested to Sophie Levine one tea-time but Sophie merely said, 'One's dealings with servants have always to be tactful. It does take experience.'

Caroline added, 'Nanny's absolutely wonderful, I think, as long as you know how to handle her. What a pretty dress, Violet. Is it new?' And, before Violet could answer, said, 'Honestly, belle-mère, I should love to go down to Farnley. I don't think I can stand any more of this sitting about all dressed up as if we were at court. What do you say?'

'Well, Caroline,' said Sophie Levine, 'perhaps we ought to set a date.'

'The fresh air's so good for the children,' continued Caroline. 'We can't sit here for ever all stuffed up like so many cockneys. Anyway, even cockneys go hop-picking, don't they? Or so I'm told . . . ' And she looked at Violet with an air of polite enquiry.

Violet, tears in her eyes, left the room.

'Really, Caroline,' said Sophie Levine. 'I think your teasing of Violet sometimes goes a little too far.' But her manner was quite easy, amounting to approval of Caroline's behaviour. Violet was daily prodded and poked to within an inch of desperation. The attacks ceased when Frederick or Laurence was about. She had managed not to react so far, knowing that if she lost her temper Frederick would soon hear about it, but would not understand. The two women would be able to pretend she was unstable. She swallowed poison daily, smiled, and wondered how long she would be able to keep it up. She left the nursery, vanquished, vowing that one day, as soon as she could, she'd get rid of Nanny.

When Frederick came in she was back in their bedroom. 'All alone, Violet,' he said. 'You always seem to be by yourself.' He picked up a book, shook his head. 'Reading, reading. You'll make your poor brain reel. Come on, I'll have a bath – you go downstairs and talk to the others.'

'Is Laurence there?' asked Violet.

'No, he stopped off at the club,' said Frederick.

Violet, knowing that without him the pin-pricks would continue until Frederick came in, set her lips and went downstairs.

Frederick gazed after her, worried. Violet, he reflected vaguely, did not seem to be fitting in. The atmosphere in the house, these days, always seemed uneasy.

When he entered the room his wife was sitting at the far end of the room, drooping on her perch like a sick bird and the atmosphere in the room was, as so often these days, mysteriously unwelcoming. He poured himself a large whisky and wished he'd joined Laurence at the club. When the plan to visit the family's house in Shropshire was suggested at dinner that night he supported it vigorously, imagining the change might benefit his wife. Violet's opinion was quite different. Frederick and Laurence would be staying in town during the week, and would come down only at weekends. During the week there would be no respite from Sophie and Caroline.

The three women and two children, and Nanny and Brough moved off to Shropshire the following week. On the train she'd imagined a big house with a garden, something like a vicarage, only in the country. But Farnley House was a long, stone, eighteenth-century house, surrounded by a large park and outside it, several farms let to tenant farmers. A housekeeper, two maids, a handyman and a gardener were there permanently, extra staff being brought in from the village of Farnley, a mile from the house when the family arrived.

Violet, her miseries already increasing, as March rain poured down outside, began to comprehend the favouritism in the nursery. When Nanny retired she would go to live in one of the estate cottages, and it would be Jo-Jo, the oldest son, who would inherit the estate and provide the cottage. She saw now that the oldest son ended up with everything, with everyone dependent on him. He had come into the world with the keys in his hands, and even if they'd tried, and they didn't, no one in the household would ever be able to forget it. She had struggled and struggled to establish herself and Pamela as authentic, legal Levines. Frederick was taking steps to adopt his illegitimate child, born before the wedding, but if he adopted her a hundred times she, a girl, would always be Jo-Jo's inferior. Meanwhile, the domestic torture went on: the fire which was not lit in her bedroom – a mistake in the instructions – the urging of fine needlework on her, and the discovery by the seemingly amazed Sophie and Caroline Levine that Violet's sewing did not include tapestry work. How could it, in the Crutchley household where there were so many clothes to make, mend, and let down, and no time or money left for making petit point chair covers or fire-screens? Then came the amusing discovery that Violet was afraid of all farm animals, even sheep. The dispute with Nanny about Pamela's rash, caused by the woollen vests, continued. Nanny would not discard the vests and was now trying unsuccessfully to treat the rash with zinc and castor oil while the child fretted and cried.

In the country, neighbours called. Violet was silent, as ladies gossiped about people she had never heard of, and discussed local events she could not understand. What did it mean to her that the Pelhams were building a hothouse, that Angela Duxbury had married Bernard Jenkins, that the son of the old farmer at the Home Farm at Lakefield was arguing about the lease on Ferry Hill? Efforts were made by curious neighbours to bring her into the conversation. They failed, but nevertheless conclusions were drawn about Frederick Levine's unusual marriage. Violet was obviously lower middle class, almost completely uneducated, quite unused to good society, so the verdict ran. Meanwhile rain poured down over the muted greens and bare trees of March. The countryside was a sea of mud. Violet got some comfort from mournful walks along sodden paths through fields and woods. At least she was left alone. She spent a good deal of time in the library, which no one used, reading bound volumes of novels, studying atlases, sometimes looking up words she didn't understand in a large dictionary.

Frederick expressed anxiety about Violet to his mother, who implied that Violet was suffering from her change of environment. Like a common plant, she hinted, his wife had not taken root properly in the richer soil to which she had been transplanted. 'She'll pick up when she gets more used to us all,' she said. Violet still managed to appear inventive and passionate in bed so Frederick was satisfied with the explanation. Sophie's real campaign continued – to break the marriage by breaking Violet.

On one particularly bad afternoon Caroline took Violet out for a ride on a horse she described as an old armchair. She promptly stimulated Violet's placid mount by manoeuvring her own healthy young mare too close, too often, until the poor gelding broke into a canter. Violet lost her seat, falling heavily on to a piece of rocky ground in a wood. She refused to remount. Ignorant of horses as she was she knew Caroline had deliberately caused the accident. After a mile and a half of rainy wood and field Caroline, sulkily leading the two horses, and Violet, drenched, muddy and hobbling, finally reached the house. There was a large car outside.

'Uncle Leopold,' declared Caroline, disconcerted. She had planned to bring the wretched Violet publicly through the main entrance, showing off her misery, then lead the horses round to the stables. But Leopold Levine frightened her. He was knowing; he had power to affect Laurence's future; he was foreign and incomprehensible. So she decided to smuggle Violet through the back of the house. But Leopold was in the hall, Sophie was coming to meet him and Brough had not yet closed the door. Leopold spotted the bedraggled women and Caroline was forced to explain what had happened.

Sophie, trying to look kind and attentive, for Leopold's sake, said, 'How very unfortunate. I hope it hasn't put you off for good, Violet? Riding is such a pleasure if you enjoy it, though I must admit, I never could.'

Violet was standing stoically on a swelling knee, where she had struck a stone, quite bruised down one side, and very muddy where she had fallen. Since she could never bear to look untidy or dirty, she felt wretchedly humiliated and said only, 'I'll see, I suppose. I'd better go up and change.'

Leopold, always tired, but no longer in so much pain, his illness being in remission, said agreeably, 'Please do. I look forward to meeting you for the first time very soon.' He already smelt trouble.

Violet smiled weakly and, upstairs, wondered if the old gentleman could be made to be on her side.

To her disappointment Leopold Levine did not come down for

tea. He was resting after the journey. Nevertheless, his presence in the house meant that her mother and sister-in-law were more polite.

At dinner Leopold drew her out and Violet was glad to talk. 'I'd like to go abroad,' she said. 'I'm learning French from a lady because it seems so many people speak it. I've been learning out of the atlas. And there's a few books about Africa in the library – I'd love to go there. And India – oh dear – that must be a place.'

'You've been reading *Kim*?' asked Leopold.

Violet nodded. She said, 'You must have been to so many places. Didn't you say you'd been to St Petersburg? I'd love to see the Tsar and Tsarina – she's English, isn't she?'

Poor little creature, thought Leopold, trying to improve herself, trying to charm him. He had left Paris in a hurry in 1870 as the Prussian army moved in. This was just before Levine-Schreft was founded in Vienna and Leopold was still trading in diamonds between London and Amsterdam for his father. He'd been twenty-one but he remembered sitting on a cart full of sacks at night, heading for the coast, and on the next sack, staring at him composedly, sat a young rat. It was of this bright-eyed little creature Violet reminded him – ready for survival, intelligent, and probably capable of giving a nasty bite if attacked. It was obvious she had not found friends in her female relatives. He looked at his sister-in-law without pleasure. Her face was still unlined, her black dress immaculate, her pearls superb, her hair smooth, black and shining. Tomorrow, she would be in her tweeds, calling on the county neighbours, subscribing to charities. Wasn't she even now describing a charity ball she was organising on behalf of the London poor? But all this aristocratic life – it mattered to her too much. Violet was the victim. He heard his father's voice warning, 'God help the Jew with a short memory.'

'I shan't be well enough to come,' he said and, as Sophie protested, 'No, I'm better, but my doctor tells me I must not start planning my hundredth birthday party.'

Sophie, who had come to terms with the fact that Leopold had not many years left to him, had been worrying about the way Leopold, major shareholder in the bank, would leave his shares when he died. Although it was not inevitable that the major shareholder would assume overall control of the three banks in London, Paris and Vienna, it was unlikely Leopold would leave the shares to a relative he thought unfit. If he had not already picked his successor, he must be considering it deeply now. He'd not told her anything about his choice of heir. The obvious contenders were her own sons, Laurence and Frederick, or his sister's children, the Waldstein twins, his brother-in-law, Joshua Schreft in Paris and Joshua's son, Louis.

Not long after he had gone to bed that evening Sophie took him a tisane, since he had mentioned that he was often troubled by indigestion. Leopold, who was, like a dying king, constantly under pressure to nominate his successor, was blunt. He said, 'I've made no decision. There's nothing to stop me, as you know, from dividing my shares, leaving no one the major shareholder.'

'If you divided them equally, Joshua Schreft would take control. He already has over twenty per cent,' said Sophie.

Her brother-in-law said, 'Sophie. You must leave this to me. If Samuel were still alive we should be deciding it between us, in the best interests of the bank.'

'What makes you think I'm not thinking of the bank's best interests?'

'My dear,' he said patiently. 'You are a mother. Your overriding concern, as is only right and proper, will be the best interests of your sons.'

Sophie, unprepared to accept that the conversation was at an end, said, 'They tell me Louis Schreft is not interested in women.' After a small pause she added, 'He may never marry.'

'If true, that would not disqualify him,' said Leopold, understanding that she was pleading for Laurence, who already had a son. 'You'd agree it is more important that the bank should be capably managed for the next thirty or forty years. We're bankers, after all, not kings.'

Sophie, having come to plead Laurence's cause, had an answer now which hinted that his chances might be worse, if anything, than she had thought. After a little more conversation about the prospective arrival of Frederick and Laurence next day and the plans for the weekend, she left the room discontented. Leopold had not revealed all his thoughts to her. He expected war with Germany. He did not think it would be short. He could not risk giving any of his prospective heirs sole control of the bank. Any one of them might be on the losing side, their interests subject to any confiscations or rearrangements the victors would decide. Moreover, any one of them, or more than one, could be killed, leaving their holdings to a wife they had married before the battle, or a small child. Unspoken arrangements about the wise distribution of shares in the family depended on men and women expecting to lead long lives, with time to order their affairs before they died. The old rough and ready arrangements would no longer do, now there was rivalry between young men and the prospect of war between the countries where the banks were based.

Leopold realised, too, that, of the people available to him to help, Frederick and his shadow Henry Sturgess would be by far the most useful in creating a series of watertight testamentary arrangements to ensure the bank's survival in almost any contingency. Since the new arrangements would mean re-distribution of Leopold's major shareholding, Frederick, if he were to help his uncle, would have to know his own chance of inheriting everything was completely gone. He would also have to keep the whole thing a secret. But Leopold believed that of all of them Frederick would be the most likely to act whole-heartedly in this business. If the rest of the family knew too soon what was going on they could start actions designed to prevent his plans. And he had no time for delay. He had no idea how long he would live. He rang for a servant, and instructed that his telegrams should be sent as early as possible next day. To Sturgess he telegraphed, 'Come to Farnley with Mr Frederick today.' To Frederick simply, 'Bring Sturgess.'

When they arrived Leopold told his sister-in-law only that there was urgent bank business to deal with. He, Frederick and Sturgess shut themselves in the library during most of Saturday and Sunday, and Monday morning. Laurence did not arrive from London until Sunday, and then took Caroline off immediately after lunch for a visit to neighbours twenty miles away. For his part Leopold scarcely gave his nephew's new wife,

Violet, a thought until Frederick and Sturgess took the train back to London late on Monday morning, carrying with them Leopold's plans for the Levine-Schreft bank's future. Sturgess took the papers immediately to Furnival's, the family solicitors in Gray's Inn. Leopold's shares, amounting to sixty-two per cent of the bank, would be divided into six equal parts among his four nephews, and Joshua and Louis Schreft. Since all shares would be the property, basically, of the bank, when any of them died their shares could only be left to each other or to their own children, the vote of a majority of the directors being needed to effect the transfer. The right of these six shareholders to purchase the shares of others was also granted. Sturgess, against the interests of his employer Frederick, questioned the term 'children' in Leopold's dispositions, suggesting Leopold might prefer to allow only male heirs to inherit. Leopold was impressed to notice that Frederick did not become annoyed at a suggestion from his own chief clerk which would disinherit his daughter, of whom, he knew, Frederick was inordinately fond.

'Women already have the right to their own money and property in Britain,' Leopold said. 'My understanding is that they will shortly have the vote here, as they have in New Zealand. I cannot say, for myself, that I have found women more foolish than men. The foolish ones are foolish in a different way, that is all. The chief reason given for refusing women rights over money is that they may be unduly influenced by the men in their lives, but I have seen many men commit acts of folly over women. In this case the ladies' husbands and sons will have no actual rights. And I trust women, even more than men, to defend their children's interests.'

As he spoke, all three men must have thought of Sophie Levine's reaction when she found Laurence would never be the major shareholder in Levine-Schreft, and none of them met each other's eyes. 'Perhaps I'd better make sure my daughter Pamela can read a balance sheet before she comes out,' Frederick said, to break the silence.

'I hope you're teaching your wife,' Leopold said. 'She seems a most intelligent young woman, as well as an agreeable one.'

Frederick said, 'Thank you, Uncle.'

'I can't imagine why you don't get yourself a nice, small

house somewhere and keep her and the baby all to yourself,' he remarked.

'Oh, Mother would be bitterly hurt, I think,' said Frederick complacently.

Find yourself and your wife a house, or your sweet-faced Violet will make you rue it, Leopold silently told his nephew.

Kate Higgins, May 5th, 1991

That morning I'd had a letter back from Wiltshire from General Levine refusing to see me or give me any information, and concluding, 'I find your idea of a biography of my Aunt Violet distasteful. I feel that until some more suitable person comes along to undertake the work it would be better to allow her to rest in peace and her actions to speak for themselves.'

He might have been disturbed by the idea of a stranger prying into his aunt's affairs but I was inclined to think he'd seen Robert Levine or Pamela Christian-Smith, and been warned off. So now on the Levine side I had as opponents Violet's two children, Robert and Pamela, Pamela's daughter Anna Schreft and now, Violet's nephew Jo-Jo Levine. Amongst the collaborators were, possibly, Pamela's son, Jack Christian-Smith, Violet's niece Jessica and her parents, and the invaluable Deep Throat, whoever or wherever he or she might be. It seemed the big guns were turned against me.

As if Joseph Levine's letter hadn't been enough, by ten I'd had a call from Roger Littlebrown. He'd had a letter of complaint from Robert Levine about my visit to his Aunt Joanna. The doctor in charge had reported to him that the disturbance had caused a worrying deterioration in his patient. Robert Levine told Roger he trusted there would be no repetition of an event which would reflect no credit on a firm for which, hitherto, he had always had considerable respect. The harassment of his aunt, he concluded, served no useful purpose since, unhappily, she was mentally unstable.

'Roger,' I said, showing a firmness which surprised me, the doctor knew why I'd gone there and he let me in. I wasn't brutal to her. What's more, I believe there's a reason why Joanna Levine is so potty, and her mother's in the story somewhere, somehow. Rosie Johnson thinks that. This letter doesn't prove I'm wrong. It means I'm getting somewhere.'

He was far from sure. He sighed. 'Okay – but leave Joanna alone in future. I can't afford to tangle with the Levines. I asked around and discovered Gordon Stone's living at Rye, by the way.'

'That's where Joanna's bin is,' I said.

'Yes,' he said consideringly, 'yes. I suppose that's a coincidence. Keep in touch. I want to know what's happening.'

Meanwhile Di had the morning off because there was no work at the print shop. She was cleaning out the spare room while I sat and looked at Leopold Levine's will. It didn't mean a lot to me other than that Leopold had a lot of friends: there were individual bequests to fifteen people outside the family, also generous bequests and thanks to his servants. Although he'd left pictures and various *objets d'art* to the family, astonishingly, all he'd left Violet was his library. Otherwise, Leopold had made sure that after his death no one outside the family could get any shares and that even the family shares couldn't be passed on without the consent of a board of directors, which consisted entirely of other members of the family. I thought about it while Di gave up cleaning in favour of home improvements; there was a series of loud bangs. I made some coffee and she came in and drank it.

'Window locks,' she explained, 'and a door lock. The break-ins are getting too much round here. Do you realise this building was broken into fifteen times last year? There are only twenty flats. Our luck won't hold for ever.' She sounded irritable, not unnaturally, since she was the one installing locks and I was reading a will dated 1914.

'What do you think of it?' I said, handing it to her. Di's father was a lawyer and she hated him, but she'd been brought up on entails, settlements and bequests.

She said, 'Well, he's made sure the wives don't get the shares. Here we are in the spring of 1914, he probably knew there'd be a war, he wouldn't risk leaving any wealthy young widows, who'd remarry, and take the money out of the family. He's worked quite hard to make certain no one would be a majority shareholder. He's still trying to balance the outcome, not knowing who'd win, or who'd live. Still,' she said, quite surprised, 'he doesn't say they have to be male heirs. That would have been quite usual then – still often is now, where big money or estates are involved. So how many of the six legatees were left when the war ended?'

'Three,' I told her.

Di put down her cup and went on with her security precautions. The only thing was, she locked the spare room door when she'd finished and she never gave me a key. I didn't think much about this at the time.

Meanwhile, Andy was stuck in Belize. No one had any news of him other than general news items on TV and radio. As predicted, the elections had produced a left-wing government including many Marxists. The USA thought a Marxist Belize, small though it was, would prove a useful bridgehead for left-wing Latin American governments. A speedy, well-armed right-wing revolution began two days after the elections. The new president, Robertson, was under siege in his own home, the seat of government was encircled so the new government could not be sworn in. Bridges were being blown up, there was a battle for the harbour at Belize City, the airport had been damaged, no one knew to what extent, but there were no flights in or out, phone lines were down, the only reports came by government-controlled radio. The British army was, as usual, peace-keeping. My husband Sam, my son's father, could be dead, or wounded, hiding under a bar, getting buried, going upriver with government troops in a flat-bottomed boat.

I watched the news with Di that evening. 'Don't worry,' she said, digging her fork into some macaroni cheese. 'The army's probably okay. As for Andy, he'll come up smelling of roses, as usual.'

'You're so sensitive, Di,' I snapped.

'Sorry,' she said, 'it's Andy. He gets my goat. It's not just the way he treats you, but there's something about him that worries me.'

'What is it?'

She shook her head. 'I don't know. I just can't work it out. I wish I could. Perhaps I'm wrong.'

'I expect so,' I said, and that was that.

I started looking at a picture from Violet's book *I Affirm*, using a magnifying glass.

Di looked over my shoulder. 'When?'

I said, looking at the group, 'September 1914, Farnley. They're already in uniform.'

Against the rhododendrons, or some big-leaved shrubs, sat Sophie Levine, Leopold, in a white suit with a panama hat, leaning back in another chair next to her. On a rug at their feet was Caroline in white, with a sturdy boy of two or three in front of her. He wore a sailor suit and a big khaki officer's cap, tilted on his small head. Violet, with her arm round a little girl in a calf-length starched dress and white bonnet, smiled maternally at the child, the child staring, it seemed, at the photographer. Beside Caroline stood a tall, fair man in khaki – Laurence. Beside Violet, also in khaki, was Frederick. Laurence was hatless, blond, Frederick had his cap under his arm, was half at attention. It was a classic picture. It said it all.

'End of long Edwardian summer,' said Di. 'I wonder what the rest of her family were doing while Violet sat there typifying things?'

'I wish I knew what Violet was doing,' I said. 'Photographs are misleading. People get photographed to conform to an image of themselves. Here they are, tea-on-the-lawn genre, it doesn't tell you anything, just that Laurence was a public school hero, Violet and Caroline were spotless young mothers, the older generation grave, kind and wise.'

'We used to have those, when we were children,' Di remarked dispassionately. 'The funny thing is, they were half-true. The acceptable face of our family. My mother used to have them made up as Christmas cards and send them out to people, like a promotional exercise. I mean, all the time Dad was having it off with his secretary, or the manageress of the hotel. The old man looks sick,' she said at my shoulder, peering through the magnifying glass. 'And the mother looks thoroughly fed up underneath. Wonder what they really felt?'

Violet Levine, 1914

Violet, in the library, which looked out over the lawn, sat scribbling her novel *A Simple Rose* on big sheets of thick paper she had ordered from London. Since the spring visit to Farnley House they had again returned to Cavendish Square. The Levines had begun to take her out in public. They had even gone to Ascot, where she had been careful to speak to no one but the family. Her accent and vocabulary were changing to meet the new circumstances and this was noticed, but not praised. Then they packed everything for the summer visit to the country. Violet was not happy about this. She had itchy feet and had tried to get Frederick to take her abroad but he had said that with his Uncle Leopold so ill, and war coming, it was a time for the family to stay together, at home. Perhaps, he said, it might be the last time it would ever be like this again.

Let's hope so, Violet thought to herself, looking sadly at him, having already decided that as far as she could see the only way for a woman in her position to have any money of her own was to write a book. Her allowance from Frederick was still small. Caroline, she was sure, got more from Laurence. She felt obliged to send money for the family to Allie from time to time, if only to keep them away from her. Although she never received a word of acknowledgment, they never returned the few pounds a week. Violet's energies were scarcely absorbed by a programme of country walks and visits. Brought up to work, lonely, not accepted by the family or their neighbours, never trained to accept boredom as a discipline, as it seemed the Levines and their neighbours had been, she often felt like screaming into the silences of the quiet country nights, or the deafening pauses at the dinner table.

When, one rainy afternoon, she announced to her mother and sister-in-law she planned to write a book, a novel, they politely agreed it might be a way to pass the time, although she knew they would laugh at her behind her back. At dinner Sophie said, 'Violet plans to write a book,' with the aim, she knew, of enlivening a table consisting of Leopold, Laurence and Caroline and their nearest acceptable neighbours, the Lloyd-Fisons.

'When do you plan to start?' Claude Lloyd-Fison asked her, smiling. He was a large, middle-aged man, who spent his winters hunting and his summers in the garden.

'I already have started,' declared Violet, 'this afternoon.'

'And your subject?' asked his wife, who was a determined, eagle-eyed cottage visitor, dreaded by the poor. She was wearing a black lace dress, in mourning for her father, and a large diamond necklace in an old-fashioned setting.

'It's about a girl who runs away from home,' Violet said, staring at Sophie. The remains of a large joint of beef were being cleared from the sideboard. It was very hot to eat fish, roast meat, then a pudding at the long polished table, while outside it was still light. They could still have swum, sat on the banks of the river or walked in the woods.

It seemed a waste to Violet. The one thing she'd never guessed when, behind her counter, she'd imagined leading the life of a lady, was exactly how much time the gentry had on their hands. It was all very well, when your feet ached, and you had petticoats and stockings to mend, a hat to trim in the evening and only half an hour to eat your dinner at midday, to imagine what it would be like having people waiting on you hand and foot, and a wardrobe full of expensive clothes laundered and mended by someone else. The question you never asked was what these lucky people found to do with all that spare time. It seemed to be a matter of entertaining, talking about other people, someone's visits to foreign countries, or plays they had been to.

During the soup the Lloyd-Fisons had discussed the harvest, over the fish Tommy Brereton's broken engagement and fresh engagement to someone else. Caroline, who could normally be relied on to keep the conversation going, had been unnaturally silent on this subject, although she had been almost brought up with the Breretons. The roast saw the topic of the wheat crop back. Next would have come someone's ball, or the increasing horrors of ugly modern art and tuneless modern music, or a neighbour cutting down a copse full of foxes. However, Violet now saw that her book would last the party through the iced pudding and perhaps the fruit and cheese, might sustain the ladies through the coffee in the drawing-room, where the subject would make a change from the normal discussion of children and domestic matters. At this season preserving fruit was on all good countrywomen's minds.

Violet thought she'd leave them to it, so, she said rudely, standing up, 'I hope you'll excuse me – I'm very keen to start chapter two.'

An hour later Leopold Levine came into the library. Violet was sitting outside the windows on the terrace in the dusk with a book, having moved the lamp from inside and put it on the paving stones. 'Gathering inspiration?' he said, looking down at the figure in a white dress, sitting on the ground.

Violet smiled up at him, 'That's right,' she agreed.

'Are you really writing a book?' he asked.

'Yes,' she replied. 'Why not? I may not be very well educated but I read a lot. Anyway, I need some extra money.'

'Oh,' he said. 'And you feel in need of cash?'

'Most do,' she answered, 'whoever they are.'

'Don't forget I'm leaving you my library,' he told her.

Violet looked at him, not sure that she wanted his books.

He added, 'If you decide to sell any books get a decent dealer.'

'Thank you,' she said.

'Good night, Violet,' he said. 'Good luck with your book. It's pleasant to think of a lady with a more original occupation than gossip and fashion.'

'Or jamming plums,' said Violet gloomily.

There was the sound of laughter and raised voices. 'Caroline's brother, and some friends, I believe,' said Leopold. His illness made them hard to bear, but Sophie Levine was too much in thrall to her favourite son's wife to forbid the visits. He made his way across the hall, greeting the visitors, three young men in light suits and panama hats, whose game of spinning them across to see who could land theirs on the hall table was interrupted at his appearance.

Violet went on reading, as dark came down. Then she heard the clink of a stopper being lifted from a decanter. Picking up her lamp she went inside. 'Ho!' said a voice. 'Thought you were a ghost.'

'No,' said Violet, putting down the lamp. 'I'm Violet Levine, Frederick's wife. Who are you?'

'Tom Brereton,' he said. 'So you're Violet. I've heard about you.'

'I expect you have,' she replied. 'I've heard a lot about you, too.'

'Concerning my caddishness in all probability,' he said. 'The world can be very harsh.'

'It can, to cads,' responded Violet.

He laughed. 'It's quite fun in here, so dark, but why do you sit alone on the terrace, away from all society?'

'What fun?' asked Violet.

'The japes, games, jokes— '

'Will there be some dancing?' Violet asked, gaining interest.

'If you say so. Come on,' he said, and, grasping her round the waist, he began to fox-trot her round the room singing, 'Everybody's doing it, doing it, doing it.' Violet giggled as she danced. He stopped, grasped her by the shoulders and gave her a kiss. 'Hm,' he said, then started to dance her round the rug again.

Caroline opened the door. 'Tommy,' she called, then saw what was going on, 'Tommy, you reprobate. Do leave Violet alone or I shall have to send telegrams to everybody saying how you've ditched Octavia in order to make up to a married woman. You'll be crossed off everybody's list. Honestly, Violet, you should never allow yourself to be alone in a room with this man. He's deplorable.'

But you've been alone in a room with him before, thought Violet, hearing the edge in Caroline's voice. And what happened? They left the room, to play charades, billiards, to sing round the piano, and ended up hunting the kitchen cat, with bugles, and Sandy Despencer's dog Roger, which he had brought down in the train. They hunted all over the house, out into the garden and down to the river.

Tommy Brereton kissed her by moonlight as they stood by the reeds. 'I adore you,' he whispered. 'Do you lock your bedroom door at night?'

'Always,' Violet told him.

'What a pity,' said Tommy.

He took her hand as she walked up the slight incline of the lawn in a dress with a soaked hem, her shoes in her hand. She glanced up to see Caroline watching from the terrace. 'This lawn is quite mad,' she said irritably as they arrived. 'Why don't they have it levelled?' Violet was in a dream on the flagstones among the vast tubs of scented flowers. She half heard Tommy Brereton reply, 'Your turn will come, Caroline.'

Next day when she came down the breakfast-room was deserted, although evidently people had been there. Then she noticed Caroline and Tommy Brereton were sitting on the window ledge, smoking, a habit which Sophie Levine disliked and had forbidden in the dining-room or breakfast-room and barely tolerated in the drawing-room and bedrooms. Violet poured herself a cup of tea, helped herself to bacon and eggs and sat down with *The Times*. Caroline and Tommy, backs to the room, were muttering to each other. Caroline's voice struck her. 'When's Frederick due, Violet?'

'About eleven,' she said. 'He said he'd catch the first train.'

'Ma-in-law's furious with him,' said Caroline. 'Know why?'

Violet shook her head.

'You must know,' Caroline went on, in her schoolgirl bully voice.

'Well, I don't, Caroline,' responded Violet. 'What's happening?'

'Row at the crack of dawn,' Caroline told her.

'Leopold, Laurence and Sophie L are now locked in the library shouting at each other in whispers,' reported Tommy.

'I thought I heard Sophie follow the morning tea in to Leopold's room,' Caroline said.

'Lying awake all night, thinking long, hard thoughts,' said Tommy in an experienced tone. 'At dawn she decides on immediate action. You can only pity Leopold.'

'What can it concern?' demanded Caroline.

Tommy, stubbing out his cigarette told her, 'Love or money, those are the only issues which keep an individual's head off the pillow at night and cause some persons to conduct dawn attacks on others.'

'Or teething babies,' Violet remarked.

Tommy grinned in her direction.

Caroline, piqued, said, 'Oh, well. There's no profit in sitting here wondering. You said you'd row me to the island if it was fine, Tom.'

'Then I will. But later, when I've gone for a stroll and checked the boat.' He dropped off the window ledge to the ground, turning to kiss his hand to her as he walked down the sunny lawn.

'Are you sure you don't know what's the matter?' Caroline asked Violet.

'Germany's declared war on Russia,' said Violet, still reading.

'There's a war closer to home than that,' Caroline told her crossly. 'I think I'd better go up and see Jo-Jo.'

Passing the library door as you go, thought Violet, wondering why Caroline wasn't more interested in the news. Her brother Sandy's leave had been cancelled. He'd been told not to leave the country in case his regiment needed him. Yet Caroline seemed concerned only with what was happening in the house. Tommy Brereton, only son of rich Lord Passe, whose mother was a lady-in-waiting to Queen Mary, must have unsettled her. Perhaps there'd been an idea, once, that they should marry, but Caroline had been forced to forget it.

Violet stepped along cool corridors to the small drawing-room to continue her writing. She had the pages she had already done in a tapestry bag beside her. She heard the car leave to collect Frederick from the station some hours later and, a little later, the library door open with a bang. There were voices in the hall – Laurence's, Sophie's, raised in protest, then Leopold's low tones. Violet lowered her head and went on writing.

Later she went down the drive and waited for the car containing Frederick. She got in and kissed him. 'Caroline says there's an argument between Laurence, your mother and Uncle Leopold. They seem to be waiting for you to arrive. I thought I'd better warn you.'

Frederick looked at her. 'Oh, yes, I see. Thank you, Violet, for coming.'

'What is it?' she asked.

Frederick considered. Then, deciding, said, 'Why shouldn't

you know? It affects you – and Pamela even more. Stop the car,' he called to the chauffeur. The car, which had been easing its way up the drive, stopped under an oak. Frederick said in a low voice, so that the chauffeur, behind his pane of glass, could not hear him, 'I imagine the argument's probably because Leopold's finally given in and told my mother about his will. Nearly everything's settled. The other banks have agreed to the changes he's suggested, the will's in here' – he tapped his briefcase – 'and Leopold only has to sign it.' He paused, saying, 'He's very ill, facing death. You'd think they'd leave him alone.'

'What's he done, left everything to you?' Violet guessed. She spoke too loudly.

Frederick hushed her. 'No, no, not at all,' and then he outlined Leopold's new arrangements for the bank, and plans for splitting his own shares equally among six members of the family. Violet, preoccupied with her own shortage of funds, realised dimly only the main facts as they concerned her. 'So who owns the houses?' she asked.

'Leopold will leave Farnley to Mother. After that, she'll make her own plans. And she already owns the house in Cavendish Square, of course, for her lifetime.'

'So Laurence gets the lot in the end,' said Violet.

'He is the elder son,' pointed out Frederick.

Violet knew by now that her own situation held no promise, just Caroline taking over more of the reins from her mother-in-law, more snubs for her and, as time went on, for her daughter too.

'Our children will be better provided for than if Leopold had put Laurence in sole charge of the bank,' Frederick told her.

His assumption that there would be more children chilled her, although she knew it was perfectly realistic. She had been lucky so far, had even wondered if Frederick was unable to father a child, but her luck might not last for ever.

'Of course,' he was saying, 'Leopold's decision doesn't reflect on Laurence. It's merely his way of safeguarding the bank in the event of war, rather the way fathers used to put one son to fight on either side of a civil war, so that whoever was the victor, one would be on the winning side. But if things had been otherwise Laurence would have had the major shareholding in Levine-Schreft, so, understandably, he's upset.' He did not mention his mother's support of Laurence, against him, nor did Violet. She had once raised the subject, knowing that if Sophie had had more respect or affection for her second son, she would be kinder to his wife, but Frederick had flinched, refused to discuss the matter and merely told her, 'Laurence is the elder son.' Now he said, 'It's getting hot in here. I've done my best to explain the situation . . .'

'Now to face the music,' said Violet, tapping on the window. The car started again. They walked across the hot area of gravel into the coolness of the hall. There was complete silence.

Brough, imported for the summer from Cavendish Square, came up saying, 'Good morning, Mr Frederick. Mrs Levine asked to be told as soon as you arrived.'

'Yes, but is there such a thing as a glass of lemonade?' asked Frederick. 'And will you tell my mother I'll be down as soon as I've changed.'

However, he met Sophie Levine on the stairs as he went up. 'Frederick, I'd like to speak to you in the drawing-room,' she said.

'Yes, Mother. I'd prefer to change first,' he replied. 'It's been a long, hot journey.'

'Now, Frederick, please,' she said.

Frederick, in his dark suit, followed her into the drawing-room.

Violet left the house. She was wandering down to the river in hot sunshine when she met Caroline and Tommy Brereton coming up.

'Is Frederick here yet?' Caroline asked.

Violet nodded.

'Where's Laurence?' she asked.

'I don't know,' said Violet.

Caroline hurried on to the house, leaving Tommy Brereton still standing, with Violet, on the lawn. Tommy regarded Caroline retreating in her white dress, the straw hat she carried swinging wildly to and fro on its ribbon.

'Difficult for a guest to know what to do in these circumstances,' he remarked.

'Not easy even when you live here,' Violet said tartly.

'And where are you heading at the moment?' he asked.

'Just away from the house,' she told him.

'Let's get in my car and have lunch in the town,' he suggested. 'They'll feel better without us at lunch.'

'Right you are,' said Violet. 'We ought to tell Brough. What about Sandy?'

'He's fishing down the river with a picnic. I don't know where. I don't propose to fight through bushes calling his name. Come on, let's escape together. Fred won't mind, will he?'

'Someone'll mind, whatever I do,' Violet said.

Over lunch in the restaurant of an inn in the small town to which they had driven, stopping only to scramble up a small hill to admire the view, where Violet had pretended not to notice Tommy was admiring her instead, she said, 'I suppose we'll have to have a war. I wonder what it'll be like.'

'It probably won't last long,' he told her. 'We'll all volunteer. Sweep the foe back where he belongs, come home heroes. It's high time we gave the Huns a bloody nose and put them back in their places.'

'Oh,' said Violet. 'I don't know much about wars. There hasn't been one for a long time.'

'I don't think there's much to know. I've learned to fly a plane – aerial combat's the coming thing, you know.'

'They seem to be very well armed, the Germans,' Violet said.

'A short, sharp shock is what they need,' Tommy Brereton replied, 'and me flying overhead showering them with lighted sticks of dynamite.'

Violet looked doubtfully into his handsome face. She imagined him going to Buckingham Palace in uniform in his smart green Benz motor-car, to get a medal.

He grinned. 'What a subject for a pleasant lunch with a beautiful woman. Tell me something about yourself. At the moment,' and he fixed her with gallant grey eyes, 'you look to me as if you think you're the ugly duckling, but you know what that particular bird became.'

'You were never an ugly duckling,' said Violet. 'You were born a swan. Now you've even learned to fly.'

'There's a well-known characteristic of swans I seem to lack,' said Tommy. 'Namely, their fidelity. I'm getting a shocking reputation for the opposite. I gather Her Majesty's mentioned me unfavourably to my mama. I shall have to be married, there's no doubt about it, but, quite honestly, Violet, I'm not sure I'll be able to stick it. I've got such bad habits.' He smiled. 'I think only you could make me forget them.'

She smiled at him. 'I'm afraid I could only be one more bad habit. Perhaps you'd forgotten I'm married.'

Tommy Brereton looked at her quizzically. 'Pie and custard?' he asked significantly.

Violet shook her head. 'I don't think so, thank you very much,' she answered.

'You're a card, Violet,' he said. 'Shall we drive about a bit after lunch?'

'I think I ought to get back.'

'I'd like to leave, drive away with you,' he said.

Later, on the brackeny hill, he took her hand and said, 'Let's go away, for a day or two.'

'How can I?' she asked.

'Violet,' he told her, 'you will one day – why not with me? In a few weeks' time, it won't matter anyway.'

'Why not?'

'We'll be at war, silly goose. Think about it, while I doze.' He leaned back and shut his eyes and seemed to be asleep. He rolled over and tried to pull her down beside him. Violet stood up and scrambled down the hill to the car. She was sitting in it when he joined her, slightly sulkily. She stuck her nose in the air and sat quite still as they drove back. In the end, ten miles and three-quarters of an hour later, he said, 'No hard feelings, Violet. You are an incredibly attractive woman, you know. And there's something else about you – you've got a bit of go in you. I don't know, Violet, but no wonder Fred married you.'

Violet, driving on winding roads through the sun-filled countryside, felt very happy in spite, or probably because, of Tommy Brereton's approaches. She condescended to say, 'It's been a lovely day, by and large.'

'Yes, by and large,' he said.

Farnley House was again silent when they entered. Violet wondered if the sign that disputes were taking place in an upper-class home weren't the exact opposite of signs in other classes. Here, instead of shouts and crashes, everyone seemed to be in a different room, not speaking to each other, and the servants were tiptoeing about to avoid disturbing or irritating the combatants. Standing at the window of the empty drawing-room Violet thought the gardener and his boy had started to cut the lawn and been told to stop. Certainly, it was only half mowed.

'Where have you been, Violet? I've been extremely worried,' said Frederick, coming in suddenly and not shutting the door before he spoke.

'I took her out to lunch, Fred,' explained Tommy Brereton, who was lolling in a chair.

'That's all very well and good.'

'I told Brough,' protested Violet. 'Surely he told you?'

'It's not good enough— '

'Keep calm, Fred,' advised Tommy, a little shocked by Frederick's outburst. 'This isn't the age of Victoria. Women are allowed to leave their homes in broad daylight without a servant in attendance you know. I hesitate to mention it, but we left for reasons of tact. I felt perhaps private family matters were under discussion and thought you might be happier for the moment to be without a guest at luncheon. I suggested we might go out to lunch and Violet kindly agreed to come with me. We had lunch and returned safe and sound as you see.'

Frederick's lips tightened. He said, 'Sorry, Tom. You're quite right. I'm sorry, Violet. The heat's making me a little short-tempered.' Still in his town suit, he had obviously been subjected to at least an hour's barrage from his mother, blaming him for having disloyally conspired with his uncle to disinherit his brother. She'd probably attempted to persuade him to put pressure on Leopold to change his decision.

Meantime, Tommy Brereton stood up and stretched. 'Frederick,' he said, 'you're a gentleman, so you are. If you'll both excuse me, I think I'll go and study form in the library.'

Frederick shook his head, embarrassed again, 'I'm afraid you might find Laurence and my uncle there . . . '

'Well, why don't we all go for a bathe in the river?' suggested Tommy.

'A good idea,' said Frederick relieved at the suggestion. 'Violet, are you coming?'

'I think I'll go and see baby,' Violet said. 'You go, Fred.'

When she went up to the nursery Nanny Thwaite and the children were not there. She went and lay down in her room and through the open windows smelt flowers and cut grass. She drowsed to the sounds of crickets on the lawn below, the occasional twitter of birds, the heavy humming of the bees. It had been a lovely afternoon driving along with Tommy, climbing the hill in the sunshine. If only there could be more such afternoons, she thought, but there couldn't be, wouldn't be. It wasn't possible, somehow.

SEVEN

Violet Levine, 1917

'Hold that lamp higher, to the right,' said the surgeon.

Violet Levine, standing by the patient's head, lifted the lamp, catching sight of a white face, stubbled chin, prominent nose. She observed a louse crawling into the pale brown hair, at the hairline. She dared not move to catch it. Her glance lowered down the blanketed body to the soldier's two bare legs, one pale white, except for the flea-bites, and thin as a stick, the other with a mass of red and pink gauze on the knee and down to the middle of the calf.

Sister Maclean was unwrapping the gauze. 'I should have preferred this to have been done earlier,' said Dr Swann.

She said, 'I'm sorry,' and went on unbandaging, but the four people in the wooden operating theatre, Sister Maclean, the two VADs, semi-trained volunteers, one of whom was Violet, even the doctor himself, knew the complaint was meaningless. One of the two men on stretchers by the wall of the hut whimpered, perhaps with pain, perhaps in a morphia dream. The layers of gauze on the soldier's wound grew redder. As they gazed at his smashed knee and upper leg, the knee a pulp, pumping out thin threads of blood with fragments of white bone poking through, the leg awkwardly broken, and black and blue with bruises, Swann said, 'I'll open the leg. If it's a clean break we'll try to save it.' But the soldier's leg was splintered vertically below a horizontal break. Swann said gloomily, 'An amputation. Can you tighten the tourniquet again, nurse, for a few minutes. Is he well under, nurse?' he asked Violet.

'Yes, doctor,' she told him.

'Scalpel then,' he said.

Plump Sister Maclean handed him a scalpel. Violet held the lamp high, her arm aching, and looked across at the other VAD, holding the lamp. She was breathing deeply. 'Don't look, Nurse Adrian. Hold the lamp steady,' instructed Sister Maclean.

Neither Violet, nor Suzanne Adrian should have been there in the operating theatre at St Luc on the Normandy coast on that May night, but patients and staff had gone down wholesale with virulent dysentery of the trenches. Half the nurses were barely able to crawl to the latrines and back to their huts. They could not have stood up for the length of one operation, let alone the twelve, or was it now thirteen operations, Violet wondered, which they'd done that evening. It had started after supper when three truck-loads containing ninety injured men, no better for having been pinned down on the roadside for five hours by enemy fire, had come in from a dressing station near Arras. The orderlies had omitted to provide water for a journey which should have taken only two hours. Since then the two operating theatres at No 53 hospital, St Luc, had been dealing with the worst injured. There had been a bombardment and half an hour after they switched on, the lights and the power had failed. Now she heard another plane approaching above the sickening sound of the surgeon's saw cutting through the thick bone below the man's knee. Violet, who had ears like a cat, was supposed to warn people of what she heard. This was not the moment, with the man's leg half off. Her arms were on fire. She prayed Dr Swann would hack the leg off quickly, just so that she could put the lamp down. There was a thump as he turned to put the leg in one of the big metal bins against the wall, a crash as the lid went back on. Violet and Suzanne Adrian moved closer, put their lamps on the operating table, handing the sister a bottle of carbolic, gauze, crêpe bandages, safety pins from the surgical trolley. In two minutes the stump of the soldier's leg was stitched, tidily bandaged, and stretcher bearers were already in the doorway.

'Next,' said Dr Swann. Violet steadied herself.

Sister Maclean said, 'I don't think the VADs can go on any longer, doctor. It's been four hours. I don't need to remind you they shouldn't be here.'

The doctor's shoulders sagged. He said, 'Can these men wait though?'

'As much as any of them can,' said Sister Maclean.

'Plane's getting closer, Sister,' said Violet.

'That's it,' said Dr Swann. 'It's probably a Hun. Ours wouldn't be flying over here at night. All right,' he said, pulling down his mask and starting to strip off his gloves, 'take these men back. I'll do them first at six thirty tomorrow. At least there'll be light. Will there be any proper nurses available, Sister?'

'I think we should have a few back on duty, doctor,' said Sister Maclean.

'I'm off then,' he said. He turned in the doorway. 'Thank you, nurses,' he said over his shoulder.

When he had gone Sister Maclean gave instructions about which huts the men should go to, and the orderlies removed the amputee, and the two soldiers who had been lying waiting for their operations, on their stretchers. Meanwhile Violet got water in buckets from the standpipe outside the hut and set them to boil on the stove in the corner. Suzanne, tall and blonde, scooped up bloodstained dressings, surgical instruments, needles, chloroform pads, pieces of bloodied shrapnel, removed bullets, which had fallen on the floor during the hours of intensive operations, and Sister Maclean swabbed the metal trolley with surgical spirit and tidied the instruments which had not been used. She shouted for an orderly to remove the bins.

Violet, on her knees, scrubbing the wooden floor with Lysol and warm water, wearing thick rubber gloves to keep the corrosive liquid from her hands, said, 'Proper nurses, indeed. We're only fit to work in operating theatres, take charge of wards of thirty men, some dying – if we're not proper nurses, who is?'

'The Voluntary Aid Detachment is like the rest of Europe, overtaken by events,' said Suzanne, pushing the instruments into a steriliser under which a small benzine-fed jet hissed. She shut the lid.

Sister Maclean straightened up and went to the door for a moment. She looked out into the darkness, breathing deeply. 'Well, thank you, girls, for what you've done. You know Dr Swann didn't mean to insult you. It was only his thoughtlessness. I'll try and get you back on the wards tomorrow, normal duties, but it depends on who's back on their feet, or who's off them.

You'd better be ready, here, at six thirty tomorrow, just in case.' She turned round and said, 'Put the soiled dressing buckets outside for the orderlies and tidy up generally for tomorrow. Then you can go off. I'm going to check the wards.'

Suzanne and Violet dropped their soiled aprons and cuffs into a bin outside the hut, walked back to the nurses' canteen past the long wooden wards each housing thirty soldiers, injured by gas, affecting lungs, eyes, kidneys by shrapnel and bullets, the men with pneumonia, tuberculosis and VD. They had survived the trenches, the field dressing stations and if they survived No 53 hospital, they would be shipped back to England on the same boats which had brought out their replacements.

Violet was almost asleep as she stared into the mug of tea next to the doorstep of bread and butter she and Suzanne had persuaded the canteen manageress to produce for them, so late at night. Suzanne's fair head was drooping on her chest.

'Suzanne,' she said loudly.

Suzanne's head jerked up. 'Oh, I was asleep.'

Violet asked herself, as well as Suzanne, 'I wonder how much longer this can go on? There was a Hundred Years War, wasn't there? How did they manage it?'

'They had bows and arrows, I suppose, not tanks and mortars,' muttered Suzanne.

Her head was sinking again. Her eyes closed. Violet thought Suzanne should go home. She was too thin, now, and she moaned at night. One of her three brothers had been killed in Italy, another was still fighting there. Yet, going home was sometimes hard, as well, a different kind of shock.

In London on leave a month before, Violet had taken a cab from Victoria Station, wondering at the quiet streets. So much had changed in three years. There were so many men in uniform and so many civilians, from old people to children, were wearing black. Everywhere she looked were tired faces, men on crutches, women in mourning – this was the third spring of the war; almost a million men had already died.

Laurence had been in France only two months when Brough carried into the drawing-room at Cavendish Square the telegram announcing his death. Sophie, Caroline and Violet were all sitting by the fire. All three looked up as he came in, at the silver tray on which lay the dreaded yellow envelope containing the telegram. All three were afraid. If Brough took the message to Violet, it meant that Frederick had been killed, injured or captured; if he took it to Caroline, it meant that something had happened to Laurence. The news that one of them had been mildly wounded or captured might be a relief – either would get them away from the fighting. Each woman waited for Brough to move towards her. He, wanting to speak, and knowing that he should, since he was the only person there who knew to whom the telegram was addressed, found his voice would not obey him.

Violet stood and asked, 'Who's the telegram for, Brough?' She moved towards him, hand outstretched, to take it.

As she did so Brough said gently, 'Mrs Laurence,' and carried it over to Caroline in her chair.

'I'll open it,' said Sophie Levine, her voice cracking. She jumped up.

Brough ignored her and bent over the motionless Caroline. She took the envelope. He went to the door, turned, and saw Sophie Levine standing over her daughter-in-law, 'Open it, Caroline.'

Caroline did so. She sat staring at it and saying nothing.

'Caroline!' cried Sophie and seized the telegram from her hand. She gave a great cry and fell, still clutching the message, to the floor, saying, 'No – no – no.'

'Oh, God!' shouted Violet. 'Brough!' Together they tried to pull her up, Violet saying, 'Sophie. He's at peace now.'

Sophie Levine wailed, 'What do you know? What do you know? Frederick's still alive.' She sounded almost angry, as if both of her sons should have died when Laurence did or, perhaps, as if she should have been allowed to choose which should live, which die. 'Think of Caroline,' urged Violet.

Caroline spoke, saying in a flat voice, 'I can't bear this. I can't bear it. Stop, Sophie. Stop.'

'Get the doctor, Brough,' said Violet, as they got Sophie to her feet and lowered the sobbing woman into a chair. 'Caroline, I'm so sorry.'

'Make her stop that noise, Violet,' Caroline said tonelessly. Then, 'Oh, Laurence – Laurence. What am I going to do without you?'

Rosalind arrived at midnight in evening dress, having found Violet's telegram telling her of Laurence's death when she came in. 'How is she?' she asked Violet in the hall.

'Desperate,' said Violet. 'She's talking and talking.'

'You don't know what it's like,' Caroline had cried at her, 'you don't know what it's like to love a man, body and soul. You don't know what I've lost, Violet.'

Violet reflected that this was the second time today she'd been told, more or less, that Frederick should have died, not Laurence. The previous months with her mother and sister-in-law had been dull and painful as the three waited – for newspapers with accounts of the war, for letters or for the announcement that one of the brothers would be coming home on leave. The next years, she calculated cruelly, could only be worse with Caroline grieving and Sophie, perhaps, inconsolable. Caroline would recover, she estimated; Sophie might never get over the death of her favourite son. And she, Violet, would have to avoid all this, somehow or other. She had to get away.

In the hall Rosalind had sympathised, 'You must be so upset yourself, Violet, but now you're all they have.'

Violet said nothing.

Rosalind gazed at her. After a pause Violet declared, 'I can't stay here.' She was on the margin of hysteria herself. 'There's some sandwiches and a thermos in the drawing-room, I think. I'm off to bed.' On the second stair, she turned and hissed at Rosalind, 'Don't think I'm stopping here out of loyalty – I'm not.'

This incident, demonstrating Violet's hard-heartedness to everyone who heard the tale, was talked much of in subsequent months, particularly when Violet joined the Voluntary Aid Detachment and embarked on training as an auxiliary nurse at a London teaching hospital – where, unlike some of the better-off volunteers who had joined under the impression that their duties would mainly consist of flower-arranging and the wiping of fevered brows, she stayed the course.

By winter Violet was nursing in France, living in a shared hut where, if the window was left open at night, snow accumulated at the ends of the beds by morning. Sea winds lashed the hospital blocks of No 53 hospital, St Luc, in Normandy. The sounds of the bombardment often came to them from inland. Convoys of sick and wounded men came in and in.

Sophie and Caroline closed up the house in London and retreated to Farnley with Joseph and Pamela. There, they were spared the worst of the food shortages. Increasingly, basic commodities like flour and potatoes became impossible to obtain. The population, though not quite starving, was severely undernourished, but at Farnley, where elderly men and landgirls were at work, hens were kept, crops grown, gardens tended and what men were left could still trap and shoot game.

Violet spent her first leave with Sophie and Caroline but she found the experience depressing. Sophie urged her to return and take up her family duties. Caroline appealed, 'For God's sake, Violet, come back. I can't get through another winter here alone.'

But she was adamant. Her conscience, she claimed, wouldn't allow her to shirk the responsibility of nursing men who had, like Laurence, sacrificed themselves for their country. In fact she saw clearly that with many of the servants gone it would be convenient for Sophie to have with her a daughter-in-law brought up to cook, clean and carry in coal. Violet wasn't going to do that, or help Caroline to grow vegetables in the garden. Apart from anything else she'd discovered she liked nursing, and was good at it. She'd been at Farnley only a week when Nanny Thwaite, furious that Violet was not planning to stay at home and take care of her child, offered her resignation, saying that the work was too much for her. Violet promptly telephoned her headquarters in London for the address of a fellow VAD who had been sent home after a series of illnesses caused by exhaustion, contacted the young woman, Jessie Oates, by telegram, got a favourable reply next day, and told Sophie that a suitable replacement for Nanny Thwaite was available. Sophie was doubtful. Nanny Thwaite, in the meanwhile, got wind of the new plan and said she might be persuaded to withdraw her resignation. Violet, aged twenty now, and suddenly conscious of the power she had acquired as the wife of the new male head of the family, sacked her.

She spent her next leave in Boulogne where Frederick

met her for the first week of his leave before he returned to England to spend the rest of his time at Farnley. Thin, very weary, louse-bitten and still haunted by his brother's death, he was less changed by what he had endured than many men Violet had seen. He told her, 'I've been a Jew at a public school, and the younger, unhandsome, ungifted brother – I suppose it imparted some intestinal fortitude not granted to other, unluckier people. Mother always told me I was born sad. Perhaps that was a blessing, to be born sad in a world like this.'

'Well, cheer up now, Fred,' Violet told him. 'Let's go out and get some dinner.' He was probably right, she thought, but she'd no patience with what she called his wailing wall attitude to life. She couldn't see how the Beethovens and Brahmses on his gramophone in the trenches could console anyone but him. The other officers would probably have preferred some cheery songs to brighten them up. She could hardly bear to read his reflective letters, though she, having seen the casualties, knew well what he was not telling her. On the whole she wondered if it was really such luck to be married to a man with so many virtues, so few vices and absolutely no go in him at all. Still, as a husband, though not much fun, he was at least alive, she reminded herself, pinning on her hat in front of the mirror in the Boulogne hotel. These days that was a merit in itself.

The same thought again occurred to her when she met Caroline for the first time after a year, during her leave in London in April 1917. The house had seemed empty when she let herself in, still in her VAD uniform, black coat, shoes and stockings, a black hat and carrying her small brown leather suitcase.

The hall was dusty, some plaster lay in heaps – a bomb must have fallen nearby. She walked down the passageway at the back of the house, down the back stairs and entered the huge, silent kitchen, hoping to find something to eat. She'd had no food since embarking at Boulogne on a ship full of returning soldiers. The huge stove, the long scrubbed kitchen table, the ranks of hanging pans, had obviously been cleaned long ago and left. However, there were some plates in the sink, and in the near-empty larder was half a pint of milk and half a loaf of bread. Someone was about, but she couldn't imagine who. She walked into the next room, the servants' dining-room, scene of her first visit when she had come in carrying a parcel of gloves for Frederick to find the staff ranged round this very table, now covered in dusty green oilcloth. She sat down wearily at the table, propping her head in one hand, hit suddenly by the exhaustion.

There had just been a massive spring assault by the Germans, a desperate attempt to break through the British lines, reach the coast and, finally, embark on the invasion of Britain. Half asleep, she saw the columns of ambulances, farm carts, wounded men on foot, reaching No 53 hospital, heard the whistling gasps of gassed men as they lay trying not to suffocate, the wounds, the blood, limbs green and puffed with gangrene, heard the screams, groans, the pleas for help, the eternal cries for water. She felt again the weariness of aching muscles, the anxiety of perpetually having to keep four orders in her head at once: send for more bandages and morphine; change the dressings every two hours on the two amputated stumps of a soldier whose legs had been crushed by a tank; replenish all the jugs of water and change the cups beside the thirty beds; take all temperatures and mark the charts. All that, and the bombardments as the enemy tried to cut the railway line which stood on the narrow strip of land between the hospital and the coast had been the background to her life for months. But now it was the silence of the big house and the growing sense that there were no demands on her, and would not be for a fortnight, which made Violet feel so tired. She wondered if there was a bed she could sleep in and whether there was any coal, so that she could light a fire.

In the library the dust-sheets covering the leather armchairs and sofa had been pushed off, and lay on the carpet. There was not only half a scuttle of coal but the grate was full of ashes – so full that, Violet thought, it looked as if someone had lit several fires, one on top of the other, until it choked. She was forced to clear the grate and, as she put the ashes in the dustbin, checked the locks and windows carefully. Obviously, from the evidence of the loaf in the kitchen and the fire in the grate, someone was using the house, but it would be better if that someone had let himself in legitimately with a doorkey. Violet had grappled with men raging with fever trying to get out of bed, or refusing to get in, had subdued groups of drunken soldiers she met occasionally walking into town during her off-duty time. She was not particularly afraid of an encounter with an intruder. But she checked the windows in the basement, seeing from the kitchen grass growing between the flagstones of the yard. Curtains drooped, discouraged, in the empty rooms opposite, above the stables. She saw no signs that anyone had come in. Even the cellar door was bolted, top and bottom. All the ground-floor rooms were empty and unused, the furniture covered by dust-sheets, cloths hanging in front of mirrors and pictures. It was from a trail of coal dust and footmarks across the carpet of the smaller drawing-room that Violet found the source of the coal in the library next door. The visitor to the house had evidently brought in a sack of coal and stored it in one of the tall cupboards which stood in alcoves on either side of the fireplace: a shovel and an empty champagne bottle stood beside the sack. Not a tidy guest, thought Violet, lighting the library fire with some of the coal and a copy of *The Times* dated earlier in April. Sophie Levine would have been annoyed. So would Brough. Upstairs in a bedroom there might be clues to the person's identity – a fellow officer of Frederick's home on leave, some refugee cousin of the Levines from Europe seeking a temporary base. She sat down by the fire. The investigation could wait, as could her own unpacking – and everything else, she realised, as she fell asleep, far from the guns and the lines of beds of wounded men.

She woke up when the library door opened. A voice said, 'Violet!' She saw Caroline, in a black coat and hat, her cheeks flushed with wind, standing in the doorway. There was a man behind her in uniform. 'Good Lord,' said Caroline, flustered.'I thought the house was empty.'

'I thought you were at Farnley,' said Violet, yawning. 'I've got leave, I only arrived a little while ago. What time is it?' She glanced at the windows. It was getting dark.

'Six o'clock, about,' said Caroline. 'Well, what a surprise.' She seemed uncertain whether to come in or not, then said, 'This is my cousin Robert Kerr – come in, Rob, and meet my sister-in-law, Violet.' A tall fair man stepped in. For a moment, still not quite awake, she thought it was Laurence, standing there in uniform with Caroline.

'Very pleased to meet you, Mrs Levine,' said the young man. 'I've heard a great deal about your wonderful exploits.'

'I'll leave you two to talk while I go and tidy,' Caroline announced.

'Caroline dashed up when she heard I was on leave in London,' Robert Kerr said, sitting down. 'I've only got three days, hardly time to get home. So she said she'd come and do a few shows with me, wonderful of her, really, in the circumstances, with Laurence dead. Dreadful loss.'

Violet asked, 'How is she now? I haven't seen her for so long.'

'She's bearing up,' said Robert. Some thought crossed his boy's face – he was no more than twenty, Violet thought, and must have joined the army straight from school. He looked slightly uncomfortable.

Then Caroline came in herself and said, 'Let's go for a stroll and then go and have dinner at the Ritz. Will you come, Violet? Shall I telephone and reserve a table?'

'Let's go to a show first,' Violet said. 'I feel like some fun.' She looked doubtfully at Caroline, still wearing deep widow's black, though Violet saw that her dress had been made by a good dressmaker, and was short enough to show black silk stockings to just below her calf and neat shoes with silver buckles.

Caroline said, 'So do I, and Robert deserves it, God knows. What about trying to get into *The Saving Grace* and hoping there isn't an air raid? Or the Byng sisters?'

Violet observed a flush on Caroline's cheeks. Her voice was pitched high, her words tumbled out faster than Violet remembered. Her manner was like that of the shocked soldiers who arrived at the hospital, sometimes seeming rational, talking, even laughing, unconscious of their wounds.

'Champagne,' Caroline declared. 'It's in the cellar. Come down with me, Robbie – it's all ghostly and covered in cobwebs.'

Robert Kerr got to his feet, looked at Violet and away from her again. 'Of course,' he said.

Violet heard Caroline's voice in the hall saying, 'How nice

to have the protection of the army, even in the wine cellar.'

Violet picked up her bag from the hall and went upstairs. The big bedroom she had shared with Frederick was dusty. Here, too, the furniture was covered with cloths, the mirrors draped. She opened her wardrobe, to see if she could find anything to wear for she only had one plain, blue woollen dress in her bag. She washed in cold water in the bathroom and put on a dark green silk dress with a V neck, green silk stockings and pale kid shoes. She took a coat and hat from the cupboard, leaving her uniform on the bed, and went downstairs.

Caroline and Robert were drinking the champagne from Sophie's prized green and white glasses which Caroline had evidently unearthed from somewhere. Violet shuddered at what Sophie would think if she knew. It was dark outside now, and the only light came from the fire, and four kitchen candles stuck in two rediscovered silver candelabra on the desk. Fire and candle flames flickered on the dark walls of the library. Violet took her glass and sat on a cushion on the floor by the fire.

'Let's drink to the end of this bloody, damned war,' said Caroline, her back turned, as she looked out of the window into the silent mews beside the house. Then she said, in an abrupt, high voice, 'Tommy Brereton died of wounds yesterday – they got him back to the Passes's house in Hertfordshire. Then one leg mortified, then the other. They cut them both off, but it was a waste of time – he died anyway. They're going to give him a medal. It won't do him much good where he is, will it? Tell me, Violet, do you think there'll be any men at all left, at the end of all this? How shall we manage, with only the women to do everything?' She turned and said, 'Sorry, Robert, not very tactful, am I?'

Violet closed her eyes and said nothing. Her eye picked up the gleam of a second bottle of champagne on the desk.

Caroline was refilling all their glasses. 'I wish I was at the front, Violet, like you. I'm useless, and I know it. But unlike you, I couldn't leave my child. How could any mother? How can I? He's all I've got left to remind me of Laurence. You've still got Frederick, haven't you, Violet? Ironical, isn't it?'

Violet stood up. 'Let's go out,' she said. 'The atmosphere's awful in this house.'

'Oh, sit down, Violet,' Caroline said. 'I like it here in the dark, just the three of us. It makes a change from Farnley. You were wise to escape. But I suppose you'd call it leaving to do your patriotic duty.' She added, 'You haven't asked me how Pamela is yet. Well, for your information, she's a year older than when you last saw her. You know Fred thinks you ought to be at home, don't you?'

'Yes,' said Violet. 'He's told me so. And I didn't mention I'd rather face the Germans than hide with you and Sophie at Farnley. I don't think he understood, but I'm sure you do, Caroline.'

'Nice way for you to spend your leave, Robbie,' Caroline said. 'Listening to bitches fighting.'

'Oh . . . ' he said uncomfortably.

'I'll go upstairs,' said Violet. 'Come and tell me when you're leaving.' She went out of the room, and up the stairs to her chilly bedroom, where she sat on her bed, hearing a car chug past below, a woman laugh. This was a bad start to a leave, here in a deserted house, with only Caroline on the verge of a nervous breakdown and a baffled young officer as companions. She'd be better off in a hotel. She went downstairs again. She heard the gramophone in the library, and looked in, planning to tell Caroline and Robbie she was going out to find a hotel. They were playing a jazz record, 'A Hot Time in the Old Town Tonight'. It came blaring out as she opened the door. Caroline was dancing by herself near the window. Her cousin Robbie was still sitting on the sofa. Violet asked, 'Is anyone ready for supper? I'm famished, so I'm going out . . . '

Robert Kerr stood up and said, 'Come on, Caroline, let's go and find some supper with Violet.'

Caroline stopped dancing, stared at him, and then at Violet, in her coat and hat in the doorway. 'All right,' she said. She blew out the candles and went upstairs for her coat.

'I'm moving into a hotel tonight,' Violet informed them in Oxford Street. 'It's too gloomy there. Isn't there somewhere else for you both to stay? I mean, there isn't even any hot water. What about Chelsea – is Rosalind still there? I know. We could go to the Café Royal, get a bite to eat and try telephoning her.'

Once they had a table Caroline left them to tidy her

hair. Robbie said to Violet, 'She's in rather an odd mood, Caroline.' An orchestra of old men and women was playing selections from Gilbert and Sullivan, the tables were full of men in khaki uniform.

Violet, looking at her work-roughened hands on the white cloth, and conscious her dress was three years out of date, felt gloomy. She said, 'I wish this war was over.'

A man in invalid blue, one trouser-leg pinned up, went past on crutches, lurched sideways, recovered, and apologised for jolting the table. Robert Kerr looked after him as he swung himself back to where an older and a younger woman, both in black, were sitting. Next to them three bejewelled women were laughing with two officers, one of whom went on laughing for too long after the others stopped. The second officer put his arm round his friend's shoulders, filled his glass with the other hand, gave it to him. Violet looked at the young man, in his brand-new uniform, opposite her. He was grave. He said, 'If you don't mind, I'll leave you alone while I go to telephone Caroline's sister. I shan't be long.'

A captain in a kilt came to the table where Violet sat alone. 'Are you alone, madam?' he asked. 'May I sit down for a moment?'

'I'm with friends,' Violet told him.

'I'm so sorry,' he said. 'My apologies.' He came to attention and saluted smartly.

Violet recognised on his khaki jacket shoulder the insignia of a Scottish regiment, half of which had been brought, cut to pieces by machine-gun fire, to No 53 hospital, a month before.

Caroline returned just as he was leaving. 'Nasty fellow – obviously drunk,' she observed. 'Where's Robbie?'

'He said he'd telephone Rosalind and try to get a bed for the night,' reported Violet, relieved that Caroline seemed to be calmer again, only very tired.

'We'll be lucky to find her in,' said Caroline. 'It's one long party, day and night, in Chelsea. Mother and Father are threatening to give up the lease so she has to go home. But it might be better there than at Cavendish Square.'

'Are you sleeping all right?' Violet asked her.

Caroline smiled. 'I've forgotten what it's like to get a good night's sleep. Jessie Oates got me a cat, to set me an example,' she said. 'She's a nice girl. Thank God you got rid of Nanny Thwaite. Even so, she's living in a cottage a mile away, with her sister, and still arrives to persecute us regularly. It's utterly grim down at Farnley. Sometimes I have to admit my only fear is that the Germans will win and we'll have to go on living there for ever.'

'I think you need some sleeping draughts and to get out of mourning,' Violet told her.

'Mama-in-law would have fifty fits if I came home in a red dress,' Caroline told her. And added, 'It would seem disloyal, somehow.'

Robbie came across the restaurant, nodding at them. 'Rosalind says yes, of course we must go there – you, too, of course, Violet – if we don't mind sofas and things. She was shocked we hadn't asked.'

Omelettes arrived, a bottle of wine and some grey bread. 'I think I'll go to a hotel anyway,' said Violet. 'I'm too tired to camp out on a sofa after the guests have gone home. I expect Rosalind'll understand.'

They went on to a variety show, where Violet fell asleep. Caroline and Robert trundled her to Claridges in a cab, where Caroline kissed her, without much enthusiasm.

I'll never like her, Violet thought, going up the stairs of the hotel. Stuck-up bitch. Ten to one, for all her present woes she'll end up married to royalty. And when she does, she'll have me thrown in the Tower for the rest of my life.

She spent most of the rest of her leave with Maria Strick, another nurse on leave from the hospital. They went to theatres and cinemas, and a dance at the Locarno full of soldiers. Violet wore her cheapest dress, resumed her old London accent, giggled, danced and flirted. At the end of the dance they played 'Keep the Home Fires Burning' and the crowd, girls and men in uniform, with their arms linked, stopped dancing and sang. Maria cried, and so did Violet, surprising herself. The young soldier she was with said in a Somerset burr, 'Cheer up, it'll soon be over, my dear,' and Violet said to this complete stranger, who, she knew, wanted to take her off into the alley behind the dance hall, and have her, standing up against a wall, 'That won't bring my brother Frank back, though, will it?' She had lost Maria, as she knew she would – some lucky soldier had found in her his companion for the alley behind the dance hall – and the kindly Somerset lad took her home, which, to his amazement, turned out to be Claridges Hotel. In the end she sneaked him in with her, but after he had, astonished, fumbled through the act of love, and then left, at her insistence – 'I'm here awaiting my husband. He arrives from York at dawn, off the night train' – she lay in the tumbled bed, remembering the brother she had forgotten about for so long. That afternoon Allie had told her Frank was dead, had been killed over a year before.

She had sent a note to the address she and Allie had been using for years. They had met at Kew. As a tall, black-clad figure walked towards her across the grass Violet did not at first recognise her sister, now nineteen. Allie was pale, rather thin, and said in a bitter, unfriendly tone, 'Hello, Violet. Saw your picture in the *Daily Sketch* – Mrs Frederick Levine, nursing heroine, bending over a wounded hero.'

'What's happened?' asked Violet.

'It's Frank. Ran away and joined the army and got killed on the Somme,' Allie told her. 'It was Dad's new wife who did it. She made his life a misery.'

'Oh, my God,' said Violet. She felt very shaken. She'd parted with twelve-year-old Frank, a rough-tongued boy in huge boots, without much regret. As long as he was alive, she hadn't given him a thought. 'I suppose you think I'm to blame,' she told Allie, seeing red cheeks, a little boy grubbing up daisies in the park.

'We're all to blame, really,' said Allie. She sounded less angry. 'All to blame – I did what I could, but then I moved out when she tried to take the strap to me one night when I came in late. I think I should have stayed, now. But in the end it was her fault, and Dad's for not stopping her from behaving like she did. The baby died too, but I expect he's best off out of it, poor little mite. Norah's husband's got invalided out, shell shock, and he's fit for nothing, or says he can't manage – I don't know. The world's gone mad. Poor little Frank just got caught in the machinery.'

'Where are you living?' asked Violet.

'With my friend Amy's family in Kennington. They're nice people – there's only Amy and I've got my own room. I've got a good job at the War Office, as a typist. I'm all right. It's poor Frank – only fifteen. He never stood a chance, after Ma died and Dad married that bitch. It's an old story, that one. I reckon he could have dodged the army, if he'd waited, if the war ended in time. But I can't find it in my heart to blame you, Violet. You got out, and then I did. Maybe if one of us had taken over when Ma died, Dad wouldn't have got married again to that woman. I don't know. What's the point of dragging it all up, going over and over it all? Everybody's got a burden to bear these days.'

They walked through avenues of trees.

'I brought a thermos of tea and some sandwiches,' said Violet. So they sat down on a bench and she unwrapped the greaseproof paper round the sandwiches, poured them both some tea.

'Your hands are in a state,' said Allie.

'I'm back scrubbing floors and fetching and carrying,' Violet responded. 'Funny, isn't it? Just what I was dying to escape.'

'I can't see why you went. You could be down at Farnley House with Mrs Levine and the Honourable Caroline.'

'You been reading the society pages?' Violet asked.

'It's a kind of hobby, where I work,' said Allie, 'keeping up with the doings of the aristocracy. None of the girls seems to talk about anything else. I never let on you're one of them, though.'

'Let me tell you,' said Violet, 'you'd go down a coal-mine rather than live down at Farnley with my mother-in-law and sister-in-law.'

'Hard to leave the baby, though, I should think,' mumbled Allie, eating a jam sandwich.

Violet, who had finished hers, lit a cigarette and said, 'Not really. Well, you might have guessed Pamela wasn't Frederick's and the worry of passing her off as his, and all that, put me right off her from the word go. That's what I think. I don't seem to have much maternal instinct at the best of times. And anyway, people like the Levines have nurses to bring up their children. You don't get very close to them. Even the mothers might as well not be there, half the time. A lot of them aren't. They make a big fuss about having children, but they don't do a lot of bringing them up, not like ordinary people, especially when the children are small, like Pamela.'

'Still, you being rich, you could have done what you liked. You didn't have to go nursing,' remarked Allie.

'Rich? I don't know where you got that from,' said Violet. 'I've got to go to my husband's confidential clerk to get money for my hotel, and something for new underclothes. That's how rich I am.'

'What – you mean you never got a legacy, or nothing?' asked Allie.

Violet laughed. 'What legacy? You *have* been reading the society pages, haven't you? You don't know what happens at all, specially in these rich families, specially where the women are concerned. I'll give you some cash when I've tapped old Sturgess.'

Still incredulous about Violet's alleged poverty, Allie said, 'I'll get them some stuff, some clothes for Ben.'

'Want to go to the pictures?' said Violet.

'Not half,' replied Allie. The sisters saw a Charlie Chaplin film, had supper and Violet saw Allie off on the bus to Kennington.

Before she left Allie said, 'Someone else is dead. Do you want to know?'

Violet considered. 'You might as well tell me,' she said.

'Tom. Tom Rawlinson,' her sister told her.

Violet breathed out.

Allie said, 'Maybe that's not the worst news you've ever heard, taking one thing with another.' Then she got on the bus.

Well, thought Violet, standing in the Strand, smelling the spring faintly through petrol fumes, hard luck on Tom, but from my point of view, it's a loose end tied up. Now there's no chance he'll ever turn up suddenly, claiming he must be Pamela's father.

Nonetheless, after the dance, and after the soldier from Somerset had struggled into his coarse khaki jacket and trousers and heavy boots and left, she fell asleep with tears on her face, though whether for her brother, or the father of her child, or just the strain of too much war and work and too many deaths, she didn't know.

The next day she went back to France, and not too long after that Violet Levine fell in love for the first time.

EIGHT

The Levines, May, 1991

Robert Levine, seventy-two but firm-moving and straight-backed, walked with his travel bag to the door of his sister's house in London and rang the bell. Having checked his identity, the maid pushed the buzzer to let him in, just as his niece Anna came lightly down the stairs. She said, 'Uncle Robert, come and have a drink,' and, preceding him into the drawing-room, told him, 'I tried to ring you in New York. I'm afraid Mother's very ill – pneumonia.'

'How serious?' asked Robert.

As she poured him a whisky she said, 'Bad enough. I've come up to look after her. A nurse comes in for part of the day. There's a night nurse. She didn't want to go to hospital. It came on very suddenly.'

'I spent a day in Frankfurt,' said her uncle. 'That's why you couldn't find me. Would it be better if I went to a hotel?'

'No. Certainly not. But I'm afraid entertaining's out of the question.'

'Of course,' he said. 'Can I go up and see her?'

'Not now. She's asleep.' There was a silence. 'She's been asking for Harry Wainwright, from Cornwall and Wallis. She wants him to come and see her, about Violet's papers. She's in a high fever, some of the time. I don't know what she's got in mind.'

'Oh, my God,' said Robert. 'That's partly why I'm here. I took a trip to Black Stump Farm, and I found the occupant as obstinate and unreasonable as ever.'

'Why did you go?' asked Anna.

'I thought it was time to change the terms of our arrangement, now Violet's dead, for obvious reasons. Apart from anything else, she's getting money from some other source, and I'd like to know what it is.'

'Mother was talking about secrets being bad,' Anna said. 'In delirium, but . . . '

Robert Levine cast his eyes up in the air. 'Oh, Lord, we'll have to put a stop to that.'

His niece nodded determinedly.

The maid came into the room to announce lunch. As they sat down in the dining-room Robert asked, 'When's Jack coming back?'

'Not for a fortnight.'

'Damn,' said Robert as the soup came in. 'I'd have liked a word with him before I left, but I can only stay a week. Whatever you do, don't get hold of Wainwright. I'll have a word with him myself – this afternoon if possible. And the doctor, when's he coming in next?'

'She,' said his niece. 'She's coming at two thirty.'

'Good.'

'So,' asked Anna, pouring some wine and handing it to him across the polished table. 'What other plans have you got for your visit?'

'This and that,' said Robert. 'These are trying times. And will you come to see *Macbeth* with me at the National, or have you already been?'

'I have. I'd love to come again,' said his niece. 'And there's a marvellous Chinese exhibition at the British Museum.'

'Wonderful,' said Robert. He paused and frowned. 'The trouble is,' he said, 'your mother's an excellent woman, but she's never been very worldly.'

Anna nodded.

'You're different,' he complimented her and she smiled.

NINE

Kate Higgins, May 28th, 1991
Violet Levine, 1917

Andy and I were lying on the grass on the bank of the Thames, behind a pub at Chiswick. My eyes were closed. I could hear the chug, chug of a motor-boat going past, the slap, slap of water against the bank, and the birds in the trees nearby were singing. I thought Andy had fallen asleep. He had got back from Belize a few days before, lifted off from a patch in the forest by British army helicopter, and landed on an American navy ship patrolling off the coast of Florida.

Andy and four other journalists had escaped the fighting in Belize City, taken off in a jeep, hidden out in a village close to a sawmill in the jungle, managed to organise a rendezvous with the helicopter and walked ten miles through forest to the pick-up point. They stayed two days there, waiting. They ran out of food and water so, leaving the other two behind, Andy and the photographer had returned to the village for supplies. They found it burning, full of machine-gunned corpses. They even saw the last of the government troops getting in their trucks and driving away. When they got back to camp with the food and water the helicopter was waiting for them. They had photographs, and the village at Sweetwater was now on all the front pages. Andy, on antibiotics for septic bites and lacerations, was writing the story of the revolution in Belize for *The Witness*.

He seemed unaffected by over two weeks in the middle of a revolution, fearing for his skin, and ending with the terrible spectacle of an entire village massacred by machine-guns in front of its own shacks. He was tired, but quite calm. I thought it must be a professional attitude. He was back, and he had work to do.

The British government was embarrassed that the army, stationed there for years to protect the country from all evil, especially Nicaragua and Cuba, was involved in a civil war. In theory Britain was bound to defend the legitimate government, but its heart wasn't in protecting a Marxist government. There was also pressure from the USA not to do so. In the confusion, British soldiers were being killed by both sides. Andy's articles all added up to advising Britain either to fulfil its obligations to the democratically elected government of Belize, or pull the army out, one or the other. His own account of the massacre at Sweetwater Village conducted by this democratically elected government didn't increase enthusiasm about supporting it. Meanwhile Andy, working, telling it like it was, seemed cool.

Dave phoned every few days to find out if I'd heard anything about Sam. This was partly concern for me and partly to try and get some news, since Commonwealth Office and Ministry of Defence communiqués were so sparse. I was going that evening to Brighton, to be with Ray and my parents. Andy wasn't happy about this, but this round of the cosmic boxing match women have to referee daily between the needs of men and the needs of children had been won by Ray. If news of his father's wounding or killing was going to arrive, his mother, at least, ought to be there. But, just for the time being, it was peaceful there at Chiswick, where the lawns and well-tended gardens of big houses opposite stretched down to the river, far from the unpainted windows of Henry Thackery House, the broken-open black rubbish bags in the streets, the stray dogs, the two long strips of roses, so patiently tended, and weeded of their daily ration of empty crisp packets and drink cans by the poor carpet-slippered old man on the ground floor. No problems here, and, somehow, no problems with Andy, who had been kind and loving, glad to be back, since he arrived from Belize. He'd even had a normal, friendly conversation with Di when he came to pick me up on his return, as if sobered by his experiences. The new Andy had even smiled nicely when Dave sent greetings through me, and I passed them on, even though Dave normally made Andy snappy for reasons I couldn't understand.

Andy, not asleep, murmured, 'Uncle Arthur's dead.'

'Your Uncle Arthur?' I asked him.

'Mm.'

'Not Roger's father?'

'No, another brother. We never saw him. There'd been a quarrel, then everyone forgot the quarrel, but he still never left Dundee. You don't feel up to getting me another half, do you?'

Keen to help the exhausted wounded hero, I got up and bought the drinks. When I got back he was sitting up.

'Thought I might buy a house,' he said. 'Then we could live together.'

'You mean Uncle Arthur's left you some money?'

'Yes. I mean, look at it. Houses sweeping down to the Thames – maybe it's time.'

'To have a home?' I asked.

'Children. All that.'

I said, 'Yes.'

'Somewhere in the country,' he said. 'On a river, like this.'

'Did he leave a lot of money?' I asked.

'Yes,' said Andy. 'He had a shoe factory, Viridian. You don't see many down here, but they're very popular in Scotland and the north. Some kind of Chinese consortium wants to buy it – Hong Kong money, I think. Nice deal.' He didn't need to look at this watch, but said, 'Let's go. I'm due at the office at four.'

As we walked to the car park he said, 'You're too old, and you're hopelessly badly dressed, but I'd like to spend your declining years with you. How about it?'

'Oh, Andy,' I said, and embraced him by the rose-covered wall of the pub, beside the car park in the sunshine. He, the man I loved, kissed me.

Violet Levine, May, 1917

Outside Blaise, the village two miles west of St Luc, a new base camp was set up while Violet was away for the Americans who had just entered the war. By the time she returned there were men marching off down the road past the hospital for their first encounters with the guns at Arras. When Violet heard a fresh contingent going past she dashed off the ward to watch. She'd never knowingly seen an American before, except at the cinema, and though at first sight the khaki men were all disappointingly unlike Douglas Fairbanks or Tom Mix, just soldiers in uniform marching down a sunny road, wearing the expressions of energy and anticipation she had seen on the faces of the British and Commonwealth troops when she arrived two years ago, before the old soldiers learned to live with steady bombardment, fear, discomfort and the loss of friends, and the new ones, arriving, had already heard at home of the horrors to greet them. But this tall contingent's optimism was well-founded. They were strong and healthy. They had come to finish the war, and they would. Some winked at her as they passed. 'Six o'clock here, don't be late,' called one, and the others laughed. A man on crutches beside Violet said, 'They've got a lot to learn.'

'There's a lot of Americans,' Violet told him. 'They won't go away till we've won.'

'Better late than never,' said the man on crutches, despondently. 'Still, I'm off. Got my Blighty one, I'm out and the Yanks are welcome to it.'

'When're you leaving?' Violet asked.

'Tomorrow, the next day – the letter with my sailing date seems to have been held up in the post,' he remarked. 'Having a cup of tea, nurse? I'd like to tell my wife I spent the war drinking tea with pretty women.'

'I shouldn't be here. I've got to get back,' Violet told him.

Swabbing a stomach full of stitches, a fellow VAD turned her head and asked, 'Are you off duty tonight? The American officers have opened the camp at Blaise to British nurses. They've got everything there – food, drink; their CO sends trucks to Brittany to bring in everything. Matron's furious. She's trying to put the camp off limits. Let's go tonight. One of the officers is coming down to pick us up.'

'Ooh,' said Violet, looking at a temperature chart attached to the bottom of the next bed.

'Please,' urged the other nurse's patient. 'All I want is to get bandaged and pull my nightshirt over my modesty.'

'Seize the chance now,' said the other nurse, 'before Matron posts a notice putting a stop to it.'

'All right,' said Violet.

The staff nurse, coming by, ordered, 'Get on with your work, nurses. Levine, how many more times do I have to tell you to adjust your cap? You look as if you'd been pulled through a hedge backwards.'

'If I hear any more about that hedge I'm supposed to have been pulled through I'll scream,' muttered Violet when she'd gone. 'My crowning glory, and this is what it all comes to.'

'If you finish the bandage, and get me done,' the patient, a small man with a ginger moustache and ginger hair said, 'I'll tell you something you'd like to know.' As they tucked his sheets and blankets in neatly he said, 'I'm blessed if I'd let my womenfolk come here and stare at a lot of strange men's bodies.'

'You'd be dead if someone's womenfolk hadn't,' pointed out Violet's companion, a tall blonde girl from Yorkshire, given to direct speech.

'I'm only saying I wouldn't let my own women do it,' said the man. 'It's bound to coarsen them, isn't it? I mean, you look as if you come from a good home. What were your parents thinking of? I mean,' he said to Violet, 'you're a married woman, so it doesn't matter quite so much. Not that I'd like my wife to be here.'

'You're a silly fool,' said the Yorkshire girl, Mabel Preston, pushing his head squarely on the middle of the pillow.

'My water jug's empty, nurse,' said the man in the next bed.

'Are you prepared to take water from the hands of a corrupt woman?' demanded Mabel.

'Well – no,' he said.

'Then I should ask your pious friend in the next bed to get it for you,' she advised, and, consulting her list, walked past him to the next bed where a patient needed her attention.

'You see,' said the man with the ginger moustache, as Violet brought water for his next-door neighbour, 'there you are – that's exactly what I mean: these young girls, bossing about a lot of helpless men, and ticking them off. They won't be fit wives when all this is over.'

'Sit on his wound, nurse,' recommended the other man, whom Violet was propping up as he drank. 'I'd marry that young woman tomorrow, if she'd have me, and if I wasn't a married man – well, twice over, truth to tell,' he said, in a lower voice.

'At the same time?' whispered Violet.

'I'm a commercial traveller in ladies' wear,' he told her. 'Don't tell, though. I know it's against the law, but I didn't have any choice. I was a victim of circumstances.'

'Still chatting on, Levine?' said the staff nurse, pushing a man past in a wheelchair. 'I don't think you're back from leave yet. Fancy another little holiday? And arrange that cap.'

'What I was going to say,' said the man with the ginger moustache, 'before that suffragette was so rude, was that the Italian fellow in the end bed used to be a West End hairdresser. He cuts off ladies' hair free and sends it back to his son, who's a wigmaker. Not that I'd like— '

'My womenfolk to have all their hair cut off,' said Violet. 'I hope you're keeping the keys to their chastity belts safe under your pillow. It wouldn't do for them to get lost.'

'Levine!' called Mabel from a bed down the ward.

'Where are you?'

'I'll come,' whispered Violet over the recumbent body of a young man with a shattered knee. 'And listen, the man in the end bed is a hairdresser.'

Mabel winked and muttered, 'If he's not dead, we'll get him up when staff nurse goes off. Staff nurse Smith's on next and she's always late. If she sends a message as usual, saying she's delayed, that's the moment.' Violet and Mabel finished the bandaging quickly, and the medicines and injections just as soon. By four, Mabel's long fair hair was neatly dressed, and Violet's long black hair lay on the sluice-room floor. The patient determinedly picked up the long locks and put them in a bag before collapsing and being carried back to bed, his head wound leaking. 'I think his wound's broken open,' muttered Mabel, in a panic.

'No it hasn't,' Violet assured her. 'Quick, you bandage him. I'll go back and sweep the rest of my hair off the floor of the sluice. Thank you, Tony,' she called over her shoulder.

'These women would kill a chap for their vanity,' said the ginger man loudly from his bed.

'Shut up,' and 'Killjoy,' called some of the men in the ward, and one or two began a ragged chorus of 'Why were you born so beautiful? Why were you born at all?' from their beds until the belated staff nurse Smith came in hurriedly and put a stop to it.

Violet, her wide VAD hat feeling very big on her short hair, which, once the weight had gone, was curling round her face, was waiting by the main gate with Mabel at six. She was not at all sure she had done the right thing; seeing her long locks on the sluice-room floor had given her a bad shock.

'You look so modern,' Mabel said, arriving in a flurry at the gate.

'Modern's all very well,' said Violet doubtfully.

'It's very nice,' Mabel told her. 'I'm getting mine done before I go back to Oxford. Just because I'm a blue-stocking, I don't want to become a complete old frump.'

A car horn tooted, and a voice called, 'Come on, girls.'

'You can get us back before ten, can't you?' Violet asked the young officer in the driving seat, as they sped through May fields, full of buttercups, to Blaise.

'Any time you like,' he assured her. He was very dark, with an aquiline nose. He had introduced himself as Landry Thomas. 'I can't tell you how much we all admire you girls, for sticking it out here. They tell me you're all volunteers.'

'We two aren't trained nurses,' Mabel told him. 'We're VADs, Voluntary Aid Detachment, attached to the Red Cross, the lowest of the low.'

'We just do light nursing duties,' said Violet.

'What're those?' he asked.

'Cutting legs off,' answered Violet. 'That sort of thing.'

After a pause, he laughed.

'What do you do, at home?' she asked.

'I work in an office,' he told her.

In the wooden hut labelled 'Officers' Mess' they were greeted by the Colonel. There were several other women there, another nurse from No 53 hospital and some French girls in best dresses and hats, one or two with mothers, others with friends, or sisters.

There were also four or five other young women, brightly dressed and talking together. It was obvious to Violet and Mabel that they were not as respectable as the other Frenchwomen, who were ignoring them. Thomas brought Violet and Mabel wine, and introduced a friend, Howard Stanton, who had left his law studies at Harvard to join up. 'Not that I was much good at it,' he said.

'Good heavens, I must apologise,' Landry said, looking at Violet's hand, 'I've been calling you Miss Levine all the time. It must be Mrs Levine, surely?'

Violet nodded. 'I have a little girl,' she said. 'She's being looked after by relatives.'

'And how does your husband feel about you being here in the thick of it?' asked Howard Stanton. 'It's worthy work, heaven knows, but even so . . . '

'My husband's at the front,' Violet said. 'Well, luckily he's just joined General Staff, so he's not fighting any more.' She added, 'But I'm sorry I'm here under false pretences. I may not be a single woman – but I can still dance.'

'And do you dance, Miss Preston?' asked Landry.

'Oh, yes,' Mabel said with enthusiasm. 'I expect you've got ragtime and jazz . . . '

'We most certainly have,' said Landry. 'But, tell me, Mrs Levine, do you think those French ladies are quite happy? Some of them seem uncomfortable. And one or two seem to be leaving.'

'A question of language, perhaps,' said Violet, tactfully.

'I'm afraid you've invited some of the local tarts,' Mabel told him. 'I'm sure it was by accident, but it might be causing difficulties.'

The two men, uneasy about her frankness, still laughed and Landry said, 'Well, I guess hospital nursing brings you close to the realities of life, Miss Preston. But it does create a problem. They must think us very boorish to put them all in the same room together. I don't know how that can have happened.'

'I speak French,' offered Violet. 'I'll tell them it was an accident.'

'Let's speak to the Colonel first,' said Landry, and they walked across the room to him.

'You must think us very stupid,' he said as they went.

'Rubbish. At least you're trying to have a nice time,' retorted Violet.

The Colonel, already beginning to see what had gone wrong, was upset at the mistake and grim about the officers who had invited the local prostitutes. He crossed the room and spoke in French to the respectable ladies. They began to leave, though smiling at the Colonel, who took their elbows to guide them, shook hands and was evidently assuring them he hoped they would meet again.

'What a diplomat!' said Violet, who was watching.

'He'll have ironed it all out,' said Landry. 'His family was originally French. He's spent some time there – here, I should say. I've been in France before a couple of times, just in Paris, but I hardly speak a word of the language. Well, your friend's got her way about those ragtime tunes – shall we dance?'

In the end it got so hot in the mess, and there were so few women left to dance with, they took the gramophone out on to the grass in front of the wooden building. Violet, staring up into Landry Thomas's face, found it very strange, dancing on grass on a May evening, in France, with an American. The whole event was dreamlike; she was claimed by other partners until, finally, she said she was tired, and must sit down, and there was Landry Thomas, at her side, with a bottle of wine and two glasses.

'Your friend's enjoying herself,' said Landry.

Mabel was passing by, waltzing, now, with a tall major. 'I think it's lucky her mother can't see her now,' said Violet. 'Her father's a Methodist minister and I don't think they'd like to think of her dancing with soldiers in that sort of way – and some of the other ladies at this ball aren't all they should be.'

'I guess she's got a good excuse. She must need to unwind, somehow. How about you?' Landry said. 'Have you actually been to the front?'

'We're not really supposed to,' said Violet. 'But I went once on the sly, to the rear lines, to visit my husband. I got a lift. It's – it's not like anything you can imagine.'

She did not tell him what she had seen, or heard, or

smelt. On the day she went it had been drizzling, and the air was thick with the smoke and fumes of gunpowder, like a fog. She had walked on a duckboard, following a soldier and, below her, ten feet down, in trenches, there were men sitting on boxes, cleaning rifles, drinking tea out of mugs, talking, smoking. They had walked to a group of three trees, the tops shot off, trunks in splinters, and there she had found Frederick. Everywhere there were men in khaki, plodding, dark as the mud that surrounded them. The light was going, on a November afternoon. There was no colour anywhere, a smell of old mud and unwashed men, the lingering smell of explosives underneath. The same long night was setting in, along four hundred miles of trenches which ran in a semi-circle from the coast of Belgium, across Picardy, Normandy, Champagne, the Bourgogne, preventing the enemy from taking the rest of France and, from the coast, launching an attack on Britain. The army's third winter there was beginning. Violet was standing, shocked, when Frederick came up, equally horrified to find her there.

Violet said to Landry through the darkness, 'He told me I shouldn't have come because of the danger of attack. But it explained a lot to me.' She had a sudden fear for the young, handsome American Captain. Would he end up, like so many, sitting shell-shocked in a garden somewhere, sobbing continually? Or permanently silent, and looking ahead of him?

Landry sat still in the darkness. He said, 'You're a strange one, Mrs Levine. A strange one. We're leaving soon, they say. Will you let me come and see you when we get some leave?'

'Of course,' said Violet.

'Well,' he said. 'This is something. This is really something. Imagine that I come three thousand miles to France, you come across to France, and we meet here, in a little village called Blaise, in Normandy. And here we sit, on the grass . . . ' His voice trailed off.

There was a slight sound of wind in the trees behind them. The stars seemed very big in a clear sky. The gramophone was taken back inside. The dancers drifted after it and the music started up again, at a distance. 'I think . . . ' said Landry, 'well . . . maybe not.'

'Maybe not what?' asked Violet.

'Just a thought – nothing. My family has Indian blood. We're very intuitive.'

Violet smiled, looking at him through the darkness. Neither of them spoke until she said, 'I must go and keep an eye on Mabel.'

'Yes,' he said, standing up. 'You're her chaperone, I suppose. You seem very young for the part.'

'I'll be twenty-one next Christmas,' Violet said. They reached the door of the hut. Neither wanted to go in. 'Well . . . ' said Violet.

'Yes,' said Landry. 'I'll think of you, in my lovely trench.'

'Trenches aren't lovely,' said Violet. 'The reverse, in fact.'

'I'll think of you anyway. Come on, then. Don't miss supper.'

Orderlies were putting heaps of food – cheeses, huge pâtés, plates of ham and beef, salads – on a long trestle table.

'Mabel,' hissed Violet as plates were loaded, 'you'll be ill if you eat all that. And you were dancing too close to that Major.'

'And you were out in the dark with a captain,' Mabel hissed back. 'And you're a married woman.'

'Girls, girls, girls,' warned Howard Stanton, coming up with the close-dancing Major, and hearing fragments of Mabel's accusation. 'No quarrelling here. Let me find you ladies some seats. Or shall we take our plates outside?'

So they picnicked on the grass, Mabel, Violet, Howard Stanton, Landry Thomas and the Major, Anton Driffield, who was obviously very taken with Mabel. 'When all this is over,' he asked her, 'where will you be? Will you go on nursing?'

'I sometimes think I'd like to do nursing training,' she said. 'But I was at Oxford for a year, and I ought to go back. My father and mother will be very disappointed if I don't.'

'It's natural they should want you at home, I dare say,' he said. 'But I think a girl should have some kind of career or occupation before she marries.'

'Anton's from Wisconsin. They let the women vote there,' said Howard Stanton.

'Only in Wisconsin?' asked Violet.

'And in Arizona and Kansas,' said Mabel.

'You're well informed,' Anton Driffield told her.

'My mother's done two spells in Holloway for the vote,' explained Mabel. 'She was forcibly fed once. Then Father said he'd rather she didn't for her own sake, and because it was causing a lot of dissension in the congregation, too. Some were for her, and some were saying they didn't want a minister whose wife behaved like that. But I think his main reason for asking her to stop attending meetings and so forth was because he thought the next time they might kill her. In case the pipe they use for forcible feeding missed, and tore her. So she stopped – she couldn't stand seeing him so worried, and the congregation saying nasty things about him.'

'It's mediaeval,' said Howard Stanton. 'When you think of England you think of hunting, and fogs, and cottage gardens, and big ships going all over the world— '

'It's got to be different, when you get close to it,' said Landry.

'Well, when we think of America we think of skyscrapers and cowboys and Indians and big plantations with slaves. I don't suppose that's much like it, either,' Violet said, but was really thinking of Landry Thomas's Indian blood. Was he serious? Did he mean his mother was a squaw, like at the pictures? Or his father a man in a feathered headdress? He didn't look like that, in his army uniform, unless his very black, shining eyes, which Violet compared with the lumps of lustrous, glistening best coal with which she had often filled the front room scuttle, were a sign of Indian blood.

The eyes were gleaming straight at her now in the darkness. 'We've got a lot to learn about each other,' he said. 'Let's drink to it.'

'A lot to learn,' they repeated, raising their glasses.

And soon it was time to leave. Violet made Mabel sit in the front of the car with Landry. She stared at his broad back. He spoke over his shoulder to her just as she spoke to him, 'You must miss your little girl. I'll get word to you when we're going,' he said. They shook hands when they got out of the car, and Landry squeezed hers. She squeezed back.

'You clicked with the Captain,' Mabel said bluntly as they walked away from the gate where he'd dropped them, towards the hospital.

'Oh, Mabel,' said Violet, 'don't be so crude.'

'Still, don't deny it. You like him,' she said. Their voices dropped as they walked past the first buildings.

'I'm married, Mabel,' said Violet. 'And they're going up the line in a day or two, maybe tomorrow. And he told me he was a Red Indian. So don't be silly.'

'Yes, but if they weren't going?' Mabel said.

'You're a young girl who knows nothing about life, and goodnight,' said Violet, walking off to the hut she shared with another VAD, who was, when she got in, asleep.

She undressed quietly and got into bed, shivered as she thought of Landry Thomas before falling asleep, and dreaming she was a squaw with two big thick plaits, and Landry was chasing her through a forest, trying to cut them off with a tomahawk.

The next day Matron posted a notice saying that in the interests of good discipline nurses, VADs and other female staff were forbidden to enter army camps without express permission from her.

'So that's that,' said Mabel, as they ate breakfast in the big nurses' canteen. 'Back to hard work and bread and marge again. She must have got up at the crack of dawn to put up that notice. Still, there's one good thing – Major Driffield and Howard Stanton are devout Episcopalians, so they'll have to go to the English church at St Luc and of course I have to go every Sunday because I promised Mother and Father to go regularly to the nearest non-Catholic church. I don't know what you can do, though, Violet, since your gentleman friend's a Red Indian. You can't really say you've got to go and dance round a totem pole with him, can you?'

Violet, reading a letter which had just arrived from Sophie, who conscientiously kept her in touch with affairs at Farnley, took no notice. 'Oh, how terrible. My husband's cousin's been killed by a sniper somewhere near Vimy and his twin brother's been taken prisoner.'

'They're deadly, those bloody snipers. Better than us,' said a nurse, sitting at the table.

Violet didn't mention that it was Frederick's Austrian cousin Rudolph who had been killed, by the British, or that his twin, Hanno, was now in the hands of the British, not the German army. She kept very quiet about her connection with the Levine family in general. There had been a flurry of interest when the *Daily Sketch* took her photograph bending over a good-looking soldier with curly hair. She saw, wryly, she had been recruited into the battalion of upper-class ladies doing their bit, and suspected her mother-in-law was behind it, keen to publicise the patriotic efforts of the British side of the family in an atmosphere hostile to people who might be seen as having divided loyalties. Nevertheless, after the photograph had been published over a year ago, the brief fuss died down. In the little world of No 53 hospital, St Luc, amid the discomforts, the alternating periods of tedium and crisis, no one was very interested in Violet's family.

In her letter Sophie also gave the news that Pamela was well, as usual. Jo-Jo, now eight, had developed measles, but Pamela had not caught it. Food was difficult to obtain – 'no sugar last week, no flour at all'. She thought that now the Americans had entered the war and there was such hope of victory Violet might, at last, contemplate coming home. Her own health, she said, was not very good and Caroline was making more frequent trips to London which she was sure did her good, but increased her own burdens a good deal. 'The work you do is vitally important, I know, dear Violet, but surely you have done enough?' she wrote. 'I feel sure, too, that Frederick would be much reassured if he knew that you were safe, and playing your part in guarding the welfare of the family at home.'

Violet folded the letter and put it in her pocket. 'Time to face men's surgical again,' she said to Mabel.

The staff nurse handed her a note which was lying on the ward table when they came in. 'I hope you won't make a practice of having your correspondence delivered here by the American army,' she said, handing it to Violet, adding, 'I'm glad to see you've solved the problem of the quarrel between your cap and your hair. It's a radical solution, but it seems to work. Before you rush to the sluice to read your letter, I should like the dressings on this list dealt with punctiliously.'

As Mabel and Violet checked the trolley containing carbolic, surgical spirit, gauze, bandages, tweezers, scissors and pins, she told them, 'Three lorry-loads of wounded, and two farm carts are on their way here from the dressing stations at the front. The lories will arrive this afternoon, the carts in the evening. No off-duty till further notice, I'm afraid. Though I think you two have had yours. Matron's not pleased,' she added.

'Who told?' Mabel demanded in an undertone as they went down the ward with the clattering trolley. 'I bet it was that Holy Joe in bed eight. I'll take his stitches out for him if I find out he ratted.'

'He'll suffer enough when he has to get up to make room for the others,' said Violet, also in an undertone. 'At least half of these men are going to have to be promoted to convalescence.'

'Yes,' said Mabel. 'There'll be about a hundred and fifty men coming in, and some'll be very bad. Might be gas cases too. I'll bet they put you back in the operating theatre again. No one likes to admit it, but you're better than some of the trained nurses.'

'I don't like it there,' said Violet, feeling a supporting warmth through her apron pocket where her letter from the American camp was lying.

'Here it doesn't matter what you like,' said Mabel, stopping the trolley. 'Well, Private Betterton, I hope you've produced a nice lot more pus for us today. We're fed up with having nowt to do.'

'Well, I'm sorry to disappoint you, nurse,' said the private, a small Yorkshire pitman who had been blown up by a faulty detonator in a tunnel he was mining near the German lines, 'I'm healing nicely, thank you very much.'

'Thanks for the news,' said Mabel, whipping back the bedclothes. 'Of course, you'd know first, having undone your own bandages in the night.'

'And so would you, if you knew it was the difference between them trying to send you back and not going.'

'Going back, it looks like,' said Mabel, bandaging.

'Not me,' he told her.

'Oh, yes, you will,' she said.

'Oh, no I won't.'

'You'd better start getting headaches, then,' she said. 'Because you'll be up today to make room for others, and after that it'll be back in the lorry and off to do your bit again.'

'Is that right?' he asked.

'As one good Yorkshireman to another, that's the way of it,' she told him. 'So if you don't want to go, headaches are the answer. You'd best start clutching your head and moaning.'

'Why should he go, and leave a widow and five children?' she said fiercely to Violet, but Violet wasn't there. She'd abandoned the trolley while Mabel was bandaging, and was standing in the sluice-room by the big enamel sink, reading her note from Landry Thomas.

> There's been a cancellation of previous plans, so, dear Violet, can you meet me at the Café des Anges in St Luc this evening? I'll be waiting from seven o'clock onwards.
>
> Ever,
> Landry

Violet's heart was thudding. And she knew the chances of getting off duty that night, with lorry-loads of wounded coming in, was very slight. 'Oh,' she said aloud, in fury. 'Oh.'

'Violet,' came Mabel's voice from the doorway. 'What are you doing?' Violet thrust the note in her apron pocket. 'Come on, Violet – you know perfectly well when we've done the temperatures, the bandages and medicine trolley we're going to have to move everybody, and do all the transfer lists and change all the beds. If we get behind now it'll be murder later on.'

From then on they were very busy, producing crutches and wheelchairs, loading the nearly recovered into lorries heading for the port, where they would be shipped home, and preparing the ward for the new patients. They had half an hour to bolt down a meal of sausages and mashed potatoes, and a cup of strong tea. They rallied themselves for the next emergency, as they had so often before. Violet often wondered how long they could all go on. By two thirty they were surveying a ward of thirty beds, containing only ten patients, all of whom had been warned by the staff nurse to cause as little trouble as possible. 'All ready for the party to start, now,' said Mabel.

At three the first lorry rolled in. After one look at the interior, Matron, a small, dark woman who, Mabel said, seemed to be worked by silent clockwork and springs, not flesh and blood, ordered a tent, with an operating table, to be set up on the grass opposite number one operating theatre, and told Violet to go to number one, so an experienced nurse, who could cope better with primitive arrangements, could be put in the tent to assist the surgeon there.

Five minutes later the surgeon at the number one theatre, Dr Swann, two nurses and Violet, were looking at the first man on the table. He was half-conscious and bleeding from a head wound, blood had soaked his tunic from his chest downwards. He could hardly breathe. 'Gassed,' said Dr Swann. 'A whiff of ether and get an orderly to hold him down. Levine, you'll have to clean up his head while we do the rest.'

One of the nurses cut the tunic and shirt from top to bottom, revealing five or six bullet wounds. 'They're still in there,' said Swann. A nurse came up to where Violet was and put ether on a pad. 'Not much,' said Swann. 'He won't be able to take it. You'd better come here and hold him,' he told an orderly. 'Hang on to his feet.' He added, 'Have any of the men you're moving been anywhere near a dressing station?'

'No, doctor,' said the orderly. 'My God,' he said, as he cut back the soldier's jacket and shirt, then made an incision in the man's chest. The man moaned, and began to move about. The orderly had him by his shoulders, until he became unconscious.

Dr Swann dropped the last bullet on the floor. 'We'll need five minutes between patients, to clear up,' he said to the senior nurse, 'otherwise it'll be an abattoir.'

She nodded. He found another bullet. Violet, holding pad after pad of gauze to the man's head, said, 'Doctor, his skull's shattered. The bleeding won't stop.'

'Describe the wound, nurse,' said one of the other nurses, holding the moaning man to the operating table.

'Two inches of cranium over the left ear shot away,' she said. 'I don't think there's anything in the wound.'

'Pack it, then,' she said. 'Then bandage.'

Violet, cutting away the man's soaked hair, packing gauze into the hole in his skull, hoped she was right that there were no shrapnel fragments in his head. If there were, it looked as if they'd be staying there. Halfway through, his head stopped moving. He'd lost consciousness, or died. She went on. Swann, breathing hard, discovered another bullet and murmured, 'Only one to go . . . ' Violet finished the packing of the man's skull and began bandaging, knowing he must still be alive. But just after his chest had been sewn up, he died. Orderlies sped his body away as the nurses cleared the floor of pieces of uniform, gauze and bullets. Violet thrust all the pieces of bloodstained gauze round her feet into the bin, got a bucket, mopped the floor. Dr Swann, who had been examining the men on stretchers outside, where nurses were trying to get them ready to be operated on, came in a minute or two later, as they were still cleaning up, too busy even to speak to each other. 'Ready?' he asked. A nurse shook her head and went on cleaning the operating table with huge sweeps of her arm. Violet put the lid on the bin with a clang.

'Quietly, Levine,' said a nurse automatically, taking the instruments from the steriliser. 'Ready now, Dr Swann.'

This man had had his boot removed and his trouser leg cut off, revealing a shattered knee and a pulped leg, where fragments of bone protruded. He lay there, staring at the ceiling, in his stained uniform. 'Leg off above the knee. Ether,' said Swann. As a nurse held the pad over the soldier's nose, Swann said, 'I'm sorry' to the man, who had probably already lost consciousness. Picking up his scalpel he said, 'The dressing stations can't manage the number of wounded. One's been completely knocked out by a shell. They're loading them into vehicles just as they are. These men have come sixty miles today. It's a miracle more aren't dead.'

And so the afternoon went on. It became hotter, the smell of fouled uniforms, stiff with clotted blood, urine and faeces, of pus and fresh blood coming from the wounds, was more suffocating. Ether fumes were not leaving the room quickly enough, on this windless May day. 'We can't go on. We've got to stop,' muttered one of the nurses. It was as she spoke that Swann, who had just sawed through the ankle bone of a boy of no more than sixteen – and Violet, dizzy, knew he was dead, and that he was her own dead brother, Frank – dropped to the floor.

'Oh, my God,' said one of the nurses. Violet, standing next to the doctor's prone body, picked the scalpel from the bloody table and cut down to the table through the flesh and skin of the boy's ankle. The foot, already red, swollen with infection, fell off the end of the table, on to the floor, on to her shoe, near Dr Swann. She stood staring at both. 'Orderly!' called the nurse opposite her. 'Orderly!' Her voice cracked but she began to stitch the stump. The orderly's mouth dropped open when he saw Dr Swann on the floor. A second later he was dragging the doctor through the mess and out of the hut.

Outside, Violet and the orderly had laid him on the grass, near six soldiers, with blankets over them, on stretchers waiting for surgery. A nurse came out of the door of the tent opposite, dragging a bin overflowing with bloodstained gauze and bandages, saw the doctor lying there, said, 'Criminy!' left the bin and went back to the tent. Matron came up, summoned, it must have been, by instinct from inside a nearby ward where soldiers were being put to bed, and said to Violet, as if she were responsible, 'What happened?'

'He collapsed. Probably the ether,' she said.

'And the patient?' asked the Matron.

'He'd finished the operation – nearly.'

Matron went straight into the operating theatre, came out, and said, 'Thank God you all kept your heads.' Dr Swann was coming round, trying to remember what happened. The Matron bent over him and said, 'You collapsed, doctor. The ether.'

'The man . . . ' he said.

'You finished the operation. The nurses put in stitches.' She glared commandingly at Violet. Violet took a deep breath and said, 'Yes, Dr Swann.'

Matron straightened up and said, 'Well, these premises don't ventilate properly. Go back inside, nurse, and clear up what you can. Then you'll take an hour's break, have a meal, go for a walk, or lie down. Back on duty in an hour. Clean uniforms.'

Violet went back to the hut. 'And do not faint there,' Matron's voice came after her. Orderlies were carrying the unconscious boy out. Violet told the other nurses what Matron had said, adding, 'She ordered us not to faint.'

'Well, if those are the orders, we won't,' said one of the nurses muzzily.

After the meal Violet detached herself from the group, due

back in the operating theatre in half an hour, and went to walk along the cliff beside the hospital. In the field beyond it she sat down. She was tired, and after another two hours of this gruelling day she would be more tired, but the bus into St Luc passed the hospital at eight, and she'd decided to be on it. They could sack her, send her home, afterwards, for all she cared. She was going to meet Landry, even if the whole army tried to stop her. When the farm carts with the wounded in them arrived, she thought, half the men would be dead anyway, and others might be gas cases, and wouldn't need surgery. In any case, she was leaving No 53 hospital tonight and going to the village to meet Landry. That was that. She stood up, looked over the sea towards England, heard the gulls crying and the distant thudding of mortars and bombardment, brought by the wind. She went back to the canteen and found the others; then they walked through the huts and the wounded men sitting on the grass to continue the ordeal.

By seven, the light was fading outside and the heat of the afternoon had given way to a cool breeze from the sea. In number one operating theatre Violet and the other two nurses had felt they were too weary to go on handing instruments, stitching, bandaging and clearing the table of blood and the floor of shell fragments, old bandages and pieces of uniform and flesh – they had felt all this, and had for a time rallied, calling up more endurance from some source which, they all knew, did not exist. As Violet and an orderly were heaving a young Australian, whose back had been lacerated in ten places by shrapnel, on to a stretcher, a cheerful, '*Bonsoir*' came from the doorway. Three nuns from the French military hospital, crisply coiffed with starched aprons over their black habits, had arrived. An appeal from the Matron to neighbouring hospitals had met with a response, though, as the nuns said, there having been a muddle over transport, they had all had to pedal to St Luc, with their fresh aprons and coifs in carpet-bags attached to the bicycle handles. 'Matron says you're off duty,' said one of the nuns.

'We're off duty,' said Violet, who was translating, to Dr Swann.

'They didn't send a surgeon on a bicycle, too, did they?'

asked Swann. His eyes were bloodshot and his face grey.

Orderlies carried out the Australian soldier and brought in a man in German uniform. 'This one's a Boche,' a man said.

'So we see,' replied Swann, tiredly.

Violet thought only of the café in St Luc, as if meeting Landry would take the ache from her legs and feet, and wipe out the memory of the afternoon's pain, mess and, in two instances, death. She stood very still with her arms by her sides, trying not to attract Dr Swann's attention in case he decided she could be of use as a translator. Four men remained to be operated on. Another cart-load could come in before they had finished. But Swann thanked the nurses and sent them off.

Violet was washing her hair in the showers when she said to Mabel, who was being given a break, but would be needed on the ward again at two in the morning, 'You'll have to cover for me. I'm going to St Luc.'

'They'll kill you if they find out. All leave's cancelled till further notice,' said Mabel, leaning against the wooden wall of the showers with a stained apron dangling from her fingers by its tape.

'That's why you've got to tell them I'm here,' said Violet.

'What am I going to say? They'll kill me too.'

'Say I'm asleep,' said Violet, 'if anyone asks.'

'That girl you share with, Helen, won't.'

'Oh, I don't care,' said Violet, putting on her camisole and, over it, a pink and green sprigged cotton dress.

Mabel made a face, seeing Violet out of uniform. 'They'll kill you.'

Violet tugged on her drawers, picked her shoes from the floor of the shower and said, 'I'm off.'

'No stockings?' asked Mabel.

'No,' returned Violet, and walked out of the shower, through the field at the outskirts of the hospital, and squeezed through the hole in a hedge which bolder nurses, and sometimes patients, used to get in after the main gate was locked at night. She stood back against the hedge until the bus for St Luc came down the road, then hopped out and flagged it down. The bus drove slowly through winding roads, with trees and hedges on either side, and drew into the square at St Luc.

The Café des Anges was crowded with soldiers and girls. A few of the elderly patrons who had always gone there in the evenings, war or no war, and would do so until they died, or the café was bombed, sat at tables drinking their wine or cognac. Standing in the entrance Violet looked for Landry, and couldn't see him. She even wondered wildly if she would be able to recognise him. Perhaps her memory of him – for she had been imagining his long, pale face and large, but very slightly slanted black eyes, throughout the day – was wrong. She had mostly seen him in the dark. It had been a consolation to be able to think of him as she'd gazed down at pained, sweating faces. There had been times, too, that day, when, tired and perhaps having inhaled too much ether, she wondered if she were to blame for all this suffering. Was that why she had to be there, at No 53 hospital, trying against all the odds to cure it? At such time the bright, healthy face of Landry Thomas, appearing before her, helped to obliterate the nightmare. But as she stared about in the thick atmosphere, she saw no one like the man she had been thinking about until a voice at her side said, 'Violet? Mrs Levine?' and she turned to see him standing beside her.

'I have a table across the square, at Mère Laclos',' he told her. 'Be quick, or someone will get it.' He took her arm and steered her out of the café and across the dark, cobbled square to a house where the ground floor was converted into a restaurant. As they went, he said, 'I realised, too late, that the Café des Anges was not for you.'

'I've been there before,' Violet said. 'And I grew up in a humble home. My father was a policeman.' This was not something she ever said and she wondered why she was admitting it now.

'I doubt if your father would like to think of you in the Café des Anges,' he told her as they went into a low room, where there were tables, and sat down. 'You must be tired.'

'It's been a dreadful day. There's been a big push near Arras . . . '

He nodded, said, 'Sh . . . I may not be able to see you tomorrow.'

She realised he was telling her his regiment was moving off next day. She realised, too, that the look of panic she gave him must have shouted how horrified she was at the thought of his departure. The woman who ran the restaurant brought them soup.

'So there were many wounded?' he asked.

She could not tell him what the afternoon had been like because she could not describe, to a man going into battle for the first time, what happened to the soldiers.

'Yes,' she said. 'But you never know whether there have been a lot of casualties, or your hospital's been sent them all, while in another military hospital the nurses are playing cards with the patients.'

'The countryside around here is so beautiful,' he murmured. 'And so old. You think the fields have been here for ever. Twenty, thirty generations have ploughed those fields, cut back those hedges, repaired those walls.'

'It's newer where you come from,' Violet said. 'Where is it?'

'New England – New York.'

'What about the Red Indians?' asked Violet.

'Some generations back,' he said, smiling. 'I suppose you must have thought I could tell you thrilling tales of the old West – about robbing trains and scalpings. I'm sorry I built up your hopes. The family's very quiet and respectable now.'

'Why did you volunteer?'

'I felt bad, reading about the casualties. And if the Germans win the war, it will be no good to the USA.'

Violet didn't understand.

'Trade,' he explained.

'Oh,' said Violet. He gazed at her. The woman took away their soup plates and brought plates of roasted rabbit. She smiled at him.

'Shall we go for a walk afterwards?' he asked.

Violet, knowing she was prepared, like any of the other girls, to lie naked on Landry Thomas's greatcoat down by the sand dunes at the edge of the forest south of St Luc, nodded.

She and Landry made love on the beach, in the dunes, to the sound of the sea coming in and out. Neither before, nor after, did they talk about the war or, for that matter, the question of Violet's husband. She lay in his arms, fairly astonished that she had felt pleasure unmixed by other thoughts. But she was still planning – she would go away with Landry whenever, if ever, she was free to leave the army. She'd leave Frederick, the Levines, even her child if she had to. She knew Landry Thomas could make her happy. No man she had ever known so far had persuaded her he could. Even at the very beginning Tom had seemed a mistake, Frederick Levine another, though lesser one. And always, with them, she'd felt restricted, required to play a part. Here, with Landry, she thought, was freedom. Shivering now, they watched the sun's tip come up over the sea, then, arm in arm, went back to Landry's purloined army van. He dropped her at the hospital, where she crept back through the hole in the hedge, got quietly into her bed, while her hut-mate still slept, and fell asleep.

Next day the rumours that the army had broken the Hindenburg Line were confirmed. 'Let's hope it's the beginning of the end,' said Mabel, but Violet's eyes were on the couple of hundred yards of mud and craters separating the two lines of trenches, the rusting barbed wire between them where a man might die screaming because no one could go out through the bombardment to rescue him until nightfall, where the bodies of the dead were sometimes not reclaimed but lay buried in mud until the next explosion brought them, or what was left of them, to the surface. She thought of that khaki and mud world, overhung with a heavy sky, which she had seen when she went to visit Frederick, that place where men arrived in their full strength and left, if they left at all, wounded in body or spirit, or both. The man she had lain with last night on the beach was due to go there that day, or the next. A few days later he might be nothing but a stiffening body on the bare soil of No Man's Land. She had seen the place, and nursed the men who came back from it. She had seen the wounds and looked into their shocked eyes. Between infatuation and a wild and uncertain hope for a future with Landry and the dreadful fear of his never returning she had no room for other thoughts. He could get a message to her today, he had promised, but all she could see was a column of men marching down from the American camp, past the hospital, and Landry with them. The fact that Frederick had refused to stay safely behind the lines on the General Staff, was now fighting in Italy, with nearly as good a chance of death or injury, troubled Violet not at all.

More wounded came in that day, but the nurses, including the nursing nuns, were sufficient to staff the operating theatres and although the work among post-operative men in the medical ward was hard, the worst part of the previous day's crisis was over. Violet went through her duties mechanically, waiting for Landry's message. Finally, after her third visit to the station at the main gate, there was a scribbled note for her.

> Plans cancelled again. On duty tonight, but can we meet tomorrow?
>
> All my love,
> Landry

She met him at St Luc the following evening, this time respectably in uniform. She had told no one about leaving the hospital to meet Landry. Now, when she saw Mabel on her way out, she said she was going into St Luc to talk to the dressmaker who was making her two new cotton dresses for the summer.

'You might have put it off until tomorrow,' complained Mabel. 'Then we could have gone in the afternoon when we're both off duty. We could have had tea there . . . '

'We can still go,' lied Violet, who planned to sleep through her off-duty time next day.

She and Landry lay on the beach later that night, staring up at the moon. He said awkwardly, 'Violet, do you really love your husband?'

'Not really,' she said. 'If I did I suppose I wouldn't be here.'

'I thought, perhaps – you haven't seen a lot of him . . . I thought I might be a kind of temporary solution.'

'No, Landry,' she replied and asked, fearing the reply, 'Have you got a girl at home?'

'Two or three,' he said. 'But you're the real thing.'

'Am I?' she said, delighted, raising herself on an arm and looking down at him.

He pulled her down. 'What did you think?' He closed his eyes. 'But, my God, I wish this was over.'

'Wish you hadn't come?' she asked.

'I wish it'd get started,' he told her.

'Oh, Landry . . . ' she began. She wanted to suggest they both left, now, before he went to the front. They could run away somewhere – Spain, Portugal, anywhere at all, and be happy until the war was over. But she knew it was not a suggestion he could accept. 'When you've done your bit,' she said, 'couldn't we go away together? I'd like it so much.'

'Let's make the most of what we've got,' he said, holding her tightly, 'while we've got the time.'

For the rest of that night, until dawn, Violet forgot herself enough not to think, or plan. But as she lay on her narrow bed in her hut, agitated, sleepless, nearly delirious with happiness and the piercing fear of that happiness ending, as it would, when Landry's regiment moved off, remembering the smell of the sea, the stars, the feel of Landry's warm body on hers, she could not prevent herself from planning, wistfully, an escape with him, a new life, in a new country.

The dream-life – snatched meetings late at night, a picnic in the forest by the sea one afternoon – went on for another five days. When it ended it came in the form of an envelope pushed under the door of her hut during the night or early morning. She noticed it as she got out of bed, pounced on it, ripped it open and read it, sitting on her bed.

My dearest Violet,

We have orders to leave today. I love you. I love you dearly, and for ever. When we meet again, we must talk about the future. Until then, I'll be thinking of you constantly. I'll write as soon as I can. I love you. I love you,

Landry

'What's that?' said the red-headed girl she shared with, waking and looking blearily across at Violet.

'Nothing,' said Violet. 'Nothing at all.'

'I've seen you, Vi,' the girl said, yawning. 'Coming in at all hours . . . ' and she fell asleep again.

What difference did it make now if she'd been seen, thought Violet, getting up wearily, picking up her clothes and heading for the showers. As the tepid water flowed over her she thought it might be all right. Not everybody dies. She got out, dried herself, got into her uniform and began the long, dreary day.

Kate Higgins, June 1st, 1991

I'd been in Brighton for four days and there was still no news of Sam. After days of confusion and sporadic fighting by the British army, and agitated diplomacy by Britain, America and the United Nations, there was now an official UN resolution stating that Britain had no right or duty to employ its army in an internal conflict in Belize. Troops were to be withdrawn immediately while the United Nations met to consider its position.

The embarrassment of the British government was over, although immediate withdrawal of the troops was not possible in reality. The airport and harbour at Belize were still being fought over, air force planes couldn't get in, British troop-carriers were cruising a mile off the coast waiting for a chance to land. Official statements said that British troops had withdrawn, or were withdrawing to their bases in Belize where they would remain until it was possible to leave. This sounded all right, unless you hadn't had news of Captain Samuel Rogers since the outbreak of the conflict.

At Brighton, mostly because of Ray, we lived the way people do when they're waiting for news – trying to be natural, sometimes even believing for hours that things were really normal, sometimes overcome with anxiety, not talking about the situation, so as not to upset each other. For my part, I felt all I needed was for Sam to die, leaving Ray fatherless, while I conducted an insecure relationship with a glamorous and heroic journalist and tried to make a dubious living in London. Selfishly, I cursed Sam, and the army, for turning me into a soldier's girl, dockside weeper, the woman whose whole life has to pay homage to heroes. I hadn't asked Sam to be a soldier. The newspaper talk of our Brave Boys in Belize didn't help. If poor Sam died a dirty death in some pathetic little war that need never have happened, I'd be the one to pick up the pieces.

I suppose this was the point where I might well have thought of Andy's proposal – but I didn't. From Brighton, it looked like a fantasy. I hadn't heard from Andy since I'd left London. When I rang the paper they said he was on leave;

the answering machine at his flat gave out the usual neutral message, that he'd ring callers back as soon as he could. Even now I can't understand why I didn't include Andy in my thoughts about the future. I can't claim to have been guided by any deep, womanly instinct, running below conscious thought. I was perfectly rational, in the way women have to be rational – weighing other people's thoughts, feelings and general trajectory, and their own, and all the practical considerations, short- and long-term, and all possibilities and probabilities attendant on all the aspects. Somehow the possibility of life with Andy didn't weigh very heavily in the scale-pan.

I just did what I could in Brighton: stayed with Ray, helped about the house, worked as much as I could on the life of Violet Levine. I borrowed the car, and by spending two afternoons searching the bookshops of the south coast, I actually found one of Violet's two thirties novels, *Carriage Paid*. It felt like luck, then, and in retrospect seems even more so.

My parents were out that evening and Ray had gone to bed. I turned the news on, low, so that he wouldn't hear it, and there, mercifully, was a picture of a troopship leaving the harbour at Belize City, full of British soldiers. The government, in control, whether temporarily or permanently, of the harbour, was assisting the troops to leave. I went up and told Ray. I said, 'It doesn't mean for certain Dad's safe, but it might. I'll ring in the morning – see if I can get more news.'

'I'll be at school,' he said.

'If I hear anything definite, I'll come and tell you,' I told him.

Then the phone rang, and I went to answer it. It was Andy. He said, 'It's been days. I'm sorry. There's been an enquiry on that Sweetwater Village affair. I've been at the Foreign Office for two days – top level stuff at *The Witness* – an epic carry-on.'

He sounded tense. 'What's it all about?' I asked.

'They're trying to get full information about which side did it.'

'It doesn't make sense,' I said. 'In a way it doesn't matter who did it. There's a war on – all sorts of horrors must be happening.'

'In the propaganda war, it's who did the atrocities that counts,' he said.

'So, who did it?' I asked.

'Obviously, the government side.'

The pictures had been horrible. A heap of bodies in the middle of the village, the body of a girl of about ten crumpled against the wooden wall of a small house, a dead woman on the body of a small child.

'The village was said to be anti-government – at any rate, the owner of the sawmill, an Englishman called Arthurs, was against the Marxist government. He thought they might nationalise the forests. And, after all, I saw the government troops leaving. Pity old Joe, the photographer, died – AIDS, would you believe it? – so I'm the only witness. Anyway, that's what's going on here. I'd like to come down. Would that be possible? Any news of Ray's father? Troopships seem to be picking up some of the army.'

'Where are you?' I asked him, I don't know why.

He paused. 'Well, a friend's flat,' he said. 'Charlie's.'

'Oh,' I said, realising that the pause and the slight change in his tone meant I couldn't believe him. I shouldn't have asked.

'Are you still there?' he said.

I said, 'Yes. Course I am. Well, when would you like to come?' And all the time I was opening the drawer of the hall table, on which the telephone stood and pulling out my address book. As soon as I'd found Charlie Garner's number I rang off, leaving Andy in mid-sentence, and rang him. I asked if I could speak to Andy.

'He's not here,' Charlie told me. 'I haven't seen him since he got back.'

'Oh dear,' I replied insincerely. 'He said he was at your place. We got cut off.'

Charlie rallied, though without enthusiasm, 'Well, he was coming over . . . '

'Perhaps he could give me a ring when he arrives,' I said.

I stood in the hall, not surprised, just jaded and fed up. Having to think that Sam might be killed had altered priorities more than I realised. At the first sign of trouble I'd instinctively gone to Brighton. I'd decided, reluctantly, but without too much difficulty, to stay there with Ray if Sam was dead. That I'd agreed to make it permanent, one way or another, with Andy didn't seem to mean anything to me. Now I'd checked up on him, found out he was lying and I didn't care.

The phone rang. It was Andy again. 'Kate, we were cut off.'

'I know,' I said. 'I rang Charlie, but you weren't there.'

'I wasn't supposed to say where I was,' he told me, using the Top Secret gambit. 'I'm going back to the flat now. I could get down tomorrow and stay a few days. I'll book in at a hotel.'

'You could stay . . . '

'No – a hotel's better,' he said. 'I'll ring when I get in. It'll be a wonderful change from all this conferring and reports and statements.'

'Good,' I said.

For all I knew he'd been at Downing Street when he rang. But I doubted it.

Then my parents came in and I told them the navy had been able to start the evacuation of the troops from Belize. Feeling easier in my mind, even though there still wasn't any news of Sam, I went off to bed and propped myself up with *Carriage Paid*, written by Violet in 1934, not, frankly, expecting to be very much excited by it. In fact I thought it might be soporific – Violet's fiction was not, it had to be said, the stuff which changes people's lives. Her biography had made a difference to many readers, mostly women, being the record of an eventful, energetic, courageous life. She'd played an active part in two world wars, started a promising career in parliament fairly late in life and even when that career came to an abrupt end she still continued to campaign for what she thought right. And although I was beginning to see by that stage that her account of herself was doubtful, to say the least, it wasn't taking away part of the essential truth of her life. Of course, at that point I didn't know the rest. The novels, though, were a different matter. The ones she'd admitted to had been reasonably well thought of in their time but they hadn't worn well, perhaps because they weren't original, too much clever imitations of what was then fashionable. So my interest in *Carriage Paid*, as I started reading, was that Violet had written it during the years she'd barely accounted for in *I Affirm*, from her divorce in 1933 to when, in 1936, she'd flung herself into the Labour movement, marched all the way from Jarrow with the hunger marchers, been arrested in violent anti-Fascist fighting, spoken against the government on every platform she could, sat on committees and written pamphlets.

I was hoping to get from this book some clues – possibly about her own life during those missing years, certainly about how she was thinking about things at the time. I half-expected it to be like her working-class novel of 1937, *Always With Us*, left-wing in its sentiments and, though set in the Depression based, I guessed, on her own early life with the Crutchleys. Of course, the glossing over of *Carriage Paid* in her autobiography ought to have warned me: I should have been able to recognise by that time the hiss of Violet's tiny skating boots skimming over thin ice. But it was a shock. Far from being put to sleep by the book I read until three in the morning, dropped off into nightmares, woke after dreams full of shouts where I was running through a jungle, trying to escape pursuit by uniformed men, being chased through a darkened aircraft hangar by heavy-booted soldiers with machine-guns, looking for the light plane which would lift me off to safety. But it was afternoon before I began fully to realise why I had been so disturbed.

Carriage Paid opened with a young suburban housewife, Celia Donaldson, sitting, bored in her garden. Married to a doctor at nineteen and now the mother of a small son, at twenty-eight she begins to feel nothing will ever happen. Suddenly, a handsome stranger, a painter, half Austrian, enters her life. His paintings are huge and powerful pictures. He is also described by Violet as having a brilliant intellect. She begins an affair with him, attracted by his strength and convictions. Andreas Haussman believes that only certain superior beings are capable of ruling and controlling the world. 'You and I,' he tells Celia in his studio, 'are strong, fierce, brave, not timid and governed by convention like the rest. Why should we live as others – we are the leaders. Together, we can make a new world.' Celia's husband sues for divorce. In court Celia expresses her feeling that what she has done is right, though it means losing custody of her child. 'Even as the judge spoke the fatal words, she knew she, a woman and a mother, could give up her adored and wondrous child to keep her lover and make a perfect world.'

Heavy speeches, titanic passions, significant weather conditions, literary bass notes rang through *Carriage Paid*. The whole book carried a crude but terrifying conviction. Before Andreas and Celia first make love they witness a fierce storm from the roof of Andreas's house. 'See the people down there, the little people, scurrying for shelter,' Andreas says, 'but we, we are different. For us the thunder and lightning give strength. They are our element.'

In the final scene Andreas and Celia have been given a vast estate in the country. It is from there they and their supporters will begin to transform the world.

The book stayed, unpleasantly, with me all day. In *I Affirm* Violet had called it a study of certain psychological types, and since almost no one, except perhaps some keen publishers of fiction written by women of the past hundred years, had read it since publication, there were few equipped to argue with her. All I could think was that such seemingly wholehearted support of the theory that only a few were fit to rule, written by Violet in the mid-thirties, with Hitler and Mussolini in power and the British Union of Fascists marching round London in black shirts, throwing Jews through shop windows, was pretty strange coming from the pen of Violet Levine, self-declared Socialist and democrat. Whatever she said afterwards my impression was that in the heated political atmosphere of the 1930s she'd got carried away by the thought of Haussman, genius and superman, and Celia, his soul-mate. And the contemporary women who'd read it with a view to reprinting it had, I guessed, thought the same and decided not to go ahead.

I forgot all this when the phone rang and we heard Sam was alive uninjured aboard the troop-carrier *Vigilant*. It was an enormous relief. Ray's face relaxed for the first time. We picnicked on the beach that evening, until it was dark, and walked home at ease. Ray went ahead up the road to the house in the lamplight, whistling.

After he'd gone to bed my parents and I had a whisky and confessed. 'Your mother and I were going to plead with you to move down here, if Sam had died,' said my father.

'I was going to come,' I told them.

Andy's phone call at ten thirty broke the relieved, united

mood of the evening. He said he was at the Grand, and asked me to join him. I went out, leaving my parents, I think, feeling a little flat, and rather mistrustful, while I felt, myself, a little guilty, rather embarrassed.

I'd told my mother Andy was coming, even added that we might get married. But I don't think she was impressed, especially because I didn't mention Ray. Nothing I said sounded quite right. We were trying to clear up the spare room at the time, in case Sam wanted to come down later to be with Ray, and clashed with a visit from my Auntie Jess. I mentioned Andy as we were pushing the wardrobe back against the wall after vacuuming under it. My mother, not only a mother of two but a teacher for thirty-five years, knew perfectly well the child's gambit of avoiding too many questions by slipping information in while the parent or teacher is distracted by another task, in this case heaving a wardrobe back into position. As I threw in more information about Andy, I started putting Windolene on the windows with a cloth and my mother said no more, which was what I'd wanted, but somehow, it didn't help.

Turning my back on England, home and beauty, I walked a mile and a half to the Grand, through a fine summer night. I looked forward to seeing Andy, why not, Your Honour and Gentlemen of the Jury? He was handsome, sexy, interesting, glamorous, I loved him.

As we were lying there, the curtains blowing in with the slight breeze from the window, the sound of the sea, and the occasional car passing by below in our ears, I asked, 'Are they going to publish a report on Sweetwater Village? Or is there going to be a question in the House of Commons?'

'Yes,' said Andy. 'A question, probably. The official answer will fix the blame on Robertson's government. That'll help the British government to wash its hands more easily over the withdrawal of the troops and justify not interfering too much about American money and arms being sent to the opposition. I don't think in the end the UN troops will be deployed in Belize. There's a strong push to keep it going as a civil war with a lot of backing from interested outsiders.'

'And this is partly because of your account of the massacre?' I asked him.

He shifted his position, his arm drooped over the edge of the bed. 'The Sweetwater affair had an effect – unfortunately. But I only said what I saw. I'd rather not talk about it. I've had to go over it again and again. And I can still see those scenes in the village. When I'd finished the last piece for *The Witness*, I thought I'd got shot of it. But I had to tell it over and over. Tell me something . . . something . . . ' he yawned, 'something nice. Not about Belize.'

The nicest thing I could tell him was about Belize – Sam wasn't dead – so I thought and thought and couldn't think of anything else. 'Wonderful weather. We can picnic on the Downs tomorrow, if you like.'

He sighed. 'Sounds ideal. We must look for a country house – the legacy.'

'Yes,' I said.

'You don't sound enthusiastic,' he said.

'I suppose I can't imagine it,' I told him, perfectly truthfully. It was mostly because of Ray. Andy and Ray had never met. Now they were supposed to live together. Or were they? Perhaps Andy assumed Ray was all right as he was. He didn't live with me now, so what difference would it make if Andy and I moved somewhere and left Ray with my parents? He could come for the holidays. So – I couldn't believe in the house we were going to buy until I knew if Ray would be there, and I didn't want to raise the subject. The invitation had to come from Andy. I thought it might be better if Ray and Andy met first, then the question of where he was going to live would arise naturally. I knew Andy couldn't stand children but I wasn't sure how he defined a child. Was it just babies and little children who needed much maternal attention he disliked – or all of them? I yawned.

He yawned, burrowed into the pillow, took my hand. 'Rog says you haven't definitely given up the biography,' he said. 'I saw him last night.'

'Might as well plod on a bit. It's interesting,' I muttered.

'Oh, no,' he said more vigorously. 'You're not going on – I don't believe it, oh no.'

I couldn't understand his alarm. It wasn't on my behalf – there was nothing dangerous about writing a biography (I then thought) and it wasn't going to hurt him. I suspected he wanted to put me in front of an Aga with a hundred pounds of plums and fifty Kilner jars, and then glance at his watch and say he was due in Bolivia in ten minutes and he'd come back, as in a fairy story, when I'd turned all the plums into jam.

I said, 'I've got to earn a living somehow. What else am I supposed to do?'

'Don't ask me what you're supposed to do,' he moaned. 'It's just that I can't believe you're going on with this ill-conceived project. Firstly, you can't do it because you haven't got the skills or the qualifications; secondly, no one is going to want to read it; thirdly, the family, far from collaborating with you, is opposed to you – you've already had Robert Levine as good as threatening you and Roger with the law. On a practical level we're supposed to be moving to the country – you'll have your hands full. Honestly, darling,' he said, in a less combative tone, turning his head on the pillow and staring at me with his beautiful blue, black-fringed eyes, 'what makes you think you can do this? You're a novelist, so write a novel. Oh, now, look, you've gone all rigid.'

He was right. I was alarmed by the thought of moving and having my hands full. What with, I wondered in a panic. Little books of carpet samples? An electric mower? A hammer and some nails? I was lying there frozen like someone in the dentist's chair, telling themselves it would be all right really. 'Andy,' I said. 'This is terrible. What are you saying?'

He turned away and burrowed his head into the pillow. 'All right, all right,' he mumbled. 'You and my cousin just go on with this doomed project, and don't blame me when it all goes wrong. Let's get some sleep.'

'Andy,' I asked, 'when you spoke to Roger, did you say this to him?'

'I don't know,' he said. 'Honestly, Kate, if I don't get some sleep I'll go mad. Can't we knock it off, just for tonight?'

I tried to be quiet, but couldn't. I went on. 'Andy, you worry me. Did I start a conversation about Violet Levine in the middle of the night? No, I didn't. You did. And exactly what have you got in mind for this house? I don't know— '

'I wish I was back in the jungle,' he declared.

'Well,' I said, knowing he would drop off if I stopped talking, leaving me alone with insomnia as a bedmate, 'life is simpler there.'

'Bugger you,' he said viciously. The threatening tone frightened me into silence. Andy fell asleep.

After a while, so did I, but I was restless and by dawn I was fed up with diving in and out of sleep, dreaming of tricky journeys involving lots of tickets, almost-missed trains and scattered baggage which had to be got out of the carriage in time, so I got up quietly and walked back through the town and down the quiet tree-lined road where my parents lived. As I went I worked out that Andy was putting more pressure on me than I could take. Someone who was on or off planes all the time, in and out of trouble spots, always trying to find a phone in the middle of a riot, used to getting along with Nigerian generals, Kurdish tribesmen and American congressmen, always meeting deadlines, might have a natural talent for challenge and change. I hadn't. Admitting that need for security embarrassed me at the time.

I let myself in to the house and made a few notes about Violet until my mother got up. I wasn't sure about confiding in her, but as she sat outside in her dressing-gown, drinking tea and smoking the first of the incredible number of cigarettes she managed to get through daily, I thought she needed to know what was going on.

She said, 'Are you sure you want to lead that kind of life? It sounds as if you'd be stuck with arranging the flowers. I don't think you're the type, Kate. And I can't see why you couldn't be going on with the biography – it all seems rather phoney and old-fashioned to me. Is that the sort of background he comes from?'

Andy's mother seemed to have been a painter on ceramics, known as Jocelyn Biggs, her maiden name, and she and Andy's father Harry, who was now dead, had always lived in a house in Bayswater, once her father's. About the turn of the century there'd been a small Littlebrown estate in Hampshire, which had gone to the eldest son, according to the usual practice, leaving the rest of the children to make their own ways. From then on it had been a tale of ups and downs and shabby gentility.

Andy's father had in fact owned a couple of garages, not all that successfully. I had the impression that if Andy hadn't been the only child there probably wouldn't have been enough money to send him to the public school which all the Littlebrowns (meaning all the Littlebrowns who hadn't emigrated, or made some fatal slip which plummeted them into the lower middle classes) always attended. And I think Andy's mother, painting her ceramics in the shabby studio at the shabby Bayswater house, had contributed a fair amount to the family finances. In short, Andy himself hadn't been brought up on a country estate.

My mother shook her head in bafflement. I could tell she was disconcerted, if not angry, when I said Ray hadn't been mentioned in the plan. All she actually said was, 'He's obviously an intelligent man. He can't have forgotten you've got a child. I suppose you'll have to wait and see.' Nevertheless, in spite of the mild and diplomatic way she was handling the matter, I knew she was sharpening her spear, ready to use it if it looked as if Ray was going to get less than his due. I knew quite well that if it came to a crisis she was perfectly capable of backing Sam's claim for custody of Ray. She'd give evidence against me, her daughter, in court, if she had to. As I looked at her she lit another cigarette, and gazed mildly at her pair of blackbirds pecking on the lawn.

I urged, 'Well, at least don't take against Andy until you've met him.'

'Of course I won't,' she assured me impatiently. 'Don't let's argue about it. Would you like to ask him to supper tonight, or tomorrow?'

Which I did, on the telephone that morning. He said tomorrow would be better, but why didn't we picnic at lunch-time as planned?

As we sat in the sunshine, high on the Downs, he asked me what it was that made me cling to the idea of going on with the biography. He was pretty sure Roger would agree to making the contract into one for a novel, if that was what I'd like. The more he went on about it the sillier it seemed to argue. I said I'd think about it. Then I told him about Violet's superman fantasies in *Carriage Paid* and he laughed.

'It's hard to believe she was serious,' he said. 'You'd have thought she was the last person to go for a strongman hero, in life or books.'

'It reads like more than fiction – she meant it,' I declared.

'Perhaps she was just a better writer than she seems,' he suggested.

I tried to get him to drive me to Ray's school to pick him up, but couldn't. He'd someone to see but he'd be back at about seven. He suggested we went out to dinner at eight.

That afternoon Dave Gottlieb rang, hoping there was good news of Sam, and I said the Ministry of Defence had promised that as soon as they had accurate news of the evacuation, which it seemed had been fairly hasty, they'd promised to ring.

He told me the background – that the evacuation had been a scramble. The government had been fighting to keep control of the harbour while the British troops got on board. Just as the last British regiment embarked there'd been rumours the rebels were winning. He told me Andy had been called to the Foreign Office to say what had happened at Sweetwater Village. I said I'd heard that from Andy who was in Brighton.

'And how's old Violet?' Dave enquired.

'Not bad,' I said. 'But – I don't know – Andy seems to think it's a rotten idea. I keep wondering, what with the Levines being so implacable about telling me anything and my sheer inexperience, is it really worthwhile going ahead?'

'I was speaking to a couple of women, last night, and they thought it was interesting. More people have heard about Violet than you think.'

'I don't know . . . ' I said.

'Well,' Dave remarked, 'the best way to find out what you want is to challenge yourself to ring Roger Littlebrown, now, and tell him the book's definitely off. Okay? Now imagine you've done it – it's over – how do you feel?'

I thought. 'Terrible,' I told him.

'There you are then,' he said. 'Now you know. Take care.' And he rang off.

From the kitchen my mother called, 'Don't you dare give it up. I'm looking forward to it. Violet was quite a figure when I was growing up. Her hats, and the mysterious story about her being dropped over France – then the Mackinnon scandal. We were all very interested in Violet. She was a bit of a heroine to me, but my mother always said you'd only to look at her to see that at bottom she was an absolutely dreadful woman.'

'A lot of people who knew her say the same,' I told her.

'Do they?' she said. 'Well, perhaps she had to be.'

My father came in, looking very glum. He was chairman of a council sub-committee set up to run the Provisional Food Programme, a system for feeding homeless people, or people with no money at all, from three relief centres in Brighton. There was a strong lobby, led by the hoteliers, who had a powerful voice as they contributed substantial amounts of left-over food to the scheme, which wanted to close one of the relief centres being run from a small hotel on the front, so that the sight of people queueing for the food would not upset the visitors. My father disagreed, but the opinions of the hoteliers and other commercial interests, were gaining ground.

'You just want people on holiday to see other people can't afford food,' my mother told him. 'That's all very well, but have you thought about the poor – do they really want to be getting their paper plates in front of the holidaymakers? Have you asked them?'

'No,' he said, a bit crestfallen. 'But if they shut that one it means a much longer walk with pushchairs and so forth. But,' he added, 'I think we can get a compromise, just close it for the holiday season. At least the weather'll be better for the walk. I just hope it isn't the thin end of the wedge. A lot of people have never liked the idea. Luckily the council and the clergy are right behind it.'

The phone rang and I answered it. I thought it might be Andy, but it wasn't. It was Dave again. 'A statement came round from the Ministry of Defence. With a list. It's all right – Sam's okay. He's aboard the *Vigilant*, safe and sound. But it looks as if they had to fight their way out. There are four casualties, one dead. A small rocket, it looks like, hit the *Vigilant*, but luckily the damage wasn't too bad. It'll be on the news I expect, but I thought I'd tell you . . . '

'The army rang, but they didn't say all that. Thanks, Dave. Thanks very much,' I said. My father was crossing the hall with two glasses, taking one to my mother in the kitchen. 'Sam's definitely all right,' I told him, 'like they said. There was fighting round the harbour before they embarked. Just in time.'

'Thank God,' said my mother from the kitchen door.

'No chance of a mistake?' I asked Dave.

'All this stuff's twenty-four, thirty-six hours late,' said Dave. 'It's vetted and monitored right to the top. By the time it gets to us there's no chance of an error – except a deliberate mistake, of course, and I dare say there've been a few of them. Don't worry.'

'Thanks, Dave,' I said.

'It must have been tough for all of you. There's not much information otherwise. "Government troops, holding off the insurgents" – that's the polite word for rebels you sympathise with – "with difficulty were assisted in keeping control of Belize Harbour by British troops of the South Staffordshire and 6th Reserve Regiments withdrawing on the advice of the United Nations." Then there's Sam's name, Captain S. R. T. Rogers. Okay?'

'Bye, and thanks . . . ' I said, but he'd already put the phone down.

'Can I come in?' came Andy's voice from the kitchen door. 'I didn't have time to ring. I thought I'd come straight on.'

I introduced him to my parents. We went into the sitting-room, where I told him about Dave's call while my father poured drinks.

'Good news,' he said. 'I'll ring my paper and see if I can get any more information. You never know with Gottlieb.'

'That would be nice,' said my mother. As Andy went off she said, 'My goodness, this place is becoming quite a nerve centre.'

'I'll reverse the charges,' called Andy.

My father turned on the news channel to see if there was a report on the evacuation and turned the sound down when he saw Adrian Critchlow was discussing the need for identity cards. Critchlow was bending forward talking to his questioner, one well-shaped hand on the table in front of him. He had a mass of straight, very well-cut black hair. He was being persuasive, but with no words you couldn't help noticing the energy and aggression under the surface. He was a bit like a dog on a lead behaving itself and waiting for the moment when the leash is slipped.

My father sighed. 'He's supposed to be the next Prime Minister.'

Andy came back into the room. 'They're doing the next leg by plane,' he said. 'They'll be back in twenty-four hours. Apparently there was a Dutch cameraman left behind when the press departed. There's some footage of the fighting round the harbour, but it's got to be passed by the Ministry of Defence.'

'I can't see why,' my mother said.

Andy, who was, I think, annoyed that the Dutchman had managed to stay on, because he liked to be first in, last out himself, remarked, 'Military secrets, I suppose.'

'We're helping to pay for this débâcle through taxes,' my mother responded stoutly. 'You can get very tired of paying and then being told it's none of your business. It's all filmed by satellites at the time, so anyone of any importance, whoever they are, knows everything. It's only the people who are paying who don't know.'

'That's absolutely true,' said Andy, glancing at the television.

My mother looked at her watch. 'Ray's late, I'd better ring and tell him to start out.' She left the room and I heard her talking in the hall.

'Identity cards,' said my father, looking at Critchlow's face. 'Well I'll never carry one. They'll have to jail me first.'

'They'll use on-the-spot fines,' suggested Andy. 'Or make it like parking tickets. In the end people pay up to avoid the hassles. Or TV licences. They can link it to passport control – no new passport if you're out of order on your ID.' He said to my mother, who had just come back into the room, 'Mrs Higgins, I'm afraid I won't be able to come to supper tomorrow. The paper's just ordered me off to Cuba. Kate, I'm sorry. Mrs Higgins, it was kind of you to invite me. This is one of the hazards of the job.'

'What a pity,' said my mother. 'Have you got to go straight back?'

'I'll have to leave for London tonight.'

'Hang on,' my father interrupted, turning back to the TV.

There were pictures taken from a helicopter of a troop-ship, the decks crammed with soldiers. Then Private Desmond Fowler's photograph, a grinning young man in a khaki tunic, someone, his father probably, shutting the door on the cameras in a street in Barnsley. 'Private Fowler, who was married, with a child, died in the fighting round Belize as anti-government troops attempted to recapture the harbour from the newly elected Marxist government of Belize.'

'I'm surprised no one predicted all this,' my father said. 'Anyone could see Robertson might get elected.'

'They knew,' Andy told him. 'Actually, Kate, if we're going to eat before I set off, perhaps we should leave now.'

'You wouldn't like to stay . . . ' suggested my mother. 'You'd be very welcome.'

'No,' said Andy. 'I've booked, and I don't want to put you out.'

'No trouble,' said my father.

I think we all knew the issue was that Andy hadn't met Ray, and ought to. I felt indignant. I couldn't force Andy to meet my son, trying to make them like each other, love me, love my dog, style. Andy must have seen this. He said, 'Shall we pick up Ray from his friend's house and ferry him back here, first?'

'That would be kind,' said my mother. 'He may be on his way by now, but you'll probably pass him if he's already left.'

Andy had hardly started the car before Ray, on skates, wheeled round the corner and up the pavement towards us. 'Just going out to dinner,' I called. 'Back later.'

He nodded.

'Hello,' called Andy.

'Hello,' said Ray and turned through the gate on to the garden path. He was carrying a stopwatch. He'd skate round the side of the house and into the kitchen, timing himself.

I sighed. The first meeting between Ray and Andy hadn't been a success. In fact, it hadn't been a meeting.

'Handsome boy,' Andy told me. 'What did Gottlieb want?'

'To give me the good news.'

'He's after you. That's what.'

'No, he's not. He's lived with a woman called Lizzie Shooter for years. She's a supervisor at Marks.' The subject of Ray had vanished from the agenda, I noticed.

'It's just the thought of you making love to a man in a woolly hat.'

Over the seafood Andy suggested I contact some house agents and check the situation as far as old manors, lodges, rectories and mills were concerned. 'Good time to buy, I heard from a banker,' he told me.

'Let's wait till you get back,' I suggested.

His face stiffened. 'What are you saying?' he demanded.

'Nothing – I'm saying I'm not sure. I don't want to do it without you.'

'Why not? We're only wasting time. Don't you love me? Look, I'm offering to buy this place – what's the matter? I can't do it from fucking Cuba, now can I? While you're at it you can start thinking about this novel. Any ideas? Have you rung Roger?'

I felt as if I might be going mad.

'Well then?' he asked. He gave me a smile, white teeth, glint of very blue eyes, and I muttered finally, 'I think you're trying to railroad me.'

'For God's sake, how old do you want to be if you're going to have a child?'

'A what?' I said. 'A what? Andy, you're mad. Who said anything about a child?'

'You've often said you wanted a child. Another one. Perhaps you meant someone else's. Perhaps I was wrong to assume that because we're in love and planning to live together you might want to have a baby. Mine.'

I was startled. I stared at him closely, the way he didn't like, and said, 'You don't like children.' Knowing him so well, I knew he was desperate. At first I thought he must have eaten a bad oyster. I couldn't imagine why he was putting himself through all this. I repeated, 'You don't like children and you're coming out in a cold sweat.'

He was furious I'd noticed. I was furious at the insult. He said, 'I've always been wary of that kind of commitment.'

'Wary?' I questioned. 'Andy, you're terrified. That's why

you're pushing. You've got to get it over with, like jumping off the top board.'

'For God's sake,' he said angrily, 'I'm doing it, aren't I? I don't do this every day. What do you want? Music and roses? Can't you just go along with me, for once? Or do you want to spend the rest of your life in that crummy flat with Diane Carter? Couldn't you try giving a little?'

'All right,' I said. 'I'm sorry.'

He urged, 'I'm asking you. Do this for me. Just tell Roger you'll write him a book, any book, but not this biography, go to the house agents, pick out some places – I'll only be away a week or ten days.' He was nearly pleading. 'Do it,' he said. 'Just do it.'

And still I couldn't say yes. For one thing, it now seemed pretty obvious Ray was to stay with my parents. More than that, I was afraid, without knowing why. I just said, 'I'll think, I really will.'

Getting angry he asked, 'How far are you prepared to damage things between us?'

'You mean, you'd be prepared to break with me?'

'Not exactly,' he said.

'But something like that?'

'Something,' he agreed.

'Well,' I said, after a pause. 'Well, now we know.'

'I'm thirty-six,' he pointed out. 'You can't keep me dangling on for ever. It's time you made an honest man of me.'

Not long after he got in his car and drove to London. I felt very tired. I couldn't face going home. I went down and sat on the beach, looking at the mass of water right up to the horizon. I felt very confused. There was something wrong. Andy was pushing me hard and, just for a moment, I had a sneaky thought about sleeping with a man in a woolly hat.

TEN

Violet Levine, 1933
Kate Higgins, June 16th, 1991

For myself, though a normal enough man in my passions, I suppose, I never saw her attractions. Yet but for a certain kind of man that air of fragility and passivity, masking a ferocity of temperament to equal Messalina's or the Empress Claudia's, perhaps, had its appeal. Her temperament itself, her sexual temperament I should say, seemed to me to be cold. Capable of anything, with iron self-control and highly intelligent, she was nevertheless basically an hysteric. The dreadful scenes which occasionally shook the household, where she behaved like a madwoman or a fiend from hell, as I have described, bear out what I say, I think. Such a nature is not and can never be a sensual nature. I believe it was only with her evil lover that she ever gained full satisfaction as a woman, and then I suspect only by means of sadism. I have been told that the scenes in the bedroom became increasingly violent as his career elsewhere became more violent. Nor do I think this relationship ceased because she saw the light, like a convert to a new religion, whatever reasons she may have given later. The Violet Levine of the barricades was not created by thought. The rupture had another cause, and even I who knew all, this time did not know what it was.

Memoirs, C. F. Lamier

Violet sat in the small drawing-room of the house in Bramwell Street, tapping her long red fingernails on the arm of the Chippendale chair, one of the pair which she had removed from her bedroom at Cavendish Square. She looked through the little crack between the net curtains and the window frame down the street in the direction of the river. If she sprawled in a more comfortable armchair she might risk crumples in her green chiffon dress, or some disarrangement of her freshly set hair. The large, famous eyes, between hazel and violet, so often featured in society magazines (Mrs Frederick Levine, sometimes with her children, sometimes without, at home, at weddings, charity balls, even heading a committee for the relief of the unemployed), had hardened. She was not conscious of that. She was only conscious of the first fine lines developing around them, of a slight coarsening of her skin here and there, a grey hair or two. These still-slight signs of age might not have troubled her so much, if she had not seen them as part of a general decline, which included a shrunken bank balance, a small house with many stairs, only two servants, a maid and a cook, in the cramped basement.

Eight months ago, at Christmas, just before her thirty-sixth birthday, she had left – been forced – from Cavendish Square, at the end of a fortnight of silence, meetings with the family solicitor, deeds and agreements. Now, she was still Mrs Frederick Levine, not Mrs Violet Levine, divorcee, only because she had refused to divorce Frederick. He would not, to avoid scandal, particularly for their children, divorce her, though he had been prepared to go to a hotel with a woman supplied by a detective agency, and endure the necessary farce of being found in bed with her there, giving Violet evidence for a quiet divorce. She had refused his offer.

She sat now in the sweltering heat of an August evening, waiting for her lover. During the summer her invitations had dropped off, partly because everyone was away (in Scotland, in the south of France, in Kenya or Rhodesia), partly because, as she well knew, the interesting, witty and well-turned-out Mrs Frederick Levine, not always with her dull, but rich and respectable husband, was more acceptable than Violet Levine, separated after a scandal, which, although the details were not fully known, it had been impossible to keep completely quiet.

There was a distant hum of traffic in the small room. Through the crack in the curtains she watched a car come down the road, but it did not stop. Out there, all over London, girls hung on men's arms, off to dances, films and parties. In the hot room Violet brooded, felt her make-up clogging and her hair going limp, saw the roses, bought only the day before, beginning to droop in their crystal vases. She, who hated looking back, began, reluctantly, to remember the past.

Landry Thomas had been killed in 1917, two days after his regiment arrived in the lines. A young officer came down from the base camp next day, with a letter Landry had written to Violet which he had been asked to deliver to her in the event of his death. Violet left her ward numbly and went along the clifftops to open it in privacy. And when she returned to the ward, still stunned, remembering the letter – 'I want you so much, Violet. If you ever get this letter I want you to know I died thinking of the future we might have had' – Frederick, in captain's uniform, was waiting for her outside her ward. For a moment she hated him. Why was he, whom she did not want, still alive, when Landry, the man she loved, was dead before they'd had any time together. Her eyes suddenly prickling with tears she said, 'Hello, Frederick.'

'You can go off, Levine. Sister says so,' a nurse appearing at the ward door told her. 'You've got till tomorrow.'

'Get out of that dreary uniform, Violet,' commanded Frederick. 'I've booked a room at the Ritz in Paris. But let's hurry. Come on, we dine in Paris.'

Paris, in that early summer of 1917, was tired, full of soldiers and tarts, weary people, young men on crutches – Violet hardly saw the desperation, gaiety, battered glamour, did not taste the food in the restaurant, where very old men served them, took no notice of the enduring elegance of the wide, tree-lined streets which bombardments and shortages had damaged little. Later she walked with Frederick in the Bois de Boulogne. British soldiers passed them, some with their arms round girls, some in groups. Frederick had tolerated Violet's silence on the train to Paris, but was becoming impatient with her wordless gloom. She could not concentrate on him, her head was filled with pain; inside her a voice was murmuring, over and over again, 'Cruel, it's so cruel. Cruel. How cruel.' She did not want anyone with her, Frederick least of all. She wanted to be alone. She wondered if the report of Landry's death was true.

Mistakes had been made, men had been reported dead and turned up unharmed, or as prisoners. As they walked she was thinking desperately, I must find out. He may be alive.

Frederick, however, was becoming angry. 'Violet,' he said, 'what's the matter? I might as well not be here. This is my leave. I've travelled hundreds of miles to be with you. Now, it seems, you'd prefer to be alone. If that's the case, please tell me.'

'I'm sorry,' she said. 'I'm so tired.'

'The life of an officer at war,' Frederick told her, 'is not as relaxing as you might believe. I also am tired. I understand. I just wish you wouldn't walk with me almost as if you wished I weren't here.'

'Don't nag me, Frederick,' said Violet. What she wanted now was to be back at St Luc, where she could go to the commanding officer at the American camp and find out how Landry had died, who had seen it. I must know, she thought, I must know. Perhaps none of it is true.

'Perhaps we should go back to the hotel,' Frederick said. There, she knew, he would expect her to make love to him. He had been away a long time. She would have to go through with it. Again, she thought that he should have died, instead of Landry. She could see no way out. In the big ornate bedroom, he did make love to her. She turned her head on the pillow, to conceal the tears in her eyes. Frederick, his arms behind his head, said, 'Violet. What's the matter with you? I think you should leave the nursing service and go back to England.'

'Yes, Frederick, yes. I may.'

'Violet, you will,' said Frederick. 'This is absurd. Your duties have overstrained you. At this rate, when the war's over you'll be fit for nothing. And you are, your main duties still are to be, a wife and mother. And quite frankly, you should be in England now. Caroline and my mother really can't manage without help. And Mother says Caroline is there less and less often, she's alone too much, and in sole charge of Jo-Jo and Pamela. I've even had a rather worrying letter from Henry Sturgess about all this which I must take seriously. Ordinarily he'd be the last man in the world to interfere. I also wonder if it was quite wise to discharge Nanny Thwaite so impulsively. Violet, darling, are you listening to me?'

But Violet was pretending to be asleep, while she remembered Landry making love to her on the beach. She lay very still, controlling her pain, until Frederick's impatient sighs and tossings to and fro ceased and he fell asleep himself. Later, he woke, to find her standing in her nightdress, looking out of the window, down on to the summer street, where a soldier and a girl were walking. If only I were the girl, she was thinking, and the soldier was Landry; I'm only twenty, I met the man I loved, too late, and now he's dead. There are women all over England, and France, who have had the man they loved with them for twenty, thirty, forty years. I had Landry for two weeks, and now I'll never have him again. It's all over. Then she sensed that Frederick had woken behind her and went back to bed.

'Violet,' he said, 'is something the matter?'

'I'll go back to England, Frederick, as you ask,' she said in a flat voice, 'in a few weeks.'

Back in England she went down to the country and lived in a dream scarcely penetrated by Sophie Levine's voice. Caroline was in London, staying with Rosalind. Her mother-in-law was now relying on Violet for support. The war had been hard on Sophie. The estate's farms were neglected, the garden overgrown, since even the fifty-year-old gardener had joined up. The house was becoming dilapidated, heating was difficult. They were living in only seven of the twenty rooms. Jessie Oates was doing most of the cooking, as well as looking after the children. Violet tried to help, but a cloud of depression hung over her. She had found, and lost, what she wanted and saw nothing good ahead.

'I'm so worried about you, Violet,' Sophie said one evening. 'You've lost your high spirits, you eat nothing. You're pale as a ghost. I think I'll ask the doctor to have a look at you. I expect you're worn out and need a tonic.'

Violet shook her head, but now, at the beginning of July she knew she was pregnant and that the child was probably Landry's. She didn't want it. There was no point, now he was dead. Only one thought penetrated her misery – how to get rid of the child. She went to London and rang Allie at her office.

'Vi,' came Allie's voice delightedly. 'Are you back?'

Violet said, 'I need some help, Allie,' and that evening

Allie took her to a middle-aged woman, once a midwife, now given to drinking and unable to work. This woman conducted an abortion by injecting a syringe of Jeyes Fluid into Violet's womb, directed firmly by Violet, lying in agony on a bed. She knew the risks she was taking.

In the cab going back to Cavendish Square she told Allie grimly, 'I don't think she ruptured anything. But I hope to God it works because I dread having to go back. I bet she's killed a few. How do you know of her?'

'How do you think?' Allie said. 'I didn't meet her while we were collecting for war orphans, did I?'

'What – you . . . ? ' asked Violet.

'Yes. Silly girl, wasn't I? Believed what the boss told me, didn't I?'

'You're still working there?'

'Funnily enough, he left,' said Allie. 'He got called up as soon as I told him I was pregnant. He didn't let on until one day I got ten guineas in the post, and a note saying he was leaving for France at six o'clock that same morning. Pretty story, isn't it?'

Violet winced. 'Phew – I think it's starting. Sooner the better. Well, we're a charming pair, aren't we? You'll have to ring Sophie up this evening and say we were at the pictures when I got taken ill.'

Later that evening, as Violet lay in bed, groaning, Allie came upstairs, with a pot of tea on a tray and said, 'She's invited me down. For a holiday.'

Violet grinned. 'Suddenly nice to my relatives – well, why not? Can you get leave?'

'I've been planning to leave the job anyway,' Allie said. 'Now's as good a time as any. I'll tell them tomorrow, get my wages and Bob's your uncle. I'd like a break, and there's always more food in the country. I can easily get another job when I come back. They're crying out for clerk-typists. You all right?' she asked in alarm, as Violet said, 'Ouch.'

'Be worse before I'm better,' Violet told her stoically. 'Christ, don't men leave women in the lurch?'

Allie hesitated, but mentioned, 'He did die in action.'

'Let's hope I don't,' said Violet.

After the abortion, from which she recovered quickly, although she was never to cease regretting Landry Thomas, she toughened herself and regained her firm grip on life. In fact, since loss and defeat never suited her, she became harsher and less merciful than she had ever been. Two years of watching seemingly pointless death and injury, culminating in Landry's death, only confirmed her existing view that in a hard world it was as well to be as hard as possible.

For the following few months at Farnley Violet stayed fairly quiet, getting over Landry's death and the abortion. Then she began to take over. By the time of her twenty-first birthday in December 1917 she was giving orders. In early 1918, while the country was reeling towards the end of the war, heedless of Zeppelin raids, she opened the house at Cavendish Square, repairing, redecorating, buying a car, filling the house with servants, paying wages which shocked other householders. Men and women in this last year of the war could get higher pay and better conditions in factories and offices than in domestic service. Violet was prepared to pay high wages, even entice away other people's servants, to get what she wanted. Eyes popped during the last gruelling year of warfare, when she began to entertain, giving dinner parties (with food for which she paid dearly), and evening parties, with dancing, all while her husband was still away at war. She left Pamela with Jo-Jo in the country, in the care of Jessie Oates.

Sophie Levine discovered when she finally came up from Farnley after the renovations that she'd been moved from the large main bedroom she'd once shared with her husband. Violet had put her in a smaller bedroom on the first floor, with a little sitting room next to it. 'Entirely your own, for you and your friends,' she told her mother-in-law sweetly, having evicted her from her position of command in the large drawing-room.

Before the war ended Violet had begun to create a social set around her, a group not composed of the old, sober Levine friends, but of the young members of well-off families, friends of Caroline Levine and Rosalind Despencer, some writers and painters, many still in uniform. At Violet Levine's, pretty women and interesting men met, talked in the drawing-room, danced in the dining-room, kissed in the conservatory or the small garden at the back of the house on warm evenings, where Violet's lamps of coloured glass hung from trees. Suddenly her now-faint Cockney accent seemed original. An excellent hostess, she was sharp-witted, good-humoured, young, pretty – and now, happy again. She was married, and therefore respectable. She was rich, hospitable, she had always been to the latest revue, or the Diaghilev ballet or the Dixieland Jazz Band, read the latest book, seen the latest paintings. She had a Decline of the West party, where everyone came dressed as an aspect of declining Europe.

As the casualty lists continued and a virulent flu swept the country in the summer, killing tens of thousands, people said Violet was running something like a mediaeval dance of death. It was unsuitable, even unpatriotic. But the guests at her parties, men who had been at the front, girls and women who had lost brothers, fiancés, husbands, had had enough of sacrifice and lost their taste for duty. They'd seen what it meant. Too many patriots had returned in wounded and shell-shocked pieces, if they'd returned at all. The survivors knew how short life could be. They wanted company, fun, a good time. The women's skirts went up; they cut off their hair; they had the vote.

Those who deplored Violet's callousness couldn't deny she had nursed for two years at the front. Often, the critics had more to say about Violet's sister-in-law Caroline, who, widowed three years before, had been living mostly in London for the past year, leaving her child in the country. She'd had two love affairs that year, one with Tom Brereton's brother, one with Claude Herries, which had ended when Claude lost half his leg, blown off in France. Caroline's parents were desperately worried about both their daughters, who were sharing the small house in Chelsea. They could seldom leave the country, where their only remaining son, Sandy, was acutely shell-shocked and needed continual care. After Laurence's death the Despencers had offered to take in Jo-Jo, if only for the duration of the war, but Caroline had refused, suspecting that once the Despencers had her four-year-old son living with them they would try to exert more control over her behaviour.

Caroline's mother, on a visit to Farnley, had tried to tell Sophie about the true state of affairs, with the idea of recruiting her in a campaign to make Caroline settle down. She'd found Sophie could not, or would not, understand her hints. 'The woman simply refuses to believe anything's wrong,' she told her husband in their bedroom that night. 'I don't think she can face facts since Laurence died. He was so much the favourite son. Now, she won't pull herself together and try to go on. It's dreadful to think of Jo-Jo, alone with her most of the time, apart from the nurse. What can we do? Should I write to Frederick, I wonder? It's such an awkward thing to put on paper.'

'I don't like this house,' Sir George had said, putting his collar on the dressing-table. 'I'm sure it's haunted.'

'I suppose it might be,' his wife agreed without interest. 'But George, I was asking what you thought we should do.'

George Despencer sat on the bed and looked keenly at his wife. He shook his head. 'Can't write to Frederick, while he's at war. I'll just have to try and catch him next time he's on leave. It might help if his wife came back. This lady-with-the-lamp stuff is all very well, but she's got a more obvious duty here.'

'I wonder how much use she would be?' asked Lady Despencer. 'After all, she's the person who discharged Nanny Thwaite.'

'An intelligent young woman with nursing experience could only be an asset,' he said, ignoring the question of Nanny Thwaite, whom he'd never liked. 'I know you're suspicious of her but I'd feel a lot happier if she were in the house. Once they give women the vote this sort of thing's going to get worse. I don't suppose from now on they'll ever be at home.'

'Violet is nursing. We are at war,' his wife told him steadily.

'A very good excuse,' said Sir George. 'I wonder which one she'll find when the war's over.'

'Oh, God,' said Lady Despencer. 'I wish it *were* over.' She paused. 'What this war has done to us all.'

And, of course, Violet's return did make some difference. When Lady Despencer consulted her, woman to woman, about the rearing of her only grandson at Farnley, Violet immediately despatched Jo-Jo Levine to his grandparents – without consulting his mother.

Her daughter Pamela, aged four by this time, was very upset at the loss of her playmate. 'She's a different girl,' Jessie Oates said to Violet over the phone. 'She's gone so quiet. And she cries at night.'

Violet, redecorating in London, told her briskly, 'She'll soon come out of it.'

Meanwhile Caroline came round to Cavendish Square and made a scene. Violet told her coolly that if she wanted her child at Farnley he could of course come back. But she assumed that once the row was over Caroline would do nothing, and she was right. Joseph stayed where he was. Lady Despencer was the only person wholly pleased by Jo-Jo's arrival. Her husband, Sir George, though happy to have his grandson with him, remarked that Violet had been clever to remove Laurence's son from under the Levine roof, thereby reducing his chances of joining the bank when older, or of figuring largely in Sophie's will. 'Violet needs to have Frederick's son, now,' he said, 'and no doubt she will.'

Violet did indeed have a son, giving birth easily to Robert a year after the war ended, and then to a daughter, Joanna, two years later. Another son would have reinforced her position, but by this time she had become an ardent supporter of Marie Stopes's birth control campaign, as had most of her friends, and planned to have no more children. Pregnancy was tedious, and still sometimes risky. She was on top now, and planned to stay so.

Down at Farnley on family holidays, or enduring the visits from the European branches of the family to Cavendish Square, when a great deal of opera-visiting, concert-going, the consumption of heavy family dinners, followed by card-playing and early nights was expected of her, she passed the time by writing novels. It provided a good excuse for avoiding, at least some of the time, Hanno and Louisa Waldstein, cousin Aimée and her husband Baron von Jurgen (himself yet another distant cousin), the Duvaliers, the Cotons and all the rest. The five books gained her, in some eyes, a reputation as an intellectual and gained her the entrée, through Didi Fraser, Louis Schreft's sister, into interesting circles in France, where she was taken to drink tea in the afternoons at Natalie Barney's, met Scott Fitzgerald, drunk at the time. She was photographed in a café-bar in Montparnasse with her arm round a man who had escaped from Devil's Island, where he had been sent for the brutal murder, in the course of a robbery, of an old woman in the rue Clichy. She saw Josephine Baker dance naked at the Casino de Paris. She bought her clothes at Mainbocher and Chanel.

During these forays she stayed in Didi Fraser's huge flat overlooking the Luxembourg Gardens. Didi's brother Louis now ran the Paris bank. Didi herself, at over forty, had been married twice, first to a respectable banker, Frederic Coton, approved of by her father, and then to a broke Englishman, shattered by war. 'Amazing how many men are now blaming their weaknesses on the war,' Violet said. Now she was alone, except for a series of lovers, from bankers to boxers, who came and went regularly. After Joshua Schreft's death in 1916, Didi had worked her way through the first half of a million pound inheritance, and was now at work on the other. Her brother Louis, though disapproving, could do or say little about this. She was ten years older than him, the money was her own and, moreover, she had borne three children, two of them sons, during her ten years with the banker, Frederic Coton. These children were the only offspring the Paris Schrefts were likely to produce since Louis was a homosexual. Therefore Didi's two sons were the future of the Levine-Schreft bank in France, although in the event it was the elder, François, sent by Louis Schreft to America in April 1930, six months after the Wall Street crash, who eventually revived the small Levine banking and brokerage house in New York turning it into Levine-Schreft-Lowenstein, one of the most powerful financial institutions in America.

But Violet, in Paris in the twenties, cared little about Louis, or the bank. In fact, she was scarcely conscious of the stock market crash, which put more lines on Frederick's face and caused him to make appeals for economy, although she did observe that as the decade ended, many of Paris's most amusing émigrés disappeared rather suddenly on liners taking them home. Whether the reasons were economic or not, Paris slowly wore itself out for Violet during the next year.

It had been a five-year-long party for Violet, to which she'd gone dressed by Chanel, smoking out of a long cigarette holder; she'd been sketched by Cocteau, fondled, she claimed, by the Princesse de Polignac and kissed by Ernest Hemingway. During the thirties the merry-go-round that was Violet's Paris began to slow down. Didi herself was too often to be found in a daze in her famous black and white drawing-room. The one-eyed man in a cap who delivered her cocaine came more and more often, and was less respectful each time. A septic abortion put Didi in a sanatorium for three months, after which she never seemed to regain her vitality. During those years Violet herself was involved with a Frenchman from a minor aristocratic family, a relationship which ended when he left her for a singer. Suddenly it seemed to her the bars began to look seedy, not gay, the music was too loud, many of the people she knew looked more desperate.

One night, lying awake at dawn in her eau-de-nil bedroom at Didi's flat, faint dawn light coming through the windows, she heard the familiar tap, tap of the one-legged ex-soldier who came each morning at five to stoke the boilers and wash the floors and was suddenly back in the shabby Paris of 1917, full of wounded soldiers, made dreadful for her by the death of Landry Thomas. She surprised herself by starting to cry.

It had not been a good night. Her lover of five months, a thickset Gascon painter, already too fond of diving into her handbag to pay for the drinks at the Select, the Coupole, the Rotonde, had, when she protested at this for the first time, parted with her, calling her a rich bitch and a Communist, a regular accusation he made when he was quarrelling with anyone. A friend had brought her home, where she found Didi, out of cash, handing a clock from the mantelpiece to the cocaine man. A row had broken out where all three women stood screaming at each other. The man in the cap disappeared with the clock. Now, at five, came the tap, tap, tap of the one-legged man and the memories of Landry. Violet, unable to stand the thought of the morning recriminations and phone calls, jumped up, packed and arrived at the Gare du Nord in time to get the boat train for London.

It was her bad luck that when the maid went into Didi's room next morning she found her mistress dead of an overdose. Violet, subduing her panic, cried and told Frederick she had been so shocked by seeing Didi and her drug-dealer that she had packed and spent the night at an hotel.

Louis Schreft, the dead woman's only brother, came to England and confronted her. The maid had told him Violet's bed had been slept in that night. He wanted to know exactly what had happened. Although under no illusions about Didi's life, he blamed Violet for his sister's death. If on that occasion she had prevented Didi from taking the cocaine, if she had only looked in during the night, he maintained, Didi would still be alive. Realising she could not afford to be connected with a scandal, Violet wept. She repeated she had not spent the night at the flat – would that she had, she told Louis sadly. Then she might have been able to prevent the tragedy. With seeming reluctance she then recounted the actual events of a previous night at Didi's. On the evening she died, Violet said, Didi had arrived with two French soldiers. They'd all been drinking. Violet had remonstrated with Didi who'd sworn at her and told her to leave. If, Violet added, a woman had slept at the flat, in another bedroom, it might have been someone brought in by one of the soldiers – she thought she'd noticed a woman she took to be a prostitute standing outside the lift as she herself got into it. It had been a dreadful evening, she told Louis. There were details she would prefer not to mention, but she was sure he could not want any further investigation into the night his sister died. Whether Louis believed her or not the story silenced him. On the night he left no one came down to dinner at Cavendish Square. Frederick spent the evening in his mother's room, where she sobbed and asked unanswerable questions. Violet did not attend the funeral at Père Lachaise, due to ill-health.

It was about that time that Frederick ceased to knock on his wife's door at night. Since the birth of Joanna, nine years before, Violet had claimed to have lost desire, through no fault of her own. The birth, she said, had been hard, and she believed had done her some damage. This was not true but Frederick could hardly ask for proof. Faced with making love to a cold wife,

Frederick felt ashamed of his own pleasure and came less and less to Violet's room. Nevertheless, for some years, he visited her occasionally at night. Violet always made it plain, though employing some charm, that she got no pleasure from sex. Relieved at having to make love so seldom, she half-expected him to take a mistress, but he did not. She concluded that she'd slowly weaned her husband away from sexual desire, as a child is weaned from the breast. After Didi's death, his rare visits ceased altogether.

It was only a fortnight later that Caroline, back permanently in the house with Jo-Jo, after a family quarrel at the Despencers, announced that she was planning to marry Julian Herries – Captain Julian Herries, as he was still calling himself thirteen years after the war. Tall, handsome and high-spirited, though not very intelligent, Julian Herries had after the war quickly spent the money left to him by his father, tried his hand at the book trade and the wine trade, failed, and was now about to leave for Malaya, to manage a rubber plantation owned by a large company.

The Despencers, who privately regarded Julian Herries as a less than solid character, and knew, as did everybody else, that Caroline had dumped his older brother, Claude, when he was crippled during the war, put a good face on the proposed marriage. After all, Caroline was not getting any younger. Her life was scandalous in their terms, although, they knew, so were many other women's these days. Proportionately more of their own class than any other had been killed because young officers had to go first into battle while often being much less experienced than their own men. They had died in great numbers, leaving the young women they would have married to spinsterhood. So it seemed to the Despencers that Caroline was lucky to find any husband at all. They had lost one son, the second being still helpless with shell-shock. Their other daughter, Rosalind, was now living in Chelsea with a female friend who, as George Despencer remarked bluntly, 'looked just like a man'. Jo-Jo Levine, therefore, might be their only grandchild unless Caroline's new marriage produced other children. He would remain in England, at Sandhurst, and then join a regiment, which pleased the Despencers. On balance, though less than enthusiastic about Julian Herries, they approved of the marriage.

The Levines did not approve. To start with, on marriage Caroline would take the large sum of money she had in her own right as Laurence's widow out of the family, virtually giving it to Herries. Effectively, too, she would be handing Jo-Jo, still under age, over to a new stepfather. Astonished, Violet watched the family machine go into action to protect itself against the new marriage. The Levines' solicitor wrote to Caroline immediately asking for the return of family jewellery. Caroline, who had never been asked personally to give it back, was outraged. 'A solicitor's letter, of all things,' she exclaimed to Violet. 'Honestly, who do they think I am, a defaulting creditor, or a dishonest tradesman? I must say it's indecent.' And after a flurry of telephone calls and conversations Jo-Jo was disinherited – by his grandmother, Sophie, in whose will he figured, by his uncle, Frederick, by his childless great-uncle in Paris, Louis Schreft. Caroline, when she discovered this, was furious. So was her family. A heated row took place between Sophie, Frederick and Sir George and Lady Despencer.

'You must see, Sir George,' Frederick said coolly in the drawing-room at Cavendish Square, 'that in the very unfortunate event of Jo-Jo's death before he reached majority, followed by his mother's death, Jo-Jo's inheritance would go to Captain Julian Herries.'

'So you disinherit the boy because his mother has remarried,' cried Sir George. 'I find that cruel and unreasonable. Did you expect my daughter to remain a widow for ever?'

This hardly answered the point, and they both knew it.

'Certainly, we wish her every happiness,' said Frederick. 'But I'm sure you see the difficulty. I imagine in the same circumstances you would consider things in the same light— '

'We certainly are not considering, as you call it, anything like that on our side,' interrupted Lady Despencer.

'That, of course, is your decision,' said Sophie Levine, somehow conveying the thought that the smaller sums involved and the half-destroyed family of the Despencers made their financial plans less important than those of the Levines.

'Our customs, perhaps, are rather different,' Lady Despencer responded, making it plain, in her turn, that the disinheriting of Jo-Jo was a typically mean, Jewish trick.

'I've already said that appropriate trusts will be set up for Joseph,' Frederick told Sir George. 'But I think you can see it would be negligent of us not to deal with matters properly now. No one supposes that anything will happen to Jo-Jo, or Caroline, in the near future – God forbid it should – but sensible people, I'm afraid, have to assume the worst.'

'I'm sorry,' said Sir George, 'but I find this ruthless, not just the matter of the wills, which is of course your affair, although I must say I do find it very unpleasant, but all this business about the jewellery. Quite frankly, it all looks extremely bad. It seems to indicate an attitude which puts family money above the family itself. How can you people bring yourselves to tear back your brother's, or son's, widow's jewellery, and disinherit his child? It defeats me, it really does.'

'I don't believe you would say that if I were, instead of Frederick Levine, an English nobleman,' Frederick replied, showing some temper. 'And I think you'd find many such families would have made sure Caroline received less of her late husband's income than ours. She is, after all, a rich woman in her own right.'

'What it amounts to is that Joseph's future now depends entirely on what you choose to do, or not do,' said Sir George.

'Unlike your own,' returned Frederick, 'where Joseph would inherit your estate, as the eldest male heir, unless your son recovered, married and had a son, in which case Joseph would get nothing and the other boy everything. We shall treat him fairly whatever happens. He will always be one of us. He's my only brother's child. He retains his rights in the bank. He will always have my consideration and if I were to die, he will have Louis Schreft, Hanno Waldstein, my own son Robert, to look after him. This consideration will not depend on a mere biological fact, whether he is the child of the son of the family, or just the daughter. He cannot be displaced. And,' Frederick added, 'I do not believe your house and land, in any circumstances, however unfortunate, will fall into the hands of Captain Julian Herries. I believe you'd make completely sure of that.'

Frederick's words, including the final slur on the character of the Despencers' future son-in-law, led to Lady Despencer's standing up. 'I don't think there's any more to say,' she told Frederick. 'We came here in good faith to discuss Joseph's future and it seems we've failed to make any impression on you. I find it difficult to believe that once Caroline is married Joseph will be properly considered.'

'I've tried to discuss this reasonably in private,' added her husband, also standing. 'I'm sorry it's come to this, but I'm afraid now all we can do is put the whole thing in the hands of solicitors.'

'That's your right, of course,' replied Frederick, 'but I imagine we both know there's nothing you can do.'

It had been an ugly encounter, with too much said on both sides. 'You must admit,' said Sir George to his wife in the car taking them back to Sussex, 'there wouldn't have been any of this fuss if Caroline had married one of them, some Abrahams or Cohen.'

'Of course not,' his wife agreed. 'They stick together like glue.'

Violet knew she was still under suspicion of having been too involved in Didi Fraser's death. Now the sight of the family moving so rapidly to protect its interests had a further sobering effect. She also recognised that the uncertain, unfavoured son she had met, deceived and married eighteen years before, had grown stronger. She no longer understood him, perhaps because he had ceased to reveal himself to her. She knew it was time to be cautious about her behaviour.

'Have I changed?' she asked Allie one day as they sat yawning in the drawing-room at Cavendish Square. Violet had given orders not to admit any of the friends who would normally come to gossip or produce invitations to parties and first nights.

Allie answered her question. 'Maybe – but you've got to keep on trying. You've been sailing too close to the wind. Frederick isn't even admitting it to himself and Sophie's just biding her time, waiting for you to put your foot in a trap. Then she'll finish you off. You've seen what happens – look at Caroline. Justice, but no mercy, that's what you get here for your transgressions. You'd better make it up to poor old Fred.

No more Paris. Take some interest in the children. Please him. You've done enough to him, and what's he ever done to you?'

'Nothing,' said Violet. 'And I'm already minding my ps and qs. Otherwise, why are we sitting here, bored to tears, wondering whether to get a dog or take Joanna to the zoo on Saturday? I'm trying. It isn't easy.'

'You'd respect Fred more if he'd been more difficult. The trouble with you, Vi, is you want a man who'll let you have all your own way, but you've got no respect for one that does.'

'Perhaps I'll go and get myself psychoanalysed,' said Violet. 'Everyone else is, and it would pass the time. I can imagine my visit to the nerve doctor becoming the high point of the week.' She sighed. 'We could at least go to see *Cavalcade* again – it's quite innocuous. There's no harm in that.'

Allie gazed at her. 'I don't think you're going to stick to the rules. I'm warning you – it's dangerous.'

Five minutes later a maid had been despatched to a ticket agency and it was that evening, at the stalls bar during the interval, that Rosalind Despencer introduced Violet, standing in her aquamarine chiffon dress, little matching satin shoes and an extremely fine double row of pearls round her neck, to her new lover-to-be, the man who effectively brought her marriage to an end.

'Polly?' enquired Violet standing there in her green dress looking up into his brown eyes.

He winked the eye where the lid slightly drooped, and said, 'See? The one-eyed monster.'

'I know you're not either one-eyed or a monster. I mean, you look like a nice, kind man to me,' said Violet, gazing up. He did not. His eyebrows were thick and black, his mouth rather full under a black moustache, his face was rather broad. He looked forceful, but not gentle, and they both knew it. 'I'm sure you're always first,' she said, 'when it comes to taking lost dogs back to their owners and helping old ladies across the road.'

'Absolutely,' he said. 'I do all that while you're in the East End running the soup kitchen for which you're so famous. I'm sure I've seen your photograph in the newspaper, sorting piles of old clothing for distribution to the poor.' He gave a wicked smile.

'Most people have seen those pictures, little as I like to be publicised for doing no more than my duty,' claimed Violet. The bell rang for the next act; the stalls audience, in evening dress, moved off towards their seats, Violet and Polly, having declared their mutual ruthlessness and indifference to charitable endeavour, parted, both feeling rather satisfied by the encounter.

He arrived next afternoon with Rosalind, for a visit, as Violet had known he would. Rosalind left after an hour, saying she was having tea with Caroline and Julian Herries, as Violet had also known she would. They were alone for an hour, and increased their understanding of each other a great deal before Allie came in with Pamela, back from school in a panama hat and grey alpaca dress.

Before dinner she came to Violet's room and said, 'Are you taking up with that man, Vi?'

'I might see him from time to time,' Violet told her.

'You're putting me in an impossible position,' her sister declared.

'You're a nice-looking woman, Allie,' said Violet. 'Isn't it about time you got yourself a fresh interest in life – it's been a long time since Norman Catterick.'

Allie was hurt. Norman Catterick had loved her and left her to become a missionary in Africa, in an area too dangerous, he said, for any white woman. Then someone had sent her the announcement of his engagement from Nairobi, a place where any white woman could live in comfort, going to parties every night and waited on hand and foot by servants. But she ignored Violet's spite and said doggedly, 'I don't like it, Vi.'

In the end, increasingly reluctantly, she stayed, because she loved her nieces and nephews, liked Frederick and was still loyal to Violet, hoping she would alter. But Violet did not alter over the next eighteen months, except to get worse than she had been before Didi's death. She danced more, disappeared for more weekends, often to places where Polly would be present. She was at Cannes, Monte Carlo. She was in nightclubs. She got more tense, more excitable as the affair progressed.

Inevitably, Frederick rebelled.

*

Frederick arrived at Farnley, around midnight. He found four people in the long drawing-room. Hugh Farraday was sitting in evening dress on the window seat at the end of the room. Charles Watts, deplorably, was playing the piano wearing an old black, beaded dress of Sophie's, Frederick's own mother, which he'd found in a wardrobe upstairs. He was painted to the eyelids, wearing powder, lipstick, mascara, even red varnish on his nails. The other two people in the room, Bea MacFarlane and Harry Lowe, were dancing cheek to cheek to the music. Frederick thought that even now Henry MacFarlane, Bea's husband, might be burning his lights late at the Foreign Office, slaving away over the terms of the No Force Declaration between Britain, France, Italy and Germany, or some other worthy attempt to secure a peaceful Europe. And he knew that, while Harry Lowe was dancing so intimately with Bea MacFarlane, his own wife was lying in labour in her home in Cavendish Square. She'd slipped on an icy patch on the steps that morning, and started to have her child in the afternoon, Brough, who'd been involved in the emergency, had told Frederick.

He'd known he'd be shocked by what he saw at Farnley. He concealed his rage about the graceless couple, even Charles Watts in Sophie's dress. He observed coolly that among the bottles and glasses on the table at the end of the drawing-room stood a bowl of white powder which he assumed must be cocaine. The dancing couple came apart suddenly, froze and stared at him as he stood in the doorway. And where, as he demanded of these guests – people he had never invited to his house, and never could have – where was Violet? No one answered. Charles Watts, initially startled rose and walked steadily towards him, murmuring, 'Hello, Frederick,' as he tried to pass him in the doorway. Frederick, horrified by the scent of Chypre from the large, blond, bedizened man who even wore pearl earrings in his ears, turned rapidly and went upstairs.

He opened the heavy door of the main bedroom, knowing what he might see, desperately hoping he would not. Violet, naked, heaving up and down, lay on top of a big man, whose mouth, opened in ecstasy, suddenly closed when his brain made the connection between the door's opening and the fact that someone unfriendly might have entered. As Frederick retreated downstairs, sickened, his heart beating wildly, he thought of Violet's naked white back, writhing buttocks and white legs, mingled with the thick, well-shaped legs of the man beneath her, the black hairs studding those legs, the black moustache, the appalled look of the man as he caught sight of Violet's husband in the doorway. He had nerved himself against what he knew he had to do and what he would find. Nevertheless, he felt ill. In the doorway of the drawing-room Bea MacFarlane, in a red gown, leaned against the doorpost, half-drunk. Charles Watts said, 'Frederick. Forgive Violet. She's – she's . . . '

'I know what she is,' said Frederick steadily. 'I've been ignoring it for years. I'll be quiet about what's happened in this house tonight for all our sakes. Although possibly you don't care. You may all be so lost to shame that gossip means nothing to you.' As he left he said from the hall, 'I assume you'll all be out of the house tomorrow.' He opened the front door and went out.

They heard his car door slam, the engine start up, then wheels on the gravel outside the house. There was a long silence.

Charles Watts said, 'That's Violet done for.'

Hugh Farraday, helping himself to a drink, said, 'She'll not get much out of the Levines. These Jews can be vindictive.'

'He may patch it up with her, I suppose,' said Charles. 'Where are you going, Harry?'

Harry Lowe was walking out of the room. 'Going to my wife,' he said. He had ignored the servant's message from Cavendish Square at four that afternoon, saying the baby was on the way.

Charles said nothing.

Bea MacFarlane's high voice cried, 'You can't leave me here, Harry. Suppose Frederick talks? What are we going to do?'

'Deny it, my dear. That's all you can do,' advised Charles, unheard, as Harry, who had paused in the doorway, continued into the hall. 'Harry!' called Bea in panic. She ran after him. 'Where are you going?'

'To pack,' he told her. He turned, with dignity, to Charles and Hugh behind her. 'I take it we'll all be respecting Frederick's desire for silence about this.' Then he turned and began to go upstairs.

Bea MacFarlane, tripping on the bottom of her long dress, ran after him shouting, 'Harry! Don't leave me here. You can't be thinking of leaving me behind?'

Charles lifted pencilled eyebrows at Hugh Farraday. 'Oho. The rat,' he said.

Hugh commented, 'Well, frankly, you and I have so little to lose.'

'I wonder what's happening upstairs,' asked Charles. 'Obviously Fred Levine caught them in flagrante. But that was some time ago.'

'I'm starving,' said Hugh. 'Let's go and make some omelettes.'

'You always think of food,' Charles told him.

Felix, who presided over these weekends, was in the kitchen with two suitcases, clearing out a drawer containing some bills and banknotes. He looked up, startled, as they came in.

'Quite Hogarthian,' said Charles. 'Where are you going, Felix, at this time of night?'

'I can get a lift to the station from the baker's cart,' Felix answered. 'Then a train.'

'Back to France?'

'You know, sir,' said Felix with some dignity, 'that in a situation like this the servants are always dismissed to prevent them from speaking, or retained so as to give evidence at the trial for divorce. I don't plan to wait which destiny will be mine. If you think I'm stealing, please be assured I'm taking no more than my wages.'

There was the sound of the car taking Bea MacFarlane and Harry Lowe away. Felix went to a cupboard against the wall, opened it and handed Charles a blue medicine bottle. 'You may need this, sir. Mrs Levine's medicine. Five drops only, on a sugar lump, if she will take it.'

'What's it for?' asked Charles.

'She becomes hysterical from time to time,' said Felix, picking up his bags and walking out.

'Wise man,' said Hugh, as the door closed. He was beating eggs in a basin in the big kitchen when another car started up. Charles ran in his beaded dress to the front door and opened it.

A car was driving away. He turned, hearing Violet screaming on the landing. Her wrapper was open. She was naked underneath. There was blood on her right hand, raised towards the open door. Her face was pale, her mouth wide open. 'No, no, no,' she was screaming.

'Oh God,' said Charles, running upstairs in his dress. He thought Violet had cut her wrists. 'Hugh!' he yelled as he ran. 'Violet!' he cried as he reached the landing. Violet turned her contorted face to him, seized the hair on the back of his head in both hands, pulled his head towards her and bit his cheek. Only at the last moment had he any idea of what she was planning to do. As she bit, he seized her shoulders, pulled her from the ground and shook her loose. Restrained by the shoulders, she began to beat at him with her arms, her hands clawing at him and yelling, 'He's left me – Polly's left me – the bastard. The bastard!' The blood on her hand wasn't her own, thought Charles. As Hugh rushed on to the landing she started to scream again. He hit her across the cheek. Violet's head went back, she drew in a sharp breath, then began to struggle and shriek again. Hugh slipped behind her and caught her from behind, pinioning her arms. He wrestled her downstairs. As he went he turned his head slightly towards Charles. 'Run for the blue bottle, Charlie dear. I think we need it now.'

In the end they had to pour what they hoped was the right dose down Violet's throat, as they pinned her to the drawing-room carpet. They held her down, talking to her until she stopped thrashing.

'Oh, my Lord, Violet,' said Charles, as she looked up at them. 'What a performance.' He was pale under his rouge.

'Well, get a blanket, Hugh,' said Charles, 'and I'll put our hostess on the sofa. Honestly, Vi, I think I've seen too much of you tonight.'

Under the blanket in the untidy room Violet said two things, 'Landry. Ring Allie. Landry . . . ' and fell into a deep sleep.

'Better let her rest,' said Charles. 'And I might just pop upstairs and change out of Mrs Levine's dress. It's rather tight, and it's never suited me. And this does look like one of those nights when anything might happen. One doesn't want to be seen at one's worst, if anyone calls.'

'I should have thought that during the last hour everything that could have happened, had happened,' Hugh told him. 'I'm not expecting any more events, myself. Still, you must attend to that bite. It could be poisonous. And perhaps we should both change. With you in that unpleasant frock and me in rumpled evening clothes, and Violet stark naked on the drawing-room sofa, I must admit an observer walking in would think the worst about standards of behaviour in this house.'

As they got dressed, they spoke through the connecting doors of their rooms.

'If you see to the fire, Charles, I'll ring Allie and do the omelettes,' said Hugh.

Charles, buttoning his shirt, said, 'Allie first, before food, I think. If Frederick drives fast, on open roads he can get back in a couple of hours. Allie needs to be warned if he's going to crash in and cause a fracas.'

'I expect he'll just go quietly to bed, and get up in the morning and go to his solicitor,' Charles said.

'I expect you're right,' Hugh said, putting on his shoes. 'I wonder what put it into his head to come tonight? It's all been going on for years – could have gone on until it stopped.'

Charles said, 'Polly's the last straw, I suppose. And Violet was going too far, let's admit it. Do you want me to disinfect that bite?'

'Done it, thanks,' replied his friend.

They went downstairs in trousers, sweaters and jackets, Hugh carrying an eiderdown to put over Violet. Later, having tidied the room, they sat by the fire eating their omelettes, talking in low voices.

'Thank God Allie took it well,' remarked Hugh. 'I was afraid she'd react like Violet. And didn't she say something about Landry? Who or what is Landry, do you suppose?'

'Landry,' replied Charles with certainty, 'is the man who would have made it all right. Every woman, duchess or tart, has a Landry in her life. It's not true to say she never forgets him. What is true is that when things go wrong, badly wrong, then she remembers him. And even if the situation is entirely her own fault, it was Landry, or rather, not having Landry, which caused the difficulty. If she'd married Landry things would have taken a different course.'

'Is that really so?' asked Hugh.

'Talk to them, my dear, and you'll find I'm right,' said Charles. 'Gentleman in the case here, old Polly, runs off, fairly obviously not having said he'll stand by her. He leaves her alone to wonder what her husband will do. Then come thoughts of the late Landry, who would never in any circumstances have behaved in that way, being always a gentleman, and if only things had been otherwise she'd have been an honest girl today, straight up, guv'nor, she would.'

'Polly was always a bastard, even at school,' reflected Hugh.

'I know it. Few have more reason than me to remember that,' said Charles.

'I wonder what he said as he jumped off the bed, jumped into his trousers and ran for it?' Hugh wondered.

'Tell anybody about this and I'll deny it and then I'll give you the biggest thrashing you've ever had,' Charlie told him. 'That's what he said to me, in identical circumstances on that patch of scrubland beside the cricket field, at the back of the pavilion. Shove a bit more coal on. We've got to keep warm if we're going to sit up all night with the little patient.'

Violet, waiting alone in her small, still house in Chelsea, remembered Landry Thomas and sighed. No point in wondering how it would have been for her if he'd lived. The past was the past and Polly was late again. Had he gone to the meeting and forgotten to tell her? Who knew? The point was that this careless treatment of her was becoming a pattern. It only confirmed for her what she already knew. He hadn't suggested marrying her. He didn't plan to.

Frederick had gone to his solicitor in the morning, after the scene at Farnley. Violet knew he wanted a divorce. His mother, Allie reported, found it hard to control her joy when she heard the news. At first, after Violet had refused to divorce him, his desire for a formal separation was so strong he contemplated divorcing her. It had been Pamela, just engaged to Harry Christian-Smith, who made him change his mind. On the evening of his visit to the solicitor she went to her father in tears, telling him the Christian-Smiths would put pressure on Harry to withdraw from the marriage if Frederick sued his wife for a divorce. 'The Christian-Smiths couldn't bear a society divorce,' she'd sobbed. 'It might ruin Harry's parliamentary career. And he says people like us, especially at this time, shouldn't drag each other's names through the dirt.' Frederick abandoned the idea of a divorce of the kind so much enjoyed by the puritanical middle classes and jumped on by Socialists as proving that, as factories and mines closed and dole queues lengthened the upper classes were still living their wealthy, immoral lives.

Frederick's decision was a relief for Violet. She would not be, for a time at least, accused of being the guilty party, the adulteress in a shocking divorce case. But it left her in an ambiguous position, neither married nor unmarried, making it easier for her lover to evade the question of whether he would stand by her, and marry her, or not. With each passing month, she knew, it became easier for him not to speak. As far as he was concerned there was no great embarrassment about being known as the lover of a Jewish banker's wife and no great pressure to make an honest woman of her when the husband found out. And Violet was no one's sister or daughter – did not belong to one of the six hundred hugely interconnected families which were said to rule Britain now, just as they had for centuries. She didn't belong now, and he did, that was what it came down to in the end. There was no one to protect her.

Polly'd been due at eight. He'd probably gone to the meeting and not told her of his change of plans. Now it was twenty past and she decided she could give him only ten more minutes, for the sake of her pride. So where could she go? She'd no invitation for the evening. The streets outside were hot, dusty, hostile to an anxious woman walking aimlessly alone. When the telephone rang she decided it must be Polly with an explanation for his absence.

Allie said, 'Violet, how are you? I'm at a loose end. Can I come over?'

'I'll come to you,' Violet told her abruptly. She wanted to get out of the house.

Allie was living in a red-brick block of flats near Queensway.

Frederick had suggested she stay at Cavendish Square after Violet moved out. She was attached to the children, he said, and they were fond of her. There was no need to go. But Allie had told him she thought it better if she went – she didn't want to be under an obligation to him now and was not really happy about the part she'd played in Violet's affairs. Allie's moving out had been painful for all of them but there'd been no real alternative. She'd accepted Frederick's offer to buy a small flat for her but had refused any other money. Now she had a job with a firm of solicitors in Hanover Square, where she typed legal documents all day. She attended LCC evening classes in law at night, and often visited Cavendish Square on Sundays, entering the house like a member of the family. She had a married lover, Donald Farrar, who was an assistant editor on a newspaper, whom she had met at one of Violet's parties a year before.

Now in her thirties, Allie, tall and blonde, looked pale. Still very pretty, with a big mouth which smiled a lot and laughed often, the long summer without a holiday and the dull job with long hours and low pay had worn her out. She was bare-legged and wearing the old print dress she had changed into when she came back from work. She'd washed off her tired make-up. Violet, who had changed out of her dining-out dress when she left her house, looked smarter in a cream dress and a small green hat, though perhaps, underneath, she was just as weary as her sister.

The sisters had scrambled eggs and a bottle of Sauternes. 'All dressed up and nowhere to go,' Violet said ruefully.

Allie burst out, 'You must get rid of Polly, Violet. He's treating you badly, and he's dangerous. Look at what's happening to the country.'

Violet said, 'I haven't much choice. What would it look like if I parted with him now?'

'You don't really love him,' Allie told her. 'It's his position, and his power.'

'I don't know what love is,' said Violet, looking across the small sitting-room to the pots of geraniums on Allie's window sills. 'I suppose I loved Landry; it was a long time ago; I was different and everything was different. And what did I get from that, in the end? Only grief. For God's sake – it's not much of a world for a woman unless you've got a man behind you, and some money. London's full of single women working for low wages, if they've got a job at all.'

Allie sighed.

'And don't say you told me so,' Violet warned her. 'I don't care. This is a new life. I'm anxious at present, but I'll get it sorted out.' She added half-ruefully, 'We had some good times, didn't we, Allie? Bright young things, eh? Do you remember me bringing the nigger band all the way from Paris for my party? I'll never know what you got up to with that big trumpeter. And the night Robert was born – all those people in fancy dress flooding down the front steps past the doctor and the midwife coming in? God, Frederick was angry. The money I spent – Lord – I wish I had some of it now. We didn't care, did we?'

Allie shook her head. 'We'd all had enough.' She stood on the mat kicking her legs out, humming and doing the Charleston. 'Oh dear, oh dear – winter's come and the butterflies are dying.' She sat down and poured some more wine.

'Where's Don?' Violet asked. 'With his wife?'

'She's ill.'

'Perhaps she'll die,' said Violet hopefully.

'Never,' declared Allie. 'She'll see us all out.'

Light faded in the little Bayswater flat and the two women, fifteen years older now than when Allie had arrived at Farnley and been persuaded to stay, opened another bottle. Both of them began to laugh. 'Can't get much worse,' said Violet.

'Are you sure?' Allie asked.

Violet became grim. 'I won't let it.'

'Disentangle yourself from that man Polly first,' her sister again advised.

'Allie, shut up,' ordered Violet. Later she asked, 'Do you think you'll really be a lawyer?'

'I can try,' said Allie. 'Look – I'm thirty-five and I'm not likely to get married. I don't want to while I'm in love with Donald. I know you think I should, but I can't marry someone I don't love. So, as I must keep myself, I'm going to try to qualify as a lawyer, and not be a secretary all my life. It'll take years though.'

'You should have let Frederick look after you,' Violet told her.

Allie shrugged. 'He put a roof over my head for fifteen years,' she said.

'You paid for your keep,' Violet pointed out. 'When Robert and Joanna had chicken pox, and Joanna was so ill, and putting up with Sophie – and all you did. I couldn't have done it. I couldn't have stood it without you.'

'I covered up for you, though, Vi, didn't I?' her sister said. 'I couldn't really take too much from Frederick after that. He must have known. I mean – the tricks we got up to . . . '

'Fred's life would have been a lot worse without you,' Violet said.

Allie was doubtful. She thought that if she hadn't been in the house, doing many of the things Violet was expected to do, as well as providing her with alibis, Frederick might have confronted his wife earlier. The idea troubled her. All she'd done, so far as she could tell, was shore up a shaky situation and make it easier for Violet to do as she liked.

Violet had used her, Allie thought, mingling charm and bribery with threat, trading on the fact that the Levines had become Allie's family and Allie didn't want to leave. In the end she'd only helped Violet to go from bad to worse, getting wilder and wilder until, perhaps in desperation as thirty was getting closer and closer to forty, she began, eighteen months before, the first serious affair of her married life – if you didn't count Landry Thomas in France. It hadn't brought her real happiness, thought Allie. Violet was fascinated by her lover, whose large, thickset body, a bruiser's physique, Rosalind Despencer called it, contrasted so strangely with her own small, light figure. His air of sheer animal strength and readiness to use it, somehow seemed to call from her admiration, even awe. But not love, as Allie understood it. She herself was repelled by him. His confidence, his swift, but ruthless intelligence, that well-knit body, determined, square-jawed face, large, brilliant black eyes, and her impression that underneath his civilised exterior lay an animal, ready to prowl, run and kill, filled her, Allie, with fear and dread. But Violet was not unique. Many women, the cultivated and well-born, hung round Polly. 'Animal magnetism' they called it and, Allie thought, if you combined the animal magnetism with his double first at Oxford and his promising political career, then perhaps it wasn't surprising that women fell for him.

The boys at his school had probably seen him more clearly than people did now. It wasn't just that one slightly drooping eyelid they were thinking of when they'd nicknamed him Polly, after Polyphemus, the Cyclops blinded by Odysseus. They'd felt the underlying menace of someone who, in the end, was never going to be inhibited by ordinary considerations. He had star quality, glamour, whatever you called it, thought Allie, but in the long run he had the instincts of the alley-fighters she'd known when she was growing up. Perhaps that was why Violet responded to him as she did. Or perhaps, she thought, looking across the room at her sister, Polly was just the male version of Violet. They both took what they wanted and asked no questions.

Allie, a little the worse for wear, due to the wine, asked, 'Why don't you just get rid of Polly, Violet, and lead a quieter life for a time? Frederick's giving you easily enough money – you could write books and articles as well.'

Violet sighed loudly. 'Oh, yes,' she said. 'I can just see myself addressing meetings on peace in a terrible hat, with a shiny nose, then back on the train to an omelette I make myself in the kitchen; up next day to interview Emerald Cunard for the *Ladies' Journal*, or some such thing. Shocking clothes and left-wing politics, articles at seven guineas. I don't think the career-woman's life is for me, really.'

Allie stared at her. She warned her tired, chicly dressed sister, 'Violet, the party's over. You've got to believe it. We're both back in the dusty streets again, in a depression. There's unemployment, pay cuts – it's a hard world, harder still for women.'

Violet leaned towards her. 'Not for me, Allie,' she said almost viciously. 'Not for little Violet.' She stood up, smoothed down her dress and took a cab back to Chelsea.

The house should have been empty. Both the cook and parlourmaid were spending the night with their families and were not due back until next morning. But as she turned on the light in the hall she heard a noise upstairs. She gasped and looked up. Leaning over the banisters, with a bruised face, his smart suit torn and bloody, was her lover. She ran upstairs saying, 'What's happened?'

'A meeting. I forgot to tell you,' he said. 'Some big chaps came to break it up – Communists, louts from the East End, dockers and men like that.' He was speaking with difficulty. His lip was swollen. Violet saw his ribs hurt. He had a cut over one eye which was still oozing blood.

She said, 'Come and sit down. I'll ring up a doctor.' She took his arm and led him into the drawing-room.

'Best not to get a doctor,' he said. 'Least said, soonest mended. You can fix me up eh, Violet? You used to be a nurse.'

'How did you get in?' she said, taking off his shirt.

'Through the pantry window,' he said. 'You ought to do something about those servants of yours.'

'What on earth happened?' asked Violet.

'Nothing new. First they shouted slogans. Then as I went on speaking they charged the platform. Our stewards couldn't hold them back. There was a fracas; they had bloody clubs – one had a meat hook – nasty thing to see brandished in your face . . . '

Violet carefully took off his shirt and let it fall on the floor where it lay on the pale carpet like a huge, black blot.

Kate Higgins, June 16th, 1991

Andy left Brighton. The days were sunny. Sam was back in England, being debriefed after the Belize débâcle. Ray was excited about his coming visit. Meanwhile the situation in Belize worsened as the arrival of the United Nations peace-keeping force was delayed, and interested parties outside the country supplied more arms to both sides. There were rumours of brutalities. Reporters were banned. In the absence of other news the material about the Sweetwater Massacre was often reproduced, demonstrating how far the government of the country was prepared to go to keep control. The Sweetwater photographs began to brand themselves on people's minds. Andy was constantly asked to comment.

One day Sam phoned to say that he was coming down to see Ray and next morning I got up, stretched, listened to the birds singing outside the window and decided it was time to start thinking about Violet Levine again. As for Andy – I couldn't really believe any reasonable man could seriously try to prevent his future wife from pursuing a harmless career as a biographer. He'd got upset and said more than he meant. Must have. Although deep down I still wondered if he might really want a marriage which could only be, in the end, a nightmare for everybody. But I realised I couldn't deal with Andy's complications and hope to lead a normal life, so on that morning I got up full of hope and enthusiasm. I decided there was nothing to stop me from marrying Andy, Ray's coming to live with us, my writing my biography, having a baby. To show I was in earnest I rang Di at work and told her I was coming back, asking if there'd been any calls or interesting-looking letters. No, said Di, giving details proving the world had not missed me much while I'd been away. She sounded strained. 'Are you okay?' I asked, with the return of the old feeling that she wanted me to leave the flat.

'Bit tired,' she said. 'I'm okay.'

I was due to have supper with Ray and my parents before leaving. We'd head for Ray's favourite spot on the Downs, where we could sit outside a restaurant watching the maximum number of aircraft of all kinds going over. If we were out of luck, or in luck as far as Ray was concerned, we could eat our chips while Harriers practised low-level flying over the Downs, over the sea, and yell to each other through the ear-splitting noise. In the meanwhile I got hold of some local directories and found, in Rye, two Gordon Stones. I remembered Dave had told me to have nothing to do with Gordon Stone, but at that point I was the fearless biographer, in search only of truth.

It was all too easy. The first Gordon Stone was a grocer, so I rang the second. An oldish voice answered. 'Is that Mr Gordon Stone?' I asked. It was. I went on, 'I've been commissioned to write the life of Violet Levine, and Mrs Rosie Johnson said she believed you knew her. I wonder if it would be possible to come and see you?'

Stone agreed, 'Yes – yes, of course. I'm busy at the moment . . . '

'Perhaps I could write to you,' I said, 'and give you more information about the book. Then we might find a convenient time to meet.'

And again he agreed. I confirmed his address, gave him my own and rang off, feeling pleased with myself. Stone might be very helpful, and with the Levine family wholly against me, I needed all the help I could get. I was still hearing from the TV company that Jack Christian-Smith, Violet's grandson, was in Latin America. Paranoically, I was beginning to suspect he was back, but like the others, didn't want to see me.

From then on, the day went mad. I was standing in the hall thinking about Gordon Stone when the doorbell rang. Dave, in a suit and tie, stood there, bright sunshine playing over lustrous blond curls. I'd seldom noticed his hair. I greeted him witlessly. 'Hello, Dave. What lovely locks – you look angelic.'

'That's why I wear a hat,' he said, 'so's to be taken seriously as a radical journalist.'

I was quite startled. I couldn't think why he'd come. 'Well, nice to see you. Come in. You on the bike?' I asked, as he stepped inside. I seemed to be hinting all the time that he was a bit peculiar, like a character in a play, always cycling about in a funny hat. That wasn't really what I thought about him at all.

'I've borrowed a car,' he told me. 'I just came down for a conference but I was early. Di gave me your address.'

We sat in the garden, chatting and my father came out of the study, made a phone call in the hall, then joined us. I couldn't get used to Dave, without the hat, wearing a smart grey suit which more or less fitted him, and an open-necked shirt. I couldn't help remembering that only a few days ago I'd been sitting on the beach after a row with Andy, quite fancying Dave. I said, by way of conversation, 'I rang Gordon Stone this morning – got his name out of the directory. He seemed willing to see me.'

It was a pity his face changed just as the sun went behind a cloud. To make it worse the cat, previously a cosy figure on the lawn, made a dash towards a blackbird and seized it. There was a dreadful squawking and flapping from the bird, its wing firmly in the cat's jaws. My mother jumped up and ran towards it, shouting. My father followed. The cat dashed into a hedge and couldn't get through into the next garden with its prey. There was a flurry in the hedge as my parents tried to grab it.

I glanced at Dave, who was looking very serious. He shook his head. 'I don't think that was a good idea, ringing Stone. I warned you not to mess with him. I told you I thought he was dangerous.'

My parents were parting the hedge and beating it.

'Honestly, Dave,' I complained, 'what's the harm? I'm only going to ask him about Violet.'

'Don't go,' he said emphatically. 'You've done enough. Now don't do any more. Please, just leave it alone – do nothing. You might be getting into trouble you can't handle.'

The bird was still screeching. The other birds were making a noise too.

I sighed. I didn't know whether to take him seriously. My mother came over and sat down. 'It's no good,' she said. 'He's got away with the bird.'

We could still hear it, faintly, several gardens up now.

'That was my favourite blackbird,' said my mother.

I thought Dave wanted to go on warning me against Stone, but not in front of my parents. And I wanted him to give me reasons. In fact, not long after that he had to get up and go off to his conference. In the doorway he said, 'Please ring me tomorrow – no, on second thoughts, can we meet tomorrow night? Do you know the Duke of Argyll, King's Cross?'

'No,' I said.

'Eight o'clock,' he told me.

'All right,' I said.

'Nice man,' my mother said vaguely after he'd gone. 'Make some sandwiches – I want to go and change into a dress. I'm broadcasting on local radio about the inspection of hostels for the homeless this afternoon.'

'Like changing into evening dress to read the news,' I said.

Later, we had supper at the aircraft-spotting restaurant up on the Downs, where the air was fresh and clear, and when the aircraft took a break, a blue sky was studded with clouds of birds, going off to roost; gulls could be seen wheeling over the sea.

When I arrived Victoria Station was blacked out due to a power failure. There were, for reasons I didn't ask, a line of soldiers in front of the station. They seemed to be watching me as I walked through the traffic to the bus stop. After Brighton everything seemed dirty and smelly and the presence of the soldiers added an air of menace. I let myself into the flat and woke Di, who was asleep on the sofa. I didn't take any notice of the gloves on the table, went into the kitchen to make a pot of tea, and it was only when I had to push them aside to put the tray down that I felt dimly it was a bit odd to find gloves hanging about in June. But Di was saying, 'Someone's rung up twice this evening for you. I think it might have been your pal, Deep Throat. I said you were on your way. You look very well.'

'You'd better go down,' I said. 'Fresh air. I even had a swim.'

She hesitated. 'I'll go if I can.' She had an open invitation from my parents, but seldom got there. Now, she looked tired, pale in her bright red T-shirt. She was wearing jeans and they'd become too big for her.

'You look as if you need a break,' I told her.

The phone rang, and she jumped for it, then came back saying, 'Deep Throat,' in a silly voice.

Deep Throat's own peculiar voice greeted me. 'I hope you enjoyed your holiday?'

'Yes, thank you. And how are you?'

By now I was used to this tactic of knowing, or pretending to know, all about me. I could even face the fact that he or she might know more than I guessed.

'I'm extremely well, as usual,' came the response. I could hear some background noise and squashed the phone to my ear, trying to hear it. It sounded like music and, perhaps, other people talking in the background. Then, very dimly, another noise I couldn't place. Then, 'How are your researches going?' asked the voice.

'So-so,' I said. An urge to confide seized me, 'The man I'm going to marry is rather against it. That makes it difficult, too.'

'What are his reasons?'

'I'm not quite sure,' I told Deep Throat. 'It's even more awkward, because my publisher is his cousin.'

My caller sounded sympathetic. 'I don't envy you. Think you'll go on? Is the publisher on your side?'

'Yes.'

'I think I knew his uncle,' brooded the voice. 'A fat man— '

I interrupted this reminiscent mood, asking quickly, 'Did you know Gordon Stone? Or anything about him?'

There was a silence. 'It's better if you don't get too close,' the voice said carefully. 'Do you know much about him? If you do, you'll see it's best to approach him cautiously, if at all.'

I felt stupid. 'I don't know anything about him. Where does he come in?'

The caller ignored the question. 'I should be careful. Anyway, I gather Jack's going to talk to you.'

'Jack Christian-Smith? That's wonderful. Why do you think he's prepared to break the family embargo?'

'You'd better ask him,' the caller told me, rather dismissing the subject, then asking more urgently, 'Have you read *Carriage Paid*?'

'I found it very odd, not like Violet. I wondered what was happening to her during those years . . . ' I felt frustrated and burst out, 'Why don't you simply tell me what you know?' At the same time I suddenly realised I knew she was a woman, though I didn't know why.

'Because these aren't my secrets,' she told me, equally bluntly. 'I promised, years ago, to say nothing.'

'So,' I said, 'you ring to check what lines I'm pursuing, sometimes you give me a little help, just as a quid pro quo. I tell you things, you tell me – is that it? But you still don't feel you can break your promise?'

'I'm frightened, also, for myself and for you. I think you're getting into deeper and deeper water.'

'I've had that feeling,' I told her.

'I wonder if I'm being wise,' came the old woman's voice. 'Someone ought to tell the story. But should it be you?' And then she broke the connection. I felt confused and suspicious.

'I don't know what the hell's going on,' said Di, when I told her all this. 'Is somebody mad? Old people sometimes have strong reactions when they think about the past, you know – old grudges and scores, and all that. It can get out of proportion.' She sounded impatient, sitting there and drinking her tea. It was the old conflict between her own urgent concern with the here-and-now and what she saw as my own preoccupation with stale old situations which no longer mattered to anyone.

Yet she was staring over my shoulder next morning as I spread out on the table five pre-war pictures of Violet which had just come in from a news agency's archives.

There was Violet, small but determined, standing on a platform, speaking, with one arm raised in a rallying gesture, a banner behind her.

'What's that?' Di asked.

'A by-election she fought in Kent in 1937 – she lost, but not badly. She wasn't expected to win.' I added, 'She'd probably have got into parliament sooner if there hadn't been a war.'

We looked at the pictures on the table: Violet in a smart suit and hat accepting a bouquet from a little girl on some steps; another platform speech where she stood with men seated on either side; one of her in a big hat, at Ascot, on the arm of a big, thickset man and, finally, one of the crowd in front of a procession. The banner behind her proclaimed the cause. I said, 'She must have nudged her way to the front like a racehorse to get in that picture. Still, she walked a lot of the way on the Jarrow March. You can tell by her shoes – low heels. Normally she wore high ones.' The little, intense face stared up at both of us. 'She's almost forty here. The strain's showing.'

'They were tough times,' Di told me. 'You can't expect her to look like a beauty queen on a hunger march. Well – I'm off.'

'Me, too.' We left together and I went to the library to check on the mysterious Gordon Stone. He wasn't in any of the major books of reference but I found him in the history section. What I read made my blood run cold. I was shocked. Partly by my own ignorance. I could see now why Dave was so interested in Stone, though I still couldn't understand why he was quite so anxious about my going to see him. Deep Throat had tried to dissuade me, too. And the real puzzle was how did he fit into Violet's life?

I met Di for lunch in the café later. She laughed when I told her about my morning and said, 'I'm surprised you had to look him up. I thought Stone was fairly common knowledge.' She added, 'I can't see why Dave's so worried about you visiting him. It was a long time ago – he's very, very old.'

'There's no such thing as a long time ago,' I told her. 'The past and present aren't separate. At least, that's what I think I'm beginning to find out.'

'Spooky, isn't it?' said Di.

'I'll tell you something else funny, as well,' I told her. 'You know we watched the last bit of a thriller last night when you came in? Well, in the morning I thought I knew what that noise at the Deep Throat end of the line was. Remember I said I was trying to hear the background noise, and I heard something faintly?'

She nodded.

'Well,' I said, 'I think it was an American police car. You know, our police sirens don't sound exactly the same?'

She shook her head. 'Do you think you can really ever write this?' she asked. 'I mean, you never seem to find anything out. It gets worse all the time.'

'I know,' I said. It was like swimming for the shore in a sea full of currents – I was being tugged all over the place, and at the same time I didn't know if the tide was taking me in, or dragging me further out.

With the effect of making me feel the tide was on my side, for once, when I got in there was a letter from Jack Christian-Smith, saying if he could help with information about Violet Levine he would be pleased to do what he could. When I rang his office he was out, so I left a message with his secretary.

Violet Levine, 1933

The great European movements of history, the rise of Fascism in Italy and of National Socialism in Germany made it hard, any longer, to stand by in merely silent support of one's beliefs. By 1936, when the Spanish Civil War was raging, I found it impossible, any longer, not to take action. I am happy to say that my house in Cheyne Walk, Chelsea (although there were those who were more than ready to criticise a committed Labour supporter for maintaining a less than simple way of life in a house some people thought far too grand) became to some extent a centre for those who were at the heart of the Labour movement, politically and intellectually. George Bernard Shaw, Harold Laski, the young Hugh Gaitskell, I am pleased to be able to say, were all guests at my home in Cheyne Walk during many stimulating evenings. I can remember, for example, an evening of animated discussion between Harold Nicolson, Herbert Morrison and C. M. Joad about the future of Socialism, which ended up at two in the morning, when the three weary word-warriors agreed that no one could easily predict the nature of a future Labour government, since no one could imagine the conditions in which it might come into power or the mood or needs of the public which would elect it. A wise, if inconclusive, ending to the discussion. Certainly, none of us could then have foreseen that the next Labour government would be elected by the British public at the end of five years of war, and how that fact would dominate the desires and requirements of the nation. And, of course, on that evening in 1936, I could not foresee that I myself would have the honour of being one of the elected MPs in that post-war Parliament.

I Affirm, Violet Levine, 1957

Violet woke up the morning after Polly had come back, and crept out of bed so as not to disturb him. Already the servants were downstairs. She smelt coffee and heard the parlourmaid rattle the fire irons in the grate as she swept. She rapidly unmade the spare room bed, to make it look as if he had slept there, bathed, dressed and made up her face. As she went downstairs the telephone was ringing. She heard the voice of Diana Gray, a woman she had not seen since she left Cavendish Square under a cloud. 'Violet, I'm just back from Antibes and about to go off to Scotland, but we must lunch. It's been far too long. Can you come today – just a few people . . . ?' She named a politician, a poet, a peer and added, 'and Rosalind, of course. Have you seen her drawings for James's book? She's bringing them with her so that we can all look at them.'

'Thank you,' said Violet, putting the phone down, and, never slow to see what was going on, realised that suddenly she was in demand again. Perhaps you had to wait for people to rearrange their thoughts about a new situation, perhaps her tide had turned in the mysterious way it sometimes did.

The phone rang again. Party headquarters wanted Polly. They understood he was resting at her house. When he was ready, they asked, would he telephone them urgently. Violet saw that Polly had told someone last night he was coming to her, the news had travelled, as such news did every morning, while women lay in bed with their trays, telephoning, exchanging gossip and making arrangements for the day. Diana Gray and everyone else, now, would readmit her to the charmed circle. She gloated. Polly had, in some way, indicated that he was firmly allied to her, and Polly was, after all, a favourite in circles where men were so much prized. A part of his generation had not survived. Those who remained were cherished as future leaders, needed by a decimated tribe.

Violet, telling her maid to note the names of other callers, sipped her coffee and, restored now to a full alertness she had lost after leaving Cavendish Square, put the final touches to a plan she had developed silently at Allie's. In view of last night and this morning's developments, it was important to implement the plan without delay. Her situation, she knew, demanded that she open a hat shop, or a dress shop, or a flower shop, where she would be innocently employed selling these items to the women she used to entertain at Cavendish Square. That was the age-old rule in all cases, she knew, with divorce or widowhood, the removal of the breadwinner – the woman was expected either to go into complete retirement or work in some humble capacity, accepting a drop in her living standards and general expectations of life. But, thought Violet, she'd come a long way since then. Violette's, she remembered, was what she'd proposed to call her little flower shop. That was an old dream now. She could do a lot better than that.

She wanted to marry Polly, partly because his rough love-making, in which blows and curses had their part, had moved her as nothing else ever had. And because he was powerful, brilliant, strong, all a man should be. And so, Violet reasoned, going upstairs to the drawing-room where she sat down at her writing desk and lit a Turkish cigarette, the first thing she needed was a better establishment and more money. Polly had little money of his own. Violet, prosperous again, would be able to help by entertaining for him, giving him the domestic base he needed for his work. She picked up her pen but then decided the business she had to conduct would be better handled in person. Therefore she telephoned Frederick at his office, saying she would like to see him at four. He said immediately he would not be available, adding coldly that perhaps Henry Sturgess could deal with what concerned her. 'I hardly think what I have to suggest is for Sturgess to decide,' Violet told him, 'or that you would particularly want him to hear it first.'

Frederick, hearing the hard note in her voice, thought it might be wiser to see her. They had not met since she left Cavendish Square.

For her part, she saw he would be hostile and difficult, and planned to be more so herself. She ordered tea to be taken up to Polly, and his breakfast prepared. She sat opposite him, talking quietly. She had already sent the parlourmaid out for the newspapers which were brought in. These he studied as he ate. 'As ever,' he said, 'our bully-boys have been assaulting the innocent audience. And two of our chaps are in hospital.'

'They'd like you to ring headquarters as soon as possible,' Violet said.

'They'll learn,' he said, putting down *Reynolds News*. 'They'll learn, when they have to submit to proper discipline, or founder. And they call themselves men. Will you send a servant to my house, Violet, and get my man to give her some clothes? I should go to Black House soon. I wonder – I'm due to speak in Lancashire today and tomorrow. Would you come with me?'

'As your nurse?' asked Violet.

'As my lover,' he told her. 'You and I are a pair, Violet, your moon to my sun.'

'I've an appointment at four, but I could join you tomorrow.'

'So be it. But in future, no more appointments but mine. When I call, you must come.'

Violet nodded submissively, knowing that with men like this, woman's weakness was a woman's chief strength. And she was rejoicing in the sense that she was being directed, led, taken care of by this masterful man. Her eyes met his intense stare over the table and she shuddered slightly, remembering how his violent lovemaking, a mixture of control and brutality, had taken her, for the first time in her life it seemed to her, from the edge of pleasure, to the heart of a storm, where pleasure and pain mingled, leaving her, afterwards, calm, bruised, grateful. Always, while he was making love to her, she could feel murder in the air. She loved the subjugation and the man who had crushed her. And there was a sort of pride she felt as, well-groomed and well-dressed, she trod ordinary ground, in an ordinary way, after their ferocious nights. No one knew, no one could tell, that underneath the well-cut frocks lay bruises on her arms and legs, that she faced the day with composure after a night of pain and delight in the arms of a man greater than other men. So she looked into Polly's eyes, trembled and told him, 'I'll do whatever you say from now on.'

He got up and left the room. He went upstairs to the drawing-room to use the telephone, while she told her maid to go and collect his clothes.

She walked into Diana Gray's house at Hyde Park Gate that lunch-time concealing her sense of triumph. She was impeccably dressed in a dove-grey dress and coat, grey suede shoes, a small plum-coloured hat with a veil on her head. She greeted her hostess with a kiss, carefully not touching her powdered cheek, giving no hint that she had not seen her for six months. There were five guests, one of whom, the poet, Jolyon Jones, was the hostess's cousin. He wore a red shirt and a piece of sticking plaster on his ear. He'd been at the Hammersmith meeting the previous night. 'The stewards had truncheons,' he told them at lunch, 'and weren't afraid to use them.'

'You might reflect,' said Lord Rillington, who was drinking whisky with his veal, 'that Mosley's men never try to break up anyone else's meetings. The boot's always on the other foot. It's your lot who go there to cause trouble.'

'I suppose you'll tell me the country needs more men like him,' said Jones.

'We could certainly do with some discipline,' said Rillington. 'It was a pity he ever left the Conservative Party in my opinion. Anyway, look around you at the state of the country – apathy, cynicism, loss of any idealism whatsoever. I see us living under grey clouds. At least the Mosley lot have got some energy, some ideas, and there are many brilliant men involved.'

'And a lot more hooligans, unemployed men, remittance men, disappointed ex-officers left over from the war, people who couldn't make a go of it in the colonies,' said Jones. 'I should know. They were attacking me last night. I didn't see any brilliance, except the stars before my eyes when one of them hit me with a life-preserver.'

'Well, not in the rank and file, obviously,' said Rillington.

'Perhaps he'll be our Prime Minister,' Diana Gray wondered. 'I shall have to invest in a well-tailored uniform and a black shirt, I suppose, just to stay in fashion. Or will it be more a case of having to stay at home and have many sons? I'm not sure how well I'd manage that. I mean, one or two would be all right, but I wouldn't like to get to cricket team proportions. What do you think, Violet?' she said, tauntingly.

'I don't think the movement really asks that of its women,' Violet said primly, adding, as a dig at Diana, who had recently left her husband, 'In any case, isn't this rather speculative in both our cases? It would hardly do for either of us to start producing even the spin bowler for the team at present.'

'Right as ever, Violet,' said Beakie Smith, who had arrived with the heavyweight boxer known jokingly as 'Beakie's pugilist'. He now sat sulkily in his chair, drinking his glass almost as soon as it was filled, not listening to the chatter around him, until Rillington asked him something about Joe Louis and they began to talk with animation. 'Anyway,' said Beakie, over the sporting conversation, 'didn't Hitler just murder an Austrian? I mean, that won't do, going around murdering other countries' politicians.'

'Hitler has nothing to do with the British Union of Fascists,' said Violet. 'I didn't know you were interested in politics, Beakie.'

'Oh, it's just something I heard,' she said.

'Don't worry, Beakie,' advised Diana. 'It's well known blonde ladies shouldn't think about these things. It turns their hair brown. Well, sorry, Jolyon, I know your friends, the lady comrades, take these things seriously, but you can't expect the rest of us to.'

'You'll have to in the end,' observed Jones. 'Is there any chance of us getting any pudding? Or an apple would do.'

'So sorry, Joly,' said Diana. 'I'm afraid it's been like this ever since the staff collectivised the household. I'm surprised you're complaining. It's far more equal these days, and that's the point. I'm only entertaining you now because it's my turn. Tomorrow, the cook's invited guests to lunch and I'm doing the cooking so don't grumble, everything here is just what you approve of . . . '

As a protest, Jolyon refused the raspberry fool when the maid brought it in moments later. 'It's very nice, Jolyon,' Diana observed, with her spoon in her hand. 'Won't you have some? It's quite a bright shade of red.'

'You'll be murdered one day, Diana,' said Violet. 'The jury won't convict.'

'If your lot get in, Violet,' Jones said, 'there won't be such a thing as a jury, only a firing squad.'

'Oh, this is so squalid,' Diana Gray declared, putting down her spoon. 'Eternal politics. It's never-ending. I wonder what's happened to Rosalind. She said she'd be a little late, but this counts as very late, I think.'

Rosalind came in as they were having coffee, followed, Violet saw with a thrill, by Polly, who said to Diana, 'I hope you don't mind. Rosalind and I met in the Strand. She was looking for a taxi so I offered her a lift.'

'You must have some lunch,' said Diana, reaching for the bell on the dining-room wall.

'No,' said Rosalind. 'I'm only eating vegetables. It's a cure I'm taking – didn't I say? I'm so sorry.'

'I've had lunch, thank you,' Polly was saying when Jolyon Jones stood up, and said, 'This is absolutely no good,' in a cold, loud voice. As he spoke Diana was still conducting the conversation about who wanted lunch while, at the same time, the boxer and Rillington, having strayed on to bodyline bowling, were back on the prospects for a Schmeling-Louis match. Jolyon went half-unheard. As they all slowly caught what he'd said and turned in his direction, he repeated, 'It's no good. I can't sit at the same table with an out-and-out Fascist and a man I saw, personally, at a meeting last night, punching an ordinary worker about the head.'

'Jolyon!' exclaimed Diana. 'What are you talking about?'

'I'll most gladly leave,' said Polly, 'although not without mentioning that a number of ordinary workers certainly punched me last night, as anyone who looks at me can see. But I certainly don't want to cause a fuss here. Diana— '

'Oh, Jolyon, sit down,' said Diana.

'Certainly not,' he said. 'Don't let me disturb you. I'm just leaving, that's all. Stay where you are, Polly. I'm going.'

'Well,' fumed Diana, when he'd gone and Polly had sat down, 'I certainly call that incredibly childish. Rosalind, you must have some coffee.'

Rosalind thanked her and asked Violet, 'How are you? We never meet. We ought to try harder.'

Rillington said, 'My father once told me never to disturb a social occasion by arguing about politics, money or a woman.'

'He was right,' the boxer agreed. 'Stick to that rule and there'd never be any trouble.'

Beakie Smith asked, 'Is that why Jolyon's gone?'

Rosalind had opened her big bag and spread her drawings on the table. 'Well, the author wanted Jean Cocteau and he got me, I'm afraid,' she told Diana. 'So he wasn't all that cordial at first, but he says he likes them now.'

Rosalind hadn't exactly made an effort with her appearance, Violet thought. Far from it. She was wearing unironed brown linen slacks, a white shirt which looked like a man's and seemed crumpled. Her face was not made up and her hands, as she opened the book she had taken from a big satchel on the floor, were ill-tended, and the nails bitten. It was probably true she'd become what they called a man-hater; her relationship with the woman friend she lived with, Arabella Crick, was probably a bit peculiar. Violet herself couldn't understand it. What could a woman do for another woman in this world? Not to mention the distaste a lot of people might feel about that sort of thing. Still, she thought, looking at the line drawings for the book of poetry Rosalind had illustrated, you had to admit they were good. She'd chosen to illustrate the poems with drawings on mythological themes, though drawn in the modern manner. The swift, sure lines took her eye. She said, 'Oh, Rosalind. Is there any chance I could buy some of the original sketches?'

'Come and have a look,' said Rosalind. 'Pick some – I was only going to throw them away, once I'd got round to it.'

But Violet, catching Polly's eye, realised she'd better be careful. He would not be keen on her showing off the work of a deviant on her walls.

Rosalind, catching the glance, winked at her. 'Anyway,' she said, 'come to tea one day. We can have a good gossip about Caroline's wedding. You've probably heard, she's put it off until November now, so's to give Pamela a chance to have her own moment to herself. Caroline's must be reckoned one of the world's longest engagements. I can't imagine why.'

Violet nodded. She hadn't heard about the wedding, but the information was useful. 'It wasn't going to be a big affair, like Pamela's, was it?' she asked. 'The last I heard, it was going to be in the country, near your parents.'

'So we thought, but the Herries lot want it in London,' Rosalind said. 'Actually no one else does, not the Levines and certainly not our side . . . ' She looked slyly at Violet and added, 'Well – really,' on an interrogatory note.

Violet's, 'Absolutely,' indicated she understood that her parting from Frederick had made everyone feel they would rather not attract too much attention.

'But there you are,' Rosalind went on. 'The Christian-Smiths want a big bash for Pamela. The Herries want one for their son when he marries Caroline. The rest of us would rather go quietly dressed to Clapham Registry office, to be followed by a high tea at Lyons Corner House. Instead it'll be the full affair – flower arrangements, organ music, ivory satin and the guests putting a good face on it. I'm going to live in Paris for a bit with Arabella so I'll just come back for the weddings. I can't face this country much longer anyway.'

Rosalind must be leaving for a variety of reasons, decided

Violet. She'd become a strong Socialist after the war so a parliament with less than fifty Labour MPs in it, and the whole country in a depression, wouldn't suit her. She might also be tempted by the famous French tolerance for men and women who preferred their own sex. Violet decided not to comment on Rosalind's announcement in case she retaliated by mentioning Violet's own renunciation of the cause they'd both believed in after the war, when it seemed that after all the sacrifice they could make a better world. It would happen, thought Violet, under the influence of her lover, but not the way Rosalind wanted. She didn't want any argument which might upset Polly, who was unnervingly silent as the women spoke.

The prospect of more political dispute made even Diana jumpy. She bent forward and said, 'Polly, you're unusually quiet. I hope you weren't upset by silly Jolyon. He's sometimes so self-important.'

'Good Lord, no,' he said easily. 'I'm used to that sort of thing. Yesterday evening I had the lefties arriving with thugs, coshes and potatoes containing hidden razor blades. Today it's been self-righteous denunciations and stalking out. Par for the course – typical of the weak and self-indulgent behaviour of a generation unconscious of its own demoralisation. What Jolyon needs is more backbone, an aim to strive for.'

'Quite right,' agreed Rillington. 'Diana, my dear, I wonder if you'd care to offer an old man a glass of brandy? I quite agree with you,' he said to Polly. 'It's absolutely shocking, all these young men from good families taking to coloured shirts and sobbing about the working classes. Just another excuse for buggery, if you ask me.' He paused. 'Forgive me, ladies.' He continued, 'Too young for the war, most of them, that's what's the matter with them. I think you saw active service yourself.'

'Yes. Still, that's behind us now, thank God,' Polly said.

Rillington and the boxer had their brandy and Violet, much as she wanted Polly in her presence, began to realise that if he had no other engagement, she might have to tell him where she was going that afternoon. Finally, to her relief, he stood up and said he had better leave to catch his train north. He bent over and kissed her as he left, saying, 'I'll see you tomorrow, then, in Preston.'

Violet left not long after. Punctually at four she was at Levine-Schreft. Quite composed, she entered Frederick's dark-panelled office, where he sat at the same big desk his father had used, and sat down.

Frederick was pale. 'I'd rather not have seen you at all, Violet,' he said. 'You've hurt both me and the family very badly— '

'You kicked me out,' Violet told him.

'If you're going to ask me if I've changed my mind . . . ' he began.

'Of course I'm not,' she told him.

'Your affair with that man is common knowledge. You could at least show a little discretion.'

'For whose sake?'

'My God,' he exclaimed. 'For ours. For everybody's sake. It's not only who he is, it's what he stands for. Are you aware there's now official persecution of Jews in Germany? – this is a logical consequence of your friend Polly's theories. The consequences for Levine-Schreft, the firm which has, and still is, keeping you, are serious— '

'The bank's in Vienna,' Violet interrupted.

'That will make very little difference . . . '

'Anyway, the Waldsteins aren't Jewish,' Violet said. She was becoming impatient. The Levine family's origins were a sensitive point in view of her relationship with Polly. She'd been assured that the British Union of Fascists did not share the Nazis' views on race. She tried to believe this, but didn't. She added, 'I don't know why you go on and on about Jews, Frederick.'

He looked at her coldly and said, 'You're a fool, Violet.' Rather as his Uncle Leopold had done twenty years before, Frederick was making plans to protect the European banks. He and Hanno Waldstein were contracting their dealings in Austria in case a sympathetic Austrian government followed the German lead. He looked at the beautiful, well-dressed woman sitting on the other side of his desk and felt that she had not only betrayed him as a wife, but now, in quite a different way, was betraying him again. 'You're a fool, Violet,' he repeated. 'And you're playing with fire yourself. Do you think that man will marry you? You're very naïve if you do.'

'Shut up, Frederick,' Violet retaliated. 'I haven't come to discuss all that.' The gloves were off. Displays of rage on her part, she'd thought, would damage her cause. Now she saw his attitude to her was uncompromising. He was surprised by her waspish tone.

'Whatever *you* feel like discussing, Violet,' he said coolly, 'I should like to talk about your present behaviour. Can't you stop flaunting yourself, with Pamela about to be married?'

'I'm not flaunting,' answered Violet, 'and I'm surprised to see you kow-towing to the Christian-Smiths' notions of respectability. Which brings me to my point.'

'What?' asked Frederick sharply. 'What now?'

'It's simple,' Violet replied. 'I want my daughter Joanna to live with me. A young girl should be with her mother.'

'Never,' Frederick declared. 'I'll never allow Joanna to live with you. You're corrupt, a thoroughly bad influence— '

'Do you think Pamela's been corrupted then?' asked Violet.

'Pamela had a household – myself, my mother, your sister, Allie. What would Joanna have? Only you and that evil man – unmarried, without honour. I dread to think what would become of her.'

'I want Joanna. I want a decent income, enough to keep a decent household for her to live in.'

'Out of the question,' Frederick said.

But Violet knew that she needed money, and the air of respectability Joanna's presence would give. Servants had tended to the children while Allie had taken over the duties of their mother. But Joanna was docile and good-natured, and now she needed her, a harmless, well-brought-up girl of twelve in her school hat – needed her giggling schoolgirl friends with their passion for cocoa and buns, films (Frankenstein, King Kong, anything with Marlene Dietrich) and their silly crushes on Ronald Colman and Douglas Fairbanks. She thought, too, that once Joanna was in a new, larger house, Allie, her sister, friend and helper, would return. She needed all that.

'Joanna comes to me,' she told Frederick.

'I refuse,' Frederick replied. He stood up. 'If that's all you've come to say . . . '

'If I don't get Joanna and a decent settlement from you,

not the present meagre allowance, then, Frederick, then,' she threatened, 'let me tell you you'll regret it.'

Frederick, pale and tense, drew a deep breath. 'I took you out of the gutter— ' he began.

'That was a long time ago,' said Violet, 'and I don't suppose even you would like to be seen throwing your wife, and the mother of your three children, back into it.'

'Sometimes I wouldn't mind,' said Frederick bitterly. 'But I don't intend to do anything so dramatic. I intend to deal fairly with you, Violet, and that is all. I haven't any more to say.'

Violet leaned back in her chair and regarded him steadily. She had trained herself not to move her face about too much – it was low-class to grimace and it created wrinkles. She said, 'A divorce would be very unfortunate for everybody at present, with Pamela's marriage coming up, not to mention this remarriage of Caroline's, especially to a man whose brother she dumped when he lost his leg. One way and another this is not the right time for the Levines to have to deal with an unpleasant divorce case. In fact, the Christian-Smiths could pull out. I gather the weddings will be close together and both will be fairly elaborate.'

Frederick stared at her. 'Well, Violet, you've never been an angel, that's true, but this takes the cake – you're prepared to wreck Pamela's marriage, break your own daughter's heart to get what you want. I thought my disillusionment with you couldn't go any further. You're unspeakable – my wife, the mother of my children. Also, of course,' he added, more coolly, 'there's absolutely nothing you can do. The only person who could start divorce proceedings is me – against you. And you already know I don't intend to do that.'

There was a silence. Violet continued to sit quietly in her chair, Frederick behind his desk. 'Well, Violet,' he said finally, 'I think this unpleasant little interview is over, don't you?'

Violet shook her head. 'No, Frederick, it isn't. This morning I visited solicitors, Henry and Watkins, in Beauchamp Place. You may check if you want to. I've discussed starting divorce proceedings against you, for adultery.'

'I've not been unfaithful, Violet,' he said, 'and therefore you have no case.'

'Oh, I have,' she assured him.

'Don't be ridiculous. To sue me for divorce you have to cite someone – the woman I'm supposed to have slept with. There's no one to cite. I think you must be insane.'

Violet licked her bottom lip. She said, 'Allie.'

Frederick fell back in his chair. 'Allie!' he exclaimed. 'What in God's name are you talking about? There's never been anything between myself and Allie. You know that. How can you be so vile? How can you even contemplate speaking of your own sister in that way? And as for citing her in a divorce case – my God. My God, Violet.' He sat back and said, as if to himself, 'I ought to throw you down the stairs of this office.'

Violet stood up. Handbag in hand she said, 'I'd advise you to talk this over with Henry Sturgess. I think he'll see it from my point of view. The choice is yours – Joanna and a settlement, or an appalling scandal.'

Frederick slumped with his elbows on the desk, his head in his hands. Violet went out and shut the door. As she went through the outside office she looked at Sturgess, who could never hear what went on in Frederick's office, and never stooped to eavesdropping. Nevertheless, the long years had given him an almost uncanny instinct for understanding what was happening out of his sight and hearing. Now he looked at Violet and knew she had won something from Frederick he did not want to part with, something more important than money. The details, thought Sturgess, would soon emerge.

'Good afternoon, Mrs Levine,' he said.

'And good afternoon to you, Mr Sturgess,' responded Violet, and left with her head high and her back straight.

As soon as she had gone Sturgess got up and knocked on Frederick's door. Frederick straightened in his chair and said only, 'I'm going home, Sturgess. I'll be in early tomorrow.'

'I'll be here at eight, Mr Levine,' said Sturgess.

When Violet got back to Bramwell Street at five thirty she was feeling better than she had for many months. She knew she'd won. She had been fairly sure from the beginning she could strike a nerve by saying she would cite Allie in the divorce. Apart from everything else, she'd always been aware that Frederick's feelings for Allie had been stronger than those of an ordinary brother-in-law. There was some hidden guilt she could work on there.

When she was told by the maid that Allie was upstairs in the drawing-room Violet felt a sudden fear. Could Allie know what she'd just done? Had Frederick telephoned her office? She went upstairs, reassuring herself that Frederick would never do any such thing. He would pay up like a gentleman, hand over Joanna, and the only person in the world who would ever know the details of what had happened between them would be Henry Sturgess, and even he might never know the whole truth. When she opened the drawing-room door, and Allie, dressed in the navy-blue costume she wore to work, turned from the window, Violet became more frightened. Allie's face was pale and furious. Her gold hair seemed to be giving off glittering sparks. Frederick must have told her. Violet quickly began to compose her defence. She'd deny everything and say Frederick had got it all wrong – she'd play on Allie's tenderness for Frederick and his for her, she'd say anything.

'Donald's in hospital,' Allie cried.

Violet, in the doorway, was taken off guard. This was not the accusation she'd expected.

'He's in hospital with a broken arm and a cracked skull. He's been unconscious since last night, when Polly's blackshirt thugs beat him up at that meeting in Hammersmith. They don't know what's going to happen to him. They must have made him a special target because of the paper he works for.'

'Well, I'm sorry, Allie,' Violet said hotly, 'but it's not my fault.' She quickly shut the door, so that the servants wouldn't hear. 'I didn't beat him up, did I? It was obviously a free-for-all.'

Allie cried, 'Violet, I've had enough of it. I've come to tell you that as long as you're associating with that bully-boy of yours, I don't want to see you any more. I don't know how you can bear to touch that man. It's perverse. Poor Don's lying in hospital now. He might never wake up, do you understand? No good'll come of associating with Polly – and this time – this time, when it all goes wrong, don't expect me to come and pick up the pieces. I've done that once too often.'

She slammed out of the room, out of the house, and

Violet sat down shakily. A few minutes later, however, she realised her solicitor must be ready to go home, so she stood up and rang Mr Watkins of Henry and Watkins, and gave him a clear and accurate account of her conversation with Frederick that afternoon.

'So you imagine he'll agree to some proposals, Mrs Levine?' enquired Watkins gently, his manner as kind as was suitable towards a lady who had discovered her husband was conducting an affair with her own sister, and of course wanted to reclaim her daughter from the man who had done something so terrible.

'Oh, I think he'll agree, Mr Watkins,' said Violet. 'But from now on, may I leave matters in your hands. I'd so much rather not deal with it myself. It's terribly upsetting, I'm sure you can see that – almost unbearable.'

'I quite understand,' Watkins said soothingly. 'Of course I understand.' Poor lady, he thought, putting down the telephone.

Violet breathed out heavily. It had been a long day. She'd better get an early night. She was due in Preston to meet Polly next day. As for Allie, she thought, as she rang the bell to ask for a light supper in an hour's time, she'd soon come round. But she was not to see her sister for almost three years, and when she did, in the worst possible circumstances.

ELEVEN

The Levines, June, 1991

Sir Christopher Jenkins, at the Ministry of Defence, said from his armchair opposite Robert Levine, 'I can only tell you we've done as much as we're prepared to do at present. Aurelia Jenks-Davidson is an independent-minded woman. But she's also a responsible one. I'm sure she can handle this situation perfectly well. Nothing she's said to me indicates that she won't. I can't give her orders about whom she chooses to see.' He added, 'Let's remember it's often more prudent to appear candid and not say all you know than appear to have something to hide. And this Miss Higgins doesn't seem to be a very high-powered person— '

'She's in with a radical journalist – a fellow called Gottlieb, from *The Mag*,' said Robert Levine. 'That's one of the things I don't like.'

'If I could have prevented Aurelia Jenks-Davidson from agreeing to meet this Higgins woman,' said Sir Christopher, 'believe me, I would.' He was slightly impatient. He could hardly refuse to see Robert Levine, an influential man and a long-standing acquaintance, but he felt the matter was more concerned with Levine's family interests than those of the government, and really demanded no more of his time. 'She doesn't know everything,' he said reassuringly. 'And as I've said, if by any chance things went in a direction we didn't want them to, then, as a last resort, we always have the law. Not that I think it will come to that.'

'There is something else, though,' said Robert Levine.

Sir Christopher looked more attentively at the thin, intelligent face of the man opposite. Plainly this second part of the story would be more interesting than the first, probably the matter Levine had really come to discuss. 'Well, Robert,' he said. 'What is it?'

'I'm not sure if it's strictly within your province, but I thought it might be useful to talk it over . . . '

'Say on,' encouraged Sir Christopher, deliberately relaxing in his chair. Robert Levine's reluctance to come to the point gave him the idea he was about to hear something disconcerting. He was under orders from his doctor to keep his adrenalin levels low.

When Robert Levine, pale and completely calm, had finished his story Sir Christopher was frowning. 'Thank you for telling me all this,' he said. 'It must have been most painful. But necessary. I imagine we'll have to compose a strategy here . . . '

'I hope you'll consult me,' said Robert Levine.

'Of course,' replied Sir Christopher smoothly, not meaning it at all. It was too serious for that.

TWELVE

Kate Higgins, June 17th, 1991
Violet Levine, 1936

I sat in the Duke of Argyll at King's Cross for an hour and a half, waiting for Dave. At one point I rang *The Mag*, but no one answered. Otherwise I watched well-dressed businessmen passing the time before catching their trains, down-at-heel men nursing their pints, the girls-together having a drink before the evening started, a couple of young girls in skin-tight shiny trousers, hoping, I think, for a couple of the businessmen to spot them and decide to get even later trains. I didn't know what had prevented Dave from coming. Finally, I gave up and went home on two buses, caught twice in showers of summer rain. The showers were quick, but not enough to dispel the stormy atmosphere. The air was heavy, the skies purple. As if to respond to the weather, I felt threatened.

Bayswater was full of prostitutes. They were very young. Men and women were sitting apathetically in the doorways of closed shops in Notting Hill. This was a night to sit in a garden with a few friends, keeping cool, then go inside and watch the storm. I didn't really fancy going back to Henry Thackery House, but lacked the initiative to go anywhere else, so I decided when I got in I'd write some passages for the book. I'd no proper information on some – most – points, but there were parts I could do, if only the background to the times. I'd write something, if only as a gesture. It made the book seem more real. It was, though I didn't study the thought, my private statement that I was committed to the book, for good or ill. It was probably the last point-of-no-return I met. And passed.

When I got in Di was sitting in the front room with a tall, thin man in jeans, about thirty-two or thirty-three; they were listening to some music.

'Thought you'd be later,' she said.

'Dave never turned up,' I told her. 'I'm going to do some work.' There was an odd silence. 'Everything all right?' I asked.

There was a pause. 'Rog says the phone's tapped,' Di said reluctantly. This seems to be the way people convey such bits of information, news of burglaries, divorces, overdoses, people suddenly having to go to hospital. It's as if they felt guilty about suddenly producing an unnecessarily dramatic note at an ordinary moment. They're as embarrassed as if you were going to accuse them of having made it up to get attention.

'The phone's tapped? Are you sure? Why would anyone want to tap our phone?' I added, 'They're welcome to listen to anything I say. I hope they enjoy my mother on the subject of her broad beans.'

I recognised Rog as Di's friend who had worked at British Telecom before he left or got sacked, I wasn't sure which.

'Routine tap, I expect,' he said. 'They do it all the time. Hundreds of thousands a year. Random checks.'

'How long does it go on for?' I asked.

'Few days. It depends if the machine picks up anything interesting.'

I went off and sat down in my room and began to look at my notes. The gaps were vast, the questions innumerable. Deep Throat had thrown doubt on Violet's own report of herself, in *I Affirm*, but had not replaced it with many other, provable, facts. Above all, I still didn't really understand. A biographer is like a policeman, who can only understand people by their actions. I began to type up the undeniable facts of Violet's life. She'd married into the Levine family though lied about the date. She'd been at No 53 hospital, St Luc, between 1915 and 1917, and been elected MP for a constituency in Sunderland in 1945. I'd read old magazines and newspapers about her successful, if brief, political career. I'd also studied all Violet's novels – and I had a reply from Ben Crutchley's daughter, in Australia, saying she didn't know very much about Violet because, as she wrote:

> The family never saw Violet after she left home to work in a shop in 1913. Apparently in those days some of the assistants lived in, like a boarding school. Apparently she sent money through her sister, but otherwise she kept them at arm's length. My father believed she wouldn't own to her family in case they let her down in front of her wealthy in-laws. He was very bitter about the fact that when his mother died, leaving him and his brother very young, Violet never did anything. He always said if it hadn't been for this his brother would never have lied about his age and joined the army, where he got killed. I suppose you want the truth. My father never had a good word to say about his sister. He used to laugh when he saw her pictures in the paper and say she was a conniving bitch. He also used to say what would people think if they knew that her daughter, who had married into a wealthy family was really the daughter of a postman. Tom Rawlins, I think his name was. He got killed in the First World War, so maybe no one will ever know the real truth. I suppose some sleeping dogs should be left. I'm sorry to give you all this bad news. I hope it won't put you off Violet. If I can give you any more help, please get in touch. Look forward to hearing the whole story of my celebrated great-aunt!

I typed on for hours, as the thunder began to roll round the flats.

When I straightened up it was late evening. I went into the living-room with a cup of coffee. Di and Rog were sitting side by side on the sofa, gazing at the TV screen. Di's face was sullen and angry. Rog was expressionless. As I walked in a voice was saying, '. . . all of us wish for nothing better than to live quietly with our families, undisturbed by crime and political violence. Nor do we wish, in our own homes, to be presented with images of crime and violence, or undesirable sexual material, or items which shock and disturb and the only effect of which is to publicise and encourage those who indulge in violence. We do not want newspapers and magazines, openly on sale in our local shops, to present us, or our children, with upsetting, distressing material, the only purpose of which is to pander to people's worst instincts.

To be forced to witness undesirable sexual material or shocking scenes of violence is an infringement of our liberty. It is for that reason that we have established the new board which, in response to complaints from the public, will have powers to seize books, newspapers and magazines of the kind I have described if it is on sale in shops, and prevent the broadcasting, on radio or TV, of this kind of material. And I'm perfectly sure,' he added, his moustached face and burning-coal eyes giving way to a flashing collage of girlie pictures, dead bodies lying shot in dusty streets, fighting men and even more girlie pictures, 'I'm perfectly sure,' he repeated, 'that in this we, the government, are responding to the decent wishes of ordinary people everywhere.'

In Henry Thackery House, North Kensington, ordinary people's decent wishes were centred on being able to walk home at night without meeting a mugger, getting their rubbish cleared, getting a paid job, managing to keep up with the bills and finding a bed in hospital when they needed one. We sat there in complete gloom with lightning flashes coming through the window. The announcer's voice, superimposed over the picture on the screen, of a dark man with good teeth, a clean shirt, maroon tie, and a big smile said, 'That was the Right Honourable Adrian Critchlow, Minister for Home Affairs.' A muted rendering of 'Land of Hope and Glory' started up as the face faded. The ads began. As a car driven by a woman in evening dress leaped a line of red buses, Di stated, 'Here is the news. There isn't any, except that everything in Britain is perfect and the Queen's corgi has given birth to five nice puppies.'

'Where's the Prime Minister these days?' I asked.

'Too unpopular,' Rog claimed. 'Critchlow's been pushed into the limelight while they polish up the leader's image. They seem to be trundling it out occasionally, like Hindenberg. Banning the news will help all that.'

'Except for the terrifying pictures of disturbances in other countries,' said Di. 'That always helps, makes you glad you're British. You missed the bit where he said women had been offended for too long by degrading pictures of themselves and how no one knew how many sexual attacks were caused by this material.'

'No one does,' I said. 'But that Critchlow looks to me as if he'd like to conduct one.'

Rog stood up. 'Why should he bother,' he said, 'when he's fucking all of us all the time?'

'He comes from near where I live,' Di remarked. 'Our local baker knows his mother. His father was a war hero, very strict. He was something to do with the coastguards. Adrian was the only child, apple of his parents' eye – piano lessons, violin, tons of homework. Now he's a self-made millionaire. They're quite proud of him, round there. Some of them.'

'Should have been drowned in the harbour,' Rog said. 'Well, come on, if we're going to the film.' They were alike, he and Di, but it was more a similarity of expression than physique – both were taut, tired, energetic, quick-eyed. Neither face looked as if it had seen a balanced meal on a plate with attendant knife and fork in a month of Sundays.

They went out in their macs, through the storm, leaving me in the darkened living-room, lit by lightning from time to time. Critchlow's face stayed with me. You can fall in love with someone you've never met, a film star or a musician and you can fall in hate with them as well. I hated Critchlow – his conman's smile, that well-cut head of black hair, nearly too long, and his fresh, well-fed face. I hated those eyes usually called 'compelling' and 'sincere', that firm, baritone voice, that air of authority and concern. According to Critchlow, we all belonged to an imaginary family in a neat house in the suburb of a large town. If we were unlucky, and didn't, by going along with Critchlow, we soon would. In this imaginary family no one ever committed a crime (but was always afraid of being the victim of one), no one needed an abortion, or wanted a divorce, no breadwinner ever absconded, there were never too many children, the breadwinner never lost his job or home, no one in the home ever wanted to be a poet, a mercenary soldier, was gay, abnormally gifted, or clinically depressed. No one was Chinese, Asian or black. Father would be a policeman, or a small businessman, Mother would stay at home washing the net curtains, looking after the old and the sick. Every son went to a fee-paying school to study science and technology, every daughter was an underpaid, but dedicated nurse.

Outside these decent homes prowled hordes of undisciplined trades unionists, black race rioters, housebreakers, proselytising gays, rampant feminists, the wilfully unemployed, hooligans and yobboes, and terrorists of all nationalities. It was Critchlow who would protect the decent home, drive off the mobs of race rioters, terrorists, gays ready to rush down Laburnum Avenue, looting, burning and mincing. Not only protect it, but somehow prevent anyone in it from falling into the same traps. It was a simple, consoling system based on the proposition that all evil lay outside the home and if you did as you were told and were quiet and didn't give Daddy a headache he'd make sure the crocodiles didn't eat you up.

Critchlow must long ago have lost his allegiance to those ordinary folk of Laburnum Avenue, from which he sprang, if he'd ever had any. He'd given his loyalty elsewhere. Still, he had his appeal. Men liked his firm and soldierly manner, women his clean and courteous bearing. He'd been decorated while doing his national service in Korea, he'd got a double first at Oxford afterwards, and a blue for badminton. He played the organ in church on Christmas Day. He had a twin son and daughter, one a nurse, the other a doctor, no prizes for guessing which. He was a man you could look up to.

Assuming the phone was tapped, I went and shouted down it, 'I hate you, Adrian Critchlow.' I felt a fool when I'd done it, and jumped childishly when the phone rang immediately afterwards, thinking it might be Critchlow, calling back. It was Andy. 'I thought you'd be away for much longer,' I said.

'There was an unpleasantness,' he said. 'Let's go out for a drink. Pop on a dress – I've got to meet some people for a nightcap in the bar at the Connaught.'

It was pouring with rain now. In the car I asked him why he'd come back so soon from Cuba. He told me shortly, 'I was asked to leave. I've no idea why. I'd got most of what I wanted anyway, so it didn't matter. I can do the rest from here.'

'Why?' I asked again.

'I don't know,' he said. 'It came like a bolt from the blue – no explanations.'

The people we were to meet were an American Democratic Senator and his wife. Andy invited them to stay with us in the country, when we were established, asking me, immediately, if I'd tracked down any suitable homes. Responding to the congratulations of the Senator and his wife I told him I hadn't found anything yet, not saying that this was because I hadn't been looking.

Andy was very quiet on the way home and not pleased with his thoughts. He seemed to relax as we got to his flat, then lost his temper because there was no milk in the fridge, and, again, when he found a note and a few messages taken down by Mrs Connelly when she was there – his answering machine had gone wrong.

'Well, at least she noticed it wasn't working,' I said.

'I'll have to get some back-up system,' he said. 'It's ridiculous to rely on one machine when you're away as often as I am.' He seemed badly rattled. I brought him a drink, but when I came back with it he was ringing a firm to organise the installation of another answering machine. He banged the phone down. 'My God,' he said, 'you'd think at least they'd have an answering machine.'

It was all mad. Andy'd been thrown out of Cuba; then, as if to compensate for all this, he'd spun me off to the Connaught, in a dress, introduced me to some strangers, and temporarily regained his good spirits; now he was in one of those states of agitation where only total order and control of circumstances will impart peace of mind.

I'd often thought Andy might be one of those very intelligent neurotics who tailor their circumstances so well to suit their neuroses that no one notices they're dotty. He'd secured a job with a built-in overload of challenge and excitement. He was well paid for never living in the same place, with the same people, for too long. He was brilliantly adapted for what he did, but then, I thought, so was a jungle animal. Like an animal, Andy dashed off hunting, used all his resources to find his prey – in his case it was information – then he ate it, and then relaxed, glutted, dashed off and did it all over again. It made me see why he was so attached to his cat, Rupert, who was out as usual.

More trouble arose when he claimed someone had been playing his stereo in his absence. Finally he sat down to relax with me on a sofa listening to a record, and as he relaxed, I began to twitch. I was getting a transfer from his own taut muscles. As the fog came down in my own brain I realised I'd never seen him quite so bad. What had happened in Cuba? Or, what else was happening?

'You're hitting the bottle,' he said, as I got up for a refill. He added, never stupid, 'Trying to blot me out?'

'You're away a lot. I have to adjust to your comings and goings.'

'Better, once we've got a more stable life.'

I heard some parrots screech in a jungle, quite clearly.

'What's new?' he asked. 'How's Di?'

'She seems fine, says the phone's tapped,' I told him. 'Her friend Rog used to work for Telecom and he said it's routine – spot checks on the entire population. I suppose it's since they got the satellites up – once you could see everything from aloft the intelligence service became useless for prowling round installations taking snaps and pretending to be bird watchers, so they had to find another way to keep themselves in work. Checking forty million phones a year, hearing all the latest about Carla's wedding and orders for copper piping and so forth keeps them nice and busy. No one has to lose their job.'

As I chatted I heard whispers in my head, then another tropical bird screamed. I knew I was going mad.

Andy didn't, of course. 'It's as good a theory as any,' he said, 'better than anything of Gottlieb's. His assumption is that what happens is being planned by malevolent geniuses, when, actually, it wasn't, or even if it was, it's turned into a complete cock-up. If they're tapping your phone at all, inevitably it'll be because they're tapping the wrong one.'

'I was meant to meet Dave,' I said, 'but he never turned up.'

'That's good news. But I must say, if life's going on here in its usual relaxed Mexican way, I can't see why you haven't managed to phone a few house agents.'

'I only got back from Brighton today,' I answered defensively. 'Late.'

'They do have phones in Brighton,' he said. 'And house agents. Still, I'll be here for a bit, so we can do it together.'

I looked into his very blue eyes, at his tanned face, the slightly beaky nose. Andy, First-in-last-out Littlebrown, the man with a head full of helicopter noise, gunfire and people shouting in foreign languages, looked at me with the eyes of a child, a boy younger than my son Ray. I was the person who was going to make it all right, make a home, be Mrs Bear in her pinny, with tea ready, when Rupert came home from one of his adventures. I was being offered a new life by this handsome and intelligent man, the thought of whom could make me nearly collapse with desire on a bus going round Hyde Park Corner. Yet I couldn't say the right words. I just kissed him. I think that made him think it was all right.

Looking back, I can see that from that moment Andy was my victim, a hard idea for me to accept even now, so much Mr Wrong had he always been. Quite hard for any woman to accept, so strong is our mythology, in fact our religion, of victimisation. The rape statistics, the income statistics, all the statistics support our victim status. But I know now that from that point on the seesaw began, imperceptibly, to tip. Andy had always sat at the top end, surveying the trees, the grass, the plain with a lordly eye, while I sat at the bottom end with my feet in a puddle. Then his end started sinking. I began to rise. Neither of us noticed it at first, and later, when we did, we both believed it would take nothing at all for Andy to bump me into the puddle again. Then suddenly it was too late. Irreversibly, my end of the seesaw went up; Andy hit the bottom with a spine-jarring smack – and fell off.

Violet Levine, 1936

Violet had fainted down the last flight of stairs at the house in Cheyne Walk. Her daughter, Joanna, a tall fifteen-year-old, was bending over her as she lay by the newel post in the hall at the bottom of the stairs. Her eyes opened. They met her bewildered daughter's eyes, then her own face filled with horror. She whispered, 'Get Allie. Get Allie.' And Allie, whom she had not seen for nearly three years since Violet moved into the Cheyne Walk house with Polly, came, horrified, to help her sister for the last time.

It had been two years since Frederick had given way to Violet's blackmail. He could not risk a scandalous divorce. In particular, he couldn't risk his daughter's marriage. It seemed unlikely that the Christian-Smiths alone could put enough pressure on their son Harry to make him withdraw from the marriage. However, Harry's own thoughts about how his marginal constituency might react to the full story of his mother-in-law's life could make the final difference. Pamela herself certainly thought so and Frederick was not prepared to gamble his daughter's happiness. So, saying nothing to his family about the reasons, he increased Violet's allowance and gave her the twenty thousand pounds she demanded.

Violet promptly moved into a large house in Chelsea, overlooking the river. She repaired it, redecorated and hired servants. Frederick then had to break the news to the twelve-year-old Joanna that she would be going to live with her mother. He attempted a matter-of-factness he did not feel, and succeeded in convincing his naïve daughter that all was well. Unaware that the sisters had quarrelled about Violet's affair with Polly, he told her that her Aunt Allie would be living in the house. Indeed, if Frederick hadn't believed Allie would be there, he might have risked the divorce to prevent Joanna from ending up in a household consisting of her mother and her mother's lover, as she did.

Meanwhile Violet told him it would be better not to see Joanna until she had settled down and Frederick, feeling he ought to give the new arrangement a proper chance, agreed.

It was therefore a whole month after Joanna and Jessie Oates, with the stuffed rabbit, her clothes and her favourite dressing-table, had all been transferred from Cavendish Square to her mother's house that he phoned and asked for Allie, planning to arrange a visit. He was horrified when told she wasn't living there. He went to see her at her flat that evening where she told him she'd quarrelled with Violet. Pressed by Frederick for the reasons, Allie told him the quarrel had been over Polly. Frederick, horrified, at last saw what Violet had been doing. 'My God,' he said to Allie, 'she claimed it was her affection for Joanna – it was only to use the child. She's nothing but a blind, to make that set-up look decent, as though I in some way approved. Now Joanna's there, with Violet, and that man. There's no one between that pair and the child but Jessie Oates. What have I done?'

Allie walked across her narrow flat, opened the sideboard and took out a whisky bottle. 'You'd better have a drink, Frederick,' she said. 'We both had. This has all gone wrong. I couldn't understand why you let Joanna go in the first place.'

'You must have wondered why I was keeping out of your way.'

'You probably wondered the same about me,' Allie replied. 'I realise I'm not Joanna's mother— '

'More of a mother to her than Violet ever was,' Frederick said violently.

There was a silence. Allie broke it by saying, 'Well, Frederick, there've been misunderstandings on both sides. That's no surprise since my sister's involved. I've been feeling very upset about not being consulted about Joanna going to Cheyne Walk. It's a detestable idea.'

But still Frederick said nothing, wishing now he had not come.

'What happened, Fred?' said Allie. She suddenly felt very embarrassed. There had always been feeling between them, more perhaps than there ought to have been. Sometimes she had been lonely at Cavendish Square, knowing that as Violet's sister, and very often without Violet in the house, she occupied an indefinable position, not a Levine, as Sophie was always ready to make plain, not the mother of Pamela, Robert and Joanna, nor their nurse or governess. Frederick had understood this and tried to make her feel more at home. In turn she knew that he was lonely and upset. In a situation where two people are being victimised by a third it is easy for a couple to fall in love. It had not happened because both were careful, more consciously in Allie's case. That history lay behind them as Allie asked again, 'What happened? Come on, Fred. At present your daughter's living with a prominent Fascist round the corner from their headquarters. God knows who comes into that house. Where will her next school holidays take place – Christmas at the

Berchtesgarten with Adolf Hitler? And she's *your* daughter. You know what's happening in Germany. Frederick, for God's sake, you've got to get her out of that house.'

He said bitterly, 'I see now that Violet wanted the money for a bigger establishment, to draw that man closer to her.'

Allie looked at him impatiently.

Reluctantly he told her, 'She threatened me with an extremely nasty divorce case, which might ruin Pamela's marriage. That was why I agreed to do what she said.'

Allie sighed. 'Typical,' she said. 'But I'd have thought you were the only one with grounds for a nasty divorce. I can't see— '

'She said she'd cite you. Presumably she'd have produced witnesses she'd bribed in one way or another – servants, Felix, malicious friends. Even if she lost, the damage would be done. You can see that once things have reached that point the result hardly matters. Mud sticks, people don't always remember the verdict, they do remember the allegations. Many people will always believe the worst. I'm sorry, Allie, I tried to keep this from you.'

Allie, who had stared at him as he spoke, her mouth half-open, and her face transfixed with amazement, said, finally, after a silence: 'That takes the cake, doesn't it? My own sister. God knows who spawned her, it can't have been Ma and Pa.'

Relieved that she had taken the news so robustly Frederick was angry.

'I should have fought her. I wanted to spare you,' he said. 'And Pamela. Even Robert.'

Allie shook her head, 'No, no,' she said. 'You acted with the best of intentions but in the end you sacrificed the weakest. Forgive me – I must say it.'

'I know what I did,' he told her grimly.

'I can't go back,' she declared. 'Violet had the nerve to ring me and ask. But I can't.'

Frederick said, 'We'll go out for a meal, Allie.'

As they walked on tree-lined pavements in the late sunshine he told her, 'I can't do anything until Pamela's married. It's only a week from now. In the meanwhile, would you ask Joanna to return? It would be easier if she came back to Cavendish Square voluntarily.'

Allie nodded but warned, 'A girl of that age can be very difficult.'

'If she won't come willingly I'll have to divorce Violet and make her,' he said firmly.

They sat down in a little restaurant in a side street, looking on to a small square, where traffic moved. He murmured, 'A case like that would make Robert's life a misery.' He added, 'If she cross-petitions, as she well might, she'll name you. You'd have to appear.'

'I know,' she said, 'but you can't use half-measures against Violet. Let's hope it doesn't come to that.'

But it did. Allie asked Joanna to tea after school one day and asked her if she'd like to go home to Cavendish Square. Joanna, still in her grey school uniform, her face ruddy and blue eyes bewildered, said she'd have to ask her mother. When Allie told her that Violet might want her to live at Cheyne Walk while Frederick might want her to live with him, Joanna gazed at her and said they would have to decide jointly, she supposed. Allie ploughed on, explaining to Joanna that she might be asked to say where she would prefer to live. At this, Joanna just burst into tears. Allie began to reproach herself for having allowed the girl to be brought up so much in the Levine nursery – a touch of something like the rough and ready atmosphere in the Crutchley kitchen might have prepared her better for this difficult situation. And this was a thought she was to have more strongly as time went on. But she could do no more now. Frederick would have to decide the matter, after Pamela's wedding.

Violet, sitting stiffly in a pew at the front, as the organ rolled out the bridal march and Frederick, with Pamela on his arm, marched to the altar, was very conscious that Sophie Levine, sitting beside her, was holding herself away so as not to touch her. She had not met her eye since she entered the church. Violet suspected she was keeping a secret and everything about her suggested she knew of bad news for Violet. Beyond Sophie, Caroline watched the service entranced, holding her fiancé's hand. No one had particularly wanted him to come, but Caroline had made a point of it, and there was no way of refusing. The couple's engagement had already lasted eighteen months and people were asking themselves if Julian Herries was really very keen to go to Malaya now he was about to marry a wealthy wife. Joseph Levine, in Guards uniform, sat beside his stepfather-to-be, carefully not betraying his dislike.

Further back in the pews was Frederick's cousin Anna Lowenstein from Berlin, with her two daughters. The young woman Frederick had known in Berlin before the First World War was now divorced. Her husband, from an old German family, being no longer in love with her, had seen the wisdom of discarding a wife from a Jewish family and marrying a younger woman who would have no complicated explanations to make about her bloodlines. The Lowensteins were still trying to get her dowry back, with little success. Hanno Waldstein, heavy-set and moustached now, sat with his wife and their eldest son, well aware that one day they might have to settle in Britain. His sister Aimée's son had become a Communist, to the distress of all his family. They were more upset now, for he had been clubbed down during a demonstration and was now half-paralysed. A week before the Waldsteins left for England the ground floor windows of their house had been broken one night, and a star of David roughly painted on their front door.

There were many reasons why the atmosphere on the Levine side of the church was not a happy one. The presence of Violet, the bride's mother, made everyone feel uncomfortable. Some knew Frederick was planning a divorce. The assembled family – Levines, Schrefts, Duvaliers, Cotons, Frames, Pattersons, Lowensteins – had by now heard about Joanna's living with her mother, and with whom her mother was living. Most were shocked. Louis Schreft, still very unhappy about Violet's part in the death of his sister, suggested that Frederick should simply abduct his daughter as soon as possible and bring her to Paris, where he would protect her from any efforts by her mother to get her back. Frederick was shaken when Hanno and his wife supported Louis's suggestion and volunteered any help they could give. He told them, 'As a last resort, perhaps. But it would be very complicated and unpleasant if Violet made a fuss and went to law. In the end she'll either give up the child voluntarily or I'll divorce her.' No one had confided any of this to Pamela Levine. The Christian-Smith party were happily unaware of the tensions on the other side of the church or of the possibility of future scandal. As the organ boomed out the march and the bride and groom left the church, satisfied, pleased by the wedding, they smiled among themselves.

Violet did not go to the reception at Cavendish Square, merely kissing Pamela outside the church and departing in a recently purchased Rolls-Royce.

'Best dressed woman in the church, though,' Sir George Despencer remarked to the groom's father, Benjamin Christian-Smith, after a few glasses of champagne.

'I don't think the new couple will be seeing a great deal of Mrs Levine in future,' he said. 'Although of course, she is Pamela's mother.'

'That much we do know,' Sir George remarked cheerfully, imagining the new bride's father-in-law to be familiar with the rumour that Pamela was not Frederick's child. If he was, he refused to admit it, saying, 'I beg your pardon,' and moving away at the same time.

'Stuffy chap, the father-in-law, very common,' Sir George later remarked to his wife, well within the groom's hearing.

'You're drunk, I'm afraid,' said Lady Despencer loudly. 'I think I'll take you home.' She turned and appeared to see Harry Christian-Smith for the first time. 'Harry!' she said. 'I'm afraid George is a little under the weather. We'll have to leave. Thank you so much – a lovely wedding – quite beautiful; and I hope we'll be seeing you at our return match next month.'

'Pamela and I have already replied to your invitation,' said Harry Christian-Smith. 'We're much looking forward to coming.'

'Good,' said Lady Despencer. 'Well, George, we must be going.'

After the bride and groom left for their honeymoon, Allie met Caroline and her fiancé coming down the steps at Cavendish Square. They walked into Oxford Street together.

'Something's up, isn't it?' asked Caroline. 'I could smell it. What is it?'

Allie told her. 'The family's up in arms. Particularly the Germans – and the Waldsteins – now Hitler's getting more and more powerful. They can't stand what Violet's done to Frederick anyway, and as for that blackshirt Polly . . . Don't say anything about all this, though. They don't want everybody talking. But if there has to be a divorce, it'll all come out.'

'My God, what a family,' exclaimed Caroline. 'It's a pleasure to leave it. Coming to my bash, aren't you, Allie?'

'No offence, Caroline,' said Allie. 'I'll wish you all the best from my office desk. This one's been enough for me.'

As she left she knew Julian Herries was asking Caroline for explanations. Allie walked back through Hyde Park, bitter about the way in which Violet had involved her in this terrible affair, reproaching herself for the many compromises and wrong decisions she'd made, all of which seemed to have dragged them to this crisis point. 'I wish I'd never gone to Farnley the first time. I should never have agreed to stay. I've spent seventeen years of my life with Violet and this is what it's all come to. I wish to God I'd never seen her again after she left home. I wish I'd stayed in south London. I'll never speak to her again.' She hung her wedding hat on a bush and strode on, fiercely.

Caroline's wedding was barely over and the couple, at last, on the voyage to Malaya, when the opening shots in the Levine divorce were fired. Violet refused to let Joanna go to live with her father. When asked, Joanna said what she had been told to say, that she wanted to stay at Cheyne Walk with her mother.

Jessie Oates came to Allie's flat, in tears, one night. 'There's something so wrong about it,' she told her. 'Joanna admires her mother too much. She lets her sit there in the mornings, making herself up with her cosmetics, and trying on her clothes. She tells her how pretty she is – and once I came in and it was going on and there he sat, on the bed in his shirt-sleeves, pulling on his horrible boots, and watching it. It might sound normal and all right – but it isn't. It's dreadful. Joanna's started to talk in her mother's voice. The same words and the same tone of voice. What can I do? I want to leave, but if I do she'll be all alone.'

Allie asked her to stay on. She reassured her, 'There'll be a divorce. And after that Joanna should be going back to her father. You can go too. I hope so.'

By the end of 1933 the case was being heard before a jury in Kensington. Frederick asked for a divorce on the grounds of Violet's adultery with three men. Violet immediately cross-petitioned, citing her sister, Alice. Two weeks of vivid interest for the reading public from Land's End to John o'Groats ensued.

Violet hired enquiry agents to find Felix, who, discovered in a lodging house in a narrow street near the Gare du Nord, was only too glad to return and give evidence for Violet, after being offered his job back at higher wages. BOARD GAMES AND COUNTRY WALKS AT FARNLEY HOUSE SAYS MAJOR DOMO, reported the *Daily Sketch* describing his evidence. MY SISTER LIES, said the *Mirror*, more than once during the case. MR F. LEVINE'S APPEAL TO HIS WIFE, said *The Times*, after Frederick from the dock had implored Violet to spare her children all this unpleasant publicity. Violet, quietly dressed in tan and cream and manifesting distress and incomprehension about the case, made a good impression. Nothing could disguise the more flamboyant looks of Allie, her head crowned with golden hair a navy felt hat could not conceal. Her slightly Cockney accent also made a bad impression – many saw a quiet and unobtrusive woman, Violet, betrayed in her own home by her flashy sister. As the story unfolded the case became a talking point in parlours and pubs throughout the land. The newspapers were seized from the mat and hidden from the children and servants of respectable homes. SHE WAS A MOTHER TO THE CHILDREN, said Brough, who had volunteered to give evidence about Violet's frequent quittings of the house, and the late hours she kept. But his stressing of Allie's worthy rôle somehow made it more likely Frederick might turn to her in an unbrotherly way. I COVERED UP HER SINS, SAYS MRS LEVINE'S SISTER; FIVE THOUSAND POUNDS A YEAR ON DRESSES; POLITICIAN SAYS MR LEVINE WAS AN UNREASONABLY JEALOUS HUSBAND went the papers, while at Eton Robert Levine died a thousand deaths. Joanna was safely in Paris with Jessie Oates, staying with her Uncle Louis. Harry Christian-Smith, mortified, refused to allow his new bride, Pamela, to attend the trial.

After a dreadful week for the Levines, the jury gave Frederick his divorce, having decided Violet was guilty. They declared he had not committed adultery with Allie. Nevertheless, the case left an abiding impression that Frederick and Allie had had an affair, perhaps understandably because of Violet's behaviour. But Frederick had won and there was no question of Joanna's being allowed to stay with her mother. She returned to the shattered family for Christmas. A fortnight later she did not come back from a visit to Violet. The chauffeur, sent to collect her next day, was sent away. Joanna, crying down the phone, told her father he had been horrible to her mother, divorced her, and she wanted to stay with her for ever. Allie took the day off work to meet Joanna after school. In the street Joanna told her aunt she wanted to stay with Violet, who let her stay up late and go to the theatre often. She had a pony on Polly's farm; life at Cavendish Square was dull, she wasn't allowed to wear nice clothes, or go out, Father was always gloomy; Mother gave wonderful parties, life was fun. Forced to go back to Cavendish Square, she'd run away again, everyone had been cruel to Violet, even her own sister, Allie. She, Joanna, would never betray Violet. She had a high flush, she spoke rapidly, and Allie was very worried. She went straight to Levine-Schreft from the school in Kensington.

'It's as if she'd been given drugs,' she told Frederick. 'It's frightening.' She paused, not knowing what she thought, what to say. 'It's like Trilby,' she said. 'As if she'd been taken over. Jessie Oates won't stay. You must do something, Frederick. The law's on your side.' Allie had come in unexpectedly, she hadn't even bothered to hold her tongue because Henry Sturgess was there. He sat on the other side of Frederick's big mahogany desk, a notebook in his hand. And Frederick had made no effort to silence Allie, or send him out.

'What will another court case do to the child?' Frederick asked, in despair at this further complication.

'Boarding school,' said Henry Sturgess. 'On that you can insist, Mr Levine.'

'Good idea, Henry,' Allie told him.

Frederick thought. 'It'd break that unhealthy atmosphere. Friends of her own age, a breath of fresh air.' And this much he was able to achieve, for now the divorce had taken place he was at least able to use money as a threat. She still had the twenty thousand pounds but he could cut Violet's allowance if she did not agree.

Allie argued that he should go to court for the return of Joanna. 'I'll come back to Cavendish Square, if you want me to,' she offered.

'No good if Joanna won't stay. If her mother continues to entice her back to Cheyne Walk and she continues to go, what can we possibly do? She's almost a young woman. I can't lock her up.'

Joanna had submitted to boarding school, but in the holidays, although she was supposed to stay with her father, she constantly ended up at Cheyne Walk, where Violet arranged a pretty, film star's bedroom for her. She stayed up for parties, wore grown-up dresses and was petted by the guests. Allie said, 'She's singing in German, while a fat Nazi plays the piano in the drawing-room. I don't know how you can stand it, Frederick. What's to become of her? She's completely changed from the girl I used to know. She's rude to me. Her eyes are insolent. She's being corrupted. For God's sake, Frederick, if you won't sue, send her to Louis in France.'

Frederick had not seen so much of Joanna's spiteful looks, which alternated with a dreamy, distanced air, where she seemed to be thinking unguessable thoughts. For her father she maintained a meek and obliging personality. Anything she had not unconsciously learned as a child watching Violet deal with her father she was now being taught, deliberately, by her mother. She enjoyed their conspiracy and made no efforts with Allie because Allie had no power over her. 'What you've done, Frederick,' Allie said grimly, 'is prove to your daughter that selfish and irresponsible behaviour pays. She's at a self-absorbed age now. She sees her mother wearing lovely clothes, dancing with a handsome man to all the latest dance tunes, going out to all the best places, thoroughly enjoying herself. She envies and admires Violet. She sees your life as thoroughly dreary; she draws her own conclusions – crime pays.'

In spite of Allie's pleas, Frederick took no further action, except to do his best, usually unsuccessfully, to prevent Joanna's constant visits to her mother.

Robert had been humiliated. Details of the Levines' lives, hitherto so private, had been exposed, their wealth brought to public attention, calling up latent anti-Semitism. At the time of the divorce, a cartoon showing a hook-nosed Jew in a top hat creeping up between two women saying, 'I don't mind vich sister I have,' was published in *Action*, the British Union of Fascists' paper.

For Frederick, a private tragedy had turned into a public one. At forty-four he looked ten years older. So, content that most of the time Joanna was away at school, at least some of the time at Cavendish Square during her holidays, he took the optimistic view that as she grew older Joanna's fascination with life at Cheyne Walk would lessen, she would become increasingly involved with friends of her own age and, not too long from now, fall in love and marry.

Domestic problems were not the only matters troubling him. Six months later, in Vienna, Hanno Waldstein had said to him what he dared not say, 'You and I both lost brothers, on different sides, in one war. Pray God we don't have to send our sons to the second.' Hanno Waldstein had been christened a Catholic, like his sisters. The Waldsteins were therefore, as he said, as Christian as the Pope, but, he told Frederick, cannibals are supposed, when eating a human being, to declare the roasted victim is a pig. Perhaps they really believe, at the time, they're eating pork. 'So, dear Frederick,' said Hanno, 'if it's convenient, we Catholic Waldsteins can be declared Jews. It's easier to eat us. This may be the start of the Terror.'

'Uncle Leopold warned us,' replied Frederick, 'twenty years ago.'

Hanno, who had not lost some of his old instincts, answered, 'To whom we drink, before going off to gamble.'

They walked down the same streets they had walked as young men. 'Remember, Frederick – Mitzi and Trudi and Johanna, all the girls. Nice to turn the clock back, eh?' As he spoke, he regretted speaking. In those days Frederick had not been married. Only a month ago he had been scandalously divorced. Now his wife was living openly with a Fascist leader, a man in a black shirt with a gang of bullies at his back. His cousin had sustained the worst kind of shock. 'But – into the glorious future,' he said, swearing to himself that tonight Frederick would win at baccarat, tomorrow he would find him a bride.

But Frederick proved unmarriable, and lived quietly with his mother and son at Cavendish Square, large and empty though it was, for the next two years. When he did remarry, in 1936, it was as much to provide a mother for Joanna, who had been returned from a clinic where she had had her appendix out and then, according to Allie, not recovered properly, because she would not eat. It was in October 1936 that Frederick, helping his tall daughter, almost sixteen by then, up the steps of Cavendish Square and feeling her bones through the thick coat she wore, resolved to court and marry his beautiful Italian.

He'd made a dreadful mistake, he knew, in letting his daughter stay with her mother. Fortunately for him he never found out exactly how dreadful a mistake that had been.

Only three people – Violet, Allie, whom Violet had called on in panic, and Joanna herself – knew exactly how dreadful it was. And Joanna forgot. But Allie could never forget that terrible summer evening, as she dug a hole in a garden and buried the evidence of what had taken place in a cottage by the sea. The gulls were wailing and screaming over her head as they swirled towards their nesting places, and the noise they made almost, but not quite, covered the horrible screams from the bedroom of the cottage.

Kate Higgins, June 18th, 1991

I got up quietly, leaving Andy sleeping, and went back to Henry Thackery House to get ready for my journey to meet Aurelia Jenks-Davidson. She'd been in two of the batch of photographs given to me in the council house in Kent by Ben Crutchley's granddaughter, both taken in war-time. One showed Violet and Miss Jenks-Davidson standing in a park, looking at some ducks. Violet was in a little hat and a cotton frock, wearing the increasingly heavy make-up she plastered on as she got older. Her companion was a tall, brown-haired young woman in ATS uniform with several pips on her shoulder. The other shot showed a lunch table – nine people, including Violet and Aurelia Jenks-Davidson – on a lawn with a big house in the background. In *Who's Who*, I'd seen that after her war service Aurelia had joined the Foreign Office where she'd had a solid career, including postings to Prague and Washington. I'd written to her, and been invited to visit her at Bleesdale House, Filton, in Yorkshire. On the map it looked like a village fairly high up in the Yorkshire Dales. I took the train to Leeds and hired a car, and got to Filton, a narrow village in a valley with a pub and a post office and small houses on either side of a street and behind them sharply rising grass and trees where a few sheep grazed. Bleesdale House was just outside the village, a small, old house with a big stone wall round it, a garden full of flowers and trees and bushes in full leaf. A duck was swimming on the stone-edged pond set in the grass, under a huge yew tree.

I rang the brass doorbell on the side of the front door. I knew that Aurelia Jenks-Davidson, as Violet's boss in Special Operations, would know about Violet's war service in the Second World War, but had no great confidence that she would tell me everything. My second letter to the Ministry of Defence hadn't been answered either. I assumed they were working on the sensible theory that sheer inattention is the best way to stop trouble: if nothing happens, nothing will. So as far as I knew, Aurelia Jenks-Davidson would tell me nothing, or might even have been set up to mislead me. I was learning. Some might say it took me a long time. My excuse is that I had a happy childhood and that's no preparation for life. No one answered the door, so I pushed the bell again.

Aurelia Jenks-Davidson came round the side of the house with a trowel in her hand. 'Miss Higgins?' she asked. 'Sorry to have kept you waiting. I thought I heard the bell from the vegetable bed.' She was a fat, sensible-looking woman in a plain blouse and a big denim skirt, espadrilles on her bulgy feet. She must have been in her mid-seventies, but didn't look it. We went through the back door, passing a woman in an apron who was preparing a casserole in the kitchen.

'Tea, Yvonne, can you? You'd like some tea, I suppose?' she asked me.

Inside the living-room, small, with a fireplace and a bow window overlooking the garden, I realised why she had asked me about tea in such a dismissive tone, for she promptly opened a cupboard, took out a glass and poured herself a gin from the array of the bottles on a lower shelf. 'Perhaps you'd like a drink?'

I declined, and she waved me into a flowered armchair by the fireplace and settled in the one opposite.

I told her more about the book than I'd included in my letter, adding that so far the family, with the exception of Jack Christian-Smith, whom I was expecting to see later, was unwilling to see me.

'Families can be difficult about things like this,' she said. Then she got up, went out and came back with the tea tray. On it was a fine old cup and saucer, a plate, a brown teapot and a milk-bottle, a large plate with a cake on it.

I drank my tea. 'I was rather wondering if you could tell me anything about Violet's war service. I've asked the Ministry of Defence, twice, but they haven't answered and I suspect that if I get a reply it will only tell me that it's still secret.'

'I believe you were in Belfast with your husband,' said Aurelia Jenks-Davidson.

I wasn't surprised. I smiled at her and said, 'Yes. I was.'

'Well then?'

'If you mean, I must know something about how intelligence works,' I told her, 'then of course I do. Not much, naturally, but I'd have to have been very stupid not to notice some things. But this must have been very different. And it was a long time ago.'

'Yes,' agreed Miss Jenks-Davidson. 'But, even now, I obviously can't tell you everything.'

'Were you in charge?' I asked.

'I was responsible for a number of agents who were working in Holland and northern France,' she told me. 'Violet wasn't official, she was a volunteer over military age – by that time she was forty-five or forty-six – and I got her chiefly, I think, because I was another woman. I was quite unhappy about it, initially. As I saw it she was too old. We're talking about small boats crossing the Channel at night, often in darkness, often in bad weather, with enemy patrols about. She faced capture, torture – it was a serious business. Imagine my feelings. I was twenty-five. She seemed as old as the hills to me. And I knew she'd been sneaked in through the back door. Through Duncan Mackinnon, I found out later. Of course, we didn't know then what he was, except that at the time he was a golden boy. He'd pulled strings to get Violet in on it all, but as the officer in charge that didn't impress me. We were in the middle of a war, inventing as we went along. It was crucial to have the right people on the spot. If they were wrong, they could get others captured and drive off all the people over there who might help us. It's pretty odd to look back on it.' She topped up her gin and looked at me questioningly. This time I nodded, and she took another glass and made me a gin and tonic.

'Anyway,' she said, 'Violet, when you looked at it, had her advantages. I must say I didn't like it. It wasn't just her age. I actually mistrusted her. But she had obvious advantages – spoke excellent French, and reasonable German – her years with the Levines hadn't been wasted. Women were less suspected in those days, I think, and one of the least suspicious, or indeed remarked-on kind of individual, as you have yet to find out, my dear, is of course a middle-aged woman. Violet claimed that, in black stockings and a black dress, with a basket on her arm, she could have walked past twenty German soldiers in Rouen while transmitting to Britain at the top of her voice, and not one would have seen anybody but the concierge, the farmer's wife with eggs to sell, the lady who ran the café on the corner. After our first interview, when she turned up in full rig – high heels, hat with a little veil, Elizabeth Arden all over her face – I was horrified that somehow I was expected to make use of her. But the fact is, she was a good actress . . . '

'Always had to be,' I said.

'I expect so,' said Aurelia. 'She had quite a career, Violet Mackinnon.' She was the first person I'd heard using the name Mackinnon. I suppose to a former intelligence officer the fact that she had married Duncan Mackinnon was the most outstanding fact about her. 'Quite a career,' Aurelia repeated. 'You do well to think about a biography, but it must be like writing the life story of an iceberg: nine-tenths of it you can't see.'

I agreed. 'I'd like as much detail as you can give me about where she went, and what she did.'

'I expect so,' said the old lady. 'Well, from what I know and understand it only went on for a year. Violet went to

France first in 1942. We landed her and a young agent named Bob Kerr on the coast, their task being to find out where the enemy was, what they had in the ways of troops and so on, where the air force was, and how many. We needed information about what was happening inland. Violet and Bob had no transmitter. They had to make contact with various local groups, get the information then rendezvous, a fortnight later, same time, same place, with the boat which was to bring them home. They did wonders, I must say, always pretending to be a mother and son. Who'd suspect a mother and her grown-up son on the bus with a basket of chickens, swapping family gossip, perhaps she nags him a bit, tells him his girlfriend's no good, where was he last night anyway? Violet and I concocted all that between us. What an intelligent woman she was.' Aurelia sighed and shook her head, sadly.

That was enough for me. 'What went wrong?' I asked.

She smiled slyly. She was enjoying me, I could tell. It was a bit like the old days, guessing what someone was up to, what made them tick. In that battle, I knew she would always win. I said I wondered if I could have another slice of cake. It was delicious but, beside that, I knew, I needed to blot up the gin or she'd run even more rings round me.

'What went wrong?' she repeated. She refilled both our glasses. I ate my cake. She said, 'It can't do any harm to tell you. Your publisher will have to check it all before publication anyway. Well – Violet came back with the young man, Bob Kerr, and it was congratulations all round. Then it was Paris, which was a good idea, because Violet knew the city well, then Paris again, and the fourth time – something went wrong. There was a bread lorry which she and Bob were supposed to take just outside Paris, pretending again to be our famous mother and son combination. This time Violet was a baker and Bob was pretending to be a bit backward – Violet was keeping the family business running while the father was away doing forced labour. They were supposed to hand the bread van over at the rendezvous and get a lift to the coast. But just before they arrived they got stopped at a German checkpoint, papers were examined, and, finally, the back of the van searched. But . . . ' and she paused. 'But, there were two people in there, who shouldn't have been. The guards arrested everybody except Bob, who just took to his heels and ran. Violet and the other two were captured, taken to local headquarters, from which only Violet emerged, free as a bird, several hours later. In time to make her way to the coast, anyway, as did Bob, and get picked up by the boat and brought back.'

'She escaped from the Gestapo,' I said in amazement.

'She didn't escape and it wasn't the Gestapo,' Aurelia told me drily. 'She was lucky. It was an ordinary post manned by an ordinary German officer. It could have been worse.'

'What happened?' I asked.

'That's what we were never sure about.'

I stared at her. 'So that put paid to her career in espionage,' I said numbly. I felt as if I had to put my brain on automatic pilot. If I tried to analyse this amazing story as we went along, I'd lose the controls. I'm not a born reporter. A real reporter can hear anything and stay calm. 'So – that was it?'

'In a nutshell, yes,' Aurelia said, still enjoying it all. And I felt she had a lot in reserve. She'd shock me into a collapse before I left, or she'd want to know the reason why. Aurelia, I reflected, was a bit like Deep Throat. Was she Deep Throat, I wondered? I didn't think so. Her voice was wrong.

'What did she tell you,' I asked, 'afterwards?'

'Said she'd talked her way out of it,' said Aurelia.

'Just that? And did you believe her?'

'Hardly.'

'Why not?'

'Well, to start with, Bob had run for it – very suspicious. She said she'd told them he was half-witted and frightened, hence his flight. So far so good but her chief problem was, obviously, the others hiding in the van.'

'What about them? Who were they?'

'We'd never put them there,' Aurelia said. 'Didn't know them from Adam.'

I could hardly believe any of it. I asked finally, 'How did they get there?'

'Violet said they must have had no papers, knew the van was leaving Paris, picked the lock and sneaked in.' She paused. 'Bob said Violet must have put them there. She had the keys all the time. He also said there was something odd about her reaction when they were found. He couldn't define it. In a way, we had to believe Violet, officially.'

'Did anyone ever find out who they were?' I asked.

'Not officially,' said Aurelia.

'And unofficially?'

'I don't know,' she told me. I didn't know whether to believe her or not. 'But it was Violet's last mission.'

'Oh,' I said weakly. This story was too much, too extraordinary and, as ever with Violet, too mysterious. I told Aurelia, 'I sometimes think she's sitting up there, watching me blunder round a labyrinth she created, laughing her head off.'

'That wouldn't surprise me,' Aurelia said.

'What did you think of her as a person?' I asked. 'How did she strike you?'

'At first I mistrusted her. Then I admired her. After her blunder I realised my first response was right. But, after all, there was no reason why a woman of her age should throw herself into these extremely dangerous situations. You can imagine the consequences of capture. But she did it, and did it successfully – that I did admire. In many ways the ideal agent, brave, with full knowledge of what she was being brave about, not rash, very orderly, intelligent and someone who enjoyed disguise, deception, a secret world.'

'You call the business of the two people in the back of the van a blunder? So nobody really thought there was anything sinister about it?'

'Not fundamentally. We had to ask ourselves, though, if she'd done the same thing before but not been caught – set up her own escape network within the organisation.'

'You must have known who the people in the van were,' I challenged. 'Otherwise you could only have thought she was smuggling German spies into Britain.'

Aurelia, sitting framed against the big yew tree which stood out darkly in the dusky garden, did not seem put out by this observation. But she did not reply. There was another whole level of information which I couldn't guess at. I didn't know the right questions to ask and it was plain that if I tried, I'd get no answers. I did, before I went, ask Aurelia about Deep Throat. It had become part of the coinage of my interviews. It always interested people to hear about it. And I thought that Aurelia, trained to think about mysterious sources of information, anonymity, and secrets, might be helpful.

She asked some questions, then said, 'Do you know, I think I could have a guess about who that must be. Only I really can't tell you, not without knowing the reason she's still clinging to her anonymity. She's told you she made a promise to stay silent. Yet even now she's half breaking the promise, and you describe her as sounding apprehensive about that. It might be unwise to tell you my guess without knowing more.'

I felt fed up about this but, as it turned out, I liked Aurelia Jenks-Davidson and I think she quite liked me. At any rate, she'd charmed me so much I didn't protest about her unwillingness to tell me who she thought Deep Throat might be. Not that she'd have told me anything she didn't want to whatever I'd said. As I put the recorder in my bag she said, 'I've enjoyed this. I think this could be an interesting book.'

'If I can do it,' I said.

'Oh, I think you can.'

I trusted her. She must have been trustworthy to have been given such heavy responsibilities for British agents when so young.

'But,' she added, 'I'm not sure what you might uncover. I should be very careful.' She got up and turned on the light. The room seemed to flood with it. She stood by the door. 'I might as well tell you that I checked, routinely, about your enquiry with my old boss. He's retired now and he simply told me that, assuming you looked all right, there was no reason to withhold any particular information. But he called me a few days later, saying he'd sent a note to the relevant Foreign Office Department in the usual way, giving brief details of a journalistic enquiry, action taken, etc. and got a prompt phone call, asking for a report on our conversation. He told me this was a new drill – perhaps. I found it unusual.' She paused. 'Perhaps,' she said again, 'I'm not sure. And I don't know if I should be telling you this, but I've always thought excessive secrecy can be as dangerous as excessive openness on occasion. It can certainly cause just as many disasters.'

I was puzzled. 'Thank you for telling me. But what do you think it means?'

'It may mean exactly what he said, new routine. The stable door being firmly shut after some horse or other has bolted. Or, it could mean you, or even someone connected with you is wandering into a minefield you're not aware of. I think it's only fair to warn you.'

With that, we said goodbye, and I left her on the step of her house and drove to Leeds.

In the train I noted down what I remembered about the interview. No wonder Violet, in *I Affirm*, had drawn something of a veil over her war service, implying it was because she was still bound by the Official Secrets Act. It looked as if she'd volunteered to do dangerous work for the sake of her country – no ambiguity there. But she hadn't mentioned she'd been manoeuvred into the job by her husband. When she wrote *I Affirm* Mackinnon's name was a dirty word, not that it was much cleaner today. Something else she hadn't mentioned was that she'd been more or less dropped from the Service. And although she might have got herself and her companion killed, the atmosphere surrounding the event seemed, officially, if Aurelia's attitude was anything to go by, very relaxed. It was as if she'd been caught shoplifting a Mars bar. Obviously, the two people in the van couldn't have been important. If they had been, the whole affair would have been taken much more seriously. Anyway, they hadn't walked away from the Germans. But why had Violet decided to freelance the escape? Who were they? A couple of friends from the old days? A couple of people she'd taken pity on? It seemed unlikely. The Violet I was discovering didn't seem the kind of woman to help any old Jacques or Jacquette out of Occupied France just because she'd known them years ago. Apart from that it would have been irresponsible – as it was she'd nearly got the other agent, the young man, killed. And how on earth had she bluffed her way out? Like almost everything involving Violet Levine, it was a mystery.

When I came to jot down Aurelia's remarks about having been asked to report on our conversation, I didn't know what to think. She'd taken it seriously, though. I stuck my folder back into my bag and went along to the buffet for a sandwich.

I was tired when I got in at about nine that evening. Before I'd left I'd noticed Di hadn't been back and it was a bit of a relief when I found she still wasn't back. She was pretty tense these days. I switched on the television, got into my pyjamas and put my feet up to open the letter I'd found on the mat when I came in. I nearly cheered – Jack Christian-Smith suggested I visit him at his office at the TV company at six p.m. in four days' time. When the phone rang I ignored it in case it was Andy, with news of a spectacular manor house on an estuary a full thirty-five miles from Lincoln, or a castle on a promontory eighteen miles from Aberdeen. I knew once he'd decided to do something, he did it. He could easily find the right place in a week, and have the contracts rushed through in six. Well before the first autumn leaves were turning brown, I'd find myself settling into Dread Manor. Thinking this brought about that familiar sharp pain between the brows. It's caused by getting what you thought you wanted and fearing to make a mistake you might regret to the end of your days.

When I woke next morning Di still wasn't there. So I confirmed my appointment with Jack Christian-Smith, then rang *The Mag* to find out what had happened to Dave. His secretary said he'd been in a traffic accident and was in Hammersmith Hospital, with a broken leg and two cracked ribs. She'd tried to ring me the day before.

I decided to spend the morning sorting out the flat. It was tidy, but a bit grimy – a place where no one was in much and nobody cared. I even included the filthy oven in my plan. After that I'd go to see Dave in hospital. So I put on jeans and a tee-shirt, went out and bought some groceries, then made a start, tidily dismantling the gas stove and putting the parts to soak in Flash in the bath; that was how serious the position had become. Di hadn't watered her plants, which were going dry because of the warm weather. I was doing this when the phone rang. When I picked up the receiver no one was there. The doorbell rang, I put the phone down and answered it. Andy came in and looked at me angrily as I stood there with the little indoor watering can in my hand.

'Where the hell have you been?' he said. 'I've rung and

rung. I thought you'd topped yourself, so I dashed round. Now I find you pottering round the flat, watering plants.'

'I went to Yorkshire to interview a woman about Violet Levine,' I said. 'Why would you think I'd killed myself?'

He kicked the front door shut and hit me a heavy blow on the side of the head. 'You stupid bitch. Why didn't you tell me? I've been phoning round the bloody house agents, when I wasn't trying to get hold of you.'

What frightened me more than the blow, which was a nasty one, was the fact that as he struck out, his expression hadn't changed. Or his eyes. Even with my hand pressed against the painful spot where his hand had landed, I was alarmed by this mask.

'What— ' I was saying, with tears in my eyes, when he hit me again. I think I stood there holding the side of my head, saying, 'Andy, Andy,' when he began talking again.

'I've begged you, I've pleaded with you to give up that damned book and marry me, try to lead a sane life. I come back from Cuba thinking you'll have had a rough look round for a house, not a large house hunt, just a few details from house agents, but no, you've been on holiday with your parents. The minute you're back here it's up and off to any part of the country but here. Jesus, if you were going to fucking Yorkshire you could have checked it out while you were there, but I'd bet any money you haven't.'

'Andy, you hit me,' I said.

He stared at me, took in what I was saying, then went on, 'Yes. I hit you. But just you try continual disappointment on top of a job which takes you out of the country all the time. For an intelligent woman you can be very stupid. I'm hurt, can't you see that? I'm hurt because you've got so little enthusiasm for living with me you can't be bothered to do anything, just go running for ever after this Levine nonsense which is going to lead you God knows where, up blind alley after blind alley, ending nowhere, wasting time, energy, money. Is that what you want? Is it? Fuck up our lives, break my heart for that bloody stupid biography?' He put his hands on my shoulders and his face to mine. 'Explain, Kate. Just tell me what's going on. That's all I want to know.'

He dropped his hands as there was the sound of a key in the lock. The door opened and Di stood on the threshold. She couldn't get in because we were blocking the hall. He seemed almost relieved to see her, as if her presence suddenly made him realise what was happening. He moved aside to let her pass. I didn't. I didn't care if she stood there for ever, listening to the row. She squeezed by and went into the front room. I didn't have rows with Andy. Andy didn't like it. He didn't like blunt statements, or questions or getting down to the nitty-gritty either. Lots of people don't. Why should they? I always thought that deadly public school full of big unsympathetic men and boys and attended by all the Littlebrowns (except the grocers), had something to do with Andy's belief that women, above all, aren't supposed to challenge you, ask awkward questions or try to discuss things. Men are the threat; women are meant to comfort you. But I was ready for a discussion, even if it meant a full-scale row, about this obsession with the country house, what sort of a life he imagined leading there, whether my son was supposed to be there, what he thought was wrong with my working on the biography – and those were only some of the questions. After that came the others: how did he see me, who did he think I was, what was I supposed to become under his régime? It sounds weak, but that was how I felt.

I tried to continue the argument, half-shouting, 'Andy, you won't explain what you want of me . . . ' but Andy, the man who could take violent hands off you and assume utter calm the moment he heard a key in the lock, just said coldly, 'I'm sorry, Kate. Give me a ring, when the situation's less fraught,' and walked out, shutting the front door quietly behind him.

Di, as if she'd seen what happened before she came in, walked out of the front room, saying, 'Bastard.'

'You can say that again,' I told her hotly, but one look at her face made me realise she was in no mood for all this. Her clothes were rumpled. It's hard to explain how a tee-shirt and jeans can look extra rumpled, but hers did. Her hair seemed a bit dirty and she was very pale. Obviously she hadn't been to work, or if she had, she'd come home not long after she got there. 'You look as if you'd slept rough.'

'I went to work,' she said. 'But I came over funny.'

'You'd better get to bed,' I told her. 'I'll make you a cup of tea. Do you want something to eat?'

'No danger of that,' she said, 'with the gas stove in the bath.'

'Sandwich? I could go to the Chinese?'

'No,' she said. 'I'll be all right soon,' and went into her room.

Ten minutes later, when I took in the tea she was fast asleep. I went on cleaning. The phone rang again, but again, the person at the other end didn't say anything. I tidied, I polished, I dusted, I cleaned the windows, and, as a finale, I cleaned under the stove, scrubbed the parts and reassembled it. I was surprisingly unmoved by the fact that my fiancé had just swiped me twice round the head and walked out. I was even rather pleased by my successful clean-up. I thought perhaps I had no talent for happiness, just taking punches and cleaning stoves. I bought a bunch of flowers and got the bus to the hospital.

Dave was lying in the ward. I'd somehow expected him to be alone, thought I'd be doing him a favour by coming to visit him, but in fact he was surrounded by people, and talking into a cell-phone. There was such a crowd I thought I might have to go and visit another patient until he was free, but I managed to push in, like someone trying to get a drink at a bar. Dave, saying into the phone, 'Must go, I've got a visitor,' poured a cocktail into a plastic cup from a plastic bottle labelled orange juice, and handed it to me. He introduced me to his mother, his girlfriend Lizzie Shooter, who had brought her little girl, and also a blonde girl and an old man holding a cap. I didn't catch their names. Ferdie Brown and Anwar Ahmed from *The Mag*, were there, too. Then Dave, all golden hair, sharp eyes and striped pyjamas, switched on his recorder, which was on the bed next to the cell-phone, and said to the old man, 'So you saw them coming through the bushes, towards the unarmed policemen, then they were shot?'

'Machine-gunned,' said the old man dourly. 'One machine-gun, and some sporadic revolver fire, that was what I heard.'

'And you were looking out of the second-floor window?'

'Bang opposite,' confirmed the old man. 'Then I hear about a battle with armed terrorists. Well I never saw any signs they were armed. And one of them was just a black lad,

I could see that. No mention of him later, but I saw him lying on the ground, hit. He was twitching, like spasms. I knew what I was seeing.'

'Thanks a lot, Mr Bentley,' said Dave, turning off the recorder.

'You seem to be well off for company,' said the old man. 'So I'll be on my way. I've told you what I saw, but I'm trusting you to keep my name confidential.' Dave nodded.

The old man walked slowly off. Dave explained, 'He saw that shooting on Clapham Common last week from his window.'

The phone rang again. It was for Ferdie Brown. Lizzie Shooter looked discontented and said, 'Honestly, Dave, how do you expect to get better?'

He answered, 'They only let me use the cell-phone in visiting hours. I've complained, but they won't give way. They say it disturbs the other patients.'

'Nice for the visitors,' she said rather crossly. 'Get out, Dave, we want to make your bed.'

He hauled himself into his chair, in his striped pyjamas. The blonde girl and Lizzie's daughter who had been sitting on the bed stood up and Dave's mother and Lizzie started to strip the sheets. Both women were fed up with Dave. You could see why. He had a double first and a PhD and he'd picked a career involving low pay, long hours and almost continual police surveillance. There was no chance of a relaxing family holiday in Portugal or of getting through Christmas dinner without a mysterious phone call and bugged stuffing in the turkey. Now he'd been run over and was a helpless nuisance.

Ferdie Brown handed back the phone and said, 'The Fenians have admitted responsibility.'

'That's three now, isn't it – Active Democrats, Fenians and that Middle Eastern group.'

Obviously there had been another bomb. I'd missed the news. Mrs Gottlieb was sliding on the pillowcases, looking worried, in an unobtrusive way. I hoped she had other children, who didn't live in big cities and weren't standing in front like Dave. I asked her. She told me, brightening a bit, 'Dave's brother Ian's a butcher and Celia teaches at a primary school just round the corner in Rotherham.' She saw the reason for the question and added, 'Out of harm's way.'

'What happened?' I asked, nodding at Dave's leg, which was in plaster to the knee.

'Run over by a bicycle, believe it or not,' she said. 'According to somebody on the pavement it swerved to avoid a taxi. The girl on the bike was very upset.'

'I'm her sister, just popped in with some flowers because she's in bed with bruises,' said the blonde girl.

'Very nice of you,' said Mrs Gottlieb.

'Just as well it was a girl on a bike,' said Lizzie Shooter, 'or he'd have thought it was the CIA.'

Mrs Gottlieb said, 'That's right,' but looked anxious. 'Back to bed, then, Dave,' she instructed. So Anwar helped him back.

I felt a bit surplus and was wondering about leaving when Dave said to me, 'Stone been in touch?'

'No,' I told him, 'but my mystery caller advised me to check his record.'

And Dave laughed. 'Meaning you hadn't? I don't believe it.'

'You might have told me,' I said. 'I was horrified.'

'I took it for granted you knew. So – you've gone off Stone as an informant?'

'I'm not rushing to meet him. But I ought to.'

'Very wise,' Dave said. 'I'm relieved to hear it. You can see now why I warned you off.'

'Wait,' I said, 'he's an old man now.'

'Don't you be so sure. He's protected. We know that.'

I felt like one woman too many round the bed. There were already Dave's girlfriend, her daughter, Dave's mother and the bicyclist's sister. Lizzie's daughter, a child of six, was looking round for something to do. When the cell-phone went again, this time for Ferdie, I said, 'Well, I'll push off. I just popped in to see how you were getting on.'

'Any progress otherwise?' asked Dave.

'Mysteriouser and mysteriouser,' I told him.

He looked puzzled. 'Maybe we could meet when I get out?'

I thought Lizzie Shooter gave me a dirty look. 'I'd like that.' I left the crowd round the bed. I heard the cell-phone ring yet again as I reached the ward door.

Di was up when I got home, saying she felt all right. She asked how Dave was. I said, 'Fine, but how are you, really?'

'Better,' she said. 'I was just tired, that's all.'

I nodded, but I wasn't very happy. I'd known her too long.

'Was that a row between you and Andy I interrupted?' she asked, to deflect any more questions, I thought.

'Yes. He's fed up because I never found our dream home. And I went to see a woman about Violet Levine. He bashed me round the side of the head, twice.'

Di was shocked. 'Charming. What did you do?'

'Nothing. I was too surprised. Then you came in.'

'He rang about twenty minutes ago,' she said.

'I've had enough,' I told her.

'You haven't. He's still got you.'

'No. The only time I've felt easy with him for years was when he lost his head completely, got angry and belted me. Like at school,' I said, 'when you'd finally got the teacher spluttering. It's to do with authority. Well, if that's the only way I can feel free with Andy, when he's yelling and hitting me, what am I saying about both of us?'

Immediately, a bunch of flowers arrived, with a card saying, 'Darling. I'm so sorry. Let's give it a few days. Your loving Andy.' Di, who was really only half all right, managed a laugh. The phone rang.

Deep Throat told me, 'Go to Somerset House and look for a certificate under the name of Crutchley, August 1st, 1936,' and rang off before I had the chance to say anything but, 'But . . . '

I stood still for a moment, puzzled and surprised. A minute later I was checking my bag, thinking I could get to the Central Registry of Births, Marriages and Deaths, St Catherine's House, before it closed. At the same time I told Di what had happened.

She observed, 'She doesn't know Somerset House is changed to St Catherine's House now.'

'That's a fact,' I said. 'Wonder what that tells us?'

Di said, 'By the way, if somebody asks where I was last night, can you say here? I don't want anyone to know where I was.'

'Why not? Where were you anyway?' I asked, looking obsessively for a pen on the mantelpiece, though I knew I must have six at the bottom of my bag.

'Oh, never mind,' she said. 'I don't want you to get involved in any scenarios – just back me up. Please.'

'Okay,' I said and left. On the tube, I reflected that whatever Di had been doing and with whom, it hadn't brought her any benefit. She seemed distracted and half dead. I should have asked myself why, but I was obsessed with following up Deep Throat's tip. She was opening up in earnest now, I thought. *And* I had a date with Jack Christian-Smith, the only living Levine, it seemed, who was prepared to talk to me, except for Joanna, who wasn't in her right mind. Suddenly, I was feeling very pleased with myself. There's a hunter with a spear buried inside all of us, padding along, charged with adrenalin, the death of his prey the only thing on his mind. I was him now. I had the map of the buried treasure, I was clutching the straight flush to my chest. I had the Rosetta stone in my pocket. I was the cat nearly up to the bird on the lawn . . . I didn't realise how much it was a question of whether I was Tom or Jerry.

St Catherine's House was hot and crowded. I charged in ruthlessly but I didn't know whether I was looking for a certificate of birth, marriage or death.

It was a birth. On August 1st, 1936, the birth of a boy on July 27th at Cobb's Cottage, Crake, Sussex, was recorded. Named John, he was the child of Alice Amelia Crutchley, of Bayswater, London, W, and Gordon Quentin Fairfield Stone, of Fairfield House, Anstruther, Cumberland.

I felt very cold as I queued behind a tall Sikh, waiting to ask for a copy of the certificate to be sent to me. I stared at his turban, anxious and thinking. Here was the mystery man again – Gordon Stone. Violet's sister Alice had had an illegitimate child by him. What did that mean? Why had Deep Throat steered me in this direction? Was she perhaps using me to revive an old scandal, pay off a score against Stone, or someone else? And where was the boy now? He was fifty-four, I supposed. And how much did this have to do with Violet?

I didn't dare take the tube back, for fear of trouble. There was trouble on the bus anyway. When we stopped at Charing

Cross a gang of five boys, none above twenty, steamed on to it. They went right along the lower deck, grabbing bags and making the passengers give up their wallets, watches and jewellery. They had knives. One kept a knife on the driver while it was going on. I had to hand over my handbag. I said to the boy staring down at me, 'Can I keep my keys, and this notebook?' I had them in my hand, so he just nodded and grabbed the bag, wanting to get away quickly. The team was on and off in two minutes, and the few people in the rush-hour crowd walking past in the street who noticed the gang robbing the bus did nothing. When it was over there was a Japanese woman in tears in front of me, being comforted by her husband. Above the cautious mumble, which became a babble as it seemed plain the team weren't coming back, I heard a little child saying, 'Why did you give that boy your bag, Mum?'

The driver closed the doors and started off for the police station. I was on a bus going the wrong way, with a woman sobbing, and the tinkling and scratching sound of someone's Walkman – how had they preserved it from the robbers? – in my ears. The whole day – the row in the hall with Andy, seeing Dave in hospital, the call from Deep Throat, my dash to St Catherine's House, which meant I'd ended up in a bus robbery – all began to feel like a dream, and not a good one.

THIRTEEN

Violet Mackinnon, 1951
Kate Higgins, June 19th, 1991

I have often been asked how it was possible for an intelligent woman to overlook what her husband must have been doing. To this question I have no answer, indeed, frequently, and sadly, to this day I ask it of myself. Perhaps neither my questioners, nor I, could ever fully imagine the skills Duncan Mackinnon must have developed over some fifteen years of practising his ugly trade, a capacity to deceive and conceal as automatic and efficient as that of any man, be he surgeon, or electrician, who has been engaged in the same profession for that length of time. However strange it might sound that Duncan Mackinnon's cunning outwitted me, it is true. I suppose I am not the only wife who has been surprised in the same sort of way. What I did observe, with distress, at the time, was his increasingly erratic and nervous behaviour, as the event came to a climax.

I Affirm, Violet Levine, 1957

I still believe, as I always shall, that there came the point where Violet Mackinnon knew what work her husband was engaged in. An accomplice she may not have been, but she knew. She prowled the house at night, like Lady Macbeth and became excessively neurotic during the winter of 1951. She relaxed only when her husband went abroad.

My Life with Violet Levine, C. F. Lamier, 1958

Violet Levine, now Violet Mackinnon, sat, at eight thirty, alone at her breakfast table, looking out over Cheyne Walk to the broad Thames, where barges moved slowly through yellow fog. Bathed, dressed, already made up for the day, she thought long, grim thoughts. That little face, which had once gazed up from the pillow in mock submission to Frederick Levine in the dubious hotel near Praed Street, was now lined under heavy make-up. But her figure remained slender, her back straight, her legs under the long, full skirt of her suit were neat and nylon-clad, her small feet trim in expensive high-heeled shoes. She was full of energy. She had never, in all her fifty-four years, been ill. But, she was thinking, I'm tired.

She'd been for nearly six years a member of what felt like the longest parliament in history. Elected after a world war, it had been both a government of post-war recovery and social reform. It had restructured much of British life, nationalising the country's main resources – transport, coal, steel – instituting a huge programme of social welfare, from free medical treatment to allowances payable to mothers for each child and all this had been achieved during the period from the Second World War, when food and clothing were still rationed and resources scarce. Now the party was split. The leaders were showing signs of strain, the rank-and-file were tired.

Violet, watching the fog thickening across the road, on the Thames, was not only tired, but anxious. Apart from her constituency and House of Commons duties, she was part of a parliamentary team working with the Ministry of War on plans for the future defence of Britain. Soviet Russia, immediately after the war, had turned from ally to potential enemy. NATO had been formed to defend the new alliance of the countries of Western Europe and the USA. Much of the Labour Party, traditionally containing a strong pacifist element and many with emotional loyalty towards the Soviet Union and the Communist Party, was unhappy about preparing again for war against the Soviet bloc, under strong pressure from the USA. Many in the government resented paying for costly rearmament, which would mean cutting social welfare payments.

Violet's own mind was made up, had been made up for her in France during two long wars. She was strongly for NATO and rearmament. She also saw, shrewdly, no hope for pacifists in the face of a huge national debt to the USA. In the briefcase beside her at her breakfast table were copies of a detailed minute from the Ministry of War on the relative merits of nuclear defence systems, as opposed to conventional forces, along the east coast of Great Britain.

Meanwhile the fog was deepening, the melancholy hooting of tugs on the river was nearly continuous and, as she put down the piece of toast she'd been eating, she sensed an anxiety she knew well, but had not experienced during the years following her election.

Those had been years filled with grinding hard work and a measure of fame based on her record in two world wars, her vitality as a public speaker – even her hats which, during glum years of rationing and general shabbiness had cheered people up, becoming a national, not unfriendly joke. Those had been good years, in a way, rather as the years at No 53 hospital, St Luc, had been good. There had been hard work and an uncomplicated sense of achievement.

Now she could feel her pulse beating and her stomach churning. This was worse than those nights in small boats taking her from the coast of England to Occupied France. It was as bad as when, a young woman, she'd been concealing her pregnancy from Frederick Levine, knowing that later on she'd have to convince him the child was his. It was almost as bad as the end of her affair with Polly before the war. That had been worst of all . . .

Two days after Polly moved out of her house he was found badly beaten up in a small street off Leicester Square in the early hours of the morning. His nose and one arm were broken. He'd lost a tooth and been repeatedly kicked as he lay on the ground. It was assumed that his assailants were political opponents. He never denied this but strangely made less capital of it than he might. And the day before the attack Allie Crutchley had called at Cheyne Walk and told Violet, 'Something's being arranged for Polly.' Violet, who had not eaten for days, and was pacing her own floor, up and down, up and down, all day and the best part of the night replied only, 'Does it matter?' Her nerve had gone, for the first and last time in her life.

It was almost a year before she began her new existence as a public speaker and a journalist. She served on many committees. Cheyne Walk was filled with refugees from the Spanish Civil

War. Now indefatigable, Violet threw herself into the struggle, speaking all over the country against unemployment, raising money for Spain. It was partly conviction. She had, after all, been close to the British Union of Fascists and over the years with Polly had learned exactly what they were like. It was partly a reprisal against Polly, who had betrayed her. One of the ways in which she sought revenge was by passing on information she had gathered about the party to those who could make best use of it – one of them a young Foreign Office official, Duncan Mackinnon. Then, just before the war, he'd arrived at her door at midnight, saying that he was passing, would she give him a nightcap? He was charming and handsome; Violet, who had admired him since they'd met, did not refuse.

They had been married in 1942 by a nervous registrar, with one ear cocked for an air-raid siren. She'd been in her mid-forties, looking years younger, and Duncan had been thirty-six. The difference in their ages had not only seemed, but actually had been, unimportant then. This was no longer true.

The war and now parliamentary life, with its regular late-night sittings, commuting to a constituency two hundred and fifty miles away, responsibility and challenge, had aged her. Even the war years before that had been harder on Violet, struggling with Felix to keep the house going. Duncan had taken his intelligence duties lightly, except for short periods of intensely hard work, sometimes abroad on missions, usually concluded with a three-day bender. During these bouts he would disappear completely with boon companions, who changed from day to day as they were called away, got lost, arrested or simply dropped out because they couldn't stand the pace. This combination of lethargy, drunken disappearances and short bursts of excitement had suited him. Violet wondered if he had ever been so happy as during the war years. Certainly their first three years had been the best for both of them. She had accepted the fact that since the war had ended, the marriage had worsened, though she didn't know if it was the ending of Duncan's war, or the beginning of her own career in parliament which caused this. The fact remained that Duncan was still effectively the same thirty-six-year-old Violet had married, while she was feeling the full weight of her years, not to mention the full financial burden of keeping the Mackinnon household in the style to which all at Cheyne Walk had become accustomed.

She put down her cup and stood up, picking up her briefcase from the floor. She left the room, her high heels clicking on the parquet. She knew Duncan must still be in bed and likely to stay there until he jumped up at eleven and shouted for black coffee, a bath and a clean shirt. With any luck he'd get to the Foreign Office by midday. He'd been up the night before until God knew when, drinking with Jolyon Jones, Walter Smith and some poet they'd picked up in a drinking club they all belonged to. One of the disadvantages of being married to the handsomest drunk in London, as Duncan Mackinnon had been described, was that you didn't see very much of him unless you, too, slept until eleven and stayed up till dawn.

'Very foggy, Mrs Mackinnon,' said her butler in the hall. 'You'll have to drive carefully.'

'I won't be the only person late today,' replied Violet. 'Would you remind Felix he's to organise a small supper next Tuesday at about ten o'clock for five people? Cold will be all right. Or something to heat. He should start scouting for food now. I know he can manage.'

'I expect so, madam,' said the servant. 'But I'll remind him.' Felix, after loyally giving false evidence for Violet in the divorce case, had stayed with her throughout the war years scandalising everyone by managing to keep up culinary standards in the household, while the rest of the nation lined its stomach with vegetable pie. Wines and spirits were mostly unavailable, even pubs flaunting signs declaring 'No Beer', but Felix, dealing out of the back door of Cheyne Walk with suspicious characters in uniform carrying suitcases, or ruddy-looking men in small cars, always managed to lay hands on a tinned ham, a hare, a dozen eggs, or a bottle of whisky, not to mention a pair of nylons for his grateful employer. Some refused to share in the results, paid for with Violet's riches. Others were amused. 'I can't stop him,' Violet would say. 'He's been in the house since the year dot and anyway he's French.' So Felix, now over seventy, still intermittently drunk as ever, continued his dubious duties, assisted in the kitchen by a young man he had imported from France, whom he called his nephew. Since the nephew asked for low wages, and Felix needed help, Violet asked no questions.

Giving her last-minute instructions to the butler, Violet had another of the nasty thoughts which seemed to be afflicting her today – was it the New Year or just because, a few weeks earlier, she'd had her fifty-fourth birthday? Or plain tiredness. Probably that, she decided, but the thought returned obstinately – how had it come about that since 1913 the only constant person in her life had been Felix?

She seldom saw her daughter Joanna, who sometimes, out of politeness, came to stay with her for a day or two, or attended one of her parties. Joanna, now thirty, was leading what Violet saw as a dull life. She had a job as a librarian, a small flat in Pimlico, one or two old friends from school with whom she went on holiday to the Loire, or occasionally to the cinema or a theatre. She had been rich since Frederick's death, but Violet knew it was only the deliberately rigid structure of the life Joanna led which kept her, most of the time, out of the clinics in which she had spent long periods over the last ten years. 'Nerve strain', they called it, and Violet knew, and dreaded the signs that another episode was about to occur. And those signs – the silences, the darting glances from side to side, the obscure, meaningless remarks – happened all too often while Joanna was with her mother at Cheyne Walk.

Violet never saw her son, Robert. After the divorce in 1933 he had declared he never wanted to see her again. He'd protested when Joanna had been allowed to come to stay with Violet after the divorce, and been self-righteous when Joanna had been returned, ill, to Cavendish Square two years later.

Sometimes Caroline, her former sister-in-law, came to stay at Cheyne Walk. She'd returned from Malaya when her husband died in 1939 and had been widowed for the third time, when her new husband was killed at Arnhem. She now lived with the Despencers in the country, staying with Violet when she occasionally came up to town. She'd put on weight, given up all but a light powdering of her coarsened complexion, and taken to wearing sensible country clothes and shoes. 'I loved all my husbands, Vi,' she'd said to Violet and her husband one evening, 'but I've given the whole thing up now, and taken up gardening. It's more predictable than matrimony and, let's face it, to have been widowed three times is almost a joke to most people. They think you must have polished them off.'

Duncan had said, 'You've had a time, though, Caroline, haven't you?' and somehow managed to make her feel better, a bit of a rogue, young again.

A sudden gaiety, like the old Caroline's, came into her face. 'Duncan. You're such a flirt. Isn't he, Violet? My goodness, even now, if I met one like you, Duncan, I could almost desert the peas and tea roses, leave them to wither on their stems. But,' she said, 'the dentist's appointment is in the morning so I'd better go to bed and get up my strength. It's all right for you, Violet – you're quite unflagging.'

'She's been a goer in her time,' remarked Duncan, after Caroline had gone upstairs. Violet had winced internally. Caroline was only four years older than she was. Fifty-three then, and married to a handsome man nine years younger, Violet didn't welcome the sight of her contemporary, Caroline, sitting there, looking such a frump and saying her only interest now lay in her garden. Nor did she want to hear her husband talk about Caroline as if she were an ancient monument, like Mrs Keppel, or Sylvia Pankhurst.

Anyway, Violet told herself on that gloomy February morning, poor old Felix had turned out to be almost her only remaining link with the past. So that was that. And Allie – Allie, she thought wistfully, had been in America with Donald Farrar since he'd decided, finally, in 1938, that his children were old enough for him to leave his wife. Not that she'd seen Allie for years before she left, anyway. Rosalind Despencer was back in the south of France with her girlfriend, Arabella Crick, part of a group of writers and artists, some ex-servicemen, who had retreated from the cold and austerity of Britain after the war. Leaving Felix, Violet thought again. She pulled herself together and said to the butler, 'Can you also get rooms ready for Mr Maidstone and Mrs Johnson? If the fog gets much worse they may want to spend the night.'

She went down the steps, in her smart suit and coat, and got into the car. As she drove slowly along the Embankment, peering through fog, she now thought of what had happened in France, which she almost never did. Nor did she usually let herself remember what had passed between herself and Sophie Levine years later, because of it. She decided she must be haunted today. But then, she asked herself, what choice did I have in France – what choice, afterwards, when Frederick died?

Violet had panicked when Frederick died, peacefully in his sleep, in 1946, loved by his new Italian wife and respected by everybody. He had been knighted after the war for his war-time work in co-ordinating military supplies and for his part in the commission set up afterwards to rebuild Germany. Therefore, when Sir Frederick Levine died at fifty-six and his obituarists claimed, using classic terms, that he had been loved by his family and friends, respected by all who knew him and honoured by his country, in his case, they spoke the truth. He left behind a grieving widow and a very worried ex-wife. His experiences with Violet in the thirties had taught him one thing: that Violet, deprived of what she wanted, could be very inventive and destructive. Abandoning any idea of justice on the one hand, or revenge on the other, he'd given her ample money.

Once Frederick was dead Violet feared the vengeance of a son who had refused to see her for more than ten years, who must still remember the experience of being a fourteen-year-old public schoolboy during his parents' scandalous divorce. What must have been said about it by parents of other boys at the school, and relayed to him by them, must have given him a cruel year. He had not wanted Joanna to live with Violet afterwards. He had been there when, half-collapsed and leaning on a nurse, she'd been brought back to Cavendish Square. Robert was now in charge of Levine-Schreft. Twenty-seven, bereaved, beset by many post-war problems Frederick had not had time to begin solving, he was not likely to be merciful to her, thought Violet.

With Frederick's allowance gone, Duncan's salary from the Foreign Office and her own from the House of Commons were not going to keep the house at Cheyne Walk functioning. Salaries had not been increased during the war, prices were rising, taxation was high with a Socialist government in power. The Mackinnons had been living to the hilt. There were no savings.

All Violet had behind her was about twenty thousand pounds worth of jewellery she'd acquired. If she had to sell it, she wouldn't get the full value. She couldn't explain where it came from and would have to sell it cheaply, as if she'd stolen it.

She knew that her husband was not, on the face of it, a man who consciously thought about money. He seemed the sort who was perfectly happy to sleep on a sofa and keep a couple of shirts in a drawer. The reality was that he expected nothing but comfort. If he wasn't looked after in a warm house, with staff, good food on the table, and accounts at a tailor, a shirtmaker and a shoemaker's, in some charming and indetectable way he would evaporate, materialising later as the husband of a younger, richer woman. Violet also knew that she wouldn't be able to function as an MP if she had to cope in a smaller house with ration books, fuel shortages and all the practical problems of a modest, post-war household. They'd had to ration bread and potatoes now. Would she be able to explain to Duncan why they were eking out slices of grey, war-time bread? Admittedly, there were women MPs who managed to run their various households with far less money. But they had in their lives mothers, sisters, husbands even, who were prepared to go out with string bags to bring in scanty provisions, fetch coal for fires, accept post-war shabbiness and difficulties. And they were not married to Duncan Mackinnon. One or two had loyal housekeepers, but Violet couldn't even imagine Duncan making do with a loyal housekeeper, eating fish pie in a small dining-room with a few worthies, while a Mrs Treadgold appeared in the doorway, asking if they'd finished, because she wanted to do the washing up. Whereupon she, Violet, would tell her she would do it, push an ashtray towards Harold Wilson to knock his pipe into and start clearing the table. A cosy scene, perhaps, but would Duncan enjoy it? Violet wondered. It was unlikely.

Frederick's will was crucial. Even before Violet found out the terms she began to complain to Joanna that things, now Frederick was dead, might become difficult for her. Joanna, deeply shaken and grieving for her father, appeared not to understand her mother. Joanna in any case was not worth much as an ally. Nor was her other daughter, Pamela, whom Violet saw twice a year, at the decree of Harry Christian-Smith. Pamela was afraid of her mother. Harry disliked her. Violet guessed that any appeal to Pamela for Frederick's money would be blocked by Harry on the grounds that Violet was divorced, had remarried, and had no claim on the Levines, dead or alive. Violet therefore took the bull by the horns, and went to see Sophie. It was 1946. They had not met since Pamela's wedding in 1933.

When Violet went into the drawing-room at Cavendish Square one afternoon, five days after Frederick's death, Sophie was drawn but composed. She sat a little straighter. 'I don't suppose you've come with condolences, Violet.'

'I'm naturally very sorry . . . '

'I'm sure,' Sophie had said drily. 'But I'm an old woman whose son has died. He might have lived longer if he'd enjoyed a long and happy marriage. However, he was not so blessed. But that's over and I don't want to go into it. And now I feel sure you've come for money. Frederick warned me years ago that you'd do this if he died while you were still comparatively young.' Sophie, upright, in black, in the chair in which she had always sat, was cold and clear-headed.

Violet was alarmed by her manner. And the last words had confirmed her worst fears. 'I'm not in his will then?' she burst out, losing composure.

Sophie didn't quite smile at Violet's alarm. She answered, 'No. You're not in the will. He wasn't prepared to acknowledge you in that way. It would look as if he'd forgiven you. He hadn't and he didn't want anyone to think he had.'

'Generous to the last,' said Violet bitterly.

'He could have broken you in various ways. You know that. He didn't, chiefly for the sake of his children. He didn't want any more of the sort of fuss and scandal he knew you were capable of producing.'

'Perhaps you should call them our children,' retorted Violet.

'Forgive me if I've violated your feelings as a mother,' Sophie said. 'Perhaps they run deeper than I, or anyone else, had ever noticed.'

'I suppose, knowing Frederick's left me nothing, you let me come here just to humiliate myself.'

'No,' Sophie told her. 'I agreed to meet you because Frederick said I should make up my own mind about what to do. He said he thought you had no means now of extorting money from the family. But I think he underestimated your capacity to make trouble. I think you're very wicked, Violet.'

Violet, not caring now about Sophie's abuse, since she saw an offer was about to be made, sat more calmly, waiting to find out what it would be. The drawing-room clock ticked on in the silence, as it had always ticked. A door shut upstairs, even the slight sound was familiar. She suddenly remembered the house, empty and dust-sheeted, during the First World War. She'd pulled things together down at Farnley when she came back from France. Sophie hadn't dared show dislike so strongly in those days.

'Wicked?' she burst out. 'Sophie, how could you know anything about it? You, who've spent your whole life doing nothing? How could you have been either good or bad? People who don't do anything, don't make any mistakes.'

Sophie ignored this. 'I don't want a discussion. Above all, I don't want an argument. I've outlived my husband, and both my sons. I'm grieving for them all now. When this is over, I never want to see you again. I'll tell you what I'm going to do. I shall sell Farnley – the farms, the house and most of the furniture. And I'm going to give you the proceeds, all of them. In return you have to do two things. Firstly, sign a paper to say that in future you'll make no further claims on this family. In that, I believe I'm doing exactly what Frederick would have thought sensible. Secondly, and this is entirely for my own satisfaction, I want your truthful account of what happened to Sonny and Germaine.'

Violet sat quite still. She had not expected this. She did not want to tell Sophie about Sonny and Germaine. She thought of the farms, the house, the furniture. Then she said, 'And if I tell you, who will you tell?'

'Just Louis Schreft,' said Sophie Levine. 'He knows you're the only person who can tell us the whole truth. And he wants to know. His sister, Didi, of course, died . . . ' and Sophie paused, looking hard at Violet. 'Sonny and Germaine must be dead, and Marcel, Germaine's husband, and there may have been a child . . . Perhaps you don't understand – Louis wants to know what really happened to his sister's children. So do I.'

'I told you when it happened— ' Violet began.

'You told me what you could get away with. I didn't expect anything else. I know you too well – you were protecting yourself. But I never believed you. You don't understand, Violet – human sympathy isn't another of your great strengths and in any case, how could you comprehend the pain of being, now, the oldest member of a family, half of which has disappeared, mostly in ways we shall never know about. All we can do is imagine, and that's terrible. You didn't tell the whole story after it happened. I need the truth. You can tell me, and above all, Louis, something about Sonny and Germaine.' She raised her head, looked straight at Violet and challenged her, 'It's quite simple. If you tell me a story which makes sense, I'll give you the proceeds from Farnley. It'll be a good deal of money, perhaps two hundred thousand pounds.'

Violet asked urgently, 'But will Louis speak? Will he tell anybody?'

'I stayed with Louis in Paris a month ago,' said Sophie. 'We agreed that not knowing what happened is worst of all. Louis won't tell. All I want is your account of what happened to Sonny and Germaine.'

'And Germaine's husband, and the baby,' Violet said determinedly.

Sophie nodded, satisfied. 'At last we come to it. So the baby was born?'

Violet became angry. 'It was you who urged me to do it. Frederick – but first you. Now, suddenly, I'm the villain of the piece. But you, Sophie, got me to do it. You were using Frederick's money as a lever.'

Sophie nodded. 'And you agreed, and we paid, didn't we? Paid you for trying. And heard how when you went to look for them, they'd been discovered and arrested, the day before. But I didn't believe you. I know you. You won't hear any reproaches from me whatever happened. I only want to know. Come along, Violet, it's the truth, or no Farnley. That house and the land will keep you nicely from now on. So – speak up.'

Violet told her the full story of what had happened to Sonny Coton, his sister Germaine, her husband and their threadlike baby, who whimpered, but could not cry, who had been born in the cellar in Occupied Paris where they'd lived in concealment for eighteen months, never able to go out. She explained how she had hidden them all in the back of the bread van due to rendezvous outside Paris with people who would get them to the coast, and then back to England. Sophie Levine listened in silence.

'So you were captured, taken for interrogation?' she said. 'What made the Germans let you go? After all, you were smuggling Jews out of the country. They ought to have shot you.'

'It was just a local post – I knew the Captain a little.'

'And . . . ?' Sophie asked.

'All right,' Violet said vigorously. 'He knew they might have money or jewellery. I told him I'd tell him where it was in exchange for my freedom. I even said I'd do it again – find more Jews wanting to escape, betray them for profit. Which we'd split. The idea appealed to him. What would you have done?' Violet said in a cold voice. 'Confessed and died? Would that have helped Sonny, or Germaine, or Marcel?'

'No,' said Sophie evenly. 'So that was the last you saw of them, as they took them away?'

Violet said, 'Yes,' repressing the memory of the grey uniforms, the rifle-butts pushing the weak Sonny, Germaine, and Marcel into a long grey corridor, Germaine clutching her undernourished baby and glancing back, just once, to look at Violet – or was it just a glance past her at the open door, showing, behind, a bit of street, the branches of a tree, a tiny piece of blue sky?

'Did you find out where they were taking them?' Sophie asked.

'They didn't tell me their plans. I didn't ask them.' She recalled her own fear, the knowledge that she was about to be interrogated, perhaps tortured. She'd only glanced at the party being pushed down that long corridor before turning to the German officer, in her character as a French bakerwoman, saying, 'Be merciful, Captain, I beg you.' She looked at Sophie and said, 'Don't judge me. This was your idea.'

'I know,' Sophie replied. 'I know.' She sighed. 'Thank you, Violet. Now, at least we know.'

After Violet had gone, her back, held so straight during

the interview, began to bow. She sat slumped in her chair, a tear rolling down her cheek. The tick of the clock seemed very loud. She imagined Violet, erect and energetic, calling a taxi and driving back to Cheyne Walk, her life on course again, as a result of telling her the truth about the deaths of three people and a four-month-old starving baby. Like a cannibal, like a cannibal, mourned Sophie. But this time, it won't profit her at all. God will make sure of that.

Violet, walking away from Cavendish Square, breathed deeply, like someone coming up from under water. She'd imagined, after giving her official report in London, when she hadn't revealed she knew the people hiding in the van, and after having told another story to Frederick and Sophie, that she'd never have to talk or think again about what had happened. Later, on the way back to Chelsea, she decided Sophie would honour her part of the bargain, give her the proceeds of the sale of Farnley. And, as a matter of fact, she still had the remainder of Germaine Coton's jewellery, hidden elsewhere in the van, at her own bank, in London.

Now, six years later, Violet peered through her foggy windscreen in Parliament Square. 'What choice did I have?' she muttered to herself, steering carefully into the House of Commons car park.

Kate Higgins, June 19th, 1991

Di wasn't in when I got back to the flat in dusty London sunshine. Rog was. He came out of the spare room when I came in, leaving the door open. The bed which I could see opposite had been slept in. There was a sleeping-bag on the floor too. Rog had a screwdriver in his hand. 'Someone kicked over the lamp,' he explained. 'I fixed it.'

'There've been a few people here while I've been away,' I said.

'Di never let them in your room,' he told me.

It wasn't the reassurance I wanted, somehow. 'Well, it's her place,' I said.

'Cup of tea?' he asked.

'Be nice.' He shut the door of the room. The lock clicked. I watched him go into the kitchen and realised I still didn't have keys to it. I felt uneasy. Up to now I'd taken a modest view of my own position in the flat, just paying my share of the rent and bills and splitting the chores but assuming Di had basic control. She paid the bills, the flat was in her name, that was the way she liked it. But in spite of my clean-up the place was looking neglected again. The plumber hadn't come to fix the dripping tap in the bathroom. There were envelopes looking like bills all over the mantelpiece. Also there was a locked room where unexplained guests slept. I didn't know them. No one told me they were there. Why not? You can't have a locked room, with a secret, in a council flat. I hadn't asked any questions about the room. Constantly betrayed by a lover, baffled by mysterious phone calls from an anonymous woman, writing my biography and living in the past, there seemed to be things I hadn't caught up with. Something funny was going on, I decided. I followed Rog into the kitchen and asked, 'What's happening? Has Di turned this place into a safe house? What's happening in that room?'

He put the kettle on the stove. 'She'll be in in a minute. She's only popped out for some eggs.'

I went cold all over. 'Oh my God,' I said, 'Oh my God.' I'd said 'safe house' as a joke.

Rog hadn't laughed, or said 'What are you talking about?' denied it in any way. Now he just looked at me, and advised, 'You'd better have a cup of tea.'

'I've got to go out soon,' I said numbly. 'I'm meeting a man about my book.'

'It's over, to all intents and purposes,' he told me, pouring the water into the teapot.

'What's over?' I asked. 'I'd like to know.'

He produced a packet of ten from the pocket of his jeans and held it out. I took one. I smoked it in the kitchen doorway, staring at him. He looked as usual, tall and lanky, old jeans and a tee-shirt.

Then the phone rang. 'Careful,' warned Rog, as I went to answer it.

'Kate Higgins?' came a gravelly voice. 'Look here, in your own interests don't ask any more questions about Violet Levine. Talk to Roger Littlebrown.'

I went and leaned up against the door of the kitchen again.

'I've been warned off,' I said, and told Rog what had happened. It was stuffy in the kitchen and the smell from the saucepan of yesterday's spaghetti bolognese was strong.

He poured me some tea and handed me the mug. 'You need this,' he told me kindly, adding, 'Threats, eh?' But, frankly, he wasn't thinking about my phone call. He was worrying about my suspicions.

I was getting annoyed. 'Don't you think you ought to tell me what's going on?'

'Best if Di does,' he replied.

I felt numb. What could I do? I went into the bathroom and ran a cool bath. I was meeting Jack Christian-Smith in an hour and a quarter. I lay in the bath, thinking hard. My dominating thought was about my own stupidity. I'd been so absorbed in uncovering old secrets I'd missed the one on the premises, which could ruin me. And still I hardly believed it. What an idiot.

Then Rog put his head round the door. 'Pardon,' he said, disappearing again.

'From what I can tell, this is no time to stand on ceremony,' I shouted.

'It's embarrassing.'

'What is?'

He came back round the door. 'Well, whatever you think, you mustn't tell anybody,' he said. 'You can see it's important . . . '

I asked, 'Am I going to? Do you really think I would? I'd be mad, wouldn't I?'

'Yeah,' he replied, retreating. 'I thought you'd see it like that.'

'No other bloody way to see it, is there?' I shouted after him. 'Not now.' The point was that although it was looking very much as if 11D Henry Thackery House had been used as some kind of safe house – for people on the run, or lying low, or illegal immigrants – I still didn't really know anything. But all the information pointed in nasty, dangerous directions, doors opening and closing, Di's frequent, unexplained absences, her distracted air, her desire to get rid of me for no reason I could see – it didn't look good.

I lay back in the water. 'Oh my God,' I was saying to myself in the bath, 'Oh my God.' I thought of Ray. I could already hear the Special Branch breaking in the front door, see the crouched marksmen on the school roof opposite, weapons pointing at our windows. I could see the trial, I could hear the prison doors banging as I lay, sleepless, on my bunk in a shared cell. I didn't think a jury would believe that underneath my superficial appearance of intelligence lay such gross stupidity. They'd assume I'd been involved. I was well and truly trapped.

Violet Mackinnon, 1951

After the slow journey to the House of Commons, Violet was late for a committee meeting. When she arrived the huge building was half empty, and full of fog, through which men moved as if in a dream. From dimly seen staircases and halls there came coughs. The committee-room contained only Bill Burgess, who said, 'Secretary's stranded at Knockholt. Looks as if we won't even have a quorum, Violet. We might as well go and get a cup of tea.'

Rosie Johnson sat down with them. 'There's more feeling than you lot know about putting charges on health care,' she said.

Violet said, 'Are you talking about a revolt? A split in the party? Resignations – what?'

'I wouldn't dismiss any of those ideas.'

Violet looked at her and asked, 'What will you do?'

Rosie told her, 'I don't know. I'm telling you and Bill because you're both so preoccupied with your bombs and stinks you don't seem to see what's going on. People are very annoyed about filling the country with planes and keeping the war-time US bases, and weapons aimed at the Soviet Union, just because the Yanks want it. They don't want revenue diverted from social welfare to pay for it.'

Violet knew in the end Rosie would join the rebels and go against the government. 'A full-scale split in the party would be a very bad idea in an election year,' she said steadily, gazing at Rosie.

'Depends how much you're prepared to compromise,' Rosie replied.

'Compromise with whom?' asked Violet. 'Half of you lot want to compromise with Joe Stalin.'

'Ladies,' warned Burgess. 'No hairpulling.'

'Shut up, Bill,' said Rosie Johnson. 'My mother carried you behind the banner when you had the arse hanging out of your trousers. Don't call us ladies. Well, call Violet one if you like. She's just called me a Communist, after all.'

'No need for any of us to name-call,' Violet told her, standing up. 'I might as well do the correspondence and go home for lunch. We'll have to meet as and when, then, Bill. It must be before Thursday. Do you need a bed at my house tonight, if it's foggy?'

Rosie shook her head. One day she'd be able to make up her mind if she could respect Violet for her hard work and believe she had genuine convictions, or just decide she was an ambitious fake who'd do anything to stay in the public eye and make a position for herself in the world. She was tough, and no mistake, thought Rosie Johnson, and just now she, Rosie, would like to give her a big kick in the back of her expensive, new, long skirt.

Finding her secretary absent from the office she shared with another MP, Violet picked up her letters, deciding to deal with them at home in the warmth, comfort and relative fog-freeness of her own study at Cheyne Walk.

As she came in the phone was ringing in the hall. The butler answered it, saying, 'Mr Mackinnon has just gone out, I'm afraid.' As Violet worked on her letters, then on notes of her meeting at the Ministry of War, then studied the report on the direction of research into atomic weapons, the telephone rang twice more, each time for Duncan, evidently, since she wasn't called to answer it.

She ate lunch alone in the foggy dining-room. After lunch she phoned her agent about two of the letters from the constituency in Sunderland. 'Tell Mr Cassidy I'll be writing to the council about the Surridge Street graveyard,' she said, 'but after I've had a look at it for myself. So, I'll see you on Saturday morning, Joe.'

'Right you are, Violet,' he replied. 'Keep up the good work.'

'Tell Madge again there's a bed here for her, when she comes down to see Tom. I don't think she believed me.'

'Too shy to come to such a big house,' Joe told her.

'Tell her not to be so stupid,' recommended Violet.

'I will,' said Joe.

Violet, back in her study, scanned the county council minutes, re-checked her notes on the meeting she'd had at the Ministry and composed a list of questions she needed to ask. Then she went downstairs. 'I'll have some tea,' she said to the butler, 'in the drawing-room.'

Duncan was lying in a chair with his long legs stretched out by the fire, a glass of whisky in his hand. Violet looked at the glass but said nothing. Duncan's intake was increasing, his hangovers were getting more frequent and more punishing. She was, in fact, tired of his drinking and the scenes which accompanied it. She was tired of telephone calls summoning him to little clubs in Soho, his sudden departures from the house and unexpected returns with drunken friends – journalists, civil servants, actors, men he had known at school and university – the calls for food at late hours, the mess in the morning, the friend who had slept in a spare bedroom without warning. Perhaps more than anything, she was tired of his blurry eyes and slurred speech.

His unpredictable behaviour was beginning to make him a liability in public, too. A visit to the theatre or a film could be ruined by Duncan, as often as not, wandering out, perhaps halfway through the act, saying loudly he was going for a pee, or a drink. He'd announced one night he couldn't stand the play, and left. The actors had heard. So had the entire audience. It wasn't so bad when they were with friends but it was awful, Violet reflected, when, as had happened not long before, they were part of a delegation entertaining Czech diplomats on a fraternal visit to this country. The situation had its comic side sometimes: Duncan sitting in the front row at a children's nativity play in her constituency, obviously drunk, and joining in the carols in his loud, bass voice; Duncan, again drunk, saying, 'How interesting, Lady Mayoress,' reaching out for the mantelpiece in the mayoral parlour, missing it, falling flat on his face, standing up and saying, 'I beg your pardon. Missed my footing. Do tell me more about the new dog-racing stadium.' But as the episodes became more and more frequent smiles faded. She had little doubt that Duncan's behaviour was reducing the number of events for which she got formal invitations from her Party. They couldn't risk Duncan. He was charming, intelligent, tactful and amusing when sober, but increasingly often these days, he was drunk and rude.

Once upon a time, in the bizarre circumstances of living in a city under constant bombardment, Duncan, for example, swooping into the cellar of a friend in the middle of a raid, carrying a bottle of slivovitz he'd won in a game of poker with some Yugoslav patriots, and box of snakes and ladders, was forgivable, in fact welcome. With his long, lean body, cowlick of fair hair, the large, capable hands which could fix anything, from a damaged pipe in the kitchen to a radio, and the bulging pockets which often contained useful but incongruous items – Turkish cigarettes, a Nazi newspaper published in Berlin, a silver snuffbox filled with sweets – Duncan had been intriguing, glamorous, exciting, a mixture of a boy scout and Douglas Fairbanks. In those days he had been fun, and recognised as someone who was doing things, although no one was supposed to know what they were. Now he was a desk-bound Foreign Office official in the Middle Eastern section, inclined to stand swaying, bored, and becoming malicious at public functions. His magic was going.

The morning after he'd come in for his nightcap and stayed all night he'd disappeared silently without disturbing her, leaving a pile of keys, small change and a Paris train ticket on the floor, where his jacket had been. He rang later, asked her out to lunch at the Ritz, stood her up and arrived, three days later, looking tired and saying there had been an emergency. He'd been driven to a certain house in the country at the orders of a certain personage from whose house no one was even allowed to telephone, for reasons of secrecy. Violet never knew if this story, implying a conference with Winston Churchill at Chequers, was true or not. Later, she thought he might have been terminating his relationship with the German Communist wife he had married in the thirties, ostensibly to provide her with a British passport which would enable her to leave Germany. Of her he said, 'Lisa – I saved her life, she responded by making mine a misery.' They had a little boy, Hans, to whom he was a fond but erratic father. When the war ended, the mother and son returned to East Germany, where Lisa was now, apparently, headmistress of a school and married to an active Communist Party member. Before that, Duncan had been married to an actress. At least, Violet thought, he had always married energetic women. When she'd decided to stand for parliament, he'd given her every encouragement. Indeed, he'd campaigned for her. The trouble was, he was not helping now.

From his chair Duncan asked, 'We're not supposed to be going out again tonight, are we?'

'I told Denis I'd meet him at Myra Brayfield's,' Violet said. 'As for going out again, as you weren't with me last night, I don't suppose you will be this time.'

'No – no. I enjoy Myra's. If you and Denis want to chat about wigs and false teeth, you can do so. I'll talk to a film star. There's often a film star at Myra's.'

'Don't forget you had a terrible argument with a man from the Bank of England last time. He wears glasses, David Kelly. If he's there again, do be careful. And if Harry Christian-Smith's there this time, try to remember he's Pamela's husband.'

'I have the impression you'd rather go without me. I know I haven't been behaving very well recently. The trouble is, I get so bored.'

'I'd rather you came, if you could mind your manners.'

He held out his glass. 'Any chance of a refill?'

Violet filled his glass and said, 'You're getting very thin, Duncan. I think you should see the doctor.'

That night at Myra Brayfield's big house in Fulham Violet was, she felt, handling a conversation with the cultural attaché from the USA very happily, when from downstairs came shouts and the sounds of breaking glass. She went on talking over the noise. 'I agree, Olivier is unique . . . ' Then she caught a glance from a friend of Duncan's who was standing in the doorway, looking for her, she imagined. She said to the American, 'Do excuse me. There's someone I must talk to.'

The short, bald man waiting for her in the doorway said, as he walked slowly down the stairs, 'Sorry, Violet. I thought it best to let you know. Duncan's laid out some chap from the Russian Embassy. Myra said she thought you'd want to persuade him to come home.'

In the large hall Duncan, his tie askew, and blood on his shirt, was struggling with two men who were trying to hold him. 'Asking me to spy for the bloody Russians, bloody bastard. Who does he think I am – Alger Hiss? I'll give him . . . ' and he began to shout in Russian. The Russian, a tall man in a grey suit, was leaning groggily against the front door holding a bloodstained handkerchief to his nose. The short man turned to Violet and urged, 'For God's sake get him out of here.'

Violet looked at Duncan at one end of the hall, struggling to get free, at the man with the bloody nose at the other, and asked the men holding her husband, 'Can you get him in the car?' and to Duncan, 'Come along – you're coming home.'

They pulled Duncan into the street and pushed him on to the back seat of the car. Then Violet realised someone else, Jolyon Jones, was also getting into the back seat. He and Duncan sang '*Otchichernya*' and 'The Volga Boat Song' all the way back.

Violet ordered black coffee and sandwiches for them, though knowing the snack would be followed by more drinking until the early hours of the morning. She went to bed furious and disturbed. It couldn't go on. This episode could be reported to the Foreign Office, where it might or might not be overlooked. You never knew. Their ways were mysterious. But tomorrow Duncan would have to see a doctor. If he refused to go, and he had before, she'd go to the Foreign Office and tell them how anxious she was. Even if they could tolerate him, she couldn't. He was becoming a liability. That grubby cuffed, charming upper-class manner did not go down well with Labour colleagues from working or lower middle-class homes. They had grown up with poverty, dole queues, narrow streets. Why should they trust a man born in a large house with a silver spoon in his mouth, even if, as Duncan did, he proclaimed left-wing views? The others in the Labour government, those whose backgrounds were more like Duncan's, had, if anything, even bigger reservations about him. They recognised him, and didn't like what they saw.

Once it had suited Violet, who believed that a woman should be respectably married, to have Duncan as a husband. But now he was becoming a nuisance. Certainly, she didn't love him any more, if she ever had. But ten years before he'd been entertaining, brave and presentable. She'd been the same, and she was also rich. They suited each other very well. He moved into Cheyne Walk easily. Later, he proposed, she accepted. After France, Violet had settled to keeping house in Cheyne Walk while Duncan came and went on intelligence work, chiefly office-based, in London, but often involving unexplained disappearances. After the war he had gone to Berlin for six months. In Britain she fought an election and began her duties as an MP in the reforming government of Clement Attlee. From then on, the marriage declined. Duncan's return from Berlin had been marked by their agreement to sleep apart, because Duncan's comings and goings and Violet's early rising caused them to disturb each other. And, as Duncan drank more, they made love less and less.

Violet was fairly sure that now there were other women. There was Jenny Holt, the long-haired painter daughter of a Cambridge don. There was Angela Garrick, who had once been a mistress of Augustus John. Now she strayed round London, having affairs and doing nothing much else in a small flat in Soho, on money provided by a wealthy father.

Jenny Holt was in love with Duncan, guessed Violet, who had found a sad note from her in Duncan's pocket: 'I waited for you, but you did not come.' She was one of the fey brigade, Violet decided, having met her once, a young woman still giving the impression of dancing in the dew on the lawn, part-nymph, part-child, part-woman, like something in a cotton frock out of J. M. Barrie. Jenny's rival, Angela Garrick, Violet thought, was in love with no one but herself, leading what she saw as a Bohemian life which meant as many rows, fights, breakages and scenes as possible. Two years before Angela had arrived at Cheyne Walk at ten in the morning with a black eye. Violet, called from her study by the maid, had found her in the drawing-room. 'Your husband gave me this,' she had announced, pointing at her eye.

Violet surveyed her from top to toe, taking in the worn-down heels on her black shoes, her bare legs and the deplorable brown coat, as well as her badly dyed blonde hair and slapped on lipstick and thought, I bet you asked for a thumping. She told Angela, 'Well, you'd better talk to him then, hadn't you? Or to your solicitor? Duncan's at his office at the moment.'

'He blacked my eye just because I wouldn't sleep with him,' Angela said.

Violet, knowing Angela wanted a drama in which she could be the main character, and would enjoy telling people about, responded, '*If* all this is true it still has nothing to do with me, I'm afraid.'

Angela's voice rose. 'Are you going to divorce him?'

Violet realised Angela wanted to marry Duncan or had persuaded herself she wanted to in order to heighten the drama. Knowing Duncan as she did, Violet doubted if he was party to the plan.

'I'm asking you – are you going to divorce him?' Angela repeated.

'I'd like you to leave,' Violet told her. 'But I'll give you my answer. It's that I have no plans to divorce my husband. As far as I know, he's not planning to divorce me. On that point, you'd better ask him for information. Please be gone before I come back.'

She turned quickly and went upstairs to her study. As she opened the door she heard a violent crash, then the sound of her visitor running through the hall and slamming the door behind her. Violet went down to find that Angela had thrown a vase at the mirror over the mantelpiece. The vase had broken, the mirror was cracked. Violet, who hated having any of her property – furniture, ornaments, her own clothing or anything belonging to her – damaged in any way, was furious, but got the maid to clear up the mess and had bought, and hung, another mirror before lunch. She never mentioned Angela's visit to Duncan, who, if he heard about it, never referred to it either.

The knowledge that Duncan was sleeping with other women gave Violet no pain as long as the marriage stayed publicly undamaged. Her desire to seem respectable had grown as she aged. She'd had to work hard to live down the still-remembered divorce and cover her tracks about her affair with Polly. She needed marriage and respectability, a husband, but not necessarily a faithful one.

Now she lay in bed, realising that all that was over – Duncan must change, or go. She couldn't afford him any longer. It was not just the scenes in public; increasingly, there were documents in the house which were either secret, or important enough to have to be kept secret briefly. And this was what she had really been anxious about, for longer than she herself knew or would admit. This was why she had been feeling so ill and nervous. At this moment, for example, there were papers on her desk, relating to future defence policy. The Americans favoured nuclear defence, half the Labour Party agreed. The rest had different views. All this could only be very interesting to the Soviet Union and almost as interesting to the USA or Britain's allies in NATO. What government or nation would want this or any other of its affairs bandied about in public by a loose-tongued drunk? Duncan had been yelling incoherently about spying to the Soviet cultural attaché that night. Violet thought, what else might he not say, drunk, about her affairs or his own? What other damage could he do?

She knew he sometimes looked over what was on her desk out of curiosity, if he happened to be in her study. Suppose, Violet thought, he was a spy? This was the unthinkable idea she'd been repressing, the source of all her hidden fear and anxiety. Now she pursued it: Duncan had done undercover work during the war – there was a point where intelligence work turned into straight espionage; these days contacts who had once been allies had become enemies; truth and lies were handed out for various reasons to various people. Spy or counter-spy, traitor, mercenary or drunk – how could she know where Duncan stood? Yet, she wondered, if his employers at the Foreign Office didn't mistrust him then why should she, his wife? Or were they using him? Or, a terrible thought, was he using them?

She lay alone in her big bed where now, with no traffic passing, she could hear an occasional slap of water against the embankment. Even now her husband was downstairs with Jolyon Jones, a former ardent Communist, a man who had fought on the Republican side during the Spanish Civil War. They were old friends. They'd been at school together. Jolyon's Communism had always, anyway, been a joke to those who knew him. She'd been at his thirty-fourth birthday, organised by Diana Gray. The cake had been decorated with a big red flag. There'd been thirty-four candles on top, all dyed red. The candles and the icing sugar, then unobtainable in Britain, had been brought from America in the diplomatic bag by a friend of Diana's, who'd been told of the joke and came to the party. But there was always a feeling, among people like that, loyal to their tribe, their customs and habits that talking was one thing but nothing would or could change. They'd thought that about Polly, Violet reflected gloomily, until war broke out. Then they'd found out they were wrong, it was impossible not to imprison the leaders of the British Union of Fascists, him among them.

Violet, sleepless, wrenched her mind away from uncomfortable thoughts of Polly, and concentrated on her present anxiety. Characteristically, she made a plan. Then she fell asleep.

Next day she cleared her desk as usual, locked her papers, as usual, in her filing cabinet and set off for a meeting with some nuclear scientists in Cambridge with Bill Burgess and the civil servant from the Ministry of War. She was back at ten that night, had a drink and a sandwich with Duncan, then left her notes of the meeting in a brown folder on her desk. As she went out of the room she glued two hairs across the crack where the study door joined the doorframe, and then went to bed. She got up at five thirty next day and found the hairs no longer in place. She thought the folder had been moved. She sat down at her desk in her nightdress, thinking that perhaps the hairs on the door had slipped, perhaps she was mistaken about the folder. That morning, there was more fog. Wisps moved about the study, veiled the lamp on the desk. Even if Duncan had read the notes, it might only have been because he was curious. She set another trap the next day, but nothing was disturbed. That Friday the other MPs who had been with her in Cambridge met over supper to decide what they would report to the Minister's private secretary; the civil servant who had accompanied them would report separately.

'It's a formality, Vi,' said Bill Burgess, who had been a physics lecturer employed by the War Ministry during the war. 'Military independence is a thing of the past. They'll do what they like. Or perhaps what they don't like. It'll be joint strategy from now on. And the Yanks are in charge. Not that I wasn't thrilled to go and talk to all those Cambridge boffins. It was a boyhood dream come true.'

'I was only ever a makeweight,' Violet said. 'Or there to watch you. No offence, Bill.'

'None taken. My impression is, you were there to see what sort of a fist you made of it. Someone's got his eye on you.' He bit into a sandwich, remarking appreciatively, 'Ham and chicken. Not to mention that good soup.'

'Some of the comrades don't approve,' she said.

'Nor do I,' he told her, taking another sandwich. 'But an army marches on its stomach. Let's get on with it before I start falling asleep. Are you all right on those rough costings?'

'I've done it, but I wouldn't like to estimate my own running costs like this. Not too clear on the present, and with no guarantee everything won't double next year and treble the next.'

'Have you put that in?'

'I've said hard questions should be asked now about the probabilities. I doubt if they will be. Do you want to see it?'

Bill took the pages. 'The figures won't mean much. I'm curious about your conclusions. Swap.'

Violet read his version. Over the next hour they organised the report. 'Can you get it typed tomorrow, Violet?' asked Bill. 'The constituency typist, i.e. my wife, is a bit too occupied with the baby. He's been yelling since he was born on Christmas Day and Mary's a shadow of her former self.'

Violet, by now not keen to keep the report in her own home, had to agree. When Bill left she decided that if Duncan was doing some dangerous snooping on her territory, she might as well test him with the report. The material it contained was serious but not vitally so – most of it had been in the house before. The recommendations, although they might carry some weight, could be ignored or only be adopted because other, more powerful voices than hers and Bill's were saying the same thing. In any case, she thought grimly, if Duncan really was spying on her, she'd have to find out by baiting the trap with something of value, and this report was, in its way, important. Nevertheless she extracted Bill's appraisal of what the Cambridge scientists had told him.

This time, in addition to sticking hairs across the study door, she scattered a faint film of her face powder between the sheets of the report, enough, when it fell off, not to be noticed in the lamplight, or if noticed, for Duncan to think she had powdered her face too close to the desk.

Upstairs, she slipped the spare pages from the report into her dressing-table drawer. She looked in the mirror and saw a pale face with dark shadows under the eyes. Bill might be right when he said she'd been given the job of helping to frame the report as a test. In reality, a woman would never get a high post in the Ministry of War, but Health or Education were open to her – if Duncan wasn't snooping on her work, talking about it publicly, or worse, much worse than that, making some wrong use of the information. If he was, she was finished. If, she added to herself, anyone found out.

She got up early again. The door of her study had been opened during the night and on her desk her papers had been moved. A little scattering of ivory face powder showed the pages had been turned. Violet went upstairs and lay down, sighing. Duncan, who, most of the time, appeared to be leading a life which must involve neglecting his own work, seemed to be taking a strong interest in hers. Unless, of course, it was one of the servants. Not impossible, she supposed, that the maid had begun an affair with a handsome Czech attaché, and sneaked into her study at night to photograph loose papers. But she knew the maid was engaged to a greengrocer, and saving up for a home. The butler was a cast-iron Ulster loyalist, and as for Felix – he could easily run a network of spies but wouldn't do so. He hated politics.

If in need of money he'd go into the black market. It wasn't a servant, decided Violet. It was Duncan, and she was fairly sure he'd been playing this game for some time. And if so, why?

Her obvious duty was to tell someone in authority of her suspicions, but she'd already decided not to do that unless she had to. She'd no solid proof Duncan was spying on her. Even if he was, he could just, for example, be tipping off a friend in the City for gain. But still Violet knew the most likely explanation was simply that Duncan was probably spying for the Soviet Union. He'd once been a Communist, though he now declared himself disillusioned. If he were a spy, that's what he would say. His comings and goings, which she'd put down to meetings with friends for a drink, or one or other of his two mistresses, suddenly looked more sinister. So did the constant phone calls. Right or wrong about him, she ought to warn the Foreign Office and the Prime Minister, Clement Attlee, and soon. She would, of course, look very stupid if she was wrong. But, far more than that, if she was right, she was done for.

There had to be another way to solve her problem, she thought, without damaging herself. A quiet, respectable answer was what she needed, something to separate herself from Duncan, and cover her in case he got found out. Someone might be watching him even now. In a way, it might be safer just to go to Attlee on her knees, immediately. But how was that going to look? She'd lived down a lot of scandal, especially her association with Polly, which too many people knew about. She didn't want any more.

First, she had to get him out of the house, where he could do no damage for a time. A discussion with the Foreign Office about Duncan's increasing drinking, his need for leave, treatment and recuperation would prove wifely concern and no involvement in his activities. Then he could go to a clinic for at least a month, out of harm's way, and, while he was gone, she might be able to find out what he was really up to, and how serious it was. She couldn't make her usual weekend visit to the constituency until the business with Duncan was at least partly resolved.

She'd been up at five thirty now for four mornings, in order to check her study before anyone else was up. Then she'd gone through her normal duties each day. But, though tired, she couldn't rest. I look a hag, I must get some sleep, she thought, but as the late February dawn began to lighten her windows, she still lay there, angry and taut with impatience, waiting for the moment when she could wake Duncan and begin to persuade him he needed rest and treatment for his drinking. She'd have to have convinced him by Monday, she decided. Then she'd get the doctor to make arrangements for his cure and inform the Foreign Office. That part would be easy. Getting Duncan to agree would be a lot harder.

Later, she phoned the constituency to say she was ill and could not come that weekend. When her tea came up she ordered breakfast for herself and a tray for Duncan.

'Mr Mackinnon isn't in his room. His bed hasn't been slept in,' reported the maid. Violet summoned up her patience, dressed, went downstairs and ate her own breakfast with little appetite. She'd wait for him, then.

She waited all day. In the evening he had still not come in and Violet, hardly able to bear the thought that he was out playing dirty tricks with the contents of a government report, was on the verge of giving up her plan of persuading him to go into a clinic and wondering if she should track him down, denounce him for infidelities she'd claim she'd only just discovered and insist he never returned to the house. But if Duncan was under surveillance, or on the verge of being uncovered, it would look better if she presented herself as a wife concerned with his habits and conduct rather than as a woman betrayed. She'd been alone, turning this over in her mind all day, unable to take any action until Duncan came back, when Allie rang up to say she'd arrived in London. It had been two years since they'd met, when Allie, over on a visit from the USA with her husband, relented and got in touch with her sister. She'd never really forgive Violet for what had happened in the past, her bitterness went too deep and Violet's lack of proper remorse appalled her. This time, she'd come without Donald, who had at the last moment been kept back by the paper he worked for. 'All right if I come over for supper?' she asked.

Violet, afraid that Duncan would come and go before she had the chance to catch him, hesitated.

'If it's inconvenient . . . ' Allie said.

'No, you might as well come,' Violet decided. She couldn't bear to be alone any longer.

Allie arrived in a smart suit, looking slim and well. Any grey hairs were lost in her still-blonde hair. She spent much of her time on a small farm in Connecticut, where she gardened and kept bees. Before she left, by patient study she'd almost qualified as a lawyer but the qualifications would have been useless in the USA and as, shortly after arriving she'd had a daughter, she settled down contentedly as a wife and mother on the farm.

'Put the light on, Vi,' she exclaimed, coming in. 'What are you doing, sitting here in the dark?'

She snapped on the light and they sat down by the fire. 'You don't look at all well,' she said. 'It's tiring, I suppose, all this work in parliament. How's it going?'

'All right,' said Violet. 'How's little Annie?'

'Couldn't be better,' declared her sister. 'Ben sends his love.'

'Ben?'

'Ben – your brother, Ben,' said Allie with a laugh. 'He's working down at Gravesend now. I went down today. He seems very content. His wife's opened a hairdresser's there, their daughter's helping. They say our stepmother's as drunk as ever.'

'Do me a favour, Allie. Spare me all these details.'

'You're such a snob, Vi,' said Allie. 'They're awe-struck about you in Gravesend. They've got a scrap album on you. But you look dreadful. You'd better call in the National Health. Is something wrong?'

'I'm a bit depressed. It's nothing,' said Violet. Allie was no longer someone to turn to. She was too angry about the past.

'I don't like to see you like this,' Allie told her. 'It's against nature for you to look crushed. That's for the rest of us. Is it Duncan?'

Violet struggled. 'Let's talk about something else.'

And for a while they did until Allie looked up from the pork pie and salad they were both eating from trays on their knees and said, 'What's up then? Duncan got another woman?'

‘Two, as far as I know,’ said Violet. ‘But I don’t care. Stop probing, Allie. You wouldn’t want to hear.’

‘I lead a quiet life,’ Allie claimed.

‘Your husband’s a senior journalist on the *New York Post,*’ Violet said. ‘You’re not that detached from the world. Anyway, you can’t help.’

‘I wouldn’t,’ Allie said with alacrity. ‘I told you that nearly fifteen years ago. I said I’d never help you again, never come near any situation you’d got involved in, and I never will. Never. But come on, Vi. Confession’s good for the soul. How many people can you talk to? Not a lot, I bet. There aren’t too many of the people you started out with left in your life.’

‘That’s what I thought, the other day,’ Violet said, remembering that it was just before the problem of Duncan’s spying settled, like a black crow on her shoulder.

‘Not like you to think long, sad thoughts,’ Allie remarked. ‘Oh well, if you don’t tell me, I’m sure I’ll find out eventually. I can wait.’

The door banged and Duncan came in. He didn’t greet Allie but stood by the door, saying, ‘Violet. I’ve got some news I hope you won’t mind – I’ve agreed to a posting to the Lebanon, only six months. Only I realise you won’t be able to come . . . ’

He was excited, nervous, and Violet had difficulty in concealing her profound relief. A wave of warmth came over her. She exulted. Duncan was leaving! He’d be out of the house, out of Britain. He’d no longer be able to spy on her, for whatever reason. Whatever he was doing, he’d have to stop. Or, if he didn’t, she reflected, she wouldn’t be involved. He’d been posted, she thought, probably because the Foreign Office had decided to get him out of London. She hardly cared about the reasons. She’d have liked to shout aloud with relief and pleasure. Instead she skilfully pretended regret that Duncan would be away for so long and told him she’d come out to see him during the parliamentary recess at Easter. She’d make an excuse for not going when the moment came.

‘When are you going?’ she asked. In a week, he told her, because the man he was replacing had left suddenly, due to ill-health. She expressed a concern she almost, at the time, really felt, as if Duncan were still the same man she'd married.

Nevertheless, after he'd gone out again, to meet yet another friend – hearing this Violet flinched – Allie said to her, 'You might have fooled him when you seemed upset that he was going, but you didn't fool me. You looked as if you'd lost sixpence and found a shilling.'

'That's not a very nice thing to say, Allie,' said her sister.

After Duncan left, Violet relaxed, believing it was probably going to be all right. She did not join him at Easter and, to separate herself still further from him, began divorce proceedings. They had not gone far when, six months later, her husband defected to the Soviet Union from Beirut. Allie said over the phone from Connecticut, 'You knew, Violet. You knew all the time.'

Violet, alone at Cheyne Walk, and knowing her career was probably ruined, still had the strength of mind to deny it. 'That's a terrible thing to say, Allie,' she told her sister.

Kate Higgins, June 19th, 1991

I went up to Jack Christian-Smith's office in the lift at six, feeling very strange indeed. Panic had given way to a feeling of unreality. My first impulse had been to run away – go down to Brighton probably. But common sense told me that if Di's activities (whatever they were, I still wasn't clear about it) were going to be detected, all I'd do was bring the police, inexorably, to my parents' doorstep. My son would be treated to the edifying spectacle of his mother, covered by armed policemen, being dragged off down the garden path. Sam might be there too. Not good for a serving officer to see his ex-wife arrested on a political charge before his very eyes, worse if Special Branch had tipped off the press they were going to make the arrest, as they were inclined to, especially if the suspect was a woman. If not Brighton, then where? They'd find me anyway. In the end it seemed wiser to stay to talk to Di and find out what was really going on. As I left the flat I'd said grimly to Rog, 'I'll be back in an hour or two. Tell Di she'd better be here.'

Now the moment I'd really wanted had come. At last I was going to talk to one of the Levines and get some facts. Unfortunately, my own circumstances were making me frantic, my mind was completely on something else, and I just hoped I could get sensibly through the meeting.

Then I was at yet another reception desk, emptied my bag in front of the third security guard since I'd gone into the building and I was asked to sit down. The wait didn't bother me. I had plenty to think about. At last a tall, tanned man in his mid-forties came out of a door and walked quickly across the floor, to shake my hand. He had very blue intelligent eyes. As he took my hand he said, 'Come into the office. I'm afraid I can't talk for too long. I'm due somewhere else about seven.'

We sat down opposite each other on two sofas, with a glass table in between. It was a very large office with a desk at the other end, under a huge window covered by a Venetian blind. I said, 'It's very good of you to speak to me. Most of your family haven't been very forthcoming.'

He said, 'I know – but I'm a journalist. I'd quite like someone to get some answers to the questions which have never been answered about my grandmother. Of course I hardly knew her. We mostly met at uneasy family celebrations, at Cavendish Square, when my parents moved there after my great-grandmother's death. Everyone was on their best behaviour, and by the time Violet herself actually moved into Cavendish Square, when she was about eighty, I was married and living elsewhere. I just feel Violet never told the truth in her autobiography and there's been a family whitewash job going on as well. You know the sort of thing . . . '

I shook my head.

He smiled. 'Many people do. It goes like this. You're bored in the school holidays. You get hold of the family album, start going through, there's a gap, and when you ask why your mother tells you the picture must have fallen out. Then another gap, same explanation, and so on. Later you wonder why a family which keeps up-to-date records of everything managed to lose so many photographs. Or, for example, there's your grandmother,

Violet, a respectable old bird in a nice dress and a lot of jewellery, covered in make-up like Elizabeth I in old age, who appears like a family totem at the Christmas gathering, but when you ask her how she met your grandfather you get a story which doesn't ring true. That's the sort of thing – the older I've got, funnily enough, the more curious I've become. It's probably feelings of mortality, or immortality – and as a journalist I've noticed the tendency of family anecdote to stray into lies, distortion and error. In our case, there are also great gaps. I'd like an accurate version. I'm relieved someone's trying to do it. Glad to help.'

I nodded, uncertain what to ask first, but Christian-Smith, a journalist himself, as he had been quick to point out, asked me, 'How are you getting along, without the family to help?'

I said, 'I think I've sensed the same thing as you. The harder I try the more I get lost in the maze. I get calls from a woman, who's never identified herself, and who gives me clues what to look for, but never enough. And the last time we spoke she told me she couldn't say much as it would be breaking a promise she'd made. But who to? Why? It never gets better, only worse. And today, before I came here, a man rang and warned me off. He said, "In your own interests, don't ask any more questions about Violet Levine." Then he told me to ring my publisher. I haven't been able to, yet, but I wonder what it's all about.'

Jack Christian-Smith, his hand on his jaw, studied me.

'I know it sounds mad,' I said, 'but I'm not making this up. And to my knowledge I haven't provoked any of this – I haven't found out anything unusual or dangerous. The only possible tricky bit, I suppose, involves Gordon Stone, but that's a pretty ancient scandal, now.'

'What – Gordon Stone?' asked Christian-Smith. 'How does he fit in?'

'I don't know,' I said, 'but his name cropped up – Rosie Johnson told me. A journalist I know told me not to go near him. Then my mystery caller directed me to St Catherine's House. Did you know he and Violet's sister Alice had a child in 1936?'

Jack Christian-Smith was astounded. 'I certainly didn't.'

'So Stone's lurking in the labyrinth somewhere, I'm pretty

sure. But can I ask you a few questions? For example, did your mother ever tell you very much about her childhood?'

'No,' he told me. 'She fudged the whole thing. There were some sentimental stories about the holidays at Farnley – as far as I can tell that was when the children saw most of their mother. In London they saw her very little. They bored her, I think. The real stories, about the dog they had, and the birthday parties and the silly accidents – the bits that were fun – involved Violet's sister, Allie. And it looks as if there was more to Allie than meets the eye. Gordon Stone – phew . . . ' He shook his head in bewilderment. He continued, 'Allie brought them up, really. Mother sort f denies it, but that's what happened. The rest was buzz-buzz noises and not-in-front-of-the-children murmurs, when I was a child. And what Mrs Wilson told me – Mrs Wilson the housekeeper.'

'Ah,' I said.

'Ah, indeed,' he affirmed. 'Who but the trusty old housekeeper? You see, she was still there at Cavendish Square when I was a child, visiting, though she retired later. But at that time she was perfectly active – irreplaceable as they say. They were lucky, really. She was about thirty around the time of the First World War, not a flighty girl who wanted to rush into a munitions factory. So she stayed on right through the twenties and thirties, and by the Second World War she was too old to do war work. When I was eight or nine there she still was.'

'What did she tell you?'

'Well,' he said, thinking, 'that Violet had married again for one thing. The divorce was never mentioned, you see. She and Mackinnon had been married for years before I found out. One day when we were on holiday there she showed me a picture of Violet with Stafford Cripps on one side and Duncan Mackinnon on the other. I asked who the two men were and she told me. I was stunned to find out Violet was married. Nothing had been said. Of course I thought it was because my grandfather had died, and said so. Then she said, "Oh well, that wouldn't make much difference would it, them being divorced all those years before." When she found out I hadn't been told about that either she clammed up – and even then I knew not to ask too many questions about Violet. I don't think my mother ever came to terms with the thought of Violet. But what I did find out, or it sounded true enough, was that Pamela, my mother that is, may very well not have been my grandfather's child. Mrs Wilson didn't exactly tell me. I was sitting in the pantry at Cavendish Square, reading comics on the sly, when I heard Mrs Wilson talking to the Spanish maid. She'd got less starchy than she must have been before, Mrs Wilson. She became a bit of an anarchist as she got older. Some of her independent remarks caused upsets from time to time. She used to lean over guests at dinner and say, "I suppose you'll be wanting another helping of that," and so forth. She once opened the door to a Minister of State who'd come to see Father while we were staying at Cavendish Square, and said, "Oh, it's you again." She got put down as a bit of a character; you know, people would always ask about Mrs Wilson's latest. My feeling is that when Grandfather died and his wife went back to Italy Mrs Wilson didn't like the situation. She never got on with Sophie. She was always praising old Frederick to me, and mentioning little things he'd done to be kind, or ease the situation or whatever. And she liked Isabella, his second wife. It must have been glum for her after he died and Isabella left.

'So there I was in the pantry one day and Mrs Wilson, no longer the old family retainer with the unspeakable family secrets locked in her bosom, also going a bit deaf and therefore inclined to speak fairly loudly, suddenly started saying, "Of course, some people always thought Pamela wasn't really Mr Levine's child." It didn't mean much to me at the time. But afterwards I thought about it. Then she went on shouting, above some saucepan banging and egg-whipping noises' – he began to imitate the old woman's voice – ' "As for that book of hers, it was all tosh. Loyal staff at Cavendish Square, indeed! I wasn't loyal to her, I can tell you. She was a dreadful woman, that's why. Mind you, they gave her hell when she arrived, Mrs Sophie Levine and Mrs Laurence. It was heartbreaking – I don't know how she stood it. But, my God, didn't she pay them back. Once she'd got the reins in her hands and she was only waiting for the chance, she was enough to make Hitler tremble. She'd hardly let her own mother-in-law in the drawing-room. She was terrible at meals. She had all the jewellery off her and her sister-in-law in the end. Sold a lot of it down Bond Street, I heard. As for the staff – she nagged them skinny. When she was in the house everyone was off on errands for her, mixing cocktails, or answering the bell to put another lump of coal on the fire. She wouldn't stir a finger. You never knew where anybody was. It was a blessing to everybody she was hardly ever in."

'Anyway,' Christian-Smith continued, 'she went on like that for half an hour. I didn't dare come out of the pantry. I can still remember the terrible smell of cheese. She was quite violent about my grandmother. She talked about parties till all hours, and goings on and how it was a thoroughly good thing that Mr Levine got rid of Violet when he did, because she was bringing the family into disgrace. Not that it made any difference, she said; once she was gone there was a worse disgrace, the divorce. Then she recounted how the butler had stepped forward and offered to give evidence to support Mr Levine's contention that his wife was a thoroughly wicked, immoral woman and how Mr Levine had refused to allow him to testify, how he'd gone independently to the solicitor concerned and persuaded him to talk my grandfather into calling him to give evidence. None of this made much sense at the time, or for years, really, until I realised that this Violet was also the Violet of *I Affirm*. By the time I was in my twenties Violet was a heroine of the women's movement. I re-read the book with much more interest; there were quite good reasons why she should have been seen as exceptional. Her unbeatable physical courage, for example. But the stories didn't match the family tales. Nor did the tiny family matriarch in the black dress, heavy jewellery and thick make-up. She was a good-looking woman at one time. You can tell from the photographs.'

'Pamela's father seems to have been a postman,' I told him. 'Violet's niece told me in a letter.'

He shouted with laughter. 'Oh God,' he said, 'that'd kill my mother if she knew – and my sister. But . . . ' he paused. 'Perhaps they do know. Poor mother, if she does. She's always been a bit of a snob. Violet never did her any good – even gave her a dubious postman for a father, it seems.'

'You can't guess who my mystery caller might be?' I asked.

He shook his head looking puzzled. Then his face lightened

and he said, 'I've been wondering as we've been speaking— ' He broke off, then told me, 'When the subject of your book first came up earlier in the year – I'd shown up at Cavendish Square on my birthday – I assumed we'd at least be considering whether to offer you some help or not. But it was obvious that they, my mother and sister and Uncle Robert, who was there too, had already made up their minds. They all started pressing me to say I'd refuse to see you when you asked. I told them I saw no harm in a book about Violet. I suggested that we should ask for some control over what you did – then everybody got angry. Robert began to make will-changing noises, Mother said it would make her ill. I gave up arguing. But I thought, to hell with all of them. They're quite happy to get nice publicity for Violet as a national heroine, for example, or their own and their children's pictures in magazines, at balls and parties. They don't admit it, but they like these things. They don't object to the royalties on Violet's book either – they're still coming in. But, I decided, when the truth starts threatening to come out and it looks as if it might not be too flattering, then publicity becomes vulgar and undesirable. Also, to be quite candid,' Christian-Smith leaned forward, 'I had a feeling there was something they're trying to hide. They wouldn't tell me. I'm not safe. But old journalists are like old policemen. They develop instincts; corny, I know, but true.'

'So,' I asked, 'who do you think is phoning me?'

He smiled. 'I'm enough of a Levine – if I am, of course – to want to be careful about that one. There may be a good reason for not telling you my guess. I'll check. Is there any chance of looking at what material you've already got?'

I hesitated.

He saw why. 'I understand. You think I might be another Levine, trying to find out what you know. Never mind, leave that. I'll crack it on my own.'

'I'm sorry . . . '

'Listen. When you've been involved in this business as long as I have, you get used to nothing being as it seems.' The phone rang. He answered it saying, 'She's still here. I don't know. Oh yes – yes, thanks, I'd forgotten. No, I won't be late.' The voice spoke again. He replied, 'She certainly did. It's about a postman.'

Smiling, he put down the phone. 'My wife,' he explained. 'She's trying to make sure I get to the party in time.'

I said, 'Well . . . '

'Don't worry,' he told me. 'There's still a minute or two. In any case, we can meet again. I'll make you a tape with what I can remember, if you like. My wife reminded me of something – I don't know whether it's worth your following it up. I was in a restaurant off Hanover Square, Le Sac d'Epingles, with my wife and some colleagues. It was a farewell party for one of them, and the meal was very good, so when the manager turned up, I said so. We chatted a bit when he suddenly asked if I was Mr Christian-Smith – he told me then that he'd worked for my grandmother for some years in Cheyne Walk during the forties and fifties. His name's Henri Clos. When I said you were coming here my wife suggested you give him a try. Jessica's on my side in this. She says the truth about Violet Levine may not be so flattering as the one she made up for herself, but it might be a lot more interesting. She did history at Somerville. She says if you don't get to the primary sources quickly, they'll all have died. In fact, she says would it be all right if she rang you? I think she plans to liaise between you and me in case I get involved in a project and try to slip away. It's a bad habit of mine. Also, I think she wants to see how you tackle the project. The children are only babies at the moment and she wanted to be at home with them, but she's already planning her next move.'

'Yes,' I agreed. I didn't like to say that studying my methods of reconstructing someone's life might only show someone else how not to do it. I did say, 'I'm not an experienced biographer, though.'

'I think she'd love to meet you, all the same. Don't worry,' he reassured me, 'she won't be spying.'

I went down in the lift and thought I ought to go back and see Di. On the way I decided to make a small detour and see if I could speak to the restaurant manager Jack had mentioned. Outside the restaurant, where two large green-uniformed men stood respectfully opening doors, I asked one if Mr Clos was in the restaurant. He gave me a very careful look. It was obvious I wasn't dressed to dine there. Then he asked me what my business was.

'Mr Jack Christian-Smith suggested I come to see Mr Clos,' I said. He went away again. When he returned he led me inside. A dark man in a dinner-jacket was standing in the expensive foyer. 'I'm Henri Clos,' he said. 'What do you want?' He looked hard and capable, but not unkind.

'I'm writing a biography of Mrs Violet Levine,' I said. 'I've just seen Jack Christian-Smith. He mentioned you might have some reminiscences . . . '

He looked at me carefully. I imagined he could sum up anyone – the clients who would get drunk, the clients whose credit was poor, the clients dining with people they shouldn't have been – then he took me into the office where, as he sat behind his desk, I explained my project as succinctly as I could. I offered to get Roger Littlebrown to telephone him and confirm my credentials. He told me this wasn't necessary and said, 'There's been a great deal of scandal. You understand my caution.'

'You were employed at Cheyne Walk when Duncan Mackinnon defected?'

He said, 'Yes. We were all interviewed. I think the Secret Service wondered if one of the domestics was an accomplice of Mr Mackinnon's. There was a lot of trouble. I was a foreigner. This seemed to interest them.'

'Yes, I see,' I said. 'I am interested in that aspect of Mrs Mackinnon's life, but the details of the defection have been explored over and over again. That isn't my first concern. I'm writing about her whole life. I'd like your impression of her – anything you can tell me, even small things, what she was like to work for, perhaps.'

He said, 'Very well. But we're moving into our busy time. Perhaps you'd like to come back tomorrow?' He was giving me an appraising look as he spoke.

'Of course,' I said, hoping he'd make it early. I might be moving out of Henry Thackery House, for all I knew.

'Eleven would be convenient.'

'Eleven it is.'

As he saw me out I glimpsed Andy and Vanessa Hume sitting in a corner of the restaurant, Andy in his white suit, Vanessa in a white Grecian-style dress, off one shoulder, her black hair shimmering down her back. They made a lovely couple. They didn't see me.

Then I took a cab back to Henry Thackery House to confront Di. The flat was empty. There was a note in the kitchen. 'Dear Kate, I'm very, very sorry. I'll be away for a few days. I'll phone tonight, briefly.'

Briefly? I thought, then I remembered the phone was bugged. For a reason probably. On impulse I shoved all my notes and tapes into a big holdall and took a short bus-ride to Julie Simmons's canal-side loft in Kensal Green. She was there with a few people in kaftans, smoking dope and pretending to be hippies. The TV was on with the sound off at the end of the black tiled floor. They were playing Ravi Shankar tapes. 'Can you keep something for me for a few days?' I asked, above the oriental sounds.

'Not a bomb, is it?' said one of the others, glancing at the TV. His hair came over the neck of his collarless jacket. The TV showed the TV centre I'd just been in. In ruins. 'Oh God,' I exclaimed. 'Can I turn the sound up? I just went there.'

As I turned up the volume Jack Christian-Smith's face appeared, talking to a reporter. The camera drew back to show him looking dishevelled, in evening dress. ' . . . into my car in the car park,' he said, 'when the explosion occurred. It threw me to the ground.'

I too sank to the ground, or rather, Julie's tiles, my bag still beside me. Christian-Smith went on with his account. There were shots of the wreckage still smoking. A man had died. I put my head in my hands. The others went on smoking. 'You okay?' asked one of the pseudo-hippies.

'No,' I replied. I called to Julie, 'I've changed my mind about the bag. Sorry to have disturbed you.' I hadn't really disturbed anybody. I turned the sound on the TV down and left. 'Peace and love,' I said in the doorway, but no one took any notice.

I went back to Henry Thackery House with my bag, sobered. The moment I'd seen that bombing on TV I'd wondered if Di was involved. It was a shocking thought, but obviously she was up to something illegal – why not that? And if she was involved, and if she got caught, how would I be able to persuade anybody that I wasn't part of it? At best it'd be assumed I'd known, even if I hadn't participated – and this was why I'd changed my mind about leaving the bag at Julie's. My only defence would be that I hadn't known what was going on. It sounded weak in the first place and wouldn't be any more convincing if it came out I'd been hiding things in other people's flats. I didn't know what had been going on but now nothing seemed impossible. I knew Di had been oppressed by the feeling she was living in a society she hated, poor, full of lies, where government power kept on increasing. She'd talked obsessively about this at one time, describing Britain as a potentially Fascist state. Then, about a year ago, she'd stopped talking. I wondered if at that point she hadn't got into something actively dangerous.

The bus ground along. Then I got out and walked to Henry Thackery House, quiet and peaceful in the dusk. The street lamp outside was already on. Hoping the place wasn't watched, I took the bag back inside, and put it in my room.

Then I sat down in the living-room and watched the end of a soap about rich people, where each shot looked like an ad for something: whisky, cars, shampoo. I was waiting for the news. I felt dreadful – tired, tense, sick. Again I thought of clearing out. If people were after Di they'd catch up with me anyway, but at least I wouldn't be under the constant strain of living at the flat. Then Di rang. 'Are you all right?' she asked.

Aware the phone could be bugged I had to restrain my anger. 'I was trying to see you. I'm not happy about you not being here.'

'I'm sorry,' she answered, equally guardedly. 'That's why I rang. To say I'm sorry.'

'I'm glad you're sorry,' I told her as evenly as I could. 'I'm absolutely counting on you to turn up and give me all the details of this holiday we're meant to be taking. I feel very insecure because I don't know what the plans are. Very insecure,' I repeated.

'Nothing to worry about, really,' she said. 'I've taken care of the details. I'll explain when I get back tomorrow or the day after.' She sounded quite calm, which reassured me. Perhaps the situation wasn't as bad as I thought. Or perhaps it was.

I said in a hard tone, 'Well, Di, I'm really looking forward to seeing you when you get back.'

She replied, 'Okay. Take care,' and put the phone down.

I was pretty angry. As I saw it we were both in trouble because of something she'd done and not told me about. I didn't even know the nature and extent of it. And now she was telling me she'd turn up in a day or two and explain. I wasn't happy and I wasn't sure that by then it wouldn't be too late. I was haunted by the idea the flat was under surveillance.

I watched the news. The usual mixed bag of terrorist organisations had claimed responsibility. After that Adrian Critchlow came on and said emergency plans to issue ID cards to everyone within a month were now in operation. He knew he would get complete co-operation, since this would assist in stamping out terrorist attacks. The House of Commons would be asking for a suspension of the rules concerning search warrants and against the holding of suspected terrorists for lengthy periods. He knew everyone would understand the necessity. I cursed Di, if she was involved in stuff like this. An innocent man had died and more civil liberties were going down the drain. Critchlow looked firm, concerned, grave and masterly. The crime rate was soaring, bomb-slinging groups were proliferating. Last Wednesday they'd found an anarchist commune on Barra with a cache of machine-guns and mortars. Belfast was regularly in flames. Six soldiers, twelve republicans and fourteen loyalists had died this year. Critchlow and his message were on all channels. I switched off, but felt he was still in the room. After all this, it was still only ten o'clock. I was tired, and so keyed up I knew I wouldn't sleep. I thought I'd read for a bit.

The phone rang and Andy said, 'I'm sorry. I'm upset you didn't get in touch. Let me apologise. At least come out for a drink at the bar.'

I really wanted to see him and I wanted to get out of the flat. I hoped there would be no discussion of Vanessa Hume. I had enough to think about.

'You look wrung out,' he told me when I sat down at the pavement table he'd bagged. I probably do, I thought. It's been a long day. I was about to describe it to Andy –

the telephone threat, my fears and worries about my flatmate, just missing a bomb at the TV centre, and other episodes from a day in the life of a working girl – when he asked innocently, 'Do you want anything to eat?' adding, 'I already have.'

I remembered where and with whom he'd eaten and the temptation to unburden myself ebbed. After all, I'd told Rog I'd keep quiet about the locked spare room and everything connected with it. If I launched into my story about meeting Jack Christian-Smith at the TV centre just before it was blown up, Andy might seize the chance to nag about the biography. The last time we'd met he'd hit me; the last time I'd seen him he'd been with another woman. Did I really want to confide in him? No – but I knew if I kept the meeting non-controversial, in an hour I'd be in bed with him. It was all I wanted, at that moment. I was done up. It only vaguely crossed my mind that three months ago I was obsessed by my relationship with Andy and that at the moment I didn't seem to care about anything but dragging him into bed.

'I'm sorry I lost my temper like that,' he said. 'It was unforgivable.'

'I didn't realise how serious you felt about it all. Perhaps I don't know what's good for me.'

An hour later we were in bed. I fell asleep the moment we'd made love. I couldn't help it. Andy woke me up: 'Talk to me.'

I said the first thing that came into my head. 'Di's gone away.'

'Big news. And the ugly Violet?'

'Not a lot.'

'Just – not a lot?'

'Mm,' I muttered. 'I saw Dave in hospital, but there was a big crowd and he kept on taking calls on a cell-phone.'

'What's wrong with him?' Andy asked.

'He got run over by a girl on a bike.'

Andy gave a laugh. 'I bet he thought it was the CIA.'

'That's what his girlfriend said.'

'Let's hope it's a motorbike next time.'

I was trying to keep my eyes open. 'Don't know what you've got against him,' I said.

'He's a pea-brain.'

I fell asleep again, hearing the word 'hospital'.

'I said, why did you go and see him?' Andy asked.

'I thought he'd be all by himself,' I mumbled.

'Oh well,' said Andy, giving up. He put his arm round me and we both went to sleep.

I went from his flat to the Sac d'Epingles. The day was clear and beautiful. On the way I bought shoes and a new cream skirt and top. I arrived feeling suitably new and fresh to get over the threshold of the Sac d'Epingles. There was only one man on the door at this time of day, and he was in jeans and shirt-sleeves. I gave my name, he went in and Henri Clos, also in his shirt-sleeves, came out and led me in. We sat in his office in two armchairs. He sent a waiter off for coffee. 'Well,' he asked, 'and how are you getting on with the book?'

'Better than at first. Though it's still a confusing story. There are a lot of dark areas.'

'Many people have them,' he commented. His face was healthy, but his eyes were those of a man who makes no judgments except where his bank accounts are concerned.

'How long did you work at Cheyne Walk?' I asked.

'Twelve years,' he said. 'From just after the war until 1958.'

'And you were the cook?'

'The under-cook. The cook had been Violet's servant for many years. He was growing old. He also drank. He needed help.'

'Oh,' I said. 'Do you know, Violet Levine hasn't struck me as a woman who would employ staff who drank, or were unreliable in any way . . . '

'Felix had been with her a long, long time,' he said.

I looked at him. 'And is he still alive?' I asked.

'He died in 1959,' said Henri Clos, studying me.

I plugged on. 'So you left in 1958 and the cook stayed on until . . . '

'We left at the same time. Mrs Mackinnon sent Felix off to his retirement down to Farnley, where the family still had a few cottages. That day I also left Mrs Mackinnon's employ. Felix would have had a better place on the estate in the old days but almost all of it had been sold. They said Mrs Mackinnon received all the money. Felix died a year later, of pneumonia, in the small cottage they gave him. The cottage was damp – it hastened his death. The damp cottage didn't worry Felix so much but he was very upset Mrs Mackinnon never visited him, especially when he was ill. Perhaps she didn't know. She never saw him after he went to Farnley. He'd been loyal, and at the last he had to recognise that she was not. A bitter truth to have to face. So . . . ' He paused, looked at me, and continued: 'Mrs Mackinnon gave him little money, after so many years of service. Three pounds a week. Then he had his old age pension.'

I was shocked. 'Too bad,' I said.

He paused, remembering, I think. 'An old man, after forty-five years of service, his reward a few pounds a week and a damp cottage in a country village in England.'

'Had he no other choice?' I asked.

Henri Clos shook his head. 'He had very little money.' Now he looked at me closely, paused and told me, 'He wrote something about her and tried to sell it. He'd read her lying account of herself in her autobiography.'

'I see,' I said, assuming calm. 'Who did he try to sell it to?'

'The Sunday papers. They refused. They said it might be libel. Felix thought Mr and Mrs Christian-Smith were preventing them from publishing the story. It was they who offered him the place at Farnley, but it was not a kind suggestion. It was easy for them, but not kind. It showed no gratitude.'

'Does this account still exist?' I asked.

Once again he measured me with his eyes.

'You've got it,' I told him.

'Yes,' he said. 'I have it. It was with his property when he died. I'm prepared to sell it.'

I'd thought as much. I nodded. 'I need to know what it's like, and how much you want for it.'

'I want five thousand pounds,' he told me.

'That's a lot for something written against an employer in anger which may be a collection of libels.'

'I know what he says is true. He told me often.'

'I'd like it,' I said, 'but five thousand pounds is a steep price. Have you got it here? Could I look at some of it?'

'All right,' he agreed. 'But read it here, not too much of it.'

He opened his desk and took out an orange cardboard

folder. He handed it to me. The contents were in two sections, the first a sheaf of handwritten papers, written, in French, in spiky handwriting. The second was about fifteen sheets of typing paper, typed, single space, in English. I read the first typed page.

> I, Felix Lamier, have an amazing story to tell, a tale of a woman's ambition, of a family's shame, of dark secrets hidden. For forty-five years I was the witness to startling events in the household of the eminent banker, the late Sir Frederick Levine, and of the Soviet spy and traitor, Duncan Mackinnon. The connecting link between these two households was a woman, the fascinating, malign Violet, wife of both men.

As I read on, to the bottom of the page, my eyes must have widened. With Henri Clos's eyes on me I daren't turn the page. I looked up at him.

'Well, Mrs Higgins?' he asked.

'May I read just a little more?'

He nodded. I opened the pages at random. Ah, I thought, the famous divorce.

> Although I spoke for Mrs Levine at her divorce case, my evidence was false. She had allowed me to go on the night of Mr Levine's discoveries at Farnley, but made no attempt to find me again until she needed me urgently a year later to demonstrate in court that she was spotless, second only to the Virgin Mary herself. She consequently hired detectives who found me living modestly in a quiet corner of Paris. They persuaded me to come back to England, where Mrs Levine put it to me that, if I wished to be re-employed by her, I needed only to deny her husband's allegations of immorality at Farnley House and present her to the public as the most respectable of women. I had also to say that her husband, Mr Frederick Levine, was having an affair with his sister-in-law. Monstrous suggestion! Of all men, Mr Levine, whose character I have already described, was the most honourable. And of all women Miss Alice, Mrs Levine's sister, was the most kind and pleasant. There was no question of wrong-doing

> in their relationship, only a little tenderness between them, easily explained by the terrible character of the woman who linked them. But – my position was not a happy one. I had responsibilities and no employment. There was a depression. Mrs Levine's bribery, my own need, and the enormous charm she was capable of exerting when it suited her, all, I am ashamed to confess, convinced me. I went to court, I swore on the name of God to tell the truth – I lied. The truth was that for more than two years before the occasion when Mr Levine burst into his own home to discover his wife in her bedroom in the arms of her foul lover, while downstairs degenerates and adulterers entertained themselves without morals or scruples, I, Felix Lamier, had cooked, cleaned and supplied, weekend after weekend, a household which in many respects was the equal of many a brothel. Cocaine, as well as alcohol, was supplied in quantity. I have seen as many as eight guests naked and pursuing each other through the grounds. Among them were . . .

And here Felix mentioned by name a noted homosexual MP of the period, a young débutante who later married a duke, a celebrated actor, later knighted, and a couple of other names I didn't know. It was hot stuff. I cheated and flipped a few pages before Henri Clos could stop me.

> There is no doubt in my mind that Mrs Mackinnon was well aware of her husband's activities for months, if not years, before he escaped to the Soviet Union.

Henri Clos coughed.

I handed the pages back. 'Phew – well, well,' was all I could say.

He was pleased by this response.

'But,' I said, 'let's face it – whether it's true or false or a bit of each, most of this can't be substantiated.'

'You need it though,' he told me.

'Yes. I'd like to have it. But I'm not sure about the price. It's a bit high for something no one else is going to want.'

He shrugged, as if to say if I wouldn't pay him he was prepared to wait until someone else would. But I was getting the idea that many of the people whom I'd interviewed about Violet weren't talking to me only because they wanted to contribute information for a wonderful and accurate biography. Some – Rosie Johnson, the MP, Aurelia Jenks-Davidson, were fairly disinterested, but Jack Christian-Smith wanted to know who his grandmother really was. So did Jessica Fellwell. And what about Deep Throat? That was personal, though I didn't know why. Henri Clos also seemed to have personal motives for supplying information. For some reason he wanted Felix avenged. Violet, and, it seemed, her daughter, had let a faithful servant die neglected. But I guessed he stood to gain five thousand pounds and his vengeance if he sold me Felix's memoirs, and neither if he didn't. So he might be prepared to negotiate a price. On the other hand, selling the Levine story to me was not going to help him professionally, if the news got out. As a restaurateur discretion was part of his stock in trade. If the clientèle of the Sac d'Epingles found out he'd split on the Levines, his reputation as a trustworthy, silent servant could easily be damaged; so he was taking a risk.

I told him, 'I'll talk to my publisher about the money,' and we shook hands cordially and parted. I thought it wasn't just an ordinary friendship for Felix which prompted him to try to sell me his story – there was more to it than that. The bitter memories of Violet's drunken cook might be invaluable to me, partly for the serious information they contained, partly for the trivia, and the general light they would throw on the woman herself. But the money was a problem. Henri Clos was asking almost exactly what I had in the bank now, to keep me, and pay my contribution to Ray's expenses, which anyway wasn't enough, until I'd finished the book. There'd be another payment when the book was published, if they liked it when I'd finished. But it might take six months or a year to complete and in the meanwhile I couldn't take on much other work, because I needed the time, so how could I give Henri Clos what he wanted? I wouldn't have any money at all left. There was only one answer – Roger Littlebrown would have to help.

I went back to the flat, expecting the front door to be swinging open, and several plain-clothes policemen waiting for me in a wrecked room, but all was well. I phoned Roger, remembering the threatening call instructing me to lay off Violet Levine and ring my publisher. He was busy so I left a message. I washed up the cups Rog and I had used yesterday, the day before the world became so threatening. Then Roger rang. He sounded irritable. He's tired, I thought charitably. What with the work, and the baby . . .

'I've been trying to get you for days,' he said.

'Listen, Roger, I've just stumbled across a man who's got what looks like some useful material for the book, but he wants money for it— '

'I've been trying to get you,' he repeated. 'The situation's changed. I've been offered another biography.' He paused.

'Of whom?' I asked, uselessly. As if I didn't know.

'Well – Violet Levine.'

I thought I wouldn't spare him. He could just tell me the whole story. 'Ah,' I said.

'It's the authorised biography.' He paused again. I said nothing. 'Simon Snow rang the day before yesterday. He said he'd been approached by Robert Levine who was prepared to allow him full access to photographs and documents, as well as every co-operation from the family to write a complete, detailed biography of Violet Levine. Naturally I mentioned our contract with you.' He seemed to stick a bit here. I left him stuck. He started up again, 'Well, obviously Snow said he needed priority on this one. I'm sure you can see that, Kate.'

'Yes,' I said. 'And you might like to know I had a threatening call yesterday, telling me, and I'm quoting exactly, "In your own interests don't ask any more questions about Violet Levine." And he told me to ring you, too. He knew what you've just told me.'

'Is that all?' he asked.

'Isn't it enough?' I was slowly sinking into the floor. My feet and ankles were already jelly on the grey, speckled carpeting Di had found on a skip two years ago. And the sensation was creeping up my legs.

'I'd better think about that one,' said Roger. 'But,' he hurried on, anxious to get to the end of the news he didn't want to tell me. 'Obviously I have to consider this offer very seriously. A full authorised biography, after all . . . We would be prepared to pay you in full on the contract, of course.'

'On condition I don't write the book.'

He said, 'Er – I know how disappointed you must feel.'

'I think I need to think about this, too,' I said.

'It's awkward, Kate. We've talked it over here, at length. Frankly, I'm a lot less than happy about it.'

I got angry. 'It must be as plain to you as it is to me that you'll get the official version, the clean one. I don't suppose either you or Snow can imagine the kind of pressure you'll be under to fudge the facts. Is that what you want? And what about my threatening call?'

It was obvious he didn't care if I'd been rung up and threatened by the Mafia. He wanted the official biography very badly. 'I really don't think Simon would be a party to anything like that,' he said without pausing. 'His reputation as a biographer is outstanding.'

And I'm a divorced woman, with no reputation for anything as far as you're concerned, except for sleeping with your cousin, I thought vengefully, as my legs weakened even more.

It's occurred to me from time to time that during the period when I was Violet Levine's biographer, some essence of the dead woman seeped into me and became part of my own personality. It's not a thought I've always welcomed. I clung to the phone and thought Violet-style, I'll get you for this, Roger. I said firmly, 'Of course I don't think Simon Snow had anything to do with the phone call and, okay, Roger, I'm disappointed, but I understand the difficulty. The Levines have made it difficult for you to back my biography. They've made you an offer you can't refuse. You know it's all a bit shady – you've got to live with the consequences, whatever they are. But don't forget I've been threatened – think about it. It must mean something. Anyway, you can send me two-thirds of the money you would have paid me if the book had been published. That's reasonable, isn't it?' Two-thirds of the money was five thousand pounds, the sum Henri Clos wanted.

'That's more than fair,' he told me. 'And I hope – well, I hope if you feel like embarking on another work like this you'll – well, you'll think of us.'

'Goodbye, Roger,' I said, and then I really did fall on the

floor, on my hands and knees, where I stared at the carpet for a bit. Then I shifted, and sat down on the carpet for a bit longer. But I'd got the five thousand pounds from Askew and Askew.

Then I rang Dave and got his mother. 'Dave can't come to the phone.'

'Can he ring me?' I asked her.

She took down my name and number. I went on sitting there, but by that time I'd had all the useful thoughts I ever would on the topic of my sacking. The good news was that I was due to get a cheque for five thousand pounds from Askew and Askew, for doing nothing at all from now on. The price of my silence. The bad news was that I'd been paid to shut up, which I resented, that I'd worked for months for nothing and, basically, that the powerful Levines had sabotaged the efforts of the little man – or woman in this case. You could argue they had a certain right, since their family reputation was involved. On the other hand, Violet hadn't just been a private woman. She'd written her own account of her life, not entirely truthfully, it seemed, and public truths were involved as well.

Roger Littlebrown hadn't truly stopped me. I could complete the book, and I might be able to sell it to another publisher. But, with an authorised biography coming out from Askew and Askew, it was uncertain that another firm would want to take on mine, when Simon Snow had access to all the information. Even if someone got interested, how did I know the long arm of the Levines wouldn't reach forward and stop me again? It looked as if I'd been a fool to launch myself into the project as I had.

I decided that, for my own satisfaction, I'd tell Jack Christian-Smith what had happened – though for all I knew he'd been working against me the whole time, just finding out what I knew. The news of the authorised biography might be no news at all. I left a message for him. Then I rang the Sac d'Epingles and left a less than honest message on Henri Clos's machine saying I'd been discussing the sale of Felix's papers with my publisher, and that there were complications. I had an idea that if Felix's memoirs were any good, someone might swoop down and get them from him, perhaps not to use but to suppress for the sake of Violet's good name.

It was hot again, and high time for some lunch, but Roger's news, that I was out of work, had shattered me. Now I'd had enough. I was smoking glumly in the front room, not knowing what to do with myself, when Di came in. She was carrying a holdall and looked tired. I didn't feel very sorry for her. 'Di,' I said, 'I think you owe me an explanation.'

She sat down on the sofa with as much of a thump as such a thin person could muster. 'I know. But it might be better for you if you didn't know too much.'

I explained, 'Until I know what's been going on, I daren't even clear out. I'm afraid your trouble might follow me. I'm afraid if I go it'll make me look as if I'm on the run. We know the phone's tapped already. I don't feel safe. It's like being locked in a building with mines in the basement.'

Di laughed. 'That used to be truer than you know,' she said.

I was furious. 'That's not funny, Di. When Rog came out of that back room, the one you had locked, holding a screwdriver and told me he'd been fixing the lamp, I believed him. But I've been thinking . . . ' I stared at her. 'What are you involved in, Di? You've been running a bomb factory in here, haven't you?'

FOURTEEN

Violet Levine, 1976
Kate Higgins, June 20th, 1991

Violet sat, a small woman in a dark green silk dress, in a chair in the window at Cheyne Walk. Sometimes her eyes wandered towards the Thames and the big modern buildings on the opposite bank, sometimes to the removal men, taking items of furniture from the sitting-room to put in her small sitting-room at Cavendish Square, the room to which she had condemned her mother-in-law when she assumed power in the Levine household sixty years before. But Violet had also insisted on taking over other rooms, one exclusively to house her books and papers. Her daughter Pamela had tried to make her go to Cavendish Square before the move. 'I'll see to everything at Cheyne Walk,' she said. 'It'll be less tiring for you, Mother.'

'Thank you,' Violet had told her, 'but I'd rather supervise it myself.'

At seventy-nine she was still forceful. Her face was deeply lined under heavy make-up, but her eyes were still dartingly alive. Her hair was still black, thanks to the weekly visits of her hairdresser. Her little wrinkled hands still bore painted red nails. In some ways age had made her more formidable, not less. She knew more: she had fewer inhibitions about what she said, she had nothing to lose. They still called her out to address large meetings at election time, because she remained a crowd-stirrer, perhaps more so now that the rallying cries came from an apparently frail old lady. The publication of *I Affirm* had increased her popularity. This story of an eventful life, led by a woman of energy and conscience, and reprinted by a feminist press, was now on sale in every bookshop.

After Duncan Mackinnon's defection she had been asked not to stand again in the election which followed four months later, and only three weeks after the government had finally confirmed what everyone suspected, that he was, in fact, in Moscow.

The Prime Minister, Clement Attlee, had reassured her. He told her he believed she had had no part in Mackinnon's activities, she had been his victim, not his accomplice. But he told her he was forced to ask her to stand down. She had lived for nine years with a man who had been passing secrets to the Soviet Union since the thirties. The Americans were appalled at the laxity of British security. The Labour Party, suspected by them, and by many in Britain, of being a nest of Communist sympathisers, could not afford to let Violet stand again for parliament. Violet expected this. It was, after all, the reason she had not exposed Duncan when she first began to suspect him. She made the best of a bad job and offered her resignation gracefully. They would, said Attlee, be happy to make use of her talents in other ways though Violet suspected she might never be fully trusted again. The Prime Minister knew how much information had been in her possession while she'd been living with the undetected Duncan Mackinnon. It suited neither of them to make this public, or even to discuss it in detail in private. But if Mackinnon had got information to pass on to the Soviet Union from his wife's desk, then, anyone might decide, Violet must clearly have been either foolish or involved. And, inevitably, some intelligent and cynical men would wonder aloud if Violet had suspected or actually known Duncan was a spy and said nothing.

Knowing the major game was up for her now Violet masked her anger and disappointment, and asked for employment at Labour Party headquarters. She indicated she would be happy to work in any capacity, however humble, where she could be useful. Inside her, though, the rage for publicity, action at the centre of things and personal importance still burned. She ended up in a central position at the publicity office between 1957 and 1964. She also wrote for the papers, undertook speaking engagements up and down the country, took part in question-and-answer programmes on radio and TV and published her memoirs, partly to assert her ignorance of any of her former husband's activities. It was necessary to be believed if she was ever to be fully reinstated. But in spite of a career which made her more famous than she might have been had she stayed on in the House of Commons, she was still in semi-exile, desperate to get back into parliament. She'd never intended to serve faithfully as a backbencher for ever. She'd her eye on promotion. In five or ten years, she'd estimated, she might have been a Minister of the Crown.

When the first Labour government for thirteen years was returned to power in 1964, Violet became very depressed. For a week at sixty-seven years of age she lay in bed like a jealous four-year-old, refusing to eat, get up, or attend to anything. She knew that, had her career in parliament continued, she might have achieved high office. This might have been her moment.

She'd known instantly that something was wrong on that terrible summer morning in 1951, when the two men in dark suits had arrived on the doorstep of Cheyne Walk, asking to see her. They identified themselves as Foreign Office officials. Violet, pretending to believe that that was all they were, thought rapidly. She took them to her office, as if assuming they had come on ordinary business. They asked her whether she'd seen her husband recently. The question was all Violet needed to confirm her worst suspicions. Duncan had run. He had left the Lebanon, they told her, on a return journey to Britain, and disappeared. Violet looked grave. He had not told her he was coming back, she told them, but that was not wholly surprising because they were estranged. She hadn't seen him for six months. Looking graver still, she asked if there was any special reason why the Foreign Office was concerned. Concealing their embarrassment they told her that it was always a matter of concern when a diplomat disappeared. Violet, seemingly reluctant, told them that Duncan's alcoholism had been one of the problems which had harmed the marriage. She reassured them that since he was inclined to vanish for days on end during drinking bouts he'd probably turn up sooner or later. They pretended to accept this suggestion and left.

After this interview Violet flung herself into a chair and cursed Duncan aloud. The men from Special Branch had gone away to dissect what she'd told them. But, unless by some miracle Duncan really was on a drunken spree, which she didn't for a moment believe, they'd be back, again and again. And she could see they knew, or suspected, more than they had told her. She'd disassociated herself from Duncan as much as possible. But unless she was very lucky it was all up with her now, she guessed. She cursed Duncan, and herself as well.

Her wisest policy, when she'd first begun to suspect him, might have been to denounce him. That way she could just have come out of the business with the reputation of a woman who had finally to put the interests of her country above her private feelings. It had probably been a bad idea to try to bluff it out. When she started investigating she discovered Duncan's transfer to Beirut, just as she was about to get him into a clinic, had not been the blessing she thought it was. Away from her he'd drunk more, acted more wildly. In the end, another enemy agent inside the British embassy had made a blunder Duncan had not been able to cover up. He had to escape to avoid investigation, then arrest. Violet saw, clearsightedly, that if her basic training in personal survival over the years hadn't involved so much covering up, evasion, manipulation and concealment, she might not have adopted the same tactics when dealing with the problem of Duncan Mackinnon. A straightforward denunciation would, in retrospect, have served her better.

For years after this catastrophe she worked and worked, always with the idea that one day a summons would come, calling her back to parliament. *I Affirm* and all her diligence never really cleared her name. Part of the reason for her collapse in 1964 was that, however hard she'd tried, no summons to stand in a general election had come. The Labour Party went out of office just after Duncan defected and when their moment of triumph came, Violet was left out. Fresh spy scandals came and went but Mackinnon's name, far from being gradually forgotten, as Violet had hoped, stayed nearly as fresh in the public mind as it had been in the days when the scandal broke. She was identified with him, as the seemingly clever wife who had not known what he was doing.

Now the old woman stood up in her sunny drawing-room as the last items were taken out of her house. She passed her daughter in the hall.

'Where are you going, Mother?' asked Pamela.

'I want to be sure any books and papers go off properly. I don't want a muddle, I'm at work on the second part of my memoirs,' Violet said, thinking irritably that Pamela, in a lemon suit with a pleated skirt, looked just like a giant canary standing in the hall. All her advantages, and no taste at all, thought the cross, famous old lady.

'Very well,' Pamela replied stiffly, barely more tolerant of her mother than her mother was of her.

Violet went up to the study on the first floor, making sure that she did not at any point use the banister to pull herself up or steady herself unduly. Not in front of Pamela.

Though Pamela had been urging her to come to Cavendish Square for some time she had not wanted to move. Violet had resisted, until the death of the housekeeper who had succeeded Felix. Only then did she decide it would be cheaper and more convenient to live at Cavendish Square. Before agreeing finally, she'd bargained for, and got the use of five rooms on the first floor, and a lift installed for her personal use.

The move over, Violet spent the afternoon organising her rooms at Cavendish Square, then took the lift down to the drawing-room, rang the bell, and asked the Filipino woman, Sylvia, who, with her husband and two daily women, constituted the whole staff, to pour her some sherry. Pamela came in while this was happening and stared soberly at the scene.

'Mother,' Pamela said, after Sylvia left, 'I think I ought to tell you we don't ring the bell very often, out of consideration for the staff, these days. There really aren't enough of them to keep running to and fro.'

'Really? You ought to have told me you were short-staffed before I let my maid Dora Davis go. I imagine I can recall her.'

'There's absolutely no need,' said Pamela.

Her mother contradicted her. 'It seems there is. I should have realised you weren't planning to add to the staff to allow for my being here. It seems hard on them to be faced with an extra person in the house without additional help. I really think I'd better phone Dora in Hove. She's an excellent person, and not a bad cook.'

'I have a cook, Mother. I also cook myself.'

'Ah, yes, of course,' Violet murmured, as if suddenly recalling a rather unpleasant experience. She held out her glass. 'Perhaps you'd refill this for me.'

'I'm quite surprised to see you down. I imagined you'd be resting.'

Violet ignored this. 'I'm so sorry,' she said. 'But I'm afraid I've been a little remiss. I took the liberty of inviting Cynthia Greenways to dinner. I hope it's not inconvenient. She's the lady who organises my luncheon club speeches and she promised to bring me the details of next month's programme.'

Pamela closed her eyes. 'Of course. But I would appreciate some notice in future.'

'Put it down to the move,' said Violet. She had fought many a campaign in this drawing-room. She would win this one eventually, too.

'Some friends are coming in after dinner,' Pamela told her. 'Perhaps you and Mrs Greenways would prefer to go upstairs after dinner to discuss your arrangements.'

'No need,' responded Violet cheerfully. 'We've very little to do. We'll be glad to join you.'

'You might not find them sympathetic, that's all. The husband is Geoffrey Biggs.'

'Oh, the MP,' exclaimed Violet. Her eyes were sharp. She sat upright in Sophie Levine's old chair. 'Please don't worry. I wouldn't dream of starting a political argument.'

She did not. The woman who arranged Violet's luncheon speaking engagements up and down the country left shortly after dinner and Violet, impressive in family diamonds, ensconced herself in a large armchair in the drawing-room, at first listening with a patient air to all that was said, then joining pleasantly in the conversation. Geoffrey Biggs was enchanted, and quite interested when she described to him why and how the present government would lose the next general election, ending, 'So both you gentlemen will shortly, I'm sure, be in the running for high office in the new Conservative government.'

Pamela, trapped with Mrs Biggs's description of a complicated illness sustained by her eleven-year-old daughter, was impatient. In bed that night she said to her husband, 'I hope Violet won't monopolise the drawing-room every night as she did tonight.'

'I thought Biggs liked her,' Harry replied. 'There certainly are occasions when I can see why your mother managed to fascinate so many people, and tonight was one of them.'

Pamela sighed irritably.

'You wanted her here,' said her husband. 'I hope you aren't going to start regretting it.'

'So do I,' she said.

Harry, tired, but trying not to yield to sleep, said, 'Pamela. I always thought – and I told you so – that your basic attitude to your mother, understandable as it is, made it inadvisable for us to take her in. She was never a particularly good mother to you. On occasions she was positively bad. She spent the early years of your life on her much-publicised nursing activities in France. Then she became a bright young thing and left your aunt and grandmother to bring you up. Neither of us will ever wholly forget that terrible divorce with which we began our married life, long ago as it was. All that's still with you.'

'That's ridiculous, Harry. You're going back years.'

He struggled with a yawn. 'I heard a great deal about formative influences when you were bringing up Jack and Anna. Now you're trying to tell me you had none, or if you had, your mother wasn't one of them.'

'We always had Allie,' said Pamela, 'and Father, of course. We weren't deprived in any way.'

'I told you before, I tell you now,' said Harry, his eyes closing, 'that in my opinion this whole business is an attempt to rub out some kind of bad memory.' He dozed briefly, then rallied and told her, 'If it doesn't work out we'll just have to ask Violet to make other arrangements.'

Pamela, remembering her husband had a board meeting at ten the next morning, let him fall asleep. Violet had been lost in that big house in Cheyne Walk, the upkeep was draining her resources, and the death of the housekeeper had been the last straw. It seemed right that her mother should come and live at Cavendish Square. People who fulfilled their family obligations naturally had elderly parents to live with them. There was, she told herself, no reason why Violet should not settle in as a normal member of the family.

The next afternoon she found Sylvia and the daily turning

out a large room on the second floor, to make room, they said, for Dora Davis, Violet's maid. She was coming up from Hove with some of her own furniture in a van that evening. Mrs Levine had given the orders.

As she watched the women pulled the mattress from the bed in the room and through the door on to the landing, she demanded, 'What are you doing?'

'Mrs Levine's maid brings her own bed,' said the Filipino woman. 'This one goes in the box-room.'

Pamela went in search of her mother. Who was not in. She went upstairs and asked where Mrs Levine was.

'She . . . ' said Sylvia.

'She's gone to Oxford,' supplied the daily, 'to talk about inflation.'

'Yes, inflation,' agreed Sylvia. 'She said she would be here for dinner.'

Pamela went downstairs, bursting with anger. How dare her mother bring a servant into the house without even consulting her? It would have to stop.

Upstairs Sylvia pulled a funny face at the daily who winked back. 'She doesn't like it,' said Sylvia. 'Inflation.' They both grinned. The daily said, 'I wouldn't be in her shoes, with a mother like that. Vi Levine – phew! I'm glad she wasn't my mum.'

'She's really a famous woman then?' asked Sylvia.

'Quite well known,' said the daily woman. 'Oh, yes, she's got quite a reputation, Mrs Levine.'

Pamela, gazing from a ground-floor window was breathing faster. She must exercise her authority over her own household firmly, now. If her mother didn't like it, she would have to leave, unseemly as a row, and Violet's moving into some small house elsewhere, might appear. Pamela had always tried to ensure the kind of unpleasantness which happened in other people's families did not occur in hers, but, after all, Violet was known to be a difficult woman. When her daughter Anna rang from Switzerland, asking how Violet's installation had gone, Pamela exploded.

'How unbearable of her, Mother,' sympathised Anna. 'If I were you, I'd just tell this woman, Dora Davis, to go away the moment she arrives. There'll be a row, but seriously, once she's in the house with all her furniture, you've as good as lost the battle.'

'It'll be awful, Anna.'

'It's the only way. You've got to show you mean business. I'm only sorry I'm not there to help.'

'Your Uncle Robert's in London and coming this evening, just to make matters worse,' her mother told her.

'I'm sure he'll be on your side.'

'Wherever she goes, trouble follows,' Pamela told her daughter.

'She is nearly eighty now,' pointed out Anna. 'She can't cause as much damage as she used to. Now do assure me that you won't let this woman, Dora Davis, set foot in the house. As soon as she arrives, tell her to go. You just must be firm.'

'I suppose so,' her mother said.

'Don't be weak,' Anna advised.

The afternoon wore on, and still Dora Davis did not arrive, nor did Violet. It was seven when Robert Levine arrived at Cavendish Square to find a small furniture van in the little road leading to the mews, and, outside it, his sister arguing with a middle-aged woman in a flowered suit and sensible black shoes.

'I'm very sorry, Miss Davis,' Pamela was saying. 'As I say, there's been a misunderstanding. My mother is not a young woman. But I'm afraid there's no question of your staying here.'

'Can I wait to see Mrs Levine?' asked the woman.

'I don't know when she'll be back.'

The woman sighed in annoyance. 'This isn't good enough.' She was about to say something else, but changed her mind. 'I'll go to my sister's in Fulham, and wait for Mrs Levine to get in touch.'

'You'll be wasting your time.'

Robert touched Pamela on the shoulder.

'Robert!' she exclaimed.

'If you've finished, shall we go inside?' he suggested.

They left Dora Davis quivering beside the van.

'Mother,' Pamela explained, going up the steps. 'She sent

for her old maid, without telling me. I'm sending her and her furniture back to where they came from.'

'Where's Mother then?'

'She disappeared this morning, to go and give an address on inflation, so I was told by Sylvia,' Pamela informed him.

Robert paused. 'Harry's going to get tired of household quarrels.'

'Do you think I'm not aware of that?' Pamela asked, leading him into the drawing-room. 'But I don't intend to keep the peace if it means Mother taking over the house.'

'She's always been wilful,' Robert said.

'Wilful?' his sister exclaimed. 'Downright rottenly selfish, I'd call it.'

Robert sat down and asked, 'I wonder if there's any chance of a small whisky?'

'Sorry,' said Pamela. 'I'm distracted. Honestly, I'm so angry.' She poured him a glass of whisky and gave it to him. 'Perhaps Harry's right. It isn't going to work.'

Robert said evenly, 'I'd be very pleased if you could make it work, Pamela.'

'Easier said than done.'

'Fairly necessary. I may drag Harry off for a quiet word after dinner. Could you distract Mother's attention, if she's here – make sure she doesn't join us?'

Pamela looked puzzled, but agreed. 'Is it about her?' she asked.

'To some extent,' he told her.

Violet came in, in her jacket and hat. 'Sylvia tells me Dora Davis came and went,' she said. 'May I ask if you had anything to do with it?'

'Pamela sent her back,' Robert said.

'Sent her back?' exclaimed Violet. 'What on earth for? Did you imagine I was going to ask you to pay her wages?' she asked Pamela.

As Pamela started to speak, her mother began to breathe very hard, and then gasp a little and began saying, 'I see now you plan to crush me. Well you won't.'

Pamela sat down as Violet, a small figure in her blue hat, face crumpled now, like a small monkey's, began to shout,

'This is what it comes to – now I'm here you want to make me miserable. What you've always wanted.'

Pamela said, 'For God's sake, Mother. Robert, do something. I can't stand this.'

Violet picked up a vase and smashed it, shouting, 'Where did Doris go?'

'Stop it, Mother!' Robert demanded.

'I'll tell you this. You can't get me – I know too much. I know enough to ruin you.' Violet moved quickly to the door, flung it open and ran into the hall, arms raised, shouting, 'I can ruin them. All of them. They don't stand a chance, the bastards.' She was moving like a woman forty years younger.

Robert caught her before she got to the front door and wrestled her back into the room. Violet went on shouting, 'I'll see you off, you bastards.'

'For God's sake, Pamela. Where's that woman – the servant you sent away – she'll know what to do,' Robert called to his sister, who was sitting still in her chair.

Pamela was blocking her ears. Her tone was low. 'I've never been able to do anything with her when she has these fits.'

Robert pushed Violet into a chair and held her there. 'Mother!' he said. 'Be quiet! Just be quiet!'

'Ha!' Violet said vindictively. 'Me to be quiet – that's what you'd like. Not what you'll get, though.' She began to scream at the top of her voice: 'I'll tell everybody what I know. Harry Christian-Smith sleeps with his research assistant, yes, he does. Respectable MP and company director and,' Violet sang, 'she wants to have his baby, oh yes, she wants to have his baby.'

'The woman,' shouted Robert at Pamela. 'Where is she?'

'She didn't say,' Pamela told him flatly.

Violet's voice went on. 'As for Pamela. She's a bastard.'

'Get the doctor,' called Robert. 'Pamela! Get the doctor! Oh, Christ,' he groaned, as Pamela did not move. He released Violet and ran to the phone. He began to dial. 'For God's sake pull yourself together,' he shouted at his sister.

Violet had seized the blue clock from the mantelpiece near Pamela's chair and raised it above her head. Robert, now speaking to the doctor, watched in horror as Pamela, suddenly moved by the sight, jumped up and grasped it. 'You can't crush me,' Violet sneered at her. In a sing-song tone, like a child in a playground she chanted, 'I know everything – you're going to get it.' She still had her hands on the clock.

'Put down the clock, Mother,' cried Pamela, her voice cracking.

'Please come immediately,' Robert said to the doctor and, putting down the phone, moved rapidly across the room to where the two women were struggling. He grasped his mother round the body and hissed at her, 'The doctor's coming. I'm taking you upstairs.'

Violet flailed, crying out, 'Let me go. Just you let me go. You're trying to kill me . . . '

Pamela, who had captured the clock, turned to the fireplace and put it back on the mantelpiece, tears streaming down her face. When Sylvia, coming in to see what the noise was, appeared in the doorway she saw Robert holding Violet's tiny, writhing body, while she yelled and screamed. 'You can't do anything to me. I can ruin you – and I will.'

Spotting her standing openmouthed, Robert shouted, 'Get out, you stupid woman. Go and stand outside and wait for the doctor.'

Sylvia turned and went. 'And shut the door!' bawled Robert.

Pamela turned round and went to her mother, still sobbing. She looked into her face. 'What did you mean, Mother? I'm a bastard? Tell me what you mean.'

Violet stopped struggling though Robert kept his grip on her. Her face contorted, she said viciously, 'Wouldn't you like to know, eh? I expect you would.' She tried to pull away from Robert. 'Wouldn't you like to know,' she repeated.

Robert wrestled her across the room, saying in a loud voice, 'Shut up – shut up – shut up.' He pushed her down on the sofa against the wall, and held her wrists.

Coming in, the doctor saw him bent over the sofa, holding Violet down as she screamed, 'Let me go, Frederick – let me go . . . ' Pamela was standing motionless in the middle of the room, staring, horrified, at both of them.

While Violet was in her room with the doctor, Harry arrived. Robert told him what had happened, while Pamela went upstairs to bathe her face. 'Violet's always done this from time to time,' Robert told him. 'But I'd never have believed she was still so strong.' He was drinking neat whisky. His face was very drawn.

'Hysteria,' suggested Harry.

'A doctor said once that during these attacks she was capable of rallying every ounce of her strength. It's as if she were possessed, almost devilish.' Robert was reliving the scene as he spoke. He turned to Harry. 'I hope you never have to witness it. The old cook, Felix, used to have a bottle of medicine he made her take when it happened. Veronal, I think it was. Or perhaps laudanum. Some sort of knock-out drops. She'd wake up perfectly normal. She'll be starting a nice sleep now.'

'Oh my God,' said Harry Christian-Smith, staring out of the drawing-room window at the evening traffic going round the square, 'if I'd known about this I don't think I'd have let Pamela invite her.'

'She'd probably forgotten. I certainly had, until it started. Then I remembered the scenes all right, Father trying to hold her and shouting for Felix, Violet swearing and breaking things, yelling abuse – she'd no idea what she was doing or saying. I don't know how he put up with it. It was madness, no doubt about it. Still is. But there was no way of treating it. She'd go on for years, perfectly rational, then there'd be one of these outbreaks. Then she'd go back to normal again. No one ever knew what triggered it, except that it was usually when she was dissatisfied.'

'Temper,' said Harry. 'But quite frankly, Robert, it isn't just this. There's already constant trouble, little things leading to rows and friction. We really can't live like this, if Pamela's always going to be upset and Violet keeps going off her head. This has been a quiet household up to now.'

Robert refilled his glass. As he did so, he said, 'I expect it'll settle down.' Harry looked as if he were about to dispute this. 'It might be best to tell you, while Violet was having this attack she shouted something about you. She seemed to be claiming you were having an affair with someone who worked for you.'

There was a pause. 'Malicious rubbish,' said Christian-Smith emphatically.

'I felt you ought to know, in case Pamela mentioned it.'

'Thank you very much.' Harry shook his head. 'It's appalling to think they seem to be unable to treat this. I hope she didn't say anything else to upset Pamela.'

He's guilty all right, thought Robert, as he replied, 'I'm afraid so. She said the woman you were supposed to be having this affair with wanted to have your child.'

'Hm,' said Harry. 'More rubbish.'

He was so transparently embarrassed that Robert, to spare him, added, 'Just to make up the weight she suggested Pamela wasn't her father's child.'

'Oh my God! That's appalling. Just the sort of thing to upset Pamela most. She's a family woman. Her mother, of course, is a monster. What makes a woman like that tick?' He hesitated. 'I'm sorry, Robert, she's your mother as well. I mean, the most extraordinary things happen in families, we both know that, but really . . . ' He blew out his breath. 'I hate the idea of her upsetting Pamela like that.'

Much of this indignation, Robert suspected, was caused by Violet's revelations about Harry's affair, but he seized this moment to say smoothly, 'I came here originally to talk to you about something. This fit of Violet's has been a bit of a distraction. On the other hand it does rather illustrate what I came— '

He broke off as Pamela appeared in the doorway. She had changed for dinner, and was freshly made up. Harry asked her, 'Have Robert and I a few minutes to talk before dinner?' Pamela, disconcerted, nodded.

'Not long, Pam,' said Robert, leading the way to the old library, now Harry's study.

Pamela looked after them, still shocked and not really wanting to be left alone. Nevertheless, she sat down patiently.

Half an hour later, after she'd twice held up dinner, her brother and husband came into the drawing-room. Both looked grave. Robert had urged Harry to keep Violet at Cavendish Square at all costs. 'I don't like to ask it,' he'd said. 'I realise it could be hard for you, but I'm afraid of these memoirs she's allegedly writing. She's addicted to being in the limelight and, on the whole, she's not any longer. She might do anything to attract attention. There are certain things she might say about events which took place in the past which could be quite embarrassing – for you as well, Harry. I'd like you to watch her.'

Harry looked cautiously at his brother-in-law. 'What sort of thing are we talking about?'

'Well, I saw some material that her old cook Felix was trying to sell to the papers twenty years ago. Scurrilous stuff written for revenge, I suppose. Some of it was very nasty – and some of it might have been true. Violet's activities in the thirties were pretty dubious. Even in the war years – trouble. To give you an example – and this is by no means the worst – there was a point where my grandmother misguidedly persuaded Violet to smuggle some relatives out of Occupied France when she was on special ops there. Understandable, but very unfortunate. They were caught, they died, must have – Violet got away. I gather that's what put paid to her career as a war heroine. She made no mention of that in her idiotic book about herself. Suppose she did now – unpleasant. And that's not all. Far from it. As I say, she's not going to take kindly to increasing age and obscurity. Look, Harry, just suppose Pamela really isn't Father's child – she was born before they married, as we know – do we really want that coming out? I can't tell you what some of that cook's stuff was like.' He paused. Harry waited. 'I'm telling you,' Robert said, 'if my mother's new memoirs come up with half – even a quarter – of the truth, it'd be a bad day for all of us. There are things I can't even tell you. But take my word for it, she's got to be stopped. Someone's got to keep an eye on her to make sure she's not doing it. It could be very damaging. To us and others.'

Harry stared at his brother-in-law. The unspoken message from Robert was that Violet's memoirs might involve a great deal more than scandal for her family. After a pause he said, 'I see. I'll do what I can.' Robert nodded.

As Pamela sat in front of her dressing-table that night she said to her husband, 'I suppose if Violet's staying, after this episode, I really have to change my mind and accept Dora Davis. Presumably she knows what to do about these tantrums. The woman'll have to take care of her when she's like that.'

'It looks like the best solution, for the time being,' agreed Harry.

'I suppose in the end it'll come to a nursing home,' continued Pamela.

'Eventually,' agreed her husband.

Pamela would have welcomed, now, his previous robust attitude, that her mother was not welcome in his house, that he was prepared to get her to move if she made life too difficult. Instead, even after the account of the scene which had taken place earlier, he wasn't even mentioning the possibility of Violet's leaving. He only said, 'I've had a word with Robert, as you know. We're both a bit worried about some of the things Violet might take it into her head to write if she had a mind to. The kind of thing which might not reflect too well on her, or any of us. Keep an eye on her, if you can. He's particularly worried about this proposed second volume of memoirs.'

'She'll never finish it,' declared Pamela.

'Probably not. But you're here most of the time, so try to keep tabs on her progress, there's a good girl. Well, time to hit the hay. It's been a long tiring day.'

He kissed her on the cheek as she sat there, then got into bed, rolled on to his side and was fairly soon asleep.

Pamela looked at herself in the glass. No one had mentioned the awful things Violet had yelled out in her frenzy. It would be too uncomfortable for all of them. But somehow her mother had found out about Harry and his research assistant. And Pamela saw no reason to disbelieve her when she'd added that the woman wanted Harry's child. So did that mean that she, Pamela, was also not her father's daughter? None of these things would ever be discussed, she knew. She also knew that she would not be able to forget them. The only person, now, who could tell her the truth was Violet, and to torment her and keep power over her, she wouldn't, even if Pamela asked. She turned to look at her husband's resting figure. She envied him his ability to sleep. She wouldn't.

Kate Higgins, June 20th, 1991

It was stuffy in the flat. I felt hot, tired and somehow unreal. Di, small, fair and shrunken, sat in her chair, legs apart. She didn't look much like the bomber I'd just accused her of being. She looked as if you could blow her over. So did Violet Levine, for that matter, I thought, and it hadn't been true of her, either. Still, Di looked worn out. One part of me was wondering what had led her into terrorism; by now I was fairly sure she was involved somewhere on the spectrum between political activism and political violence.

Di came from a nice enough home in a nice part of the country. Her parents, James Carter, bluff country solicitor, and Helen Carter, well-brought-up but slightly benumbed wife, were both phonies, I thought, but parents like that didn't create terrorists – or I supposed they didn't. Di's brother, the horrible Sebastian, was a local property speculator, who had the borough surveyor in his pocket. Sebastian built expensive so-called town houses in beauty spots all over the county; the surveyor drove a Lamborghini. Di's sister was living with a religious group in California. Just a typical late twentieth-century middle-class family, in short. It wasn't as if she'd grown up in religious conflict and semi-civil war, like the women in Ireland. Agreed, she hated the government, but so did many. She also had a lot of physical courage. But still, I couldn't believe it. Not really. If it was true, it was sad. I didn't let her see I felt that. I just showed her how angry I was.

'If you had anything to do with this TV centre stuff,' I told her, 'just consider that you've not only left an innocent man dead – that security guard, just an ordinary working man, wife and three grown-up children – but I was there half an hour before, talking to the documentary-maker. He barely got away in time. You nearly got me, too. You'll have to tell me the truth. I know you don't want to – you're afraid I'll turn you in, or I'll just blab it around and someone else will. But you've got to tell me. I'm in trouble too because of you and what you're up to. You didn't have any right to go on with what you were doing without warning me.'

She was cast down. 'I should have asked you to go. I tried at one time to get you to leave.'

'I know, but you didn't, did you? I feel betrayed, frankly.' A fly was buzzing round the room. And I'd just lost my job – I didn't know what to do.

'Put it like this – something was happening, and it's over,' she said.

'Oh well,' I said derisively, 'now you've told me that I feel much better. I won't ask any more questions. I'll be able to tell the cops when they come for me, "Don't worry, my friend says it's over." Come off it, Di,' I said angrily. 'Tell me the truth. I think you and Rog are in the Active Democrats. You're responsible for some of these bombings. You probably did the TV centre. Perhaps you thought the building was empty. It wasn't. You didn't want to hurt anybody – but you did.'

She opened her mouth to speak. I wouldn't let her.

'You stupid cow – can't you see we could get shot the next time we walk out of this building, suspected of being armed terrorists? Who'd ask any questions? Loudly enough?' The doorbell rang and Di jumped. I put my head in my hands. 'Is there anything incriminating still here?' I asked.

She didn't answer. I knew there must be some evidence still in that room beside the front door. A screw, someone's hair or fingerprints which would match with some they had on record. Traces of explosives? The doorbell rang again. Di said, 'I might as well open it.'

I sat there frozen. She came back with an envelope in her hand. I opened it. It was the cheque for five thousand pounds, two-thirds of the money I would have received for the delivery and publication of my book on Violet Levine. An enclosed letter from Roger Littlebrown stated that this was the sum agreed on termination of our contract for the book. He must have sent it before he left the office that night. He hadn't wasted much time. Probably one of the conditions was that he couldn't sign up with the Levines until I was out of the way.

I looked at the cheque and thought, no more Violet, possibly. At the same time I knew what to do. I told Di, 'We've got to clean up and redecorate that room, get the carpet on a skip miles away. We've got to get rid of every trace as fast as possible. It'll look better if we chuck out all the carpets.'

'You're getting in deeper here,' said Di.

'I don't want to go to prison, or worse. Anyway Roger's sacked me. I'll have plenty of time for emulsioning the walls and picking out tasteful shades of carpet, generally getting rid of the smell of explosives and terrorists' armpits. It's funny how quick you can be when you're afraid for your skin.'

Di looked guilty. I knew the thought of that dead, perfectly innocent security guard kept on hitting her.

'Ring up that friend of yours who knows those brothers who do carpet-laying in the evenings,' I suggested. She went out wordlessly, but before she got to the phone, it rang. It was Henri Clos. We arranged to meet next morning. I told Di I'd buy the carpet on the way to see him.

We were on our hands and knees measuring the floors in silence when the phone went again. It was Dave. He was ringing from *The Mag*, sounding rather numb. I said I'd see him next day and we went on measuring. We didn't speak, apart from saying, 'Is the tape straight?' and checking each other's figures. Di, I suppose, felt terrible. It looked as if she'd been involved in killing a man. But I couldn't guess at the world she'd been living in for so long or what it did to you. It was a different reality. Had to be. And I hadn't noticed not only what had been going on, but how she'd changed. I'd been an idiot, but for the time being I didn't care. If we could get every betraying fingerprint, hair, screw and scrap of paper out of 11D Henry Thackery House there'd be nothing for the police to find, if they came. I hadn't asked if she thought the police or Special Branch were close to the group. Our phone was tapped but nothing else had happened. We probably had a chance.

We finished the measuring and I put the piece of paper with the floor measurements in my bag. 'All right. I'll get the carpet tomorrow while I'm seeing Dave and another man.' She looked wary. I told her, 'Don't worry. I won't tell Dave anything.'

'What did you mean when you said Roger'd sacked you?' she asked.

I told her, briefly. 'He shopped me, really. He got a better offer.'

Miraculously, I slept like a stone. Di, too, I suppose. There wasn't a sound in the flat all night and she was still asleep when I got up. A lovely sunny day. I began to enjoy it as I walked to the underground station. Standing up in the crowded train on the way to *The Mag*'s office I wondered if, once we'd cleaned up the evidence at Henry Thackery House, Di would still be going out in the middle of the night to destabilise society. Because, if she got caught, even if I'd left the flat, I'd still be retrospectively implicated. I hoped for her sake as well as mine she'd given it all up. There were questions I'd have to ask her. Should have asked already.

In Dave's office, there were four desks in a space about twelve feet by twelve. The small sound of telephones and patter of word processors went on all the time. Dave, in jeans and an unironed white shirt said, 'Sit down. Don't kick my plaster.'

I looked under the desk and saw that the leg of his jeans was ripped open to accommodate his plaster cast. He looked a wreck, probably working too hard after the accident. 'Dave, I know you're busy. Can I just tell you what's happened over Violet? I feel an idiot. You've got enough on your plate . . . '

'Come on, my policy is to listen,' he said. 'If I don't, I never find anything out.' Then he mouthed something at me. I shook my head. He scribbled something on a piece of paper, with his arm hooked round the page, like a child trying to stop the child in the next desk from copying. Did he think people on the next floor were spying on him through holes in the ceiling? Or were they? After what had happened at 11D Henry Thackery House I could believe anything. He handed me the page. 'Don't mention Gordon S,' it read. I shrugged, meaning, 'All right, but I don't understand.'

Then I launched into my story about the threatening phone call and later news of the authorised biography. When it came to relating the tale of Deep Throat's tip-off and the trip to St Catherine's House, where I'd found the birth certificate of a son born to Violet's sister and Gordon Stone, I remembered Dave's caution about anything to do with Stone, so I took a sheet of paper from the other side of the desk, Dave's side, and started to write it down in case the place was bugged.

He stopped me by saying quickly, 'Let's go to a film tonight?'

'All right,' I agreed, suddenly looking forward to the outing. Would Andy mind my date with Dave, I wondered? He might if he found out, I thought, so I'd make sure he didn't.

Before I'd seen Dave I hadn't been certain what I was going to do about Felix's memoirs. After all, if I bought them from Henri Clos and didn't use them, it was five thousand pounds down the drain. But, quickly selecting a carpet in a big store, the priority being speed rather than decorating a dream home, I decided I'd just tell the whole story to Henri Clos and buy Felix Lamier's memoirs anyway. Then perhaps I'd do the book. An odd book, about a woman of decision, by a woman of none. Still, I was angry with the Levines – I'd had the idea in the first place, gone to Roger with it, done the work. Now I'd been elbowed out. It wasn't fair.

So when I sat down with Henri Clos I told him everything, and concluded, 'There's a chance you could sell Felix Lamier's story to Simon Snow, who's doing the authorised biography. You might get more money there. But they might suppress the contents. In fact, it could put him in a very awkward position. He'll be constructing an act of piety, fed with suitable information by the Levines; reading Felix's story, from what I've seen of it, might make that impossible.'

'So you believe the Levine family has conspired against you to prevent you from finishing your book?'

'What would you think?' I asked him. 'Anyway, the point is, I'm ready to buy your papers, and see what I can make of it all. I can't promise there'll be a book – or anything.'

'I understand,' Henri Clos said. And it seemed to me that he did. He was silent, thinking. Suddenly he told me, 'I'll lend you Felix's memoirs, if you write the book.'

I was startled. 'That's generous. But the book may not be published.'

'Oh, I don't know. We have clients here who are publishers. Sometimes I talk to them. What a scandal when your version is so different from the official story – someone might be interested. And Mr Snow himself comes to this restaurant. He's an honest man. He may find himself unable to continue without asking difficult questions. I would think it by no means certain your Mr Littlebrown will get the book he wants. Shall we take the risk?' And he pulled the old battered pages from his desk drawer. 'So . . . ?' he asked.

I drew a deep breath and said, 'I'll do my best. If you lend me those pages I'll continue, as I would if I'd still got a publisher. I'll try to get a new one. And I'm very grateful to you . . . '

He stared at me and decided, I supposed, to tell me. 'I'm Felix Lamier's natural son,' he said.

I nodded.

'I was born while he was in France, before he went back to England in 1933 to give evidence in Mrs Levine's divorce case – she rescued him from the dump where he was living, unable to find a job. He says this in the memoirs. My mother worked in a restaurant. I think she became the boss's mistress; anyway, she was able to look after me. But she was shot by the Germans in 1941 and I was put in an orphanage run by nuns. You can imagine the life of a small boy, bereaved of his only real parent, in an orphanage during those years. But immediately after the war, as soon as it was possible to travel, Felix arrived to see me, unaware my mother was dead. He found me and took me first to his sister in Normandy, then, when I was old enough, he brought me to England and palmed me off on the household of Mrs Mackinnon. Remember that by then they were both mistress and servant and fellow-conspirators, an odd alliance, but it meant she trusted him, in her way, and he was allowed to do what he liked. He called me his nephew and he taught me his trade. Felix was a good man, in many ways. I loved him. Of course, my position was difficult when Mr Mackinnon defected. We were all suspected of being his accomplices, and I had no papers. The interrogation was tricky for me.

'You see,' said Henri, 'Felix was loyal to Mrs Mackinnon, as he had been to me, but she used him, as she used everybody. She was a rich woman. She could have done so much, but he ended his days in a damp cottage. I was working as a waiter. I had a wife, and a baby. We were living in one room. When he died, Felix left me his savings, about two hundred pounds, and, learning from his experience, that loyalty is not repaid, I borrowed more money and started a small café, in a street off Tottenham Court Road. I prospered. I only wish I had prospered in his lifetime.'

I imagined, though I didn't ask, that he had some kind of a share in this smart restaurant.

'So . . . ' he said, and handed me Felix's memoirs.

'Mr Clos,' I said, 'thank you very much, for your explanation and for your help. I'll do my best. I'll have this copied, and return it to you.'

He stood up. 'Good luck, Miss Higgins.'

'Thank you again, Mr Clos.'

And with the pages in my bag I hurried off. I had two copies of Felix's manuscript made, got to the Post Office at the last moment and registered one copy to Henri Clos and one to myself at Henry Thackery House. In case I lost the original. My experience on the bus, when my bag had been snatched, had made me cautious.

Then I sat in the park in the sunshine and read Felix's story right through. Though there were questions to which he did not know the answers, the information he did produce was staggering. But as I finished reading I realised calmly that I had the key to Violet Levine. It answered half the questions I'd been asking myself all this time. It gave clues to the answering of the rest. Perhaps, above all, it gave me the first view of Violet's whole personality I'd had so far. Not a pretty sight, Violet's personality, but after so many lies, including her own distortions in *I Affirm*, the truth was refreshing.

Then I hurried off to meet Dave. I went to the bar we were meeting in and was grinning over my lager when he hobbled in on his crutches, looking more like an unmade bed than ever. I got him a drink. 'It's on me. So's the film. I've just been given this.' And I produced Felix Lamier's memoirs, explaining how I'd come by them.

He had a quick look and said, 'Phew – is all this true?'

'Fairly true,' I said. 'If I described my day to you it wouldn't be completely true. Like this.' If I described my day to you, I thought, you're one of the few people who'd believe it. You and the Metropolitan Police.

'You're cracking this case, Inspector Higgins,' he said. 'But, be careful.'

'There's more,' I said and told him about the birth certificate.

Dave whistled. 'Gordon Stone's involved with nasty people,' he said. 'Neo-Nazis. Some are high-ups who see Communism, even Socialist régimes as a threat. The people who're backing the rebels in Belize, for example – with many currencies, not just dollars. Pounds, for example. Stone looks like a silly little man but some of his supporters are true internationalists – their ideal world involves a few friends running countries with minimal involvement from the rest of the population. Those are Stone's big supporters. Down at the bottom are the yobs, beating up Asians. He publishes a little magazine from his house in Rye, with news items about black crime and white supremacy and articles about how there weren't any concentration camps. Nice pictures of tough young men, all in black uniforms, drilling on the estates of various sympathisers. There's a regular Nazi get-together every year for Hitler's birthday in Paris or Holland, usually. Stone always goes. He's a bad man. If you're really going to see him, would you like me to come too? As a witness. Just in case.'

'Thanks, Dave,' I said. I wasn't sure how seriously to take all this. I told him, 'I think I know who my anonymous caller is. I spoke to Jack Christian-Smith, Violet's grandson, and he said he thought he knew but he didn't want to tell me yet, if at all. Felix's account makes it look as if it can only be one or two people.'

'Who is it, then?' he asked.

'My money's on Alice Crutchley. According to her great-niece Violet took her in during the First World War. She lived with the Levines for years. But significantly, I think, Violet doesn't mention her. There's no record of her death at St Catherine's House. She'd be very old, but after all Violet's not been dead long. She was ninety-three. It was a long-lived family. Felix says she married and went to Connecticut. Allie could be alive, and in the USA. One thing's certain – all the mysterious calls come in the afternoons or evenings. Never the mornings. Perhaps because of the time difference. And she's told me she promised someone to keep quiet. So who would this mysterious caller promise to be silent for, presumably out of loyalty? It could be her former in-laws, the Levines. She was very close to them, closer than Violet ever revealed. Where this baby comes in I don't know.'

Dave said, 'Kate, keep me informed about all this as you go on. I'm not trying to butt in but it's like mountain walking. You have to tell someone where you're going.'

'In case you fall down a cliff.'

He nodded. 'That's right.'

We went off for a snack, then walked through Leicester Square, swarming as usual with pickpockets, and rough trade, beggars, prostitutes and plain-clothes men. We saw a film about the French revolution, all in soft focus and very nostalgic. Even the guillotine looked like a charming antique, beautifully carved. I held Dave's hand. I got a taxi outside so he didn't have to go down the underground with his bad leg, which might have made him a prey to thieves. People in side-streets were already settling down in doorways. Someone was lying on the pavement, spreadeagled, looking dead, but I didn't dare get out of the cab to check. The driver, who had a gun in his pocket, wouldn't have stopped anyway. The streets were infernal in that particular neighbourhood. Dave and I went on holding hands. I wondered what was going on, then I fell asleep.

The next thing I knew, Dave was getting out. 'Do you want to come in and stay?' he asked, but I said I'd go home. 'Keep in touch,' he said. He looked strained.

'Are you okay?' I asked. 'Can I do anything?'

'Lizzie's left me,' he said. 'She couldn't take it any more. I don't blame her.'

I thought tenderly of Dave for the rest of the journey but the moment I got back to the flat I lost my temper. There were Di and Rog merrily painting walls together. Rog, Di's fellow terrorist, was someone I didn't want to see much of ever again, especially in company with Di, especially removing the traces at 11D Henry Thackery House. No doubt there was something between them. No doubt they loved to be together, popping out for a quiet drink, or painting a flat, or when creeping through the streets with a bomb in a plastic bag. But I thought if we were being watched it was a mistake to stick together. I pointed this out. They told me more or less to mind my own business and I went nervously to bed with Felix's manuscript in the bag on the floor beside me.

I felt no better in the morning. The events of the last few days since I'd got back from Brighton had caught up with me, but I'd have to get the decorating done, clean the flat of any traces, or there'd be no peace of mind. When I got up I found Di and Rog cooking breakfast and kissing each other in the kitchen. I felt like an intruder. I had to ask, 'I've got a question. Have you and the rest of the guys ceased your activities? And, second part of the question, for ten points, if so, is this temporary or permanent?'

There was a silence. Guarded looks were exchanged.

In the end Di replied angrily, 'All right. All right. Put it like this. Active Democracy has disbanded. Possibly for ever. There've been some arguments. We're pretty sure one of us is being watched. The phone's tapped here. It's getting too risky so, as far as you're concerned, it's over. I'm going round this afternoon to make my peace with the print shop. They slung me out for being unreliable. But I think they got suspicious. Same applies to Rog. He's looking for a job from now on.' She looked at him. He nodded. 'That's it.'

No wonder they were united. They were in love. They'd faced danger together. Now they'd had to decide to pack it in, go back, I supposed, to local politics, agendas, meetings, resolutions, and in some ways they felt bad about it, as if they'd lost something. They also knew they'd killed an innocent man in the last explosion.

I said, 'Right. That's all I wanted to know.' I made myself a cup of instant coffee, feeling like the wet liberal who knew nothing of the dedicated, dangerous life of the activist. You could see how it could take you over – the fear, the adrenalin, the feeling you were striking for the right, countering tyranny, the sheer practicalities of doing it and not getting caught.

Perhaps I should have gone to the nearest police station to turn Di and Rog in. All I can say is I was afraid of what would happen to them and possibly me. I was afraid of a forty-eight hour questioning, and all it might involve. I didn't want my family dragged in.

We spent the morning pulling up the carpets and putting them in Roger's van. We decided the safest thing to do was put them on the council dump. Driving them out of London and putting them in a hole in the woods, or over a cliff might arouse more suspicion, bearing in mind that in the country there's always someone watching. The dump, on the other hand, was constantly raided, and within twenty-four hours our rugs and carpets would almost certainly be carried off and laid on floors elsewhere.

While Rog was off dumping the rugs, Di and I had a quick cup of tea, before starting to paint again. Then, as I approached the ladder in the hall, the phone rang. It was Jack Christian-Smith. I told him my story of how Askew and Askew had pushed me out so that they'd get full co-operation from his family for Violet's authorised biography. I still wasn't sure he wasn't a spy within my camp, but he seemed genuinely shocked.

'I haven't heard anything about all this,' he said. 'It's disgraceful. If they wanted to do it, they could at least have got hold of another publisher. That would have put you at a disadvantage. This is a deliberate attempt to silence you. Are you going to let it happen?'

I didn't know what to tell him. All I said was, 'There's something you might be able to help about – is your great-aunt alive? And if so, can you give me her address and phone number?'

'Oh – you worked it out. At least, I assume you have . . . '

'The mystery caller is Alice, Violet's sister,' I stated.

'I think so,' he told me. 'I wanted to find out if there was any good reason why she'd be asked not to speak before I told you my guess. I asked my sister, Anna, but she went berserk when she heard I'd even spoken to you. There was a row – no proper answers. I say to hell with them. I don't see why you shouldn't talk to Alice, if she wants to talk to you. Truth's usually better.'

So he gave me Alice Crutchley's married name and an address in Connecticut. He said, 'I haven't got the phone number. We exchange Christmas cards with a little bit of news. Well, Jessica does it. Sends pictures of the children, and so forth. The last card Alice sent was perfectly sensible, in firm handwriting. It's remarkable, though. She must be over ninety.'

'So will you be, if you've got the Crutchley genes,' I told him.

'God forbid,' he said. 'Let me know how you get on; give her my love.'

'I will.' I went on to tell him about Felix's memoirs, and something of the contents.

'I'll be damned,' he said. 'You'll let me see them, won't you? How would it be if I talked to a publisher I know?'

'Please,' I said. 'I'd be glad.'

'That near-miss at the TV centre makes me all the keener to get this story told,' he said, 'while I've got time to read it. Okay then – all the luck in the world,' he said cheerfully, then paused and said, 'I wonder if Violet's own second lot of memoirs will ever turn up.'

'What?'

'After *I Affirm*, many years later, she said she'd embarked on a second lot of memoirs. *I Committed Perjury*, they sound like . . . '

'Tell me,' I said.

Jack Christian-Smith told me.

FIFTEEN

The Levines, 1990

The organ of the handsome eighteenth-century church in Trafalgar Square swelled out 'Oh God Our Help In Ages Past' as the men and women attending the memorial service of Violet Levine Mackinnon walked down the aisle to take their seats. It had been Anna Schreft who had suggested this compromise name for the woman known, during most of her adult life, as Violet Levine. Her daughter Pamela had opposed the idea, describing it as vulgar and American. 'She had no right to the name Levine after her remarriage,' said Pamela. 'It was simply that there was no way of preventing her using it.'

Robert, appealed to by telephone, had said wearily from New York, 'Look, we don't want to hold this ceremony. I certainly resent having to come back to England just to attend it. But since the family's stuck with arranging it, then Violet might as well use the family name, as she did in life, entitled or not. For God's sake, Pamela, women these days call themselves anything they please.'

At the church door Robert Levine stood shaking hands with the guests as they came in while, opposite him, Jack Christian-Smith also welcomed those invited and helped people to their seats.

As the hymn went on Jack looked down the crowded church and estimated there were about a hundred and fifty people in the black pews. He glanced uneasily at his uncle, took the arm of a very old lady, accompanied by a woman, her daughter perhaps, who seemed scarcely any younger than she was, helped her to a seat. Robert's face, when Jack returned to the door, was still as stiff as a poker. He wasn't putting a very good face on the situation, thought Jack. The truth was that Violet's will, when opened, had been inordinately long and complicated. Pamela had tried to suggest that her mother had been on the verge of senility when she'd composed it, but the document, though irritating to the family, made perfect sense. In it Violet had suggested her own memorial service (with an appended list of guests), to be held at St Clement Dane's or St Martin-in-the-Fields, both churches connected with the arts and politics. Pamela, scanning the list, had thrown up her eyes. 'They won't come,' she'd declared. Jack, having been at the door of the church, knew now that many of them had.

Violet had also left the bulk of her money, which totalled seventy thousand pounds, to her daughter Joanna. Robert, relaying this information to members of the family assembled at Cavendish Square, showed his anger. 'Joanna's sixty-nine,' he'd said. 'She's childless and she's been in a nursing home for nearly forty years. It's highly doubtful if she's competent to make a will herself. Why Joanna?'

'It's very wounding to Mother, who took care of Grandmother for so long,' Anna Schreft declared.

'Oh, I don't mind,' Pamela had said.

'Well, you should,' Anna told her forcefully. 'That's true, isn't it, Joe?'

Joe Schreft, her husband and second cousin, a stocky man with a thick black moustache, said, 'It isn't very pleasant.'

'The whole thing's a challenge,' Robert had observed from the chair where he sat scanning the seven-page document, typed and correctly witnessed by a solicitor and Violet's old maid, Dora Davis. He wished his sister had taken the will herself from Violet's desk, and read it before his arrival from the States. Instead, he'd been forced into a family reading and, since the will was Violet's, there was almost bound to be trouble. Pamela hadn't dared face it on her own, he imagined. Her husband was in Jamaica, and showing no signs of rushing back to help. He, too, gave up. 'I can't face reading it all out. Would everyone like to look for themselves? Pamela?'

Pamela said, 'I'll leave it to Harry, when he comes back.'

Anna walked across the room and took it. She sat down and began to read. Jack crossed the room and turned the light on. 'Gets dark, these afternoons.'

'The days'll lengthen from now on,' Joe Schreft said, watching his wife. He didn't much like his brother-in-law, especially since a recent unfavourable television investigation, directed by Jack, into some Bolivian mines in which Joe was a major shareholder. But both men recognised in each other a deep dislike for the Byzantine family relationships and fierce, long-lasting passions of the Levines. He added, 'I suppose it was only to be expected that Violet would produce some lengthy and trouble-making document.'

'I'm afraid she'll have wanted to create as many problems after her death as she did during her life,' Pamela remarked bitterly. 'I wish she hadn't died while Harry was away. It was all such a shock.'

There was a silence. It was generally known that Harry Christian-Smith, chairman of a quango connected in some way with urban renewal, had organised yet another fact-finding visit to the West Indies, gone there with his mistress of many years and did not plan to return until the funeral. No one in the room wished to make any comment, just as no one wished to go into the details of Violet's death. An old woman should die peacefully in bed, it was thought, and not by falling, goodness knew how, out of her bedroom window, only to be discovered on the pavement, neck broken and nightdress up to her thighs. There'd been an ambulance, a crowd on the pavement and two police cars. The situation had not been made any quieter or more dignified by a vigilant policeman who had spotted Violet's nurse, Damian, walking casually away from the house with a large airline bag over his shoulder and asked him to open it. The discovery of a small Dutch painting, a silver teapot, and some other items led to Damian's arrest. He was now on remand, awaiting trial. The knowledge of all this hung over the group in the drawing-room at Cavendish Square.

Robert reflected, 'She must have gone through a million and a half in her lifetime – and that's going back to the days when money was worth twenty times as much as it is now. She did herself well.'

'Oh, really,' Anna cried from her chair. 'I've never read such rubbish. We can't do it. And look what she's left me – seed pearls, I ask you. And you won't like this bit, Jack. She's left nearly all her jewellery to your ex-wife.'

'A real trouble-maker,' groaned Jack. 'World class.'

'She says, "because Gillian has suffered so much in her life",' Anna read.

'Who? Gilly?' exclaimed Jack. 'I wouldn't have said she'd suffered much.'

'She wants her memoirs published. What memoirs?' asked Anna, still reading.

'We haven't found any,' said Robert. 'You didn't, did you, Pamela?'

'No,' answered his sister.

'It was a delusion of hers, I think,' Robert told them.

'Just as well,' said Joe Schreft.

'If this will's anything to go by, the memoirs would have started the Third World War,' observed Jack.

'I'm afraid you'll have to speak to Gillian about the jewellery,' instructed Robert. 'I mean, it should really go to Anna – or your wife . . . '

'I don't know. Is there any chance of a drink? Then, if there's nothing else I can do I ought to get back to the office.'

In the end he and Joe Schreft walked down the steps together, leaving the others in the house still discussing the will and the funeral arrangements. They were struck by icy blasts.

'Dreadful woman,' said Jack with feeling. 'I had the idea she quite liked me. Now I've got to go to my ex-wife and ask her to sacrifice the family sparklers. It's not easy to part the nicest of women from good jewellery and it has to be said that my ex-wife isn't the nicest of women.'

'There'll be a little bombshell in that document for all of us,' Joe consoled him.

'I'm going into that pub,' said Jack. 'I can't face going back to work without a drink. Join me?'

'Oh, all right,' said Joe. 'The whisky Anna poured me was pretty small.'

Jack cheered up in the pub. 'Well,' he said, 'here's to Violet.'

'To Violet,' responded Joe, lifting his glass. 'A remarkable woman.'

Jack also managed to abandon the family party following Violet's funeral a week later, this time with his Uncle Robert. Together they left Cavendish Square where some twenty-five

Levines, Schrefts, Waldsteins and Lowensteins and Cotons had assembled after Violet's interment near the gloomy family vault, surrounded by tangled weeds and leafless brambles, at Kensal Green cemetery. The mausoleum, a hundred years old and topped with marble angels, had been unusable for years. Attempting a clear-up, the day before the funeral, Anna Schreft had evicted two tramps who had been living in it.

The two men headed for Robert's club where, sinking into a large leather chair Jack said, 'I suppose you've done this before, Robert. I must say I find it all a bit difficult.'

'I'd no idea so many would come,' Robert told him. 'I think there's still a tradition of making a big event of these ceremonies on the European side of the family. One lot had flown in from Budapest. I'd never seen them or even heard of them but Pamela said they were perfectly authentic. She explained the connection to me but I got lost in the family tree.'

'Poor mother,' Jack said. 'How's she going to manage? I thought she and Anna were mad when they started to prepare to feed the five thousand.'

Robert shook his head. 'Oh no. They'll be there in the morning, many of them.'

Jack, taking a gin and tonic from the waiter's tray, slumped.

'You can go,' said Robert. 'It's different for me. There are some members of the family I should like to talk to anyway.'

Jack gave an enquiring look but Robert failed to answer the unspoken question. From an early age Jack had taken no interest, indeed, seemed bored by, the banking house of Levine-Schreft and it had been plain he never had any idea of making it his future career. 'Harry won't thank me,' Robert now said, 'for leaving him with all the foreign in-laws. But it's his turn to take over.'

'He doesn't look well,' observed Jack.

'I'm not surprised. A man of his age— ' He broke off, realising it was unsuitable to speak too frankly to Harry's son.

Jack, however, remained placid. 'Mother knows, doesn't she?' he asked.

'It's been going on for twenty years. But she prefers not to know and I'm sure your father has made it plain that there's no question of a divorce. Pamela's sensitive. Not like her mother.

Violet could always look after herself.' He remembered his sister, Joanna, in her mental hospital, remembered his parents' divorce. 'And now this will,' he added. 'And the memorial service. Of course we didn't follow her instructions about the funeral to the letter . . . '

Jack smiled. 'Involving her cremation, her ashes to be strewn in three places, at Kensal Green, at St Luc in Normandy and in her old constituency in Sunderland.'

'And plaques, in two languages, wording supplied by Violet. The one in French was particularly awful. She called herself a British heroine. We couldn't have done it. Her egotism was extraordinary.'

Jack noted that Robert, like so many of the offspring of vivid and energetic parents, viewed his mother with intense dislike. Grandchildren, like him, were often more tolerant. The children, he supposed, had bitter, personal memories. Violet had produced, in his mother, a timid and unselfconfident woman. Robert was confident but for some reason he had never married or, so far as Jack knew, formed any permanent relationship with another person. If Jack had been asked to guess about his uncle's life he would have imagined Robert having discreet, short-term relationships with young working-class men, nothing to prevent his arrival at the Levine-Schreft building in New York early next day, ready to bankrupt the Seychelles or take a scrambled call from the White House. And then there was Joanna who had not even been told of Violet's death. 'It wouldn't mean anything to her anyway,' Robert had said and Pamela had agreed. One way and another, he thought, it looked as if Violet had been a less-than-perfect mother.

When they left the club to go back to Cavendish Square, Jack wondered why he hadn't told his uncle about his last visit to Violet, one summer evening six months before. Perhaps it was because the old lady, then ninety-two, had been sitting up in her bedroom at Cavendish Square against a huge pile of lace pillows, saying vindictively that she knew they'd ignore the instructions for her cremation as given in her will (she hadn't mentioned that trouble-making bequest of jewellery to his ex-wife, Jack thought sourly). She'd told him she knew they'd bury her with the family at Kensal Green. This thought seemed to give her pleasure. 'I'd have preferred the Abbey,' said the old egotist, smiling, 'but this'll do. Right near Sophie Levine, who hated my guts, and Frederick, who thought I was deplorable, and all the others hating the idea of lying next to me when their time comes.' And she'd given a laugh. Not an encounter to report to the late woman's son, thought Jack. He could still hear her voice. 'They won't like it, especially with my being divorced from Frederick anyway, but I'm Robert's mother and that's that. They'll be spinning in their graves when they put me in beside them.'

The room was sunny and full of flowers and pictures. A table next to the huge television set was laden with booty. The drawing-room clock was on it in front of a sketch by Cocteau, Jack guessed, showing a small, chic woman with a long cigarette holder. That was probably Violet herself. A pair of very old Chinese vases stood on either side of the table, one crammed with roses. There was a sketch of Sophie Levine, signed by Sickert. There was a small engraved box, which looked like gold, with some necklaces trailing out of it. And were the pair of Russian icons on the wall by the window as old as they looked, wondered Jack. And was the nurse allowing her to smoke the Balkan Sobranies beside her on the bedside table? And did his mother know that Violet was using a large embossed silver platter, which looked several hundred years old, as an ashtray? Beside the plate stood a Lalique vase containing a lily and a mounted photograph of Violet Levine embracing an ex-Prime Minister, Harold Wilson. She had his pipe in her hand. In the middle of this Aladdin's cave sat Violet, like a shrunken little monkey, some lipstick smeared inaccurately on her tiny wrinkled lips, now saying, 'I want you to know this. They'll burn my memoirs as soon as they get hold of them but I've allowed for that. I've made provision for that eventuality: Violet Levine, The Naked Truth,' she added, laughing aloud, then, getting out of breath, coughing heavily.

Jack had heard several times about Violet's illusory memoirs. They were, his mother said, just a way of threatening people and making sure she got her own way. People who annoyed her were told they would be unfavourably mentioned in Violet's new autobiography but, said Pamela, this manuscript did not exist;

Violet had never written a word. They merely humoured her by pretending to believe in it. Curious, he asked the old woman, propped up in bed like a bad, wrinkled child sent to bed for a misdemeanour, 'What have you done with your memoirs?'

'That's for me to know and you to find out,' Violet told him provokingly.

'Granny, you're a dreadful woman,' Jack said.

'Maybe,' she replied, 'but, oh my God, this is an awful business.'

'What?'

'Getting so old,' she moaned.

He thought she was trying to squeeze him for sympathy. 'You've had little old age, Granny, and it arrived late,' he told her. She gave him a nasty look. Later he wondered if his response had caused her, when altering her will, which she did frequently, to put in the clause giving her jewellery to his ex-wife. It was true, however, that Violet had been up and about until the beginning of the year, when she'd suffered a bout of pneumonia from which she hadn't fully recovered. Up to that point she'd been capable of small trips, visits to the theatre, sitting up to dinner with guests. Now she was more or less bedridden but nevertheless, feeling slightly better a few months earlier, she'd sacked her nurse and hired one who flattered her and made her laugh. He now came in and looking pointedly at Jack asked, 'Still here?'

'Yes, Damian,' replied Jack. 'After a full fifteen minutes. Am I wearing out my welcome?'

'Well . . . ' Damian drawled. 'If you want to tire her . . . anyway, you're going to miss *The Jeffersons*,' he said to Violet. 'You remember, Julie's just going to tell who pushed Bimbo off the pier.'

'Oh, yes,' said Violet, looking at the large television screen.

'Who's Bimbo?' asked Jack, reluctant to be ignored.

'The dog,' Damian told him. He wore a white coat, like a doctor, and tight jeans.

As Jack stood up the television went on immediately. 'Well, goodbye, Granny,' said Jack, bending over and kissing her withered cheek. But Violet was watching the screen.

'There, I told you so,' Damian was saying to Violet as Jack left the room. 'It was Amelia – what did I say?'

Downstairs Jack's mother poured him a cup of tea. 'She seems very alert,' he said.

'Oh, she's alert enough,' Pamela said wearily. 'But I wonder how long we have to put up with Damian. He does nothing but watch television with her. I just hope he's honest. She's got half the house up there. I suppose she hasn't got long.' And Pamela sighed.

Walking back to Cavendish Square in flurries of snow Jack murmured, 'I can't think how Mother put up with it for all that time.'

'Fourteen years,' Robert answered. 'And then she left her money to Joanna – how ungrateful. Like an insult to Pamela, really, delivered after death.'

'What about all the papers? That autobiography and the letters. Some of the stuff might be of interest.'

'I think I said there wasn't a sign of any memoirs,' Robert told him. 'I'll appoint someone to sort out all the rest.' As they approached the house he told his nephew, 'I've got some jewellery of Violet's to give to François Coton. I'll hand it over now and join you later.' He parted from Jack in the hall, found François just inside the drawing-room and took him into the library.

'So she had the jewellery all along,' said François, a very thin man of seventy. Louis Schreft, his uncle, had told him, during his final illness, about the capture of Germaine, Sonny and her husband by Germans outside Paris, how they had been found in a van driven by Violet. François never saw his sister and brother again. No one ever discovered what had happened to them.

Robert took the old suede bag from his safe and handed it to François. 'I'm sorry,' he said.

'Well, thank you, Robert,' replied François Coton. 'I'm grateful. In your shoes I might have been tempted . . . ' He paused.

'To say nothing and not reveal what my mother had done,' supplied Robert. 'The thought crossed my mind, I must admit.'

François pulled the old leather thong round the bag open with difficulty and tipped the contents on the desk. There were several strings of pearls, a large brooch made of precious stones in the shape of a leopard, some rings, a bracelet of square emeralds.

'There's a photograph of Germaine wearing the bracelet,' murmured François.

'I'd be grateful if you wouldn't tell too many people,' Robert said.

'Of course not,' his cousin agreed. 'The past is the past. We have to put it behind us.'

The two bankers regarded each other steadily.

'As to our meeting, would tomorrow morning suit you?' asked Robert.

'Yes. We're going back to Zurich in the afternoon.'

'Ten, at Levine-Schreft,' said Robert.

François, pushing the jewellery back into the bag, nodded.

'Would you like me to return that to the safe until you're ready to go?' asked Robert.

François pushed the bag into his pocket and smiled. 'My wife and daughter are waiting eagerly for it. I've called it a legacy.'

'And what a legacy,' said Robert.

His cousin smiled reassuringly. 'The past is the past,' he said.

In the drawing-room Robert found about fifteen members of the family. Pamela, in black, was talking to Julie Waldstein's granddaughter, Anita Valentine. Hanno Waldstein and his wife and children, and his sister Julie and her husband had all come to Britain in 1938. Julie and her husband had never returned to Austria. Anita, a small pretty woman in her early twenties, told Pamela, 'I'd better take the baby home.' The large child in her arms was squirming and pointing at the floor, wanting to get down. Anita's brother David came up and offered to drive her back to Swiss Cottage, where she lived. She grinned and refused.

After she'd left David Valentine told Robert, 'She's expecting another baby by that black chap. Told me today.'

Robert shook his head. 'I'd have thought one was enough,' he said. 'I don't know whether I'm glad or sorry they're not married.'

'I'm glad,' David said. 'Unless you want to end up with

a Rastafarian sitting on the board of Levine-Schreft.'

Robert did not reply. David looked at him sharply. An MP, he also sat on the Levine-Schreft board. Robert was aware that this ambitious young relative had his eye on the chairmanship.

Pamela interrupted, saying, 'Such a pretty child, though. Don't tell Harry I said so.'

'What aren't you going to tell Father?' Anna Schreft, large and handsome, asked. She and her husband Joe joined the group by the fireplace.

'Only that I thought Anita's little girl was so nice. But you know what your father feels . . . '

'Oh, yes,' Anna said. 'I do.'

'I can't say I'm all that thrilled myself,' David said.

'Congratulations on your new appointment, by the way. Does this mean an end to all strikes?'

'I can't promise you that, I'm afraid,' he told her. 'I'm fairly junior. I doubt if I'll be authorised to call out the army to man the oil rigs.'

'More's the pity,' remarked Robert.

'Shoot them down, Uncle Robert?' suggested Anna.

'Solve a lot of problems.'

'They're an international rabble,' David told her, with vigour. 'And the British are the worst.'

In the car going home Anna Schreft remarked to her husband, who was driving, that David seemed pleased about his new appointment at the Department of Employment. 'What they used to call "a coming man",' she added.

Joe, looking tired, said short-temperedly, 'That's what he thinks, the cocky little bastard. In some respects he's the going man, though he doesn't know it yet.'

'Is this to do with the meeting you're having tomorrow?' asked Anna, who had picked up whispers at the party.

'Yes,' Joe Schreft replied shortly.

'Don't you think it's time to tell me what it's all about?'

Joe Schreft, waiting for the lights to change, said nothing.

'Joe! I'm involved,' his wife protested. 'And if it'll affect the children . . . '

'Just let me get out of the worst of the traffic,' he said at last. As they drove through south London he told her what she wanted to know. Anna was silent for the rest of the journey. There was a coating of snow on the large lawn of their long suburban house as Joe entered the drive and parked in front of the house.

Anna opened the door. They went in and sat in the living-room. Anna said, 'You'd better put the pool heater on. The water could freeze tonight.'

When Joe came back she said, 'Does Marcus know?'

Joe shook his head. 'We agreed to tell only the principal people involved.' Anna opened her mouth to speak. Joe forestalled her.

'Anna, it's not the end of the world for Marcus, you know. He's not going to have to join a dole queue. And frankly, having met David Valentine again for the first time for fourteen years I don't mind Marcus having to put more energy into his career than that little shit. Valentine's pretty obviously coasted into his present position using the family firm as a kind of credit card. The previous generation, your father and mine, had to work at it. The four horsemen of the Apocalypse were close behind. I don't think everything should be handed to you on a plate.'

'Easy for you to talk,' said Anna.

'It took backbone growing up with my father,' Joe responded. 'The place was full of beautiful young men telling me what a big success I'd be as a ballet dancer. Father agreed, that was the joke.' Anna smiled. Her husband, a thickset man, was famous for his clumsiness. 'It was like growing up at the court of Tiberius,' he added.

At fifty, shortly after the war ended, Louis Schreft, head of the Paris bank, and a homosexual, had caused surprise by marrying the widow of a distinguished Frenchman, killed as a Partisan, and even more surprise by fathering a son, Joe. His wife had not lived long and after her death Louis reverted to having male lovers. The young Joseph Schreft had grown up happily enough in this environment, much as he complained about it.

Later Joe said, sitting with his arm round his wife on the sofa, 'Between ourselves, although I don't like what's happening – who would? – there are one or two aspects of the business I won't miss. There's too much politics these days.

It's inevitable to some extent, with this kind of banking. But Robert enjoys it. He believes he knows how countries ought to be run and he's manipulating banking matters accordingly. That's dangerous and I don't like it. He's an old man with a lot of power and at least now he'll be held in check – the new lot may be worse, of course. I hope not.'

And Anna, privy to the family secrets and knowing, perhaps, more about Robert Levine, in some ways, than her husband, stayed silent. Joe glanced sideways at her and reflected that from now on he would have no reason, himself, to worry about what she knew.

Jack Christian-Smith, settled at the end of his pew by the door glanced at his uncle, seated across the aisle from him. As the last notes of the hymn died away, leaving the church in silence, he gazed up at the ornate plaster of the domed ceiling above and heard the footsteps of someone at the other end of the church ascending the wooden steps of the pulpit.

'It is hard to describe the great quiet which fell over the country after that day in November 1918,' began the beautiful voice of the actress who had played the part of Violet in a television series some years before. 'It was as if the sound of the guns of northern France and Belgium had been audible in Britain for four years, and their ceasing had caused this silence.'

Jack closed his eyes and leaned back against the pew, letting the words of Violet's elegy to the dead of the First World War waft over him. 'They were stilled in doing their duty, so that we might live on and do ours,' the actress read. It crossed his mind that this service represented, for the Levines, more than just the end of a troublesome relative.

Certainly there'd been a big turn-out for her. Half the opposition front bench was there and a good few of the government's. There were MPs who'd been in their cradles when Violet had been shot out of the Commons because of Mackinnon's defection, young women to whom she was a heroine, people she had worked with in the BBC, a group from her old constituency, old ladies who could not have known Violet in the suffragette movement (since Violet was not in it, being too busy at the time persuading Frederick to marry her) but had perhaps known her on committees connected with women's causes. It was a crowd, thought Jack, and to all these people Violet represented something.

Yet, there was another aspect to the memorial service. There was a big move coming at Levine-Schreft, of that Jack was sure. It had begun with those odd silences at the party after Violet's funeral.

Three months later, having talked to friends in the City, politicians, journalists, picked up an item of information here and a nod or a wink there, Jack was fairly convinced that the bank was selling out to a Far Eastern consortium, based on Hong Kong. Perhaps the deal was already done. Robert looked as if he'd been drained of the vital force which had kept him going long after another man would have begun to settle into old age. David Valentine had not come to the service, perhaps because he wanted to distance himself from his dubious left-wing relative, Red Vi Levine. But when Jack had last seen him, in a restaurant the week before, Valentine had seemed a sour and resentful man, responding to Jack's greeting from another table by looking at him as if he had done him some great harm. The bank was being taken over, for sure, Jack decided, and although there'd be seats on the board for some – Joe Schreft was a certainty, Robert would stay on in a nominal way – for others, Valentine among them, it would be the end. David Valentine would never succeed Robert Levine.

Without realising he was doing it, Jack looked over at his uncle, to see an old man in a black suit come in and sit down beside him. Robert Levine, unwillingly, moved along the pew to make room for him. 'Yet, in those black-clad streets,' read the actress in the pulpit, 'some vitality, as with a lightning-struck tree which in spring produces, from its blackened branches a shoot, a bud, a flower, began to emerge . . . ' Jack saw, rather than heard, his uncle say something, not pleasantly, to the old man in his sagging black suit. Had he said, 'Stone'? During a pause in the reading, while the actress turned over a page, Jack heard the man beside Robert say reproachfully, 'She was part of my life, after all.' Robert Levine's face betrayed anger at this remark. Jack leaned back and shut his eyes again.

What was all that about? It wasn't like Robert to betray temper but, of course, he must be feeling upset. His father, grandfather, great-uncle, even his great-grandfather, old Isak Levine, had died in harness in their own bank. But Robert would not be in charge to the end or select his successor from the ambitious young men of his own family. It was the end of family control based on a big European tribe which had survived wars, moved easily from country to country, even shifted, without difficulty from Europe to America when it was necessary. Whatever the pressures, external or internal, the family had somehow always pulled up the shutters, opened for business early in the morning, stayed open all day and every day for a century.

The church smelt of wood, and women's scent. Outside the jobless and homeless tucked themselves into corners of the stonework to avoid the cold. Getting to his feet for the final hymn Jack saw the old man beside Robert quietly leave the church. Singing 'Jerusalem' from his sheet Jack thought that after a funeral and a memorial service Violet ought to seem truly dead and done with. But she didn't.

SIXTEEN

Kate Higgins, June 22nd, 1991–

I said goodbye to Jack Christian-Smith and put the phone down.

'What's all that about?' asked Di from her ladder by the front door.

I moved the phone into the sitting-room and said, 'I know who Deep Throat is.'

'No! Who?' asked Di.

'It's Alice. Violet Levine's sister. She lives in Connecticut.'

'She must be very old. What a peculiar story.'

'Not as peculiar as this one,' I said, pointing at the floorboards, and the furniture everywhere. Then Di had to get down to answer the front door. The carpet delivery men stuck the rolls of carpet on the landing outside the front door. By then we'd done the dreaded spare room and half the hall. During the afternoon we finished that, had a beer and a sandwich Rog brought in on the way back from the council dump.

'They were converging like flies on those carpets as I drove away,' he said. 'There's acres of rubbish out there. It's being picked over like a slag heap in a strike. There was even a woman with a baby on her back.'

Di had an idea. 'Why don't we put some light stuff downstairs in the Bells' flat? They're away for a week and I've got the keys.'

We carried cases, bags, bedding and lighter bits of furniture downstairs. Then we ate, finished painting the hall and Rog and Di started on her bedroom while I washed the walls down in mine. By seven we'd finished both bedrooms and were exhausted.

'Maybe we can get away with just washing the kitchen and sitting-room walls down, and giving the bathroom a good scrub,' Rog said weakly. 'I can't do much more.' After doing that, they crawled to the pub for a drink. I watched TV, fell asleep, woke up when they brought in some fish and chips, ate a couple of chips and went to bed.

And that morning, at three a.m., we were raided. Unceremoniously, as was the local custom, they broke the door in. The first I knew of it was when, coming out of sleep, I felt something land on me. I opened my eyes to the fierce lights they'd brought in with them, and saw the muzzle of an Alsatian dog, jaws open and teeth at the ready, staring down at me. Some of its saliva dropped on my face. Swivelling my eyes, I saw a uniform jacket and trousers, a pistol pointing at my head. I could even see the man's erection. 'Don't move,' he said, but the warning wasn't necessary with a gun at my head and a dog standing on me ready to tear my throat out.

From all over the flat came the sounds of men searching. They must be kicking cans of paint over. Of course they had their problems too because nothing was where you'd expect it to be, except the kitchen cupboards and their contents, which I could hear smashing to the floor. They must have been chucking the furniture about, to get at the contents of the chest of drawers and the desk, both of which were turned to the wall. I lay there rigid, with my eyes shut, though the light of the arc lamps shone through my closed lids and I could hear the dog panting and smell its breath. If they find anything, I was thinking, this is going to get a lot worse. I couldn't hear anything from Di and Rog, who were sleeping on a mattress in the sitting-room. They were probably lying as still as I was, for the same reasons. Then I heard men come in and open my wardrobe, which was the only bit of furniture left in the room. I heard the drawers crash out, the hangers rattling, some tearing sounds. They didn't speak to one another. Then close to me there was the sound of an axe coming down on wood, and loud splintering noises. They were tearing my wardrobe apart. Now there were several men in the room, an axe and a loaded gun pointing at me, not to mention the dog.

'Get them up,' said somebody.

'Off. Up you,' said the man with the gun. The dog jumped off the bed and I jumped up. It was nothing to him if he shot me. He could say I'd a gun under the pillow. There weren't any witnesses. Up and blinking, I saw what was left of the wardrobe.

Matchwood. My clothes were everywhere. I saw one of my shoes, with the sole wrenched off. 'In with the others,' said the man with the pistol.

In the sitting-room everything was flung about, books, clothes, drawers. Violet's wedding picture which I'd had blown up, framed and hung on the wall, lay, glass smashed, picture torn, frame broken. Di and Rog, both naked, were standing against another wall. Di stared at me expressionlessly and slightly closed one eye. A uniformed policeman was covering them with a gun. Others were tearing the mattress to pieces. One man was ripping the pillows apart. The man nodded at me and I joined Di and Rog against the wall. 'Anything?' said a young man with a crew cut, in jeans. The policeman didn't reply. 'Get her in the bathroom,' he ordered and a woman in a cotton dress and high-heeled shoes, with nicely cut black hair and a pistol in her hand, nodded me in the direction of the bathroom.

I walked in front of her, carefully, through the hall, where bits of crockery and foam lay on the boards. The foam came from my pillows, as I saw when I passed the bedroom door. They'd gutted the mattress, too. Now there were two policemen, with spanners, unscrewing my bed. 'Take off the tee-shirt,' said the woman, though I couldn't see why I was being searched in privacy, when Di was standing stark naked in the front room. I was shaking. I took off the tee-shirt and held it. She took it and looked at it, shook it and threw it on the floor. In a minute, I thought, she'll have her fingers in my vagina. But her boss put his head round the door. 'We're off now.' She left. There was the sound of feet over the crockery in the hall, uniforms brushing the walls as they crowded along, the dogs pattering and panting and padding – then silence. I sat on the lavatory, shaking, trying to put my tee-shirt on.

Rog came in and said, 'You okay? Mind if I have a pee.' Di came in, shivering. She'd put on a dress she must have found on my bedroom floor. Then she passed out and I just caught her before she fell against the bath. It was only half past three. Later, we sat on the floor in the wreckage.

It was Di who voiced what we were all thinking. 'Why didn't they arrest us? It's standard in these situations. It doesn't matter whether they've found anything.'

'I don't know,' Rog said. 'They can't really be hoping we'll lead them to anyone else. After all, we've been warned they're on to us.' He pointed at the wreckage.

'They've certainly given us a hint,' said Di. 'Do you know, I think they've taken every scrap of paper in this flat. Nothing else. I watched them collecting it and putting it in bags. They cleared the desk in one sweep – the whole lot, bills, letters, envelopes. Look,' she said, 'they've even taken the calendar.' It was one Di's firm had printed for a local butcher. It showed scenes from country life. It had been last year's. 'Did you see them take anything else, Kate?'

'No,' I said. 'I had my eyes shut most of the time. Too scared to look.'

Di told herself, 'You don't know where to start, do you? We haven't got enough rubbish bags.' No one responded. Much later we did start clearing up. It seemed to be the only thing to do at half past four in the morning when we were too afraid to go and stay with anyone else, in case we were followed there and brought trouble on them. We moved like zombies until Di said suddenly, 'One good thing – we've got all that stuff downstairs. They can't have gone in there. We'd have heard them.'

We were weakly pleased. It seemed like a little victory over the wreckers. I crept down to check the door of the Bells' flat, to see if it was still shut. I couldn't believe the searchers had really gone away. But they hadn't been in there.

Then we started clearing up, as best we could. When we'd got everything which would have to be thrown away into the spare room, there was practically nothing left.

The man from downstairs came up at six thirty, on his way to work. 'Sorry about the noise,' said Di. 'We've been raided.'

He replied placidly, 'I thought so.'

'Don't know why,' claimed Di.

'They didn't find what they wanted. I heard one of them say, "I don't think there was anything in the flat." '

To have heard that, he must have been standing with his ear pressed to his front door.

Di shrugged, and he said, 'Probably went to the wrong address. It's not unheard of. They haven't left you much, though.'

No one replied, and he went.

'He probably fingered us,' remarked Rog, 'for money.'

'You can't say that,' Di said.

I muttered, 'Why aren't we in prison? That man looked surprised to see us. He knows after a search like that you're not there in the morning. I bet he only came up to see if he could salvage something for himself.'

'I'll see if I can get the door back on its hinges,' Rog volunteered.

Di and I went down to get our stuff out of the flat downstairs. All the bedding was there, quite a lot of cushions, the single mattress from the other bed, some cases of clothes, two sleeping bags, boxes of books and kitchen stuff and my bag with all the books, notes and tapes about Violet Levine inside. I told her this, as we lugged the cases back upstairs. 'I'd rather it was my stereo,' Di said, gloomily. 'Mind you,' she added, elbowing the front door open, 'they did take every scrap of paper away. It wouldn't have been that they were after all the time, would it? Just a thought.'

I shook my head. 'Of course not.'

'There was that guy Mackinnon. Perhaps there was a cover-up. What do you think? Did someone name the fifth man to you?'

I was very tired. 'Don't be ridiculous,' I said.

We put the mattress and the cushions on the front room floor and sat down. I lay down to rest and fell asleep. The traffic started up two hours later, and I woke up, had a rough wash, went to the bank and got some money, leaving Di and Rog lying side by side asleep on the narrow mattress. My handbag had gone with the police, as had Di's, Rog's wallet and the contents of his jacket pockets. Feeling weak, I bought myself some breakfast in a café. While I ate my sausages two men were pasting up squares of poster on the big hoarding opposite. As if in a nightmare, first a square of hair and forehead appeared, then the rest of a face, burning eyes, moustache and all. Adrian Critchlow. Then they did the next section. That bit started to look like the Prime Minister. After that I bought some of the many things we needed and went back. Di and Rog were up, clearing the wreckage out of the spare room.

Di and I sat on the stairs, smoking, while Rog put the lock back on the front door. The carpet layers had turned up and were philosophically laying the carpet. They didn't seem surprised.

'Are you sure there's nothing in that Violet Levine suitcase?' Di said, returning to her idea.

This made me impatient. It looked like a feeble attempt to lay the responsibility for the raid at my door, when it was perfectly obvious which of us was the most likely to attract official attention.

It only needed Andy to come up in a tropical suit while Rog was carrying down the shattered stereo, with the shattered record player on top, and Di and I were on the landing, putting small pieces of smashed furniture in bags, and stacking larger pieces against the wall. Andy leapt up the remaining stairs saying, 'What happened? A raid?'

'No,' I returned. 'I just lost my temper.'

He looked very shocked. 'Jesus Christ,' he said, and then started to help clear up. He got filthy but he didn't mention it. When we'd finished we went round the corner for a cup of tea. The poster opposite the café was finished now. There was Critchlow, confidently embracing the PM, who was giving a strained smile and beside the picture in big, black letters, the moral, WORKING TOGETHER FOR WEALTH AND STABILITY. 'I'm too tired to laugh,' I said.

'So they didn't take you in for questioning,' Andy said.

'Halfway through they probably realised they were at the wrong address,' Di responded. 'We're going to register a complaint this afternoon. Much good will it do.'

'Did you salvage anything?'

'Not a lot,' Di said. I didn't add that we'd had some stuff in the empty flat downstairs. Even after all that, I dreaded his reaction to discovering part of what we'd reclaimed was the Violet Levine material.

'We'd better get in the van and go to the dump,' Di said. 'Do you want to stay, Kate?'

'No,' I said. 'I'll come round with you.'

There was a lot to do. And all the time we were expecting to feel hands on our collars. We weren't telling each other how scared we were. I suppose the difference was that Rog and Di had already thought about it, lived with it for months.

'Dinner tonight?' Andy said. 'You could do with it.'

I was at his flat that night, when they hit us again. Luckily Rog and Di were at Rog's mother's in Wimbledon. The first I heard of the raid was at ten next morning when Di rang Andy's flat, sounding hysterical. 'They've done it again,' she said, 'my flat.' I couldn't believe her. 'They've smashed the bathroom, torn up the carpets, and the floorboards.' She began to cry.

'I'll meet you in the café,' I said. Andy came with me.

Di was shattered. Rog was fairly calm, but frightened. 'I don't believe it,' he said.

'What did they get this time?' Andy asked.

'There wasn't much left. Ripped up what there was, smashed the fixtures. I don't understand it. Two raids, and still no arrests. Why weren't they waiting for us when we came in? If they think there's something in the flat, and they can't find it, the next step is to get hold of us and make us tell them where it is. What else?'

Andy stood up. 'I've really got to go. Can I do anything? Kate, come and stay with me at the flat. I suppose you two'll go to Wimbledon.'

'Oh no,' said Rog. 'They'll do over my mother's place next. I'm going nowhere but here. My mate who's a builder is bringing over a spare toilet this afternoon and he's going to fix it in for nothing. Then I'm going to sort it out, then I'm going to wait. I'm trying to get Di to go somewhere else . . . '

'You're crazy.'

'What else can I do?'

After Andy left he said to me, 'Not to worry. We put a lot of stuff back in the Bells' flat before we went to Wimbledon. It's . . . ' He nodded at the van parked in the street. We weren't sure now if we were being overheard. After two raids you can't be sure of anything.

Di looked at me and said quietly, 'Only it was your bed they took to pieces. And your suitcase with all your notes in it they didn't get the last time. And I wouldn't run to Andy, either, because he's been too close to this. It was his cousin who sold you out.'

'You're mad,' I told her.

Rog shook his head. 'She's not.'

The face of Adrian Critchlow and his puppet Prime Minister caught my eye. I felt frightened. 'Can I have the keys to the van?' I took them, climbed in the back, got the bag containing my notes and tapes and Felix Lamier's story. I went back into the café and asked if the phone was on at the flat. Rog told me it was.

'They've made a neater job of it this time. The phone survived.'

I picked up the plastic bag which contained the rest of my property and said, 'Look, I've had enough. I'm going to make one long expensive call from the flat and after that I've got a feeling there might not be any more raids.'

'What are you going to do?' Di asked in alarm. 'Don't put yourself in any danger.'

'Look who's talking,' I retorted and, hoping my bold gesture wasn't going to be a fiasco, as such gestures often are, I walked out of the café, shot a malicious glance at the poster of Adrian Critchlow and went back to Henry Thackery House. I was angry now. I'd been terrified during the first raid; who wouldn't have been? This second was too much and the thought, this time, that I was the target made it worse.

Inside the flat the searchers had pulled up all the new carpet, which lay like waves, all over the place. They'd pulled down the lampshades and ceiling fitments, torn all the fittings away from the walls in the bathroom and the sink and the units from the kitchen walls. They'd taken Di's desk and the chest of drawers to pieces but left the bits in tidy heaps. As Rog had said this wasn't a big smashing-up job like the last one. This search had been methodical, as if done by tidy workmen. They hadn't even broken the lock on the front door, just picked it to get in.

The telephone sat on a heap of carpet in the hall. I sat down and got Alice Crutchley's – now Alice Farrar – number from the operator and dialled. The phone rang at the other end. I bit my lip and stared up at the dangling wire where the light had been. What had the searchers been after? Why hadn't they just asked me for what they wanted? That way they wouldn't have had to wreck the place – twice – apparently to get hold of my notes about the life of an old woman who'd died over a year ago.

As the phone went on ringing I thought the only person who could help now was Alice Crutchley. Through the kitchen door I watched a tap dripping on to the edge of the kitchen sink. Answer the phone, I urged the residents of Black Stump Farm, Alnick, Connecticut. Answer – and then someone did, a young American, by her voice.

I said, 'Could I speak to Mrs Farrar? My name's Kate Higgins. I'm ringing from England and it's important.'

'Oh,' said the voice, 'my grandmother's in bed. She's very old. I can't disturb her. Could you call back?'

'Please tell her it's urgent,' I said. 'It's about events connected with your great-aunt Violet Levine.'

She must have heard panic in my voice. She said, 'Oh God, it's you. Well, I don't mean that quite the way it sounds but, please, if she speaks to you, will you be careful. She's very old . . .'

'I know she's very old, but things are complicated here. I'm writing a biography.'

'Yeah, I know,' said the young woman. 'I know what you mean. I must tell you, I advised her not to interfere. I knew there'd be trouble.' She hesitated. 'Don't think I'm rude. I'll go and talk to her.'

There was a silence while I listened to the tap dripping. Finally the phone was lifted. I could hear a canary singing.

'You tracked me down then, Miss Higgins,' said that familiar, slightly cracked voice.

'I had to. I hate to disturb you, but I must have the answers to some questions and I haven't much time. The flat I'm living in has been raided by the police twice in two days. I think they might be after my material on your sister, particularly the reminiscences of Felix Lamier.'

'Felix?' said the voice. 'Have you got some reminiscences by Felix? They'd be very revealing.'

I went on desperately, 'Felix was very angry about the way he was treated by your sister at the end of his life. He wrote what he knew of her, which was almost everything, of course. He tried to sell it to the papers, but they wouldn't buy it. I got his account from his son – but there've been these raids, phone-tappings. The truth is I don't know what to do.' If she didn't tell me the final bits of the story, which I was sure she knew, I'd never find out what was going on. 'You've got to tell me what you know.'

There was a long silence. Then Alice Crutchley spoke. 'You realise Robert, my nephew, has been keeping me for many years. It's very difficult, when you're old, to live without money. But I recently sold some paintings given to me years ago by Rosalind Despencer. Did you know she was for years the lover of Arabella Crick, the painter? The Crick paintings were very valuable. I didn't realise it. My granddaughter spotted it and told me.'

When would she tell me, I wondered.

She went on, 'This released me from my dependence on Robert. I'd been bribed but also I wasn't sure how much of this dark story I ought to reveal. I wanted it out in the open, in some ways. Harm had been done to innocent people. And the terrible thing about the past is that – sometimes it doesn't stop.'

'As I've found out . . . '

'I've made many mistakes, where my sister's been concerned,' said the old voice. 'I'm praying you aren't another.'

'Gordon Stone?' I asked, saying the name with some relief.

'Stone,' I heard. She paused for a long time. I held my breath. I was weak with anticipation. She started to speak again. 'I registered the child as my own.'

'It wasn't yours? I wondered at one point if it mightn't have been Violet's.'

'If only it had been,' she said. 'A filthy business.'

'Whose?'

'Joanna's,' she told me.

I was speechless.

She went on. 'We went to a cottage, Violet, Joanna and I. To hide the birth. We did it in secret, buried everything in the garden. I expect a lot of it's still there, even after fifty years.'

I felt very dizzy. Yet still I couldn't see how this old horror story could connect with what was happening now, in 1991.

'She was only fifteen. Stone seduced her. I should never have brought her up to be so silly. She was over-protected. Stone was a fascinating man, just the sort of vital, all-conquering hero a young girl might be attracted to. Violet didn't know. When she found out, the girl was six months pregnant; she asked for my help. I'd finished with her, over Stone, but how could I refuse? Violet was panic-stricken – apart from anything else, her income depended on Frederick. If he'd found out what had happened he'd have broken her. I'm not sure he wouldn't have killed her. Frederick, the most gentle man in the world.' She paused. 'We Crutchleys never did him any good. I ought to have told him and let Violet take the consequences. But Stone was threatening her, too. And he was a terrifying man. So I helped,' she said, her voice seeming low and weak. 'And after that dreadful ordeal – I think Joanna only half-knew what was happening to her – Violet blustered and threatened and said she should never tell. And I, to my shame, backed her. Violet persuaded her, in the end, that nothing had happened.'

'Oh my God,' I said. I could hear Joanna's voice, even now. 'I'll never talk about him, never, never. Mother was a dreadful woman. She was a Nazi – Duncan made her do it. He was a German agent – I won't say anything. I promise I won't say anything.' They'd muddled her up all right. She knew something had happened, but not what or who'd done it.

'I'll never forgive myself for my part in it,' said Alice. 'Joanna became very ill after that. You see, we wouldn't let her speak about it. We told her it hadn't happened.'

I heard Joanna's voice again. 'I won't say anything, I promise I won't say anything.' She'd been handed a nightmare lasting fifty years by Stone, then by Violet, and by Alice, her kindly aunt, as well.

Then the American girl's voice came on the phone. 'She's very tired. She's upset. Can you give her a moment?'

'Yes,' I said.

'She says there's more. You have to know everything,' said the girl.

I knew there must be more. That Violet's daughter had been seduced and had a baby by Hitler's friend and Mosley's henchman was horrible enough, but that was all in the past, not enough to bring so much trouble now. I realised I was breathing shallowly because of the suspense.

The girl was back. 'She's okay now. I'm Veronica, by the way.'

'Hello,' I said. 'Thanks for what you're doing.'

'Don't mention it – here she is,' said the cheerful voice and Alice Crutchley's voice resumed, sounding stronger.

'Can you come here?'

'To the States?'

'We could take care of you.'

'They've got my passport,' I said.

'Ah,' she replied gravely. 'That's too bad.'

'What happened to the baby?' I asked, to get her started again.

'He went for adoption. He was taken by a family in Cornwall. I'm afraid that's the problem. The family in Cornwall – their name was Critchlow. The boy grew up to be Adrian Critchlow.'

'Oh no,' was all I could manage. Then, 'Does he know? Of course he does. And I suppose Stone knows what happened to his son?'

'Yes.'

'Everybody knew but me. The Levines? Yes of course they knew.' Except seventy-year-old Joanna, I thought, in her private asylum along the coast. 'Mother was a dreadful woman – she was a Nazi – she knew Hitler – Duncan made her do it – I saw him, in the dark . . . '

'Don't go near Stone,' Alice said promptly. 'He's still dangerous. I don't want you to get hurt. There's been too much damage.'

'Yes,' I said. 'There certainly has.' The enormity of it was beginning to sink in. There was a conspiracy of silence. Stone knew he was Critchlow's father, Critchlow knew he was Stone's son. The Levines all knew. My best bet was to join the conspiracy, if they'd let me. I didn't know how far Critchlow, Stone, the lot of them, would go to keep their little secret. It wouldn't do Critchlow any good if it came out he was the fruit of a seduced fifteen-year-old and a leader of the old British Union of Fascists. And like so many secrets, it stank worse now than it had when it was fresh.

'I've helped to construct a situation where you're in danger,' she said.

'At least I know, now. And I don't think anyone who came near Violet Levine didn't get compromised, one way or another. I'm just one more.'

Alice, in Connecticut, sighed. She said, 'I must go now.'

Then I was talking to her granddaughter, Veronica, again. 'Isn't there any way you could get here?' she asked.

'Without a passport? I'm not going to get one from the Home Office, controlled by Critchlow, am I? Anyway, I've a family here. Also friends. I'm afraid of what might happen to them if I just disappeared.'

'What are you planning to do?'

'I'd tell, but this phone's bugged,' I told her.

She groaned. 'Oh, no.' Then she added, 'Grandmother says good luck. I do, too. You'll keep in touch?'

'Of course I will. Thanks a lot. I've got to go . . . '

I put the phone down, picked up my bags and left the flat quickly. I got a cab to the station. I found one straight away. Sitting there I thought that during the whole course of this business I'd had my phone tapped, Roger Littlebrown had sacked me and Di's flat had been raided twice. I'd been pushed around by people I didn't know for reasons I didn't understand for too long. Now at least I was beginning to see the truth, and though I was frightened – no doubt I was now in the classic position of knowing too much – at the same time I was angry. I didn't think I was being followed and if they hadn't got me staked out already they'd never guess where I was going. Why not? Because it was crazy, that's why. But I couldn't see any alternative.

I also reflected that for years I'd been keeping my head down and doing my best, with the one ambition, really, of establishing myself, emotionally as well as financially, so that I could bring Ray to London. I hadn't made spectacular progress. I'd made some though. My relationship with Andy reflected this I'm-a-good-girl-I-am mentality as, in a way, was deciding to write the biography of Violet Levine, heroine and woman of integrity – as she then seemed. No mad ideas of intense creative effort on my part, just the desire to produce a useful and edifying study.

And the result was that unwittingly I was now in more trouble than Di Carter, girl terrorist. So much for a policy of keeping your head down and not bothering anybody.

At the station I phoned Dave, thinking I ought to let someone know where I was going. He wasn't at his office or his flat. So as I waited for the train I wrote two letters, one to my parents and one to Di. I hadn't time for flourishes. I wrote:

> Dear Mum and Dad,
>
> While I was doing research for Violet Levine's biography I discovered that Adrian Critchlow is the son of Gordon Stone, Sir Oswald Mosley's old second-in-command in the British Union of Fascists, and Violet Levine's daughter, Joanna, who was fifteen years old when she had the baby. I imagine Critchlow knows I'm aware of this. Stone's still an active Fascist. It's possible I'm in danger from Critchlow. I don't think anything will happen to me but I'm on my way to Rye to confront Stone. If I go missing, will you tell Dave Gottlieb and Jack Christian-Smith. Love to you both, and Ray.

Di's letter was roughly the same. Imagining that the post could be scrutinised for names and addresses and intercepted, I addressed one to my father under his official title at the Town Hall and the other to Di as co-ordinator at her print shop. I bought some stamps from a couple at the next table and posted the letters before I got on the train. It clacked through London. I was relieved it wasn't a corridor train. At least no one was going to come round the door and push me out.

I couldn't see why Adrian Critchlow wouldn't do it. He was the Home Secretary after all. He gave the orders. And if the story of his birth came out he wouldn't be Home Secretary very much longer, certainly never Prime Minister, which was what he wanted. It shouldn't matter who a person's parents were but in his case it would. That his father had been a committed Fascist, imprisoned during the war as a potential enemy of the state would be meat to his enemies and repulsive to many of his supporters. The supporters it didn't repel, but in fact attracted, were not those with whom he'd wish to associate himself publicly. He might just have been able to get away with his father's political record, but the villainous behaviour towards Violet's fifteen-year-old daughter would damn him.

In the end it all came down to how far Critchlow would go to silence me. Secrets have varying lifespans. Some come out in a day, some in a year, some in twenty years and some, of course, never. Would Critchlow decide that his little secret had had its day, couldn't be kept any longer? Would he resign himself to losing his job and his chance of becoming Prime Minister? I doubted it. Professional politicians are tough. Confronted with disgrace, I thought, Critchlow would hang in there and try to beat it. He could stop my story with injunctions and threats of libel but he certainly wouldn't face a real libel suit with all the details coming out in court. And I didn't think he could even afford the rumours which always surround the threat of a suit for libel, or risk publicity in foreign newspapers. So what else could he do?

As we journeyed through fields and orchards on the way to Rye I felt very unhappy. He'd already started a persecution, with his raids and phone-taps. What would his next step be? He'd either frame me on a false charge or arrange a nasty accident. This was why I had to see Stone. I wasn't going to sit waiting for the next blow to fall and I certainly wasn't going to appear at the Home Office, asking to see Critchlow for explanations and negotiations. I felt I might not get safely out of the building. My best bet was to get to Stone quickly and try to sort something out with him. I had elderly parents and a young son – I couldn't afford to be too proud.

Still, as the train arrived I felt unconfident enough to wish I'd taken Dave up on his offer to come with me to see Stone. I was feeling lonely as I got out. I didn't of course know what was happening to Dave . . .

The telephone had rung at mid-morning in his flat. An American voice said, 'Dave? Bill Blow from PA. I thought you'd like the latest from Belize. Sweetwater Village – we've just had a report in that a woman and two men, one the local priest, have turned up. Witnesses to the massacre. When the troops came in and started shooting everybody they climbed up and into a stack of logs outside the sawmill. From where they were hidden they could see everything. The point is, they're claiming the men they saw weren't government troops at all – they were the opposition. And they saw two men in the trees opposite, Europeans, one taking pictures. What do you think? Apparently it took them a long time to tell their story. First they had to bury the dead. The priest did the ceremonies. Then they had a three-day walk. But I'd like to know why Littlebrown tells such a different story. The other account seems fairly reliable. Do you know where I can get hold of him? He seems to have disappeared. His paper wants him, too, obviously.'

Gottlieb thought.

'Dave?' came the other man's voice.

Then he said, 'You wouldn't like to leave this with me for a little while, Bill?'

'God, Dave. I wanted you to help me, not the other way around.'

'Come on. This one isn't going to go all round the world. You've put out what you've got already, I suppose. After that what do you bet Andy Littlebrown says the villagers were mistaken? They got the uniforms wrong. Most people'll believe simple villagers couldn't tell one lot from the other.'

'You're saying you can take it further?'

'I might. If I do, you'll be the first to know.'

Putting the phone down he went to the computer and began checking, occasionally making some notes on a pad. Twenty minutes later he breathed a sigh of satisfaction, thought of something, went to the phone and rang Kate, getting no reply. Then he rang Andy and got his answering machine. He left no message. He tried Kate's mother, in Brighton, who said Kate wasn't there. He made some more calls, tried Kate and Andy again. Kate's flat was still empty but Andy's line was engaged and, he suspected, would be for a long time. He'd have the press on to him for comment, and explanations to make at *The Witness*. The politicians to whom he'd related his story would want to know what had happened. And really, Dave thought, he wanted to know what Andy was going to do, not what he was going to say. He rang a friend, asking him to go to Andy's and keep an eye on his movements.

An hour later the friend called back. Andy, he said, had

come out of the flat, got in his car and driven off. He'd spoken to Andy's daily, pretending to be from his paper with an urgent message. The daily had told him where Andy was headed. 'This bloody great cat sank its claws in my leg,' he added with feeling.

'Yes,' Dave said. 'That's right. I know exactly where he's going.'

'Then it sunk its teeth in,' said the other man. 'Dave?'

'Thanks,' Dave answered. 'Got to go.' And put the phone down.

He rang Kate again and this time got Rog. 'Gone? Where is she?'

'Don't know. She didn't say,' Rog replied laconically.

'Snap out of it – this is important.'

'Sorry,' he relented. 'This place has just been done over for the second time. Look, she got grim, came back here, saying she was going to make a long, expensive phone call, then we'd never have the boys in blue here uninvited again. I don't know what she meant. Should I have stopped her?'

'I don't know,' replied Dave. 'But if she gets in touch can you ring me? I'll give you my cell-phone number. And if she rings tell her to stay where she is, do nothing and not, in any circumstances, talk to Andy Littlebrown. Whatever he says or does . . . '

'Got it,' agreed Rog. 'Di already told her that, before she made the phone call. What's it about?'

'It isn't at all clear. What's Di got against Andy?'

'She just seemed to think he'd been around too much while things were going wrong. It's an instinct, really. She's never liked him.'

'She could be right.'

Dave put the phone down, then rang a car hire firm and his magazine. He slowly made his way downstairs, his crutches under one arm, leaning on the banisters. All I need, he thought, at this moment, is a broken leg. He wondered where Kate had gone.

In the car he looked over the notes he'd made from his computer records. In the previous May he'd had a call from a man who'd been paid to fly over a big area of the Matto Grosso, dropping a defoliating agent. This had made the local Indians leave an area wanted by a large minerals consortium. The only thing was, the guilty pilot had already told Andy Littlebrown about this, six months before. Just after that Andy had tracked down London arms dealers supplying arms illicitly to various groups all over the world. He'd named, among the purchasers, a group of terrorists working inside South Africa. Dave knew he was wrong. Two years before that Andy had exposed the President of a small Caribbean island as an orgy-organiser and drug-runner. He'd had to go, chiefly because of Andy's intervention, which had enabled a law forbidding the sale of land on the island to foreigners to be overturned. A large tract of land was now being used by a multinational pharmaceuticals firm, careless about its safety arrangements and testing procedures. The drugs business had also fallen into international hands. On another occasion when the leading litigants in a case against a large chemicals firm in Thailand had been shot, Andy had made a strong case for the government's being involved, although the killers were later proved to have been hired by the American firm who owned the company.

Dave read on. It all began to add up. Taken in the context of what else he'd done, these episodes didn't form a pattern. When you took them all together it began to look as if on rather too many occasions Andy Littlebrown had fearlessly espoused the cause of the dictator and the multinational corporation against the little man. He'd done it again over this Sweetwater Massacre business. The elected government was planning to transfer land to the peasants and would probably ally itself with other left-wing régimes in Latin America. It might nationalise foreign interests in the country. Andy, exposing the new régime as brutal murderers had tipped the scales of opinion against them. Perhaps he was right, and the government had done it, thought Dave. On the other hand, perhaps this time he'd gone too far.

I took a cab from the station to Gordon Stone's house, still clutching the bag containing my notes and tapes. It wasn't too far from here that I'd visited poor, mad Joanna. I could still hear her voice: 'I won't say anything. I promise I won't say anything.'

We drove up a road of tidy-windowed bungalows, each with a garden in front. It didn't look like a place for old Nazis. Funny to think that if things had worked out the way he wanted he'd have been a top-ranking Nazi leader by now, working out of Buckingham Palace. Did he grow sprouts in his back garden, I wondered, shop in the little supermarket we'd just passed? Did the neighbours know? Then I sat upright, staring. I couldn't believe it. Andy's car was ahead, parked outside one of the bungalows. Inevitably, as we reached the car my cab slowed down. 'This looks like it,' observed the driver. We parked just behind.

As I got out and paid I felt quite cheerful. I couldn't imagine why Andy was here but at least I'd have somebody on my side when I talked to Stone.

I couldn't have been more wrong. I went through a garden gate and up a path that led between straggling rose-bushes. The bungalow had a neglected air. It needed a fresh coat of paint and the net curtains in the windows sagged and wanted washing. The lonely pint of milk on the step hadn't been taken in. I rang the bell and Andy, tall and handsome in a cream suit answered it. Behind him was the stooped figure of an old man, wearing a cardigan, his bowed legs in corduroy trousers. I scarcely noticed him, so horrified was I by the expression on Andy's face when he saw me on the step. Complete incredulity was quickly replaced by one of utter rage. It crossed my mind at that moment that he was going to step forward and grab me by the throat. I'd expected a surprised welcome and instead was facing a murderously angry man. It didn't reassure me much when he quickly got his feelings under control and open anger was replaced with calm. He said contemptuously, 'You stupid bitch. What have you come here for?'

I pulled myself together. 'To have it out with Gordon Stone,' I told him. 'What are you doing here?'

'That's my business.' There was a big dog somewhere in the house, barking incessantly.

Stone came forward. He had a long lined face, a straggling moustache and dead eyes. I could see through an open door off the hall behind him piles of heaped up newspapers and pamphlets. His propaganda, I assumed. Stone wasn't a nice old man at all. He was a bitter old man. He spoke to me as if he knew me.

'What do you want?'

I looked him in the eye with difficulty and said as firmly as I could manage, 'I've talked to Alice Crutchley and she's told me how you seduced her niece. Adrian Critchlow is the son she had – your son.' They didn't look surprised. Someone tapping our phone had obviously told Stone I'd been talking to Alice. He'd told Andy – well, he would, wouldn't he? As they stood there like father and son I suddenly realised they'd no secrets from each other, only from everyone else in the world. I, as it happened, was thinking about my own son and how I had to make sure he'd be safe from the wrath of Stone and Critchlow – and, I was now beginning to see, from Andy. Shocked and frightened, I hurried on, 'The flat's been wrecked twice and I think it's something to do with all this. I need to find out— '

Andy interrupted, saying coldly and viciously, 'I tried to protect you all along. I tried to steer you away from all this. I even offered to marry you. But by that time, you weren't going to marry me – oh no. For years you took what I dished out to you, then, just when you really needed to have me, you changed your mind about marriage. You didn't want to know. And all the time you've been tightening the noose round your own neck, going deeper and deeper into this stupid Violet Levine business. You've been a silly girl, Kate, but I tried, God knows— '

I burst out, 'You bastard.' But my eyes were burning, for along with the rage I felt humiliation. And betrayal. The proposal, the I-love-yous, they'd been a sham.

He ignored me. 'God knows, I tried. I fought for you— '

'Against your friends? But who are they?' I looked at Stone. 'Is he one? Is he, Andy?' My voice was rising.

Stone said, 'I think we should go inside and talk.'

Andy shot him a look. I stared at both of them, the old man and the young. Confused as I was, even disbelieving, I knew for certain I wasn't going to enter that house. It might be just a seaside bungalow on a nice summer day, but it was too dangerous for me.

Andy put his hand out, intending to take me by the shoulder and draw me in. The dog inside went on barking and scrabbling at a door. I stepped back quickly. 'I'm not coming in,' I told them, hearing the panic in my own voice.

Stone asked harshly, 'Why did you come?'

'I wanted to talk to you. I want to sort something out. I'm sure Adrian Critchlow doesn't want to broadcast the news of who his parents are. I'm worried about what he's going to do next.'

Stone smiled. 'I should think you are.'

'Well, what's he going to do?'

'Suppose I said I don't know what you're talking about?' he suggested. Andy, beside him, stared at me stonily.

I didn't know what to answer. I said childishly, 'Well, Alice Crutchley knows.'

He just looked at me as Andy said coolly, 'A senile old woman and a journalist of the loony-left variety . . . '

I told him desperately, 'Andy, if I thought it could be stopped . . . That's why I'm here. I don't want any trouble. If I thought I could trust you to persuade Critchlow to leave me alone. I mean, for God's sake, I'm only writing a biography of Violet Levine. I don't have to mention who Critchlow is. It's got nothing to do with the book.'

'Well . . . ' Andy said consideringly.

'If you don't want to tell the story,' Stone remarked easily, 'then I don't think there's much of a problem.'

'I'd have to have some guarantees,' I told him. 'Since I arrived the thing's got worse, with what Andy's said about trying to stop me – all that. There seem to be a lot of people involved. I'll need a document from you that I can leave at a solicitor's, in case anything happens to me.'

They didn't want that. Andy asked suddenly, 'Does Gottlieb know about this?'

Uncertain of the right answer, I didn't reply.

Andy turned to Stone and told him, 'He does.' There was a silence, while the dog went on barking itself hoarse. It was hurling itself against the closed door, now.

I said to Stone, 'I recognise you. You're the man who was walking his dog on the beach outside where Joanna Crutchley's kept. That must help her frame of mind. Totally confused, she's always seeing you on patrol. No wonder she's not making much progress.' Inwardly I despaired. It seemed plain they were prepared to tell me I was safe as long as I didn't publish anything about Critchlow's antecedents but they weren't prepared to supply anything with which I could protect myself. I could almost hear the phone call to Critchlow just after I left. Then there'd be motiveless killing in a quiet street in Rye – the gunman would escape; or a car would mount the pavement somewhere, knock me over and drive off; or I'd interrupt a burglar at the flat and get hit over the head. The police files would open and close again quickly due to lack of evidence. I'd be another statistic proving the mounting level of violence in our society – violence and statistics both supplied by the Home Secretary.

I said, 'So, you aren't going to be able to give me any guarantees?' There was a silence while they looked at each other again. 'All right.' I turned round and started to walk down the path.

Andy called, 'Kate, we can work something out . . . ' But I knew even if he wanted to he couldn't. He didn't have the power. Stone and his chums were the bosses. He said loudly, 'Kate! You're in trouble. Don't be a bloody fool. Come back.'

Stone cried, 'Andy! Be quiet.'

I hadn't heard the car drive up and stop on the other side of the road. I hadn't seen it because there were tears in my eyes. Then suddenly Andy stopped shouting at me and yelled, instead, 'Gottlieb!'

At the gate now, I wiped my eyes with my sleeve and saw Dave coming surprisingly fast across the road on his crutches. He'd spotted me and was looking amazed. As he reached the gate he said, 'What's going on?'

Andy, now on the path behind me broke in. 'Clear off. You're not wanted here. Kate and I are trying to come to an agreement about something.'

'Sounded like it,' observed Dave, leaning on one of the crutches.

Stone came up and asked, 'Who's this?'

'Dave Gottlieb,' Andy told him, without pleasure. Stone sighed.

'I don't know what's happening here,' Dave said. 'I just

came to ask about this Sweetwater business. You've heard about these other witnesses appearing?' He looked hard at Andy, then at Stone. 'Yes, I thought so . . . '

'Shall we go in the house, if you want to talk?' Stone asked. His invitations were destined to be refused that day.

'I don't think I'm quick enough to get out of the way,' Dave replied. 'I think I'll stay out here.' Stone turned and began to walk back to the open front door. Dave called after him, 'My magazine knows I'm here, and why. If I'm suddenly arrested or meet with an accident . . . ' But Stone had gone in. He turned to Andy. 'Come here to avoid the publicity? Or is it to decide what you're going to do next? You've gone too far this time, that's my opinion. You planted the blame for that massacre on the government and the holes are beginning to show. I think I know who you're working for.'

'Oh, for Christ's sake, Gottlieb,' Andy retorted. 'What are you talking about – some new conspiracy theory you've invented? You want to grow up. Those people are peasants. They got it wrong.'

'You said AFO was buying arms from British dealers, when they weren't; there was that defoliation campaign in the Matto Grosso you never heard about; the exposure of Northcott; those death statistics from Bolivia you discredited; it does add up, you know, Andy. Now you're switching the names of the villains at Sweetwater. I've got a lot of details. You've been helping your friend in there' – he gestured at the house – 'and others for a long, long time, now. I'm not surprised to find you here.' He sounded mild, even reproachful.

Andy responded, 'I'm not here about that. Why should I be? I'm here trying to help Kate, though she doesn't seem to think so.'

'When I arrived you didn't know I was coming,' I said.

Andy shook his head at me, disappointed.

'He and Stone are old friends,' I told Dave. 'You can tell. I came here because I'm frightened. Adrian Critchlow's Stone's son. He doesn't want anyone to know.'

Dave said, 'It's over, Andy.'

Stone came out of the bungalow with the Alsatian straining on a lead. It tried to lunge at Dave and me. Stone was old and tired, now. I hoped he'd restrain the dog. He told Andy, 'There's no point in prolonging this. There are things I'd like to discuss.' He jerked the dog back with difficulty. It knew who his master disliked.

'Any comments on Sweetwater, before you go?' Dave asked.

As we were walking across to the hired car Andy called, 'I tried, Kate. I did all I could.' He added, 'And it wasn't easy.'

'Bastard!' The dog barked once more, then they went inside.

As Dave struggled into the car he asked me, 'What did he mean?'

'He was making love to me to find out how I was getting on with the Violet Levine story. He proposed, in fact, to get me to stop,' I muttered. It hurt and Andy's parting remark just rubbed salt in the wound. The car started up.

'Don't let it worry you. It must have been bad for him. He had to do what he half-wanted to do anyway, but under orders. The conflict must have shaken him. Then it began to look as if he hadn't enough power over you to make you stop researching the biography. He was in trouble with the Critchlow mob by then, especially as he'd suggested the idea to you in the first place, and his cousin was publishing the book. And it must have been demoralising when he found you wouldn't go along with him. I'd have thought so,' he added, looking at me. 'But to do him justice,' he added, 'he must have been very concerned about you. Anyway, by that stage he was getting burned-out. Ten years of being a top-rank journalist, sometimes being straight, sometimes suppressing information or producing disinformation, never getting caught – he must have been tired. Perhaps his career was over. I wonder if that was why he was asked to leave Cuba. The Cubans had caught some whispers.'

We were on the road back to London. 'What am I going to do?' I groaned. 'They're out to get me, I know.'

'Shout the story from the rooftops,' he advised. 'The louder you shout the safer you are. Once it's out they'll have no more reason to silence you.'

'That was always the only other choice,' I said. 'Maybe we should stop the car somewhere. I think I ought to talk to Alice again.'

I phoned her from a pub and now we turned the car back,

going along the coast until we found the cottage she'd directed us to. This was where she and Violet had taken Joanna to have her baby in secret. It must have been in one of the upstairs bedrooms that she screamed through the birth of her child and where, I suppose, they took the baby from her and brainwashed her, so she lost any clear memory of what had happened.

It was a pretty place with a long green lawn sloping towards the sea which was, that evening, blue and still. We dug until it was almost dark and we'd found what Alice had said was there – the rotting remains of a sheet, stained with brown and a tin box containing a baby's placenta and umbilical cord, now dry and withered. Dave, putting his coat over these remains of an old crime said, 'There are the genetic fingerprints, I suppose. Sad, though.'

The gulls were going off to roost, crying overhead.

We sat in silence for a while, then we kissed and went back to London.

I rented the cottage, to write Violet Levine's biography. I stayed there to have my baby. I go there a lot, to write, but not biographies. You can have too much of living with the past, present and future, all at once, and in violent collision. I've planted a tree where Alice buried the gruesome reminders of Joanna's ordeal. Her baby, Adrian, resigned from the House of Commons on grounds of ill-health not long after our visit to Gordon Stone. Andy, proved to have lied about the Sweetwater Village massacre, was wafted away by the many friends he had accumulated during a lengthy career of speaking for the poor and helping the rich. What I held against him at the last, I suppose, was that wherever he went, he didn't take his ginger cat, Rupert. I found Rupert's body in the road outside his flat one day. Andy was long gone, and Rupert had been run over.

If I'd never tried to write the story of Violet Levine, I might never have had Dave or the baby, never got my son back, never got a career, however minor, going. I've been sitting here in the garden of the cottage on sunny days writing and minding the baby and watching my tree grow. It's surprising how often, while I'm here, I silently thank Violet Levine for the strange legacy she never knew she'd left me.

But is it over? I just don't know – because Violet's grandson, Jack Christian-Smith, is on the trail of the autobiography they all said she hadn't written. He thinks he's almost found it and if he's right, then what else will come out about Violet Levine, that tiny, energetic woman whose fierce clutch on life led to such extraordinary consequences? I look out of over the sea and wonder – is it, is she, really over? Is Violet Levine's legacy paid in full, or was my part of it only the first instalment.